Trapped in the Den of Alphas

BOOK ONE IN THE TRAPPED SERIES

BY

MOLLY CAMBRIA

Trapped in the Den of Alphas

Copyright © 2023 by Molly Cambria.

ISBN: 978-1-3999-5963-6

CONTENTS

Prisoner

Eden

My consciousness is stirring, yelling at me to wake up. However, I can't meet its demands no matter how hard I try. Instead, I lie there. Still and silent as the raised voices grow from a small, tittering whisper in my mind to a loud, unforgiving avalanche. One that washes over me completely, pinning me to the ground, buried with no hope.

Or so I thought.

Slowly, my brain takes in the mishmash of brutal growls, grunts and snarls. Slotting them together like pieces of a puzzle. Connecting them to create some sort of meaning. Now, with my wits about me again, I have to decide which situation is worse. The empty nothingness that consumed me only moments ago or this. The clarity that has now descended upon me, starting in my thoughts and raging through every nerve ending in my tired, weak body.

"Why the fuck did you bring her here, Mateo?"

"What was I supposed to do, Henrick?! She saw me shift and had been tracking me for Goddess knows how long! Was I supposed to leave her to return and tell the others?"

"You should have just wrung her neck and saved us all the damn hassle, you idiot."

"Get fucked, Rocco. I've never killed a woman, and I'm not about to start now, you piece of shit!"

"First of all, THAT is not a woman. It's an elf. Second of all, what the fuck did you just call me? You little runt!"

"You heard!"

"Hey! Break it up, assholes!"

"She's here now, so there's no point arguing about it, Goddess above. Sometimes I wonder if there are enough brain cells in this house to rub together."

"Shut up, Jarek."

"You know he will be pissed when he sees this, right Mateo? This is an epic fuck up."

"Con will understand, Hunter. I had no other option!"

As I listen to their heated discussion unfolding around me, it's clear that I can no longer deny the cold, hard truth. My chest constricts against the solid wooden floor, and my breath catches in my throat as all my senses return to my body like a lightning bolt.

I have been captured by *them*.

Of course, with hindsight, I know that I should have been more careful. I should have taken heed of the countless warnings drummed into me since I was small. However, after going one hundred and twenty-seven years without ever seeing one of *them*, there comes a time when you grow complacent. And that's exactly what I was when I stumbled into this mess, complacent with an added sprinkling of stupid.

Werewolves.

They were the most violent, savage and brutal species in our world and one we thought was eradicated long ago. But as the years rolled on after *The Culling*, it became clear that this perhaps wasn't the case. Now, unluckily, I am the elf to discover this for certain.

"Well, Mateo, what should we do with her now? What was your big plan after bringing her here?"

"I didn't have one, Evan! But like I've said, for the millionth time, I had no fucking option!"

"Shhh! She just moved."

"No, she didn't. Trust me, I knocked her out cold."

"No one trusts you, Mateo! That's the problem. How did you get caught shifting anyway, you half-witted asshole?!"

At that exact moment, the noise level kicks up a notch. The once-heated exchange turns chaotic as the beasts fight amongst themselves like the uncivilized devils they are. Seizing the opportunity, I open one eye to assess the situation.

Wolfmen. A whole room full of them.

My eyes flick between them in turn, and I realize that each one looks different in their own way, with various combinations of skin, hair and eye colors. Some masquerade their brutality with handsome features, while others wear their scars like a badge of honor. However, despite their apparent differences, there are also some attributes that every single one has in abundance: huge, towering statures, muscular physiques, and perhaps most worryingly of all, powerful auras.

Quickly, I consider my options.

Do I continue to lie here and wait for them to decide what to do with me? Or do I try to escape?

Either way, I'm savvy enough to know that my chances are dire. So I choose to wait for the opportune moment, and when it arrives, I don't hesitate. Bouncing onto my feet, I run for the window, which looks out into the sanctuary and protection of the thick, dark forest. I know I'll be alright if I can just make it there.

"Shut up, you pricks! She's making a run for it! Catch her!" a voice booms out from behind me.

Frantically, my hand reaches for the window latch, and I twist it just a little before my arm is ripped backward with such force that it sends me spinning around on the balls of my feet.

Then I see it. The backside of a massive hand as it gets ready to smack me across the face. I let my head fall to one side defensively while the building chaos continues.

"What the hell, Rocco?! There's no need for that!" Mateo, the one I have now identified as my kidnapper, shouts amongst the fray.

I know that I should remain still, but the burning hatred in my heart is not ready to relent just yet. Instead, I lift my head defiantly to look into my would-be attacker's eyes. My bold glare immediately provokes a reaction, and before I know it, his hand comes toward me as if in slow motion. There is no escaping it now. All I can do is prepare myself for the blow, but when I close my eyes again and wait... I am met with nothing but complete silence. A tense and weight-filled silence that makes my heart threaten to stop dead in my chest.

Every voice in the room has ceased. All movement around me has stopped. The sudden shift in dynamics sends a strange, nervous tingle shooting up my spine.

☐

What on earth has caused this?

The atmosphere has changed in the blink of an eye, and I must know why. My eyelids flicker open one at a time to take in the sight before me.

There, my attacker stands. His hand still poised and ready but suspended mid-air, held in place by a strong, unmovable fist. My eyes slowly make the journey upward to the owner. And as they do so, my breathing intensifies. I swear I can hear it amplify tenfold against the tense silence that fills the air.

Then I find him. The owner of the fist and the owner of two intense, penetrating, honey-colored eyes. Eyes that hold onto my gaze, taking my body and mind prisoner. I can't help but swallow a strange kind of gasp. I could have sworn he wasn't here only a few moments ago when the arguments and insults were flying around this hellhole.

"Fucking let go of me!" the dog I now know to be Rocco growls as he tugs his arm away defiantly from the iron grip that holds him steady.

The man with honey-colored eyes doesn't react. Instead, his eyes stay firmly on mine for what feels like an eternity. My lips part, and suddenly his intense gaze snaps away, now settling on Rocco.

"Control yourself or leave," he states with a deadly kind of calm that has the other men in the room looking at each other in quiet anticipation.

I can instantly sense their uncertainty from the looks that cover their faces. This man, the one they all seem to be wary of, is unpredictable. Unreadable. They seem just as tense as I am standing in this room alongside him.

"You've got to be kidding me?" Rocco questions furiously, with a stunned expression plastered over his awful face.

The man doesn't bother to reply. Instead, he stares back threateningly, cocking his head to one side while his dark eyebrows knit together. And just like that... Rocco's question has been answered. Without words, without actions, but with one look alone.

"This is bullshit!" Rocco seethes under his breath, yanking his arm free and stepping backward into the wall of towering, silent onlookers.

My eyes scan them all once again. Only mere moments ago, the competing auras of the men in this room seemed so powerful. But compared with his, the man with the honey-colored eyes, they now pale into insignificance. Standing before him, I feel his power slip under my skin, rushing through me without my consent. The tingling electric current makes me squeeze my eyes shut briefly before I return to see those piercing eyes looking straight into mine. I have his undivided attention, yet still, he says nothing. Not a word before his invasive gaze travels over me, leaving a burning trail in its wake. My heart pounds hard in my chest. My breathing turns ragged and uneven as I stand there at his mercy.

This is pathetic!

I decide I can't take it any longer and step back to escape his suffocating presence. His eyes narrow slightly, and finally, the silence is broken by the sound of his low, composed voice.

"What is your name...elf?"

The authority in his voice almost compels me to answer, but my stubborn nature won't yield.

"My name?" I ask while trying to gain control of myself.

He doesn't respond, and the intensity in his glare doesn't falter for a second. In the short time I've been in his presence, I have now determined that he won't ask the same question twice. He is challenging me outright, bringing my rebellious nature to the surface to push past the nervousness and burst out in a small but powerful explosion.

"Why the hell should I tell you?"

We continue to stare at each other in disdain, and this time, I try, oh how I try, to match his intensity with my own. He's a beast, after all. A filthy barbarian and I need him to see that I'm not afraid.

His left eye twitches. The slight movement is almost unnoticeable to the naked eye, but I don't miss it. He's not used to someone talking back to him. The realization makes my confidence grow, and my chin rises higher. He takes a step closer, and I remain steady in my resolve. However, the air between us rapidly becomes charged as his aura reluctantly mingles with mine. Still, I don't dare to back down.

Standing so close to him, I now have no option but to take in his appearance, and I have to say, I've never seen a creature like him. Elven men typically have a smooth kind of ethereal beauty. Their skin is unblemished by nature, their features are soft and delicate, and their outfits are strategically placed and considered. But standing in front of me right now, this beast bears no resemblance to this image. In many ways, he is the complete and utter opposite. His jaw is strong and covered with rough, manly-looking stubble. His tanned skin isn't perfect at all. Small lines penetrate the skin around his eyes and forehead; however, I'm surprised to discover the effect strangely isn't unpleasant. Instead, they add to the deep, intense look on his face. His hair isn't long nor sleek, like many elves. Instead, it's short, messy and textured. Then there's his body... His frame is broad and imposing, yet chiseled with well-defined muscles poking through the thin material of his black shirt. As I examine him, I can't help but think that a high elf wouldn't be caught dead in such a state of undress.

This is a barbarian alright... A rough, wild, ill-mannered, sexy...

Fuck. What's going on?

I feel my skin tingle as I am drawn closer to him like a moth to the flame. I suck in some air desperately. His eyes flick to my mouth, and the strange tension between us suddenly reaches boiling point without warning. A shaky breath leaves my lips before I can stop it.

"She's just a wood elf," he then states matter-of-factly, cutting through the thick tension. "Take her back into the forest." His face moves closer to mine, and every nerve in my body stands to attention. "Take her back...and let her go."

My heart jolts upon hearing those words leave his lips.

"But Conall, she's seen this place. She might tell someone!" Mateo protests, stepping out from the crowd.

"Then what would you have me do?" the man with the honey-colored eyes asks casually without moving a muscle. "Kill her?"

I glance to the side anxiously to see Mateo shaking his head in defeat before swallowing and looking down at the floor.

"Wood elves are no danger to us," his calm voice continues. "Just let her go."

My eyes snap back to meet his, and the room instantly vibrates with intense chatter as the other men speak in hushed voices. But I have yet to hear a word of what they are saying. I'm entirely focused on the beast in front of me.

He can't be serious...can he?

Suddenly, a blond man leans forward. "Wood elves can still talk, Con," he whispers cautiously under his breath. "Are you sure about this?"

The man doesn't answer the question. He's too busy studying me, and after a few seconds of silence, I wonder if he even heard it all.

"Con—"

"Don't worry about it, Zeke," he answers, nodding toward me. "Wood elves are the most simpleminded creatures in existence. I can tell this one is no different."

His taunting words extract an automatic reaction from me. My fist flies out for his face on instinct, but instead of reaching him, it lands square in the palm of his hand. Before I can react, his fingers curl around it, dragging me closer. Our bodies clash against one another, our heaving chests pressed together as he holds me tightly in place. His eyes lock with mine for a split second longer before they migrate toward my hand in his. His grip is so tight that it borders on painful, yet a strange magnetic energy emanates from the area where our skin touches. The look on his face doesn't change as he examines our position, but something in the atmosphere around us does. It's a subtle shift that only he and I can detect. His honey eyes flick back to me again, and then he speaks.

"You exposed yourself, elf," he mutters, his breath fanning my face. "You have the looks of a wood elf but the fighting temperament of a high elf."

I blink quickly but don't respond to the accusations laid against me. How can I? I fucked up and exposed myself, as he said. I have no defense. I fell straight into his trap, and now I feel like a damn idiot for allowing it.

He lets go of my hand abruptly as though nothing happened, and I tense my jaw, snatching it back to my side. His eyes break contact with mine first, but his calm demeanor remains fixed as he issues his next order. "Zeke, put her somewhere secure until I figure out what I'm going to fucking do with her," he demands coldly, stepping away to turn his back on me and head for the door.

"You can't do this!" I scream in protest, the anger inside me reaching new scorching levels. "They will look for me! You won't get away with this, you filthy fucking dog!"

He doesn't turn around and the last ugly word leaves my frantic lips just as Zeke takes hold of my wrists. The door closes and the room filled with beastly men watch on as I am led away, kicking and screaming in a state of pure, desperate, unfiltered rage.

Azealea

Eden

EARLIER THAT DAY

I close my eyes and breathe in deeply. The scent of the forest soothes my soul in so many ways. The delicate whisper of morning dew hangs in the air, clinging to my skin, wrapping me in its fresh, cool embrace. I listen to the sound of robins and blackbirds gleefully twittering and tweeting their morning tunes. The forest replays their glorious chorus, with every chirp bouncing off the grand, towering trees overhead. I open my eyes and smile a smile that's just for me as I watch a bright yellow butterfly land on a nearby oak tree.

I like to be alone.

In many ways, I prefer it. It wasn't always this way, but perhaps after one hundred and twenty-seven years of living, one does become accustomed to the sound of their own internal voice.

I bend down to examine the contents in the basket by my feet before gently selecting the delicate blooming flowers around the base of the large tree.

White Spike Weed.

It only blooms this way at dawn, so it's the best time to find it. I place the flowers in the basket and cast my eyes over the other beautiful flowers nature offers me this morning. My attention settles on a little Bluenette that has unfortunately seen better days, its petals beginning to turn from a vibrant blue to a dull shade of gray. I frown as I look at the little guy. The flower itself is pretty worthless in terms of its magical or medicinal properties; however, it's always one I have admired for its sheer beauty. I place my fingertips on the decaying petals and channel my energy towards them, letting myself feel nature's powerful lifeblood run through me. After a few seconds, the flower's stem strengthens, and it stands to attention like a proud member of the Elven Guard, its petals bursting with vivid color once again. "That will do." I smile, taking one last look around to make sure I have everything I need. I pick up my haul for this morning, three rabbits and a selection of some of the rarest plants and flowers in this ancient forest, and take off for the village. Considering how I planned my morning route, it isn't all that far. Before too long, I arrive in the heart of Azealea, which is now coming to life to begin a new day.

"Eden, you're early today!" Findell calls out as he sets up his produce cart.

"Just my lucky morning, Findell!" I call back with a smile, lifting the basket into the air triumphantly as he chuckles in return.

I carry on my journey with a smile, nodding at all the friendly faces who greet me as I pass by. Wood elves, such as those here in Azealea, are peaceful and friendly by nature. They keep themselves busy by caring for each other and the enchanted forest they call home. Their lives are simple, but they have plenty of heart, as my father always says. If I had to guess, I'd say he misses living here just as much as I do sometimes, although he would never say the words out loud. After all, being invited to live amongst the high elves by the king and queen personally is a great honor for someone of his humble upbringing. He wouldn't dare dishonor them by admitting that he misses his old life here in Azealea.

That's where my father and I differ. I, for one, can't help but appreciate the simple, uncomplicated beauty of this place and all the fantastic elves living within it. Occasionally, I think I would like to live here again. To spend my time hunting, studying herb enchantment and healing alongside my father and grandma. I daydream about it sometimes when life is hard at the palace. When the scheming, rumors, royal politics, and other shit gets out of control. I can't say the thoughts haven't prompted me to consider moving back here alone, but I know that would humiliate my mother and father, which is the last thing I want to do. There's also the fact that I am not the typical wood elf myself anyway. They are gentle beings, passive and kind to a fault. Both are traits which I can't honestly say that I possess. I know in my heart that I can be stubborn, headstrong and argumentative. All with good reason, of course!

Pia Náre

That's what my father called me growing up. It means little flame, which I suppose was a pretty apt nickname.

So here I am. Eden Nestoriel. The Nowhere Elf.

Neither a wood elf nor a high elf, just somewhere in between!

☐

Eventually, I reach my destination at the village's edge and enthusiastically knock on the small cottage door.

"Come in, Eden!"

I open the door and duck as I enter the cozy living room, looking around to see the fire roaring with a large iron pot hanging over it. I enjoy these weekly visits to see my grandparents with supplies. They tell me I don't have to bring anything when visiting, but I want to help out.

"You're early this morning!" Grandpa Erwin smiles, walking toward me to help with the supplies.

"Yes! I got an early start. Lots to do today."

He nods knowingly but says nothing else as he places the game meat on the kitchen table. The action draws my attention to the shiny, golden envelope lying nearby. I'm not entirely surprised to see it remains unopened. Every year my grandparents are invited to the Palace of Morween to celebrate the anniversary of *The Culling,* and every year they fail to show up. Despite being the only wood elves to receive such an invitation, I know already there is zero chance they will attend tonight.

"Morning, Eden." Grandma smiles as she enters the kitchen, walking over to give me a gentle kiss.

"Hi, Grandma, you are looking beautiful this morning."

She chuckles as she pours me a fresh cup of daisy tea, and I sit at the wooden table as she passes me the cup.

"Ahh...a bountiful hunt this morning, I see," she says, examining the mini natural treasure trove.

"I managed to get some White Spike Weed by the gully. I know you have been using it a lot lately."

"Thanks, dear. This will come in useful."

"What kind of enchantment are you working on anyway? I'd love to help out."

She laughs as she reaches across to pat my hand. "Oh, that's okay, my dear, you know me. I'm always experimenting with this or that. You have enough to do at the palace."

I smile in return, but I can't help the slight tinge of disappointment that nags at my insides. Grandma took great pride in teaching me her craft when I was little. Her enchanted potions and medicines have helped the villagers countless times, and I have always been fascinated by her gift. A gift that she also passed down to my father. But since he took a job working within Morween, Grandma rarely includes me in her work anymore. Most of what I have learned in my studies has come from my father; however, even he would admit that my grandma's talent, magic, intellect and intuition are entirely different. They are a blessing from Ira, the Goddess of Nature herself.

"Anyone for breakfast?" Grandpa Erwin asks eagerly as he pulls some bread from the stone- fire oven.

I nod gratefully, and he gets to work cutting the thick bread into slices.

"So...are we just not opening the invitations anymore?" I ask, bringing the cup of tea to my lips innocently.

Grandpa stops in his tracks, glancing at Grandma Citrine, who sighs softly. "Oh Eden, Morween is not a place for elves like us. We have no interest in going there."

"But I'm there...and so are Mother and Father. I know they would love to see you—"

"No, no. It's not the place for us, dear."

"What about the celebration? The end of the war with the wolves. It's an important part of our history, is it not?"

Her eyebrows rise slightly as she shakes her head from side to side. "It's just like the high elves to remember war and death as if they are a cause of celebration."

I frown in annoyance. "But Grandma, it *is* a cause to celebrate or at least a time to reflect. The wolves almost tore our lands apart! My Aunt Felou, your own daughter, died at their hands. Not to mention countless others! Men, women and children! When the Elven Guard finally defeated them, it brought peace to the kingdom and every creature within it—"

"Enough," she interrupts abruptly, in a harsh tone I have never heard her use. From the look on her face, I can see there's no point in me carrying on my rant. Instead, I take a deep breath, swallow my burning hatred for now and nod my head.

For a few seconds, an awkward silence hangs in the air.

"So...how about that breakfast then?" Grandpa asks brightly, placing the wooden bowl filled with delicious bread in the center of the table.

Erix

Eden

I hear a knock on my door just as I fix the last tendril of my lilac-colored hair in place. "Come in!"

Swiftly the door opens, and my mother appears inside the room. "You look beautiful, Pia Náre," she coos as she looks over my gown for this evening. "And I love that you kept your natural hair color tonight."

"Thanks, Mother. Yours is pretty too. I love the blue on you."

"You think?" she asks, fluffing up her voluminous up-do. "I'm not sure about it."

I watch as she walks toward my dressing table, touching the petals of the Violet Sipple flower, which stands in its white marble plant pot. Within a few seconds, her hair color begins to change, and I shake my head in amusement as every strand flits from vibrant bright blue to soft purple.

"Perhaps I just fancy matching my daughter tonight," she shrugs with a grin. "Are you ready to go?"

I take a deep breath and nod as she examines me with obvious skepticism.

"I'm fine. I promise."

She walks over and lifts her hand to my face sympathetically. "You're sure? I know you always find this occasion difficult—"

"It's been seventy years, Mother. Trust me, I can handle it," I reassure her gratefully, placing my hand on top of hers.

"We had better go then," she adds, finally dropping her hand to walk with me to the door.

After a few minutes of walking through the enormous stone palace, we reach the bottom floor of the building. The grand ballroom is decorated with elaborate floral displays, and it's immediately evident that the queen has decided to go with a striking, colorful theme this year. I can't help but smile in wonder as I cast my eyes up to the tall ceilings, which are reminiscent of the forest canopy itself. Dangling green vines and leaves of every shape and size are adorned with brightly colored flowers which catch the light like little multi-colored stars. The room is filled with large circular tables with pink willow trees as their centerpieces. When I look closely, I can see each little tree buzzing with life, its branches swaying as though they are being moved by the forest breeze.

"It appears Queen Siofra has outdone herself this year," my mother comments, taking in the general splendor. "The ballroom looks more beautiful than I have ever seen it!"

On this occasion, I have to agree.

Beauty is often viewed differently here in Morween. Wood elves value nature, whereas high elves lean more toward opulence and grandiosity. It's never really been a style that has interested me.

"If I didn't know any better, I'd say Queen Siofra has taken inspiration from the wood elves of Azealea for her decor tonight," I whisper to my mother, who gives me a stern look.

"Oh, I wouldn't share that opinion with anyone else if I were you, my love," she warns before spotting one of her friends across the ballroom. "I'll be back soon, Eden."

I watch as she disappears through the crowd of well-dressed high elves, deciding to go for another wander around before heading to our table.

I let my fingers graze against the walls of the stone fountain positioned in the center of the room and gaze upward at the sparking silver streams of water as they lash down upon the multi-colored rocks below.

It's then that my eyes lock with a familiar pair from across the room, and my whole body freezes in place. I wasn't lying earlier when I said I would be fine this evening. It's been a long time since we lost him. Still, every year...every single year, when I see his face again, the hurt and the pain come flooding back into my heart in one fell swoop, and the heavy emotions leave me paralyzed temporarily. Eventually, I summon the courage to amble toward the center stage, and I tilt my head to the side as I look up at his handsome face.

His skin is smooth. His bright eyes are gleaming. His smile is beautiful. He's exactly how I remember him.

Then, I feel a presence by my side and see Aubrun standing shoulder-to-shoulder with me. "You miss him?" he asks quietly, nodding at the painting of Erix, which stands proudly before us.

"Of course, don't you?"

He lets out a heavy sigh and nods in reply. "Every day."

I turn to him and smile sadly.

"How are you, Eden? I came by your father's study this morning, but you weren't there."

"No. I was out," I answer vaguely, looking back at the painting once again.

"Azealea?"

I roll my eyes and shake my head from side to side. "Don't start tonight, please, Aubrun."

He lifts his hands in surrender. "I know that you can take care of yourself. I've seen you fight and hunt. I'm just looking out for you because I care about you, Eden. Deeply."

I shift uncomfortably as I feel his gaze burn into the side of my face. "Well, you don't need to worry—"

"It's my job as a High Elven Guard," he snaps back, cutting me off mid-sentence.

I decide to nod dismissively rather than argue. I just don't have the energy tonight.

Although we aren't exactly best friends, Aubrun and I have known each other for a long time. Ever since I moved here around eighty years ago, he has been a part of my life. It was inevitable really as he was best friends with Erix, and Erix and I were inseparable before... Well, before he was gone.

"Erix would want you to move on, you know, Eden. He would want you to be happy," Aubrun says quietly as he watches me admire the painting.

"I know," I whisper, my eyes connecting with the pools of deep blue.

Erix was a beautiful person in every way and perhaps the only high elf I didn't think was a pompous prick with entitlement issues when I arrived here. He made time for everyone. Was generous and kind. In fact, I used to joke that perhaps he was a wood elf in disguise.

Aubrun then turns to me and lifts my hand gently to hold it between his palms.

Shit.

Panic settles over me as I take in the serious expression on his face.

He isn't about to do this... is he?

"I was going to ask if you'd allow me to take you—"

Suddenly, a gong rings through the hall, which then falls into silence as everyone hurriedly makes their way to their tables for the entrance of King Ciridan and Queen Siofra. I must admit that I'm one hundred percent grateful for the interruption. I glance at Aubrun again cautiously and slip my hand from his. "I better go to my table."

"Of course, you must," he agrees insistently, checking over his formal attire to ensure everything is in place.

I escape to join my mother and father at their table near the front as everyone claps for the king and queen.

As they make their way to the front, I have to admire Siofra. The woman doesn't do anything by halves. Her dress and hairstyle reflect the evening decor down to a tee. On the other hand, the king doesn't look entirely himself. Despite his elaborate tunic of bright colors, I notice the pale hue of his skin, the bags under his eyes and the general heaviness in his step as he follows the radiant Siofra to take their thrones. I look around the room briefly, wondering if anyone else has noticed the subtle changes in his appearance.

The crowd quietens, and everyone sits, waiting patiently for their king's speech. Ciridan looks around the room slowly, nodding to the many notable lords and high elves. My father also receives a respectful nod that catches the attention of others around us.

A lowly wood elf being acknowledged by the king? Oh, how very uncouth.

Urgg, you would think these snobs would have gotten used to our presence here by now.

King Ciridan then stands up and holds his hands in the air. "Good evening! Thank you all for coming tonight to celebrate the anniversary of *The Culling* and the end of the war that plagued our lands for too many dreadful years," he begins loudly. "On this day seventy years ago, our enemies finally met their demise. Their wicked, evil, violent intentions no longer hang over us because of the actions of the brave elves in this very room. We can now sleep soundly at night. Our children can play and grow. Our women are safe and protected."

The room erupts into applause, and I join in, just as thankful as anyone here that the days of war are far behind us.

"However, this is not only a day of celebration. For we also remember those we have lost...such as my son, your prince, Erix of Morween."

A knot forms in my stomach as he gestures toward the large portrait on the stage behind him.

"I do not doubt he would have led this kingdom with great dignity and strength. We honor him tonight by remembering his sacrifice and the sacrifice of your own sons, daughters, sisters, brothers, mothers and fathers. Let's fondly remember them and celebrate their lives with joy in our hearts!"

Again the room comes alive as everyone shows their gratitude in abundance. However, while everyone seems focused on the celebrations, I keep my eyes on the king, watching as he flops down onto his chair with an air of exhaustion. Queen Siofra glances at him from the corner of her eye before reaching across to grab his hand.

"Now, everyone! Let's eat!" a voice at the table calls out, breaking me from my trance and thrusting me back into the present.

Captured

Eden

"This is all very exciting! We have never been treated to an after-dinner show before." my mother says as we take our seats in the open-air theatre.

I take a moment to look around the circular structure, which is now rapidly filling up with the citizens of Morween. Rows upon rows of high elves. Men, women and children who have come out tonight to be entertained by the first-ever *Culling* stage performance.

The stage, set up in the center circle, is lit with a soft glow but remains empty at the moment. Just then, I see a swish of color appear before us, and I rise to my feet to greet Queen Siofra.

"Your Majesty, this a wonderful celebration," my mother compliments sincerely.

"Thank you, Iriel. I hope you and Haleth enjoyed the feast?" the queen enquires with a kind smile.

"Absolutely, Your Majesty."

Then, the queen turns her attention to me, and I bow my head respectfully before she takes both of my hands in hers.

"Eden, you grow more beautiful by the year. Tell me, how are your studies coming along?"

"Very well, thank you, Your Majesty."

She smiles, giving my hands a light squeeze.

"That is good to hear. Another few decades, and I think you may just be the new number-one healer and herbologist in Morween!"

"Perhaps my father might disagree." I joke, causing her to laugh lightly in return.

"You are a fine young woman, Eden," she finishes before winking with a glint in her sapphire-colored eyes.

☐

She then takes her leave, and I breathe in relief as we retake our seats.

"Haleth! The show is about to begin!" my mother calls out to my father, who is chatting with his colleagues a few feet away.

He turns to acknowledge us and begins to head toward his seat. "Are you still doing okay there, Pia Náre?" he asks me dotingly as he sits on my right-hand side.

"Hanging in there." I smile as he nudges his shoulder against mine.

Suddenly, the lights in the outdoor theatre disappear entirely, and the place is plunged into partial darkness. Only the light of the moon and the sparking stars remain.

The crowd goes silent, watching with interest as the stage now fills with actors. The first scene begins with the sound of a roaring fire. The stage is illuminated orange by the flames that lick against the background scene, which has been set up to look like an Elven village. Ear-piercing, harrowing screams emanate through the air as giant wolf beasts ravage the Elven town, the dramatic music adding to the atmospheric horror of it all.

I watch the entire thing with my eyes wide open. Elves falling to the ground in death, children being ripped from their mother's arms and killed as they attempt to flee, and wild beasts attacking innocents with zero hesitation. Those vile, horrific, loathsome creatures! The unprovoked atrocities those poor elves suffered make my blood boil with anger!

The play then tells the story of those brutal years at war. The actors playing King Ciridan and Queen Siofra do so quite convincingly; they have even altered their appearances to look alike.

And then it hits me like a punch to the gut.

Erix.

There he is in all his glory, walking to the center of the stage to take a staring roll in the next act. The crowd is treated to seeing him fight valiantly on the battlefield, and tears threaten to spill from my eyes as I take in his every move. It all seems so real. Too real, in fact.

I look into the crowd, where my eyes meet with Aubrun's as he watches me intently. "Are you okay?" his lips mouth subtly while a look of concern covers his face. I nod and quickly try to pull myself together, looking back to the stage at the exact moment that signifies Erix's death.

The death of a valiant young prince who was taken far too soon.

I watch as the stage turns silent and solemn. The colors around us turn dark and gray. Even the temperature in the air seems to drop by a few degrees. I swallow hard as a few gentle sobs ring through the theatre. Reliving his death again like this is not something I thought I would ever have to do.

Thankfully, the scene comes to an end, and their final act depicts the moment of *The Culling*. Relief washes over me when I realize that we are almost near the end of this horror show.

The last act depicts the king and his advisors setting their plan in motion by releasing a deadly series of toxins around the kingdom, designed to protect our people from more horrific attacks by *them*. Cheers ring out around me as the "wolves" on stage fall to their demise, breathing in the toxic air and dropping like flies. The chants and cheers get louder as the rowdy crowd rejoices in their memories of our victory, but I stay silent. Rooted to the spot as my eyes focus on one actor in particular. A child actor. A little wolf who falls to the ground to land unceremoniously by their dead mother's side.

Bile threatens to rise in my throat. Somewhere in my hazy mind, I see my father look away from the stage, closing his eyes and dropping his head.

The sounds of laughing and cheering become overwhelming, making me feel like I am drowning.

It's then that something inside of me snaps, and I realize that I can't take this anymore. I stand up abruptly, taking my parents by surprise.

My mother tugs on my hand. "Eden?"

"I'm not feeling well. I'm going to bed. I'll see you both in the morning."

"I'll walk you back—" my father begins, but I shake my head insistently, my fiery will winning the fight without much effort.

Quickly, I shuffle out of my seat, navigating the boisterous crowd to make my way toward the exit. I take off in a run, gasping for air as laughter and cheers echo in the night. I cannot even consider returning to my bedroom; instead, I take the path to the forest. Its calming silence is precisely what I need right now. The further away I get from the palace, the greater my ability to breathe again. My heart begins to slow down, my stomach returns to normal, and my head no longer feels like it is about to explode. I come to a halt in the middle of a small clearing and lean back against the cool bark of a colossal tree, closing my eyes as I breathe in the fresh air.

What an *awful* evening.

Reliving the mass killing of innocent elves, the memories of my aunt and Erix's death were all so distressing and unnecessary. But what is more surprising is my reaction to seeing the scenes portraying *The Culling*. In my mind, I have never for one moment doubted that wolves are vicious creatures. My people were tormented and killed at their hands for years. My own future happiness was stolen from me because of them. But when I saw it with my own eyes...when I saw that little wolf child fall... It made me sick to my stomach.

Just then, I hear the snap of twigs and the rustling of leaves a few feet away. I frown in confusion, carefully turning around to press my chest against the tree as I peek around its thick trunk.

My eyes widen at the sight of a man in the distance. I can't make out his features from this far away, but I can see him looking toward the palace through the trees, watching and listening intently.

I stay frozen for a moment as I consider the possibilities.

Perhaps he is a wood elf, curious about the festivities going on in Morween or maybe he— I stifle a gasp as my thoughts are interrupted by what I see next. The shadow of the man's body morphs and changes, rearranging itself into the shape of something horrific.

Something unmistakable.

A *wolf.*

It can't be! I shake my head to try to wake myself up from this nightmare.

I'm seeing things! The stress of the evening has caused me to invent this horrid scenario in my head. I'm all but sure of it!

I watch with bated breath as the beast turns away from the palace, taking off in a trot in the opposite direction. I stay completely still for a few more seconds, glancing over my shoulder at the castle.

What if I'm not wrong? What if what I am seeing here tonight with my own two eyes is real? What if the wolves never did die out?

What if...one survived?

My insides fill with dread, but something inside me tells me I must find out more. I make my way out from behind the tree, following the beast from afar, using all my skills from years of hunting and navigating this ancient forest. I follow him over a gully, briefly losing sight of him for a while before I pick up his tracks on the forest floor. I continue hot on his trail, all the while wondering what I will do if it turns out I am right about all of this.

He reaches the brow of a hill up ahead, and I hang back until it's safe to proceed after him. He seems pretty set in his route. If I had to hazard a guess,

I'd say he's heading back toward wherever it is that he calls home.

A moment of clarity makes me stop and look at the ever-growing darkness around me.

What if he isn't the only one?

What if he isn't alone?

Quickly, I reconsider my options: I either continue to follow him and potentially land myself in a tricky situation, I run for the hills and go straight to King Ciridan with my accusations, or I seek the advice of the wisest person I know.

My Grandma. She'll know what to do!

Having made my decision, I veer right for the village of Azealea, hiking my dress up to run barefoot across the wet forest floor. Then, out of nowhere, a figure steps out in front of me, and I run straight into its path, colliding with what feels like a wall of solid rock. I bounce back and land on my ass, my eyes traveling upward to see the shadowy figure of him. The wolf man.

"Stay away from me," I growl as I shuffle backward on the muddy ground.

I stumble to my feet just as he lunges for me, and I lift my knee to connect it with his jaw. He lets out a yelp as his head jolts back, but he grabs hold of my ankle with his strong hand, dragging me back down to the ground with a thud. I thrash around wildly as he tries to pin me in place.

"Fucking stay still, elf!"

"Get off of me!" I grit out between my teeth, unwilling to surrender or give up fighting.

He then reaches behind my head, and the last thing I see is a large rock as it comes hurtling down toward my head, knocking me out completely.

Hopeless

Eden

PRESENT

My eyes widen as the door in front of me is thrown open, I try to turn around, but the dog's grip on my wrists is so fucking tight that I can't move.

"Come on... in you go, elf," he says calmly, releasing my arms and giving me a firm nudge inside the room.

I stumble a little over the hem of my soaked, muddy dress and then spin around quickly to see the blond man look at me one last time before he reaches for the door handle. "NO, DON'T! NO, PLEASE DON'T!" I cry out, making toward the door in a desperate run. It slams in my face, rocking the foundations of the old, crumbly stone walls in the process. "YOU FUCKING ASSHOLE!!" I scream furiously, battering my balled-up fists against the solid wood. "LET ME OUT!! LET ME OUT NOW!! YOU ARE GOING TO REGRET THIS!!"

There is no reply.

Of course, I'm not entirely stupid. I know in my heart that my efforts are in vain, but this rage inside me needs an outlet, somewhere to go before my brain explodes within my skull. So, I continue to kick and batter the door in a savage rampage, yelling obscenities as I grab hold of the handle and yank it violently.

Nothing.

It doesn't budge an inch.

I try to catch my breath, standing back to scrutinize it carefully. I can tell the faded wood was once painted green. I dare say it might have even been pretty at one point in time, but now it stands in the way of my freedom. Perhaps even my life.

My eyes then scan the derelict room in a panic and settle on an old wooden chair in the corner. I snatch it up quickly, holding it to my chest as the four legs poke out in front of me. I let out a fierce growl, running full pelt toward the faded green barrier. An almighty clash rings around the room, but the door remains perfectly intact. I toss the useless piece of furniture to the side in anger. The echo as it clashes against the uneven floorboards pretty much solidifies the fact that I am now completely alone.

I'm trapped here. In this place. With these vicious creatures.

Despite my internal panic, I dare not break down. From all my years of hunting, I know that when an animal loses its senses altogether, it becomes truly helpless.

I pause to breathe in a lung full of dusty air and cast my eyes around the place again. It's a bedroom, if you can even call it that. The single bed in the center is grubby-looking and unused, and it appears as though no one has gone near the thing in years. The furniture, a long dresser and a tall, wonky wardrobe, are old and dusty. Their once grand appearance now dilapidated after years of obvious neglect. Despite the damage, I can tell that this room, and this building in general, are not Elven in the slightest. The style is all wrong.

The moon's light pours in from a window in the corner, and I run toward it eagerly, placing my fingertips under the wooden frame as I attempt to pull it upward. It doesn't move, and I find that I'm not surprised. It wouldn't matter even if it did open. The long, steel bars on the outside rule it out as a possible escape route anyway.

From the corner of my eye, I then spot a closed door and open it to find a small, windowless bathroom equipped with only a toilet and a cracked porcelain sink. I don't even bother to check if they work or not. Instead, I walk back over to the window as the reality of my situation begins to settle in, and I look out over the dark, thick forest below. After being knocked out for most of the journey here, it's impossible to know how far away from Morween I have traveled.

Is this it for me?

Am I too far beyond the reach of my people to be rescued?

Will my family ever suspect that I have been kidnapped? Or will they just assume I have run off to lick my wounds somewhere after the so-called celebration show?

After all, there have been many stories over the years that there may have been some wolves left behind after *The Culling*, but that's all they ever were. Stories.

Aubrun used to tell them to me all the time, but no one truly believed them. Not really.

No, the chances of anyone finding me here are not good. If I'm going to get out of here, I'll have to figure it out on my own, and the only trait I have on my side, the only thing I have over them, is magic.

Don't get me wrong; my Elven powers are limited. It seems the Goddess of Nature blessed me with more modest abilities compared with others like my grandmother. Nevertheless, there are a small number of tricks I have learned along the way. The only problem is that I won't be able to access these powers while stuck in this awful room. I need nature's lifeblood—the energy of the earth itself to draw upon. I look around the room again in search of anything living. A single plant or flower that might give me some hope, but as expected, I find none.

Shit.

I'll have to improvise.

I spend the next few hours trying out other useless escape attempts. I try detaching the curtain pole, using it as a battering ram against the impenetrable windows, before using a pin from my hair to pick the door lock. I even snap off a sharp piece of wood from the dresser and attempt to use it to pry up the uneven floorboards! I don't know why. I guess people do silly shit when they are desperate.

Eventually, giving up, I close my eyes and let out a faint sigh before lying down on the dusty, beige sheets. I bring my legs up to curl into a tight ball, hugging my knees while wondering what horrors lie ahead. Before the commotion started, it was clear that many of the beasts downstairs favored getting rid of me. And the others, well, they didn't seem to know what the hell to do with me.

My mind then drifts back to when their leader stepped into the room. He may have stopped the beating I was about to receive, but when he looked at me the way he did, I saw no sympathy in his eyes. No compassion or empathy. It was something else entirely. Perhaps he hates my kind as much as I hate his. Probably even more so. One thing's for sure is that *he* is the most dangerous one of them all. I already know my fate lies in this mysterious beast's hands, and the thought utterly terrifies me.

Nuisance

Eden

I stand by the sink as the pipes reluctantly splutter to life. A small burst of water explodes from the faucet, followed by a steady trickle. I desperately cup my hands underneath, waiting for them to collect just enough liquid to bring it to my lips. I drink it down without a thought, the overwhelming thirst taking over any worries I might have had about its cleanliness. Thankfully, it tastes fresh enough, and my shoulders drop in relief as I press my wet hands against my face.

It's been a few hours since I woke to see the sunlight beaming in the window. Unfortunately, my failed escapades with the curtain pole last night have left me with little shade against the heat that circulates the suffocating room.

I turn the tap off and wonder if this is all part of their plan. Maybe none of them wants to be the one to kill me, so they have left it up to nature to decide my fate instead. Be it starve to death or boil alive in this unbearable heat.

I look down over the muddy rags that were once my gown. The thin material is torn in random places, and the bodice is barely holding together. Still, with no other options, it will have to do.

Just then, I hear a key grind inside the lock on the door, and I waste zero time rushing back into the room to see what's going on. It's the same blond guy from yesterday. The one who was ordered to put me here. I might have heard his name is Zeke, but I can't be sure. "What's going on? I need to speak with your leader immediately to negotiate my release," I say adamantly, charging toward him.

"Don't come any closer," he snaps back harshly, stopping me in my tracks.

I watch as he lays a tray on the floor before rising to his feet again.

"So you are going to feed me, but you won't let me speak to the one in charge?" I snarl.

"Yes. That's right," he answers without missing a beat, reaching for the door

□

handle to close it again.

I grit my teeth and fold my arms across my chest as I walk over to the tray on the floor, eyeing it suspiciously from above. It looks like some sort of fried eggs with slices of bread on the side. The stubborn part of me wants to ignore the food completely; however, my hungry stomach won't allow it. It groans in loud protest to the thoughts running through my head, so I pick up the food tray in defeat, bringing it to the bed to devour it like a wild animal.

* * *

The hours pass by at great length. The day turned to night and then back to day all over again. Still, there's been nothing. No disturbance in the forest and no contact with any of the other wolf-men. The blond one, Zeke, has periodically brought food, leaving it at the door as he ignores my incessant badgering.

Although it's only been a short while, the isolation is already beginning to take its toll on me mentally, and all I have left now to pass the time are my dark thoughts. There's no worse thing for an elf than to be kept from nature. Spending so long without contact with it makes my body feel weak and powerless.

As the door opens, and what I assume to be lunch appears, I decide that enough is enough. I stand up from the bed and wait for the blonde man to show his face before I launch into my speech. "Zeke? It's Zeke, isn't it? That's your name." He doesn't bother to answer me. "You know, I'd rather you just fucking kill me than leave me here in this room to rot!" I grit out as he places the tray on the floor once again.

"Hmm," he mumbles, standing back up to take in my pitiful state.

"Why don't you tell your almighty leader that from me, huh? Tell him he might as well kill me now!" I add, taking a determined step forward. "Or is he too chicken-shit to do the deed himself?!"

The man's eyebrows rise as he takes in my serious demeanor. "I'll be sure to pass along your message," he says with a slight hint of amusement, gripping the old tray in one hand and pulling the door closed.

Rage bubbles up inside me, and before I know it, my temper spikes. I rush forward to grab the tray and toss it against the wall, where it clatters against the wooden dresser before finally settling on the floor.

It's then that it hits me. If they won't talk to me, then I'll make it damn impossible for these bastards to ignore my presence here any longer. It's childish tactics, I know, but it's the only idea I have right now.

I pick up the tray again and beat it against the door repeatedly, using my anger to fuel my tired body. I then couple the loud bangs with screams that could pierce the ears of an elf five miles away. "LET ME OUTTTTT!"

My onslaught of high-pitched sound is relentless. I take only small breaks to sip water from the faucet before going again even louder. Once the tray has served its purpose, I grab hold of the heavy wooden curtain pole and batter it against the walls, shaking them enough to cause dust to descend from the cracks in the ceiling. "COME ON, YOU COWARDS!" I taunt them loudly, my voice now hoarse but nowhere near done. "LET ME OUT!!"

My endless tirade is beginning to wear me out, but I won't give in now. Not when I've come this far. Suddenly, I hear voices outside, and I rush to the window to see a couple of the wolf-men I recognize from the other night have made their way outside. One is shouting and swearing angrily, while another is holding onto his ear with one hand and massaging his forehead with the other.

I did read once before that wolves have heightened senses, hearing included.

The first grin I have smiled since I got here spreads across my face, and I step back from the window to continue my one-woman band of all things so fucking irritating, annoying and loud that they cannot possibly be ignored.

A few minutes later, the key clatters against the lock, and the door opens to afford me a soundbite of what's happening in the hallway.

"SOMEONE SHUT HER THE FUCK UP!"

"I SWEAR I'LL CHOKE HER MYSELF IF SHE KEEPS—"

Zeke closes the door behind him and folds his arms across his chest as he stands there with a look of annoyance on his face. "I think you made your point. Are you quite finished?" he asks sternly as if dealing with a naughty child.

"That depends. Will you take me to your leader?"

"No—"

The word barely leaves his lips, and I'm already banging the legs of the wooden chair off of the creaky floorboards again.

□

"For fuck sake, wait a damn minute," he growls, closing the door to leave me alone once again.

I decide to do as he says. Timing the minute by counting the seconds in my head. Right on time, the door opens again, and I hold my breath in anticipation. If it's him, their leader, then I'll have to have my wits about me. I straighten myself upright and hold my head high. I then can't hide the wave of disappointment that washes over me as I take in the appearance of the man who has entered the room. It's not the leader at all. Nor is it the blond second-in-command, but it's the one I know as Mateo. I take in his appearance for a few moments in silence. He is tall and tanned with brown eyes and has a mop of chocolate-colored curls that bounce around playfully on his head when he moves. Despite his pleasant appearance, I can't look past the fact that he is the asshole wolf that brought me to this dump in the first place.

"YOU!" I snap angrily, moving around the chair to step toward him.

He holds his hands up in surrender, his brown, apologetic eyes flicking over me. "Cool it. I'm not here to hurt you."

My eyebrows knit together in confusion. "What are you doing here then?" I ask scathingly.

He shrugs his shoulders. "Well. It seems that you are causing quite a nuisance, and I'm the only one who can be trusted not to choke you to death to shut you up."

"So you are telling me that I should trust you? Is that some kind of joke?"

"Hey... I took a lot of heat for sticking up for you!"

"When?!"

"When you first got here!"

My mouth drops open in complete shock. "You are the one who brought me to this place! Should I be thanking you for it?!"

"But did I kill you, though?"

"No, but you *did* smash me over the head with a rock. A pretty big rock!"

He frowns a little before taking a deep breath. "I panicked...that's on me."

I examine him critically for a few moments. I can't trust him, but I'm hardly in any position to burn my bridges with potential allies in this place.

"So you don't want me dead?" I ask suspiciously.

He shakes his head from side to side, but I have to say he doesn't look all too sure.

I fold my arms over my chest. "So what do you want?"

He walks further into the room. "It would be good if you would stop the noise—"

"Then take me to the one in charge." I interrupt quickly.

A look of shock covers his face as he lets out a puff of air. "I wouldn't be asking for that if I were you," he says in warning, shaking his head.

"Why?"

"It would be better for you to stay out of his way. Trust me."

"Then no deal." I shrug, laying my hands down on the chair, ready to go again.

"Look, woman! He's not going to let you go, so there's no point!"

"Maybe I can offer him some kind of deal? I don't have much in the way of money, but—"

Mateo begins to laugh in disbelief, throwing his arms out. "You think he cares about money? Do you think any of us do?"

"Well, perhaps if you just tell him to come here, then I can at least suggest—"

"Yeah, right. I'll just march into Conall's room and tell him you want an audience with him."

"Why the hell not? Why does everyone seem so afraid of him?!"

He doesn't answer my question; instead, a look of defeat covers his face as he falls silent.

The atmosphere suddenly changes, and it becomes clear that there won't be any compromise.

"I'm not getting out of here anytime soon, am I?"

"No, you're not," he answers honestly.

I lift my hand to my face to pinch the bridge of my nose before I turn away to look back out of the window.

"But you might have a chance of at least staying alive so long as you behave."

I shake my head, not bothering to turn around.

"I'm not kidding. You need to keep your head down. Make yourself useful. Don't try any funny business and most importantly of all...."

I turn around to look him in the eye.

"Keep out of Con's way."

I finally relent to the feeling of defeat that creeps up on me and walk over to the bed to take a seat. Mateo hangs around by the door, watching me. Neither of us uttering a word.

"What am I supposed to do?" I ask quietly, looking around the room. "I'll go mad if I'm kept inside this tiny room day in, day out."

He steps forward, grabbing the wooden chair, which he drags across the floorboards to sit in front of me.

"I might have a solution for you, but you're probably not going to like it."

I frown, and his facial expression softens. "Look, there was a meeting last night. It was suggested, by me, that your presence here might be useful. I volunteered you to do chores around the house."

"So I'm to be a slave?"

"I told you you wouldn't like it, but Con didn't say that you couldn't."

"What did he say?"

"Not much, but then he never does."

I nod my head in silent understanding.

"It would at least get you out of this room for a bit."

I think it over while he clasps his hands together, watching me closely. "It's a take it or leave it kinda situation."

My eyes drift toward the door, and I nod in agreement.

"Good," he answers, slapping his hands together before standing up. "Let's get going then?"

"In this?" I ask, glancing down at my torn dress.

"Um, for now, yes, but I'll see what I can do."

"Wait!" I call out, the burning unanswered questions swirling around in the forefront of my mind forcing their way out of my mouth one after the other. "What is this place? How did you all get here? The wolves...they died out after the war."

He looks away shiftily and clears his throat. "As you can see...we didn't."

I shake my head in disbelief. "But there are so many of you; you're all so young. Under forty years old, I would guess? I don't understand how—"

"Can we just get a move on? Let's go," he interrupts, gesturing to the door.

I get up from the bed and follow him, but I don't give up my line of questioning. "Where are all the women? Surely, if wolves survived the war, they would have produced males and females? Can I talk to one of the women?"

"There are no women. Only men," he answers vaguely, with an air of awkwardness.

"No women? But how? And that's another thing...why do all the men have such strong auras? I've read about wolves, and it's usually only the leaders, the Alphas, that have—"

"You ask too many questions," he interrupts for the last time, giving me a glare that causes me to drop the subject altogether.

If I'm going to be here for the long haul, I guess I'll just have to figure out the answers on my own.

Slave

Eden

"What's your name anyway?" Mateo asks, opening the door that leads out into the hallway.

"Eden,"

"Okay, I'm Mateo."

"Yes, I know. I heard the others say it the night I was brought here."

"Yeah, I bet you did," he scoffs. "They were pretty pissed at me...."

I become distracted as I look around the semi-familiar hallway. It really does appear different in the daylight. I can now see that the thick walls are paneled with dark mahogany wood and decorated with various oil paintings of all shapes and sizes. The floorboards have elaborate red and black patterns that worn over the years. The ceilings are high, indicating the sheer size of this place. Of course, it's not anywhere near the size of the Palace of Morween, but it's not an average house either. A mansion might be a better description. This floor of the house seems to be rectangular. I stop momentarily to look over the balcony that stretches around the whole corridor. It looks down onto the floor below, where there is a large sitting room with patterned, dusty sofas and old, antique furniture positioned around a grand fireplace.

"Come on," Mateo says quietly, hurrying me along again.

I tear my eyes away and follow him down a secluded corridor. We stop at the end of the hallway, and I notice a set of narrow steps leading upward and a set leading down. "Where do these go?" I ask, pointing up at the more intriguing option of the two.

Mateo follows my gaze but looks slightly shifty as his voice lowers to a whisper. "Con's quarters. Don't go up there," he says quietly, gesturing to the other stairs instead. "You take these stairs down to the kitchens and the storage cupboards where we keep the cleaning supplies."

He begins his descent, and I can't help but stare upward one last time before following on. "Cleaning supplies?!" I then scoff as Mateo leads the way. "This place doesn't look like it's seen a feather duster in years."

He turns his head to look up at me. "I'm afraid that's where you come in, Eden."

I roll my eyes but don't bother fighting him on it. I've already agreed to this deal anyway. We get closer to the kitchen, and men's loud, gruff voices and intermittent laughter fill the air. I swallow nervously as Mateo pushes the door open into a big kitchen with a square wooden table and some chairs. The chairs are currently occupied by *them*. The wolf-men.

Immediately, the room descends into silence, and just like that, all eyes are on me. I look around at the faces of the men slowly. There aren't as many here as the night I was captured. In fact, there can't be more than five in the room, but their expressions haven't changed much since that first encounter.

"I see the elf has finally stopped causing a fucking racket," one of the men growls, looking me up and down in contempt.

I instantly recognize him as the man who tried to smack me across the face on the night I was captured. Rocco. That was his name. I made sure at the time to burn the damn thing into my memory.

"She's just here to get some cleaning supplies," Mateo states, glancing at me over his shoulder.

"We should be sending that pretty little head of hers back to Morween in a box!"

"Then you take that up with Con, Rocco. You know his orders on this." Mateo hits back.

Rocco's jaw clenches angrily, but he doesn't reply. Then, one of the men purposely knocks a jug of milk off the edge of the table. The noise makes me jump as it smashes upon contact with the stone floor, and I stare at the mess for a moment as my heart sinks in my chest.

"Well...good luck, elf," Rocco says with a sneer, standing up to leave the room as the others follow behind, each one looking at me suspiciously on the way.

Once the room has cleared, Mateo walks over to a cupboard to open it up for me. "This is where you'll find everything you need. You'll be responsible for cleaning and perhaps even cooking soon if they learn to trust you enough—"

"They shouldn't," I answer under my breath, picking up a bottle of toxic-looking liquid to examine it.

"Fucking hell...whatever you do, don't let them hear you say that shit, Eden."

I place the bottle back on the shelf and turn around quickly to look at him.

"Why would they *ever* trust me, Mateo?" I question. "I'm under no illusions. It's probably high time we address the elephant in the room."

He crosses his arms and leans against the doorframe, his body growing stiff.

"I know that all of you here wouldn't have been around for the war, but—"

He immediately shakes his head and holds up his hand to stop me mid-sentence. "Let's leave the elephant in peace for now," he says insistently.

"But—"

"I said we should leave it,"

I swallow carefully and nod my head before he takes a step backward.

"Well, I'll leave you to it. Clean until your heart's content, but like I said, don't try anything, Eden. There are plenty of uhh...safeguards in place around the house. No one in or out without Con's say so. If you try to leave, not only will you fail, but I won't be able to stop them. You'll be on your own."

"Okay," I answer, realizing that he's right.

He turns to leave, and I reach out to touch his arm. "Mateo," I say, causing him to pause for a second. "Thanks."

He nods and then disappears to leave me alone in the closet.

I can't believe I just thanked someone for making me a literal servant, but anything is better than being stuck in that room for another long day. I turn my head to look at the supplies on the grimy shelves. I'm no stranger to hard work. Even after moving to the palace where being waited on by servants is a normal part of life, I still prefer to do my own cleaning and chores. However, I can't deny a house as vast and neglected as this is overwhelming. The place is falling apart!

I grab a bucket and scrubbing brush, heading back into the kitchen. I start by cleaning up the spilled milk and then the broken jug, sweeping it into the trash. I look up to the small narrow window above the sink and catch sight of the green, overgrown grass outside.

What kind of safeguards do they have in place?

Have they used some sort of magic to keep this place secure?

I have no idea, but I'm not stupid enough to try my luck until I know all the facts.

After cleaning the rest of the kitchen, I grab a broom and make my way back up the stone steps. This time I head along the corridor and downstairs to the main sitting room in the center of the house. Again, I hear the familiar sound of male voices, but I try to pay them no mind, starting in a quiet corner of the room where I begin sweeping the floor. Despite my best efforts, the hateful stares have me on edge. One of these beasts may choose to attack at any given moment, and I'd be powerless to stop it.

I lift my hand to tuck my loose hair behind my ears and hazard a look sideways at my unnerving audience. A few are still watching me, but others have thankfully moved on to other activities. Some are playing cards in the opposite corner of the room, and a couple are napping on the dusty sofas. A few more are scattered around, chatting or reading, and I hear footsteps overhead, letting me know that some are upstairs too.

My eyes are drawn up to the balcony of the next floor, and it's then that I see *him*.

Their leader. The man with those honey-colored eyes. Those eyes that are trained on me at this very second.

I stare back at him as if in some kind of trance, unable to look away from his imposing figure. If possible, he looks even more intimidating and intense than the night I arrived. His large hands grip the wooden barrier in front of him, his body tense and still.

I swallow nervously, unsure of what to do. It's ironic, really. After all of my blatant attempts to get his attention earlier, you'd think that I'd be jumping up and down like a lunatic right now, but I'm not. Now I have it...his full attention...I have no idea what the hell to do with myself.

His dark brows furrow as he watches me, and I notice his eyes flick over my disheveled appearance. The intensity of his gaze leaves me squirming inside. Suddenly, he tears his eyes away from mine, looking around the men one last time before turning and heading for the stone steps leading to his quarters.

Dinner

Eden

I tuck the broom in the corner of the cleaning closet and wipe the sweat from my brow before looking back into the kitchen. Sighing heavily, I mumble insults under my breath when I see the mess left behind by the two great oafs who prepared dinner in here earlier. "Disgusting pricks," I groan, lifting the tray with remnants of a few chicken carcasses to toss it in the trash.

I have already cleaned this part of the house today. Well, if you can even call it cleaning. I spent at least three hours mopping and scrubbing for it to look only marginally better at the end of it all. It seems that looking after this house is going to be a lot harder than I expected. More than a few times, I almost threatened to give up. To head back to my room/prison cell and pretend I never made the stupid deal with Mateo in the first place! But I know for a fact that I would regret it soon enough. Allowing my body some freedom to move today has made me feel slightly better.

After washing my hands, I glance at the wooden table to see a plate lying there with some chicken meat and bread. "I assume this is mine..." I say to no one in particular, slouching down onto the seat to begin eating.

It's not unpleasant but a little bland for my tastes. From what I've noticed already in this place, the food is pretty dull, with bread and some kind of meat being the staple of every meal. Seasoning also seems to be non-existent, but for now, I'm not going to complain. I'm too damn hungry for that!

"How has your day been?" a voice asks from behind.

I turn around to see Mateo standing in the doorway. "Awful," I answer without delay. "But better than yesterday."

"At least that's something," he says, folding his arms over his chest as he gives me a sympathetic look.

"What is it now?" I ask suspiciously, raising an eyebrow.

"They wanted me to tell you that dinner is almost over upstairs, and the plates are waiting to be cleared."

I tut in annoyance and roll my eyes. "Never saw that one coming," I groan sarcastically, finishing the last piece of bread. "This evening just keeps getting better and better!"

It's then that I notice the pensive look on Mateo's face as he stares off into space. "Are you alright?" I ask curiously.

"Huh? Yeah fine... I guess I just know the feeling," he shrugs.

"You've had a bad day?" I enquire, picking up a cloth to take with me upstairs.

"Not really, but I'm about to," he answers cryptically. "Never mind."

My eyebrows crease, and I open my mouth to question him further, just as a gruff voice disturbs the silence. "ELF! WHERE ARE YOU? COME. NOW."

I turn to look up the stone steps, and my shoulders slump. "I'll see you later," I grumble to Mateo, taking the route to the main living area as quickly as possible.

As I round the corner, I cast my eyes over the long rectangular dining table set out down the side of the room. There are a few empty chairs here and there. However, the majority are occupied by the beasts who are still eating, drinking and laughing together. It doesn't escape my notice that *he* isn't here.

Does the leader ever eat with the rest of them?

I hold my head high and walk toward the men, starting at the top of the table, where I begin piling the finished dinner plates in my arms. "About time, elf," one of them snorts. I stare at him blankly for a moment taking in his red hair and scruffy beard before I decide to ignore his taunts completely. My jaw begins to ache under the pressure of gritting my teeth together, but what would be the point in arguing back anyway. It will only land me in more shit. I continue working my way down the row of men until I have just about as much crockery as I can carry before returning it downstairs.

The cleanup process takes more than a few trips, but I'm relieved to be left alone for most of it, save for a few snappy comments here and there.

Finally, the men disperse from the table, allowing me some breathing space from the thick tension. It appears it's not only me who is having a hard time adjusting to this new arrangement; it seems like perhaps some of the wolf-men are too. Of course, there are the mouthy ones who seem to enjoy partaking in my misery, but there are also a number of them who can barely look me in the eye. Who tend to just ignore me altogether. It's as though my presence here makes them uncomfortable. I prefer this. I'm happy to be ignored if it means I can go about my business in peace.

On my final trip to the kitchen, I am stopped by a voice from behind.

"Elf!"

I turn to see the blond man, Zeke, looking back at me. "My name is Eden," I retort, narrowing my eyes.

He nods but doesn't bother to correct himself. Instead, he points to the narrow staircase, the one which I have been warned not to go near.

"Conall had dinner in his quarters. You should remove the plates. They will be outside his door," Zeke explains matter-of-factly before heading off on another mission.

I watch him leave for a few seconds and briefly wonder what he does around here all day. I didn't see him relaxing with the other men earlier, and he always seems to be charging around with great intention. Still, I have no idea why or what he is actually doing.

Quickly, I scurry into the kitchen and get rid of the stuff in my hands before I begin making the journey up the narrow set of forbidden stairs.

Liar

Eden

As I get nearer to the top, I realize that my heart is beating a little faster, my senses heightened as I take in the sight in front of me. A long dark corridor with a few closed doors on either side.

This part of the house is completely silent. Isolated from the noise and the hustle and bustle of the busy floors below. My eyes finally settle on the door at the end of the corridor. The largest of them all. I already know that it's his. Why wouldn't it be? Clearly, this man holds all of the authority in this place. It would be his prerogative to take whatever the hell he desires, the biggest room included.

I begin walking forward, my light footsteps still causing the old floorboards underneath to creak intermittently. Finally, I reach my destination, and my shoulders drop when I realize there are no dinner plates here for me to take.

I bite my lip nervously, contemplating my next move.

Should I go downstairs and return later or knock on the door and ask if he's finished eating?

It seems that the latter option fills me with a strange kind of dread, and it's this fear that pushes me to make my choice. Hurriedly, I begin walking back down the hallway. I am just about to reach the top of the steps when suddenly, my stubborn spirit begins to nag at my insides, taunting me for being too fearful to ask a damn man a simple question.

Is this who I am now? A woman who is afraid and meek?

No! I simply won't allow it.

I come to an abrupt halt and twist around determinedly, stalking back toward the door and giving it a firm knock before I can change my mind.

The sound of my knuckles hitting the wood reverberates through my tense body, but I stand to attention, waiting for his reply anyway. The sound of his deep voice then carries through the barrier between us, seeping out through the cracks around the doorframe. "Come back later."

☐

My brows knit together in annoyance, and I rattle the door louder than before. "Actually, I am just about to finish cleaning the dishes, so I would prefer if I could take them now," I reply stubbornly, holding steady despite my obvious nerves.

After a few seconds of silence, I hear his slow, heavy footsteps heading in my direction. I draw breath as the door opens and stand as still as a statue when I come face-to-face with him.

He rests one hand on the heavy door, staring down at me with a blank, unreadable expression as the light of his softly lit bedroom filters into the corridor all around me.

I clear my throat awkwardly. "Can I—"

He turns away, stepping back to hold the door open for me. I let out a shaky breath before walking through the doorway with all the bravado I can muster. It's then that I accidentally look up at him as my body passes his, and I see that he is watching me intently. Our eyes connect like magnets, and a strange tingle works its way up from the base of my spine.

Hastily, I turn my attention to the enormous bedroom, its decor in keeping with the rest of the house. Tapestries in rich shades of red, brown and black hang over the mahogany-clad walls. Old, worn, textured materials of the same colors adorn the four-poster bed and the various other soft furnishings around the room, including the elaborately patterned carpets.

I'm so busy taking it all in that, for a moment, I forget why I'm here.

"They're on the desk," he says, breaking me out of my trance.

I nod nonchalantly, walking in the direction of the large wooden desk that is positioned by a roaring fireplace. Thankfully, the crackle and hiss of the glowing, orange flames help to fill the silence between us. I focus on each individual sound in turn as I stack the various dishes on top of one another. I hear him move and then, unable to help myself, glance upward in his direction.

He closes the door as I stand gawping at his large back, clad in a loose-fitting black shirt that rests against his huge frame, pulled in at his waist by a pair of tight-fitting black trousers. My eyes unwittingly settle on his ass as my curiosity gets the better of me, and now, no matter how hard I try, I can't seem to look away.

Elven men don't dress in such a way that you can see their bodies. Their forms usually are well-hidden beneath elaborate robes or tunics that signify their wealth and importance. But the men in this house don't seem to care much about their clothing. Its only intention is to serve a practical purpose. I can't help but notice how his shirt pulls up at the elbows, displaying his solid and muscular forearms. I feel my cheeks warm and quickly swallow as my brows knit together in confusion. I *need* to get the hell out of here and fast.

I begin to rush the job at hand, and a wayward fork accidentally slips out of my grasp, bouncing against the floorboards with a clang. "Shit," I groan under my breath, walking across the room to retrieve it. But before I can get there, he lifts it from the floor, rising back onto his feet to tower over me. I gulp as he reaches past my body to place it back on the table, and it's then that our eyes meet again.

"Thank—"

"Are you being treated well?" he interrupts dismissively.

I stare at him with wide eyes for a moment.

Is he serious?

"No," I answer back with steely determination.

He nods his head, taking a step forward. "You need clothes?" he questions.

"I do. As you can see," I answer, glancing down at my torn dress.

His eyes flick over my chest, and I swear I see their honey-colored shade darkening in the glow of the roaring flames. "You can have whatever is in the box," he says, returning his gaze to mine again.

I tear my eyes away from him and look toward the four-poster bed, where I see a small wooden box. "I also need somewhere to bathe. I see there's a large bathroom downstairs. Perhaps I can—"

"No," he snarls quickly as I study the look of anger that spreads across his face. The moment takes me by surprise, and I jolt a little in fright.

"You'll bathe here tonight. I'll be out anyway, so you'll have privacy," he states gruffly, gesturing to the door beside the bed. "You'll find whatever you need in there."

I shake my head in refusal.

"I'd rather—"

"It's not up for discussion, elf," he snaps, stalking toward me.

"Eden," I hit back sharply, lifting my chin to face him directly. "My name is Eden."

He doesn't respond at first, and then I see him swallow. His left eye twitching as it did the first time we met. "And tell me, Eden...where do you come from?" he asks in a low, demanding voice.

My mind races with a range of possible answers. Something tells me that in order to protect myself, I must be as vague as possible. I must pretend that my disappearance will be of no consequence to anyone of great importance. If I tell them the truth, it may put a target on my back.

"Azealea," I answer finally.

A smirk touches his lips.

"You're no wood elf."

"I can assure you, I am."

He closes the gap between us, and I move backward to maintain my defiant stance.

"And this dress?" he asks, nodding to my body. "This is standard wood elf clothing?"

"I...uhh—"

"You were there. The night of *The Culling* celebration in Morween. Tell me how a mere wood elf gets invited to an event like this. You must run in powerful circles?"

"I do not."

"So you do not know the king and queen? You don't know anyone in the Elven Guard?"

I scoff for effect, attempting to seem convincing as I stare into his eyes. "No, I work in the palace," I answer, bending the truth to my will.

His face moves closer to mine, and my chest rises and falls quickly. "I know exactly what wood elves are used for in the castle... Are you a palace whore?"

My temper flares in response to the sheer cheek of the man.

How dare he?!

I lift my hand rapidly and smack him hard across the face, showing him exactly what I think of his damn disrespect. His head dips to the side, but he barely flinches. And I stand there. I stand there in total shock at what I have just done. I must be out of my damn mind!

Fear rises in my chest, but I push past it, squaring my small body up to his. "I'm not a whore," I snarl. "You disgusting dog."

He lifts his hand quickly to grip my chin, holding it firmly as we stare at each other hatefully. Our bodies move against one another under the weight of our heavy breaths. "No..." he mutters almost inaudibly, as his nose brushes against mine ever so slightly. "You're not a whore...but you *are* a liar."

My wide eyes stare into his, and then his gaze drops to my lips. My body turns weak as a barrage of confusing emotions hit me simultaneously. Fear, anger, and, most worryingly of all...lust. I've never had a man look at me so intensely before. It's wrong. It's wrong in so many ways, and yet my core throbs unexpectedly in anticipation. I should kick and scream. Fight him off in some kind of way, but my limbs simply refuse to move.

My chin jerks as he lets me go abruptly, releasing his grip to take a step away. "The room is yours for the rest of the night," he says lowly, pointing to the clock on the fireplace behind me. "Be out of here by midnight."

I stand rooted to the spot, blinking furiously as he turns, leaving me in the middle of his empty bedroom.

Punished

Eden

I wriggle my toes again, watching them through the haze of steam that clouds the bathtub around me. The hot water goes a long way to soothe the aches and pains of the day. I have to admit that a tiny part of me is shamelessly glad that I ended up in his bathroom in the first place. I look around at the worn but grand space, my eyes scanning the marble sink area and moving up over the ornate gold mirror hanging directly above it. Again, it's not my style, but it is pretty in a way. The dark maroon-colored walls against the contrasting white marble give the place a rather grand feel. The whole bathroom is a damn sight better than the communal one. Not to mention a LOT cleaner. Don't get me wrong, though, despite the stray suspect hairs and stains, I would have taken my chances downstairs. There's something uneasy about being here, about being in *his* space, knowing he could show up at any second.

The intrusive thought pretty much tramples my peaceful moment, and I decide that I need to get out of here sooner rather than later.

I stand up carefully, allowing the water to cascade from my body down into the spacious tub. I glance at the door, listening for any signs of life. The lack of a lock on the door makes it impossible for me not to be on my guard the whole time. I lean over and snatch a cloth towel from the gold rail on the wall, wrapping it around my body while giving it a firm rub down at the same time.

Tiptoeing to the door, I press my ear against the wood for a few moments to listen intently. I determine that the coast is clear and throw the door open into the fiery warmth of the bedroom. The sight of the brown wooden box immediately grabs my attention, and I make my way toward it, opening it to peer inside at its contents. "You have got to be kidding me..." I mumble, pulling out a faded, loose black shirt. One not unlike the shirt that he was wearing this evening.

I glance around the room before bringing it to my nose for a sniff. It smells like him. That enticing masculine scent of musk, forest and firewood all rolled into one.

I hold the enormous shirt up to examine it critically. Sure, I didn't expect them to be able to give me women's clothing, but this won't work. Out of all the men who live here in this house, at least half of them are a lot smaller than Conall. I roll my eyes as I shake my head from side to side. It's not ideal, but I refuse to spend another moment naked in his room. I pull the massive shirt over my head and let it fall over my body, unraveling the cloth towel underneath to place it on the bed. I look down to see the hem floating around my thighs.

Fantastic.

I pull the other items out of the box to take a closer look. A few shirts for daytime wear, a white shirt that could do for sleeping in and two pairs of enormous pants.

What the hell am I supposed to do with these?!

I poke my legs inside and hold them up by the waist as I look around the room for something that might help. I then spy the ropes tied around each corner of the four-poster bed holding the heavy, drawn-back curtains in place. I unravel one of the ropes, letting the curtain drape freely at one corner of the bed. I'm sure he will be pissed, but I couldn't care less right now. I loop the rope around my waist and tie it tightly to secure the loose pants in place. I'll have to make it work. I have no other option. There is no way that my torn dress can handle another day of chores in this hellhole.

I gather the remaining clothes in a bundle and stick them in the box, heading down the dark, narrow hallway back to my room. The eerie silence sends a curious feeling running through me.

Where are they? What are they up to now?

All day the house was filled with their noisy banter and loud conversations that filled all corners of the creaky, old house. There's no way they have all gone to bed at this hour. Maybe they have gone hunting or changed into one of those blood-thirsty beasts I heard many stories about as a child. I decide not to think too much about the terrifying prospect. Instead, I open the door to my little bedroom and place the wooden box on the floor.

The moonlight pours in from the window in the corner, and the stars twinkle brightly in the obsidian-colored sky. I can't help it when my mind wanders reluctantly to my parents. By now, they are sure to know that something is seriously wrong. Although I am a fully grown woman, they know that I'd never take off without telling them where I was going first. I can just imagine how frantic with worry they must be right now, and I desperately wish there was some way for them to know that I'm still alive. That I'm out here waiting for the right opportunity to get back to them. The depressing thought brings a painful headache, and I walk over to the lumpy bed to sit on the edge.

Suddenly, the sound of male voices grabs my attention.

What the hell are they doing out there?

I rush over to the window eagerly, my eyes widening at the sight below.

All of them are outside in the clearing at the front of the house, where there is a bonfire of some sort blazing and flickering into the night air. The sounds of heightened laughter and slurred voices immediately indicate that they have been drinking. Pretty heavily, by the sounds of things. I watch as some sit around on large logs next to the fire while others stand in smaller groups talking. I scan the scene slowly until my eyes settle on him.

Conall.

Unlike the others, he wears the same serious expression as usual, his arms folded over his chest as he stands in deep conversation with his second-in-command, Zeke.

It's then that they all begin to make a move, congregating in a large semi-circle around the base of a tall tree. My view becomes semi-blocked by the thick leafy branches, but I strain my neck to see a shirtless Mateo walking out from the crowd toward the center of the circle.

My mouth drops open in shock as I watch his hands being bound together with rope before he is shoved down firmly onto his knees. The noise from the men dies down, and silence takes over as one of them steps forward, holding a long, black whip.

My eyes widen again as the whip is tossed back into the darkness, and a gasp leaves my lips as it comes down, slicing through the air to lash against Mateo's smooth back. He grunts in agony, his body jolting forward, his pain made known by the moonlight shining down upon his scrunched-up face.

What the fuck?!

Fury

Eden

I slap my hand over my mouth in shock and utter disgust when it dawns on me what is happening. Mateo is being punished.

Because of me. Because he brought me here.

Suddenly, everything he said earlier this evening makes sense.

Immediately, I lift my arms to begin beating my fists against the window, but it does nothing to stop the horror transpiring below. Another lash lands with an almighty crack, and Mateo's pain-filled cries ring out loudly against the harsh silence. Before I know it, I'm already running full speed out of my room and down the corridor to the staircase. I fly down the stairs like a bat out of hell, heading straight for the front door.

Safeguards? I don't give two shits about their damn safeguards!

I have to do something! Anything that I can to try and stop this!

I throw the door open, my view of Mateo still obscured by the backs of the large men circled around him. "STOP!!" I yell at the top of my lungs as I try to step forward. My path is blocked, and I realize that an invisible barrier stands between me and the rest of the world. "NO!!" I scream, lifting my hands again to beat them against the invisible pane of glass. "STOP! PLEASE STOP!"

Nothing.

Not a single one of those beasts turn around. In fact, it's as though they can't hear me at all. My voice doesn't seem to be penetrating the barrier.

Instead, it just bounces back into the empty living room behind me.

The torture continues with another crack of the whip, and I scream and kick desperately in pointless protest. "YOU FILTHY BEASTS!! YOU *DISGUSTING* BARBARIANS!! STOP!! STOP!!"

I hear another loud grunt pierce the air, and my fists clench harder. "YOU BASTARDS! STOP!!"

Then, I see the outline of one of the men turn to look directly at me.

□

Conall.

His eyes remain lifeless, his face completely stoic as his arms stay folded over his chest.

"YOU ARE EVIL!" I yell in anger, refusing to back down from his intimidating glare. "YOU CRUEL BASTARD!"

Eventually, he turns back around, muttering something to Zeke, who is standing by his side attentively. Zeke nods his head, holding his hand up in the air, and just like that, the silence disappears, and a ruckus round of drunken cheers commence.

What the fuck is wrong with these beasts?!

My mind boggles at the whole strange situation. Still, I bat my thoughts to the side for now, standing on my tiptoes to try and catch sight of Mateo between the drunken bodies surrounding him. "MATEO!" I shout, my eyes wide as the crowd parts to reveal his wounded form. He's being propped up by two other men, supported on shaky legs as they all begin to make their way back to the house.

I take a few tentative steps backward, but the boiling rage in my blood has yet to calm. I'll tell these assholes exactly what I think of their barbaric punishments!

A few drunken men enter the house first, their eyes settling on me in both surprise and contempt. "What the fuck are you doing here, elf? Go to your bedroom," one of the delightful men barks at me. It's the redhead one from earlier, Samuel. I grit my teeth and ignore him, my eyes trained on the entrance waiting for Mateo's arrival.

"Mateo!" I yell in concern as he is practically dragged into the room. "What on earth have they done to you?" I rush forward just as his bouncing curls move upward to reveal his tired-looking face.

"Eden... I'm fine," he croaks out breathlessly.

"Course he is!" one of the men supporting his weight grins, patting him on the shoulder. "You took them like a fucking champ, Matty!"

My brows scrunch in confusion, and I reach out to place my hand on Mateo's sweaty face. "He's not fine! Look at the state of him!"

I step back to hastily cast my eyes over his back, which is dripping with fresh, crimson blood.

"This doesn't concern you, elf," another asshole chuckles in amusement, breezing past me to throw himself onto the sofa. Steadily the room fills up around me, and I stand in complete awe of their indifference. A moment ago, they witnessed and took part in such brutal torture, and not one of them appears fazed by it.

"We have to get him medicine right away! These cuts can become infected and—"

"Ahhh, he'll be fine! Won't you, Matty?" the man I now know as Hunter laughs as he pours a drink over in the corner. "And now he's learned his fucking lesson too."

I glance at Mateo, whose expression begs me to drop it, but my stubborn nature refuses to yield. The last men enter the room, and my eyes immediately find *him*. "YOU CALL THIS LEADERSHIP?!" I fume, storming through the other men to make my way toward Conall.

He doesn't bother answering me, and my yelling quickly crosses the line from irate to all-out fury. Before I know it, I'm beating my fists against his hard chest. "If you want to punish someone, then punish me! Punish me, you fucking COWARD!" I scream before my entire body lifts off the floor. My world is thrown off its axis as I am tossed over his massive shoulder.

"LET ME DOWN!!" I demand, kicking and screaming like an overgrown toddler as I am carried upstairs and back down the corridor toward my room. The laughing of the men down on the floor below only fuels my vicious temper, and I wriggle and writhe around as the door to my bedroom is thrown open.

The sound of his heavy boots on the uneven floorboards pounds in my ears. The door slamming behind him spikes my adrenaline, and I am now in full fight mode as I continue my wild attack.

Suddenly, I'm thrown down roughly onto the bed, my back hitting the hard mattress with a thump. His solid body smothers mine entirely, towering over me as one of his hands yanks my wrists above my head.

"YOU ASS—"

His free hand covers my mouth, his hot skin pressing against my lips.

"Stop," he seethes, his teeth gritted as his face comes down to meet mine. "Fucking stop now, elf!"

I scream fiercely, my body pushing against his, my back arching as I try with all my might to release myself.

"Calm down," he commands. "Or Goddess help me, I'll tie you to this FUCKING bed!"

□

My eyes stare into his, the stormy black irises holding me hostage momentarily. My body slows just a little, and he releases his hand from my mouth to support his weight over my heaving body.

"I'd like to see you try...wolf!" I retort in a wild snarl.

His eyes connect with mine again, and his jaw tightens as his hand reaches down to yank the rope off from around my waist.

"Hey!! What the—"

"Don't fucking test me, Eden," he warns, holding the rope in his tight fist threateningly as he stares into my eyes. "Don't."

I focus my steely gaze on his but close my mouth in compliance. After seeing what was just done to poor Mateo, I know this man isn't joking. It goes against every instinct I have, but I back down and do as I'm told.

We stay like this for a few tense moments, both our uneven breaths filling the air around us. Then, he lets go of my wrists, hoisting himself upward.

He steps away from the bed, but his eyes don't break contact with mine for one single second. I sit bolt upright to glare at him in utter hatred as he tosses the rope onto the bed beside me.

"I need to see to Mateo's wounds."

"You take great interest in his well-be—"

"Why wouldn't I? He's the only one who has shown me any kind of decency," I interrupt determinedly.

His eyes narrow, his jaw clenching as he lifts his hand to point his finger at me. "Get some sleep, Eden," he growls before leaving the room.

Alphas

Eden

I fix my hair into a tight knot at the base of my neck and look back at my tired eyes in the mirror. After Conall left last night, it was impossible to fall asleep. I'm practically wrapped in the man's scent and it's fair to say his presence here certainly left an impression.

Who does that asshole think he is? Who the hell died and made him king of this run-down castle?

Today is the day that I find out.

I fix a determined look on my face and head out into the corridor, making my way to Mateo's room, which he happened to point out to me yesterday in passing.

I can already hear the men downstairs eating, but something tells me he won't be joining them this morning. I lift my hand to rattle the door, and I'm greeted immediately with a weary voice. "Come in."

I swing the door open and see him lying face down on the double bed, his sheets covering his body up to the waist. His head swings around, and a crooked smile appears on his face. "Morning," he groans, lifting his arm to give me a meager wave.

"Goddess, look at you," I tut, closing the door behind me. "You're a mess!"

"Yeah, thanks for that," he retorts, laughing just a little before wincing in pain.

I walk over to his bedside, casting my eyes around the place as I move.

The room is definitely bigger than mine, but it's not much more inviting. The old paint is still peeling off the walls, and the furniture is still tired-looking. "Yeah, I know...it's not quite the Palace of Morween, is it?" he taunts.

I ignore his joke and come to a stop, examining the soaked dressings that are covering his wounds. I can already tell by the scent in the air that they have been doused in Emerdas sap which I guess is somewhat of a relief.

"Well, at least someone had the decency to fix you up last night," I mutter, dragging a chair over to sit beside him. "Who was it?"

"I don't know," Mateo answers with a shrug. "I was out of it. Probably Jarek, though. He's the only one here who knows about medicines and shit. I guess I'll have to thank him."

"This should never have happened. What they did to you was terrible! Why aren't you angry? That asshole Conall ordered your punishment!"

"Eden..."

"I mean, where does he get off handing out these kinds of punishments to his own men? It's disgusting! Does he get some sort of joy out of watching someone else's misery?"

"You must stop trying to battle Con, Eden; it's a battle you'll lose. Trust me. Let it go and stay away from him."

"What? But it's not right."

"Maybe not...but this decision wasn't up to him anyway. The code is the code, and that's all there is to it."

"Code? You are trying to tell me that a man like him isn't able to overrule some silly code?" I question, straightening up in my chair.

"Eden, listen. When a lot of men, a lot of men like us, live under the same roof, we *must* have a code. A set of rules that we stick to no matter what. The rules apply to us all. As do the punishments, whether we like it or not. We can't pick and choose."

I stare at him as I begin to piece the puzzle together. "So what happened last night...you already knew that it was coming? You knew the minute you brought me here?"

He nods his head.

My shoulders slump, and I take a deep breath. "Mateo, I'm so sorry. I didn't know."

"You're sorry that I bashed you over the head and made you a slave?"

"Hmmm, well, when you put it like that, maybe you deserved the lashing after all,"

He grins in return.

"So why did you bring me back here? If it's against this code or whatever?"

"There was nothing heroic in it, Eden. I'd like to say there was," he admits with a shrug.

"At least you're honest," I answer, folding my arms over my chest.

"The truth is I'd have been punished either way. One of our rules is that we don't expose ourselves to others, especially elves. I broke that rule the second I shifted in front of you—"

"But you could have killed me."

"Then I would have been breaking an even bigger rule."

I scrunch my face in confusion.

"We aren't the monsters you think we are, Eden. Not anymore..." he adds quietly.

I must admit that everything I've learned in my life and everything I've seen in this house so far has taught me otherwise. However, I keep my mouth shut on the subject for now, having caused enough drama for one day.

"Well, for what it's worth, I'm sorry you had to go through that."

"Ahh, it wasn't so bad. I was pretty wasted," he laughs, his body bobbing up and down.

"Yeah, it smells like it!" I answer, pinching my nose for dramatic effect. "The stench of alcohol in here could kill a little wood elf like me stone dead!"

He raises an eyebrow at me. "You aren't fooling anyone with that wood elf story. That freakout last night could rival the fiercest Luna. I kid you not."

As soon as the words are out of his mouth, his eyes turn sad, and his smile disappears.

My curiosity gets the better of me, and I can't help but press further. "Luna...that's a female leader, yes?" I ask for clarification.

He nods his head cautiously.

"Did you ever meet one?" I whisper, my eyes opening wide.

He snorts just a little. "Meet one? My mother was the most badass Luna you could ever meet."

"Your mom? But wouldn't that make you—"

"An Alpha," he answers for me.

I blink a few times before swallowing. "Mateo, if you're an Alpha, then maybe you could take over here. Perhaps you could do something good—"

"Eden, you don't understand," he states exhaustedly, shaking his head.

"Then help me to understand. Why is Con the one in charge?"

"Because he's an Alpha too," he snaps back, clearly irritated by my probing questions. "We all are!"

My mouth drops open a little in shock. Of course, I knew these men were powerful but every one of them an Alpha?

How is it even possible?

"You are all Alpha males, yet he is in charge? I don't get it—"

"Every pack needs a leader," he explains plainly. "Without one, we fall apart."

"You all chose him as your leader?"

"Not exactly."

Before he can elaborate, the door knocks loudly from behind, causing me to jump in fright.

"Come in," Mateo calls out, wincing again.

The door opens, and one of the men walks inside, his eyes flicking between Mateo and I from beneath his glasses.

"Jarek, hey man," Mateo says, moving to sit up.

"No, don't get up. I just came to check if you need anything?" Jarek answers with a look of genuine concern.

"Wouldn't mind a couple of your magic pain pills, Doc," Mateo answers with a weak chuckle.

"Coming up," he answers, his eyes then gravitating toward me.

"Jarek, her name is Eden," Mateo says.

I'm surprised when the man nods at me, his face not entirely filled with contempt. "I'll go get those pills."

He makes for the door, and I stand up, ready to join him. I do have places to be, unfortunately. "I'll stop in with some lunch for you later if you'd like, Mateo?" I offer with some uncertainty. "If they'll let me touch the food, that is."

"Wouldn't count on it, Eden! Also... please don't do anything fucking stupid while I'm out of it."

"I can't promise anything."

I give him a small smile before leaving, walking past Jarek on the way.

"Hey man, I meant to say thanks for the bandages."

"Bandages?"

The door closes behind me, and I walk over to the peer over the balcony's edge. The breakfast table is now empty, but I can see a mass of plates have indeed been left behind just for me.

Here we go...

Training

Eden

The morning and afternoon pass by uneventfully. I was, of course, rejected in my offer to cook lunch for Mateo. Apparently, Zeke seems to reckon that I still can't be trusted to prepare anyone's food. He's probably right to be concerned, if I'm honest. With the mood that I'm in today, I'm not sure that I'd even think twice about poisoning their bland plates of meat and bread.

I place the little teapot on the stove, and the flicker of the orange flame catches my eye. Suddenly another crazy plan begins to form in my mind. Perhaps if I can't get out of this place...then I could destroy it. Raise the entire building to the ground.

Despite my initial excitement, I quickly rubbish the idea. How would I make my escape if I can't leave? I can't count on any of these assholes to take me with them. Not without Con's approval, anyway. There's also the thought of what might happen to anyone left behind. Unfortunately, I'm not so sure that I want charred men on my conscience. No matter how beastly they are.

The sound of multiple moans, groans, and grunts then make their way to my ears, and I'm left wondering what they are doing. After lunch, the Alphas all disappeared into the forest to hunt for fresh meat, and I was more than grateful for the peace and quiet. I've already managed to scrub down the dusty sofas in the main living room and tackle the dreaded communal bathroom, which hopefully will make it at least useable later this evening. Sure, Conall forbade me to bathe there, but why should I listen to a word he says? After last night, I'm convinced that the last place I need to be is anywhere near his damn bathroom!

"Get out, elf." The order comes from behind me, and I turn around to see the two colossal chefs themselves, have come to cook dinner for the rest of the men.

"Fine, she's all yours," I grumble, breezing past them to investigate the noise outside.

□

Taking some cleaning supplies with me, I arrive in the living room to find the front door wide open, offering me a perfect view of the yard. I sweep the floor absentmindedly as I begin spying on their unconventional activities.

The men seem to be engaging in some kind of combat lesson. Which I know in itself isn't highly unusual. Even in Morween, the guards have training sessions, but this is different.

The men are paired off, each couple locked in a battle of flying fists and wayward limbs as rainwater smacks against their bare, muscular chests. I hardly realize I'm doing it, but somewhere in the back of my mind, I'm acutely aware that I'm getting closer and closer to the door, too mesmerized to look away. The sheer amount of bare flesh on display leaves me feeling more than a little...strange. I swallow hard as I nibble on the edge of my lip.

Elven guards are very skilled in fighting by hand and by the sword. There is beauty and precise choreography in their every move. But these men fight with something else entirely. Their style is much more instinctive and animalistic. I'm one part terrified and one part fascinated, all at the same time.

It's then that I hone in on one physique in particular that stands out from the rest. The broad back of a man so physically dominant and powerful that the sight of him makes my breath hitch. I watch in a trance as the rain beats off his tanned skin, slipping between the grooves of the sculpted muscles on his back. His skilled hands pull back into tight fists, swinging outward to assault his attacker in calculated yet wild strikes. His arms, huge and bulging, could no doubt crush me to death, but I oddly find myself wondering what they would feel like to touch. What they would feel like under my fingertips. He pushes his attacker away, and his hand lifts in the air as he pushes his fingers through his wet hair, slicking it back to reveal his handsome face.

I'm not at all surprised to see that the beast I've been ogling is Conall.

Of course, it is.

Since last night, I've had to stop my mind from drifting to the moment he pinned me down on the bed. The weight of his heavy body on top of mine. The untamed animalistic look in his ever-changing eyes. The feel of his hand against my lips.

I hated it.

Every second of it...or at least I tell myself that I did.

I shake my head in annoyance, downright furious at myself for allowing these strange thoughts to plague me like this. Just as I am about to tear my eyes away, he looks in my direction, water droplets running down his serious face. His attacker takes advantage of his distracted state, grabbing him by the waist to wrestle him to the ground. I gasp just a little, walking forward to stand in the doorway. The fight turns intense in the blink of an eye as Con begins defending himself with a flurry of powerful, targeted punches. The broom drops from my hand, and my eyes widen as he takes a blow to the stomach.

This only angers him even more.

Suddenly, he flips positions with his sparring partner, who he now has pinned beneath him by the neck. His arm stretches back to land strike after strike repeatedly. The rain beats down harder. Thudding off of his body and the muddy grass around him. The men nearby stop what they are doing to take in the nasty one-sided fight. My breathing begins to get faster. My heart is pounding in my chest.

Look Away, Eden, I order myself privately in my fucked up head. *You know that he's an animal. A ruthless savage.*

Look. Away. Now.

Suddenly, everything goes quiet.

Con lets his victim go, standing up straight as his taut body rises and falls rhythmically.

His neck twists.

He looks straight at me, and I at him.

The rain bounces aggressively off the ground between us as he stalks toward the door, coming straight for me.

The men part to let him through unhindered.

I stumble back and brace myself as he walks through the doorway, his sexy as fuck, yet dangerous body dripping wet.

A low growl leaves his chest as his wild eyes flick over me hungrily, and a throbbing delicious feeling aches between my legs.

I hardly know whether I want to fight him or fuck him.

My lips part to let out a small breath, and his eyes catch the subtle movement.

And it's then the dam bursts.

He races for me.

His solid body crashes against mine before his huge arms lock me in their iron grip. He lifts me clear off the ground, his hand gripping the back of my

□

neck, tangling in my hair as he pulls me forward to smash his lips against mine—

"Eden...."

All of a sudden, my senses jump back into my body with a startle, and my eyes find Con standing by the doorway, staring at me with a scowl on his face.

What the fuck just happened? Did I just drop off into a sexual daydream right in front of him? In front of this asshole?

I lift my hand to my head to feel that it's slightly damp. "Huh?" I ask in a daze.

He narrows his eyes, his glistening body dripping large water droplets onto the creaky floorboards.

"What do you want?" I ask more assertively, trying to push my confusing innermost thoughts aside.

"I said...I'm going to wash up. I'll take dinner in my bedroom," he states coldly.

"Fine," I answer, trying to maintain the same air of indifference, however, the truth is I can barely focus on anything I'm so damn flustered.

I turn around quickly, rushing back downstairs to the relative safety of the kitchens. I burst through the door and walk over to the wooden table, clinging to the edge tightly while squeezing my eyes shut. It's rare for me to have erotic dreams. I can't remember the last time I had one. I'm not exactly what you would call experienced in that area... Well, not since Erix, anyway. Immediately, I picture his handsome face smiling down on me the first time we made love. His gentle hand lifting to sweep a stray hair from my face.

The memory knocks the air out of me, and a sudden pang of guilt fills my heart. Even after all these years, it hurts. It hurts to remember our time together. To betray his memory by thinking about another man in that way. Especially a man like him.

"Elf, take these plates upstairs for dinner."

I snap my head to the side in surprise to see the two cooks staring at me.

Damn, I forgot they were fucking here! I swallow hard and wipe my sweaty palms against my shirt. "Oh? I thought I wasn't allowed to touch the food?"

They give each other a look indicating they have already discussed the matter.

"Seems the orders have changed. You better just get a move on," one of them growls before turning around to carry on spooning out the rest of the food.

I lift four plates, balancing them in my shaky arms before I begin to climb the stairs from the kitchen.

My ears fill with voices from the living room as the men take their usual seats around the table. Clearly, dinner etiquette and proper hygiene aren't exactly big priorities in this house. Some men have put shirts on while others just sit there. Wet and bare-chested. I begin setting the plates down, my mind too preoccupied to care.

"Did you like what you saw out there, elf?" Hunter asks jokingly, lifting a piece of bread from the center of the table. "I saw you watching."

"Watching was she?" Rocco snorts, shaking his head. "More like spying."

I roll my eyes in return. "Perhaps if you'd just let me go, you wouldn't have to worry about me spying on you."

"Hey, don't ask me, *Sweetie*. If I had my way, you wouldn't be here in the first place," he answers, his icy blue eyes staring into mine.

"She's serving us food now?" a man named William asks uncomfortably, directing his question to Zeke, who is sitting near the head of the table.

My eyes drift to Zeke, and he glances at me before shrugging nonchalantly. "As you can see."

"But I thought we discussed it and agreed that wouldn't happen? I don't want no one messing with my food!" William says defensively, looking me up and down with suspicion.

"Come on, Will. It's not like she can do much damage anyway," Hunter snorts, earning him a warning look from the other men at the table. "Who knows, maybe a sprinkling of rat poison will help spice this shitty food up!"

"That's not the point," William argues. "She hates us. How can we trust anything that she has prepared?"

Zeke casually tears off a piece of bread, leaning forward to place his elbows on the table. "Then don't eat," he answers simply, sticking the bread into his mouth.

William shakes his head in annoyance but doesn't say anything more. The tense interaction lingers in the air for a few moments before the men begin to speak again, changing the subject. I take the chance to turn on my heels and return to the kitchen to collect more plates.

"We've got the rest," one of the cooks says as I am about to fill my arms again. "You take this one to Conall's room."

☐

He hands me a plate and some cutlery while I stand there like an idiot, frozen on the spot.

How will I look him in the eye after what just happened?

"Hello? Wakey, fucking wakey, elf. Get a move on."

I snap out of it and make for those forbidden stairs once again.

Honesty

Eden

With my free hand, I knock on the door, tapping my foot on the floor nervously as I wait for a reply. There is none.

Shit.

I know he's in there, so perhaps he's still getting cleaned up. Maybe if I'm quick, I can be in and out before he even sees me.

I decide to take my chances, opening the door into the familiar bedroom. It looks and feels just as it did last night. Dark, warm, and strangely inviting compared to the rest of the house. Luckily, it seems I was correct in my assumption, and the room is empty with the bathroom door closed.

I head for the desk in a hurry, placing down the plate of food and laying the cutlery out beside it. I am just about to step away to make my escape when the bathroom door opens, releasing a cloud of steam into the air.

I stop dead as he walks into the room, one cloth towel wrapped around his waist while he rubs the hair on his head with another.

I clear my throat awkwardly, giving him a curt nod as I avoid looking at his naked torso. "Your food is on the table."

He stops what he's doing, placing the second cloth towel on the bed as he bobs his head in response.

I make for the door and am just about to reach it when he stops me. "What happened to you earlier?"

My stomach twists in knots in response to his question. There's no way on this earth that I'd admit the truth. Not to anybody, but least of all him.

"What do you mean?" I ask dismissively, spinning around to face him.

He takes a step forward, and his eyebrows knit together as he examines me, but he doesn't challenge me any further. "You watched us train...I'm curious to know what you think?" he then asks, walking away casually to his desk.

My shoulders relax when he lets the subject go while my eyes continue to avoid scanning his body at all costs. "I'm not sure why you'd care what I think?" I eventually snap back in reply.

He stares back at me, unimpressed, as he drags his chair out to take a seat. "Working at the palace, I would assume you've seen the Elven Guard train many times?"

The question immediately puts me on the defensive. "So?"

"So how do we compare?" he asks, not bothering to look up at me as he cuts a slice of steak. He leans back in his chair and watches me intently as he eats.

"It doesn't compare," I answer angrily. "You really think I'm going to tell you anything about the Elven Guard? About the palace? If that's why you are keeping me here, then you are wasting your time," I say passionately. "I'm not a traitor."

He places his fist on the table and nods his head slowly. "I gathered that."

I scrunch my brows. "You did?"

He shrugs before leaning forward to cut another piece of food. "Well, since we are now being honest with one another... I know that you have a higher station within the palace than you are letting on, and the fact that you haven't tried to use that to secure your release tells me something about you."

"And what's that?" I question.

"That you're loyal."

I nod my head, taking a deep breath. "It's not a bad thing," I say defensively.

"I never said that it was," he answers, taking another mouthful of food.

"Okay...since we are being honest, as you put it," I begin with narrowed eyes. "Why are you interested in the activities of the Elven Guard? Are you planning some sort of attack?"

He smirks slightly as he looks at me. "Do you believe an army of less than twenty wolves can take on the entire Elven Guard?" he asks, raising an eyebrow.

"There may be a small number of you here, but I'm not stupid. Who knows how many more of you are out there? If some wolves survived *The Culling*, then there could be hundreds by now for all we know."

He shakes his head. "Afraid not," he says casually. "Only us."

I stare at him as the unanswered questions run through my head. "Care to explain to me why?"

"We are a pack of men. I assume you know how breeding works?" he asks passive-aggressively.

I don't even bother to answer.

"Fine. You want to know why there aren't more of us?" he asks for confirmation.

"Yes."

"You already know the answer, Eden," he says, pushing the chair back to stand and walk toward me.

My body begins to tingle the closer he gets, but I do my best to ignore it completely. "I do?"

"The elves killed the rest of our people in *The Culling*, as you call it. Wiped an entire species out... just like that," he says, stopping in front of me.

"Yet here *you* stand," I hit back sarcastically.

"You think that it's some kind of joke?" he asks, his expression darkening. "The indiscriminate death of men, women and children? That's a joke to you?"

Flashes of the stage performance in Morween begin to flicker through my mind. The wolf child. The Elven towns being ransacked. My hazy memories of those dark days of the war. Memories of my aunt dying. Of our neighboring village being burnt to the ground. It makes me feel damn sick.

"No, of course I don't. Do you?" I ask, turning the question around on him. "Many innocents were killed in the fighting, Elven women and children included—"

"It's not the same," he snaps, jutting his face closer to mine.

"You don't know anything. You don't know what my people endured," I hit back angrily, staring into his stormy eyes. "You weren't there!"

"Well, that, Eden, is where you are wrong."

My eyes widen as confusion eclipses my anger. Wolves have a lifespan of around one hundred years, and the battle ended seventy years ago. If he were telling the truth, he would be nearing one hundred years old by now.

"You were there?" I ask in clear disbelief. "How can that be possible? You're lying."

"I don't lie, but perhaps you need to ask your Elven leaders that question. After all, it was them who left us here. Stranded in time," he states firmly, his eyes running over my face.

I open my mouth to retaliate, but I'm so blindsided that nothing comes out.

"I've known more pain and suffering than someone like you will ever comprehend. You look around this place and judge us, but you know nothing about what *we* have gone through. What we have lost. What do you know of real pain, elf?" he asks, his every word steeped in anger and disdain.

"You don't know a damn thing about me," I reply, matching his intensity with my own as Erix's image comes springing to the forefront of my mind once again. "I've lost in this life too—"

"But did you lose everyone?!" he interrupts in a rage, taking a threatening step forward as I begin to back away. "Did you lose your entire family? Every single last one of your friends? Every individual you had ever met in your lifetime?"

I cannot answer, and he knows it. I clamp my lips together as my heart pounds.

"Because I did," he snarls, aggressively stabbing his finger into his bare chest. "I lost it all. I lost it all because of fucking elves just like you," he finishes accusingly.

The hatred for my kind runs so deep that I can feel the anger radiate from him in waves. Waves threatening to drown me any minute if I don't get the hell out of here.

"Then maybe I'll do you a favor and stay out of your way, and you can stay out of mine," I whisper, tearing my eyes from his to barge past his shoulder.

He catches my wrist, and I tug on it fiercely.

"I can't do that," he says adamantly, his jaw tightening.

"And why is that?" I snarl in reply.

"Again... you know why," he answers before silence falls between us.

My breathing begins to speed up as his eyes stare into mine. His words all but confirm it. These strange conflicting emotions I feel towards him, the tension I feel every time he's around, he feels it too.

"Then let me go," I say determinedly. "Let me go free, and I'll forget this place ever existed. You'll have my word."

"Your word means *nothing* to me," he answers harshly, dropping my wrist.

I watch as he stalks back to his desk, taking a seat again. "Don't bother coming back for the plate. The room will be free for you to bathe shortly," he adds with icy cold dismissal.

I turn away from him without reply, making my way to the door.

"Midnight, Eden."

I close the door behind me, knowing that I don't have a single intention of coming back here tonight.

Mate

Conall

I sit there with my eyes firmly on my plate until I hear the door click shut behind her. "Fuck!" I groan, tossing the fork on the table and pushing the chair back. I take a few seconds to pace the floor, closing my eyes to try and regain my composure.

I lose it every time she's around, and I'm well aware of it. In fact, I fucking despise what her presence does to me. One hundred years on this earth, and I've never met a woman who does those things to me, who makes me forget what the hell I'm about to say, or who makes me feel so on edge.

I walk over to the fireplace and lean on the mantel with one hand as I stare at the flames.

What the fuck am I going to do about her?

I've been racking my brain for days and still haven't come up with the answer.

How could the moon goddess put me in this situation? Haven't I fucking sacrificed enough in this lifetime?

An elf as a mate... I've never heard of anything so ridiculous in all my life. Even when I was young, growing up with the rest of my pack, it was rare for wolves to be mated outside their own species. It wasn't unheard of, but I never knew anyone who was.

And now, even after everything, after all the shit we have been through, the Goddess decides to let this happen. If I didn't already believe that she had abandoned us, I sure as hell would believe it now.

An elf, for fuck sake!

I loathe the creatures with every fiber of my being; however irrational that might sound, I can't help it. For this reason, part of me wonders if it's all some fucking big mistake. If the sparks I feel when I touch her skin and the way her scent drives me wild with sex-crazed lust are just signs that I am indeed going crazy. After all, seventy years is a long time to live in isolation.

To live without connection. I'd like to think that's the case. That I'm just losing my damn mind, but every time I come face-to-face with her again, it only confirms the opposite.

I lift my hand and swipe it over my face. I've always been a man who is sure of himself. Who makes decisions and sticks to them no matter what anyone else thinks, but this situation is different.

Letting her go isn't an option. Sure, it gets rid of temptation on my part, but I can't afford to jeopardize the lives of my men. Not when we are now at this stage. Not when there is a slither of hope within our grasp. My men wouldn't allow it, and I wouldn't fucking blame them. They would rather see her dead than on her way back to Morween. However, I also know that killing her isn't an option either. It never was and never will be.

All that's left is for her to stay here. To live under this roof and partake in this grim reality that we call life. I already know that the pain of resisting her every damn day will be hard to bear. Especially when she feels this pull too, but no matter what, I won't back down. I will not betray the memory of all the people I have lost to satisfy my own sexual desires.

Because that's all it is.

Desire.

She's beautiful. An elf...she's a damn elf, but she's the most stunning woman I have ever seen. The soft lilac hue of her hair reminds me of the heather that used to surround this pack house back in its heyday. Back when I used to visit Lincoln here as a child. The silvery-purple color of her eyes can capture me in an instant, rendering me completely and utterly fucking useless. Then there is her attitude. Stubborn and headstrong, but oh so fearless and sexy. It turns me on against my better judgment.

Against my will.

Shit.

It's then that I remember that I need to make myself scarce. I don't particularly feel like going for a run; however, it might do me some good, and I know I can't be anywhere near her naked body right now. If I get too close, I'm not sure that I'd be able to stand it. That I'd be able to stop myself from taking her over and over again, making her scream my name, knotting her fingers in my hair and coming hard while she takes my aching, solid cock inside her.

"Con."

The knock on the door kicks me out of my forbidden fantasy, which is probably just as well.

"Wait," I answer, already knowing who it is. I walk over to the dresser and pull out a shirt and pants to put on.

After getting dressed, I call out for Zeke to come in.

"You're going for a run? At this hour?" he asks, eyeing me up and down as I sit on the edge of the bed to pull on my boots. I don't bother answering.

"Everything alright?" I ask, glancing up at him.

He shrugs his shoulders, placing his hands on his hips. "As predicted...they aren't happy. They think she's being granted too much freedom."

I shake my head from side to side and let out a breath before standing up to face him. "And what do you think?"

He snorts and throws me a smirk. "Since when have you cared what anyone else thinks?"

"True," I answer, heading for the door with him following behind. "But I'm asking anyway."

"Well, honestly, I think you were right in what you said earlier. If she is going to be here for the long haul, then we can't keep her locked in her room. It doesn't mean we shouldn't still keep an eye on her, though, Con. As you've noticed, she's got some fire."

I stop when we arrive in the empty hallway. "Are the men behaving around her?"

"There have been comments, but nothing she can't handle. None of them would dare lay a finger on her if that's what you mean," he states assuredly.

"Good. Keep an eye on her. I'm going out for a few hours."

He nods his head, accepting my command before his eyebrows crease.

"You think that's wise, Con? Henrick and Evan spotted an Elven patrol ten miles west of here only this morning. You know they are looking for her."

I shake off his concerns dismissively. "I'm not Mateo. I'll be fucking careful, at least."

He laughs a little as he nods his head. "You're not going to forgive the kid, are you?"

"For being fucking stupid? For putting us all in danger? No, I won't." I answer in annoyance.

"Why are they looking for her, Con?" he presses, looking at me with suspicious eyes. "If she's just a wood elf working in the palace, then surely they

□

wouldn't send a unit out searching for her."

I can't help the hint of protectiveness that swells within my chest. If any of the men in this place knew what I knew, if they guessed that she wasn't just some nobody, then you're damn right it would change things.

I look around and lower my voice before looking into his eyes. "It doesn't matter if she's a peasant girl, Zeke. The Elven Guard already knows that there are wolves in these woods. We saw to that. They don't want that information getting out. They will try to track her down to protect their secrets...it's just our job to make sure they don't get anywhere."

He nods in agreement, and I head for the stairs.

"You'll need to visit your contact again soon. We need those safeguards now more than ever."

"It's under control," I answer before changing the subject. "I want a patrol ready to go out in the morning for surveillance, and we might need to consider canceling tomorrow night—"

"Hey, hey, hey, no fucking way, Con," he answers, stopping dead in his tracks. "You cancel tomorrow night, I swear you'll have a fucking riot on your hands, and I'll be first in line," he grins.

I shake my head, knowing that he's right. "Fine. But don't fuck this up. Same precautions as always."

"You got it," he smiles widely, saluting me goodbye.

I continue my journey through the house and walk through the busy living room, not bothering to stop and talk to anyone. I rarely do, anyway.

When I open the door, I fill my lungs with the fresh evening air and head for the trees, determined to run off some of this pent-up energy that rages inside me.

* * *

I enter the quiet living room and look around to see that it's near enough empty except for Jarek, who is in his usual spot reading.

"Evening, Conall," he states, lowering his glasses to give me a nod.

I nod in return, my eyes finding the clock on the wall. Two minutes to midnight.

"Mateo is recovering well, by the way," Jarek says as I walk toward him, where he sits by the large bookcase. "I think he will be on his feet again by tomorrow, but then we all know that's probably only because he doesn't want to miss out on all the fun."

"Fine, that's good to know," I answer distractedly, lifting a glass from the table to pour myself a drink.

"The Emerdas sap was a good healer. I believe you saved him from a painful day indeed."

I knock the drink back in one, ignoring his insinuation. "How is your research going?" I ask, nodding toward the books on the small table by his side.

"Alright," he answers with a shrug. "The new ones that you acquired have been useful. It may have taken me seventy years, but I'd like to think I have reached pack doctor status by now," he chuckles.

"Good," I answer bluntly, my eyes returning to the clock. "I'll see you in the morning."

"Night, Con."

I head for the stairs, stalking toward my quarters. The run cleared my mind completely, and I feel more determined than ever. I've been through much worse things than resisting a little temptation. I *can* and *will* handle this.

I throw open the bedroom door and look around critically, walking into the bathroom to see it is undisturbed. "Goddess fucking help me," I seethe through gritted teeth, knowing she hasn't been here tonight.

She hasn't been in this room, which means she disobeyed me.

I charge back downstairs, heat rising around my neck when I take in the sight ahead of me. Four of my men standing in the hallway outside the communal bathroom, laughing like fucking little girls. My animal urge to rip their fucking heads off of their shoulders threatens to consume me, my rage boiling dangerously beneath the surface.

They hear me approach, standing up straight and to attention.

"Con—" Hunter begins before I cut him off.

"What the fuck are you doing here?" I snarl, taking them all by surprise.

Hunter's mouth opens, but he has no witty remark to make. He can see I'm not in the fucking mood.

"Nothing, we were just curious. You've got to admit it...an elf woman...it would be interesting to see," he states with a semi-joking smile.

☐

"All of you, fuck off. Now," I answer, looking between each man in turn.

"We didn't mean any harm. Honestly, I was just kidding around. We weren't planning on—"

I give him a look that tells him I'm not interested. Hunter lifts his hands in surrender, nudging Evan with his shoulder before they hurry off down the hallway.

Then I turn my attention to Rocco, leaning against the opposite wall.

Neither of us says anything. Instead, I stand in front of the bathroom door defensively, folding my arms over my chest as we stare each other down.

Eventually, he breaks first and takes a step forward. "You give this elf a lot of your attention," he says slyly, tilting his head slightly as he glares at me.

I narrow my eyes in return. "Leave."

"You know, some of us aren't quite on board with how you are choosing to handle this one, Conall," he says, shooting a glance to his buddy Samuel who is by his side as usual.

I lean in closer to look him directly in the eye. "If you don't like it, you know what you have to do."

I watch his jaw tighten, and he steps back in reluctant defeat. "Come on, looks like we won't see much of the elf tonight after all."

I watch them both in disgust as they leave, rounding the corner to disappear.

I unfold my arms and look down at my hands, which are bleeding from the pressure of my protruding claws, and I wipe them against my pants hurriedly.

Fucking hell...

It took everything in me not to kill the asshole. Goddess knows it's not the first time I've wanted to, and I'm sure it won't be the last.

I turn my head to look at the closed door, and a surge of anger rises within me again. I beat my fist against the door in rapid thumps.

"Hang on, damn it! I'm almost finished!" she calls back, clearly unaware that it's me behind the door.

I rattle the door again, and she doesn't bother to answer this time. Before I can help myself, I'm pressing on the handle to find that it's stuck in place. It appears she had the foresight to jam something in front of the door. At least, that's something.

A few seconds later, it clicks open behind me, and I swing around to see her standing there with a shocked look covering her face.

I flick my eyes down over her body, clad in my white shirt with her creamy legs on full display.

"Con? What the fu—"

I don't bother waiting for her to finish her sentence. I grab her roughly by the arm, lead her out of the bathroom, and back down the corridor, practically dragging her alongside me. My heart thuds in my chest as I scan the empty hallways, ensuring no one is around.

It's then that Mateo's bedroom door opens, and he sticks his head out curiously. "Get back in the fucking room now," I demand, pointing at him with my free hand.

He closes the door swiftly as I carry on toward her bedroom.

"How dare you touch me like this?! Let me go, you ASSHOLE!" she demands angrily as I open the door to drag her inside.

I let her go, slamming the door shut behind me.

"Who do you think you are?!" she questions, lifting her hand to her arm.

"When you are under this fucking roof, Eden, I'm your Alpha. You take orders from me."

She pushes her long wet hair out of her face. "HA!! You are no Alpha of mine!" she seethes, her narrow silvery-purple eyes filled with fiery rage.

We stare at each other for a few seconds as I back away towards the door.

"You'll bathe where I tell you to—"

"I will not!"

"Then every time you walk into that bathroom, I'll drag you back out again. Believe me. I will."

She swallows hard, folding her arms over her chest.

"Are we clear?" I ask in finality, my voice low and serious.

"Crystal," she snipes back.

Goddess knows how I do it, but I turn around without so much as a glance at her tempting body. I open the door and head back to my room.

Angry.

Horny.

And back to fucking square one.

☐

Downtime

Eden

"Shit!" I catch myself just in time before falling on my ass; however, my dangling legs accidentally kick over an old rusty mop bucket in the process. I hold still, wincing as the metal clangs against the stone floor. When the noise stops, I breathe a sigh of relief and try once again to open up the long, narrow window. "Come on...come on," I grit through my teeth, tugging the latch violently until it eventually gives way. "Yesss."

I use my upper body strength to pull myself onto the narrow window ledge, peering out at the overgrown grass. I then reach my hand forward to try to touch it with my fingertips, but instead of the cool, fresh earth, they are met with a solid invisible wall.

"Urggggg!!" I groan in annoyance, my head dropping in defeat.

Assholes!

I shuffle myself from the high ledge, dropping my dangling body back down to solid ground, looking down at my dusty clothes and patting them with my equally dusty hands.

Suddenly, the basement door swings open, and I jump in fright as a large figure appears in the doorway. "Eden?"

"Mateo? You're out of bed!" I say, grabbing the old bucket by my feet.

His eyes run over me carefully. "Yeah," he smirks, taking in my flustered state. "What are you doing in the basement? And why are you up so early?"

"Me? Uh, I'm just fetching another bucket. I want to get a good jump start on the day. Lots to do!"

He raises his eyebrow at me.

I'm possibly over-egging it a little. Acting has never been my strong suit, so I quickly change the subject. "So, how are your wounds?"

He follows behind me as we make the journey back to the kitchens.

"I'm still fucking sore, don't get me wrong, but I'll be okay. Our wolves help us heal."

I place the bucket on the floor and swing around to face him. It's always intrigued me how a wolf's healing ability works. I cannot deny that I would be thoroughly interested to learn more. "Fascinating...how long does it take for your wolf to heal you?"

"Depends on the severity of the wound, I suppose," he answers, sitting at the wooden table. "These might take another two to three days to disappear completely."

"Amazing," I whisper truthfully, walking over to the sink to wash my hands. "Shouldn't you still be in bed recovering if you aren't one hundred percent better yet?"

"I'll be fine. I'm well enough."

"Okay...."

Then, the two huge chefs make their way into the kitchen. "Morning," one of them mutters before walking to the stove to start the breakfast.

I stare at him in utter disbelief. "Were you talking to me?"

He glances over his shoulder at me in annoyance. "Who else would I be talking to?!" he snaps, returning his attention to the job at hand.

I look at Mateo, who stifles a scoff, shaking his head from side to side. It's then that I realize how good he looks this morning. His shirt is clean and looks more pressed than usual. His messy, curly, wayward hair has been styled carefully. Heck, even the great oafs next to me have combed their hair this morning too.

Am I missing something?

"So, what are the plans today?" Mateo asks.

I shrug my shoulders. "Perhaps I'll go for a run down by the lake. Head to the market to buy some fresh fruit. I might even have time to stop in and visit some friends for a quick drink and a chit-chat!" I answer sarcastically.

He holds his hands up defensively with a grin. "Okay, okay. I deserved that." He stands up to make himself a cup of tea, and I help the great oafs prepare breakfast.

Sure, they watch my every move like overgrown hawks, but I have to admit that it's nice to be doing something that I at least enjoy to some degree. Back in Azealea, Grandma and I would cook together all the time. It's one of the many things I missed about home after moving to Morween. I also discover that the two burly chefs have names! Anton and Neville. So, all things considered, it hasn't been my worst morning here despite my disappointing failure to escape.

I carry the plates of scrambled eggs upstairs, convincing Mateo to help me. As soon as I walk into the living room, I can tell there is a definite buzz in the air. These men, who are typically so pissed off and mad at the world, actually seem to be in good spirits for a change.

"About time, elf! We are starving over here!" Henrick states, moving his cup out of the way as I lay down his plate.

"Whatever," I mutter, continuing around the busy table.

"Matty, I didn't know you were such a good waitress." Hunter laughs, mocking Mateo as he places down some knives and forks.

"Yeah, yeah, just being a decent person. You assholes should try it sometime," he laughs.

Some of the men laugh in reply, and I can't help looking at Mateo with a grateful smile. "Thank you," I mouth at him subtly, causing him to wink back.

Just then, I hear footsteps from behind me and turn around to see Conall descending the staircase. Our eyes meet immediately, but I look away quickly, clearing my throat as I continue serving.

The buzz around the table quietens substantially, many of the men fixing their game face back in place as their leader takes a seat. From the way they watch him intently, I get the feeling that this situation is a rarity.

"Con, it's good of you to join us this morning," Jarek says genuinely.

I hazard a glance to the side to see Conall's eyes still on me for a brief second before he directs his gaze elsewhere. "Has the patrol already set off?" he asks, leaning back in his chair to lift a glass of water to his lips.

"Zeke, William and Rocco left a couple of hours ago," Jarek answers dutifully.

Con nods, his serious expression remaining fixed in place.

"I get the feeling they will be cutting patrol short today, don't you agree, lads?" Hunter jokes, looking around at the others knowingly.

"What's going on today?" I ask innocently, placing the jug of water down in the center of the table.

I watch in confusion as they look at each other like naughty little boys.

"I don't think it's your scene, elf. You might want to turn in early tonight," Hunter replies, pointing his fork at me before taking a spoonful of the hot eggs.

"Who knows, maybe she'll want to join in," Henrick grins, wriggling his eyebrows.

"That's enough." Conall cuts in abruptly, ceasing the banter with little more than a stern look.

Everyone looks at one another awkwardly, and I step away from the table in irritation. With so many unknowns already, it bothers me not knowing what is happening in this damn house today.

"Uhh, the eggs are fucking awesome this morning. Does this have anything to do with you, elf?" Henrick asks.

Just as I'm about to reply, Mateo interrupts first. "Her name is Eden," he says calmly.

The table grows quiet yet again, and I can't help but notice how Conall stares at Mateo in disapproval. I guess he would prefer it if everyone remained an asshole in my presence since it's the same tact he has adopted thus far.

"Okay..." Henrick concedes, looking at me and pointing at the eggs again. "This was you, Eden?"

I shrug a little as I begin to head back toward the kitchen. "Must be all the rat poison, huh?" I state with a devious smile.

Hunter laughs and claps his hands together as I disappear downstairs.

* * *

The rest of the morning flies by, and I keep myself busy washing some sheets from the men's bedrooms per Zeke's request. Most of them seem like they haven't been washed this side of the decade.

Gross.

After soaking them thoroughly, Mateo and a few others take them outside to be dried by the warm spring sun that shines brightly in the clear sky. I can't help but stare out the window at them in sheer jealousy. I'd do almost anything right now to feel the breeze catch my hair or the sun's rays touch my skin. The thought alone is enough to change my mood entirely.

"You miss the outdoors?"

I turn to see Jarek sitting in his usual chair over by the bookcase. It surprises me that he is trying to strike up a conversation, but with the loneliness I now suddenly feel, I am grateful for it. "Yes. I do," I answer honestly, wandering closer to him.

He nods with a hint of sympathy before his eyes return to his book. I tilt my head slightly to read the title.

'Medicinal Purposes of Vevilium Plants'

"Good choice," I compliment, nodding my head toward it.

He glances up at me over his glasses. "You have read it?"

I nod, folding my arms across my chest. I don't intend to give *too* much away about myself, but the temptation to talk about my passion in life is difficult to pass up. "I like learning about plants. It's kind of a hobby of mine." I lie.

"I find them very interesting myself. I have discovered that there is never an end to what you can learn about them."

"Oh, I know." I grin. "My grandma, though, she knows just about everything there is to know, trust me. Vevilium plants are one of her specialties."

"She sounds like an interesting woman."

I nod my head with a small smile.

"Eden."

I glance up at the balcony to see Conall looking down at me from above.

"Can I have a word?"

"I've got to clean the—"

"Now," he cuts in rudely.

Before I can respond, I see him heading to my room.

Fantastic.

I wave Jarek goodbye and head upstairs, nerves coursing through me the closer I get to him. He stands with his arms folded, looking away while waiting for my arrival.

"Yes?" I ask with a hint of attitude left over from his shocking behavior last night.

His eyes find mine, and we scowl at each other with equal frostiness. "You'll take the rest of the day off. No more chores," he states plainly.

"What? But I still have to redress the beds—"

"I'll have it taken care of."

"Then there's dinner—"

"There won't be dinner tonight. Take the evening off."

I frown, waiting for the catch.

"My room is empty. Make sure you use it this time." He gives me a stern glare before turning his back to walk away.

It seems strange that I would be given the night off, considering these men seem to have gotten used to me waiting on them hand and foot, but I guess I shouldn't complain.

I watch as Conall disappears downstairs, and I decide that if I am going to use his room to bathe, it might as well be now while I still have daylight on my side.

* * *

I pull a clean shirt over my body and tie it around the middle using some rope. It is beginning to get dark now, and the glow of the fire illuminates the cozy room around me. I walk along the edge of his bed, gently running my fingers across it. My eyes are then drawn to the bookshelf over in the corner, and I make toward it to have a closer look. Most of the books are centered on the history of the wolf species. I select one at random, its leather cover showing its advanced age. I blow off some dust and open it up to look inside.

Chapter One- The Moon Goddess

Of course, I've heard of her, but in Elven culture, we worship a variety of deities—the most important of all being the Goddess of Nature. I become so engrossed in reading the first paragraph that I barely notice when I sit on the edge of the bed. I must admit that it feels so good to feel something more luxurious against my skin. My old bedsheets are not exactly the most comfortable after all.

I decide to throw caution to the wind, wriggling myself back to rest my head on the pillow and stretch my legs out. The action makes me smile a little before I realize how pathetic that is. I turn my attention back to the book and continue reading.

Chapter Two- Mates

□

Nymph

I stretch my arms out above my head lazily before yawning. Opening one eye at a time, the realization of what I have done hits me like a ton of bricks. "Oh fuck!" I mutter, looking around the empty room frantically.

Did I fall asleep here? How could I be so stupid?

I quickly bounce onto my feet and gather my dirty work clothes into my arms when suddenly, the sound of a woman's laugh greets my ears.

I abandon the pile of clothes and rush to the door, heading down the corridor with eager anticipation. The closer I get to the center of the house, the louder the sound becomes, and I can now identify more than one woman's voice through the mixture of male guffaws.

What the fuck is going on?!

There are no female wolves! Mateo and Conall both confirmed as much!

I arrive in the hallway overlooking the living room and tiptoe forward to peer over the balcony at the scene below. My eyes widen in shock at the sight before me.

The Alpha men are spread out around the room. My gaze first locks on a group of men sitting on the sofas around the roaring fire, howling with laughter as one of them tells a very vulgar joke. This isn't a rare occurrence, but what takes me by surprise are the scantily-clad women that hang over them.

Nymphs.

A very beautiful all-female species and one I have always found highly interesting. I've never met one in person, of course. They were thrown out of Morween territories hundreds of years ago upon the ruling of an old Elven queen. It is said that she grew tired of the attention the beautiful creatures would attract from the high elf men, particularly her husband, King Tiewin. It is said that he grew so fond of one nymph that he threw himself to his death from the top of the palace after she was banished from the kingdom.

Since then, they have lived in the distant mountains. Their scorn for the Elven race is well known and, in this case, highly justified.

I examine each one curiously in detail. They all have various hair, skin and eye colors; however, each shares the same desirable feminine allure. Luscious lips, twinkly eyes, bodies that seem to curve and dip in all the right places, and, above all else, a bizarre serene quality.

The giant burly men are like putty in their hands. Their eyes glued to the women as they move around the room. Some are seated in the men's laps, fawning over them giddily, running their hands over their chests and through their hair. While others stand behind their chosen Alpha male, rubbing his shoulders attentively. Some men even have two women or more catering to their every whim!

My eyes drift outward where other men are scattered around, sitting on high-backed chairs. Most are either drinking or smoking a cigar, but almost all have a woman already in their lap or a woman delighting them with some sort of tempting dance.

"Pour me another drink, Sweetheart," Rocco orders demandingly, watching his nymph as she sashays away to fulfill his request.

Hunter seems to already be in the midst of a full-on make-out session with his chosen woman, who straddles his body in her tiny pink negligee that barely reaches past her pert buttocks. I stare at their interaction for way longer than I probably should. My attention caught by how his hands reach into her hair and how she grinds herself gently against his crotch. I'm just not used to seeing such sexuality on full display; my naturally curious nature can't help but observe. The sound of a loud woman's voice then meets my ears, and I glance to the fireplace once again to see a slightly older woman laughing heartily with a glass of liquor in her hand. She is more modestly dressed than the rest, but her clothing is made of expensive silks and velvets.

Is she their Madam of sorts?

After looking around a little more, I spot Mateo at a table playing cards while a large cigar hangs out of his mouth. I tilt my head as I examine the blonde beauty who rubs his shoulders, watching as she periodically leans down to whisper in his ear or land gentle kisses against his neck. He looks highly impressed by the whole thing. In fact, every single one of these men are on cloud nine right now.

Suddenly it all makes sense. The combed hair, the jovial spirits, and, dare I say, the clean sheets.

I find myself wondering how often this sort of thing happens. I would have thought it would be dangerous for the wolves to expose themselves in such a way, but then again, I doubt that the nymphs would lift a single finger to help the Elven Guard. I'm pretty sure the long-standing banishment burned any chances of that.

I walk along the hallway, still staring at the scene, when it dawns on me that I have yet to see Conall in all of this. I stop and examine the men again. Everyone is accounted for. Hell, even Zeke is currently being delighted by three nymphs unbuttoning his shirt with gleeful enthusiasm.

Surely Conall wouldn't miss this? Would he?

I am about to enter my room when another sudden question arises.

How the hell did these nymphs get inside the house?!

I rush back to the balcony, and my eyes find the closed door as a pang of excitement bubbles up in my stomach. Perhaps these horny assholes dropped the safeguards which enchant this house. They would have to, surely, to allow all of these women to enter freely!

A renewed sense of determination settles over me, and I instantly decide to investigate. I head for the stairs, walking confidently into the center of the room. I see a few of the nymphs look my way, their pretty faces scrunching in a mixture of confusion and disapproval. Luckily for me, most of the men are oblivious to my presence which is just how I need them right now. I wander over to the cards table and watch in amusement as Mateo shakes off the blonde nymph attached to his shoulders. "Eden... I, uh, thought you had gone to bed?"

"I'm about to, but I thought I'd grab something to eat first."

"Oh, do you want some help?" he asks to the annoyance of his petite admirer.

"Nope, I can handle it." I smile. "You have fun now."

He swallows carefully before nodding and lifting the cards that Jarek has just dealt.

I continue my wander through the room, my body quivering just a little as I take in the erotic scenes. The closer up I am, the more intense it all becomes, and I find myself more than a little distracted.

I scold myself internally, reaching the stairs for the kitchen and rushing down.

As soon as I arrive, I run over to the kitchen counter and haul myself up on top, reaching up to open the narrow window. For just one second, I believe that this could be it. For one second, I genuinely believe that freedom is within my grasp. But the notion is ripped away from me as quickly as I came. The invisible wall remains in place. As impenetrable as ever.

"NO!" I screech as tears sting the back of my eyes. I close the window and return to the kitchen floor, sitting at the table in hopeless despair.

Just then, I hear footsteps coming from the stone staircase. "Oh...hello..."

My eyes meet with those of a nymph, and we stare at each other for a second in mutual curiosity.

"Uh, are you okay?" I ask, standing up to face her.

"Yes, I am, thank you," she answers in a soft, delicate voice. "I have been sent by Madam Piffnel to retrieve some more alcohol for the Alphas,"

"Ahh," I answer, smiling in return. "Well, I can give you a hand?"

"I'd like that," she beams back.

I nod toward the storage cupboard, and she follows behind me, her red eyes giving me a thorough examination.

"Is everything okay?"

"You are an elf, yes?"

"Yes."

"You have very full breasts, and your bone structure is sublime," she comments kindly.

"Ohh," I reply, laughing a little in shock. "Thank you, you are very beautiful yourself."

"I know!" she nods, accepting my compliment as I lean into the cupboard to pick up a bottle of home-brewed alcohol.

"Here. They do go through this stuff,"

"Yes, aren't they wonderful?!" she gushes enthusiastically. "We look forward to visiting the Den of Alphas every three months. It is truly a delight!"

I raise my eyebrow but decide to keep my opinions to myself. "Erm, well, I'm glad you're having fun..."

"I was, although it is time for most of us to leave," she states in disappointment.

"You're leaving now?" I ask interestedly, closing the cupboard door.

"Midnight, yes. Each man will choose his woman to spend the night with him, and Madam Piffnel will take the rest of us home. She will return for the

□

other women in the morning!" she answers brightly, turning around to head back toward the stairs.

My mind starts ticking over like crazy. If these women are leaving, then perhaps I can go with them! All I have to do is figure out how to blend in!

Then, the woman turns to me again, her small hand outstretched toward mine. "It was nice to meet you!"

I can barely form a response. I'm too busy scanning over her in a panic.

Her body is clad in a tiny, white lacy dress covered by an equally tiny, white silk robe. The pure color contrasts greatly against her mane of striking bright, red, wavy hair.

It's then that my eyes settle on it. My savior. The damn lifeline that I have been waiting for.

A pretty red rose hanging out of the little pocket on her silky robe.

Mine

Eden

The nymph follows my line of sight as I stare at the rose, touching it gently with her hand. "Do you like it?"

"Yes," I whisper in reply.

She smiles at me kindly as she pulls the rose out. I take it from her hands and examine its velvety soft petals with my fingertips.

It's a long shot. A total and utter long shot, but I know that it's something that I just have to try. My eyes return to the nymph, now staring at me with a worried expression. "Is everything okay?"

Without delay, I pounce on top of her, wrestling her weak, unsuspecting body to the ground as she squeals in fear. I clamp my hand over her mouth while reaching around the floor with the other. Frantically, I grab the edge of the rusty metal bucket and smack it against her head with moderate force. Her struggling stops, and I look down at her still body guiltily. "I'm so so so sorry!" I whisper breathlessly, dragging myself back up onto my feet. "Please forgive me! I'm so sorry!"

I look around the kitchen and stop at the cupboard. Gripping her hand, I drag her toward to stuff her inside. I gently undress her, pulling off her white, lacy dress to expose her body. Guilt threatens to stop me, but I know I must carry on. She'll wake up in a couple of hours with a sore head. By then, I will be long gone, and she can leave with the rest of the women! She'll be okay.

I remove my baggy shirt and pull it over her body before dressing myself in her very revealing attire instead. I also put on her high-heeled shoes, wobbling a little before I find my balance.

I take a second to close my eyes and catch my breath. If the illusion that my mother taught me is going to work in the slightest, then I will need every ounce of energy and concentration that I have. I pick up the rose and hold it in my cupped hands, letting its energy fill me up from the tips of my toes. In my mind's eye, I picture the nymph before me. The red color of her irises, the bright hue of her red hair, her alabaster, buttery-soft skin. I conjure the image in my head and hold onto it for dear life. As the illusion falls into place, I feel my body begin to tingle and spark, and I wait as patiently as I can before opening my eyes to examine the outcome.

I stare at the nymph lying peacefully on the floor and then down over my body. My skin tone has lightened a little, and my hair has turned a fiery shade of red.

"Yes!" I exclaim excitedly, closing the cupboard door and locking it behind me. I run over to the sink and pull out a silver platter, using it as a mirror to examine my face. It's not a total match, but it's enough to be convincing! My hands begin to shake as I contemplate what is to come next.

You can do this. I encourage myself sternly. *You need to do this.*

I turn around and head over to the stairs, bending down to grab the bottle of alcohol on the way. I carefully navigate the narrow staircase, my heart thudding in my chest as I enter the busy living room again.

"There you are, Rose! Do hurry along now, girl! The men are waiting!"

I nod my head anxiously, making my way to the fireplace. Madam Piffnel watches as I approach, and for a second, I wonder if I have been caught out already.

"Didn't I say to hurry, girl? Come on now! Pour these handsome men a drink."

"Of course, Madam Piffnel," I answer in my most pleasant voice.

I glance to the side to see Evan, a glass nestled in his outstretched hand, as he looks at me expectantly. I pull the top off the bottle and begin to pour, my nerves making the bottle rattle off the rim of the glass just a little. He eyes me carefully but doesn't say a word, only nods in thanks before he goes back to showering his chosen nymph with passionate kisses.

I make my way around the group, filling up the glasses of each man with precision. I know that I can't afford to fuck this up.

Just then, Mateo walks over casually to take an empty seat, and my heart skips a damn beat. If anyone were to see through this illusion, it would be him.

"Rose!" Madam Piffnel calls out authoritatively, causing me to swing around in surprise.

"Uh, yes?"

She looks at me with wide eyes, clearly annoyed for some reason. "Won't you see to this, Alpha?"

"Oh, yes," I answer, walking over to Mateo with all the courage I can muster.

Play the part, Eden… you have to play the damn part! My consciousness screams internally.

I lift my chin upward and try to inject more confidence into my demeanor. Mateo watches me approach, his eyes running up the length of my body hungrily before settling on my face. I give him a playful smile before I walk around behind him, rubbing his shoulders gently. His blonde nymph from earlier walks over to join us, settling herself down on his lap.

The conversation continues, and I'm thankful I am no longer the center of attention. I steal a moment to glance up at the clock above the fireplace.

With any luck, Madam Piffnel will soon announce that it's time to leave, and I'll be out of here without a hitch.

"Well, gentlemen…we will now leave you to enjoy your night!" Madam Piffnel states happily, downing the rest of her wine in one go. "I know you have all chosen wisely from my beautiful ladies!"

There is a hearty chorus of approval as the unchosen nymphs begin to say their goodbyes, kissing the cheeks of the Alpha men and their fellow ladies alike. I join in the act, playing my role well as I bend down to land a gentle kiss on Mateo's cheek and a further kiss on his blonde plaything.

"Come on now, ladies! Chop chop! The Alphas have many plans, I am sure."

The room comes alive as some of the burly men scoop up their giggling women to haul them off toward the bedrooms, and Madam Piffnel begins to gather the rest of us together to head for the exit.

My heart thumps in my chest as I watch a half-dressed Zeke head over to the doorway, waving his hand over it and muttering an inaudible incantation. He opens the door, and the fresh night air blows through the room to waft against my skin.

I can practically taste freedom! I grow giddy with both excitement and sheer, desperate relief. The nightmare is now over. Once I'm past this threshold, I can leave this place forever. Forget it, and never, ever look back!

"I shall meet you tomorrow, Alpha Zeke? To come back for my ladies?"

"Of course, Madam Piffnel. Until tomorrow," he answers as she leans in to kiss his cheek.

"Excellent! Have a delightful eve—"

"WAIT."

The rough voice cuts through the chatter, bringing the entire room to a complete standstill.

Shit.

I blink quickly, turning around with the rest of the nymphs to look back into the house.

There he stands. Silent and stoic as he looks over the crowd of women.

"Oh, Alpha Conall! How wonderful of you to come along this evening!" Madam Piffnel gushes in surprise. "I am so pleased to see you again!"

He glances at her briefly and nods before his eyes make their way back to examine us.

"Will you be choosing Alpha?" Madam Piffnel asks curiously as Conall steps forward, ignoring her. "Ladies! Make a line immediately!"

The women all begin to giggle excitedly and do as they are asked, fluffing up their hair and patting down their tiny negligees in preparation. I shuffle into place between two gorgeous women, my heart racing in my chest as he begins to make his way down the line of ladies, casting his eyes over each one slowly.

I wait with bated breath as he draws nearer, his honey-colored eyes finally reaching me and carefully drifting over my entire body.

Shit, shit, shit.

My heart fucking stops in my chest.

I've never been so nervous in my whole damn life.

Then his eyes shift to the next woman as he continues walking down the line.

I am about to breathe a sigh of relief when he suddenly stops, turning his head to look straight into my eyes.

My quivering body grows tense and still, as he turns around and walks back, coming to a stop directly in front of me. We stare at each other, and just like that, I am pulled into his orbit once again.

Unable to escape him.

Unable to break free from the bizarre, inexplicable connection that we share.

The silent room watches as he lifts his hand to envelop mine in his tight grasp, leading me forward to stand directly in front of his muscular chest.

"This one," he says in a dangerously low voice that makes my core tighten. "Tonight, this one is mine."

Deception

Eden

Walking across this silent living room is one of the longest walks I have ever had to take. Every single soul is staring at me. Or perhaps I should say, staring at us.

The grip Conall has on my hand can only be described as iron-tight. I try to wriggle my fingers subtly to loosen his grasp, but it only makes the situation worse. His large hand squeezing my fingers almost painfully.

I glance at him from the corner of my eye to see his sights are firmly focused on the staircase in front of us. He doesn't once look at me, and I have to ask myself why.

Rose is a beautiful nymph.

Isn't he pleased with his choice?

Whatever the reason, it does help a little not to have his penetrating gaze burning through me right at this very second as I try to collect my thoughts.

"Yes, Con!" Hunter encourages enthusiastically as we pass by him and his raven-haired nymph. "I knew someone would catch his eye," he whispers to William, who is watching us with interest, a glass of whiskey in his hand.

The living room comes to life when we reach the top of the staircase. The remaining Alphas rush to their bedrooms, and Madam Piffnel declares her departure again. Con and I walk along the corridor hand in hand, and I can't help but stare as she takes her leave, ushering the unchosen nymphs outside into the moonlit evening. My heart completely sinks at the sight. So close and yet so fucking far! All because of this asshole...

I take another covert look in his direction to see that he is also watching Madam Piffnel leave the house. His unreadable eyes then turn their attention to me, burning into my skin. I pretend not to notice, instead looking straight ahead as we pass the noisy bedrooms.

A chaotic yet extremely erotic mixture of uninhibited sounds linger in the hallway. Screams of euphoric delight. Whimpers of pure satisfaction.

☐

And delicious moans so sensuous that they send a shiver running up my spine.

It's then that I realize the full scale of my current situation. He chose Rose— he chose *me* for this reason. To bring him pleasure. To cater to his every whim. To hand my body over to him freely, allowing him to do whatever he desires with it. The prospect leaves me both alarmed and disturbingly intrigued all at the same time.

Can I keep up this illusion until morning?

Do I still have a shot at this?

How far am I willing to go to secure my freedom?

The decision is not easy, and I find myself at a loss regarding what I should do next.

We reach the forbidden stairs, and he gestures for me to go ahead first. My heels click against the rough stone steps as the sounds of the erotic chorus accompanying our journey here disappear. We now find ourselves in total silence. I stop at the bottom of the hallway, my eyes fixated on the closed door ahead. My breath hitches when I feel his body press against my back gently. "It's the room at the end," he says in a dangerously calm voice. I nod, feigning ignorance as I try to ignore the wave of nerves that shake me to the center of my being.

This is it. Decision time.

If I'm going to confess, I'd better do it now.

I take a few steps forward, pulling myself together as quickly as possible. I fix a determined look on my face and straighten off my shoulders.

I am *not* a quitter.

Whatever happens, I will find a way to keep this fight alive.

Deception is not a game for the faint of heart. I must be strong. I must be unbreakable. I must do whatever it takes...

When I reach the door, I twist the knob to let myself in. Everything is just as I left it a short time ago. My eyes find the abandoned pile of clothes on the floor and the book I was reading still lying open on the bed.

Fuck. I forgot all about them.

The door clicks shut behind me, and I turn just in time to face him head-on.

Neither of us says a word. His eyes narrow slightly.

Shit.

94

Panic settles over me, and I know then that I must commit to the act. If this is going to work, then despite my nerves, I'll have to be the most convincing nymph anyone could ever lay eyes on. I let a slow smile spread across my face and bring my hand up to brush it through my thick mane of red curls teasingly. I shake them out, flicking them around until tousled. He watches my every move intently, his now dark eyes filled with unmistakable want.

"How about a drink, *Alpha*?" I ask in my most seductive tone.

I immediately surprise myself with the sound of my own fake confidence. The words hardly seem as though they are coming from my own mouth!

Maybe they aren't at all. Perhaps these are not the words of Eden but those of Rose, the Alpha's dedicated servant for one night and one night only.

Conall nods before lifting his hand from his pocket to point to a bottle of amber liquid on his desk. I giggle playfully, swaying my hips from side to side as I wander over to pour him an overly generous glass.

Perhaps I can stall him long enough to get him incredibly drunk?

The thought crosses my mind, but I'm not so sure that Conall is the type of man to let himself get too inebriated in the first place. I kick off my heeled shoes and tiptoe over the floorboards toward him, staring into his eyes as I hand over the drink.

"Here you go, Alpha," I simper, fluttering my eyelashes.

He tilts the glass to me in thanks, lifting it to his lips to take a drink. I watch carefully as he swallows, the rugged stubble on his handsome face hypnotizing me momentarily. He then holds the glass out insistently, and I take it from him, my fingers lightly brushing against his in the process. The brief contact sends a pleasurable ripple racing over the surface of my skin, but I ignore it. Keeping my wits about me will be necessary. Especially if I am to come up with my next move anytime soon.

"Thank you." I smile, lifting the drink to take a sip. The strong alcohol burns my throat, warming my cheeks even more so than they are already.

He watches me closely, and then he speaks. "You seem nervous."

My eyes widen slightly in response to his observation. Damn.

"Me? Only a little, Alpha," I answer, biting the edge of my lip. "Perhaps it is because you are the leader... I do not wish to let you down," I answer, hoping that my lie is convincing.

I take another sip of the burning liquid and pout at him coyly for good measure.

He nods, taking the glass back from me. He takes another drink before placing it down on a nearby table. "What is your name, nymph?" he asks curiously, his eyebrows knitting together.

"Rose," I answer without hesitation.

"Hmm..." his gaze lowers to my chest, causing me to pause. "I should have guessed," he says, reaching for my white satin robe.

He plucks the fresh flower from my pocket and holds it between us as he examines it carefully. I swallow down a bubble of wayward nerves. Keeping the rose close to me is vital. Especially if I must keep this illusion going for longer than expected.

"Beautiful," he states, tearing his eyes away from the flower to look back at me.

Fuck.

I feel my temperature rise, a long-forgotten ache beginning to radiate between my thighs. The feeling is unwanted and unwelcome, but I cannot control it. My body reacts to him of its own accord, and there is nothing I can do to stop it.

He tucks the flower in his back pocket, his gaze then drifting down over my body. I stand there as still as a statue as his fingers silently reach out for the knot of the belted white robe. My chest begins to rise and fall, but still, I don't dare to move. His skilled fingers make light work of the job, and the robe tumbles open freely to reveal the tiny white negligee underneath. I hear a low, almost inaudible grunt come from his chest before he lifts his hands to slide the soft material down my arms. It falls in a gentle heap by my feet.

His eyes travel back up my body slowly to meet mine, and he waits. He waits patiently for my next move.

I focus on keeping my hands steady as I reach for the buttons on his shirt, unhooking each one, in turn, to uncover the hard, sculpted body beneath. My fingers brush lightly against the grooves of his solid, warm abdomen before I drift them over his chest to push the black material from his broad shoulders. Still, his eyes remain focused on my face. His searing gaze doing nothing to douse these strange, confusing feelings that now rack my body, setting every nerve ending alight.

The shirt falls to the floor to join the white silk robe.

The tension between us is almost too much to bear, and eventually, I take a small step back, disguising my uncomfortableness for passing curiosity.

"You have a wonderful room, Alpha. Was this always your home?" I ask, wandering to the fireplace to watch the flickering flames dancing sensually.

"No. The house belonged to someone I knew a long time ago."

"Oh?" I question, glancing at him over my shoulder. "And where is this person now?"

"Gone," he answers plainly.

I examine his serious face, knowing now that this house has more significance than he cares to let on.

"I see," I state, continuing to wander around the room. I slowly head over to the bookcase, running my fingers along the dusty spines. "Have you read these books?" I ask, purposely stalling, but at the same time interested to hear his response.

He nods, and I watch as he walks to the bed, picking up the book I carelessly left lying there earlier this evening. My chest tightens as he holds it open, examining the page.

"Tell me, nymph...do you know much of wolves?" he asks, closing the book over in his hand.

I shake my head a little and giggle. "Only what I have learned here, Alpha,"

He nods, walking over to join me. I stay perfectly still as he stands by my side, reaching up to replace the book on the shelf.

"Then let me enlighten you further..." he murmurs in a hushed tone.

My mouth opens just a little, but I have no words. He gestures his hand toward the bed, and I gulp.

Part of me wants to throw in the towel right now. Stop this charade before it passes the point of no return. But then there is a more dominant part of me that refuses to back down. A part of me that willingly accepts his challenge.

I walk forward slowly, stopping when my thighs graze against the red, thick material of the bedspread.

I do not need to watch his approach. I can feel his every move in the air that sparks between us. I close my eyes, and his bare chest presses against the skin of my back. He feels so warm. So devilishly inviting that I cannot bring myself to move. His hands gently peel the straps of the lacy dress from my shoulders one by one, allowing it to slip down further. My hardened nipples poking through the sheer material as his hands reach for my breasts, grasping them roughly. A long breath leaves my lungs in response. Oh my....

I then feel his hand lift to brush my hair to one side, his hot breath fanning against the tingling skin of my neck as he leans inward. "You see, nymph, wolves are both equally cursed and blessed with a mate," he states lowly, his voice like smooth, dripping honey pouring down the spine of my arched back.

"A mate...who belongs to no one but them," he continues, his hands now resting on my waist as his nose touches the tender spot below my ear. "A mate...who is destined to be theirs forever."

I gasp a little as his hands grip the smooth material of the negligee, tugging it upward at a painstakingly slow pace.

"Theirs to kiss...theirs to touch...theirs to claim...theirs to fuck."

The bundle of nerves I feel now mingle in perfect harmony with the lust that clouds my judgment, creating the perfect storm of sheer wanton desire and indescribable need.

My head leans against his chest, my breathing quickening as the silk material rises toward my midriff upon his demand.

"You see, the thing about wolves, nymph, is that they would know their mate anywhere."

His nose grazes the skin of my neck before his lips press against me.

An accidental moan escapes my lips on contact. He pulls me tighter against his body, his hard cock now pressing against my ass. I can't help but grind desperately against him.

"Her scent calls out to him. Filling him with so much fucking unbelievable need that it drives him to the brink of insanity."

His lips touch my neck again, this time with more delicious pressure and vigor.

I whimper in ecstasy, every inch of my body blazing with fire as he slides his finger down my soaking wet slit.

"Con...."

"To touch her skin...to touch her incredible body...is to touch the doors of Elysium...of paradise itself."

My breath gets stuck in my throat as his firm but tender touch sends shockwaves through my body, from the tips of my toes to my fingertips. I find myself reaching one hand down to cover his as he fondles my pussy.

Caressing it.

Stroking it.

Worshipping it.

"A wolf always knows his mate," he continues, his pace quickening as he circles the small bud over and over again teasingly.

"He knows every move that she makes."

Without warning, his finger pushes inside me, and I groan in a mixture of delight and delirious need.

"He knows every fucking sound that leaves her lips."

His other hand tugs my hair to twist my head.

I stare up into his eyes, writhing against his hardness as he pumps his finger inside me.

"He knows exactly how she fucking tastes."

Two fingers slip inside my sopping core, his lips crashing against mine in a frantic kiss that has me completely reeling inside.

He tears his lips away, and I instantly crave their return.

"He knows how to make her come like no one else can."

My mouth drops open as I press my head against his shoulder again, the pressure between my thighs beginning to build...and build...and build.

"A wolf knows his mate anywhere...*Eden.*"

My eyes snap open upon hearing my name leave his lips, and before I know it, his free hand wraps around my neck tightly, squeezing my air supply for a couple of manic, magical, heavenly moments in time.

"Change...back..." he grits out between his teeth as his fingers pull out to press my clit forcefully. "Change back. Now."

The dangerous growl leaves his chest, and my whole body explodes like never before. An orgasm ripping through me that's so intense, so thrilling, that I can't focus on anything else.

Nothing else matters but this rapturous, all-consuming pleasure.

Nothing I have ever felt compares.

I jolt and shiver as I begin to descend back down to earth. His hands grip my waist, holding onto me firmly as I lean against his broad chest for support.

And then it comes.

Realization.

I open my eyes, listening to the sound of both our labored breaths tangling together as one.

Then he nudges me away from him. I fall forward, my hands gripping the sheets for support as my weak arms wobble slightly under my weight.

I breathe in deeply, and I hear him step back.

□

My head flops, and my long lilac hair spills over my shoulders around me.

Fuck.

I twist myself to look up at his heaving body towering over me. I shift backward, shuffling away from him.

Our eyes meet once again and stay connected like magnets.

Only this time, we both know for sure.

The connection between us is deadly.

A toxic abomination.

A wicked and cruel mistake.

Unwanted and loathsome.

But damn, is it real...and damn, is it fucking exhilarating.

Cover-up

Conall

She stares at me wide-eyed, shuffling herself backward on the bed. My wolf claws at my brain ferociously. To see her as her true self once again only makes the desperation to claim her even more intense. Even more unbearable. I fight the urge with everything I have inside me, my body heaving from my erratic breathing.

But it's no use.

I need more of her.

I need to feel her lips on my skin.

I need to taste her dripping wet pussy.

Devour every inch of her body.

To make her come again.

Fuck her until she's ruined for all other men.

Until she's mine and mine alone.

The thought drives me fucking wild, and I can't help myself. I stalk toward her, and her legs part to allow me access to her incredible body. I hold myself up with my hands on either side of her head while she lies beneath me. She says nothing. Her silvery-lilac eyes still searching mine. My cock swells as it grazes against her bare pussy, and all I can think about is filling her up, feeling those silky legs wrapped around my body while she writhes in pleasure.

My gaze moves down to her plump lips. So inviting is the sight of them that I can't help but picture them wrapped around my cock. I'm losing my fucking mind. I can feel the little sanity I had left slipping away from me.

Lifting my hand to her chin, I capture her bottom lip with the rough pad of my thumb, pulling it down slightly. A labored breath leaves her chest, and her eyes close as her back arches against the bed. Her hardened nipples grazing against my chest through the thin material of her stolen dress.

She enjoys the feeling of my touch as much as I enjoy hers. Knowing this makes it impossible to fucking stop. My face moves closer to hers, and her hands reach up to snake around my neck, sending sparks radiating down my back. Our noses brush against each other, her warm, sweet breath drawing my lips ever closer.

Fucking hell. What am I doing?

I clench my jaw and squeeze my eyes shut, forcing myself to move abruptly, break out of her spell, and stand up again. I lift my hand to rub it over my face, taking a few steps away from the bed to pull myself together. The scent of her arousal threatens to reel me back in, but I know I can't let it.

Her eyes shoot open, the initial look of shock draining to leave behind the look of pure betrayal. She sits up quickly to examine me, and her face contorts in anger. "You knew it was me all along? From the second you saw me downstairs?" she asks breathlessly. "You knew?!"

I don't respond. Instead, I turn my back on her and lift the glass of whiskey by the fire, tossing it back in one go.

My head is all over the place, a jumbled mess as I try to rein in my wolf.

"ANSWER ME!" she yells, jumping off the bed to storm closer to me.

I twist around, and my pent-up frustrations erupt like a violent volcano. "Of course, I knew it was fucking you, Eden." I snarl coldly.

Her petite frame rises and falls as she stares into my eyes. "So it's true. All of that stuff you just said? About what this *thing* is between us. It's the mate bond?"

I walk over to the desk to pour myself another drink.

How the fuck could I be so stupid to tell her?

What was going through my mind?

As soon as I scented her in amongst those nymphs, I decided to bring her here and expose her the second I got her into the privacy of this room, but my fucking cock had other ideas. The second she touched me and became turned on in my presence, I lost all sense. Part of me was curious to see how far she would take her little rouse. To see how far she was willing to go to trick me. I have to admit that there was a large part of me that wanted her to try. I became weak. A slave to the mate bond that draws me to her.

"CON, is it true?!"

"Yes," I answer, inserting calmness back into my voice. It makes no sense for the both of us to be furious. She has enough fire for us both.

I turn around slowly to see her face fall, her brows scrunching in confusion. "It can't be...you must have made some sort of mistake! I'm not your mate!"

"It's no mistake, Eden," I reply with certainty. "I knew it the moment I set eyes on you."

She brings her hand up to her face and shakes her head from side to side in disbelief. "But it's wrong. It's SO wrong!!" she declares.

"I know that. I have no intention of acting on it. As far as I'm concerned, it's not an issue."

"Not an issue? Of course, it's an issue! Or don't you remember the part where we almost fucked each other?! What can we do about it? Surely there's a way to fix this?"

Her eyes immediately drift to the bookcase in the corner, and I know I have to act fast. There's no way I can risk her finding out the truth. I need to be at the top of my game and can't go through the rejection process. Not right now, anyway. It will have to wait. "There isn't. We just have to fucking deal with it. Keep a clear head around one another," I lie, watching as her eyes make their way back to me.

She shakes her head and walks away with her hands on her hips, clearly trying to come to terms with the reality of our situation. "You shouldn't have done that," she then mutters lowly, folding her arms over her chest as she nods at the bed, the scene of our mutual crime.

I take a drink quickly and place down the glass before stepping in her direction. "I shouldn't have?"

She nods defiantly. "If you knew it was me from the start, you should have just said something!"

"And you shouldn't have tried to fucking trick me in the first place," I hit back in return.

"I had no option," she snarls. "I saw a chance to leave this hellhole behind, and I took it. I have to look out for myself, Conall!"

"And I have to look out for every man in this house, Eden. There is no way I'd let you leave—"

"I've already told you I would never say anything!"

"And I've already told you your word doesn't mean shit to me! Let alone to the others!"

I see a hint of hurt linger in her eyes for a second before she nods. "Fine... congratulations, Con. You win," she says, rushing to the door.

"Where are you going?" I question, as she glares at me over her shoulder.

"Back to my room. You said we need to keep a clear mind, and I need to be out of here. Now."

I shake my head in refusal. "You can't leave. Not yet."

"Like hell I can't!"

"The men saw you come to this room with me as the nymph."

"And? I'm sure you'll all have a good laugh about my failed escape attempt in the morning," she shrugs in annoyance.

"You think it's that easy?" I growl, closing the gap between us. "If the men realize you accessed Elven powers under their roof...if they figure out that you tried and almost managed to escape, they will call for your fucking head."

Her mouth falls open a little in shock. "Surely, they wouldn't—"

"Just because they tolerate you now doesn't mean they trust you, Eden. These men have lost almost everything they have because of your kind. They aren't going to risk what little they have left for anyone. Not even you. When you were brought here, I chose to let you live. It was only agreed by the others under the condition that if you tried to escape, if you used magic of any kind, then you would be punished."

"But you can tell them—"

"I can't tell them shit, Eden. This pack is a brotherhood. Not a dictatorship. The code is the code, and that's all there is to it. I thought Mateo explained this to you, told you not to try anything fucking stupid."

"He did, but...." her voice trails off at the end, and I watch her shoulders slump in defeat. "I didn't realize."

The look of pain in her eyes hits me harder than I expected.

"Look, no one will find out about this," I say determinedly. "Not if you do as I say."

She rubs her forehead gently before giving me a reluctant nod. "What do you need me to do?"

I study her face for a second, batting away the dirty thoughts that try to enter my head once again. There's plenty that I need her to do, but I have to focus on the situation at hand. "Where is the nymph? The real one," I question.

She sucks in her bottom lip guiltily.

"Where, Eden?"

"In the storage closet in the kitchen," she concedes.

I walk across the creaky floor to lift my shirt and throw it over my head.

She watches me get dressed, her arms now covering her exposed body uncomfortably as she tugs the dress back into place.

"I'll be back in a minute. Stay here," I order in a warning tone, striding over to the door.

"Oh, just a warning, she *may* still be unconscious, and if not, then I'm guessing she'll be more than a little pissed."

I twist my neck to look at her. "Seriously? Goddess, fuck." I groan, reaching for the doorknob to leave.

As I quietly make my way down the corridor, I use my hearing to detect any potential movement in the hallways. Luckily, the coast seems to be clear for now. I find myself now wondering how the hell I'm going to handle this situation. Nymphs are pleasant little beings, but they are not the most resilient, and I'm not sure how this one will react when I break her free from the fucking closet!

As soon as I enter the kitchen, I hear her faint squawking from behind the door, which all but confirms my suspicions. I reach for the keys on the counter and open the door to reveal the strange sight. The nymph, the redhead one I had wrapped in my arms only a few minutes ago, stands staring back at me with wide, bloodshot eyes and disheveled hair.

"OH, ALPHA! YOU HEARD ME!" she cries, running to throw her arms around me.

Her tiny frame vibrates against me as she sobs into my shirt. I roll my eyes in irritation. Goddess above....

I curse Eden under my breath, peeling the distraught woman from my chest to hold her firmly by the shoulders.

"Alpha! It was horrible! An elf woman hit me over the head and—"

"I know," I tell her quietly, looking into her strangely familiar, yet somehow unfamiliar, eyes. "I know what happened to you. Now I need you to be calm. Be as quiet as you can and follow me. Can you do that?"

She sniffles a little before nodding and lifting her hands to wipe away her tears. I examine her carefully to see she has a small red bump on her head. It's noticeable but not entirely obvious.

"Come on," I whisper, taking her hand to tug her alongside me back up the stone steps that lead out of the kitchen and then up the passageway to my room.

"Where are we going, Alpha?" she whispers meekly as I open the door to usher her inside.

The second she enters the bedroom and sets eyes on Eden, she hits the fucking roof.

"THAT'S HER!! THE ONE WHO ATTACKED ME!! IT'S HER!" she screams wildly.

I put my hand over her mouth to silence her squeals while Eden holds her hands up apologetically in surrender.

"Listen, Rose, she won't hurt you. You have my word but you must be quiet and calm down. Do you understand me?"

It's not in my nature to be gentle, but I already know it's the right way to deal with this situation. I can see Eden raise one eyebrow in disbelief as she watches me calm the nymph down with my uncharacteristic approach.

Rose nods, her wide eyes staring into mine. Slowly, I remove my hand from her mouth, and her head shoots to the side to glare at Eden scornfully. She then leaps at me, burying her head in my chest. "Oh, Alpha, it was horrible. She is horrid! Please don't let her touch me! Please protect me!"

"She won't hurt you. She's sorry for what she did to you. Isn't that right?" I ask Eden, who is watching us both intently.

"Yes. I am. I'm sorry, Rose. I shouldn't have hurt you. It wasn't personal, and I really do hope you're okay."

Rose doesn't respond; her hands grip my shirt tightly as she squeezes her body against mine.

"Now, Rose, I have to ask you to do something for me. It's important," I say, drawing her attention back to my face.

Her head tilts to the side curiously. "Anything you need, Alpha."

I hear Eden tut just a little as she folds her arms over her chest.

"I need you to spend the night here. I need you to keep what happened last night a secret."

She nods, but I can see that she's still not wholly convinced. "I have something for you to thank you for your help," I add, lifting my hands to remove her from my chest.

My eyes connect with Eden's as I walk across the room, opening a drawer to pull out a small velvet box. "This is for you," I say, turning to Rose and pulling out the diamond necklace.

Her red eyes light up as she watched it dangle from my fingertips, twinkling and shining by the light of the fire.

"Oh, I love it, Alpha! Thank you! Thank you!" she gushes, turning around to swoop her hair out of the way with eager enthusiasm.

I clear my throat awkwardly as I set the velvet box on the table, reaching around the nymph's neck to fasten the clasp. She giggles and bounces a little on the spot as she looks down upon her new trinket. I turn my head to look back at Eden, who has a blank, unreadable expression on her face.

"Both of you will have to swap clothes again."

I gesture to the corner of the room, and Eden walks over, waiting for Rose to join her. Rose only stares at her with a childish pout. "Oh, but Alpha, I'm afraid," she whispers. "Perhaps I need you to come with me."

I don't miss how Eden rolls her eyes, clearly losing patience with the needy nymph.

"It will be fine. Remember I said she won't hurt you."

A small smile covers her face, and she nods her head at me sweetly. I turn my back to face the wall, waiting patiently as the two women silently exchange clothes. I find myself picturing Eden's body once again. The way her lilac curls tumbled around her bare, creamy shoulders. The soft skin of her slender neck which had me itching to claim her. My eyes close as I remember exactly how her warm pussy felt wrapped around my fingers—

"Finished," Eden declares after a few seconds, breaking me from my memory.

Fuck.

I cough to clear my throat, then twist around to see her standing in my battered old shirt, now stained with dust from the kitchen closet. She approaches me slowly, and I lift my hand to pull her over to the corner of the room, ignoring the sparks that dance across my fingertips.

"You have to get back to your bedroom without anyone seeing you. Can you do it alone?"

"Yes," she answers determinedly.

We stare at each other for a moment. I realize it's time to gain some perspective and man the fuck up... To close myself off to the possibility of ever getting this close to her again. When she leaves this room, so does all the drama of this crazy night.

"Good. Go back to bed and forget this night ever fucking happened."

"Oh, I will. Gladly," she answers with narrowed eyes.

It's all meaningless words, and we both know it. There's no way either of us will forget what happened here tonight. I already know that her touch is seared into my memory forever more.

She takes a step away from me to head for the door, her eyes making their way over to the bed where Rose has shuffled her body under the bedspread. "Enjoy the rest of your evening, Alpha," she finishes, disappearing into the empty hallway without a second glance.

I exhale and shut the door behind her, closing my eyes for a second to get my thoughts in order.

"Are you coming to bed, Alpha?" Rose's voice asks expectantly from behind.

I examine her for a moment and realize just how unappealing the sight of her is to me now.

There's only one woman that my body aches for. That I crave like a fucking drug, and it's not her. "No. I have things to take care of, and you need to get some sleep."

She pouts at me in disappointment but follows this with a dutiful nod.

I walk over to my desk and throw myself down into my chair, staring at the fire once again. Immediately, I fall back into that same forbidden memory, replaying every second of what it felt like to hold my mate in my arms.

Help

Eden

I make my way to the messy living room where most of the men are sitting around with their nymphs. There is still a definite buzz in the air, and I can tell by the looks on their faces that the men are thoroughly happy with how their night has played out.

Lucky for some, I guess.

I ignore the hustle and bustle and begin tidying, putting everything back in its original place. Just then, the front door knocks, and Zeke opens it to reveal Madam Piffnel wearing another elaborate velvet outfit. "Good morning, my dears!!" she announces loudly, leaning in to kiss Zeke on the cheek.

"Morning," he replies, gesturing for her to move inside before standing guard next to the closed door.

"How are my lovely ladies? Thoroughly satisfied, I see!" Madam Piffnel laughs.

Urgh!

I look away, deciding to get back to work.

"Eden."

I glance to the side to see Mateo standing there with a rather guilty-looking expression on his face. "How are you?"

"I'm fine, thanks," I reply, offering him a small smile.

He frowns a little but doesn't say much else. His blonde plaything demands his attention as she drags him over to the door with the others. I watch them leave, and that's when I see them. Conall and Rose walking downstairs hand-in-hand to join the others.

I can't help but stare wide-eyed at their display that has the whole room stopping mid-conversation to watch. I study Rose's confident attitude. She sure looks like the cat that got the cream. Perhaps after I left last night, they had some fun of their own.

Did they sleep together in his bed?

It immediately bothers me that I care so much.

His eyes snap toward me, and I divert my gaze quickly, my body growing tense as he passes me by. Damn it, whatever this mate bond is, it's intense. Even when I can't stand him, my body has other ideas.

"Rose! Alpha Conall! Don't you both look great together? I hope you enjoyed a lovely evening?" Madam Piffnel asks excitedly.

"We did!" Rose squeals in delight, grabbing Con's arm. "It was perfect." she coos, looking up into his eyes.

You have got to be kidding me?

I shake my head, lifting a wooden chair to place it back at the dining table. Con looks over his shoulder at me but doesn't move, his arm still wrapped securely around his nymph.

"Look what Alpha Conall gave me! Isn't it beautiful?" Rose questions as the other nymphs crowd around her eagerly.

From what I can see, a fair few of them look rather jealous.

"Goddess, Con. That must have been one hell of a night you had," Hunter observes with a loud laugh as he eyes the diamond necklace.

Conall looks at me again, our eyes connecting briefly before he nods his head. "It was."

The excited chatter continues for another few minutes before Madam Piffnel instructs her nymphs to say their goodbyes. Before long, they are all gone, and the house returns to normal.

"Eden, any chance of some more of those eggs? I've worked up quite the appetite!" Hunter laughs, taking a seat at the table.

"You're telling me... Mine was the most energetic one I've had yet. Barely slept a wink," William grins as the rest of the men join in with a chuckle.

"Sure, I'm starting breakfast now," I say, heading for the staircase.

"Hey, never mind you, Will. We all want to hear from Con." Evan says as the men turn their attention to him.

I try not to look, but I can't help steal a glance at him.

He shrugs his shoulders. "It's no one's business. You've all had your fun. Now get back to work," he orders, turning his back to head upstairs.

* * *

"Need any help?" Mateo asks, bending down beside me as I scrub the dirty staircase with a scrubbing brush.

"Be my guest!" I grin, watching as he drops his hand into the bucket of water to retrieve the other brush.

We work in silence, and I can see him examine me closely from the corner of his eye. "You're quiet today. Are you okay?"

"I'm fine." I shrug.

The truth is I'm anything but. After my complete and utter failure last night, I feel pretty low. Not only was it extremely humiliating, but it was an eye-opening experience too. I was reminded once again of the dangers of this place. Despite settling in, I don't belong and never will.

"You know, the woman last night...she uh...it's not anything deep. Sometimes we just need to blow off steam, and it's the only chance we get to—"

I lift my hand to stop him in his tracks. "Mateo, you don't have to explain yourself to me."

He smiles a little in return. "Okay, well, I just wanted you to know—"

"Oh, I don't think I need to know!" I laugh, standing up to stretch out my sore limbs.

His brows knit together curiously. "I never did see you again after you went to get some food?"

"Oh, I went straight to bed. Decided it wasn't my *scene* after all."

"AHHHHH FUCK! IT FUCKING BURNS!"

Frantic yells enter the room, and Mateo stands to attention. I look to the doorway and see Evan and Hunter hauling Henrick into the room, his body dragging along the floor and his face contorted in pain as his arms hang limply around their shoulders.

"QUICK, MATTY! GET JAREK! NOW!"

Mateo nods and takes the stairs two at a time. I run over to the sofa and clear a space as Evan and Hunter lay Henrick down, stepping back to catch their breath. Speedily the room begins to fill up as the other men appear to find out what the commotion is.

"What the hell is going on?" Con's voice enquires as he storms in to examine the scene.

"I don't know, Con. One minute we were hunting in the forest, then the next, he was screaming in agony. By the time we got to him, he couldn't walk," Hunter pants.

Just then, Jarek appears at the bottom of the stairs and runs for the sofa.

I watch in stunned silence as Henrick writhes around in pain, his face scrunching as labored gasps leave his wheezing chest.

"Where is the pain?" Jarek asks, pushing his glasses into place.

"My leg! My fucking leg!"

Jarek reaches for his pants, yanking the material upwards to reveal the problem. The rest of the men wince and shoot their eyes away at the sight. Bright blue burns are scorching through Henrick's skin, eating away at the mangled flesh.

"Fucking hell...what is that?" Anton exclaims gruffly, looking over my shoulder.

Jarek examines it, and Conall glances at him expectantly. "Well, Jarek?"

"Ehm, I'm not so sure. I haven't come across this before. Give me a second," he replies, trying his best to come up with the answers.

There's silence for a few tense moments before I decide to intervene. "It's Blue Thistle burn," I state clearly, immediately drawing everyone's attention to me.

"What?" William asks. "Blue Thistle burn? Never heard of it."

"It's because it's extremely rare," I answer in return. "The plant only blooms at certain times of the year and must come into direct contact with the bloodstream to cause an injury like this," I say, nodding my head down at Henrick.

"Is she right, Jarek?" Hunter asks demandingly.

"Ehm, it may ring a bell, but I'm not well acquainted enough to know."

"I know how to treat the wound," I say determinedly, looking at Conall, who eyes me suspiciously. "All I need are some basic plants and herbs from the forest."

His eyes stay firmly with mine as the men around the room grumble in disapproval.

"How do we know she's telling the truth?!" Rocco snarls. "We can't trust her. I say we just leave the wound be. It's not like it will kill him anyway, fuck sake."

The rest of the men nod in agreement, and I furrow my brows. "It can kill him."

They shrug nonchalantly, seemingly unbothered by my revelation. "He'll be fine, won't you, Henrick?" Samuel asks, patting him on the shoulder.

I fold my arms over my chest and shake my head. "Fine, but even if the poison doesn't kill him he will lose the leg."

"What?!" Henrick gasps in shock, hauling himself up on the sofa. "Con! I can't lose my fucking leg!"

Conall looks at me again, and I shrug my shoulder. "I just need a few things."

The room grows quiet as everyone waits for his judgment.

"Conall, we do need her help," Jarek admits in defeat. "I'm not sure what to do."

Eventually, Con nods his head in agreement. "You'll stay by my side the entire time."

My eyes widen as he heads for the door, and I scurry off after him, grabbing an old basket on the way. I watch as he lifts his hand to the door, and the warm air wafts into the room, washing over my body.

He turns to look at me as I stand there completely frozen, my senses overcome.

"Well, let's get a move on," he states, gesturing for me to go first.

□

Chemistry

Eden

I follow Conall across the grassy front yard, my eyes focused on the thick trees up ahead. I vaguely notice him turn to look at me, but I'm too distracted by the beauty of the outdoors to care about our strange entanglement right now.

As soon as we step inside the forest, my heart swells in my chest, feeling like it might burst at any moment. I close my eyes and revel in the feeling of having nature surround me once again. My ears fill with the sounds of various birds fluttering around in the trees. Birds whose species I can determine by the sound of their tweets alone. The sun's rays have disappeared for the day, but the evening dusk brings its own pleasures. A cooling sensation trickles across the surface of my skin while the fresh air blows through my hair, lifting it up to billow wildly around my face. I begin to smile.

"Eden..."

I drop down to the forest floor, reaching my hand out to touch the nearest plant. A Marabell Daisy. An otherwise common and insignificant little flower, but one that now holds so much meaning.

"Eden."

I shoot my head toward the interrupting voice to see Conall looking down at me with a furrowed brow. "Are you okay?"

"Wha-"

It's then that I realize I'm crying. Full, fat tears roll down my cheeks, leaving cool trails in their wake. "Yes, I'm fine," I answer determinedly, shaking my head a little to break from my reverie.

I reluctantly let the flower go and stand up again to face him. His eyes sweep my face silently, a look of bewildered curiosity swirling around in their depths. My breath hitches as his hand unexpectedly lifts to my face, his thumb swiping away a stray tear from the outer corner of my lips with gentle care. I stare at him in wide-eyed astonishment for a second before he takes a slow step away from me, turning his back to look around the trees. "Where do we begin? What do you need?" he asks, slipping back into his usual frosty default setting.

I allow myself to breathe again and try my best to refocus my attention on the task at hand. A Blue Thistle burn can be deadly; however, I'm confident I know the correct plants and herbs to counteract the poison.

"We need to find water," I begin, scanning the forest alongside him. "Two of the plants I need are found near a water source. I can pick up the rest of the things on the way."

He nods his head, gesturing for me to walk with him. As we walk in silence, I can sense him staring at me. I make a few stops to pick the various herbs and plants I need, and he watches every move I make. At first, I try to ignore it, but his gaze makes me squirm in ways that cloud my already overwhelmed mind. "You don't have to worry. I'm not going to run," I say honestly as we carry on the journey side-by-side.

"I know that," he answers, shrugging his huge shoulders. "You wouldn't get very far anyway."

I roll my eyes in response to his sheer arrogance. "I do know the forest well. I'm sure I'd be fine."

"You were captured by Mateo... I'm not worried," he answers with an infuriating, dismissive tone.

"Then why keep such a close eye on me? You haven't stopped staring at me since we left the house."

He comes to a stop, and we turn to face one another.

"Well?" I ask, raising my eyebrow in challenge.

He doesn't respond at first. His strong jaw remains tight.

"There's your water," he says, finally breaking the silence and flicking his head to the right.

It takes me a second, but I manage to tear my eyes away from him to find the source myself. "Good," I say plainly, trudging off through the grass away from him.

The closer I get, the louder the sound of babbling water becomes. It's not a river but a rather pretty-looking stream instead.

"Is this what you had in mind?" Con asks, looking around to scan the trees.

"Yes, it's perfect," I reply, placing the basket on the ground. "I need a Willop flower. We should find one down near the water's edge."

I take off carefully down the small hill, steadying myself on the muddy ground as I approach the edge of the fast-flowing little stream. I turn my head to see him standing there watching me with his arms folded. "Well, don't just stand there! Help me look!"

"I have no idea what a fucking Willop flower is, Eden."

"Oh...well, it's red and has blue spots on the petals. You can't miss it."

He huffs a little but edges down the side of the bank to join me anyway.

We both begin to search, raking through the tall grass with our fingers for a few minutes.

"Wait, is this it?" Conall asks, plucking a flower from the ground to bring it over for inspection.

"Gently!" I hiss, watching how he grips the flower in his enormous hand without any care whatsoever.

He stops in front of me and opens his palm.

"Look what you've done to the poor thing," I grumble, placing my hand under his to cup it gently. "Always hold them delicately. Like this," I explain quietly. "Some flowers lose their properties if they are squashed and squeezed."

His hand rests on top of mine for a second longer, and I feel the muscles in his tight fist begin to relax.

"That's better," I say in approval, watching the flower's petals rest peacefully against his skin.

It's then I feel his gaze on me again. I look up into his honey eyes which seem to pin me in place despite my best efforts. A strange energy surrounds us, and I gulp before stepping back. "It's the right flower. You can put it in the basket."

His eye twitches slightly and he clears his throat, doing as I ask. I then begin to instruct him on our next mission. "Now I need a Vivillium plant. Its stalk is long, with two heart-shaped leaves hanging from the top."

"Vivillium? Like in the book Jarek was reading?" he asks while looking around.

I stop for a moment in surprise. "Yes...have you read it too?!"

He scoffs and shakes his head. "No, I just bring him the books," he explains. "It's not my thing."

"Hmmm," I answer before beginning my search once again.

"So this is your thing then. Plants and flowers and shit?" he asks gruffly with a hint of uncomfortableness.

"Uhh...."

I know I have to be careful how I answer this question. After all, the wolves were wiped out through the use of dark Elven herb and plant enchantments. It makes sense that they would find it threatening.

The silence stretches for a few seconds before he fills the void for me. "You should keep it secret for now," he says insistently, causing me to stop and look at his serious expression. "From the others... If you possess some kind of talent for this stuff, you'll need to downplay it."

I swallow nervously and stand up to face him. "And what if I do? Would you want me to keep it secret from you too?"

His eyes connect with mine. "You don't need to hide anything from me."

The tension between us is powerful enough to make me look the other way, my vision captured by the sight of the tall plant poking out of the water in the middle of the stream.

"Over there!" I exclaim, pointing to it in triumph. "It's in the water!"

I immediately begin to pull my boots off as Con watches.

"I'll get it," he says, shaking his head as he bends down to loosen his own footwear.

"No, I can manage!" I call back, already wading through the cold rushing water.

It sloshes around my knees, soaking the edges of my pants. I stop where I am and reach out to touch the plant with my fingertips. "Come on, little guy. Come...to...mama."

Suddenly I lose my balance, falling forward into the running water with an embarrassing splash.

My hands settle on the rocky bottom of the stream, and I begin to push myself back onto my feet.

"Fucking hell," Conall's voice cuts in from above as he grabs hold of me under my arms to hoist me upright.

"I've got it!" I protest, wriggling myself free of his hold.

"Yeah, you sure look like you have everything under control," he snaps back as the water splashes around us.

I pull my arm away from him and inch closer to the plant, snapping its stem to pluck it from the water. "I don't need you to rescue me, you know," I mutter, mortified that I made the silly misstep in the first place.

"Really? Because that's twice in twenty-four hours by my count," he answers in irritation, turning away from me to trudge back through the water.

□

"You think that you saved me last night? Wow... That's some slant to put on what actually transpired."

"I saved your ass, and you know it. You should be fucking thanking me," he hits back, stepping out of the water before turning around to yank my hand, pulling me up onto the muddy bank alongside him.

"HA! You're kidding, right? So I should thank you for keeping me under lock and key as your slave? Besides, you say that like I'm the only one that gained anything from last night," I snipe back in return.

His eyes run over my face to settle on my lips. "Fair enough. I think it's fair to say we both did," he answers suggestively.

I immediately begin to picture the moment when his hand wrapped around my throat. The feeling of his hot, tantalizing body pressed against mine while I came undone by his touch.

"Don't look at me like that..." he mutters gutturally, breaking me free of the memory.

"Like what?" I ask between slightly labored breaths.

His grip on my hand tightens, and he pulls me closer to him. My wet chest meets his, soaking through the thin material of his shirt. Our bodies seem to writhe against one another in perfect sync. My breasts tingle in response to the sensation, and I can't help but crave the same delicious skin-to-skin contact that we enjoyed last night. I can tell he is having the same struggles, his hard body rising and falling more violently as his breathing intensifies.

"Look at what you do to me, Eden," he murmurs, lifting his hands to place them firmly on either side of my face.

The rough pads of his thumbs graze my cheeks before he drags one along my lower lip. Before I can help myself, I kiss it in reply, allowing the tip to dip inside my mouth just a fraction.

His hungry eyes widen slightly at the sight. "That's it...." he whispers, his husky voice awakening those same familiar feelings inside me.

The lust, the passion, the want.

It's undeniable.

But then it hits me.

The flashback of Rose lying comfortably in his bed last night. The sight of her gleeful display this morning as she hung off his arm like some kind of trophy. I can't help the sudden rush of irrational jealousy that ripples through me. I won't be a bed warmer for some ladies' man. "Perhaps some of us had more fun than others last night, though. Isn't that right, Alpha?" I question, separating my body from his.

His eyes flick back to mine, and his brows knit together, but he doesn't reply.

"It seems you had a very enjoyable night after I left. So maybe *you* should be the one thanking me?"

He doesn't deny my accusation; instead, he lets me go, allowing me to take a step back.

I cannot deny that part of me is disappointed, while another part is relieved. Relieved that I now have a renewed resolve and a more solid reason to stay well clear of him.

"Conall."

Both of us snap our heads in the direction of the trees where Mateo stands, watching us.

"What?" Conall barks, taking a step away from me.

Mateo's eyes flick to me awkwardly before he clears his throat. "It's Henrick. The poison seems to be spreading, and he's freaking the fuck out back there."

Conall looks at me, and I nod my head. "It's fine. I have everything I need now," I reply confidently, walking over to the basket to place the Vivillium plant inside.

"Go back and tell them we are on our way," Conall orders Mateo, who runs back through the trees.

I cast my eyes over the basket's contents for a moment while Conall shoves his boots back on. I take advantage of his distracted state, examining a little patch of flowers by my side.

Maybe I could—

"Don't even fucking think about it, Eden," he snaps, not bothering to lift his head.

Remedy

Eden

As we enter back through the door of the old house, a sense of sadness washes over me. I had prepared myself for it the whole journey back, but it still cuts deep. I turn to see Conall close the door behind us. He looks at me briefly before nodding over my shoulder towards the chaos.

It's then that I register the frantic shouting and yelling as three men pin Henrick to the sofa. He thrashes around wildly against them, his screams of agony filling up the large house.

"Eden!" Jarek calls. "We need that remedy, and we need it quick!"

Shit.

I run over to examine the damage. Henrick is now lying in his underwear. The Blue Thistle burn has spread up over his muscular thigh, turning almost every inch of skin bright blue. "It's moving faster than I thought," I say to Jarek. "I need a pestle and mortar. Now," I order Anton, who takes off toward the kitchen, to fetch them for me.

I unpack the basket, laying out the various things I need to double-check everything is accounted for. Within a few seconds, the pestle and mortar appear, and I get to work meticulously building the complicated concoction. The amounts needed of each item are highly specific and must be added to the bowl in a certain order. Despite this, I'm not concerned. I have had this remedy in my head for a long time now. In fact, I'm almost slightly excited to try it out on a real-life subject for the first time.

Half the men crowd around to watch what I'm doing, but I pay them no mind. I can hear them mumbling to one another, partly disturbed and partly intrigued by my actions. Finally, I'm happy with the mixture I have created, and I stop to hold my hand over the small bowl.

"What the fuck is she doing now?"

"I don't like this...I don't like this one fucking bit, you know."

"Conall, this isn't normal."

I shut everyone and everything out, closing my eyes to concentrate on the energy that runs through my body. I focus all of it on the remedy, knowing it needs this final touch to make it just right. The sound of gasps are audible all around me, and I open my eyes to see the stunned looks on the mens' faces. Conall's included.

Good. That means it worked. I look down to see the concoction glowing a pale shade of yellow.

"It's ready," I declare, lifting the bowl to head for the sofa.

A small crowd rushes after me to watch on while those who are more dubious hang back a few paces. Henrick stares up at me, his forehead covered with beads of sweat.

"Do it," he grits out, nodding in permission.

I begin to pour the glowing liquid over his skin, ensuring every part of the infected area is covered. He winces in pain, gritting his teeth together as he throws his head back violently. And then he passes out.

"What did you do to him, elf!?" Rocco demands, stepping forward to stand over me. "Whatever that stuff is, it doesn't help—"

"Shut the fuck up."

I glance upward to see Conall step in front of Rocco, shielding my body defensively.

"Are you serious?! Conall, look at him!"

"I said...shut the fuck up," he repeats.

They both glare at each other in mutual disdain.

"Yeah, let her work, you asshole," Mateo adds supportively. "I'm sure this is part of the recovery. Isn't it, Eden?"

I nod my head, looking around the men confidently.

"Yes. His body has shut down for a bit while it battles the infection. He'll be awake soon and as good as new," I shrug, standing up with the bowl in my hand.

"Look! The poison! It's beginning to retreat!" Hunter calls out, pointing to the disease-ridden leg that is already losing its vibrant blue color.

The men look at each other with unspoken suspicion mixed with a slight hint of awe. I practically feel Conall's body tense as he stands by my side, and I already know the reason why. The questions are coming.

"How do you know how to do that shit? That kind of magic?" Samuel questions through narrowed eyes.

I shrug with an air of nonchalance. "All wood elves of Azealea know the remedy for Blue Thistle burns. It grows down by the gully that we played on as children." I lie.

His brows knit together, unconvinced, but no one questions me further.

"We should get him to his room to rest," Conall states, looking to me for confirmation.

"Yes, of course," I say with a nod of permission.

Zeke and Hunter move forward just as Henrick begins to come to, groaning lightly with his eyes still closed.

"Come on, man. Let's get you to bed," Hunter says as they haul him to his bedroom.

Thankfully, the room comes to life again, and the men break apart, discussing what they have just witnessed.

"That was amazing, Eden!" Mateo laughs, clapping his hands. "I've never seen anything like it. Fucking awesome!"

His infectious enthusiasm makes me smile.

"Well, thank you," I reply as he hugs me tightly.

"Eden," Conall's voice says from behind.

I turn around, finding him glaring at Mateo in warning before his eyes return to me. "Thanks for your help. You can use the room now to get cleaned up. You'll want to get out of those wet clothes."

My core tightens just a little at the mere suggestion leaving his lips.

He gives Mateo another look before following Zeke, Hunter, and Henrick.

I swing around and smile at Mateo again.

"Well, you seem to have cheered up!" he observes with a grin.

"A little fresh air does that to a person," I laugh, throwing him a wink. "However, I guess it's back to reality, and the stove is calling—"

"That's fine, Eden," Anton interjects roughly from the other side of the room. "We've got it tonight."

My mouth drops open a little in shock, but I don't dare question his unexpected generosity.

"Oh, thanks," I mutter in return as he nods respectfully.

"Hey, maybe they'll warm up to you yet?" Mateo whispers, causing me to laugh lightly.

"Maybe...."

* * *

I grab a cloth towel from the gold rail and wrap it around my body before climbing out of the large bathtub. I have to admit that I spent a lot longer bathing than I intended, but I found myself completely lost in my thoughts for most of the time. Being at one with nature again gave me such a sense of purpose. Such a rush. It brought me some much-needed peace at a time when I required it the most.

I dry myself off quickly and tiptoe to the door to peek into the warm, dimly lit bedroom. It's empty as I had hoped it would be. My shoulders drop in relief, and I walk into the room, heading to the bed to lift the clean white shirt. I throw it over my head and use the cloth to dry my hair a little. Then, my eyes catch sight of the bookshelf, and I walk towards it, casting my eyes over the spines of the dusty old books once again. I find the one I'm looking for almost straight away. The same book I had been reading last night before I fell asleep. I pull it out carefully and open it up where I left off.

"Chapter Two- Mates"

Curiosity consumes me, and I climb onto the bed, sitting cross-legged as I begin reading.

"The wolf may smell his mate long before he even sets eyes on her. Her scent has a spectacular hold over him already. Bewitching his mind and taking over his senses from the moment of realization. The wolf will seek out his mate without delay. His instincts will guide him in quickly tracking her down and claiming her as his own, which he should do immediately. Upon touching his mate for the first time, the wolf will feel his skin tingle. His mind will be overcome with sexual desire. His beast eager to be set free to begin the mating process. These reactions are perfectly normal and impossible to ignore. The mate bond is a gift from the moon goddess herself and, therefore, cannot be forged nor forsaken."

I snap the book closed and take a deep breath, closing my eyes as I fall backward onto the bed.

Why did it have to be me?

Of all the elves in this realm, I have been chosen for this so-called "blessing"?

If I didn't know any better, I would assume that the Goddess of love has had it out for me all along.

Immediately, I am bombarded with images from our interaction in the forest earlier. As soon as he touched me, I was under his spell, ready to hand myself over to him at his command.

I lift my hand to rest my fingers against my lips, remembering his firm but gentle touch. I picture myself kissing his thumb, grazing it with my teeth as his eyes penetrate through me.

My hand quivers slightly as I lightly suck on my fingertips, making them wet and slippery. A delicious ache begins to build between my legs, which part slightly of their own accord.

My back arches against the bed, burying my head deeper into the thick bedspread. My hand drifts down over my writhing body, settling between my legs. I suck in my bottom lip to stifle a low moan as my wet fingertips find my waiting pussy, stroking it slowly. My mind continues to throw me images of my most forbidden desires.

Pictures of him.

I picture him towering over me, his bare chest pressed against mine as he leans down to kiss my neck with wild, reckless abandon.

My free hand closes into a tight fist, gripping the sheets. My speed increases a little as I imagine him positioning his cock against my wet, aching slit. His hands grabbing at my breast roughly. His wild, frantic kisses as he captures my nipple between his lips. I picture myself pulling him closer. Begging him to put me out of my misery and give me what I want.

Because I *do* want it.

I want it more than anything, and he knows it.

I want him inside me.

I want him to fuck me.

To ruin me.

To claim me.

Shit!

Suddenly, the door in the corner of the room opens, and I jump in fright, pulling my legs back quickly and shuffling myself up on the bed. Conall's eyes connect with mine where I sit, and we stare at each other in silence.

Stripped

Eden

The sound of my erratic breath fills the quiet room until he pushes the door closed, walking toward me slowly.

I lift my hand up and shake my head, stopping him in his tracks.

"Don't come any closer," I pant out. "You can't."

My core still throbs demandingly, my wetness coating the skin between my thighs. If he comes closer...I know that I won't be able to stop myself. That I'll be powerless to resist.

His jaw tightens, his chest rising and falling as he stares into my eyes for a moment. He then turns away, walking over to his desk.

I watch with a mixture of pent-up desire and nervous energy as he pours a drink, lifting it to his lips. The tension in the room is palpable. Encircling us both like an invisible, silent, deadly whirlwind. Then, he sits down on his chair, leaning back to look into my eyes once again.

I bite my lip and wait for him to say something... Anything....

"You don't want me to touch you?" he asks lowly.

I manage to shake my head slowly in reply.

He lifts his glass to take another drink. "Then I won't,"

My breathing quickens once again as I find myself staring at him wantonly. I cannot bring myself to back down. Slowly, I move onto my knees, gripping the shirt to tug it over my head, revealing my naked body underneath.

Still, he doesn't move. But he watches. He watches my every move with undivided attention.

I lift my fingertips to my mouth, sucking on them gently before sliding my hand down my body. Already I can feel every single nerve standing to attention. My blood coursing through my body like a rush of sheer desire running through my veins. My middle finger touches my clit, and I moan in pleasure, closing my eyes as I bite my lip hard.

"Let me hear you, Eden," he demands, again drawing my eyes to him.

☐

I begin to moan lightly as I pleasure myself, my hips grinding rhythmically back and forth. He doesn't move. Instead, his eyes travel over me, turning impossibly black. The sight only fuels my delirious, ravenous lust. I throw my head back in ecstasy as my movements get faster.

"Yesss," I whisper, running my other hand over my body to grasp my breasts.

My hips move quicker, my core tightening and releasing in a pattern that has me climbing closer to my release. I slip one finger inside my pussy, groaning in satisfaction as I slide it out again to run over my clit.

My mouth drops open a little as I look at him again. His eyes watching me intently. He leans forward a little in his chair, his hand lifting to swipe over his face. His body tense and rigid.

He's struggling to keep it together.

The thought makes me even hotter and wetter than before.

I lift my fingertips gently to my mouth, tasting myself on the tip of my tongue as I flutter my lashes at him seductively.

His brows knit together in a look of pure lust.

"Go faster for me, Eden," he orders.

I happily oblige, closing my eyes and slipping my fingers between my legs to tease my needy clit again. My muscles grow tense, and my hips thrust desperately. I chase this orgasm as though it's the air I need to breathe. My moans become louder. I open my eyes as the feeling builds and builds. They connect with his, and I can't help but utter the word. "Please...."

He stands up quickly, walking over to the edge of the bed, and I yelp in pleasure as his large hand grips my chin, pulling my face upward to look into his eyes.

"Come, Eden."

And at his command, I combust on the spot. My orgasm ebbs and flows through every part of my body while my hips jerk slightly back and forth.

I close my eyes and try to catch my breath, my mind all over the place as it tries to catch up with what I have just done. I sit further back on my knees, my bare ass resting on the bed as I float back down to earth.

It's then that I open my eyes to see him staring at me. His tight grip on my chin releases to set me free.

I'm so stunned that I can't bring myself to speak; instead, I only watch as he steps back, running his hand over his face again.

"I- I'm sorry. I—"

He shakes his head, stopping my incoherent mumbling.

"You... You're fucking beautiful," he says, swallowing hard.

He shakes his head, rubbing the back of his neck before he turns his back to walk over to the desk.

I quickly reach for the white shirt in a daze, throwing it over my head. I position it in place and hop off the bed, walking over to the door as he watches me.

"Eden."

I turn to look at him.

"Nothing happened with the nymph," he says, a look of sincerity in his eyes. "Nothing."

I nod in reply before leaving the room.

As soon as the door closes behind me, a burst of air leaves my lungs, and I take off quickly down the hallway, rushing down the forbidden steps. Then, I run slap-bang into a hard body that almost knocks me backward.

"Eden? Are you okay?"

I find myself looking directly at Mateo as he eyes me up and down with a worried expression.

"Yeah, I'm fine," I smile, lifting my hair to tuck it behind my ear casually. "Excuse me, I was just heading to bed."

I move around his body to make my escape when suddenly he grips me by the arm.

"Hey, Mateo! What are you—?"

"Shhh, I need to talk to you," he says impatiently, looking around before tugging me down the hallway to my bedroom.

"Mateo, what the hell is going on?" I ask in confusion, sitting down on the edge of my bed.

He puts his hands on his hips and begins to pace the floor. "Eden, I don't know what's going on with you and Conall, but it has to stop. You need to stay away from him. He's dangerous."

"You keep saying that! But he's just as dangerous as any other man here!"

"That's not true, Eden," he says, shaking his head adamantly.

"Then tell me!" I demand.

He takes a seat next to me on the bed. "He's ruthless. More ruthless than any wolf I've ever met."

"In what way?" I ask nervously, my eyes scanning his worried face.

He looks reluctant for a second, but I know I can't let him stop there. I need to know what he is talking about.

"Please tell me."

He looks into my eyes and nods. "It's about how Con became the leader in the first place."

My brows knit together questioningly.

"You see, it was written in the code since the beginning that if you want to become the leader of this pack, then you must challenge the current Alpha in charge in a fight to the death."

My eyes widen in horror. "He killed one of your own?" I ask quietly.

"Yes, but it's more than that, Eden. After *The Culling*, we had nowhere to go, and the responsibility fell on Lincoln to be the leader of the pack. He owned this house," he explains, looking around briefly.

I follow his gaze and then nod in understanding.

"Lincoln was Conall's best friend and closest confidant. They had known each other since they were kids. They did everything together. When we formed the Den of Alphas, Con acted almost as Beta for Lincoln. He was his right hand—his second-in-command."

A horrible feeling begins to bubble in my chest as I silently predict the next words that will leave Mateo's lips.

"And that's why no one saw it coming when Conall challenged him for the role of pack leader. He challenged his oldest friend, the man who trusted him implicitly, in a fight to the death. A fight that he knew he would win. He's unpredictable. Dangerous. He won't bat an eyelid using you to get what he wants. Just as he did to Lincoln."

I swallow the bile that rises in my throat and bring my hand up to rest it on my chest.

What sort of monster have I been tethered to?

The thought leaves me both disturbed and terrified all at the same time.

"That's why you must keep your distance from him, Eden. You must stay away from him at all costs."

Suspicion

Eden

SEVENTY YEARS AGO

A slow, satisfied smile touches my lips as he brings his hand to my face, gliding his soft fingertips down my cheek.

"You've no idea how much I will miss this face."

"Then don't go," I plead, already knowing full well that it isn't an option.

He lifts my hand to kiss my palm gently. "I wish I didn't have to. You know that," he whispers before giving me a sympathetic look.

I pout a little, and he leans forward to land a kiss on my lips. I laugh softly against his mouth and throw my arms around his neck, holding him close to my naked chest. His lips break away from mine as he raises his hand to tug me off playfully. I reluctantly let him go, watching him pull his naked body upright to stand beside the bed.

Automatically, my eyes drift to the unique gold medallion around his neck, the symbol of his status. I can't help but wonder how much simpler life would be if he were just an average elf like myself. But the fact of the matter is that he is not. Not even close. A future king has responsibilities. I'm well aware of and fully understand this, but it doesn't make his leaving any easier.

"Hey, listen. Don't look so worried, Eden. I won't be gone long. A couple of days at the most. Besides, you'll be so busy with all your studies that you'll hardly even realize I'm gone," Erix shrugs with a handsome grin.

"I know," I smile, sitting upright in bed and running a hand through my wayward hair.

He reaches down to the floor to pick up his pants, shoving them on quickly. The clock on top of the mantle begins to chime, and I roll my eyes at its rude interruption.

"I'm late for a meeting with my father and his advisors," he says worriedly, sitting on the bed to pull on his shoes.

I slowly move onto my knees, pressing my naked body against his back while kissing his neck teasingly. He laughs, twisting his neck to give me his best stern look. "Now, this is highly distracting. Especially when I'm about to head into a meeting with both of our fathers. Come on... Let me get myself together a little," he jokes.

I press my forehead against his shoulder blade in defeat. "Okay, I'm sorry." I smile cheekily, watching him walk to the mirror to fix his tunic.

"Do you think anyone knows about us?" I ask, raising an eyebrow at him.

He nods his head as his eyes connect with mine through the mirror.

"How could they not? We spend practically every second together!"

"I guess you're right," I laugh.

He turns around and walks over to me, resting his hand on my face. "I'll marry you someday, Eden Nestoriel."

"Is that right?" I question with a grin. "Even though I am but a humble wood elf?"

He shrugs his shoulders. "That doesn't matter to me, and when I'm king, I'll do whatever the hell I like."

I wink in reply as he puts on his array of gold, gemmed rings.

"So what's this meeting about?" I ask, trying to sound casual.

He examines his hand as he places each item on his fingers strategically. "Tomorrow, we will attack a pack of wolves just north of Gildroy. We must discuss the plan of action."

I furrow my brows. "You're going to attack the entire pack? That sounds like an ambush rather than a battle—"

"That's because it is an ambush, Eden," he states matter-of-factly, his serious eyes connecting with mine again.

I swallow a little, and my shoulders slump. The bitter feud between elves and wolves has been raging for decades, but it is now that the fight has truly reached boiling point. It's hard to believe that it all escalated over some unclaimed land. The whole thing seems so silly to me... Yet here we are. Years later and nothing has been gained by either side. Nothing but hatred, bitterness, and death. The raging war is the main reason we moved here a few years ago from Azealea. News of my father's talent for herbology and natural enchantments had reached King Ciridan here in Morween. He insisted that my father move here immediately to serve his duty to the entire Elven race.

I can't say it's a decision that I particularly agree with. I liked my life in Azealea, but at least I now have Erix here to keep me sane. Well, when he isn't off fighting, that is.

"Don't give me that look," he says quietly, sitting on the edge of the bed. "You know we don't have any options now. They aren't fighting fairly anymore, which means we can't either. The wolves' attacks are becoming more ruthless each time. Look at what happened to your Aunt Felou's village! There was no need for her and others to die so brutally. They are attacking defenseless women and children! It's now time to begin fighting fire with fire."

I nod in understanding, the memories of my Aunt's death still fresh in my mind.

"You get it, don't you?" Erix asks insistently. "I don't take any pleasure in this, but I will show them mercy no longer. I must protect my people. My future kingdom."

"I understand," I reply, shrugging my shoulders. "I just wish there was a peaceful resolution."

"The time for that has passed now, Eden," he answers dismissively. "Now I've got to go, or my dad will send out a search party, namely Aubrun, to track me down—"

Just then, the door knocks, and we look at each other as we begin to laugh.

"Erix! You are needed now! Come on!" Aubrun calls out from the other side of the door.

Erix stands up, and I stand with him, wrapping my long silk robe around myself tightly. He takes hold of my hand, lifting it to his lips to kiss it once again as we walk to the door.

As soon as it opens, Aubrun jumps with a slight startle.

"Hi, Aubrun," I chuckle as he gives me an awkward nod.

"Hey, Eden," he replies, clearing his throat and looking the other way nervously.

"I'll be back before you know it." Erix winks, leaning in to kiss me on the cheek one last time before he walks away from me forever.

* * *

□

PRESENT

All thoughts of Erix drift far away from me as I hear a fist thumping on my old wooden door.

"EDEN!! Do you know what time it is? Get up, lazy ass!" Anton's gruff voice calls out loudly.

I groan, throwing the sheets off my body to trudge to the door. I open it just enough to peer out into the hallway.

"You had your time off last night. Come on, get moving. Now elf!" he grumbles.

"Oh, so its elf again, is it?" I question, raising my brow. "Keep your hair on. I'll be down as soon as I can."

He shakes his head and stomps off like an overgrown man-child.

I click the door closed and lean against it, shutting my tired eyes for a few seconds. I hardly slept a wink last night after Mateo revealed the truth of Con's character to me. Sure, I have always known that he is a dangerous man. A man to be feared. But yesterday, I saw a glimpse of humanity in his eyes. I felt a hint of gentleness in his touch and protectiveness in his manner.

I let it cloud my judgment. I let myself give in to the desperate pull that I feel toward him. In short, I let myself down.

To make matters worse, the only moments of rest I managed to get last night were filled with memories of Erix.

What would he think of me if he saw my behavior last night?

I push the thought from my mind quickly, afraid to face up to the glaringly obvious answer.

All night I thought of ways to confront Conall if I could. How I would ask him what happened all those years ago with Lincoln. However, I know that I can't. The last thing I want is to get Mateo into any more trouble.

I walk over to the dresser to pull out some clothes for the day when suddenly, the door rattles again.

"You know, I would think by now that you would have mastered the art of boiling a fucking egg!" I call out in irritation.

The door opens, and I snap my head to the side to see Con enter the room. I look away quickly, trying to keep my breathing steady as I fiddle with the old handles of the drawer.

The door closes, and I can feel his eyes on my back, waiting for me to turn around. The silence between us is deafening.

"Eden."

"Mhmm?" I reply, silently scolding myself for sounding so unnatural.

"Will you turn around?"

My shoulders tense painfully as I twist my body in his direction. I try not to make eye contact, but I can already see from the corner of my vision that he is wearing a confused scowl on his face.

"I brought you something," he says, breaking the tense silence.

I examine the faded black leather bag in his hand and reach out to take it from him. My skin grazes against his accidentally, and I snap my hand back quickly. I swear the mere touch of the man sends shockwaves through my body.

"What is it?" I ask, trying to remain focused.

"I meant to give it to you yesterday. I asked Madam Piffnel to bring you some clothes," he explains. "I know the ones you have been wearing aren't suitable."

My brows knit together a little as I finally meet his gaze. "Ohh," I say, taking the bag to set it on the bed. "Thanks."

I face away from him as I open the bag, closing my eyes and praying that he takes the hint and leaves.

It seems my prayers have fallen on deaf ears. The next thing I hear is the sound of his boots against the floorboards as he walks closer to me. I feel every movement of his body in the suffocating air around us, my temperature rising as my cheeks begin to warm. I have to imagine that they are now glowing a bright shade of pink. His footsteps stop, and I feel his breath against my shoulder.

"You're angry with me," he says calmly, his smooth voice making my skin tingle in anticipation.

I grit my back teeth together and open my eyes, fighting every instinct in my body. Every urge I have to press my body into his. To pull his lips down to meet my neck.

"Uh, no. Last night is on me. It was my fault."

Without warning, his hands lift to rest on my waist, gripping it firmly.

My pitiful attempt at an apology is interrupted when my breath catches in my throat. My pussy throbs again. My body and mind are now locked in a fierce battle of wills.

Why is this so damn difficult?

"I can't stop thinking about you," he says quietly.

I suck in my bottom lip to stop it from quivering as his hands begin to move upward over the curves of my waist, dragging the loose shirt along with them.

Fuck! Will power, Eden!

I turn quickly, and his hands drop from my body as I stare up into his eyes. "Last night was a mistake. It won't happen again," I say sternly.

"If that's what you want," he answers without a hint of emotion on his handsome face.

"It is," I reply adamantly.

His eyes travel over my face for a moment before he juts his head forward. "I don't believe you."

The daring look he gives me almost causes my weak resolve to snap.

He steps away from me, his eyes leaving mine to work their way around the room suspiciously. "I'll see you downstairs," he finishes, heading for the door.

I nod robotically, watching him leave without a second glance.

I sit down on the edge of the bed and bring my hand up to my head in exhaustion. Despite everything Mateo told me, my feelings for Erix, and my loyalty to my own people... I just can't seem to help myself around him.

At that moment, I hook my finger around a tiny negligee, pulling it from the leather bag to hold it up in front of me.

Oh... shit. I do not stand a chance.

Bedroom

Conall

As soon as I close the door behind me, I take a second to compose myself. It's getting harder to be closer to her. Harder to resist touching her at any opportunity I get.

Last night just about fucking killed me. Watching her sit there in front of my very eyes, finding her release without my help, left me both hard as fuck and completely frustrated.

I needed her last night. I needed to feel her skin beneath my fingertips. I needed to be the one to bring her pleasure. To make her moan in ecstasy.

I can't deny that I was shocked when I walked into the room to the scent of her arousal. The sight of her silky legs spread out across my bed almost broke me, but I somehow managed to keep my cool. Partially anyway. Fuck, it was only yesterday morning I was telling myself that I had to stay away from her. To keep my distance and fucking focus on my work. My fucking job!

But I couldn't help it. Being in the forest with her and seeing her get lost in her own little world amongst the trees left me speechless. Nature isn't just something that she loves. It's part of her. She's never looked more beautiful than she did at that moment. The moment when the wind caught her hair and a crystal clear tear dropped onto her pink cheek.

After I saw her in this way, I was racked with guilt. Guilt that I was the one who was taking it all away from her. I was the one who was denying her from being her whole self. It messed with my fucking head!

I stride down the hallway, looking over the balcony to catch sight of Mateo as he sits at the breakfast table. Fucking kid. As soon as I walked into her bedroom this morning, I scented him. I can already tell that he is attached to her. That he cares for her in some kind of way. I try to stop myself from thinking about it. If I do, I might fucking kill the kid where he stands. I wonder if Eden's sudden change of heart this morning has anything to do with him.

□

Did he say something to her that made her decide to take a step back?

I stop and walk over to the banister, gripping the solid oak tightly as I think it over. It's then that he glances up at me, his startled expression giving him away instantly. He looks away quickly, and I narrow my eyes.

It has never been a priority of mine to make friends in this house. I'm not here to win any fucking popularity contests. After all, most of these assholes I would never have even associated with in my old life, but it's now my job to keep them safe. To stop them from getting themselves killed in their attempts to exact revenge on those who took everything from them. As long as I have their faith as a strong leader, then that's all I need.

"Con."

I look to the side to see Zeke standing to attention. "How did this morning go?"

"Fine. We spotted an Elven patrol to the east, but nothing too close to the base. We left some tracks to draw them away in the opposite direction."

"Good."

"I've made the preparations for tomorrow. Hunter, Evan and William will come with me," he adds.

I nod, tearing my eyes away from Mateo to face him. "I'm going to move Eden to the top floor," I say, taking him by surprise.

"Really? To *that* bedroom?"

"Yes. Have it prepared while I'm out. I have to pick some things up from our contact. Our stock is running low."

"Sure," he nods, examining me suspiciously for a moment. "Eden's a fine woman, huh, Con?" he then asks, raising his eyebrow. "You know...for an elf," he adds with a jovial laugh.

I give him a warning look that causes the smile to leave his lips.

"I'll be back later."

* * *

Eden

I smile to myself as I look down at the meal I have prepared for this evening. I have been working on a rabbit stew for most of the afternoon. To be quite honest, I needed a distraction. It also allowed me to hide out down here for most of the day, out of the way of a certain someone.

"Smells fucking amazing," Neville says, placing bowls on the wooden table.

"It should," I answer with a grin.

Zeke steps into the kitchen, looking around until his eyes find me by the stove.

"Eden."

"Yeah?"

"Can you come with me for a minute?"

I give him a questioning look but follow his lead anyway, handing over the wooden spoon to Anton to begin plating up for dinner.

"What's up?" I ask as we make our way up the stone steps.

He doesn't bother answering. Instead, he continues, heading toward the steps that lead to Con's wing of the house.

"Zeke, what is this about?" I ask stubbornly, folding my arms over my chest.

He turns around to give me an exasperated look. "Listen, I'm just the messenger. I've been told to move your things upstairs."

"Upstairs?!" I ask in a panic, practically running after him as he strides up the dark steps.

"That's what I said."

Panic overwhelms me as I consider what this means. It did say in the book that a wolf will seek to claim his mate—to possess her—to make her his own.

Will Con try to force me to stay in his bedroom from now on?

Although I never considered myself in danger from him, the events of last night have made me think twice.

I don't get a chance to finish the thought as Zeke stops at the very first bedroom. I glance briefly at Con's closed door at the end of the hallway and swallow hard.

"This is your new room," he states, opening the door and nodding inside.

I glance at him sideways before I walk in. I cannot deny that I'm immediately shocked by what I find. A large room, possibly bigger than Conall's, complete with a marble dresser and four-poster bed draped in heavy, teal-colored fabric. It looks nice. Aged, like every other part of the house, but it's a world away from my dinky little bedroom downstairs. I wonder to myself why no one has claimed it already.

"Why am I being moved here?" I ask Zeke.

He shrugs his shoulders. "Like I said...messenger," he answers, giving me a curt nod before closing the door.

I rush over to the large bay windows and stare at the lush, dark forest now covered in a sheet of storm clouds. Despite this, I can still see its beauty, making my heart soar.

I look around the room again and walk over to the bed, glancing to the side to see the leather bag filled with my new clothes. I sit beside it, bouncing up and down a little on the firm but somewhat comfortable mattress. I let out a breath as I think over my next move. Marching straight to Con's room to demand he tell me what game he is playing may not end as I expect it to. In fact, with the way I've been acting lately, I might just end up landing myself in another compromising position.

I decide to leave it alone for now, rushing out of the room and back down to the kitchen to begin serving dinner. I follow Anton and Neville upstairs with the last of the bowls, heading for the dining table, which is already filled with the rowdy group of men.

Surrender

Eden

The hearty laughter and loud conversation continue as Neville, Anton, and I place the bowls of stew on the table.

"Goddess, what the hell is this?!" Hunter demands in his usual over-the-top fashion. "You can't have cooked this, Anton. It looks like proper fucking food for a change!"

Everyone laughs, and I smile a little, watching the men prod at their meal or lift it to their noses to give it a whiff.

"Eden, this tastes amazing," Mateo declares, pointing his fork at me before he does a dramatic chef's kiss.

"Well, thank you," I reply, placing my hands on my hips. "It's about time you guys gave me a little credit around here."

"Yeah, yeah!" Evan laughs, shaking his head in amusement as he reaches for the bread in the middle of the table.

Suddenly, the front door opens, causing the sound of heavy rainfall and thunder to echo through the room. Con walks inside, running his hand through his wet hair as he stalks across the room to the bookcase in the corner. He lifts the pile of soggy books in his hands to place them on the shelf.

Swifty, my gaze drifts over his back, which is clad in a soaking wet black shirt that clings to his massive shoulders. My eyes then meet Mateo's accidentally, and he frowns just a little. I lift the jug of water and begin pouring, keeping my hands and mind busy while Con makes his way over to the head of the table.

"You need to try this supper tonight, Con. It's delicious. Just like my old grandma used to make," William states between mouthfuls.

Con nods, pulling out a chair as he looks in my direction.

"Sounds good," he replies, sitting down to pull his bowl closer to him.

The chatter continues all around me, but it doesn't seem to matter.

☐

Whenever he and I are in the same room, there is only one thing on my mind. I force myself to focus back in on the conversation.

"Did you hear me, Eden?" Hunter asks for clarification.

"What?" I ask in surprise. "Sorry, I missed that."

"It's not just the food that looks good tonight. I see you've got yourself some new clothes."

I laugh lightly as I look down over the tight-fitted tunic and snug black pants. "Thank Goddess for Madam Piffnel, huh?" I say with a grin, leaning forward to top up the next glass, each one bringing me closer to Con at the end of the table.

"Thank the Goddess indeed," Anton chimes in as Evan lets out a loud wolf whistle.

"Assholes," I mutter in amusement.

"Don't listen to them, Eden. You look beautiful. Like always," Mateo says kindly.

"The ass isn't half bad, elf," Samuel adds, lifting his hand to smack my ass hard.

I hardly have a chance to react when Samuel suddenly yells in pain.

My mouth drops in complete shock when I see the offending hand, bloodied and nailed to the table, the hilt of a knife poking out from the skin.

The whole table falls into shocked silence, and my heart thunders against my chest as my eyes connect with Conall's where he sits, his large frame heaving up and down with rage.

What the fuck did he just do?

Then all hell breaks loose.

Immediately, Rocco jumps out of his seat like a shot, his eyes black with fury as he shouts obscenities at the top of his lungs. Samuel pulls the knife from his hand with a pain-filled grunt, standing up to point its bloody blade at Con wildly.

I gasp in horror as he lunges for Con, who gets out of his chair to punch Samuel in the face. The whole room descends into chaos after that as plates of food and chairs fall to the floor. Yelling permeates the air as others jump into the fray. Hunter has Rocco pinned to the table, brutally exchanging punches that send splatters of blood flying all over the place.

I look on in utter disbelief, my eyes wide as I see Con punch Samuel in the stomach before snatching the knife out of his hand to toss it away. Both men fight savagely against one another while some of the others try to hold them back.

Just then, a tight hand grips my arm, and I am dragged away from the carnage.

"STOP!" I yell in protest, thrashing against Zeke as he hauls me off to the staircase. "Let me go!!"

He doesn't answer my requests. Instead, he wraps his arm around my waist, practically carrying me with one arm as he charges upstairs.

"WE NEED TO STOP THIS!" I scream, kicking my legs out erratically. "CON!! CON!!"

Finally, we reach the forbidden staircase, and Zeke grabs my hand tightly, tugging me upwards.

The sounds of manic yelling and tossed furniture grow further into the distance as my new bedroom door is opened. Zeke thrusts me inside the dark room, and I stumble a little before swinging around to run for the door. He lifts his finger to point it straight at me.

"Stop," he orders, looking into my eyes seriously. "Con's wolf has taken over. You have to let him come back around. Your scent in the room will only make things worse."

My eyes widen in surprise when I realize that he has figured out the secret. The one Con and I have been keeping from everyone in this house. He knows we are mates.

"Stay here, Eden," he says adamantly, closing the door behind him.

A burst of air leaves my lungs, and I lift my shaking hand to my head.

Fuck, fuck, fuck.

I feel something wet and quickly examine my hand to see it is covered in tiny blood splatters. Blood that doesn't even belong to me. In a frenzy, I wipe it against my pants, rushing to the door to press my ear against the solid wood. I still hear the sound of faint shouting, but I cannot figure out what the hell is now happening down there.

I lean my head against the door and close my eyes. The look on Con's face after he stabbed his knife through Samuel's hand is like nothing I've ever seen. His expression was...dark...savage even.

Is this what happens to him when his wolf takes over?

I push myself away from the door and begin to pace back and forth, my jittery nerves causing me to breathe in and out erratically.

☐

I can no longer hear any shouting in the house. Only the sounds of the raging thunderstorm outside. The lightning snaps through the obsidian skies and flashes intermittently in the dark room.

A few tense minutes pass, but my high adrenaline remains intact. Until I know what's going on, there's absolutely no way I can relax. Not for one second.

Finally, the door flies open to reveal Con, who steps inside, slamming it shut behind him. I take a step back, my adrenaline spiking even further as I stare at his large imposing figure in the darkness.

"Eden—"

"What the hell happened down there?! Has the fighting stopped?!" I demand, my voice shaking just a little as I yell at him.

"It's over," he confirms.

The thunder rocks the foundations of the old house, the lightning flashing through the room to afford me a view of his face. He has a cut above his eyebrow and a trickle of blood running down the side of his face.

"WHAT THE HELL WERE YOU THINKING?!" I snarl in anger, my rage now taking over the initial shock.

"I wasn't," he answers, taking a step forward.

"You stay the hell away from me!" I scream, pointing my finger at him threateningly.

His eyes narrow, and he strides forward defiantly, grabbing my wrist to pull me close to his chest. "No man will ever touch a fucking hair on your head, Eden. No man will ever put his hands on you...not while there is still breath in my fucking body."

"That's not your choice!" I seethe back in return.

"You're *mine*," he replies possessively, his dark stormy eyes looking down at me.

I breathe heavily as I stare back at him. "I belonged to someone else!" I snap back quickly.

His grip on me tightens ever so slightly.

"He loved me. He treated me with grace and respect. He touched me with care and tenderness."

His face gets closer to mine as his gaze falls on my lips.

"I don't want that from you," I finish adamantly, my voice low and determined. "You're not him, and you never will be!"

"Then what do you want?" he snaps, his lips edging closer to mine.

My muddled thoughts all mash together as I stare at him. Nothing makes sense anymore. Nothing except this burning, all-consuming need.

"Do you want courser treatment from me?" he asks, letting go of my wrist to grip the back of my neck tightly. "Do you?"

My body jolts with a delicious mixture of mild pain and sheer sexual desire.

"Is that what you want, Eden?" he demands, his black eyes looking straight into my fucking soul. "Tell me!"

I nod my head in admission as his nose skims mine.

"Say it," he grits out wantonly, his grip tightening again.

"I want you to fuck me...and I want you to fuck me hard."

The filthy words leave my lips like a weight being lifted from my shoulders.

Immediately, he pulls me forward, his mouth smashing against mine as he devours my lips, forcing them to part for him. The electrifying feeling that courses through my body right now feels like fucking heaven. I throw my arms around his neck, letting him lift me off my feet to slam me against the wall forcefully. A loose picture frame falls, smashing unceremoniously against the floorboards. There's nothing gentle in his touch. No restraint. It's wild and passionate just as I hoped it would be.

Neither of us stops to draw breath. My legs wrap around his waist as he pushes his hard body against mine, the crushing feeling only adding to my crazed, filthy appetite. A growing, all-consuming appetite that can only be satisfied by him alone. My fingernails claw at his shirt, and his lips leave mine as he puts his hand down to help me tug it over his head. A second away from his lips proves to be one second too many, and I tangle my fingers in his wet hair as I pull him to me once again. I moan against his mouth as his hardness strains through his pants, pinning me to the wall. My pussy demands his cock like never before. Throbbing and pulsing between my legs in a way that can no longer be ignored. He seems to read my mind, his lips leaving mine to cover my neck desperately as he tugs my hair roughly to the side. The slight graze of his teeth against my hot skin causes me to groan loudly, squeezing my eyes closed as I enjoy the rush of delirious pleasure that falls over me.

He grips the edge of my tunic, pulling it over my head and throwing it away. He pins me to the wall again as his tongue finds my hard nipple, swirling around it and tugging it like the wild beast that he is.

"Yesss..." I grit out, arching my back out toward him shamelessly.

☐

His arm wraps around my waist, his lips meeting mine again as he sits me down on the nearby marble dressing table, knocking over the old knick-knacks which clang and clatter together. I lean back on my hands and watch as he bends down on one knee to unbutton my pants, my chest rising and falling violently. I lift my ass to help him slide the pants down my legs, and he tosses them to the side.

His eyes connect with mine briefly as he throws my legs open. His head dives between my thighs, and I yell out in ecstasy as his tongue plunges inside me.

"Fuck!" I scream, my hips thrusting against him as I grip his hair.

His hands wrap around my thighs, pulling me closer to him as his nose and lips bury themselves deep in my throbbing pussy. My mouth drops open as I watch him. Hungry and rampant. His sheer carnal, savage behavior only making me wetter. Lightning flashes through the window against us, its power somehow insignificant when measured with the beast between my legs.

His hands grab my ass tighter, his fingers digging into my skin. Marking me. Turning my creamy flesh red raw. I don't care a single bit. In fact, I relish the feeling of his harsh, unforgiving touch.

I moan out loud as his tongue circles and flicks expertly against my clit. I can already feel my orgasm building, but I'm not ready to let go yet.

Tonight I want it all.

I want everything he has to give, and I don't care about anything else. There are no other thoughts in my mind.

Only him.

Only this.

I throw my head back, and he rises to his feet, biting my neck as he fists my hair. His fingers work against my soaking wet core, eliciting sounds from my lips that I never thought possible. His finger slips inside me, and he begins to work it back and forth at a rhythmic yet firm pace.

"Look at me, Eden," he demands in a growl that sends a shooting bolt of electricity down my spine.

I snap my head forward to look into his eyes, jolting my hips forward to ride his finger. It's no longer enough. I know what I want, and he knows it too.

He lifts me from the dressing table in one strong swoop, carrying my naked body over to the bed to throw me onto the mattress.

My legs spread wide as he tugs his pants down, kicking them off to tower

144

over me. I wrap my hands around the nape of his neck as he positions his solid cock against me, and my hands spread over the sides of his strong, stubbled jaw. He leans in to kiss me fiercely, his tongue moving in perfect sync with my own.

He notches his dick at my entrance, running the tip over my soaking wet clit. I whimper as my body jolts, my eyes glued to his handsome face which contorts in pleasure. Finally pushes his cock inside me, filling me up slowly at first before a satisfied grunt vibrates in his chest. He plunges inside, and I yell out in ecstasy. His head pulls back to look at me as my hands stay on his face. We stare into each other's eyes as he fucks me, his cock making me feel full in every sense of the word.

"Yes...Con, yesss," I moan through gritted teeth.

His thrusts grow more frantic as his nose touches mine. My mouth opens, but the screams get caught in my throat. My pussy throbs in a mixture of stinging pleasure and pain as he pounds into me again and again. Over and over without fucking mercy.

He lifts my hips to drive into me deeper, one of his hands smacking my ass hard. I yelp when he then leans down on top of me, his heavy weight pressing down on me as he kisses and nips my neck, his rough, manly hands gripping my tits.

I push myself into his touch, reaching my arms above my head as I savor every second. He seizes the opportunity immediately, holding my wrists in place tightly with one hand as he fucks me even harder.

My orgasm is so close I can practically feel it bursting at the seams already. My muscles begin to tense one body part at a time. My breathing intensifies. I scream out his name as my legs wrap around him desperately.

He lets go of my wrists, his hand now slipping down to my neck. The rough passion ignites the fire inside me, and I can hold on no longer.

My orgasm hits like a strike of lightning. My eyes connect with his, and he watches me in complete fascination as I unravel beneath him. My body vibrates and shudders with the intensity of my release. A release that is followed by a state of such utter contentment and satisfaction that it spreads over me from head to toe.

His thrusts become slower, his eyebrows knitting together as he pulls away from me to finish. I reach my hand down to assist, feeling his warm cum as it meets the skin of my navel. His eyes close, his jaw tenses, and I watch him intently. Every groove and curve of his handsome face has me captured. His muscled shoulders begin to relax, and his head drops, touching my chest as we both breathe deeply.

I lift my arms to hold his head against me. His lips kiss my hot skin gently, leaving tingles in their wake.

His head lifts, and his eyes look into mine, but neither of us dares to say a word.

We lost the battle. That much is clear.

But right now—at this moment—none of it seems to matter.

Aubrun

I remove my wet cape, tossing it aside as my men filter in through the doorway behind me.

"All of you, please be ready to search again tomorrow. Early morning, same time," I say, turning to look around the group.

Each one nods their head in turn, proceeding down the stone hallway to the armory to store their bows and swords.

I take the steps two at a time as I rush towards the royal wing of the household. It's a journey I know well, having grown up here all my life, but for the past few days, it is a journey that I have come to dread.

How can I tell king ciridan that I have failed my mission again?

A mission that was trusted only to me and the men I command.

How on earth do I look haleth in the eye and tell him that his daughter is still out there somewhere?

Most likely captured by those disgusting beasts. The mere notion of it leaves me sick to my stomach. After all, it is as though I predicted the whole scenario. There have been rumblings for a while amongst the Elven Guard that wolf tracks have been spotted in the forest. A few men even claimed to have seen one of the beasts with their own eyes in recent years, but King Ciridan and his advisors always assured us that this was nonsense. Despite this, I always had my doubts. Some sneaking suspicion in the back of my mind that they would return one day to wreak havoc and throw our kingdom into disarray once again.

I should have insisted that Eden stay out of the forest, and I should have followed her on the night of *The Culling* Celebration. I could see she was upset after the play. I should have known the forest would be her first port of call! Because of this, I must conclude that her disappearance is partly my fault.

I reach the door of the king's study and give it a firm knock. As I wait to be granted entry, I hear the sound of raised voices, muffled by the solid oak. The door then opens, and Queen Siofra gives me a gentle smile.

"Aubrun, come in, please," she says, stepping back to allow me to pass through.

I bow my head to her respectfully on the way and cast my eyes around the room to see the king sitting at the head of his intricately carved mahogany table, surrounded by at least ten of his advisors.

The room's warmth contrasts with the thundering rain beating off the stained glass windows, the glowing light of the fireplace adding to the already tense atmosphere.

I walk over to the desk as everyone falls silent and bow to my king before glancing sideways to nod at Haleth standing by the fireplace.

"Well, Aubrun. Please tell us you have some news for us?" King Ciridan asks.

"Unfortunately, I have no news, Your Majesty," I admit shamefully, looking down at the floor in disgrace.

Eden's mother lets out a pained whimper, and I look to the side to see her gripping Haleth desperately as she cries into his tunic.

"Now, now, Iriel. You must be strong," Queen Siofra states in an almost stern tone, walking over to pat Iriel on the back and offer her a glass of water. "It is perfectly within the realm of possibility that Eden is unharmed and safe."

"How can she be?" Iriel questions through tears, reaching her shaky hand out to take the glass. "Who knows what those beasts will do to her!"

"Do not think that way, my dear," Haleth says softly, guiding her onto a chair by the fireplace. "We must have hope."

I tear my eyes away from their emotional display and look back at King Ciridan. "Your Majesty, we found tracks in the forest heading east. We followed them for some miles before they trailed off."

He lifts his hand to his chin, nodding in deep thought.

"Your Majesty, perhaps if we engage the whole of the Elven Guard and increase our numbers—"

Immediately, the table of advisors begin to grumble in disapproval of my suggestion.

"Impossible, Aubrun," the king interrupts, shaking his head from side to side. "As I told you only days ago, this situation must be handled with the utmost discretion. There would be widespread panic if Morween and the wider Elven realm discovered that wolves had somehow returned to our lands.

148

Our people do not need this worry placed upon them."

"There is no guarantee that the girl has even been taken in the first place! The wolf sightings are still unproven! She may very well have left Morween of her own accord!" Lord Faenor chimes in, his loud voice attempting to dominate the room. "All this search is going to do is arouse suspicion amongst our people. It ought to be called off immediately."

"Nonsense, Lord Faenor!" Haleth protests. "My daughter would not leave without informing us first. A scrap of material from her gown was found in the woods, stained with droplets of her blood! Your Majesty, under no circumstances, should—"

The king holds up his hand to demand silence.

"The search will continue, Haleth, for now. Although, I cannot put the future of this kingdom at risk. We must contain this information. Each person in this room has agreed to do so under enchantment, as have Aubrun's men. Not another soul will know the truth. We will maintain the story that Eden has gone to study in Galnethas for the time being. The search will resume tomorrow, and we shall hope for better results."

As he finishes the last sentence, his eyes fall on me to give me a steely look.

"Yes, Your Majesty." I nod dutifully in return.

"In the meantime, Sire, we should be looking at ways to eradicate the last of these abominable beasts for good if they still reside in our forest. We honor the Goddess of Nature by doing so," Lord Algar says decisively.

Everyone then looks at Haleth, who swallows carefully, his face awash with clear reluctance.

"Haleth will work on this," King Ciridan agrees, drawing the attention in the room back to him. "He got rid of them once. I am sure he can do it again."

Both men stare at each other, an unspoken understanding lingering in the air between them.

"Aubrun, that will be all for now," King Ciridan states, dismissing me from the room.

I bow in return, making my way to the door to take my leave. As it closes behind me, I let out a frustrated breath, walking back through the hallways to my bedroom. I decide to take a last-minute detour, taking the path that I have trodden many times. Many times in the hope of running into *her*.

I arrive outside Eden's bedroom door, looking around cautiously before entering. The faint scent of her still lingers in the air, and I close my eyes to breathe her in for just a few seconds. I walk over to her little desk in the corner, running my fingers along the scattered books that rest undisturbed. She always was a bookworm. Devoted to her studies, as I was too, at the time when she first arrived in Morween. As soon as I set eyes on her, I was captured by her beauty. Unfortunately, so was Erix. Whereas I was shy and retiring, he was bold and dashing. It wasn't a surprise when he swept her off her feet, taking her from me before I could make my move. Despite this, I still loved him as a brother. I said nothing when they fell in love because I had missed my chance, and they were both so happy together.

After he died, I daren't picture a future with her in it. Not for a long time. Not until I was sure she was over him once and for all.

I walk over to the window and look over the kingdom below. When I return her to these lands, I will no longer remain silent, fading into the background.

I will create my own legacy.

This time I will not fail. I will make Eden my wife by any means necessary.

Loyalty

Conall

I leave the bathroom to find her curled up on an armchair beside the fire. Her damp lilac hair is pushed over one shoulder, her long legs on full display in one of my shirts. She's staring at the flames in deep thought, and I can't help but wonder what is going through her mind.

She hardly acknowledges my entrance into the room; honestly, I'm not surprised. Since we fucked, we have barely said two words to one another. Neither of us really knowing what the hell to say.

It was the most intense sexual experience of my life. To let go of every inhibition. To follow my primal instincts and take her as I have longed to do since the second I set eyes on her. But it doesn't change the fact that our situation is complicated as fuck. I walk over to the dresser and put on some pants before throwing a shirt over my head. As I turn around in her direction, I notice she remains completely unmoved. I'd be surprised if she has even blinked.

I clear my throat and walk over to my desk, sitting in my chair. I lean back and fold my arms over my chest, watching her as I try to think of something to say, fucking anything to break this silence.

My mouth opens, but she beats me to it, swinging her head around to look straight at me.

"Zeke knows," she says quietly, watching me carefully for my reaction.

"I thought so," I answer with a nod.

She stares at the fire again, and the silence continues.

"What are we going to do, Con?" she whispers.

I don't respond at first. I have no fucking answers to give her. There is no magic solution that I can think of to solve all of our problems.

"What do you want to do?" I ask, leaning forward to rest my forearms on my knees.

She looks back at me with a surprised expression on her face. "Me?" she asks quietly.

I nod my head.

She thinks for a moment before taking a deep breath. "I don't think we should tell anyone else we are mates. Will Zeke keep it a secret?" she asks with concern.

"If I tell him to,"

"Good." She nods self-assuredly. "No good can come of everyone knowing. Rocco and his little gang would probably demand my head on a pike—"

Her words immediately crawl under my skin, igniting the embers of rage again.

"He won't touch you, Eden. He wouldn't fucking dare," I reassure her insistently. "Trust me."

My words don't seem to dispel her worry as she nervously looks down at her fidgety hands.

"But if you'd rather we kept it a secret, that's what we'll do."

Her eyes snap up to meet mine.

"The only issue is...this is an old house, Eden. The walls are thin—"

"I know," she groans, wincing a little as her cheeks tinge pink. "Sorry."

The word immediately brings an unexpected and rare smile to my face, and she tilts her head to the side as she looks at me curiously. "Are you making fun of me, Con?" she asks, raising her perfectly shaped brow.

I shake my head and hold my hands up defensively. "Not one bit."

She smiles just a little, bringing her thumb to her mouth to nibble on her nail anxiously. "So they know we had sex... That's all they need to know," she shrugs, doing her best to sound casual. "It's not like it's anything more than that. It's just sex, right?"

I stare at her for a second, her words stirring a strange feeling inside me.

However, she's right. Of course, she is.

We were both pumped full of adrenaline. Crazed. Deprived. We snapped. But the sex was different, and we both know it. Even if we aren't going to admit it to one another.

"Just sex," I confirm.

"Then tell them that," she says decisively.

We look at each other intensely for another moment when suddenly my eyes are drawn to her pale legs where the top of her thighs are marred with tiny purple bruises. I frown, and she tugs the shirt down further to cover herself up.

"I hurt you," I state matter-of-factly, gesturing to the marks left behind by my wild behavior.

She shakes her head with a determined look fixed on her face. "No...no, you didn't," she replies adamantly. "I wanted it that way," she insists.

We stare into each other's eyes as I battle the guilt that rises in my chest, and it's then that I remember her words before we gave in to the pull.

"I belonged to someone else."

"He touched me with tenderness."

"I don't want that from you."

She wanted her experience with me to be different from her experience with this man. This man who was, or perhaps still is, the love of her life.

Jealously fiercely tugs at my brain, but I do my best to keep it at bay. To remain calm as I usually do.

"Con?" she asks. Those deep pools of purple pulling me deep into their depths. "Did you enjoy it?"

Her voice is now nothing more than a gentle whisper. The soft melodic sound makes me freeze and my cock twitches as the memory of her, her body and her incredible pussy all come back to flood my thoughts.

"Yes," I answer without a doubt in my mind. "More than you'll ever fucking know."

She sucks in her bottom lip for a moment. "I did too."

I feel the heat rising around my neck after her admission. Now I've had a taste of her, I'm not sure if I'll be able to give her up.

Not yet.

The door knocks, interrupting my thoughts and breaking the tension between us.

"Con, are you ready?" Zeke calls out from the hallway.

"On the way," I answer in return, waiting for his footsteps to trail off down the corridor.

Eden looks at me questioningly as I stand up.

"I called an emergency meeting about what happened at dinner earlier. It's starting now."

"Con..." she begins worriedly, standing up. "What's going to happen? What if Rocco—"

"This wasn't the first fight in this house, and it won't be the last," I interrupt.

She nods her head with a low sigh. "What should I do then?"

"Get some rest, you get up tomorrow, and you don't worry about this. I'll handle it."

She pinches the bridge of her nose for a second before putting her hands on her hips. Her signature determined expression returning to her stunning face. "Okay, but I'm going back to my own room," she says with conviction. "I think it's for the best." She straightens her shoulders and holds her head high.

"Fine," I answer in agreement, my eyes drifting to her plump lips. "Just don't get too comfortable. You won't be there for much longer."

Her eyes widen, lighting up as I make my dirty intentions crystal clear. I lean down to the crook of her neck as her eyes close gently. "I want you all over again, Eden, and I know you want me too."

I take a step back, and we look at each other for a second longer before I turn to leave the room, following Zeke downstairs.

* * *

I make my way down to the living room, where everyone is already sitting around the table waiting for me. I lock eyes with Samuel as he glares at me with hatred, his jaw clenched as he rests his bandaged hand on the table in front of him. I can tell by looking around that someone has cleaned up the mess. The scattered food and broken furniture are now completely gone.

The men fall into silence as I take a seat at the head of the table. Each of them looks at me expectantly, clearly waiting for me to begin, but I don't bother to say a word. If they have questions, they can go ahead and ask.

"Did you lose your fucking mind tonight, Conall?" Rocco growls, directing a sneer at me before he looks around the other men. "Is this the kind of leader we can have faith in? A man who fucking protects one of *them*?! Who puts his little elf whore before his brothers?!"

"No, it is not," Samuel adds in support, narrowing his eyes at me.

I rest my fist on the table, leaning back in my chair before speaking. "You put your hand on a woman in this house, then you leave me no choice but to put you in your fucking place," I say, looking around each man in turn before settling on Samuel.

"A woman? She's a fucking elf! She's one of them!" Rocco snaps hatefully.

"She's not like the others. Eden has a heart. You've all seen it," Mateo says in her defense.

The others nod in agreement while I try to ignore his evident affection for my mate to focus on the matter at hand.

"It's true. Eden is a good one," Hunter adds. "She shouldn't have to be felt up by a smelly fucker like you, Samuel."

"What did you just call me?!"

"Enough," I demand, drawing their attention back to me.

They all wait patiently for my next speech.

"Eden has not to be touched. If I hear that any of you assholes have laid a finger on her... I'll kill you," I say with unwavering resolve. "That is a fucking promise."

Rocco shakes his head slowly from side to side. "All this drama is because you didn't have the balls to slit her throat the minute she came through the door. You've grown attached to her! Soft! I bet you've been fucking her since her first night here!"

The men all look to me curiously for confirmation, and I shake my head in answer, rubbishing his claims.

"Come on, Con. We all have ears. We know what was going on up there tonight," William says, clearing his throat awkwardly while a hint of fear lingers in his eyes.

I shrug nonchalantly, the conversation I had with Eden a few minutes ago now replaying in my head. "No, I wasn't fucking her. But I am now," I answer, getting straight to the point.

They look around each other in slight shock at my revelation. Mateo shakes his head and drops his gaze down to the table.

I've always been a man to keep my cards close to my chest. To never really reveal anything about my private life, but now I don't give a fuck who knows about it. Eden and I tried not to give in to the pull, but it proved almost impossible. I'm already itching to be inside her again, and I can't deny it to myself any longer. There is no other way to handle this situation anyway. To deny what we did tonight would be pointless and a waste of time.

Zeke's eyes connect with mine, and I can tell what he is thinking. He knows there is more to tell. I give him a look, and he nods a little in confirmation,

☐

assuring me of his silence without a single word.

"How can you be fit to lead us now?! To be the one in charge when we finally get our revenge on those fuckers who took everything from us," Rocco demands, standing up to point at me accusingly. "You sleep with one of them, then as far as I am concerned, you are fraternizing with the damn enemy!! You've made your choice! Your loyalty is no longer with us!!" he finishes, slamming himself back down into his chair.

I look around the silent table at the faces of the men, and I can see that even those loyal to me look doubtful.

I cannot blame them.

I rise to my feet, resting my fists on the table. "Does anyone else question my loyalty?"

No one answers.

I look down as I prepare myself to go to that place again. The place that threatens to swallow me whole whenever I allow myself to visit.

"Three hundred and twelve," I say quietly, lifting my head to look around the room at each of them. "Three hundred and fucking twelve..."

They nod in understanding, and I turn my attention to Rocco.

"Don't ever fucking question my loyalty. If you come at me again, lay down the challenge outright because I won't be stepped down."

He grits his teeth in anger, but he has no response to give.

"Now let this rest. My sex life is none of your concern, and we have shit to do," I say, looking to Zeke to carry on the meeting with other items on the agenda.

He gives me a nod and stands up to take over.

Quickly, his voice fades into the background as my thoughts take over, my eyes drifting upward to the staircase. Every word that I said tonight is true. I won't let a single person touch her. I will protect her with my life. But I will remain loyal to my men and the loved ones I have lost.

By this time next week, the Elven king, along with every single one of his heartless scheming advisors, will finally die for their crimes.

Vengeance, at long last, will be ours.

Pancakes

Eden

I hear the sound of footsteps behind me, and my body tenses automatically. The pep talk I gave myself this morning before coming down here clearly hasn't settled my nerves entirely.

"Morning," I say cautiously, my eyes still on the batter in the bowl in front of me.

I continue to stir as the footsteps draw closer, the shadow of the enormous man finally settling over me.

"Morning," he says in his usual grumpy tone. No more or less pleasant than usual.

My shoulders drop in relief as I glance to the side, still mixing the batter as I look at the two great oafs who have come to help prepare for breakfast. Anton picks up a sharp knife, beginning to cut through the freshly baked loaf of bread. "Sleep well?" he asks, a smug grin inching itself over his face.

I can't help but smile, narrowing my eyes at him as Neville scoffs.

"*Very* well, actually," I reply, twisting around with the bowl in my arms.

Both of them laugh, and I shake my head from side to side. I know they are teasing me, but I'd rather have their playful, insinuating banter than awkward silence any day of the week.

"What is that anyway?" Neville asks, nodding his head to the bowl in my arms.

"Pancakes!" I declare happily.

"Really?" Anton asks, taking a bite from a slice of bread. "I haven't had them in...well, fuck knows how many years."

"They aren't that difficult," I chuckle in amusement.

"What you forget, Eden, is before we ended up in this place, Anton and I had never cooked a single meal in our lives," Neville answers, taking the bowl from my hands to beat the mixture for me.

"Seriously? Not ever?" I ask, smiling as I fold my arms over my chest.

"Nooo," Anton answers immediately. "We had cooks. Everyone had a role to play in my pack. Mine was being Alpha, of course."

"So being Alpha means everything is done for you?" I ask, raising my eyebrow.

"Of course, it was one of the perks of the job. Haven't you realized that most of us assholes are used to getting our own way?" Neville replies, handing the bowl back to me.

"Oh, can't say I have," I answer sarcastically.

"Now, what do we do with it?" Neville asks, looking down at the batter, his tone reminding me of a curious child.

"Now, the fun part." I laugh, grabbing a ladle to spoon some of the mixture into the hot pan.

Both men watch as I wait until the right moment, flicking my wrist to flip the pancake upside down. "There it goes!" I say, happy with my successful flip.

Anton claps his hands together, peeking over my shoulder at the golden pancake. "That one is mine... Fuck, look at that," he says, his stomach groaning in hunger. "It's glorious."

To hear them both so enthusiastic about a damn pancake does wonders to improve my overall mood. Don't get me wrong, I'm not the type of woman to shy away from anyone, but I can't say I haven't spent the whole night dreading this morning and what it would bring. Things have changed now. They were bound to as soon as everyone learned about Conall and I and our...well, whatever you would call it.

I must look a million miles away because Neville snaps his fingers at me to break me out of my stupor.

"Come on, I'm starving. Let's get a move on."

We continue the job at hand until we have a pile of pancakes stacked on each plate ready for serving. I grab the first few dishes and take a deep breath before heading for the steps.

"Eden," Anton calls out. "Pay no attention to Rocco. He doesn't speak for all of us; remember that," he says, his brutish face turning softer than I've seen it before.

A swell of emotion rises in my chest, and I give him a nod in thanks. I return to the stairs, his words giving me strength as I hold my head high to begin my day as always.

After stepping foot into the living room, the chatter amongst the men automatically quietens. I scan my eyes over them, trying to remain calm and confident amidst the tension. Con isn't here. Neither is Zeke. I don't know whether their absence makes this situation more or less daunting.

"Morning," I say plainly, placing a plate in front of Henrick and Evan, who both give each other a knowing glance. "Morning, Eden," Henrick answers brightly.

"How's the leg?"

"Good as new, thanks to you."

"Hey, I helped a little too!" Jarek interjects, pushing his loose glasses up his nose.

"Good. I'm glad it's on the mend, Henrick," I add, continuing around the table.

"Well, you bunch of assholes. Don't we have a treat for you this morning," Neville says proudly, placing down a few more plates. "Fucking pancakes!"

The joyful and enthusiastic chorus of approval is like music to my ears.

"Eden, even if you weren't our prisoner, you could never leave us now," Hunter says in a comment which I know is meant to be a joke. "We would miss this food too much."

"Yeah, I couldn't possibly let you all go back to that meat and bread diet you had going on," I joke in return.

"This...now *this* is hitting the spot," William mumbles as he stuffs his face.

"The elf would know all about that, wouldn't she?" Rocco pipes in, his snarky comment instantly dampening the mood.

Samuel scoffs, and I can't help but feel a little embarrassed.

Hunter glares at him in warning before he looks at me. "So what? You get yours, Eden," he winks with a wide smile. "Con's a lucky man if you ask me."

"I wouldn't comment on his woman unless you want a knife in your fucking eyeball," Henrick says with a grin, nudging Hunter playfully.

"Yeah, so maybe no one tells him I said that."

They begin to laugh, and I push my hair from my face awkwardly, thankful for Jarek, who changes the subject, talking the guys' ears off about the importance of them bathing more regularly. I'm not about to interrupt this well-needed speech for more than one reason.

My eyes then settle on Mateo, who hasn't said a single word since I entered the room. He's looking down at his plate, eating silently.

"Hey..." I say gently, filling up his cup with water. "Are you okay?"

"I'm fine," he answers grumpily, snatching the cup of water to gulp it down.

I decide to ignore his attitude. After all, I think I know why he is pissed, and I don't blame him. He went out of his way to warn me off Conall. He took a chance when he revealed the truth to me, and I repaid him by ignoring his advice completely.

I head for the stairs, leaving the men to eat in peace. I'd rather be alone after the intense emotions of the morning anyway. Damn, who knew living in a house filled with men would be so drama filled!

I sit down at the table and take a sip of hot tea, lifting my hand to soothe my aching forehead. I don't know what the hell to do next.

Last night with Conall, it was utterly mind-blowing. I can't lie. He read my body in ways that I have never experienced before. Even with Erix, who I loved dearly, the sex wasn't nearly as good.

It was raw and intense in many ways, but it also felt...*right*. Like giving myself up to him was what I was supposed to do from the very start.

But I know that Mateo's warnings also has merit.

How can I, in good conscience, sleep with a cold-blooded killer? Does it make me a bad person? But then, aren't all these men killers?

I have yet to learn the part each of them played in the war.

I fold my arms on the table and place my head down to close my eyes.

"Hard morning?"

I jolt upright in my seat, looking to Conall, who stands in the doorway watching me.

"Uhhh, it's been fine," I reply vaguely, fixing my wavy hair behind my ear.

He nods, picking up the little kettle from the stove and pouring some tea. His eyes meet mine as he turns to lean against the countertop. "Has anyone said anything to you?" he asks, a hint of steely determination lingering in his gaze as he drinks.

"No," I answer quickly, shaking my head.

I'm not about to start any more drama today. I don't think my nerves could take it!

"Good," he says, putting the cup down to roll up his sleeves. "I knocked on your door this morning before going on patrol."

"I must have still been asleep," I lie.

A smirk touches his lips, and he nods his head. "Hmm. Right," he answers, raising his eyebrow.

Fuck, he's so good-looking. The sight of him already has me shuffling uncomfortably in my seat.

What the hell is he doing to me?

"There's pancakes if you want to eat?" I say, gesturing to the leftover stack.

"No, I had something else in mind," he answers, walking over to the storage closet to open it wide.

"Con..." I say breathlessly in a mixture of disapproval and forbidden excitement. "We can't."

His brows knit together, and he shrugs his large shoulders. "Goddess knows what you are thinking. I was only going to suggest we go outside."

"Outside?" I question, practically spitting out my tea in surprise.

"But I understand if you...can't," he says challengingly, his eyes drifting over me.

A slow grin spreads across my face, and he smirks a little in return, bending down inside the cupboard to grab a basket. "Come on."

I shoot up from the chair as he strides back through the kitchen, taking the steps two at a time. I practically jog to keep up with his pace as he makes his way to the locked closet at the end of the hall. I've always wondered what they keep in here.

"So you hunt?" he asks, taking a key from his pocket to open the door.

"How did you know?"

"I've seen how you look at my men when they come back from a hunting trip."

I open my mouth in protest. "I haven't said a word!"

"You don't have to. It's written over your face," he answers. "You think you can do better."

He then steps back from the closet, and I freeze when I see the weapon in his hands.

A bow and arrow.

My eyes scan over it with mixed emotions before I return my gaze to meet his. "Con, what the hell?"

"You wouldn't shoot me now, would you, Eden?"

"I- uh." I can't formulate an answer, my brain scrambling as he pushes the weapon into my hands.

He leans in closer, his breath fanning my neck, creating tingles that ripple down my spine. "I think I'll take my chances," he husks.

☐

I swallow hard, looking up into his honey eyes. "I don't like your odds, Alpha," I whisper.

Delicious excitement creeps up on me, and I have no idea what causes it. Perhaps it's the knowledge that I'll soon be outdoors again, the feeling of the weapon in my hand, or the thrill of his challenging tone.

Whichever one it is, I'm strangely ready to embrace it.

Hunt

Conall

As soon as we step outside, I see Zeke, Hunter, Evan and William preparing to leave. I nod to them as we pass them by, not missing how they examine Eden standing next to me with a bow in her hands. I'm sure they probably think I'm fucking out of my mind. Maybe I am.

As soon as I saw her this morning, I had this urge to be near her. To find out more about her. Making conversation doesn't come naturally to me, so taking her out hunting was the first thing that sprung to my mind.

I carry on toward the trees regardless of the guys' stares, Eden at my side as we enter the thick of the forest.

"Where are the others going? Not another patrol at this time?" she asks, glancing back over her shoulder curiously.

"No, they have work to do," I answer vaguely. "They'll be back in a couple of days."

"Couple of days?" she asks in shock. "I haven't noticed anyone leaving the house for that amount of time before."

I ignore her comments completely, instead stopping to drop the basket by my feet. "So are you going to keep asking questions, or are you going to hunt?"

Her once shocked expression switches to determined, and she turns away, closing her eyes as she breathes in deeply. I watch, fascinated, as the sunlight seeps through the gaps in the trees, falling on her stunning face. A slight smile touches her lips, and a few moments later, she tosses the arrows over her shoulder, pulling one from the quiver. Her fingers run along it gently before she positions it against her bow, raising her arms to aim straight ahead.

I watch as she pulls the string back, stilling her body and closing one eye in preparation. Her fingers release the arrow, setting it free to pierce a large tree around twenty yards away. I smirk as I examine its position, wedged in the trunk.

"Maybe our hunting reputation is safe after all," I tease.

"Practice shot," she declares with a shrug. "It's been a little while. Since I've been busy, you know, locked up washing dishes for a bunch of man-children."

"Point taken," I answer, folding my arms as she readies another arrow.

"This way," she demands, walking off away from me.

I follow her, and we walk together in silence as she stalks the trees around us for her prey.

"Do you hunt?" she asks, glancing at me sideways.

"When I need to," I answer. "Usually in my wolf form. I can show you."

She swallows a little, and I can tell the thought makes her uncomfortable.

"No...no, it's alright," she answers, her brow scrunching.

We stop at the crest of a hill, and she peers over the edge. "Doesn't look too steep; we'll have more luck down here," she says decisively.

I follow her lead deeper into the forest. It's cooler down here, the trees blocking out most of the sun's powerful rays.

"So, is last night the reason for your sudden invitation this morning?" she asks, changing the subject.

"It would seem like it."

Her head turns towards me, and she looks me up and down. "Perhaps if I had known, I would have slept with you sooner."

Her bold words both surprise me and turn me the fuck on. "You think I can be so easily manipulated?" I ask, watching as she comes to a stop, her gaze almost burning through my skin where I stand.

"You?" she says, tilting her head to the side. "No... I have the feeling I could know a man like you for a hundred years and never really know what's going on in your head."

"What do you want to know?" I question, stepping closer to her.

I can tell she is feeling the pull as I am, but it seems my offer of openness is too tempting for her to resist.

"Where are you from?" she queries, examining my face carefully. "Is it far?"

I shake my head. "Not that far."

She stares at me in clear demand of more details.

"West of here. Evercrest was the name of my pack."

"Oh," she replies quietly. "I've never heard of it."

"Well, you wouldn't have. It's now an Elven town," I answer scornfully.

Her eyes drift away from mine, and she turns to continue walking.

"So you were in the war?" she asks, now with a hint of caution in her voice. "Yes."

"How did you survive *The Culling*? How did any of you survive?" she asks. The question lingers in the air between us for a few moments.

"Because of our genes... The thing we share in common."

"Because you are Alphas," she concludes.

I nod in confirmation.

"But you are all still alive seventy years later? And you haven't aged? How?" she questions, glancing at me sideways.

"I ask myself the same question every day," I answer truthfully.

The weight of our conversation begins to take its toll, and I know I must change the subject. "You left Azealea to work at the palace?"

"As I've said," she replies with a nonchalant shrug.

"Getting to know each other only works when we are both honest," I hit back in irritation.

There is a moment of silence before she concedes. "Fine... I went there during war times to study. I still am."

"Still studying?" I ask with a judgmental smirk.

"Yes," she snaps back defensively. "It takes at least two hundred years to become efficient in my field, and even then, I still won't know it all."

"Two hundred years to study plants and shit?" I ask. The silliness of it piques my interest, I have to admit.

"It's more than just *plants*," she says, stopping in her tracks. "It's the energy of the earth itself. The sheer gift of nature!"

Her words show her passion, and I can tell her studies mean a lot to her. It's sort of sexy in an odd kind of way. To be totally devoted to something. To pursue it no matter how long it takes. However, my admiration doesn't last all that long when I think about what her talents entail... Magic and sorcery.

"But nature can also be deadly if you will it to be," I counter, looking into her eyes challengingly.

I can tell that she's well aware of my meaning.

"I am sorry about what happened to your people," she says. "Truly. When I think on it now... It makes me sick."

I can detect sympathy in her words, her kind heart is as plain as the nose on her face, but she still has no real sense of what we went through. The sheer magnitude of the loss we have suffered.

□

I nod, and she swallows, turning around to keep walking toward a stream up ahead.

Suddenly she stops, bending down to place her bow on the ground as she cups a crinkled little white flower in her hands. Her eyes close, and I watch in both confusion and disbelief as the grass around her sways in a sudden, gentle wind. The flower in her hand begins to glow a light shade of blue before the petals turn back to pure white, flourishing in front of my very eyes. The wind disappears, and she lets the little flower go, rising to her feet to look down upon it.

"How do you do that?" I ask, trying my best to understand.

"You study for a helluva long time," she answers sarcastically.

"Hmm," I answer as we continue our journey to the river, falling back into silence again.

The topic of *The Culling* hasn't exactly afforded us an easy conversation. The silence between us now feels even heavier and more awkward.

She suddenly stops to listen, and we hear some faint movements amongst the trees. She holds her bow up, ready to shoot.

"So you love nature but have no problem killing other living things?" I ask in a low voice.

"We've all got to eat," she answers, never breaking concentration.

"Still...it's surprising."

"I'm good at it, but I wouldn't say I enjoy killing," she adds, stopping to bend down on one knee. "Perhaps not like some people..."

I frown as her arrow flies across the forest, taking a pheasant down with one clean shot.

"You believe I enjoy taking lives?" I ask as she stands back up to face me.

"I don't know, do you? You have taken lives, I'm assuming? Elven lives?"

Her eyes are fixed on mine, trying to figure me out.

"Many," I answer without a hint of hesitation or remorse.

"I thought so," she seethes as I brush past her, walking over to collect her kill.

Just as I am about to bend down to lift the unfortunate beast, I hear the rustle of leaves behind me. I stop, slowly turning to see her standing a few feet away with her arrow pointed squarely at my chest.

Her beautiful face is devoid of emotion as she stares into my eyes, and I stare back.

"Why don't you do it?" I ask, opening my arms out as I take a step forward. "No one would see you. You could make a run for it."

Her brows twitch a little in confusion. "As I said, killing brings me no pleasure. Now maiming, on the other hand...." she continues, pointing her bow at my right thigh.

I scoff a little taking another step closer; she pulls the string of her bow back tighter.

"How far would you get before I captured you again?" I wonder out loud, looking her up and down. "Before I caught up with you and dragged you back to the den."

"Don't move a muscle," she orders as I get closer.

"Are you sure that's what you want?" I ask, my mind beginning to run away with me as a strange, addictive mixture of adrenaline and lust creeps through my body. "I don't think it is, Eden," I add confidently.

"You don't know what I want," she growls in return.

I stop in front of her arrow that maintains its aim, but I can see the slight shudder of her hand.

"That's where you are wrong because you want the same thing I do," I state, looking into her lilac eyes. "You want to feel alive again."

Her jaw clenches, but there is a blazing fire in her eyes that she cannot hide from me...her mate.

I step forward again, gaining distance to close the gap between us.

"Put the bow down, Eden... Put it down, and let me fuck you."

□

Alive

Eden

His words light me on fire.

They fall from his lips so effortlessly that even with this bow in my hands, I am the one playing catch up. My arrow is pointed at him, ready and waiting, yet I am not the one in charge.

His body language. His face. His eyes. He embodies dominant masculinity in a way that leaves me feeling powerless against his raw, commanding energy.

He takes another step forward, and my resolve wanes further, my grip on the string of my bow faltering just a little. He lifts his hand to push the bow slowly to his left, his determined eyes never leaving mine.

My arms drop, and the weapon falls from my hands, landing on the leafy forest floor with a gentle thud.

My heart races away from me, but I have no desire to catch it. Instead, I'm frozen. Frozen as he begins to circle my body. His closeness sets off a chain reaction. The same crazy, stupid, amazingly tantalizing reaction that leaves my knees weak and my guard all but diminished.

Every inch of my skin trembles for his touch. Every cell is awake and focused on him. His chest brushes against my back, and my eyes close automatically, my lips parting to let go of a heavy gasp when his lips press against my neck.

His kisses run upward while my breathing begins to intensify. My body is unwittingly encouraging him to go further. My hips swinging subtly back and forth against his dick. It begins to swell on contact, the solid feeling of his arousal possessing me at once, making me lose my damn senses yet again. I reach my arm up behind me, hooking my hand around his neck to pull him in closer. He slams my hips against him hard, his kisses growing wilder.

I throw my head back against his chest, and his hands move up from my waist, squeezing my tits with delicious vigor. I can't help but look down. The brawn of his large, rough hands makes me wetter and even more desperate.

My mouth drops open as my intense breaths begin to mingle with the sounds of the forest. One of his hands moves up to grab my jaw firmly, twisting my neck around for his lips to capture mine.

The power in his kiss blows me the fuck away.

I turn around to face him, and our bodies attach like magnets that can no longer withstand the pull. My hands reach into the dark hair at the nape of his neck while his work their way up to my face, holding me in place as his willing prisoner. His tongue explores my mouth like never before, its erotic dance leaving me wanting for more. Our mouths smother one another as though breathing has no meaning anymore.

All we need is this.

All we need is each other.

His hands move down to my shoulders, and he unbuckles the quiver, causing it to fall to the ground, scattering the arrows at my feet. I reach for his shirt, tugging it out from his pants and pushing it up over his fucking incredible body. We break apart for a moment as he pulls it over his head, discarding it on the ground. His eyes are now black with lust as he stares at me in that same animalistic way. A look that would have once struck fear in me now only brings sheer excitement and desire. I want to be savaged by this man in every way possible.

"Take them off," he orders, his eyes running down my clothes with disdain.

I do as I am told without question, pulling the tunic over my head to release my breasts. His eyes fixate on me, watching my every move as I reach for the waistband of my pants, pushing them down to the ground. I step out of them along with my boots, my bare feet resting on the grassy forest floor. The cool spring air lashes at my skin, making it feel almost too sensitive to touch. Despite this, it's one of the most exhilarating feelings I've ever had. I close my eyes and feel a burst of pure energy running through me. I feel as though I could float away into the ether at any given second.

Then I feel them. The warmth of his arms wrapping around me, anchoring me in place on this earth. His lips find mine again, moving with wild passion as my hands explore the ripples of his muscled chest.

Fuck, his body is hard like solid marble and yet so damn warm and inviting. To feel his huge frame engulf mine feels so right. As though we fit together like two missing pieces of a complicated puzzle.

One of his hands has a tight grip around my waist, while the other holds the back of my head, his fingers tangled in my wild hair. He begins to move forward, backing me up against a tree until the rough bark grazes my skin.

His hand leaves my head, hooking under my chin tenderly.

I reach for his pants to push them downward. They squeeze down over his firm ass, and my hands grab at him, pulling him closer. The feeling of his cock against the bare skin of my midriff makes me hiss in pleasure, and I can't wait to have him inside me. He steps out of the pants and presses against me harder, driving his hips forward to meet my untamed thrusts.

Despite my desperate need, an alarm bell rings in my head. His hand, which was positioned against my cheek, turns softly. The back of his fingers lightly drifting across my skin as they make their way down my neck and chest. My body shivers at his tender touch, and I fall deeper into him.

I am lost.

Completely and utterly lost in a man who I swore to hate. Who I swore I would never fall for under any circumstances.

I lift my hand to still his touch. His chest rises and falls against mine as he leans back to look down at me. I shake my head slightly, my eyes pleading as I stare back at him. His brows knit together briefly, then he lifts his hand to squeeze my neck roughly. His head falls, and his warm breath ripples against my skin.

"If rough is what you need, then it's what I'll give you."

My legs begin to quake at his declaration, and we throw ourselves at each other wildly. I watch in a lust-filled haze as he lifts his hand to his mouth, soaking the tips of his fingers before he reaches down to drive two inside my aching pussy. I yell out in ecstasy, holding onto his shoulders as he continues to please me. His fingers fill me repeatedly while the pad of his thumb presses against my clit, rubbing it with forceful yet delicious speed and power.

My eyes roll in my head as I become wetter...delirious...needy.

He pulls his fingers from me, lifting his hand to push them between my lips. My tongue swirls of its own accord, and I grip his wrist with both hands while he watches me through dangerous, feral eyes.

I wanted the beast. I begged for him, and now I've got him.

He pulls his hand from me and wraps his fist in my hair, tugging me downward forcefully. I crouch in front of him, opening my mouth wide to take his thick, solid cock in my mouth.

"Fuckkk," he groans in pleasure, watching me intently as I begin to move back and forth over his impressive length. "That's it, Eden. Take it," he encourages, driving my head back and forth with his hand.

His grip pulls on my hair somewhat painfully, but it only adds to my wild insatiableness. I force myself to take him deeper, gagging a little as he repeatedly hits the back of my throat.

His eyes close, and I can't help but stare up at him in awe through watery eyes. His muscles tense. His handsome face is overcome with satisfaction. Knowing I am making him feel this way sends self-gratifying pangs of pleasure to my throbbing core.

I reach a hand down to caress my pussy while my other plays with his balls, my touch switching from gentle to rough in a way that has him driving his cock into me harder. His hands reach down to hold my face as he plunges into me, and I groan against him as I begin to build my orgasm.

The sound tears him from his lust-filled trance, and he tugs my wrist, pulling me back onto my feet. He spins me around before I know what the hell is going on, his hand pushing my body forward, as I grip the tree for support.

I look back at him, and he pauses as he positions his cock against my slit.

"Now, Conall," I demand, barely even finishing his name before he rams inside me.

My eyes roll back in my head once again as glorious satisfaction fills me from head to toe.

"Yes... yessss," I moan through gritted teeth, watching as he holds me in place. One hand is on my back while another grips my waist.

His relentless pace is unforgiving, brutal, and commanding, but I wouldn't have it any other way. My walls surround him so perfectly, pulling him in again and again, never wishing to let the feeling go.

To let him go.

My orgasm is already within reach, my moans growing louder to make him well aware of the fact. He gentles his pace to pull me back from the brink, and I narrow my eyes to growl at him needily.

He doesn't seem to care. He pulls out of me, landing a hard smack on my ass, and I almost crumble to my knees.

He steps away from me, wrapping his hand around his cock to pump it back and forth a few strokes.

I watch. Hypnotized.

"Lie down," he orders me in his commanding tone.

I twist my body around to face him, my eyes staying firmly with his as I lie back on the cool grass.

His shadow falls over me before his body follows. I automatically open my legs to invite him in, gasping when I feel his solid length enter me again. His hands rest on the ground at either side of my head as fucks me. My body jolting with the force of his thrusts, my insides clenching with delight.

I hook my arms around his neck, and he kisses me long and hard while he is burrowed within me. Then he pulls back just enough to watch himself slide in and out of my body. We both watch together in mutual awe and appreciation.

The sight drives me closer to my end, but it's clear he's not done with me yet. His strong arm hooks around my waist, and he sits back on his knees, pulling my body up to straddle his lap. My breasts press against his chest as his hands run over my back, grabbing my sensitive skin. His head buries in the crook of my neck, landing frantic kisses, and I writhe against him, moving up and down his dick over and over.

He moans against my skin, his breaths becoming more labored. I hold onto his head, pulling his hair back to bring his gaze up to meet mine. We stare into each other's eyes as my orgasm explodes, shattering me into a million tiny pieces.

I barely have the capacity to call out or scream; I am so overcome. He holds my body steady to keep me from falling, and my movements begin to slow as the rush of pleasure runs through me.

He then pulls me up, laying me back down beneath him as his breath hitches, and he comes on my stomach.

I lie there in shock, my heart racing, my body hot and sweaty.

He slumps down onto the grass beside me, and we both stare into the canopy of trees. The sounds of the forest competing with our ragged breaths.

Eventually, my head falls to the side to find him already looking straight at me.

Neither of us says a word.

Then he stands abruptly, and I sit up to rest my hands on the grass behind me. I watch in confusion as he bends down to scoop me up, yelping just a little as he pulls me in against his chest, one arm hooked under my legs and the other below my shoulders.

I hold onto his neck as he walks forward, our eyes entirely focused on one another.

I hear the water splash against his legs as he brings us deeper into the cold, flowing river. The cool water eventually reaches my body, enveloping us both until we are in deep up to our shoulders.

He lets my legs go, but my arms remain hooked around his neck as he drags my body in closer to his. Our chests press together, and he leans in until his nose grazes against mine. He closes his eyes, and mine follow suit before our lips meet again.

We stay like this.

The minutes pass, but I have no idea how long he has held me in his arms. I have no concept of time whatsoever.

Finally, our lips break apart, and his forehead rests against mine as the cool water washes over us, soothing us and bringing us back to reality.

My eyes open, and I am greeted with the color of warm honey. His hand lifts to my face, his thumb rubbing against the skin gently.

"You have consumed me, Eden. How can I give you up?" he asks quietly. "It won't ever be possible."

I stare back at him for a second, unsure how to respond.

"Then don't."

The words escape before I have a chance to stop them, and his nose nudges against mine as our lips touch again.

Suddenly, his body stills and his grip on me tightens.

"Conall, what—"

His hand covers my mouth as I frown in confusion. I struggle against him, twisting around to see movement in the trees behind us.

It's then that a familiar voice echoes through the forest, causing my body to go completely stiff.

"You four with me to the river! The rest of you head for the gully, and we will meet you there!"

The voice.

It belongs to Aubrun.

Choices

Eden

Aubrun's voice carries on the wind through the quiet forest. He's close. Close enough that he is sure to arrive through the thick of the trees at any given moment.

One hundred and one thoughts run through my mind simultaneously as I stand here frozen in Con's arms.

Is this it? The moment that I've been waiting for?

Is this the end to this whole ordeal? The route back to my old life?

The questions come thick and fast, but I don't have the brain capacity to come up with the answers.

Con's narrowed, focused eyes scan the trees behind me, and then he looks down, his intense gaze meeting mine. He slowly removes his hand from my mouth. There are no words needed between us. He knows what's going on in my mind. He can practically feel my nerves. See the conflicting ideas racing through my brain.

"You can run," I whisper sincerely, cutting through the silence. "I'll stall them. You can go home. You know I'll never say a word about the den to anyone. Please tell me you know that?"

He looks at me intently for a second longer before he shakes his head, his solid body remaining rooted to the spot.

"No."

"But, Con—"

"Eden, I won't leave your side," he says decisively. "I can't let you leave with them."

My brows knit together as I consider his words. With each passing day, I have felt less and less like a prisoner, but the fact remains that I am just that.

A prisoner.

I'm a threat to their entire way of life. They won't ever allow me to leave. Not willingly.

"Con—"

"You have a choice to make," he interrupts plainly. "Come with me now, or we stay here. Together."

I open my mouth to respond, but I have no words. I have no clue what to fucking do!

Do I want to go home? To my parents, my friends, and my studies? Of course I do, but if I allow this, if I allow Aubrun and his men to find us, then Conall will surely be killed.

His eye twitches subtly as he studies me with uncertainty. "Will you come with me?" he asks.

I can sense a slight hint of hopefulness in his tone, and it makes me wonder if there is more to this...perhaps more to us.

It's the final push that I need to make my choice. I take a deep breath, looking over my shoulder hastily before nodding at him. The choice I have made seems to shock us both in equal measure because the second our eyes connect, it feels like the first time we met all over again. Only this time, instead of running from him, I'm running *with* him.

A determined look covers his face, and he squeezes my hand in his. "Come on," he grunts, tugging me back toward the river's edge.

He puts his hands around my waist and lifts me out, my naked body dripping water onto the grass while the cool air wafts over me.

I crane my neck to look across the river nervously, my heart jolting when I hear Aubrun's voice again. "This way. We haven't checked this portion of the forest yet!" he calls out loudly.

He's getting closer.

Conall hauls himself out of the water, grabbing my hand again to tug me over to our clothes. He lifts his shirt from the ground and thrusts it into my arms, and I throw it over my body, my eyes darting back to the tree line again.

Conall pulls his pants up over his muscled thighs quickly. However, he doesn't seem half as panicked as I am.

Doesn't he realize what is about to emerge from the trees?!

The Elven Guard are highly trained, skilled fighters. If they see him, they could kill him on sight!

"Con, we need to go. Now!" I whisper impatiently.

That's when I hear it. Aubrun's voice as soon as he lays eyes on me from across the river.

"EDEN!!" he yells, his frantic tone filled with a mixture of both worry and relief.

My eyes find him, and he stares at me in complete shock for half a second before he reaches for a bow from his quiver. The two men on either side of him do the same.

"Too late," Con growls, pulling me back forcefully behind the thick tree trunk.

Immediately after, I hear the whoosh and thud of the arrow as it sinks into the tree bark at Con's right-hand side.

"Shit, shit, shit!" I squeal, looking around as a flurry of arrows speeds past us. Smashing into the ground and nearby trees, poking through the earth like tiny but deadly spears.

"Cover us! You there! Come with me!" I hear Aubrun order, the sound of splashing water following soon after as he and one of his men enter the river.

Con peeks around the edge of the tree and jolts his head back just in time to escape another flying arrow.

"Con, what the hell are we going to do?" I ask, panic-stricken.

"Stay here and be ready," he orders me sternly.

"What?!" He doesn't answer. "Ready for what?!"

The question leaves my lips at the exact moment Con shoots out from behind the tree, colliding with the guard to tackle him to the ground. He punches the man with such force that he is knocked unconscious instantly.

I scream in pure fright and horror as I watch Aubrun reach for an arrow, managing to take aim before Conall launches at him viciously. They hit the ground with an almighty thud, the wayward arrow disappearing aimlessly into the canopy of trees overhead. They roll around on the forest floor, throwing wild punches at one another.

"STOP!!" I shriek like a banshee, looking around the edge of the tree to see that the flying arrows have now stopped temporarily while the remaining guard makes his way down to the river's edge.

"You disgusting beast! Get off of me! Get off of me now or die!!" Aubrun shouts out as Con cranes his arm back to land a brutal, defiant strike to his face, causing blood to explode from his nose.

"STOP!!" I scream again, racing toward Conall to pull his solid, heaving body from Aubrun's, but it's useless. He's holding Aubrun by the scruff of the neck in a trance-like state. His black eyes filled with venom as he unleashes his fury in the most savage way I have ever seen.

Aubrun's face becomes more dazed by the second, his eyes beginning to swell from the intensity of the beating. My face turns bright red as I struggle desperately against the brute of a man before me.

"PLEASE! PLEASE STOP!" I bawl in utter distress and disgust.

However, it's what I see next that truly terrifies me.

Claws. Razor-sharp claws suddenly protruding from the knuckles of Conall's clenched fist.

He hauls Aubrun up by the neck like a rag doll, slamming him against the tree. Aubrun's eyes widen in fear as Con gets ready to strike.

"NOOO!! CONALL, NO!!" I scream out with every fiber of my being, desperate to get through to him somehow.

Just then, I hear the sound of footsteps behind me, and I twist to see the guard raise his bow, his arrow pointed at Con's broad back.

I lift my hand in the air defensively. "CON, LOOK OUT!"

The arrow flies past me, grazing my upper arm before it burrows in the tree by Con's head.

The guard reaches for the next arrow, and Con turns around, his wild eyes connecting with mine for the first time since the fight started. He drops his shaking fist, and within the blink of an eye, his body as I know it combusts, leaving a large black wolf standing in his stead.

Aubrun slumps against the tree. "Eden! Run!" he splutters in exhaustion, blood dripping from his mouth.

The giant wolf takes an arrow to the leg as it charges for the Elven guard, knocking him to the ground and snapping viciously at his leg. The guard writhes around in pain, and I run to Aubrun as he falls to his knees on the forest floor.

"You're going to be okay. Please be okay! Go back to Morween, Aubrun! Do you hear me? Stay safe, please!" I beg, gripping him by the shoulders.

His eyes, although swollen, cannot hide the confusion lurking in their depths. "We can't leave you, Eden."

"You have to! I want you to!" I yell, turning my head to see the rest of the Elven Guard now appearing on the other side of the river. "Go! Go home now and don't come back! Please don't come back!" I plead, just as the large wolf runs toward me.

Without a second thought, I already know what I have to do. It stops beside me, and I climb on its back, pressing my chest down and gripping handfuls of its fur as it takes off at lightning speed through the trees. Arrows whizz past us as the beast dodges and weaves expertly to avoid them. Its massive paws thundering against the ground as it gathers even more momentum. Wind smacks against my face, and my wet hair flies around in all different directions as I hold on for dear life. I open my eyes, and up ahead, I see the safety of the familiar forest landscape that surrounds the old house. However, strangely, the den is nowhere in sight.

Just as I am trying to wrap my head around what the hell is going on, the beast leaps into the air and comes to a sudden stop. I lose my grip on its fur and tumble head over heels onto the grass in a heap. Throwing my head back, I then stare up at the stone steps of the house that seems to have appeared from nowhere as if by magic.

"Get her inside. Now!"

My head snaps to the right to see Con striding toward me determinedly before hauling me onto my feet to pass me into Anton's waiting arms.

Anton holds me in his tight grip.

"MATEO, HENRICK, JAREK! With me now!" Con orders, reaching down to his bloody, bare thigh to snap off the stem of the arrow piercing his flesh.

"Con, where are you going?! Please don't fight! Don't go back out there!" I beg, shaking my head and struggling to reach out for him.

"The defenses are up!" Samuel declares, emerging from the doorway in a rush.

"Good. We will lead them away from the house. The rest of you, stay inside," Conall finishes.

He finally looks me in the eyes, and I plead silently for him to stay, but I already know that he has made up his mind. He turns away and runs after the others, his wolf form taking over his body once again as he disappears through the trees.

Confessions

Eden

I lie back on the bed, staring at the ceiling.

Unmoving.

Unblinking.

The events of the day have left me completely numb, and I blame myself. After all, when push came to shove, it was I who chose to come back here.

I *chose* him.

But after seeing the man I chose to act so savagely, I have to admit that I'm now more confused than ever. The man that beat Aubrun to a pulp, who was seconds away from killing him, isn't the same man who held me in his arms only moments before.

He was cold.

Harsh.

Brutal.

The realization was a complete smack in the face. It's what Mateo had been warning me about all along, but instead of being wary as he told me to be, I let myself fall victim to the bond. Yet here I am, despite everything, lying here, worried sick about him. It's dark now, and still, neither he, Jarek, Henrick, nor Mateo have returned.

What if they were cornered by the Elven Guard?

Four beasts, even as strong as they are, could have been captured or perhaps even worse.

I close my eyes and lift my hand to pinch the bridge of my nose, guilt washing over me when I think of my parents and how they will react to the news of my defecting.

Will they cast me out when they find out what I did? Call me a traitor and disown me?

A part of me hopes so. Seeing Aubrun battle with Con was gut-wrenching enough, and I do not wish my parents to bear the brunt of the backlash this

☐

could cause.

Suddenly, I hear voices outside and rush to the window to see four wolves emerge from the trees. My vision zeros in on the largest wolf. Its sleek black fur shining under the light of the moon.

In an instant, the beasts disappear to reveal the men. Silent and stoic, they make their way back to the front of the house. At that moment, Con looks up at my window, his face unreadable as usual, and I clench my jaw. We both know what's coming next. The enviable messy aftermath of a day gone completely awry.

I fold my arms over my chest and pace the floor. Waiting. Trying to come up with the words that I want to say. Ten whole minutes prove insufficient because when he opens the door, I'm left with nothing. We stare at each other with matching intensity before he closes the door behind him.

The atmosphere immediately switches. The tension between us is so palpable that it almost feels like its own damn presence.

He steps forward, and my eyes flick to his leg, where blood is seeping from his arrow wound through the material of his pants.

"You're bleeding."

"So are you."

"It's a scratch."

He nods his head silently.

"What happened out there?" I ask.

He doesn't answer. Instead, he walks over to the window, turning his back on me to look out over the forest.

I stand there like an idiot for a moment longer before my eyes narrow. "Con—"

"Is it him?" he suddenly interrupts.

"What?"

"Is he the man that you are in love with?" he asks bluntly.

"Aubrun? Of course, he isn't!"

"Then why defend him so fiercely?" he snaps back, turning around to face me with suspicion written all over his face.

My mouth drops open in indignation. "I defended him, Conall, because I know him. He's a friend from home."

"You said you didn't know anyone from the Guard," he interrupts, taking a step forward.

"Are you kidding right now?" I snarl in return. "You almost beat a man to death in front of my face, and then you have the gall to turn this around on me?!"

"If that asshole is not the man you love, then who is?" he demands, jealously practically leaping from his body.

"None of your business!"

"It is my fucking business now! It's my business because you're my mate. I deserve to know if this man is still out there waiting for you."

"No, he's not!!" I shout, scorching anger bubbling up inside me. "He's not here anymore because I lost him! I lost him in the war all those years ago, and yes, I was devastated because I loved him! I wanted to spend the rest of my life with him!" I finish, shrugging my shoulders as pain fills my heart.

He looks down at the floor guiltily, his tough facade dropping just a little. However, I can't seem to stop myself. The floodgates have opened, and I'm not about to back down now.

"But all of that is beside the point, Conall. That isn't the reason we are fighting!"

"Then what is the reason, Eden? Because you chose to come back here with me. You chose this."

"You didn't exactly leave me much choice!" I yell in reply. "Do you think I wanted you to be captured?! Of course not! There was no way I was going to let that happen!"

"So that's the only reason you agreed to come with me?" he asks, his jaw tensing as he stares into my eyes.

My shoulders slump a little, and I shake my head. "No," I answer in defeat. "You know it isn't the only reason."

Silence lingers between us as we both consider what this means. My admission, coupled with his back in the forest, confirms what we both feared from the beginning. That we have grown attached to one another in some way.

How could we have let it go this far?

I shake my head, sighing as I head for the door.

"Where are you going?" he demands sternly.

"I need to think!" I snap back. "I can't be here right now!"

He chases after me and grabs my wrist to stop me from leaving. "You can't be here with me? Why? Because I almost killed the fucking elf?"

"YES! Conall, you beat him half to death! That isn't normal!"

His expression turns dark once again as he glares back at me. "Do you want me to say I wouldn't have done it? That I wouldn't have killed him? Because I would be fucking lying to you if I did," he grits out between his teeth. "If you hadn't been there, Eden, I would have torn him limb from fucking limb and I would have enjoyed every second of it."

My eyes widen as I stare up at him in shock. "You *are* a monster," I say quietly. "How could I have been so blind?"

"You know what, you're right. I am a monster. And you...you are blind! Blind and fucking naive!" he argues. "Naive if you think that a wolf and an elf would ever be able to be anything other than enemies. I am loyal only to my own kind—"

"And what about me? Am I your enemy?" I snap, pulling my wrist from his grip.

He glares down at me in return.

"Answer me!" I order adamantly.

His chest rises and falls against mine. "That's different."

"Okay, so you almost beat Aubrun to death because he is an elf, but what's your excuse for your other past behaviors, huh?" I ask, the question that has been plaguing my mind spewing to the surface before I can stop it.

His brows immediately crease, and realization covers his face.

Shit. My all-out fury made me completely fuck up. To reveal my knowledge of what happened between him and Lincoln all those years ago.

"He told you," Con mutters under his breath, looking past me toward the door determinedly. "Fucking kid!"

"Don't even think about it!" I yell before he sidesteps around me. "Conall, no!! It's not Mateo's fucking fault! He was trying to help me."

I grab him by the arm, and he shrugs me off, anger radiating from his body in overpowering waves. "Help you? More like fuck you!" he growls. "I've seen the way he looks at you. How he follows you around. I'll strangle the little bastard."

He reaches for the door handle, and I stomp my foot in desperation.

"THEN YOU WILL PROVE HIS POINT ONCE AND FOR ALL," I yell. "DON'T BE A COWARD! TELL ME THE TRUTH! WHY DID YOU DO IT?! WHY DID YOU KILL YOUR BEST FRIEND?!" I demand, watching as he freezes in place. "Go on, tell me! Tell me why, if you are so loyal to your kind, would you do such a heinous thing?!" I question challengingly.

He turns around to look at me. His body is tense. His face devoid of emotion. "Don't, Eden," he warns lowly, but I'm too far gone to stop now.

"NO! Come on!! You want to talk loyalty, Conall! Let's talk! Why did you do it?!" I ask, stepping forward to push against his hard chest. "Was it for the power? For the glory? For the chance to be top of the food chain? What sort of man did I choose tonight? Who are you?! Come on, tell me?! WHY DID YOU DO—"

"BECAUSE HE FUCKING BEGGED ME TO!" he roars, his chest heaving with the enormity of his admission.

We stare at each other. My eyes are wide in surprise. My intense, sharp breaths filling the air.

He steps forward, pointing his finger out the window, his body rigid and unyielding. "And that's why I wouldn't think twice about tearing those bastard elves apart. Because they took everything from me! EVERYTHING!" he yells, his wild, untamed emotion washing over me completely. "You lost people in the war, Eden; I understand that. But do you want to know what the last image is that I see up here every fucking night?" he questions, jabbing his finger against his temple aggressively.

My mouth drops open. "Con, I—"

"It's him!" he snaps back. "My best friend. My fucking brother. I see him...lying at my feet. Dead. His fucking wide-open eyes staring up at me."

My heart pounds, running away from me as I stand there stunned. Not knowing what to say or how to react to such a confession.

"He was the last piece of home I had left, and then, then he was fucking gone, and I...it haunts me every minute of every damn fucking day," he admits in anguish. "But I can't let it show because these men need me. They need me to be at the top of my game. To be the ruthless asshole. To be their leader," he says, pointing to his chest. "But in here... I am fucking broken, Eden. I am in pieces. Pieces that can never be put back together again."

The sheer raw emotion in his voice takes me aback, and a tear drops from my eye without warning. I quickly lift my hand to swipe it away.

His eyes leave mine, and he drops his head down in defeat, walking over to sit on the edge of the bed. I watch as he leans forward, resting his head in the palms of his hands.

Curse

Eden

As I look over him, my heart aches, and I suddenly have the overwhelming need to go to him. To comfort him. To be there for him. I walk over to the bed cautiously and sit by his side. I reach my hand up to take his, and he gives it to me willingly, lifting his head to look at me.

My eyes convey what my words cannot express. He leans forward to lean his forehead against mine, and I lift my other hand to rest it on the back of his neck.

We stay like this momentarily before I open my eyes to study his face. "Why?" I ask in a quiet whisper, my eyes sympathetic but curious. "Why would your friend ask you to do something like that?"

He holds my hand tightly, looking down at our intertwined fingers as he clears his throat. "Lincoln and I knew each other for as long as I can remember," he begins. "Our fathers were good friends and allies, so when we were children, we were often around each other. We struck up a bond that never really left us, I suppose. We were asshole teenagers together. Thick as thieves. Learning our craft and acting like a couple of cocky little shits."

I smile softly, my thumb stroking his hand in encouragement.

"Eventually, we grew up, taking over responsibilities for our packs. Doing our jobs and working together just as our fathers did before us," he continues. "Then he met Fern..."

It's then that a rare and truly beautiful smile flashes across his lips as he falls back into the memory, his eyes drifting off elsewhere.

"Lincoln's mate?" I ask gently.

He nods his head. "Yeah, and man, he fell hard. And I mean *hard*. They both mated and married within the week, you know," he chuckles, shaking his head from side to side.

I smile back in return.

"I was best man at their wedding... Got pissed at the reception, of course,

184

and Fern told me off for telling too many rude jokes during my speech, but she could never stay mad at me for long. She was like the sister I never had."

As he talks about Lincoln and Fern, I can't help but marvel at the way his whole personality shifts. It's hard to imagine him like this. So carefree. So open and sociable. It seems like a different man entirely.

"They were the perfect Alpha and Luna. Everybody that knew them thought so. They ran this house expertly together," he says, looking around. "This was their room."

I gulp a little, finally realizing why it had been lying here empty all along. It was too painful for him to see anyone in here. It holds too many memories.

My brows crease a little as I squeeze his hand. "They sound like they were a great couple."

"They were," he nods, looking straight ahead. "Then they had the kids,"

At that point, his body tenses again, his pain clear to see. He leans his elbows on his knees again, his hand then reaching up to swipe over his mouth and chin. His vulnerability at this moment hits me hard as I watch his hand tremble, his eyes growing slightly glassy in the moonlight.

I shuffle in closer to him. "Conall, you don't have to—"

"Their oldest kid, Lilly, was my little princess. I doted on her as any good uncle should. Then the twins came along, Zara and May and Lincoln was completely outnumbered after that," he says with a sad laugh.

Suddenly, his head drops to the ground, and he takes a deep breath. I already know what's coming, and my blood runs cold at the thought, tears springing to my eyes.

"The day of *The Culling*, after I lost everyone in my pack, I ran here. I ran here through the night and...and when I walked into this house, I saw them."

My heart pounds in my chest, and I reach my arm around his body, laying my head on his shoulder as I squeeze my eyes shut in preparation.

"Lincoln, he was on the floor...." he begins, his voice shaking just a fraction before he pauses for a second to get himself together. "He was holding his girls in his arms. They were...they were gone, and he...he was sobbing uncontrollably. Destroyed"

The sheer horror of it all causes bile to rise in my throat. I cannot fathom such a sight. Such pain. Such loss. Such unimaginable suffering.

"And I, I couldn't do anything to help. I just had to stand there and watch. Watch as the world crumbled to pieces around us."

I intertwine his fingers with mine once again. "I'm so sorry," I say shamefully, tears rolling down my cheeks. "I'm so so sorry."

He shakes his head, pulling himself back into the present as best he can. He rubs his hand over his face, taking another deep breath as he sits up straight. "It wasn't long after that we realized that only the current Alpha wolves in the surrounding areas survived. This was the most central and secluded place, so we all ended up here. In hiding," he explains. "Lincoln was an amazing Alpha. He had this way about him, and the others could see it too. There wasn't any question that he should be the one in charge. He was the logical choice."

I nod my head in understanding. "But he didn't want to be in charge?"

Con shakes his head. "He tried. For years. We set up the den. Put protection in place through contacts we made who were sympathetic to our circumstances. The rest of us were kept going by our hatred. Fueled by it. But Lincoln was different. All he wanted was to be free. To join his girls and be with them again."

"That's awful... I can't imagine what you all went through. Especially losing children like that. He must have been in so much pain."

"He was."

"And so he asked you to kill him? So he could be with his family?"

Con nods in confirmation.

"But why? Why you?" I ask carefully, trying desperately to understand.

"Because whatever curse is upon us, Eden, means that there's only one way we can die."

My brows crease questioningly.

"The only way we can die is if we are killed by another Alpha."

I stare at him for a moment in shock. "Wow- uhh."

"I know," he says, shaking his head exhaustedly. "Anyway, Lincoln tried everything he could to defy the curse. Fucking threw himself off a cliff. Cut his own damn throat. You name it, he did it. But hell, nothing worked. You have no idea how many times I tried to pull him back from his darkest moments. I tried my damn hardest, but it wasn't good enough."

"You can't blame yourself," I say sincerely.

He nods his head, but I can tell that he does anyway.

"It wasn't long until Rocco started to sniff around. Lincoln tried to hide it, but the cracks were showing. Eventually, there was talk that Rocco would challenge Lincoln for leadership. Lincoln knew that in his state of mind, he wouldn't win, nor did he want to."

"So why didn't he let Rocco kill him?" I ask carefully.

"Because then he would be in charge. He would have fucked everything up that we had built here, and Lincoln couldn't stand the thought of it. He begged me to challenge him instead," he recalls, shaking his head. "And I refused. Goddess knows how many times I told him no, but he never let up. Said if he was going to die, he would rather it be by my hands. The hands of his brother. He said he would die happy knowing he would see his girls again and that everything here would remain stable and the men would be safe. Then Zeke told us one evening that Rocco was about to make his move and... that...that was the night I gave him his wish."

"Con, I'm so sorry," I whisper again, unable to think of anything else to say.

"It was a long time ago now," he replies, looking out the window.

"But that doesn't matter, does it?" I say knowingly.

"No, it doesn't," he answers honestly.

"Why didn't you tell the others?" I ask. "Do any of them know the truth?"

He shrugs his shoulders. "Zeke suspects, I think, but we have never talked about it. Lincoln knew I needed to appear ruthless. It needed to look like I earned my place as their leader. The truth is; I didn't earn shit."

"That's not true. Trust me, I've gotten to know these men. If they didn't have anyone keeping them in line, they would have torn each other to shreds by now," I say without a doubt. "But that's not the only reason you keep it secret, is it?"

He wipes his brow and exhales. "I don't want anyone to think less of him," he says, looking at me seriously. "To think of him as weak because he wasn't. Not in the slightest. Lincoln was the strongest person I ever knew," he adds adamantly. "He was a warrior, and I won't have anyone think or say otherwise."

I nod reassuringly, resting my head on his shoulder.

"He was my brother, Eden. And he deserved so much more. They all did."

The man I chose tonight is so much more than he appears to be; he sacrificed so much, suffered beyond words, and I know then that he *is* a good man. Even if he doesn't let anyone close enough to see it.

We sit there together in silence before his head rests on top of mine, our bodies melting together as one.

King

I look over my tired, battered and bruised appearance in the mirror and feel utterly disgusted. Disgusted by the hideous creature that did this to me. Disgusted to see him with Eden in such a state of undress. But most of all, I am disgusted with myself.

How can I be deemed a worthy leader within the Elven Guard when I cannot take down one of these beasts on my own? When I cannot defend the woman that I care about so deeply?

Perhaps I let my affection for Eden distract me. The near-fatal mistake almost cost me my life.

I straighten my tunic and take a deep breath, my broken rib sending shooting pain through my entire body. Wincing in pain, I hold my hand over my chest and close my eyes for a moment. After I was brought back here yesterday, I spent the night in the hospital wing of the palace, barely conscious as they pumped me full of medicines and potions. I should probably still be there right now, but the king has requested my presence this morning as a matter of urgency. I can only assume he wishes to demote me from my role as commander. The thought fills me with unimaginable sadness, but I cannot argue with his decision when I messed up so badly. I will accept the punishment bestowed upon me as any loyal subject should.

The door knocks, and I pull my hand from my aching chest, walking over to open it. "Yes?" I ask the king's servant.

She bows her head at me respectfully. "His Majesty wishes you to meet him in his chambers immediately."

I nod my head in return, my curiosity peaked. If he indeed wishes to demote me, as I suspect, it is the procedure to do this with his advisors present. I must admit to being completely dumbfounded.

I follow the servant to the king and queen's quarters, a part of the castle I have not seen since Erix was alive. We walk through the enormous solid oak doors, and I examine the surroundings, my memory suddenly triggered by what I see. The decadent furnishings positioned strategically around the vast room strike up a vivid picture of Erix in my head when we were small elflings, running around pretending to fight with the Guard.

"One moment, please," the servant says, her voice echoing through the marble room.

She then slips away through one of the stone archways to our left. I watch her leave and then cast my eyes around once again, my eyes settling on the set of thrones sitting proudly at the end of the long room. The sun shines through the enormous windows, bestowing its glorious light upon them. A sense of shame immediately consumes me when I consider how I have failed my people and how I have failed my king and queen. If by some miracle I am not cast aside this morn, then I shall step aside gracefully. It's the most honorable thing to do.

"Come this way, please," the servant's voice calls to me from the archway, gesturing for me to follow her again.

We walk silently down a long marble corridor before stopping outside the bedroom door.

"You may enter now. His Majesty is expecting you," she states, nodding in finality.

I swallow heavily before reaching for the door to open it slowly. I look around the room in confusion for a moment before I see him.

King Ciridan is lying in bed, cocooned by large pillows that seem to almost consume his body. "Aubrun," he says, his voice little more than a weak whisper. "Come forward, my boy."

I do as I am asked, walking through the bedroom to stand at the foot of the huge four-poster bed. The sight shocks me to my very core. The man in front of me is King Ciridan, to be sure, but he is a shadow of himself. Without all of his elaborate robes and tunic, his body looks small and weak against the backdrop of pillows, his skin pale and sweaty. His expression is one of defeat, although I still see a hint of determination lingering in his eyes.

"Sire, I was unaware that you were unwell. Please do not let me trouble you today. I fully accept the consequences of my failure—"

He holds his hand up to stop me in my tracks, and I do so immediately. I stand there silently as he opens his mouth to speak. Instead, he lets out a hoarse cough that seems to take over his entire body. He leans forward, and I see droplets of blood fall from his mouth to land on the sheets wrapped around him.

"Your Majesty, I'll get help," I say hurriedly, ready to make for the door.

"No need, Aubrun," he splutters, shaking his head.

I then look to the side to see Haleth and Queen Siofra walking into the bedroom from the long balcony that runs alongside the room. It does not take a genius to work out that their interaction was not a positive one. The tension in the air is thick, the temperature frosty despite the spring sunshine peering through the archways.

"My dearest," Queen Siofra coos gently, sitting by the king's side to lift a cloth to his sweating brow. "You must be careful not to push yourself too hard."

"I am fine, my love," King Ciridan replies, lowering her hand.

I hazard a glance at Haleth, who is watching them both with an unreadable expression. He doesn't once look in my direction, and I can only assume that he has heard of yesterday's events.

"Aubrun," the king begins again, straightening himself up. "You misunderstand my reason for bringing you here today."

"Forgive me, Your Majesty, I assumed you had heard from my men what happened in the forest yesterday."

"Yes, I did," he answers with a nod. "I was very saddened to hear it. Not only does it seem the rumors of wolves in our forest are true, but we now have confirmation that our once very dear young friend, Eden, is living with them willingly. It is an awful shame," he concludes, looking at Haleth, whose eyes drop down to the floor.

I cannot deny that I feel sympathy for him. His daughter has betrayed him. She has betrayed us all. It does not make any sense in the slightest.

"Sire, perhaps Eden's actions were not entirely as they seemed. We do not know what these barbarians are doing to her. They may have manipulated her."

"We know enough to know that she is a traitor," Queen Siofra cuts in abruptly, standing up to walk toward me slowly.

She gently places her hands on my shoulders, and her eyes turn sympathetic. "Believe me. No one is more shocked than I am, but we cannot deny facts. Unfortunately, she is now lost to us all. You know this to be true. Don't you?"

I nod in sad reluctance.

"Haleth knows this too," Queen Siofra finishes.

He doesn't respond.

"Aubrun, we have called you here for more pressing matters," King Ciridan says as the queen walks back to his bedside. "What we are about to tell you may be a lot to take in."

My brows knit together, but I bow my head respectfully and wait patiently for his explanation.

"The truth is, this news that the wolves have resurfaced on our lands could not have come at a worse time. For a long while now, my health has been deteriorating."

My mouth drops open a little in shock. I had noticed his step was a bit heavier than usual, particularly at the *The Culling* celebrations, but I had put it down to both age and the stress of the evening rather than anything more sinister.

"We have managed to hide this illness thanks to Haleth. He has kept me alive for these past years using powerful remedies, but alas, even his talents have their limitations," he states sadly. "My boy, my body shall be returned to Mother Nature within the next day or so."

The news hits me hard, and I swallow as I try to comprehend his words. King Ciridan's rule is all I have ever known. Finding out that it will be ending in such a way seems cruel.

"I'm sorry to hear that, Your Majesty. I wish there was something I could do to help."

"Well, actually, there is," he says, looking to Queen Siofra to take her hand in his. She looks down at him with a loving, tender smile.

"As you are aware, I have no children to succeed me, and my queen will not be able to rule in my place either as per Elven law. We have discussed this together and decided that the throne must pass to someone we know will rule the kingdom with *our* values and Morween's best interests at heart."

I nod in agreement while everyone in the room stares at me.

"Aubrun, you shall be my successor. The new Elven King of Morween."

The words instantly steal the wind out of my lungs, and I stand there in complete disbelief.

Silence fills the air. Their expectant stares still upon me.

"What? Why?" I stutter out breathlessly, looking between the king and queen in turn. "Sire, I do not understand. I am not worthy to sit in your place upon the throne."

"You are more than worthy and very capable, Aubrun. I know this may come as a shock, but it is the best decision for our kingdom. Siofra will be your right hand. She knows how to rule and will support you in your new role. She will be your chief advisor and confidant. She will help you navigate Court and uphold the rule of this land. You need not worry about taking over; she will make the transition as smooth as possible."

I look at her thankfully, but the fact remains that I am still not sure why it is I who has been chosen for such an honor.

"Your Majesty, Respectfully, I must ask—"

"Aubrun, my son Erix would have made an excellent king. We do not doubt it. Since he was unjustly taken from us, we knew we had to find a young man with the same love for his people and the same love for this family. You are a perfect choice. Now...you have heard my wishes. Will you serve our people? Protect them from this looming threat, these wretched beasts, and restore peace to our lands?"

My mind is overcome with thoughts and questions, but if there is one thing I am sure of, it is that I would do anything for the People of Morween. Without hesitation, I would lay down my life for every man, woman and child in our kingdom.

"Yes, Your Majesty. As your faithful subject, I live to serve you, our queen and the People of Morween. If this is your wish, then I humbly accept," I say sincerely, bowing my head as I take a knee.

"Then it is settled," King Ciridan says decisively as I rise back onto my feet. "Your bravery and loyalty will be rewarded, both in this life and the next. May your reign be long and successful, my boy."

"Thank you, Your Majesty," I say sincerely.

"Now I'm afraid you must both leave us," he says calmly, looking between Haleth and I. "What little time I have left in this realm shall be spent with my darling wife."

I nod in return, my eyes connecting with his in silent promise before I leave the room, Haleth following behind me.

As soon as I step out into the empty corridor, I let out a puff of air, closing my eyes briefly as I try to decompress.

King of Morween.

How am I to undertake such a mammoth task? How am I to know where to begin?

Thank goodness I have Queen Siofra to guide me.

"Are you okay, Aubrun?" I turn to see Haleth examining me.

"Yes, I am just—"

"You must help her." he interrupts quietly, his blank face suddenly filled with worry.

"Haleth—"

"You know her." he snaps desperately, stepping forward to pull me to one side. "You know that she would not hurt a fly. She is not with them."

It is then that I allow myself to picture her once again. To picture her as the beautiful woman that I have come to admire so much. I visualize her clearly in my mind's eye. Her lilac hair tumbling over her shoulder to graze the pages of the thick dusty book sitting in front of her while she studies.

She is all beauty personified.

"Haleth, perhaps I do believe that myself, but I now have a job to do."

"I respect that, Aubrun, I do, but please promise me that when you are king, you will look upon her mercifully for her actions. They are not within her control right now. Please promise me this?" his eyes look into mine pleadingly, and I nod in agreement.

"I will do what I can to bring her home safely, but I will not spare a shred of mercy for the beasts that she protects, and I will not jeopardize the safety of my people."

"I understand," he says adamantly.

I get ready to take my leave when he put his hand up to stop me.

"Aubrun..."

I look at him questioningly.

"Be careful who you trust. Follow your instincts and be your own man." he says in a hushed tone, looking around cautiously before he walks down the hallway, leaving me alone to contemplate his words.

Code

Conall

I open my eyes to birds chirping in the trees and look at the sun through the window as it rises, its rays sending soft orange streaks across the misty, blue sky.

My head drops to see Eden lying by my side. Her head nestled against my chest, her right hand resting gently across my stomach. I stay completely still as I study her up close. Her dainty little nose is covered in a light spattering of freckles that I hadn't noticed before; her skin is as smooth as pure silk. Then, my eyes settle on her ear, small and pointed at the top. I can't help the curiosity that takes over my body, and to my surprise, my hand lifts to touch it gently with my fingertips.

I never once thought I'd be here right now... Staring at an Elven woman with so much wonder, but I can't help it. Every facet of her body and face leave me captivated to the point where it's hard to focus on anything else but her.

My hand moves to her face, and I curl my fingers into my palm to lay the back of my fingers against her, the soft blush of her cheeks stealing my attention for another long moment. She stirs a little, wriggling her body as she presses herself against me for warmth. I pull my hand back slowly, lifting it to my face to rub my brow.

What the hell happened last night?

After our fight, it was as though something inside me snapped. The façade I have spent years cultivating cracked upon her request, spilling out secrets I swore would follow me to my grave someday.

How does she do this to me?

My mind tells me I should be wary and stay guarded, but my heart tells me otherwise. It's relentless in its mission to make me open up to her.

To make me feel our bond.

To give in to it.

To embrace it.

It's one of the most powerful feelings I've ever had.

Pain, regret, anger... Those emotions have been my constant companions these past decades, but these new feelings have left me blindsided. Awe, interest, contentment, affection... I had resigned myself to the fact that they would never enter my life again. Yet here I am. Staring at her with all those feelings pulsing through my veins with such intensity that they are becoming impossible to ignore. Despite this, I can't let myself get carried away. There are good reasons why I must keep her at arm's length. I still have so much left to achieve here, and it's not just my own interests that are on the line.

I carefully maneuver myself from under her body, slipping off the edge of the bed. Her arm spreads out over the sheets, but thankfully, her eyes remain closed.

It briefly crosses my mind that I should wake her. Ask her to completely forget my confessions from last night. However, I rubbish the idea quickly. Something inside tells me I can trust her with this secret. My instincts could be wrong, but I choose to follow them on this occasion just as I did yesterday in the forest when I asked her to come back here with me.

It was a gamble. One that ultimately paid off in the end.

She's here.

With me.

Now I just have to figure out what to fucking do next.

* * *

I walk through the doorway towards the table, scanning the room for any sign of her.

"Where's Eden?" I ask, my nose breathing in her soft scent in the air.

"Downstairs cleaning up," Neville answers. "How was patrol? Did you see anything?"

"Nothing at all. We are in the clear," Jarek confirms as he walks through the doorway behind me.

"Yeah, for now," Rocco adds, following after him.

"There's no sign of any guards in the forest today at all?" Anton enquires. "I thought they would be all over it like flies around shit now they have a confirmed sighting."

"Well, they got more than that, didn't they?" Samuel snaps, turning his attention to me. "They got a whole damn introduction."

"You have something to say?" I ask, taking a seat at the table. "Then say it."

"Fine, I will," he replies determinedly, dragging his chair out across the floorboards to take a seat.

I watch as he throws himself down into the chair, glaring at me as he waits for the other men to join the meeting.

"You could have been captured yesterday. All because you wanted to go skinny dipping with your little plaything. If that had happened, where would that have left us?"

I shrug my shoulders nonchalantly. "You are all aware of the plan we have in place. You know your roles."

"And what about rescuing you? Huh? Because I know some of these assholes would have suggested it," he growls, looking around the table accusingly.

"We have a code for a reason," Jarek interjects, looking at me. "It applies to us all. Conall would not have expected us to jeopardize the plan to come to his aid. We agreed a long time ago that the plan comes first. Always."

I nod my head in agreement, my eyes flicking back to Samuel. "Satisfied?"

"What happened anyway?" Neville asks cautiously.

The rest of the men look at me through curious yet demanding eyes, and I know they have the right to know the truth.

"Eden and I were hunting in the woods and ran into the Elven Guard. She could have given up our position. She could have led them to us before I had the chance to act, but she didn't," I confirm, a slight sense of pride filling my chest as the words leave my lips. "She chose to come back here without a fight."

They all look at each other with raised eyebrows, and I watch as a small smile stretches over Anton's face.

"Don't get carried away, you bunch of idiots," Rocco snaps in irritation. "So the elf wants to play Alpha's pet for a little longer. It doesn't mean she's one of us," he snarls, standing up to drive his point home. "She is not part of this pack. We can't tell her about the plan under ANY circumstances."

The men nod in agreement before they look to me for my say.

"The plan stays between us," I answer in confirmation.

"Then swear it right here in front of your brothers," Rocco states, leaning his fists on the table. "Swear by the code. Swear it on your life."

The tense silence continues as everyone stares at me expectantly. "You have my word."

He glares at me for another second before sitting back down again.

"Well, now that that's sorted," Henrick begins, cautiously looking between Rocco and I. "What do we do if the elves step up their search?"

"It doesn't change anything," I answer. "We are well protected here. We continue what we were doing, leaving tracks to keep them at bay."

"Won't we have to get word to Zeke and the others somehow before they journey back here from Harmony? They might run into some trouble on the way."

"They won't. Zeke's not stupid. He follows the protocols we have in place," I answer with confidence. "Now, if there's nothing else?"

In turn, I cast my eyes around each man to see them shake their head; however, when I get to Mateo, I find he isn't looking at me at all.

The men begin to chat amongst themselves as I leave the table, making my way to the stairs leading to the kitchens. Immediately, as predicted, I sense his presence behind me.

"You want something from me, Mateo?"

He looks around before nodding his head. "Not here."

He begins to head towards his bedroom, and I follow him, closing the door behind me.

He takes a deep breath, and I can see a hint of fear in his expression as he psyches himself up. "I didn't want to say this in front of the others, but I care about Eden," he begins.

I take a step forward, and he flinches.

"As a friend," he adds hastily.

I fold my arms over my chest, and he looks down at the ground nervously before he looks up again. "I think you should break things off with her. Not because I think you'll betray us, but because I don't want her to get hurt."

"I'll save you the worry. I would never hurt her," I reply, my jaw tensing as I try to keep hold of my temper.

"I don't mean it like that. What happens after we carry out our plan? When she finds out we killed her king and his advisors right under her nose? Do you think she'll be okay with that? She'll be devastated."

My brows knit together as I consider his words. "She'll understand once I've told her what really happened during the war. Like the other elves in Morween, she has been fed the story they told her."

"She won't believe you."

"She will," I answer with confidence.

"It doesn't mean she'll forgive you...or any of us," he says, a hint of sadness tinging his voice. "Death is death. She'll never see us the same way again."

I know in my heart that he makes a good point. Eden doesn't know the king. Probably doesn't know his advisors either, but that doesn't mean she won't be mad as hell when she hears what we have done.

Will she change her mind about me yet again?

The answer is probably yes.

"Then what would you have me do, Mateo? Cancel our plan?" I ask with a raised eyebrow.

"No," he replies adamantly. "Of course not, but she *will* be hurt. More so when she finds out that you, the man she invited into her bed, set this whole thing in motion. I think you should take a step back from her."

I glare at him in silence. Damn, if he wasn't such an irritating, opportunist little shit, I might respect him just a little for having the balls to say this to me right now.

"And if I take a step back...." I begin stepping forward. "Tell me, Mateo...what will you do?"

He swallows, his eyes as wide as saucers. "I... I—"

I decide I can't be here one second longer. If I don't leave, I might tear his fucking head off.

Different

Eden

I stand there with my hands in the sink, thinking of everything else *but* the dirty dishes right now.

Yesterday was intense.

Not only because of what happened with Aubrun, but because of Conall's confession. I wasn't expecting him to open up to me the way that he did. There's no doubt that I pushed him into it, and when I woke up this morning to find him gone, I immediately began to wonder if he regretted the whole thing. After all, how we were with each other last night was different in every possible way.

We listened. Really listened to one another. And for the first time, we spoke not as enemies but as equals. The barrier that has remained between us since the beginning had all but disappeared, and what was left were two people who wanted to be there for each other. Who needed each other for comfort. Trust isn't something that he does easily. I knew it from the very second I met him, but last night, I felt him put his trust in me.

The conversation has already changed things between us whether we meant it to or not. It brings our connection past the physical, adding a new and even more complicated layer to this whole messy situation.

Lincoln's story had my heart aching in my chest. How he lost his whole family in the blink of an eye is truly the most horrifying part of this whole thing. However, when I close my eyes, I can't help but imagine what it must have been like for Conall all those years ago. To have to kill a person that he loved in order to save them from themselves. To maintain their legacy and fulfill their wishes. The actions don't seem like those of a barbarian.

His confession gives me a greater understanding of him. Why he is the way that he is. The mystery of him is unraveling with each new interaction, and I cannot deny that I'm more than curious to know more.

In Morween, we were taught that *The Culling* was a brutal but very

☐

necessary act of war. An extreme measure that ultimately saved the Elven species from being wiped out by the savage beasts who were determined to destroy us, but I can now see that there is much more to this story. Another side that must be heard. Not just by me but by everyone.

However, there is still one part of this that does not add up. I immediately promise myself that when the time is right, I'll ask Conall about the wolf attacks during the war.

Why did they target innocent villagers?

Why did good, kind, salt of the earth people like my aunt Felou have to die?

And perhaps the most terrifying question of all....

Was he involved in any of these attacks?

After last night, my heart screams no with the fire of a thousand suns, but I cannot be sure unless I look him in the eyes and ask.

"Morning."

"Shit!" I squeal with a startle, dropping the cup back into the sink to splash water over my chest. "You need to stop doing that," I grumble accusingly, turning my head to watch Conall walk toward me.

He stops at my side, leaning against the kitchen counter as he folds his arms over his muscular chest. It seems that I am getting a little better at reading him because the anger seeping out of his every pore right now is hard to miss.

"So you do regret last night," I say, plunging my hands into the soapy water again.

He doesn't respond at first, and my chest tightens. I should have known.

It's always one step forward and two steps back—

"No," he says, interrupting my thoughts.

I turn to look at him with wide eyes. "You don't regret it?"

He shakes his head, his honey eyes staring into mine. "I don't want to fight with you anymore, Eden. It's not doing either of us any good."

"Oh," I answer quietly. "I don't want to fight either."

Then, he surprises me, picking up a cloth to shuffle his body in beside mine. He reaches into the sink, and I watch in shock as he grabs a dirty plate.

"You don't have to do these things anymore," he says without looking up, furiously scrubbing away.

I can't help it when a smile edges its way onto my lips. "Really? One heart-to-heart conversation, and suddenly I'm not a slave anymore?"

"I thought we were going to try this no-fighting thing?" he answers, lifting the soapy plate out of the sink to fumble it onto the kitchen counter.

I smile, watching as he takes hold of a spoon next. "I've gotten used to it, actually. It keeps me busy around here."

He nods, thoroughly focused on the task at hand. The look of concentration on his face has me ready to burst out laughing. I don't think I've ever seen him so damn focused.

"Please don't tell me this is the first time you have washed dishes."

He turns to look at me, and his mouth curls at the edge to reveal a sexy smirk.

"Fine. I won't."

I shake my head in disbelief as I laugh gently. "You Alpha men were real spoiled, huh? I mean, Goddess forbid you should have to cook and clean up after yourselves!"

He shrugs his shoulders. "I apologize that my dishwashing skills aren't up to your Elven standards," he says jokingly, placing the spoon by his successfully washed plate.

"That's okay. Maybe later I can teach you how to wash your clothes. You know...really blow your mind," I retort, nudging his arm with my elbow.

"Deal," he answers.

"Then it's a date!"

I curse the words as they leave my lips.

"It's a date?" Really?!

I sense his eyes on me still, and I look to the side to meet his gaze.

"What?" I ask, my eyebrows knitting together, my insides clenching with awkwardness.

"Nothing," he answers, lifting his soapy hand from the water to itch his nose. "I was just thinking that sounds like the saddest date in fucking history."

I begin to laugh in relief, nodding furiously in agreement. "It does, doesn't it?"

"We could go hunting again?" he suggests, a surprising hint of playfulness in his voice.

I raise my eyebrow at him, and his smirk turns to an all-out grin.

"Too soon?"

"Much too soon," I reply, washing the last cup and letting the water out. I grab a cloth to dry my hands and lean back on the counter as I examine him carefully.

☐

He's different today.

Don't get me wrong, he's the same gruff Alpha he has always been, but he's trying. I guess you could say that I'm trying too.

"You've got soap all over you." I smile, reaching my hand up to wipe it away carefully. He remains still as my thumb swipes across his skin, his eyes focused on me entirely. "There. It's gone."

He shakes his head slowly. "I don't think it is."

The way he is looking at me leaves me flushed in the cheeks once again. "It's gone!" I repeat playfully, pulling my hand away from his face.

"Maybe you should check again," he says, moving closer until his chest brushes against mine.

I stare up into his eyes that immediately dart to my lips, and I can't help it when my hands reach up behind his neck. He exhales slightly in response to my touch, his shoulders tensing as he blinks slowly. I watch his face curiously for a second before his body pushes against mine hard as his lips find mine in an intensely passionate kiss. I fall into it without thought or restraint, relishing the feel of his skin against mine. I don't bother to fight it. I don't try to push him away. I give in to the sheer magic of it all, and in truth, giving in has never felt so good.

His hands reach around my back, his fingers spread as he pulls me closer to him. We can't be close enough. There's no feeling like it, and we both know it.

I feel his need within his touch, which, although sexy and rough, carries something new and unexplored. Something I can't quite put my finger on.

I drop my head to the side to allow him easy access to my neck, on which he leaves hot, trailing, open-mouth kisses. My excitement rises as he bends swiftly, lifting me behind the thighs to sit me on the counter. I hold his face in my hands.

"Con, what are you doing?" I question in both excitement and slight embarrassment.

He looks down, reaching his hand to my boot to slip it from my foot suggestively.

"Not here! We can't," I say with a strange giggle, shaking my head.

"Am I doing it wrong? As you said... I'm really fucking bad at doing the dishes."

"Very funny," I smile, throwing my head back as he attacks my neck again.

I can feel him smirk against my skin before he lands those addictive kisses, and I already know that if he wanted me here and now, he could take me, no questions asked.

Suddenly, a bang breaks us apart, and our eyes dart to the door to meet with Anton's as he awkwardly averts his stunned gaze. "Fuck, I didn't mean to disturb. Was just coming to tell Con that training has started. As you were." he says, bending down to pick up the fallen bucket before heading back upstairs.

I begin to laugh, and Con follows, leaning forward to rest his forehead on my chest.

I run my hands through his hair before he steps away from me, then we look at each other in a strange, giddy nervousness.

Hearing him laugh, even for a few seconds, leaves me aghast, and I can tell he is thinking the same thing.

"I did tell you," I grin, narrowing my eyes.

"You did," he concedes, folding his arms over his chest.

I jump down from the counter, grab my boot, and place my foot back inside.

"Still...if that was doing the dishes, then maybe cleaning the clothes won't be so bad after all."

I pick up the wet, dirty rag and toss it at him. He catches it in his hand with that same smug, sexy smile. I don't know what is going on between us, but it appears neither of us quite understands it.

"Well, I better go. I'll leave you to it," he says reluctantly.

I decide to take a chance.

"So if you say I don't need to do these chores anymore, does that mean I can train?" I blurt out, hopefully.

He twists around and raises his eyebrow at me. "You want to train?"

I shrug my shoulders, chewing the edge of my lip. "I could do with the exercise."

He takes a moment before nodding. "Alright then, elf. Let's see what you've got."

I half hide my smile in reply as he turns to head upstairs.

"But I'm not giving you a fucking bow this time!" he calls back as he disappears from sight.

Flirt

Eden

I stand in the doorway and look out into the bright front yard. The sun is shining today, and I can't help but notice how it shows the men off at their very best. Their muscular bodies glisten in the sunlight as they throw wild punches at one another. It's funny how I have now come to appreciate their rugged form. Especially the build and physique of one man in particular. My eyes are drawn to him yet again, but unlike the last time I watched him train, I don't feel dread. I don't feel frightened by the pull.

I feel...excited.

Excited to be close to him. To find out what sensations his touch will bring with this new experience.

Suddenly, he drops his fists, nodding his head at Neville before he turns to face me. He gestures for me to come out, and I kick my boots off before lifting my hand to the threshold to find it open for me to walk through. As I approach him, my eyes stay locked with his. I barely acknowledge the other men but can sense their gaze upon me, most likely wondering what the hell I'm doing out here. I stop in front of him, and he puts his hands on his waist, looking down at me with those penetrating eyes.

I carefully trail my gaze down from his strong jaw to the curves and grooves of his sculpted torso, which is rising and falling gently from physical exertion.

"I take it shirts are not required out here?" I ask, raising my eyebrow jokingly before looking around the yard.

"For you...they are always required out here," he answers dryly.

The air of possessiveness in his voice takes me by surprise, but I cannot deny that a small part of me enjoys it. His words ripple down my spine, creating this odd yet highly satisfying feeling. It's been a long time since I've desired this kind of attention from a man, let alone a man like him. It's fair to say I'm completely out of practice.

"So what are you all doing anyway?" I ask, changing the subject in an attempt to control my urges.

"You missed the warm-up," Neville says matter-of-factly. "Isn't that right, Con?"

"You did," he says, his eyes connecting with mine again. "You need some time to catch up?"

"I think I'll manage," I smirk.

"Ooooo, fighting talk," Anton chimes in, taking a break from sparring with Mateo.

Con and I stare each other down, and Neville takes a step away from us. "Uhhh...looks like I'll be finding a new partner. Go easy on him, Eden," he says, his voice laced with intrigue.

"I'll try." I shrug casually, walking across the grass to stand opposite Conall.

He disguises an amused smile as he looks down, his eyes then flicking back up to meet mine. Looking into his eyes, the strangest feeling suddenly takes over my body. There's something in his demeanor right now that turns me on. That same hint of playfulness he had in the kitchen earlier, mixed with his own unique brand of "brooding asshole," turns out to be quite an intoxicating combination.

It does things to me...things that I cannot explain.

I do my best to refocus quickly. He takes a fighting stance, and I do too, readying myself for an attack.

"Are you ready for me, wolf?" I ask him airily, disguising the hint of nerves in my voice.

He pauses for a long moment, and his eye twitches slightly in response to my seemingly innocent question. "Try me. Elf," he answers, his tone somehow gentle yet firm at the same time.

We begin to circle one another, and as we do, I concentrate on my bare feet, feeling the earth's energy rush through my body. While I remain entirely focused, he steps forward and reaches out to grab my wrist. I swiftly lift my other arm to aim a punch straight at his jaw. He dodges his head out of the way just in time.

"Ooooo. The elf didn't come to play," Anton laughs, clapping his hands together.

A few of the men join in, and by now, most are so engrossed in what's going on that they have abandoned their own training session.

"So that's how it is?" Conall asks with a hint of a grin, lifting his fists defensively.

"Mhmm," I reply challengingly, cocking my head to one side.

After a few seconds, I make the first move this time, jabbing my fist forward in a smooth, precise motion. He grabs my arm, moving around my body speedily to twist it up my back, his pressure firm but restrained.

"Seems I've got you exactly where I want you now...." he says lowly, his voice dripping with desire as I wriggle against his hold.

"You think?" I ask, immediately stamping on his foot and throwing a sharp elbow into his abdomen. His weak hold falters, and I free myself, spinning around to face him again. "Don't go easy on me. I can handle it."

"Oh, I know you can handle it," he answers quietly, his statement a clear double entendre.

I narrow my eyes at him in return.

"Less flirting, more fighting!" Henrick calls out over my shoulder, earning him a few guffaws from the others.

It's then that Con makes a run at me, and I wait patiently for the right moment. His body comes within inches of mine, and I leap upward into the air, using the energy beneath my feet to propel my movements. I wrap my leg around his neck and pull him back onto the ground. We both hit the grass with a thud, and I tighten my grip on him, squeezing his neck between my thighs while my hands reach down to grab him under the chin.

"How the fuck did she do that!" Henrick exclaims loudly.

"Did you see how high she jumped? Is that a fucking elf power?" Neville asks in both disbelief and admiration.

Conall's arms reach up to secure themselves around my thighs, and he pries them apart, swiftly releasing himself.

I try to hop back onto my feet, but he grabs me around the waist, pulling my body down on top of his. He rolls over me, pressing my chest into the grass as he pins me to the ground.

He hovers above me. His bare, fucking perfect chest pressing down on my back. "Can't say I don't enjoy being between your thighs...but all good things must come to an end," he whispers against my ear. "You are good, elf, but not quite good enough," he adds smugly.

I can almost sense his smirk, and it makes me more determined than ever.

He lets me go, hopping back up onto his feet.

"Better luck next time, Eden," Jarek says, clapping his hands.

"You almost had him!" Henrick adds supportively. "Valiant effort."

I twist around and sit up on the grass, gripping the fresh, green blades between my fingers. I look up at Con in defeat, buying myself time to gather more energy.

He raises an eyebrow at me in mock sympathy. "What can I say? You should have warmed up."

I scowl at him playfully, and he leans forward on one leg, reaching his hand out to help me up. I snatch it straight away, using it to hold my weight while my foot swipes out at his standing leg. The sudden hit causes him to lose balance and fall to his knees.

I let go of his hand, flipping my body backward to land gracefully on two feet. He remains on his knees as I walk forward to hook my finger under his chin. He lets me do so without a fight, a reluctant but impressed smile touching his lips as he stares up at me.

"Is that warm enough for you?" I ask with a wink.

I feel him swallow hard, and the look in his eye tells me he is feeling the same way I am. He wants me. He wants me like I want him.

The other guys begin to cheer, but I can barely focus. My mind is too busy conjuring images of Con pinning me down on the grass and taking me wildly. Having his way with me. Over and over again.

"Come on, Eden! Take a bow!" Neville calls out, lifting his fingers to his mouth to whistle.

I finally manage to tear my eyes away from Con's and bow to our audience, unable to help the joyous burst of laughter that leaves my lips.

Con stands up and joins the others, clapping his hands as he looks over me with a sexy smirk.

I walk over to him slowly as the men return to their training. "You think I don't know you were still going easy on me?" I whisper accusingly.

He shrugs his shoulders. "What sort of man would I be if I didn't?"

"Are you going soft on me, wolf?"

"Never...elf."

I smile, taking a few steps back from him to clear my head. If I'm not careful, I'll end up jumping his damn bones right here and now.

"Well, if you want to take this to the next level—"

"I do," he interrupts without hesitation.

I laugh gently and shake my head. "I was going to say...I actually learned to fight using weapons."

"What did I say about the bow?" he asks, folding his arms.

"Oh, I know. I was wondering if you happened to have any swords in that mystery closet of wonders?"

He can't help but laugh, nodding in reply. "I think you might be in luck."

"Good, it's time for me to teach you a thing or two, Alpha," I reply cockily.

"Looking forward to it." He steps back, his eyes remaining with mine until the last possible second. "Anton!"

I watch as he walks over to give him the key to the closet and feel my heart flutter softly.

Shit...

This is not good.

This is *so* not good.

Content

Eden

"Who taught you how to fight anyway?" Conall asks, interrupting my thoughts.

"My dad," I answer fondly, a smile touching my lips as the memories return in a flood. "He isn't much of a fighter though; he taught me how to use the earth's energy for strength."

Con nods interestedly. "And the sword skills?"

The smile drains from my face, and I look awkwardly at the ground. The truth is that I have another man to thank for those combat lessons, and that man is not my father.

Con's brows knit together a little, and he steps closer to me. "You can say his name, you know."

I look up at him in surprise. I can sense the uncomfortable edge in his tone, but his expression remains genuine. Perhaps now that he has opened up to me, he wants me to do the same.

But is he ready to hear the whole truth?

Am I ready to tell it?

I open my mouth to reply when Anton appears at our side. "Ladies first!"

I turn to him in a daze and look down at his hands, where he holds two swords with ornate steel handles. I immediately recognize them as Elven, and I cannot deny that I'm left wondering where they came from. I push the worrying thought aside as quickly as I can.

"Eden? Are you okay?"

"Huh?"

Con watches me suspiciously, and I nod my head frantically. "Of course! I'll have this one," I say, choosing the smaller and lighter of the two swords.

He takes the other and swings it around while I do the same. I can tell straight away that he is no stranger to the weapon.

"I thought wolves didn't use weapons?" I question curiously.

☐

"We don't."

"You look pretty handy to me?"

He holds up the blade to examine it. "My father believed that to defeat the enemy, you have to learn to fight like them," he answers plainly, his eyes meeting mine.

"I see," I reply, clearing my throat as silence settles between us.

Con drops the sword, and his playful smirk returns once again to thankfully cut through the awkward tension. "Come on then. Let's see what you've got."

I nod in determination and get to work, showing the guys some moves I learned from both Erix and Aubrun over the years. I spent many evenings watching them train with the Guard, and occasionally, Erix would allow me to join them. The other guards weren't pleased, but Erix didn't care. He took great pleasure in training me.

Conal and I fight for a while, and I'm thoroughly impressed with his skills. He's a little more heavy-handed than an elf and lacks some grace, but he makes up for it with his speed and sheer brute strength.

Anton then begs to have a go and subsequently has the whole yard laughing out loud as he falls on his ass with my blade pointed at his throat.

"Fucking Bravo, Eden!" Neville laughs, gesturing to Anton rudely as he stands up to dust himself off.

"Yeah, yeah! Let's see you try it!"

I join in with their laughter when suddenly, a fierce snarl pierces the air. The sound makes me freeze stiff on the spot and causes my breath to catch in my throat. My eyes widen in horror as I watch them. Two wolves snapping at each other viciously as they roll around on the grass, locked in battle.

Their sharp teeth glint in the sunlight.

Their razor-like claws scratching at each other's flesh.

Their noses crinkled as deep growls emirate from their chests.

My breathing begins to quicken, and before I know it, I find myself back in Morween on the night of *The Culling* ceremony. Watching helplessly as Erix is embroiled in a ferocious battle to the death.

"STOP," Conall orders, his commanding tone making the yard fall into silence instantly.

The two beasts halt, their eyes making their way to me accusingly.

I swallow, flicking my eyes to Conall to find him looking right at me. We stare at each other for a second before he looks away, walking toward the two wolves.

"Shift," he commands.

Without hesitation, the beasts disappear to reveal Samuel and Rocco in all their naked glory.

"What the fuck? We can't train in wolf form now? Does that threaten the elf too much?" Rocco snaps angrily. "If she's going to live here, she should get fucking used to it!"

Conall folds his arms over his chest, but he doesn't bother to reply to Rocco directly.

"That's enough for today. You're all dismissed," he calls out over the yard. "Leave. Now."

The men all nod in acceptance, picking up their things before returning to the house. I stand there, still as a statue, as Anton carefully slides the sword out of my grip, offering me a sympathetic look before following the others inside.

Soon after, the yard is empty. The door is closed, and only Con and I remain.

I immediately rush forward, making a run for it. "Uhh... I better go too. I've got to think about dinner and—"

He puts his arm out to block my path, and I stop dead in front of him. "You're not going anywhere, Eden."

I look up at him questioningly. "Excuse me?"

"Rocco may be a prick, but he's right," he answers calmly. "If you are going to live here, then you have to know our wolves too."

My brows scrunch before my gaze drops down to the grass. "I know... I didn't mean to freak out. It's just—"

"I get it," he interrupts. "I had the same reservations with your magic, but I realize now that it's part of who you are."

"And your wolf is part of you," I whisper.

"We are one and the same."

"I'm sorry. I'm trying to understand. "

"Let me show you."

"Con... I don't know if I—"

"You can," he interrupts adamantly, taking a step back. "Just stay calm."

When I saw his wolf yesterday, I didn't have the chance to stay calm or to get to know the beast inside of him. I can't say that I wanted to either.

☐

I stand there watching, adrenaline rushing, my heart thundering in my chest as he kicks off his boots, loosening his pants to slide them down his thighs.

He stands in front of me. His eyes connected with mine.

I cannot deny that fear is threatening to take over right now, but I push it to one side, focusing all my attention on him alone.

He would never hurt me.

My *mate* would never hurt me.

It's then that his body transforms. The man disappears to leave the beast standing in his stead. I do my best to hold my ground. To stay rooted to the spot as the beast begins to stalk forward, its sleek, predatory-like movements causing my fingernails to dig into my palms.

Still, I remain frozen as it draws closer, finally arriving by my side. Its large head nudges against my waist, its black fur surprisingly soft against my wrist.

I look down at it as its nose lifts into the air. Its familiar honey eyes searching mine. I lift my hand shakily and place it on the beast's head, watching as it blinks slowly under my tender touch.

The vicious beast doesn't seem so vicious anymore. In fact, its soft and gentle demeanor encourages my confidence to grow. "Do you like that?" I ask curiously, gingerly running my fingers through the fur on its head.

It grunts in confirmation, its large head pushing further into my touch. I exhale in relief, and the wolf moves around my body, pressing against me before nudging my hand again with its nose. I smile a little, giving its head another scratch. Then, my next move completely takes me by surprise. I find myself slowly bending down to sit on the grass as the wolf watches my every move. It then sits by my side, its stance protective as it scans the forest around us.

We stay like this for a while, and with each passing second, I feel my racing heartbeat even out, returning to normal. I breathe in the spring air and close my eyes as I lift my face to the sun's warmth. Then, pure peace falls over me for a few blissful minutes. My troubles and worries floating away. Temporarily carried off on the gentle breeze.

"You know, I might even like you better like this," I say quietly, a small smile taking over my face as the wolf's head tilts to one side.

I laugh gently as *he* places his giant head on my lap, and I realize I feel more content at this moment than I have done in a very, very long time.

Truth

"Oh, there she is," Anton snickers, raising his eyebrow at me as he finishes slicing bread. "Thought you were too important to help out down here now."

I make a face in his direction. "Oh, shut up."

He laughs as I walk over to dip a spoon into the large pot of stew.

"Well, what do you think?" Neville asks as they both look at me expectantly.

"Not bad!" I answer honestly, nodding my head in approval. "I might make half-decent cooks out of you yet!"

"I'm taking that as a compliment," Anton shrugs.

I smile as I pick up a tray to begin filling it with bread.

"Where did you get off to anyway?" Neville asks curiously.

"Oh," I stutter, shaking my head nonchalantly. "Conall introduced me to his wolf then I went to get cleaned up after training."

"He introduced you to his wolf, and you didn't freak out?" Neville blurts out, earning him an elbow in the ribs from Anton.

"No. I didn't," I laugh, rolling my eyes. "Come on guys. I hardly freaked out at training! I was just—"

"Terrified?" Anton interjects.

I let out a puff of air, unable to keep the charade up any longer. "Okay, maybe a little, but I'm fine now. I actually enjoyed meeting Con's wolf properly."

"Well, you would love mine," Anton grins. "He is a big fucking softy."

"Somehow, I can see that!" I answer, filling my arms with plates before following them upstairs.

I instantly flick my eyes to Conall, sitting at the end of the table.

"Smells delicious as usual, Eden," Jarek says kindly as I lay a plate in front of him.

"Excuse me?!" Neville butts in. "This is an Ant and Nev special tonight. No elf supervision required."

"Don't believe you," Henrick calls out, shaking his head. "You two idiots couldn't put a meal like this together if your life depended on it. I've eaten enough of your shitty food to know that by now."

"Eden!" Anton protests, holding his arms out to me for backup.

I can't help but giggle. "No, guys, I have to be honest. I had nothing to do with this."

"Thank you!" Neville states triumphantly, taking his seat.

I look to Con, who gives me a subtle smile.

"Well...enjoy everyone," I say sincerely, turning around to head back to the kitchen.

"Where are you going?" Conall's voice asks, causing the table to quieten down.

"What?" I ask, twisting around to look at him.

"Sit," he insists, his honey eyes looking into mine seriously.

"Oh, I don't know if—"

He immediately stands up to pull out the empty chair by his side, the one usually reserved for Zeke. I watch as he nods at it commandingly. "Sit with us and eat."

I look around the table of men watching me in silence, not knowing what to do or how I should react. My gaze lands on Rocco, his nostrils flaring as he glances at Samuel. However, after a few drawn-out moments of awkwardness, it's Mateo who speaks first.

"Go on, Eden," he says encouragingly. "Take a seat."

I smile at him gratefully just as the room kicks back into life once more.

"Get over here!" Henrick adds, his voice muffled as he scoffs a piece of bread.

"Yeah, sit on your fucking ass already. I'm starving!" Anton demands, pointing his fork at my chair.

The other men nod and grunt in approval, digging into their food as I walk over to Con. When I get closer, I offer him a small smile taking the seat before he pushes it in gently. I look around the table at the faces of the beaming men, and the warmth of the moment fills my heart. If someone had told me that first day that I arrived here that I would be sitting down to eat with these assholes, I would have called them a liar, but here I am. I twist my head to see Con watching me with a knowing smirk. He winks at me subtly before lifting his glass to take a drink.

214

"Wine, Eden?" Jarek asks politely, lifting the bottle to my glass.

"Don't mind if I do," I reply with a grin.

✳ ✳ ✳

Conall

"You didn't have to walk me to my room," Eden smiles, leaning against the wall, her eyes filled with desire. "It's very gentlemanly of you."

"Well..." I say with a shrug, nodding toward my bedroom at the end of the hallway. "... it's fair to say I was headed in this direction anyway."

"Hmmm," she laughs, biting the edge of her lip. "Then I guess you are no gentleman at all."

"You know me well enough by now, elf."

"Do I, wolf?" she asks, her question hanging between us.

It's true that in the grand scheme of things, we are practically still strangers, yet at the same time, I feel like she's seen more of me in these past twenty-four hours than I've ever cared to show anyone before. We stare into each other's eyes for a moment before I take a step closer. Her breath hitches ever so slightly.

"I'm not opposed to knowing more," she whispers, lifting her hand to press it against my chest. "Do you want to come in? Maybe we can talk. Get to know one another."

The sultry tone of her voice immediately has my adrenaline climbing again, just as it did out on the training field earlier today. The truth is there hasn't been a single minute since this afternoon that I haven't thought about having her in my arms again. Thoughts of her consume my mind, and I cannot deny it to myself anymore. Neither do I want to.

She waits for my answer, a hint of nervousness lingering in her gaze.

"That depends," I answer slowly.

"On what?" she asks, raising her brow.

"On how drunk you are," I smirk in reply.

Her mouth immediately falls open as she lifts her hand to smack my arm. "I am not drunk!"

□

"Really? That empty bottle of wine might tell a different story," I answer, placing my hand on the wall by her head as I examine her carefully.

"Uhh, Jarek and I shared that bottle!" she protests, pushing her face closer to mine.

"Oh yeah?" I ask tauntingly, unable to help the smile that touches my lips.

"Yes! Besides, you had much more to drink than I did."

I shrug my shoulders casually. "That's because I can handle my liquor. Plenty years of practice."

"Need I remind you that technically I'm older than you?" she states, narrowing her eyes playfully.

"You are, aren't you?" I grin, unable to stop my gaze from lingering on her soft, plump lips. "I've never been a toy boy before."

She laughs melodically, her beautiful face lighting up.

Fuck, how I want to kiss her.

I can tell that she senses my desire, and for the first time, she encourages it, slowly lifting her hands to rest them on my chest. I look down as they run over my shirt, her hungry eyes following their movements. My cock hardens in response to her teasing touch, but I resist the urge to slam her against the wall and fuck her senseless. Something inside me wants to see what she will do next. Wants to follow her lead and let her make the first move for a change.

Her hands press firmly against me as she runs them up my shoulders, her fingers knitting their way through the hair at the base of my neck. Her eyes flick back to mine wantonly before she stands on the tips of her toes. My eyes close when I feel her body graze mine as she leans forward, her soft breath landing gently against my jaw.

"Stay with me tonight."

My jaw clenches as I try to keep hold of my self-control.

She pulls back to look at me challengingly, her request triggering a reaction inside me that cannot be stopped.

I need her. I fucking need her, and I can't take it any longer.

We launch into a frenzied kiss. One that sets my whole body on fucking fire. Kissing her is like nothing I've ever experienced before. A wild cocktail of emotions rages through my body and mind. Yet, at the same time, my instincts lead the way, directing my every movement. Her lips moving in sync with mine feels as natural as breathing itself. As though we were both made for this very reason.

We were both made for each other.

She drags me with her as she backs up against her door, fumbling with the handle. The door swings open, and we practically fall inside the room, my lips refusing to leave hers as I kick the door shut behind me. It slams hard, rocking the old foundations and causing dust to fall from the ancient ceilings. Fuck me, this house could collapse around me right now, and I wouldn't give a shit. I wouldn't even bat an eyelid. My every ounce of focus is on her and her alone.

My arms wrap around her waist as she lifts her leg, driving her hips against me greedily. I pick her up instantly, squeezing her ass hard as she grinds against my solid cock. She throws her head back, and I lift my fist to wrap it around her hair, tugging on it firmly as my lips meet the smooth skin of her neck. Suddenly, an almost overpowering and unexpected urge hits me like a ton of bricks.

The urge to *mark* her.

To make her mine.

I fight it with everything in me, but I want it more than fucking anything. My tongue runs up the column of her neck causing her to gasp and dig her nails into my skin. My hands return to her waist, pulling her in harder against me. Goddess, I can already feel her pussy wrapped around me. The memory of it is engrained in my brain. She lets out a moan, moving her head closer to press her nose against mine. Our eyes stay deeply connected as we kiss once again. I can't bear to look away even for a second, those lilac irises captivate me completely.

I walk toward the bed, laying her down beneath me before I press my body against hers. She lifts her hands to pull off my shirt, and I help her, tossing it to one side before I return the favor. As soon as my eyes fall on her bare, perfect tits, I am a man possessed. The pink blush of her nipples invites my tongue to explore her. She arches her back against the mattress, pushing herself further into my mouth as I flick and swirl my tongue around the hardened buds. Her hips begin to thrust again, her desperation now as apparent as mine. My lips smash against hers again as she pushes her pants down, lifting her ass to push them over her silky thighs. I stand back up, reaching for her pants to tug them off quickly.

My eyes run up her body and settle on her face, framed by her messy, lilac hair.

Goddess, she's fucking perfect in every way.

She's so damn beautiful that the moment paralyzes me temporarily.

"Are you okay?" she asks breathlessly, a hint of confusion in her voice.

"I don't know," I answer truthfully.

I lift my hands above my head, leaning on the bedpost as she wriggles further onto the mattress. She smiles at me coyly for a second, gently lifting her finger to curl it at me. I shake my head in reply. I'm not finished admiring her. Every single inch of her.

Her hands lift to her breasts, and she kneads them gently as she watches me. I stay completely still as my eyes ravage her from afar.

My cock presses against my pants achingly now. I'm so fucking turned on; I could come at the mere sight of her alone.

Is that fucking normal?

Her teasing smile grows before she bites her bottom lip, her legs separating slowly.

My chest rises and falls under the weight of my heavy breaths. My eyes stalk her hand, which moves down over her midriff. Her fingers graze against her pussy, and a look of satisfaction covers her beautiful face. I hardly know which sight intrigues me more. The image of her stunning face overcome with pleasure or the view of her open, wet pussy waiting for me.

My jaw locks stiff as she pleasures herself, her eyes fluttering open to connect with mine again. I reach down to my waist to push my pants down over my thighs, stepping out of them to kick them aside. Her eyes widen, scanning over my body as a long, low moan leaves her lips.

"Turn around," I demand quietly, watching as she spins onto her hands and knees before me.

Fuck...

I rest my hands on either side of her ass, lifting it further into the air. I press my mouth against her hot, wet pussy, relishing the taste of her as my tongue parts her folds. She yelps in delight, her fists curling around the bedsheets as I wildly drive my tongue inside her. She pushes herself against my face unashamedly, and I love every fucking second of it. I flick my tongue over her clit repeatedly while raw, intense sounds tumble from her lips, creating music for my ears.

Her delicious symphony is all mine.

She's all mine.

I drag my tongue upward, feeling her shudder beneath me with desire. I take a second to admire her up close, her pussy glistening with a mixture of her arousal and my saliva.

Fuck.

I press my thumb against her clit, circling it slowly as she buries her face into the bed in an attempt to muffle her moans. My hands squeeze her ass, my teeth grazing the skin of her asscheek as I kiss it frantically. My kisses move up her back before I take my place to kneel behind her. She kneels to meet me, her back pressing against my chest as she twists her slender neck to look up at me. I grab her jaw, bringing her lips forward to meet mine. Her tongue plunges inside my mouth, her ass grinding against my cock as we fall into a mind-blowing kiss. My arms encircle her body, grasping her tits again, causing her to groan in approval against my mouth. One hand then drops down to her core, which I begin to rub in teasing circles.

She pauses briefly, her mouth dropping open before she presses her lips together to stifle another loud moan.

"Don't," I order her sharply, looking into her eyes. "Don't you dare hold back," I growl through gritted teeth. "Let me hear you. Let them all fucking hear you, I don't care."

A burst of air leaves her lungs, followed by a loud, satisfied moan. "Yesss..." she mutters between labored breaths.

I lift one hand to her neck, gripping it firmly as my fingers rub against her faster. "That's it...Con...yess," she encourages, her ass grinding against me harder. "Fuck me. Please fuck me!"

Her words break me, and I let her go, pushing her forward to thrust myself inside her.

"YES!" she screams in delight, pushing back against me.

I bury myself inside her, and a grunt leaves my chest as her wetness consumes me. It feels so un-fucking-real that I can hardly think straight.

I close my eyes and focus on feeling her surround me, her walls pulling me in deeper with each thrust. My fingers dig into the silky skin of her hips, tugging her back toward me aggressively.

I can't help it.

This woman drives me utterly insane in every possible way.

She pushes herself back against me hard, her ass slapping against me as I

☐

drive my cock into her. Her enthusiasm and vigor only make us both more delirious. I groan with each movement, threatening to fucking explode inside of her at any given moment.

Then, her moans melt into one long, continuous, earth-shattering orgasm. Her pussy tightens around me, and I hold on for dear fucking life, not ready to give her up just yet.

I can't.

I've not had enough of her yet.

There will never be enough.

Her head sinks onto the pillow as she tries to catch her breath, and I slow down a little to afford her the chance.

She glances at me accusingly, unhappy with my change of pace. She pulls away from me, turning around on her knees to kiss me hard. Her hand wraps around my cock firmly, and I look down as she pumps it back and forth over my length.

I break forward for another kiss, and she stops me.

"Lie down," she commands sternly.

She lifts her hand to my chest, guiding me to rest against the pillow. I watch her with anticipation as she throws her leg over my waist, straddling me. Her hand lets go of my cock when she positions it against her pussy. She inches down slowly. Her eyes on my face as she tortures me. Seeing myself disappear inside her makes me so horny it's unreal. She lifts herself off me swiftly, leaning forward to capture my bottom lip with her teeth. She tugs on it gently before kissing me hard, her hair tumbling over us both.

"Eden..." I warn desperately as she hovers above me. "Don't tease me."

A smirk touches her lips. "What are you going to do about it...Alpha?"

Without hesitation, I grab her hips, forcefully slamming her pussy down on top of me.

She screams in ecstasy, grinding her hips up and down my cock in an automatic reaction.

I lift one hand to pull her head closer to me. "This pussy is mine," I growl possessively. "This body...is mine."

She lets go of another loud moan of approval, her hips picking up speed.

"You... *You* are mine."

Her head lifts, and our eyes connect.

"I'm yours," she murmurs in agreement.

My cock grows impossibly hard, her declaration speaking to every part of me. The animal inside has always wanted her; now the man does too.

Unequivocally.

The once conflicting counterparts come together in this life-changing moment of pure clarity.

I'll keep her forever.

I'll never let her go.

I hold her hips as she sits back, continuing her rhythmic movements, fondling her breasts as she rides me. I watch her in complete and utter wonder.

My muscles tense as I edge closer and closer to coming. She falls onto my chest, and I hold her close, kissing her, frenzied, as I thrust into her. Her body freezes, her hands resting on either side of my face as she looks into my eyes.

Her brows knit together, and her mouth opens to release a noise so damn erotic that it pushes me over the edge with her. Her orgasm rockets through her body, and euphoria hits me soon after.

Fuck knows how I manage it, but I pull out of her, finding my end while losing all sense of reality at the same time.

Her body shudders above mine, and her knees shake unsteadily, her body then collapsing on top of mine in a heap. We lie there panting in exhaustion for a few seconds before I search for her lips again. They meet mine in a hard kiss which gradually softens as our wild, erratic breathing returns to normal. I gently lift my hand to the back of her head, and our lips part before her forehead rests against mine.

* * *

I open one eye to look across the darkened room, her silhouette outlined against the moonlight that pours in the window.

"Eden," I call out quietly, but there is no reply.

Instead, she stands there. Completely still. Her frame draped in my shirt, her arms hugging her body protectively as she looks out over the forest.

Shit.

Maybe I was wrong to say what I did earlier. Perhaps I freaked her the fuck out. I lean over the side of the bed to grab my pants, pulling them on before I walk over to her slowly. She barely flinches as I approach. Her eyes laser-focused straight ahead as I come to a stop behind her.

"Eden, if this is about what I said when we were—"

"I need to know, Con," she interrupts, her voice laced with both nerves and uncertainty. She turns around to look up at me with glistening eyes. "I need to know what happened all those years ago during the war. I need to understand why. Why the wolves broke the treaty and attacked Elven villages?"

I exhale, lifting my hand to rub my fingers through my hair. "I'll tell you if you are ready to hear it," I answer.

"I am," she answers adamantly.

"Even though you won't like the answer?"

She nods her head insistently. "Please, start from the beginning."

I nod, readying myself to revisit that dark place.

The dark place that now exists only in my memories.

Attacks

SEVENTY YEARS AGO

"You're late," Lincoln states as I walk into his office.

"Hardly. Fucking hell," I grin, checking the clock before taking a seat opposite him. "You were always the late one. I never gave you any shit about it."

"How times have changed, huh?" he laughs, pushing away some parchment to throw his feet onto the desk.

"You can say that again." I chuckle, listening to the chaos fast approaching us.

"Uncle Conall!" Lilly screams excitedly, bounding into the room.

"Hey, kiddo!" I stand to scoop her up, twisting her upside down to dangle her by her feet.

"Ahhhhh! Stop it! Daddy tell him!" she screams through belly laughs.

"I'd appreciate it if you didn't drop my daughter on her head." Lincoln shrugs, standing up to walk toward Fern, who has just entered the room with their screaming twins in her arms.

"She knows I'd never let anything happen to her. Isn't that right, Princess?" I ask, lifting Lilly upright in the air.

"Right!" she giggles back, throwing her arms around my neck.

"Here...go to Daddy!" Fern says hurriedly, her voice stressed as she hands over the wailing toddlers. "Mummy needs a break."

"Tough day?" I laugh as she kisses me on the cheek.

"Oh, you have no idea!"

"Of course, he doesn't! He has no responsibilities." Lincoln grins accusingly while jostling the twins in his arms in an attempt to soothe them both.

"Yeah, because looking after a pack of three hundred and twelve wolves in wartimes is no responsibility at all," I answer sarcastically.

"Nah, babies are tougher," Lincoln says, amused. "Take my word for it."

"Speaking of babies... How about you stop by my book club before you go home tonight, Con? We have a couple of newcomers I'd like you to meet," Fern says airily.

"Book club? Not really my scene, Fern," I answer with a knowing grin.

"She wants you to find your mate, Uncle Conall!" Lilly laughs, pointing at her mom.

Fern shakes her head innocently. "Me? Interfering? Never!"

"Even our daughter sees through you, Fern. Who are you kidding?" Lincoln adds, finally managing to settle the screaming twins in his arms.

"Fine! But what sort of thirty-two-year-old Alpha isn't out there searching for his mate?! It's unheard of!" she scolds, giving me a stern look.

"Hey, I'm doing alright," I shrug, grinning at her as she rolls her eyes. "Listen, if she's out there somewhere, then I'm more than happy to meet her, but I'm not sure that she will be hanging around your book club."

"What's wrong with my book club?"

"Nothing," I laugh, watching her pout in annoyance.

"Fine, we will have a ball then!"

"I'm not planning a ball in the middle of a war!" Lincoln cuts in.

Fern twists around to glare at him. "Why? We got married during one, didn't we? This feud has been going on for decades, and it will probably still be going when Con's an old man! We are having the ball."

"Alright, don't mind me. I'm only the Alpha around here," Lincoln grumbles.

"You know that title means nothing when there's a Luna, right?" I say matter-of-factly.

"Don't I know it!" he laughs as Fern takes Lilly's hand.

"Okay, now that's settled...we'll go and let you two very important Alphas get back to work," she says jokingly. "Alphas are already arriving downstairs for the meeting, by the way."

Lilly waves at me frantically, and I give her a little wink as Lincoln walks over to the door with Fern.

He hands the twins back, kissing them both on the forehead before giving Fern a brief peck on the cheek.

"I love you."

"Love you too," she smiles brightly in return.

The door closes, and peace descends on the office again.

"Ready?" he asks, switching from Dad to Alpha mode in the blink of an eye.

"Yeah, let's go."

I follow him through the hallways of the pack house, looking around as I go. I've always liked this place. Even as a kid, the grand old house was always more interesting to me than my own. Lincoln comes from a long line of Alphas that dates back thousands of years, whereas my pack is relatively new.

As soon as we walk inside the meeting room, we are greeted with the sound of frantic voices and arguing.

"Hey, hey, what the fuck is going on?" Lincoln demands, heading for the chair at the head of the long table.

I scan the room, sitting beside Alpha Zeke, who gives me a respectful nod. "Con."

"Zeke."

"I was telling them that I received word last night that an army of wolves attacked two Elven villages yesterday," Alpha Jarek states worriedly.

"Elven villages?" I ask for clarification. "You mean civilians?"

Jarek nods. "Unfortunately, yes."

"Casualties?" Lincoln asks quickly.

"I believe there was vast loss of life. Including women and children."

"Shit... Which towns?" I ask.

"One of them is near Morween. It is mainly populated by wood elves."

"What? That's not how we operate!" Lincoln answers in confusion, screwing up his face. "We have a battle arranged for a month from now. Who sanctioned this attack?!" he questions, standing up to rest his fists on the table. "Who the fuck in this room is attacking peaceful wood elves?!"

Silence falls over us all, and Lincoln looks straight at Alpha Rocco, the new dickhead in charge of Whiteclaw, a pack just north of the Elven city, Gildroy.

"What the fuck are you looking at me for?! I didn't fucking do it!" he snaps in outrage at the assumption.

"You've been pretty outspoken about wanting to start these kinds of attacks, Rocco," Lincoln states accusingly.

"Yeah, because I'm sick of these pointy-eared bastards encroaching on my land! Sorry if my heart isn't fucking bleeding that some Elven town was trampled, but it wasn't me. You'd know it if it was. I wouldn't deny it."

☐

Rocco is indeed an asshole, but even he wouldn't go against the rest of us so blatantly. He knows Lincoln would kill him.

"So no one is going to own up to this?" Lincoln seethes, looking around the table.

Jarek clears his throat. "Lincoln, there is another possible explanation—"

"Rogues," I say immediately, finishing his sentence.

Jarek nods as the table falls into silence again.

"Rogues? Why the fuck would they suddenly get involved in this fight?" Zeke asks. "We went to them years ago to ask them to bolster our ranks, and they refused. They don't give a shit about helping us fight the elves."

"Exactly! It doesn't make sense!" Young Alpha Mateo adds. "The Elves will only hit us back even harder. Their armies are bigger than ours. We won't stand a chance if they start attacking individual packs with mainly innocent civilians."

"There's only one reason rogues do anything," I answer, looking at Lincoln.

"Coin," he says in understanding, shaking his head. "Someone is paying them to attack innocent Elven villagers."

"The question is who?" Jarek says, looking around the room. "Who would do that?"

No one says a word.

"Well, one thing is for fucking sure. A retaliation is imminent," I say with certainty.

The room descends into chaos as the Alphas all begin to panic in tandem.

"You best believe if they come after my pack. I'm going to rip every one of them to shreds!" Rocco growls, earning a few grunts in agreement.

"Mine too! We won't show any mercy," Alpha Samuel adds.

"Stop," Lincoln demands, holding his hands up to the room. "We can't make any rash moves until we get to the bottom of this."

"Then what are we going to do?" Samuel demands. "Sit around and wait to be attacked? I say we hit another Elven village ourselves. Maybe the rogues are onto something."

"Are you fucking stupid?" I question in disbelief. "What good would that do?"

"NO! No one in this room will sanction an attack. I'll kill you myself if I hear of it," Lincoln promises, pointing his finger at Samuel. "We handle this like men. I, for one, won't touch a hair on a fucking woman or child's head, and neither will any of you assholes! Understood?"

"Then what do we do?" Alpha Anton asks, leaning back in his chair.

Lincoln puts his hands on his hips as he thinks. "We go to King Ciridan directly. We tell him this recent, blatant attack on innocents had nothing to do with us. We will tell him that we will take care of the rogues ourselves. We honor the rules of warfare."

"He won't believe you," Rocco says, shaking his head angrily. "You go to Morween; you're as good as dead."

"If we come to him for negotiations, he cannot kill or detain us as per the treaty that has stood for thousands of years. King Ciridan may be many things, but he's not a madman."

"Bullshit. He's an asshole! He's been trying to get his grubby hands on our lands for years!" Rocco states.

"From what I hear, it's his heartless bitch of a queen that's the ambitious one," Alpha Hunter adds. "Goddess, forgive me for speaking like that about a woman, but it's true."

"Then we shouldn't bow down to them!" Rocco shouts.

"And what is the alternative?" Lincoln snaps. "You are full of fucking big ideas, Rocco, but if an Elven army was to march to your pack, they would kill everyone without difficulty! The fact is, all of our packs are vulnerable. We only stand a chance when we stand together on the battlefield."

The facts make me feel sick, but I know them to be true. Of my three hundred and twelve pack members, only ninety are highly trained warriors. The elves have the advantage, whether the others want to admit it or not.

"So what next?" Alpha Henrick asks.

"I'll go to Morween myself. Conall and Zeke will come with me. I'll speak to Ciridan and explain that the attack didn't come from us. Anton, Henrick, and Hunter, you track down the rogues. Set up a meeting. I don't care what the fuck you have to do, but make sure you find out who put them up to this."

Everyone nods in response to Lincoln's orders except Rocco. "You'll look weak as shit if you go to him begging for mercy."

"I won't beg for anything," Lincoln answers. "But I'm not too hard-headed to put my pride before the safety of our women and children. Now, if Con and I are going to have any chance of smoothing things over, I need you all to be on high alert. And for Goddess sake...don't do anything stupid."

Talks

Conall

At least thirty Elven guards surround us as we are taken through the back doors of the Palace of Morween under cover of darkness. As soon as the door closes, we find ourselves standing in a dark corridor, lit only by the torches on either side of the stone walls.

"Well, this is cozy," Zeke mutters under his breath.

We are then guided down the corridor, which leads directly into the dungeons.

"What the fuck is this?!" Lincoln demands angrily. "We are here to talk terms with King Ciridan, not become prisoners."

"You will wait here for the time being until the king is ready to receive you—"

"Like hell we will," I snap. "You'll take us to the king, and you'll take us now."

The guard stares at me, gulping as I take a defiant step forward.

"That's enough."

I turn around to see a man standing there, surrounded by his own personal guards. I can tell by the detailed tunic and expensive rings on his fingers that he is a man of importance around here. Even if he does look like a fucking eighteen-year-old kid.

"Follow me," he says dryly, his voice filled with lingering hatred.

"And you are?" I question, taking a step toward him.

His guards move in front of him defensively, which only appears to irritate him. He moves between them, walking over to stand in front of me. "My name is Erix. Heir to the throne of Morween...wolf."

I nod, unfazed by his speech. "Then lead the way... *prince.*"

The word tumbles from my lips like an insult which he clearly picks up on.

He doesn't like to be underestimated. To be thought of as his daddy's little prince. It's written all over his damn face.

His jaw tightens before he swings around to pace back through the corridors. We follow behind them silently, and Lincoln gives me a stern look in warning. I shrug my shoulders nonchalantly. He's always been the diplomatic one. Not fucking me.

We find ourselves climbing a spiral staircase, the door at the top opening into a room made of polished marble. I immediately identify it as the throne room. The two elaborate high-backed chairs tell me as much.

We are led over to the bottom of the steps in front of the towering windows, which allow the light of the moon to pour inside.

The guards step back, and the prince stands at the edge of the stairs, waiting. I take a moment to examine the eyes that are upon us. As well as the guards, Elven lords are lining the edges of the room in silent judgment. Their hate-filled expressions adding to the overall tension. I scrutinize them in turn. Each one standing there adorned in their expensive garments and jewels.

Fucking assholes.

This whole war is fuelled by them. By their greed and want for more. Yet here we are, ready to ask for their mercy. The whole thing makes me fucking sick.

Just then, the large oak doors behind us open wide, and the king appears beside his queen. Everyone watches in silence, and as they approach, the elves begin to kneel down, bowing their head in respect.

Thank goddess, I wasn't born one of these fuckers.

Lincoln, Zeke, and I remain standing as they pass us by, walking up the marble steps to take their thrones. King Ciridan looks down upon us with a blank expression. He doesn't say a word.

"Your Majesty—" Lincoln begins before the king raises his hand.

"In my palace, it is I who shall speak first."

Lincoln gives me a side-eye, his chest rising and falling slightly as he struggles to maintain his composure.

"You may proceed, Alpha Lincoln," the king says pompously.

Damn, this asshole is full of his own self-importance.

Lincoln nods, taking a step forward. "I'm here to negotiate terms on behalf of the wolf packs of the realm—"

"Excuse me, Alpha, but you lost the right to negotiate as soon as you targeted a peaceful Elven village. You lost that right as soon as you killed innocent women and children in your attacks a couple of weeks ago!" the prince snaps back in anger. "Many lives were lost! People in this very room have had to lay their loved ones to rest!"

The prince then looks to the side at one of the king's advisors. I recognize him straight away as a wood elf. No elaborate tunic can hide the fact.

"Erix..." the king says in a scolding tone before he turns to face Lincoln again. "Forgive my son's outburst, Alpha, but he is not wrong. Your attacks were needless and brutal. Morween will never negotiate with wolves from this day forth."

"King Ciridan," Lincoln begins. "I have been trying to arrange this meeting with you for some time now to tell you that these attacks were not sanctioned by any Alpha within the realm."

Eric screws his face up in disbelief. "Then who are you suggesting—"

"Rogues," I answer, staring him in the eye.

"Rogue wolves? Whoever heard of such nonsense?" Queen Siofra barks, narrowing her eyes at us. "There is no such thing! Your kind are liars! Unpredictable and uncivilized. You maimed and killed innocent elves, and now that you fear retaliation, you are here to deny it like the cowards that you are!"

"I am no liar, nor am I a coward," Lincoln snarls back in reply, turning his attention to the king. "Would I be here tonight without an army if I was?"

The king's brows knit together slightly as he listens. "Then tell me, Alpha. Why would these rogues, as you call them, attack our people without your say-so?"

"We're not sure yet," Lincoln answers. "We have been trying to track them down, but our efforts have been unsuccessful so far."

A low murmur emanates around us as the lords begin to tut and shake their heads in disbelief.

"Rogue wolves do not share the same values we do," I interject, standing beside Lincoln. "They value only self-preservation and coin."

"You are suggesting these creatures were paid to attack us?" the king asks.

"That is what we are going to find out," Lincoln adds.

The king stares at us as he considers our words. "I am unsure who would benefit from an attack such as this, if not one of your own Alphas—"

"Perhaps it was one of your people, King Ciridan," I suggest bitterly, looking around the scumbag lords again. "After all, it is they who benefit the most from all-out war."

The angry lords begin to jeer and curse as they loudly deny my claims.

"How dare you?!" Queen Siofra squeals, springing to her feet. "You have the gall to suggest that someone here would harm their own citizens? The very elves they serve and protect?! My dear, we should not hear of this!" she protests, turning to the king. "These animals should be arrested straight away! They should be executed for their crimes!"

King Ciridan holds up his hand, and the room quietens upon his request. "My queen is correct. I will not stand for my advisors being called into question without a shred of evidence."

"Then give us a chance to handle the rogue wolves ourselves," Lincoln states. "Halt any retaliation attacks you may have planned on innocent packs. Once the matter is sorted, we will resolve to end this war together, once and for all."

"My dear! They have fabricated these lies and—"

"Despite my better judgment, I will give you time," King Ciridan interrupts. "However, if I am not provided with evidence, I will no longer hold back my armies. My people are calling for justice. They are afraid for their lives. You will feel our full force if any more of them should die. We will show *no* mercy."

I do not miss how his final ominous words are spoken like a promise.

"Now, you will leave us."

I stare at him in disdain before my eyes flick to the prince, who is seething where he stands. Lincoln grabs my arm, pulling me away to head for the door, surrounded by our armed escorts.

"Well, that didn't exactly go to plan," Zeke states quietly. "Sounds like they are moments away from an attack. Their prince will probably lead the fucking charge."

"At least we bought a bit of time. Did you spot the wood elf advisor?" I ask Lincoln lowly.

"I did," he answers.

"What's that got to do with anything?" Zeke asks curiously.

"High elves look down on wood elves. They are only valued for one thing," I reply.

"Their magic," Lincoln adds, his voice laced with worry. "We need to find these rogue wolves, and we need to find them fast."

Secrets

Conall

PRESENT

"You... you mean to tell me that it wasn't any of you who attacked Elven people?" she asks, her chest rising and falling.

I nod in reply.

She lifts her shaky hand to her head. "What happened next?" she asks, wide-eyed. "Did you find the rogues?"

"We didn't get a chance," I answer, anger weaving through my every word.

"What do you mean? The king gave you his word."

"And it didn't mean shit, Eden!" I snap back. "Two days later, the Elven Guard, led by the fucking prince, attacked Whiteclaw—"

"Whiteclaw?" she interrupts, looking at me in shock. "Didn't you say that was the name of Rocco's pack?"

I nod, watching her as she paces over the creaky floorboards.

"They attacked the pack. Rocco killed the prince instead of taking him fucking hostage like Lincoln told him to."

"Rocco killed him?" she asks, stopping in her tracks. "Rocco killed the prince?"

"He did."

She closes her eyes, bringing her hand up to pinch the bridge of her nose.

"After that, there was no option for peace. The king had gone back on his word, and the prince was dead. It was only a matter of time before all hell broke loose."

"*The Culling,*" she answers, slumping back onto the mattress.

"Three days later, every last wolf perished. Innocent men, women, and children. All dead. Eden, *The Culling* was not carried out to protect the elves from wolves but to win them the war fast. It was to hide their own crimes."

"You still believe the lords paid the rogues to attack their own villagers?"

"I don't just believe it, Eden, I fucking know it. As soon as the wolves died out, the lords scrambled to pick off our lands one by one. Most of them are now at least ten times wealthier than they were back then. They orchestrated this whole thing, and their king was too stupid and inept to see it. He was their puppet, and they played him like they played the Elven people. I'm also convinced the queen was also involved somehow. She was hungry for war. I could see it in her eyes."

She gulps, taking a deep breath before she pushes her hand through her hair. "Then why not expose them?" she asks, looking into my eyes. "Our people need to hear this!! They have to know that they have been tricked! That their queen and their lords are corrupt on every level!"

"Do you think the people would have believed us?" I ask, looking into her tear-filled eyes. "They saw their loved ones killed by wolves, their beloved prince slain. Not to mention we have no proof."

"Because the rogues were culled too," she murmurs in realization.

"They thought of everything. I have to give them that."

Eden takes a moment to think, tears spilling onto her cheeks. "All those people, elves and wolves, dead because of greed! And not only that, the realm has no idea who is truly responsible. It's so cruel!"

I place my hand on her face and swipe my thumb over her cheek to wipe away her tears. To see her hurting so much makes me feel fucking awful. It's been a long time since I've felt this way. Since I've cared about anyone the way I care about her.

"Con, I'm so sorry. I had no idea."

I frown before I pull her into my chest to hold her close.

"I wish I had known," she sobs.

"It's not your fault, Eden. The ones who are responsible are the king and his lords."

"Then we have to find a way to bring them to justice. We have to find a way to tell the truth about what happened. Maybe I can help—"

"You can't," I say, leaning back to place my hands on her arms. "I wouldn't put you at risk."

"But Conall, you don't understand. I can get access to the castle."

"The answer is no, Eden."

Her head drops in defeat, a look of pure devastation covering her beautiful

□

face. "Con... I need to tell—"

"You need to sleep." I insist, taking her hand in mine.

She looks up at me, exhausted, finally nodding in agreement.

* * *

Eden

I open my eyes to the light of morning, the sun hovering over the trees.

My brain feels too big for my head.

My muscles ache as though I've run for miles on end.

And most of all, my heart aches in my chest.

Last night, I discovered everything I believed and understood to be true was built on lies.

I knew my father played a role in *The Culling*. It's a fact that has always played on my mind, but I always believed him to be a good man. That he did what he did to protect the Elven people from evil. To hear that he was in the room the night Conall and Lincoln went to King Ciridan for mercy makes me sick. Then there's Erix. I always believed that he was a man of his word. That he wouldn't harm a soul unless it was truly necessary, but it was he who led the attack on the wolves, even after he heard their pleas for help.

How am I to fathom such devastating crimes?

I feel utterly betrayed in every possible way.

I look to the side to find the bed empty beside me, and I close my eyes to keep from crying once again.

How am I to tell conall that the men I have loved in my life are responsible for his pain?

How will he see me when I tell him the truth?

I cannot help but feel ashamed. Ashamed of my previous opinions on *The Culling*. Ashamed of my family and the part that they played. But most of all, I'm ashamed that when I had the chance to tell Conall the truth last night, I didn't.

I was scared, and I was selfish.

I wanted him to hold me in his arms. To tell me everything would be okay,

234

but in the cold light of day, I can see it's not.

It never will be. Because once he knows who I am, who I'm related to, we can never go back. Any connection between us will surely be lost.

I sit up in bed and sigh, throwing the sheets off me to prepare for the day.

After leaving the room, I glance over the balcony at the full breakfast table below, my chest tightening when I see that Conall isn't there. I'm pretty sure it's not his morning for patrol.

Where the hell is he?

Perhaps it's better that he's not around. The space might allow me time to think about how I will drop this bomb on him.

I spend the day keeping myself busy with work downstairs, out of sight. Cleaning old silverware and reorganizing the entirety of the dusty old basement.

"What the hell are you doing in here?" Anton asks in amusement, opening the door to examine me curiously. "I've been looking for you all over the place."

"Oh, sorry. I've been meaning to do this for a while," I shrug.

He frowns a little before taking a step closer. "Are you alright?"

"Sure," I answer a little too defensively. "Do you need something?"

He shakes his head with a grin. "No, just came to tell you dinner is ready. Come on."

"I think I might just eat in the kitchen tonight."

"Why?"

"I'm tired," I lie. "All this cleaning, I guess."

He nods his head suspiciously. "Okay, well, I'll leave you a plate."

I nod my head, watching him turn his back to leave.

I slouch down to sit on a rusty bucket contemplating my next move. I can't stay down here all night. Sooner or later, I have to speak with Con and tell him the truth once and for all.

My stomach groans in protest, and I give in to its requests, dragging myself down to the kitchen, which thankfully is empty. I sit at the table and lift my fork when I hear footsteps descend the stairs behind me.

Shit.

I turn around to look at Conall as he folds his arms over his chest. "What are you doing, Eden?"

I open my mouth, but the words get stuck in my throat as I look into his

□

eyes. "I just don't think it's right for me to sit at the table. I don't belong there."

"Don't do this," he says, shaking his head.

"I—"

"You belong with me," he says adamantly.

His words tug my heartstrings.

"Come on," he continues, lifting my plate from the table and taking my hand.

I let him lead me upstairs into the living room and over to the table, where the other men are oblivious to my internal turmoil. He places the food down and pulls a chair out for me.

Suddenly, the front door swings open, and I jump as Zeke, Hunter, Evan, and William appear through the threshold.

"Good evening fuckers!" Hunter calls out loudly.

The other men laugh, and Anton tosses a bread roll at him.

I watch as they approach the table, greeting everyone with handshakes and pats on the back.

"Ahhh, we have a new addition to the table, I see," Hunter laughs, jerking his head to me.

I try my best to offer him a smile in return.

"We have missed you all," he says sarcastically, throwing himself on a seat.

"Well, we enjoyed the peace and quiet," Neville answers with a chuckle.

Zeke then approaches, bending down to Con's ear to whisper something.

I watch them both curiously as Conall stands up, tossing his drink back before he looks down at me. "I have to go catch up on some work. Will you be okay?" he asks.

I nod my head in reply.

"Good. Come to my room after dinner. Whenever you're ready."

"Sure," I reply quietly.

I watch as he and Zeke disappear, all the while wondering what business is so important that they must discuss it immediately. My head twists back to look between Hunter and the other returning men.

Where have they been for the past two days?

The questions swirl around in my head, adding to my uneasiness.

Then, I lock eyes with Rocco, who glares at me across the table. It was him. He was the one who took Erix from me all those years ago. Justified or not... I feel completely sick. Losing my appetite, I push the plate away, the men's loud banter drifting into the back of my mind as my thoughts take over once again.

* * *

I step inside Con's dimly lit bedroom, my eyes drifting to the bathroom, where I can hear some movement. I walk over to the bed, lifting his shirt to my nose to breathe in his scent. I let out a deep sigh, and my eyes again meet the closed bathroom door.

Stop being such a coward, Eden. You know you have to do this. Just tell him.

"Con! We have to talk!" I call out nervously, moving his clothes to one side.

Just then, I'm distracted by the sight of a small piece of parchment, floating from his pants to land gently at my feet. I bend slowly, lifting the parchment between my fingertips to turn it over.

*

*

He's dead.

*

*

I frown in confusion.

Who's dead?

The door opens, and Conall walks in with a cloth towel wrapped around his waist. "I was hoping you would come in to join me—" he begins before his eyes settle on the note in my hand. "Eden..."

"Who's dead?" I ask quietly, searching his face for answers.

He doesn't reply. He only stares back at me.

"Con?" I ask, stepping forward. "Who is this about? Where did you get this?"

He shrugs his shoulders, walking over to his desk to pour himself a drink. "Leave it, Eden. It's nothing that concerns you."

"Are you serious?" I ask in confusion. "I don't understand, Conall. Why can't you tell me?"

He doesn't answer. He throws back the drink as he completely ignores me instead.

"Where did you go today? Where have Zeke and the others been for the last two days?" I ask.

"I can't tell you that."

"Why?!"

"Haven't I told you enough?!" he snaps, twisting around to look at me. "I gave you the answers you wanted last night! You know what you need to know, and now you have to drop it!"

"How can I drop it, Conall? How can I live here and not know what is happening around me?! I can't deal with any more damn secrets!"

"So you have told me everything there is to know about you?" he counters accusingly.

I stare back at him with no defense.

"That's what I thought," he says, shaking his head.

A deafening silence falls between us both. One so heavy that it forces me to realize we are living in a fantasy world, and it's time to face facts.

"It will *always* be this way," I whisper.

His eyes stay connected with mine.

"There will always be this space between us that can never be filled. Because I am me, and you are you. Enemies...with secrets that neither of us can give up."

"Eden..."

"Will I ever be allowed to leave this house on my own? To see my family again?" I ask desperately. "Will I ever be privy to what goes on around here? Will I ever be anything more than a lover?"

"You know that's not how I think of you," he argues, taking a step forward.

"But as long as there is distrust between us, we are not partners, Con. We are not mates."

His head drops to the floor. It's the truth, and he knows it as well as I do.

Reluctantly, I leave him behind to go to my own bedroom.

Even if I tell him who I really am, what good will it do when he still harbors more secrets of his own?

I lie on the soft mattress and squeeze my eyes shut, trying to block out the pain that eats away at me.

I awake with a startle, looking up to see Conall standing by the edge of my bed. "What are you do—?"

"Come with me," he says calmly.

"Where?" I ask, pushing myself up to look outside at the new day dawning.

"I have to show you something, but we must leave right now."

He puts his hand out to me, and I look at it doubtfully for a second.

"Please."

The softness of his voice takes me by surprise, and I look up into his beautiful honey eyes, nodding my head as I place my hand in his.

Harmony

Eden

We walk through the yard silently, Con scanning the surroundings as we go. The sky is hazy with morning mist, the fresh scent of dew hanging in the air. I can already tell that it's going to be a beautiful day. The sort of day which would usually bring a smile to my face and put a spring in my step; however, this day is different.

I glance at Conall from the corner of my eye to see him focused on the trees in front of us. "Are you going to tell me where we are going?"

He doesn't answer at first, then shakes his head from side to side. "It's better if you see it for yourself."

We come to a stop once in the safety of the trees, and it's then that he drops the bag to the floor, beginning to pull his shirt off.

"What are you doing?"

He stuffs his shirt in the bag, standing back up to look at me. "I need to shift. The forest isn't safe, and we need to be quick."

Images of what happened a couple of days ago with the Guard flash through my mind, and I anxiously run my finger through my hair. "Then maybe we shouldn't go into the forest. If this is about what I said last night, I shouldn't have—"

"What you said last night was true," he interrupts plainly.

My shoulders drop as guilt gnaws at my insides. "Con, I had no right to demand honesty from you when there is so much I still have to say. Let's go back to the house. We can—"

"Talk?" he asks. "That didn't go well last time we tried it, Eden. I don't know if you've noticed, but talking...it's hard for me. So let me show you instead."

I look around the quiet forest before my eyes meet his again. "What do you need me to do?" I ask gently.

He pulls off his pants and stuffs them inside the bag, which he then hands to me. "Just hold on tight and stay alert. I'll take care of the rest."

I nod, stepping back to watch him transition from man to wolf. His large head nudges against me tenderly, and I stroke his fur before tossing the bag across my body. He lets me climb on his back, and I do so carefully, leaning my body forward to grip his fur. I close my eyes as I listen to his strong heartbeat. "I'm ready," I whisper.

He moves cautiously, trotting along the grass before he takes off, running through the trees so fast that I can't keep watch properly. I do my best to scan the forest around us but give up quickly. He knows exactly what he is doing anyway; his movements tell me as much. I never thought for a moment that I would feel safe under the protection of a wolf, but it turns out that I do. I trust him with my life.

We journey through the uneven terrain, his wolf tackling uphill climbs, large, jagged rocks, and gullies with no problems whatsoever. The longer we travel, the more I wonder where he could be taking me. As far as I can tell, we are heading to the mountains in the opposite direction of Morween.

The sun rises in the sky fully, burning brightly to bestow its rays upon us. The misty haze is long gone, and the bright blue is now clearly visible through the gaps in the trees. Still, we continue in silence.

The minutes tick by, and my body grows numb from sitting in the same position for so long, but I don't say a word. His pace remains relentless despite the length of the journey so far. Surely he must be exhausted!

Finally, we reach the base of a mountain, and I hold on tight as he takes the well-trodden path winding around it. His pace slows down, now hindered by the steep climb.

"I can walk," I suggest softly, stroking the fur at the base of his neck, but he doesn't respond. Instead, he keeps moving, taking us further around the mountainside. Eventually, he stops, and his body drops to the ground to let me climb off him.

I do so carefully, leaving the bag on the ground before taking a few steps away from him.

Where are we?

I look around in confusion. First up at the cloudless sky, then at the grass and steep rock surrounding us. I glance back at the forest in the distance, the thick trees stretching as far as the eye can see. Then, I focus on Con, watching patiently as he pulls his shirt over his head.

"Are you okay?" he asks.

"Maybe I should be asking you that question," I reply, raising my eyebrow.

A subtle smile touches his lips before he shakes his head. "You get used to the route after a while."

I stare at him questioningly, and he clears his throat with a hint of nerves I have never seen from him before. He's always so confident, stoic and self-assured.

"Last night, when you left my room. I couldn't stop thinking about what you said."

"Con, I shouldn't have—"

"Just listen," he insists, causing me to close my lips. "I need to get this out."

I nod softly.

"It's hard for me to admit this, but it would be stupid of me to try and deny it any longer."

I gulp as he takes my hand in his.

"I care about you a lot, and I know that I don't always know how to show it," he says quietly, stoking his thumb over my skin. "I once told you that I'm broken. That I'm a man in pieces," he says, his eyes flicking up to meet mine. "But there's not a doubt in my mind, Eden that every single one of those pieces now belong to you."

I stare at him with wide eyes.

"You were wrong about one thing last night. I don't see you as my enemy anymore. I might not be able to give you all the answers you need right now, but I will soon, and I brought you here today as a promise. A way to show you how much I trust you. Eden, I brought you here because despite everything, I *want* us to be mates. I *want* us to be together."

"I want that too," I whisper honestly in return.

I hardly know what else to say; I'm so blindsided.

The beauty in his words.

The vulnerability in his expression.

The care in his eyes.

All of it tugs at my heart, causing tears to spring to my eyes.

"Come on."

I let him lead me to a small, rocky ledge that juts out over the valley below.

We stop, and I watch his handsome face as he looks straight ahead. I then follow his gaze, peering over the edge to take in the magnificent sight.

It's a village.

A small village with quaint houses of all shapes and sizes scattered over the landscape, dotted between trees and rocks. Among the houses are people. Some travel in groups, others alone, but all seem to be busy going about their daily lives. Carrying baskets of food, chatting with one another, and washing clothes in the river, all oblivious to the fact that they are being watched from afar.

"What is this place?" I ask softly, turning my head to look at Conall again.

"Harmony," he answers in return.

"Harmony?"

"The only pack of wolves still in existence."

"W-what?" I splutter, a shocked exhale leaving my lungs. "Wolves? I don't understand."

"Eden...this...this is my everything. The reason why I get up in the morning. The reason why I'm still here on this earth. My purpose is to protect these people."

My mouth falls open in utter disbelief, and I turn again to watch the villagers below. It's then that my eyes land on a small group of children chasing each other across a little stretch of grass, laughing and playing together. I lift my hand to my mouth, and tears of pure, unfiltered emotion spill from my eyes.

"There were more survivors," I say, my voice quivering as the realization sets in.

I feel Conall move, standing with me side-by-side.

"Yes," he answers gently.

"How?"

"We don't know how or why. All we can gather is that the spell missed them for some reason, and so did the curse that fell on us," he answers. "After *The Culling*, we assumed that we were the only survivors until one day Lincoln and I stumbled upon a little kid wandering close to one of the old pack lands. His mother died, but for some reason, he didn't. We found out later he was a hybrid of some sort. His genetics must have saved him from the same fate as his family."

"What happened after that?" I ask in wonderment.

☐

"Well, once we knew there could be more survivors, we spent the next few years scouring the realm. Bringing together as many remaining wolves as we could."

"How many did you find?"

"Around eighty," he answers.

"Woah," I whisper, the revelation taking my breath away. "So you brought them all here?"

He nods. "We knew we had to find them a safe place to live, far away from the eyes of Morween. We built this village piece by piece over the decades. Survivors aged. New children were born. The pack began to grow and flourish. There are now over two hundred and eighty wolves living here. With more distant pockets of survivors arriving all of the time."

I shake my head gently as I try to take everything in. "I can't believe it. This place...it's amazing," I say sincerely.

Conall smiles. "That's why we call it Harmony."

"Why don't you all live here with your people?" I question in confusion.

"Because twenty Alphas living here would ruin the peace. It's in our blood to try and lead. Eventually, some would try to take over and divide the pack. Lincoln and I knew the pack needed time to build itself up without conflict. Splitting up into smaller factions would have been harder for us to protect. The safest thing for us to do was to keep our distance," he explains. "To use our skills instead to keep the Elven Guard distracted and at bay."

"That's why you patrol every morning. To ensure no one gets too close?"

"Yes, we leave trails purposely for the Guard, drawing their attention away from here. Protecting this place has been our main concern for seventy years. It's written in our code. We swore that we wouldn't mate with any of the villagers or procreate while the pack remained hidden in secret. It wouldn't be right. Not with the curse we have on us. We still have no idea of the impact it could have."

Strong magic can sometimes leave a subtle trail. A calling card for those gifted enough to find it, so it's no wonder the Alphas have decided to be guardians from afar. I admire both their sacrifice and restraint now more than ever. They put the survival of this pack before their own needs. I'm not sure I've ever witnessed such selflessness.

"You didn't want to risk putting them in jeopardy," I say in understanding.

"With the help of enchantments, the pack is well protected here anyway.

We check in on them regularly to make sure their needs are met. We provide protection for them to go out and hunt for food, and Jarek has become a kind of pack doctor."

It then all begins to click into place, and I let out a breath. "This is where Zeke and the others have been the past few days. Checking in on Harmony?"

"Yes," he answers. "We rotate our watch but never stay longer than a couple of days. It's better that we don't interfere too much."

I look down over the land again, completely overcome with what they have managed to achieve here.

It's beautiful.

This man in front of me...

He is beautiful.

Guilt falls over me like a dark shadow, and before I know it, I begin to hyperventilate, the enormity of his gesture beginning to settle in.

"Are you okay—"

"You shouldn't have brought me here!" I pant, shaking my head in a panic, turning to walk back the way we came.

"What? What the hell are you talking about?" he demands, following after me. "Eden, I brought you here to show you that I trust you! Are you saying that I can't?"

I spin around to face him, looking deeply into his confused eyes. "Conall, I'd die before I would tell a living soul about this place!" I hit back passionately, meaning every single word.

"Then what's the problem?!"

"The problem is me, Conall!" I shout, my frustration at myself boiling over. "I've kept something from you this whole time! Something that has been eating me alive. "

He shrugs dismissively. "You think I care now that you lived in the palace? Or that you used to be in love or engaged or whatever the fuck your secret is—"

A painful feeling twists in my gut, and I shake my head. "No...no, it's more than that!"

"Then we will get over it. Just fucking tell me—"

"My real name is Eden Nestoriel!" I blurt out, the admission jumping out of my mouth like word vomit.

As soon as the words leave my lips, I see his face fall, telling me that he already knows the significance of my name. I step forward, ready to lay it all out on the table. "Conall, I'm the daughter of Haleth Nestoriel, Chief Enchantment and Herbology advisor to the king. He is the wood elf you saw that night at the palace. He...he's my father."

He puts his hands on his hips, his jaw tightening before he looks down at the ground. His eyes close as he shakes his head from side to side. His sheer disappointment evident to see.

A heavy weight presses down on my chest, making me feel physically sick. "I'm so sorry, Con."

"You should have told me this sooner," he says, pointing his finger at me accusingly.

I nod my head frantically in agreement. "I know that, but I didn't tell you at first because I was afraid. I knew my father was involved all those years ago, but I had no idea how or to what extent. I still don't! I was afraid that if I revealed who I was, you and the other men would turn on me!" I answer in total honesty. "Conall...I was trying to survive."

He doesn't reply. He just stares into my eyes.

The same feeling of shame I had last night creeps up on me like a disease, spreading through my insides.

He turns his back, lifting his hands to rest them behind his head. He takes a few steps away, and silence falls on the mountain again before he yells aggressively.

"FUCK!"

I jump slightly at the sound of his voice, which echoes all around us, but no matter how nervous I feel, I know I can't stop now.

"There's more."

He turns around to look at me, and I swallow hard.

"More?" he asks in disbelief.

"The man I was in love with. It was Erix."

He doesn't say anything, but the expression on his face at this moment is worth one thousand words.

"I was with him the morning he left to attack Whiteclaw. I knew that he was leading an ambush against innocents, and I- I didn't stop him." I explain honestly, tears rolling down my cheeks.

He nods his head, swallowing hard before his eyes make their way back over to the village.

"But Conall, I swear, if I had known then what I know now, I would have done everything I could have to stop—"

"We need to get back," he interrupts, staring at me blankly in a way that takes me back to the first moment we set eyes on each other in the den.

He begins to walk toward me, and I reach out for his arm, which he moves out of my way.

"Conall, please. Who I am...it doesn't change how I feel about you! Please, can you talk to me?"

He doesn't reply.

And I stand there...watching as he walks away.

Flowers

Eden

I stand awkwardly, looking at the house as he puts his clothes back on. My brain desperately tries to pull together something I can say to make this whole situation better, but I already know that there isn't anything I can do. I am who I am, and there's no changing that fact.

From the corner of my eye, I see him silently walking over to stand beside me, and I work up the courage to speak first. "What happens now?"

He pauses. "You should eat," he answers robotically, making a move to leave.

I grab his forearm, and he freezes but doesn't turn around. "Then what?"

"I have some work to do," he replies, his cold eyes flicking to my hand.

Slowly, I release him, and he walks to the house, disappearing inside.

I feel totally numb.

The man who opened up his heart to me seems to be all but gone, and now all that remains is the shell. The tough, impenetrable exterior that he shows the rest of the world.

I'm so caught up in my thoughts that it takes me a moment to realize that he left me out here all alone. At first, it makes me feel strangely rejected. As though he no longer cares if I choose to leave. But then, a small hopeful notion floats through my mind. Perhaps he has left me here because he trusts that I won't.

I trudge over to the house, opening the door to find the living room pretty busy. This is typical in the early evenings; however, there is something different in the air today. Instead of lounging or joking around, the men are huddled together in smaller groups talking intensely.

I look around, and the chatter stops. Eyes wander over to me in equal curiosity while others look wary of my sudden appearance in the room.

I don't even have the energy to speculate what they are up to or what they are thinking right now. Instead, I head straight for the stairs to my quiet place. The kitchen.

As soon as I walk in, I sense their presence. Their beautiful energy filling up the space. I lift my hand over my heart, and again, for what feels like the millionth time these past couple of days, I begin to tear up.

I walk to the table and sit, lifting my fingers to touch one of the perfect flowers in the old intricate vase.

It isn't long before I hear footsteps coming down the staircase behind me, and I quickly wipe my cheeks dry.

"Hey," Mateo's soft voice says cautiously.

"Hi," I answer, turning around to give him a small nod of acknowledgment.

His brows crease briefly before he rushes over to sit at my side. "Eden, are you okay?" he asks, looking between the flowers and my pink-tinged eyes. "They were supposed to be a gesture. I'm sorry if they upset you."

"They didn't," I say with a sad smile, reassuringly reaching out to pat his hand. "They are amazing. Did you do this?"

He shrugs with a proud grin. "Not just me. Anton, Hunter and I were on patrol this morning and thought you might like them."

As soon as he finishes speaking, I break down in tears. Damn, how I wish I wasn't a crier, but I am, and there's no holding it in. It wasn't so long ago these men were frightened to let me anywhere near nature, and now they are bringing me flowers. Willingly!

If only they knew what I had just told Con.

Would they instantly change their mind about me the way that he has?

Would they hate me?

"Eden, what's wrong?" Mateo asks, lifting his hand to rest it on my shoulder.

"Nothing. Please. I don't want to ruin your evening."

"You aren't ruining anything," he says adamantly before realization settles over his face. "This isn't about the flowers at all, is it? It's about him."

"Mateo...."

"He upset you. He's let you down already."

I shake my head in refute of his claims, but I can see the determined look in his eye.

"I knew this would happen! Where have you been all day? What did he say to you?!"

"He hasn't said anything, Mateo."

□

"Clearly, he has, or you wouldn't be so upset! I told you this might—"

"I don't need a lecture from you!" I snap back, my tear-filled eyes meeting his. "This was on me!" I admit, pointing my finger at my chest. "I did something. I was the one who hurt him!"

Mateo looks at me in shock for a moment. "What did you do?" he asks, concern evident in his tone.

I half considered blurting out the truth. It's on the tip of my tongue to do so, but given how Con reacted, I know I can't. Not right now, anyway.

I shake my head, wiping away my tears to pull myself together.

"I'll be fine."

Then, he grabs my hand, squeezing it supportively in his. "I'm sorry I pushed you. I just wanted to know you were okay."

I give him a grateful smile just as Zeke walks into the kitchen. His eyes immediately drift down to our hands, and Mateo lets me go, awkwardly clearing his throat.

"Don't mind me..." Zeke says, his eyebrow twitching slightly. "Mateo, they need you."

Mateo nods, getting out of his chair to give me a hesitant glance before heading upstairs.

Zeke stands there with his arms folded over his chest, glaring at me.

I look away quickly. "He wasn't doing anything wrong, Zeke," I say sincerely.

"Oh, I know," he answers, leaning against the doorway. "He wouldn't dare step on Con's toes like that."

I shake my head from side to side. "Con won't care."

Zeke snorts in response. "You already know that isn't true."

My eyebrows crease a little in confusion as I turn to look at him.

"Listen, Eden. If Con took you to see Harmony, then you best believe he cares."

"He told you about taking me to Harmony?" I ask quietly.

"He didn't have to."

"And you aren't mad?"

He shakes his head in reply. "I trust his judgment, and what's more, I understand why he did it."

"Because he trusts me," I answer, looking down guiltily for a moment.

"Well, that...and because he loves you."

My eyes flick back up to meet his, unable to hide my utter surprise.
"Nice flowers, by the way," he says casually before sauntering off.

* * *

Conall

How the fuck can this be possible?

First, the Moon Goddess pairs me with an elf, and somehow, against all the fucking odds, we manage to overcome our differences. Then she smacks me in the face with this! The elf is not only the daughter of one of those gutless cockroaches, but she was in love with one too!

How are we to move forward from this?

How can we be together when the reality of our situation makes it fucking impossible?

I'm so angry that I barely know how to function right now.

She kept this from me. All this time, she knew these insurmountable barriers existed, and she said nothing! The betrayal gnaws at me, and yet, despite everything, when I looked at her today on that mountain with pain in her eyes...all I wanted was to take it away.

I wanted to hold her in my arms. To protect her from it all. To shield her from having to suffer any more than she has done already in this lifetime, but how the fuck can I be the one to do that?

How can I hold her and comfort her, knowing that this time tomorrow, we plan to tear her father to shreds for his crimes? Along with every single one of those Elven bastards who did this to us. How can I tell her everything is going to be alright when I know that I'll be the one to break her heart all over again tomorrow?

I walk over to my desk, pouring a drink before I sit down. My eyes immediately fall on the note I received yesterday, and I pick it up to look over it again.

*

He's dead.

*

☐

When I heard the news of King Ciridan from my contact, I almost fucking jumped for joy. I knew it was coming. I engineered it, after all. But knowing our plan was finally falling into place was a weight off my shoulders.

Now, the thought of it gives me a headache.

The door knocks, and Zeke walks inside before I have time to reply.

"Come in," I mutter sarcastically, leaning back in my chair.

"I just came to let you know the men are going over the plan one last time, but everyone knows what they have to do."

"Good," I answer, throwing my drink back.

"Really? You're happy? Could have fooled me..."

"What?" I snap back in irritation.

"Well, first, I run into Eden, who seems distraught about something. Then there's you...sitting there looking fucking miserable even though we've waited for this moment for seventy years."

"It's nothing," I lie. "Eden and I had a fight. I'll handle it."

He nods, taking a step forward. "You should. She's a good one, Con."

"And how would you know that?" I ask interestedly, pouring out another drink to push it toward him.

"Because you wouldn't have taken her to Harmony otherwise," he answers, lifting the glass.

I stare at him for a moment, and he smirks. "I also heard about the thing with the Elven Guard in the forest. If she didn't try to run from you when she had the perfect opportunity, then she won't run now."

My chest tightens in response to his words. That may have been true up until the moment I found out who she really was. Now I'm not sure about anything.

"So you trust her?" I ask.

He shrugs his shoulders. "It doesn't really matter. I trust you, Con."

I nod, appreciating his loyalty more than he will ever know.

"Did you tell her about what happened with Lincoln too?"

I can't help but raise my eyebrow at him. "More than fifty years you haven't said one word about that, now you're choosing to bring it up?" I ask.

He grins a little, but a note of sadness lingers in his expression. "It's none of my business, but fuck it. Tomorrow will change everything anyway, right?"

"It will," I answer pensively, my mind drifting back to Eden once again.

"Right, well, I'll leave you in peace. Clearly, you have some shit to work out.

We all need to get a good sleep tonight."

"Zeke..."

He nods at me curiously as I stand behind the desk to meet him.

"I need to know that if I'm ever not here for any reason, you've got all of this. The den. Harmony. I need to know if you can handle it."

He frowns slightly. "Nothing will happen to you, Con," he chuckles. "Or to any of us. We have planned this attack to perfec—"

"I just need to know," I interrupt seriously.

He looks into my eyes, his hand reaching out to mine to shake it firmly.

"I've got this," he says with total confidence.

I give him a respectful nod, and he disappears, leaving me alone again to battle with my conflicting thoughts.

Connection

Eden

I toss and turn, throwing myself back onto the mattress.

I can't sleep.

Every time I close my eyes, I see his face. His disappointment when I told him the truth. I know logically that he needs time to process my admission, but I'd be lying if I said it wasn't killing me, not knowing what's going through his head. I finally decide that I just can't wait any longer.

Throwing the covers to one side, I jump out of bed and head for the door, entering the corridor. There is not a sound to be heard throughout the whole house, and I briefly wonder why it's so quiet at this time when usually there are always a few men who stay up late into the night.

I look at Conall's door, striding toward it determinedly before I have time to change my mind. However, just as I'm about to knock, it opens wide, and I come to an abrupt halt in front of his chest, my eyes flicking up to the serious expression on his face.

"I was just—"

"Me too," he interrupts, stepping back to open the door wide. "Come in."

I do as he asks, my body shivering slightly as I pass him by.

Once inside, I linger awkwardly while he closes the door and pours a drink for us both. I watch him intently as he lifts the glass to hand it to me.

"Thanks," I say gently.

He nods, taking a drink before leaning against the edge of his desk, folding his arms.

I take a sip from the glass, my eyes staying with his, before placing it on the table.

"I uhh. I couldn't sleep." I admit, shrugging my shoulders.

His eyes wander over my body, which is clad in a small red garment from Madam Piffnel's bag of wonders.

"Me either," he answers, looking down at the floor.

I take a step forward, summoning all the strength I have to say what I have to say. "Con, I was telling the truth today when I said that who I am does not change my feelings about you. The connection we have...it's still strong. I can feel it whenever we are near and even now when we are not. I understand if you don't feel the same way I do anymore, but you should know that I cannot change who I am or where I have come from."

"I know that," he answers. "I'm not mad at you."

"You're not?"

"How could I be?" he replies, his brows knitting together. "Eden, you're special," he whispers, stepping forward. "You're kind, loyal, and intelligent. You're beautiful. Inside and out."

He stops right in front of me, and I stare up at him in shock. "Oh, I thought after today that you had changed your mind."

"About you?" he asks, lifting my chin. "Never."

He moves his warm body closer to mine, his large hands now resting on either side of my face. "I was an asshole for reacting the way that I did earlier. I just needed time to take it all in, but I should have said right from the beginning... You are the most amazing woman I have ever met. *Nothing* will ever change that."

A small wave of relief washes over me, but I can tell from the look in his eyes that there is more. "But...?" I whisper.

He swallows, his hands dropping back down by his sides. "But no matter how much we want it to work. It can't."

He steps away from me, turning his back to make his way over to the desk.

"Why Con?"

He sits on his chair, looking at the flames of the raging fire instead of me.

"I asked why?"

"Because how can we be together, Eden, when I could never so much as look your father in the eye? Or be in the same room as him?"

I exhale, nodding as I've spent the whole day wondering the same thing. "I understand. I do, but I can talk to him. He will listen to me; I know that he will. Whatever he did back then, I know there must be more to it. There has to be a reason. My father isn't an evil man! Something must have happened. Perhaps he was forced or—"

He holds up his hand to stop me, shaking his head from side to side. "Eden, I can't. I can't listen to you defend him."

☐

"I'm not!" I protest sadly. "But he's my father. The man who raised me, and I need to understand exactly what happened. Then when I know, I can explain the truth to him. I know I can get him to help us," I say adamantly, kneeling in front of him to take his hands in mine. "Con, we can get justice for your people. We can find a way to set the truth free. No matter how hard it is, no matter how long it takes, I'm in this with you."

A painful expression is written over his face as he places his head in his hands. "We can't. It's not as simple as that."

"Stop pushing me away! We can! You just have to believe in us!" I say sincerely. "Believe in me."

He removes his hands from his face, his eyes looking deeply into mine. "I don't deserve you, Eden."

He reaches for me again, pulling me forward gently to rest his forehead against mine.

Despite our closeness, I feel his reluctance and sadness through our bond. He thinks our circumstances make this challenge impossible, but I don't see it that way. Together we can achieve even more. We can make real change. Perhaps one day, the people of Harmony can live freely, without fear. Perhaps one day, life could be full of happiness for us.

I lean forward slowly, our eyes connecting as my lips softly brush his. At first, he barely reacts, his face soft and still.

I lift my hands to place them on top of his where they rest on my face, and this time, I apply more pressure, my lips expressing what words cannot.

His honey eyes flicker closed, and his chest rises and falls as his fingers spread into the hair behind my ears. His lips press against mine harder, with more feeling and emotion than I've ever felt before. Our kiss becomes deeper, and with every passing second, I give more of myself away to him.

If I already own the pieces of his soul, then by the end of this night, he shall own mine.

One of his hands moves around the back of my head, and he holds me in place as though I might slip through his fingers and disappear at any moment. I tear my lips from his to stare into his beautiful eyes.

"I'm not going anywhere, Con," I say sincerely. "There's nowhere I'd rather be."

His eyes run over my face before he pulls me up from the floor to guide me onto his lap. I straddle him where he sits, my lips moving with his as his hands spread over my back, gripping the red silk. Our chests press together, and I grind against him slowly, feeling him get harder and harder beneath me. The feeling excites me as much as ever, and my movements get faster, my grip on his stubbled face intensifying. But as I begin to fall into our usual pattern, he stops. He pulls his head back to stare up at me, and I look back questioningly before he lifts his hand to sweep my dangling hair behind my ear. I watch as his eyes then drop down, his hands following as he tugs the silk slip up over the curves of my body. He pulls it over my breasts, and I lift my arms in the air to allow him to discard it completely. The garment drops to the floor, and he leans forward, kissing my chest tenderly. My eyes close as tingles begin to run up and down my spine. He then makes his way up my neck, his lips reaching mine again in an entirely new way. His fingertips drift over the bare skin of my back, his touch more delicate and affectionate than I have ever felt before. I reach down for his pants, which he pulls down just enough, and then next, I reach for him. Sliding myself down his length slowly, feeling every part of him inside me. Relishing every moment.

I pull back to look into his eyes.

And it's then, with a single look, we fall in love.

□

Love

I lie in his arms, and the world no longer frightens me. My worries now are nothing but faint whispers in the back of my mind. I choose to ignore them. Focusing instead on the gentle rhythm of his heartbeat, which pulses against my ear.

I look down to see his fingers intertwined with mine, where he holds my hand, rubbing the rough pad of his thumb over my skin.

"Are you okay?" he asks softly, interrupting the silence.

I lift my head from his chest to look up into his waiting eyes. "Of course," I whisper back, a gentle smile touching my lips. "Conall, that was...."

"Everything," he answers, finishing the sentence for me.

I nod my head as he continues to look at me intently.

"Tell me about him," he says calmly.

I frown, pulling myself up to lean on my elbow. "What?"

"Tell me about him."

There is no need to question who he is talking about, but the shock of him asking to hear the story in the first place renders me entirely speechless.

"I told you once that you didn't have to hide anything from me," he says, examining my face. "I meant it."

His words take me back to that moment by the river when we collected flowers for the remedy that healed Henrick's injured leg. It seems so long ago now. It's truly crazy how much things can change in such a short period of time.

"I don't mean to push you. You don't have to—"

"I want to."

For the first time since it all happened, I find myself able to contemplate talking about it. I am ready and willing to open up about what happened all those years ago.

"Are you sure?"

"You've been open with me. I want to be open with you too," I reply sincerely.

He nods, his hand tightening around mine as I take a deep breath. I lay back down on his chest, his heartbeat comforting me as I trawl through old, painful memories. Memories that I tried to shut out a long time ago.

"I met Erix when my family first moved from Azealea to Morween. My life when we first moved was pretty miserable. The fact that I was a wood elf meant that everywhere I went in the castle, I was treated like an outsider. People would stop and stare. They would whisper insults to one another directly in front of my face."

"Sounds like a fantastic place," Con says sarcastically.

I smile a little and squeeze his hand.

"I was lonely, and I didn't have any friends. That was until I met Erix. Whenever he would pass me by, he would always smile this beaming smile and make time to talk to me. At first, it was just simple greetings and everyday chit-chat, but eventually, our conversations grew longer," I explain. "He started to come by my father's study more often, and he would try to take an interest in my studies, even though he didn't have the faintest idea what the hell he was talking about," I laugh softly, the memory unlocking the full weight of my emotions. "He was kind, and he was sweet. It wasn't long until he became my boyfriend and the only person in Morween who didn't look down on me for who I was or where I came from. We fell so much in love that we agreed to spend our lives together. Someday he would inherit the throne and make me his queen. Not that any of that mattered to me; all I wanted was to be happy. All I wanted was him."

I glance at Con to see his eyes fixed firmly on my hand, which rests in his palm.

"We talked about our future together all the time. What it would look like. Our dreams and our aspirations."

It's then that the familiar feeling of gut-wrenching pain swoops in over me, doing its best to take hold. However, this time, I have Conall to keep me from falling into the abyss. He holds me closer to him, leaning down to land a gentle, encouraging kiss on my head. I smile slightly in reply, my heart thudding as I embrace his comforting touch. His touch that gives me the courage and the strength to keep going.

"The day they brought him back to Morween was the hardest day of my life," I say honestly. "I remember standing there on the palace balcony, watching from afar as they took his body inside the royal mausoleum. I had to stand there and watch them close the doors for good. Those stuck-up lords who didn't give two shits about him followed the coffin inside, yet I wasn't allowed to say goodbye to him properly. Me... The woman he loved. The woman he was supposed to spend the rest of his life with."

"I'm sorry," Con says quietly, lifting his hand to rest on my upper arm.

"My father left a white rose on the coffin for me, but it wasn't enough," I say, shaking my head as tears spring to my eyes. "I had lost the one person who seemed to understand me. I lost my future, my way in the world, and I... I wasn't sure how I would go on in this life without him."

Con kisses me again just as a tear lands on his chest.

"I'm sorry. You don't want to hear this, Con. Not after everything you told me about him. Not after what he did."

"I do," he answers adamantly. "Because your past is part of who you are. Just as mine is."

Love swells in my heart as I look over his handsome, understanding face. Somehow life has given me a second chance at happiness in the most unlikely place.

Here...with him.

"Now the heartache can finally stop," I whisper to him hopefully. "I can find peace again. We can find it together."

He looks into my eyes, but he doesn't say a word. Instead, he kisses my head gently. "You should get some sleep."

I nod as my eyes begin to droop, laying my head on him again while my hand rests over his strong, beating heart.

* * *

I awake to an empty bed, stretching my arms above my head. I look over to see Con standing by the petering flames of the fire.

"What are you doing?" I ask softly. "It's early. Come back to bed."

He doesn't answer me, and I frown, looking to the side to see clothes set out for me on the chair. My gut instincts kick in, and immediately, I know that there's something wrong. It's evident in the way he is transfixed on the fire, deep in thought, and it's clear in the expression on his face when he finally turns his head.

"I need you to get dressed," he says in a quiet, demanding tone.

An ominous feeling settles in the pit of my stomach. "Why?" I question, sliding off the edge of the bed. "Is it Harmony?"

"It's not Harmony, but I need you to get dressed now. We don't have much time until the others wake up."

I swallow the lump in my throat, glancing at the clothes again before standing up. "What do you mean?"

He rests his hand on the wall, closing his eyes as he shakes his head. "Can't you just do what I'm asking?"

"No! Not until you tell me what the hell is going on!" I hit back in return.

It's then that he moves, striding toward me with intensity. "Eden, just do it. Please." His pained eyes look into mine pleadingly.

I reach for the shirt to pull it over my head, and he turns his back on me as I finish getting ready.

I open my mouth to speak, and he twists, grabbing my hand to tug me to the door. Just as he is about to open it, he stops and looks at me seriously. "Don't say a word. We can't risk waking anyone."

I nod, unable to decipher what is happening. Don't get me wrong, I always knew that he was unpredictable. We've played this game of cat and mouse since the moment we met, but this rapid change in his demeanor catches me off guard.

Last night had been so perfect. So special in every way, and I thought he felt it too.

Did I get it all so wrong?

Did I misread what happened between us?

He leads me through the empty house, navigating the hallways stealthily until we reach the living room, where he heads straight for the door. As soon as we enter the cool morning air, I let out a shaky breath, glancing back at the den. We break through the barrier of the trees, but Con doesn't stop. By now, he's practically dragging me alongside him as we enter deeper into the forest.

Eventually, I snap and stop dead, yanking my arm from his tight grip. "Enough!" I snarl. "I'm not taking one more step until you tell me what the fuck is going on!"

His jaw tenses, and he looks around us warily, thoroughly scanning the forest. I wait for him to speak, but he doesn't say anything.

"Well?! Why are you acting like this?! Why did you bring me out here?!" I question angrily.

He blinks slowly before his eyes connect with mine. "I brought you out here, Eden, because I'm letting you go."

My mouth drops open in shock. "You're what?" I gasp, the pit in my stomach growing exponentially.

"I'm letting you go home," he repeats calmly.

I shake my head slowly. "I don't understand... You want me to leave the den?"

He looks at me for a moment before nodding his head. "Yes."

"No! I don't believe you!" I protest passionately. "You can't be serious, Con, not after everything that happened last night. Don't try to deny it. Something happened between us, and I know you felt it too!"

"Eden...." he begins, reaching for my arms to hold me in place. "I need you to do this. I need you to go home. To forget about me and pick your life up where you left off—"

"The answer is no!" I yell furiously, pulling myself from his grip and stepping back. "How can you say that? Were you lying when you told me that you wanted me? That you wanted us to be mates?"

At first, he doesn't reply, and then he shakes his head in frustration. "No, I wasn't lying. I meant every single word."

"Then what is this, Con?!" I demand. "If this is because of my father, I told you I will find out the truth. I will do anything to help you get justice. I'm with you on this. Please, let me help you!"

He closes his eyes, turning away from me as he puts his hands behind his head. "You can't help me."

"I can," I say confidently. "I have some connections. We can work something out—"

"NO, WE CAN'T!" he snaps, turning to look into my eyes as he takes me by the shoulders again. "Eden, if you don't leave today and don't do what I'm telling you to do, then you'll lose your father! He'll be fucking dead by nightfall!"

My eyes widen in shock. "What?"

He briefly drops his head to the forest floor before looking back up in defeat. "The note that you found...it was about King Ciridan. He's the one who's dead. He's dead because I planned it this way."

I have no words. Instead, I stare at him in plain shock. Unable to move.

"This evening, his body will be taken to the royal mausoleum, which will bring together every Elven lord from every corner of the realm as well as Ciridan's closest advisors."

"Including my father," I whisper.

He nods his head, swallowing hard. "It's our only chance to get them all together in one place. Without their guards, without their enchantments and protections—"

"You're going to attack," I interrupt. "This is what you all have been planning?"

"Yes," he answers honestly. "Harmony is growing bigger than we ever imagined. It's getting harder to protect. Now is the time to strike. We need to remove these assholes from power and hopefully gain freedom for my kind in this realm once again."

"So you're going to kill them all?"

He looks at me seriously for a few seconds before answering. "We will, Eden, and before you ask, I couldn't stop the attack even if I wanted to. These men have waited for this moment for seventy years, and I won't be the one to take it from them. Tonight we will go to Morween, and we will have our vengeance once and for all."

I close my eyes, a tear falling to stream down my cheek. "Why are you telling me this?" I ask, opening my tear-filled eyes to look into his.

"I'm telling you because of everything I said last night...because of everything we felt. Eden, it was real."

My heart tugs in my chest at the sound of his words.

"I won't have you lose anyone else you love. I won't break your heart again."

"You're letting me go to save him? To save my father?"

He nods, his hands reaching up to rest on my face. "I couldn't live with myself if I didn't do this for you."

I don't want to leave his side. Everything in me wants to stay here with him, but how can I let my father die when I have the power to change it?

I lift my hand to cover his, tears now falling fast as I lean my head to the side to kiss the palm of his hand. "Thank you," I whisper softly.

"You don't have to thank me," he says, holding my cheek. "Morween is twenty-five miles south of here. Can you get into the castle discretely without being seen?"

"Yes, I know a way. There's a tunnel that Erix showed me years ago."

"Then take it," he says hurriedly. "Go straight to your father and keep him from going to that gathering, but you must do it quietly. Do you understand? No one must find out about the attack. No one."

"I understand. You can trust me to do this," I say determinedly.

"I know I can," he answers, pulling me close to kiss the top of my head.

I sob into his chest as he holds me tightly in his embrace, and it's then that a disturbing thought enters my head.

"Conall, what will happen when the others realize I'm gone?"

He pauses for a second before answering. "Don't worry about it. Let me sort that out."

I pull away from him and look up into his eyes. "You should tell them that I escaped. Tell them that I ran. Then do what you have to do tonight. Have your vengeance, and then I'll come back to you. I'll come back, and we can be together."

"You can't come back. It won't be safe. You should try to move on—"

"I don't care if it's dangerous! Once you have completed this mission, then there is nothing that can stand in our way!" I say in distress.

He looks over my face, his eyes softening. "Eden..."

"No! Don't try to stop me. I won't—"

"I love you," he says with conviction, his hands cupping my face.

"Wha-"

"I just needed you to know that. I'll never regret that you came into my life. My only regret will be not holding you for longer—not taking you into my arms the second I saw you. There was no light for me left in this world until there was you, Eden, and no matter where we find ourselves from this day on... I'll be forever grateful that I found you. Do you understand?"

"Y-yes," I stutter.

He leans forward to press his lips against mine, and I fall into his kiss instantly, my hands reaching up around his neck in this moment of pure love. A moment that simultaneously fills my heart and breaks it all at the same time.

Our lips part, and he rests his head against mine. "Con, I love—"

"Be careful out there," he interrupts, his hands still holding my face tenderly.

"I will," I reply. "Please tell me that you will be careful too."

He nods, his hands taking mine. "You have to go now if you're going to make the journey back in time."

Reluctantly, I take a step away from him while still holding his hands tightly.

"Go," he says calmly, releasing his grip to give me a sad but reassuring smile.

I hold his gaze for a few seconds longer before turning my back to begin heading south toward Morween. I break out into a run, my feet shuffling through the leaves as I pick up the pace.

My heart longs for him already, and I glance over my shoulder one last time. But there is now only an empty space where he once stood.

He's gone.

Vengeance

Conall

We stop in a remote spot by the edge of Morween territory, shifting back to our human form one by one.

Zeke and I examine the castle from afar. "White smoke...." he says quietly, looking upward into the air.

"It means the funeral is almost ready to begin," I answer in return.

The rest of the men stand in silence, each of us watching as the darkening sky gradually fills with a white haze. I face them, and they stand to attention, ready for their orders. I had anticipated nerves at this point in the mission. After all, it has been years since we have faced combat of any kind. However, when I look around each and every one of them, I feel nothing but their strength and courage. I feel proud to stand among them. Proud to be their leader while we fulfill the promise we made all those years ago to avenge those who died on that fateful day.

"Years of planning and sacrifice have brought us to this moment. Tonight we make those assholes pay and pave the way for the survival of our species," I say, looking around the group again. "So when you fight tonight, remember why we are here. For the living and the dead. Be their warrior. Take your vengeance and win them the retribution they deserve!"

They nod their heads in determination, the fire evident in their eyes.

"Two hundred and sixty-eight," Zeke says, looking around intensely.

"Two hundred and thirty," Mateo adds, looking up to the sky.

"One hundred and forty-nine."

"Seventy-seven."

"Two hundred and eleven."

"One hundred and fifty-two."

Each number adds a new layer of purpose. A new level of fearlessness and drive.

We are ready for this.

We have been ready for the longest time.

The men fall silent, and their focus falls on me again.

If this is to be my last night on this earth, then you better believe I will fight tooth and nail to make it count. Every last one of those bastards will die tonight. There can be no survivors. We cannot afford to leave a single lord behind. For Harmony's sake and for Eden's.

"Three hundred and twelve," I add in finality, thoughts of everyone I have loved and lost appearing in my mind's eye.

I turn back to the palace and narrow my eyes before giving the order. "Go."

As soon as the word leaves my lips, the men shift, dispersing in different directions as they head off to complete their own individual missions. I look to my left to see Zeke, Mateo and Evan by my side, each of them shifting and taking off straight ahead in the direction of Morween. I follow on, ready to face whatever is thrown at us.

We take the route we have spent years plotting. The most difficult route there is toward the palace. Narrow pathways run along the edge of steep cliffs with multiple obstacles in our way. We navigate the rocky terrain as though second nature. The result of countless trial runs. Every fallen tree, every gap in the path, and every steep ridge is accounted for.

Before long, we find ourselves in the danger zone around the palace grounds—the area which is patrolled by the Guard at all times. However, I'm not worried. We have monitored their movements for years. Their security always increases for significant events, as is taking place tonight, but the pattern is always the same. I look sideways at the others and nod, each of us stalking off to take cover in the darkness of the trees.

Within seconds, I see my own targets walking into my vicinity. Two guards armed with bows and swords walk side by side as they examine the forest. I wait for the opportune moment to strike, jumping out onto the first guard to take him down to the ground. He struggles under my snarling body, but I'm in no mood for a drawn-out fight, so I sink my teeth into his shoulder with enough power to subdue him completely. He cries out in pain before I stamp my foot over his face causing him to pass out immediately. The other guard draws his sword, swinging it at me with a loud shriek. I dodge the blade, gripping his ankle with my teeth to drag him to the ground. He thrashes around wildly before his voice rings out through the quiet.

"Hel—"

I sink my claws into his chest before he has the chance to finish, dragging both elves into the trees before continuing on. I run past Zeke, who has taken out the next level of protection, and we move together to Mateo's position. He has one guard by the throat while another is aiming at him, his arrow poised and ready to release. I immediately speed up, my paws pounding off the ground as the elf turns his attention to me. I swerve to avoid the flying arrow, leaping through the air to land on top of the sorry son-of-a-bitch, ending his life for good.

There can be no mercy tonight. No hesitation.

Mateo finishes with his guard, and we keep moving, finding Evan, who is keeping watch in our next position across from the royal mausoleum. He nods east, and I look over to see the signal. A tree branch waving in a known pattern. Rocco, Henrick, Hunter and Anton have made it to their hiding place. As we wait, I scan the trees for the rest of the men's signals which come one by one. All except Neville, Jarek and William's.

Zeke glances at me sideways as we wait.

Something is wrong. Their route was shorter than the others, so they should be in position by now.

I give Zeke a nod, knowing that he will understand what to do, and I take off through the trees to help. As I get closer, I see them in their human form. William and Neville are kneeling on the ground around Jarek's limp body.

I immediately shift to greet them, looking around cautiously as I do. "What happened?"

"He took two arrows to the chest," William answers. "He's completely out."

"Fuck," I grit out between my teeth.

At least I know that he isn't fucking dead. It's impossible, but an injury like this will keep him down and unable to shift with the rest of us.

"One of you will have to take his bag, and one of you take him back to the house. We can't risk leaving him here, or he may be captured."

"I'm not fucking missing this, Con," William protests in a quiet snarl. "Please."

"I'll take him," Neville interjects. "I've got this."

I pat his shoulder, waiting for him to shift before William and I pick up an unconscious Jarek and toss him over Neville's back.

It's then that an arrow flies past my head, sinking into a nearby tree.

"Go!" I order Neville, who takes off through the trees back to the den.

William grabs the bag, slinging it over his shoulder, and I take cover as a flurry of arrows head our way. I manage to look around the tree trunk to find the source of the attack—a lone guard.

"I'll draw his fire, and you get the bastard from behind. We need to get out of here," I instruct William quietly.

He nods, and I shift, taking off between the thick trunks of the trees. I'm moving so fast that I can't see the guard anymore; my other senses lead the way as I dodge the onslaught of arrows. Every sound in the air is amplified. I feel every brush of the gentle wind. I hear it before I see it, the arrow racing for my body, I leap into the air allowing it to pass beneath me, and by the time I land, I hear the faint yelp of the guard as William does his job.

I make my way back over to him, and we reach our position, sending the signal to Zeke.

It seems our arrival has come just in time as we hear the music play in the distance. The sound of trumpets indicates the arrival of King Ciridan, followed by his queen and his lords.

The white haze surrounds the circular building as its multiple doors open slowly. A small army of elves march forward in front of the coffin, each of them filtering into their positions to stand to attention around the mausoleum. They aren't allowed to enter inside. Only those assholes of noble birth or rank have the right to do so. As the coffin draws closer, I frantically examine the followers. The queen leads the way, her blank and cold expression visible through her sheer veil. I then look to the men who follow her; their familiar faces have been seared into my brain since that night in Morween when we went to talk with Ciridan. One by one, hundreds of the cruel bastards filter inside the building, and I continue looking for the one man who I chose to spare.

The wood elf.

Eden's father.

There's no sign of him.

The fact makes my shoulders relax a fraction. His absence means she got to him in time. I had not a single doubt in her capabilities or her loyalty. She's clever and resourceful, not to mention damn right stubborn and fierce when she needs to be. From how she speaks of her father, I know he loves her. He'll protect her here as long as I take out every other threat in her way. Every fucker who could stand to try to punish her for her so-called "treason." Sheer venom flows through my veins, but I know I cannot let it distract me. I have a job to do, and now is the time.

The pompous crowd disappears inside the circular stone structure, and the doors close, cutting off the music to plunge the forest back into silence.

The guards stand like statues in position, some already with bows poised. Some with swords drawn. They aren't taking any chances, but neither am I. We get into a raging battle with these men; it will only allow the lords the opportunity to scarper. It will create a scene so loud that it will alert the rest of the guards that remain at the palace for the second round of funeral ceremonies.

No... It wouldn't make sense to attack this way.

I decided long ago to take my father's advice in this instance.

"To defeat the enemy, you must learn to fight like them."

I look to William, and we both shift back to human form. He lays out Jarek's bag on the ground and opens it to reveal the vials of liquid. We grab half each, nodding at each other before heading in different directions.

I make the first move, tossing one of the thin glass vials at the mausoleum. It smacks the stone wall with a quiet thwack, immediately combusting into pieces to release the toxic substance inside.

It won't kill them, but it will certainly knock them the fuck out.

The nearby guard twists his head to investigate the sound, but he drops to the ground before he can raise the alarm. The others around him move to his aid, but they soon follow suit, falling onto the stone steps. I toss the next vial, now running at speed. I can tell William is doing the same as the guards now begin to fall one by one like silent dominoes. A few stragglers try to run, one even reaching the mausoleum's doors. I freeze on the spot, then, to my relief; the guard falls face-first to the ground, the hilt of a knife protruding from his back. That kind of aim can only be the work of Zeke. I continue until the last vial leaves my hands, scanning the building to ensure every bastard is down. One of the remaining guards lifts his bow to the forest in a panic, his voice echoing through the woods as he shouts a warning in Elvish. He doesn't finish the sentence before Anton's wolf breaks from the trees to silence him.

The action begins our attack, and I shift back to my wolf form, emerging from the trees in a determined run. I look sideways to see my brothers at my side, pushing forward to the stone building.

Nothing stands in our way now. Not a single thing can stop us.

I barrel through the doorway to find myself in the middle of the mausoleum. Screams ring through the air as the crowd inside scarpers in fear. Men in expensive robes run around in terror like the good-for-nothing cowards that they are.

"GUARDS! GUARDS!" the crooked queen screams from beside the coffin, but it's useless. No one is coming to their rescue.

Evan and Henrick shift into human form to close the doors, locking our victims inside. I look around, securing my first target, the Elven lord who took over my land after *The Culling*. He spots my determined run and takes off in the opposite direction toward the rest of the carnage, but he can't outrun me. I grab him by the leg, tripping him to the ground. He yells and grunts in pain as he pulls a dagger from his robes, slashing the air in wild, imprecise movements. It takes seconds for me to sink my teeth through his wrist, causing the dagger to rattle off the stone floor. My claws dig through his chest, and blood pours from his mouth as the life drains from his eyes.

I look up, scanning the chaotic scene for my next target, Lord Faenor, one of the most outspoken wolf-haters from the days of the war. I set my sights on him, and his eyes widen in fear as he begins to run, pushing others out of the way as he tries to make it to one of the exits. I'm gaining on him with each passing second, but just as I reach the tails of his robe, a warning howl enters the air. My head snaps back to see Henrick's wolf by the central door, and within milliseconds, arrows begin flying through the air, followed by the presence of guards. Seeping into the building from every direction.

Where the fuck did they come from?!

We anticipated their arrival at some point but not this soon.

I barrel through the nearest guards knocking them off their feet before I hear the howl of my fellow brothers as some are caught with flying arrows. We are fighting with everything we have in us, but the sheer volume of guards begins to swamp us. If it were up to me, I'd stay and take out every single one of these bastards, but I know that to do so would result in our eventual capture and imprisonment. Something that we cannot risk is leaving Harmony without protection. Capture is not an option. It becomes clear that we have no choice but to abandon the mission altogether.

Pure anger rages through me, but I remain focused as I howl into the air, the signal for us to get the fuck out of here. The men follow my orders, each battling through the frantic crowd to make their way back outside into the cover of the forest.

Then I hear a familiar yell, and spot Samuel being dragged along the stone floor by guards as two arrows poke out of his leg. The injury won't allow him to shift back, and I know what I have to do. I shift into human form, navigating the fleeing crowd before grabbing one of the guards from behind. I break his neck before he can fight back. The other drops Samuel's arm and swings a punch at my face. I duck out of the way, dropping to one knee to lift a discarded sword from the ground and drive it through him. He drops to the floor, and I lift Samuel's arm, slinging it around my shoulder as I carry him out into the carnage that awaits outside. All around me, wolves battle with the guards, taking as many of them down as they can as they gain ground toward the trees.

Mateo's wolf stops by my side. I throw Samuel's limp body over his back, hurriedly allowing them to take off to safety.

I look up at the palace, watching with wide eyes as hundred's more guards pour down the hill in our direction.

"MOVE!! NOW!!" I order, readying myself to shift, but it's then that I spot her, and I freeze stiff.

Eden.

I see her lilac hair in the distance as she stands on the stone balcony of the palace that overlooks us.

Her father stands to her right side, and then the asshole from the forest is on her left. The one I almost tore to shreds—her friend she defended fiercely that day.

I stand there staring at her as she looks back with a blank expression. The asshole throws his arm around her protectively to kiss the side of her head.

I look back to the sea of guards heading our way, the pain in my chest rendering me useless. An arrow pierces the skin of my shoulder, but I barely flinch. It's nothing in comparison with her apparent betrayal.

"CON! MOVE!" Zeke demands, nudging me in the direction of the forest. "Fucking shift now! We need to get out of here!"

I do as he says, my wolf taking over as I follow him through the trees, making our escape.

Sentence

Conall

"WHAT THE FUCK WAS THAT SHIT SHOW!?!" Rocco screams in rage, blood pouring from a wound on his head.

"WE SHOULD GET IN THE HOUSE!" Mateo yells in warning, bending over to catch his breath.

Rocco runs over to Samuel, who is rolling around the grass in pain.

"PULL THEM FUCKING OUT!" he demands, tugging at the arrows buried deeply in his thigh.

"WE NEED JAREK!"

"He's still out of it!" Neville shouts, emerging from the house. "What the hell happened?!"

I shift to my human form, striding across the yard as I count the men shifting around me. "WAS ANYONE FOLLOWED?" I bellow.

They shake their heads, every single one of them exhausted from the run back here.

"Wait...where is Henrick?" Hunter asks, scanning the trees.

"I can't see Evan either!" William pants, wincing as he pulls an arrow from his side.

"Fuck!" I grit out between my teeth. "I'm going back for them."

"I'm coming," Zeke adds, following on behind me.

"No, I need you to stay here. Make sure the house is secure and get everyone inside," I order him.

He nods in compliance, springing into action.

I shift again, running through the trees until pained growls hit my ears. Then I see Henrick's wolf stumbling onto the ground with an injured Evan on his back.

Shit!

I approach them, shifting to my human form as Henrick collapses in an exhausted heap.

"Can you walk?" I ask him, scanning the trees again.

His human form takes over, and he looks up at me and nods. I then examine Evan to see a huge bleeding sore in his neck. The sight makes me fucking sick to my stomach. I bend down to pick him up, summoning every last ounce of strength I have to throw his heavy body over my shoulder.

"Come on. We have to get out of the forest," I say through gritted teeth, taking off in a labored jog. The weight of the man on top of me threatens to buckle the legs from under me, but I won't fucking give up. Not until I make sure everyone gets back to the den safely.

We finally burst through the trees, the moonlight illuminating the way to the front door. It swings open, and Neville and Anton emerge, running downstairs to support Henrick before reaching for Evan, who is gradually coming around, groaning in agony.

It's then that Zeke appears, running downstairs toward me quickly. He grabs my arm, pulling me backward. "You need to leave, Con. They know she's missing," he says in a frantic whisper, his voice steeped in worry, his eyes piercing mine. "If you go now, you'll at least have a head start."

I shake my head in refusal. "I'm not going anywhere, Zeke," I answer, pulling my arm from his.

"Are you fucking crazy?! You broke the code. You know what this means. I can't let you do this!" he says, standing in my way.

I lift my hand and place it on his shoulder. "I won't run away, Zeke. Remember what you told me last night? You've got this. Now that I've failed, you have to be the one to step up."

He gulps, his eyes closing in defeat.

"THERE HE IS!" Rocco yells from the doorway, making his way out into the moonlit yard, already armed with a knife. "DON'T LET HIM RUN!"

"Does it look like I'm fucking going anywhere?" I answer calmly in return.

Zeke stands by my side, and we watch as the others filter out into the yard.

A suffocating silence fills the air around us where we stand. Looking around at their faces, I can tell there are mixed emotions.

Disappointment.

Anger.

Sadness.

Betrayal.

I can't act as though I'm surprised. The second I let Eden go free, I accepted my fate. I accepted that my punishment for breaking the code would be my death, and I made my peace with it. However, I had hoped that the circumstances would be different and that we would be standing here victorious. Our revenge fulfilled. Our bloodlust is satisfied.

"The elf is fucking gone, Conall," Rocco growls, stepping forward to narrow his eyes at me.

"She must have escaped while we were away," Zeke interjects on my behalf.

Rocco glares at him before his eyes shift back to me. "Is that what happened?" he asks, his eyebrow raised.

"You already know that's not what happened," I reply honestly.

As soon as my admission leaves my lips, I see the men look at each other in defeat. Some turn away from me to gather themselves, others sweep their hand over their face, and some shake their heads.

"Fucking hell, Con," Hunter breathes out in disappointment, his head dropping to the ground.

"How could you do this to us?! You traitor!" Samuel snarls, hobbling forward on one leg.

"Traitor? If it wasn't for this fucking "traitor," your ass would be rotting in a Morween cell right now!" Zeke snaps back angrily.

"Are you fucking kidding?" Rocco snarls. "The whole plan went to shit because of him and that little slut bitch!!"

I step forward, my blood boiling in my veins to hear him speak of Eden like that. "Don't you dare," I say lowly, pointing my finger at him.

"Why did you do it, Con? We deserve to know why?!" Mateo asks.

Everyone stares at me. Waiting.

"Because I love her," I answer honestly.

The stunned men stand in silence.

"And look where that got us! She set them on us! She told them we were coming!" Samuel yells furiously.

"Eden wouldn't do that!" Mateo protests vehemently. "She's loyal to us!"

"Really? Then why don't you ask lover boy here why she was standing on the palace balcony with high elves? Don't deny that you saw her! I know you fucking did!" Samuel accuses me.

It's then that I picture her once again. Standing there staring back at me from the palace. The thought of her betrayal tears me apart, but in the end, I'm not sure I can blame her for how this has played out. I let her go, and I must take fucking responsibility.

"Shit..." Mateo frowns as he looks at Anton.

"You broke the code!" Rocco continues. "No matter what the reason. No matter if you were fucking tricked. The code is the code. No exceptions," he says through gritted teeth. "We will not treat you differently—"

"I'm not asking you to," I interrupt, looking him dead in the eye. "I knew what I was doing."

The silence continues as I take a step forward, taking a deep breath.

"Despite the outcome tonight, you all fought like warriors," I call out around the men. "And I was proud of every last one of you. You did your jobs, but it was I who didn't do mine. I let you down." I say, ashamed. "I don't have a problem admitting my faults. I took a gamble for the woman I loved. A gamble that backfired on all of you...and so for that, I'm sorry and accept my fate at your hands."

Rocco nods, his hand tightening around the hilt of his blade. "The code is clear on this, men!" he yells. "The punishment for breaking it is death. Without the code, we have no honor! Our leader has proved himself unworthy, and now he must die and a new leader elected immediately!"

The men stand silently, neither in agreement nor protest.

"So none of you bastards have the balls to do it?" Rocco questions in disgust. "Fine. I'll do it myself. Turn around! And don't try anything!" he demands.

I look around the men one last time, each of them giving me a respectful nod, their reluctance written over their faces.

Finally, I reach Zeke and look into his eyes. "Look after them."

He nods, his jaw tense and his eyes glassy.

I turn to look up at the moon.

I hear Rocco make a move toward me, but before he can get close, Zeke sinks a long blade into my lower back. One hand holds it in place while his other rests on my shoulder, squeezing it firmly.

It's now so damn quiet you could hear a pin drop.

He pulls the blade from my body, its absence causing searing pain to rush up my spine. My eyes begin to grow hazy, and my legs collapse from under me, dropping me to my knees. I lift my hands to my stomach, my eyes drifting down to the bright red blood that now covers them.

I feel myself begin to slip away.

The pages of my life have now come to an end, and I know, despite it all, she was the one who brought me the most beautiful chapters.

And in the end, it is her that I see.

Her lilac hair spills over her shoulder as she straddles my lap. Her eyes look into mine. I reach out my hand to touch her soft skin.

My light after the darkness.

My love.

My mate.

Journey

Eden

EARLIER THAT EVENING

My legs ache from being on the move for hours on end. My body growing weaker and weaker by the second. However, I know that I can't stop.

I have the palace in my sights, but I still have a dangerously long route to travel. I knew coming back here discretely would be challenging. The palace is patrolled at all times, and if the king is to be buried this evening, then security will be tight around Morween. I had no option but to venture into less traveled areas of the forest, where the landscape is a lot less forgiving and the journey longer than usual. I've trekked through knee-high sink mud and climbed over treetops to avoid large patches of poisoned Hipplegriff. Now, if I'm one hundred percent honest, I'm not entirely sure where I'm going. It's been over seventy years since Erix showed me the passageway leading into the castle, and my memory of that day is vague at best.

Think, Eden, think!

I'm forced to pause and draw breath while I decide which way to go. At that moment, I hear voices ahead, and without hesitation, I sprint to the nearest tree, pressing myself against its thick trunk.

I listen carefully as the footsteps draw closer, using them to guide my movements around the base of the tree.

"Are you on duty later?"

"Of course, isn't everyone?"

"Yes, but not everyone gets to protect the mausoleum..."

The footsteps stop momentarily.

"That's a cushy assignment."

"What are you doing?"

"Guarding our new king-in-waiting at the ceremony in the palace."

"Ha! I still can't quite believe that you know."

"Tell me about it."

"What makes him better than the rest of us anyway?"

"Connections, my friend, it's all about connections in Morween."

"That's true."

Their voices trail off into the distance as they walk further into the forest, and my brows knit together in confusion.

Has a new king been selected already?

The question plays on my mind for a moment as I consider how different things might be right now if Erix was still here and about to take over.

Would he hear me out?

Would he listen to what I have to say about The Culling?

Part of me still likes to think that he would. That deep down, he really was the decent man I had always thought he was.

The prospect of a new king is worrying on so many levels. The chosen man must be incredibly fearless and dominant. Perhaps he hates the werewolf kind as much as his predecessor.

I quickly decide to head east of the palace, my fuzzy brain finally giving me some well-needed clarity. I must locate the tunnel near Hollowood River, where I would often take Erix to look for Lemoncrest weeds. I can always rely on my knowledge of plants and flowers to lead the way when I'm lost.

After a while, I hear the sound of a waterfall up ahead, the rushing water giving me hope that I'm finally getting closer. I stop before a steep decline, peering over the edge to identify the river.

I close my eyes, my jaw tightening in frustration. If I try another route, it will add yet more time to this journey. Time that I just cannot afford to waste. Instead, I sit on the ground and shuffle my ass toward the edge of the rock face. My legs dangle over the side, catching the breeze as they swing freely in the air. I must really be out of my damn mind!

I take a deep breath and muster all the courage I can to turn around and lower myself down, my fingers still gripping the grassy edge for dear life. My feet scramble around in search of a foothold. Eventually, I find one secure enough to take my weight. I carefully drop one hand down to cling to another piece of solid rock jutting out from the wall, and slowly but surely, I climb down the rock face, my chest pressed against the cool stone.

The sound of flowing water intensifies, and I feel water droplets wafting around me, touching my skin. Then I make the mistake of looking down, and the sight of the terrifying drop makes me lose concentration for a split second. My foot slips, and I yelp in surprise before the echo of my own voice mocks me loudly for making such a stupid error.

I continue my descent when suddenly a spattering of dust and small rocks rain down on my head from above. I glance up through narrowed eyes to see a guard's helmet emerge over the edge.

Fuck!

Desperately, I look left to right, spotting a small alcove in the rock face. I frantically maneuver into the tiny space, latching onto a thick vine to hold myself in place. I stay as still as possible, looking over my shoulder as the dust and small debris continue falling.

"Must have been an animal, Ethin. There's nothing here!"

My entire body shakes as my burning muscles fight against me violently. My knuckles begin to turn white from the sheer intensity of my grip, but I don't dare let go. Funnily enough, it is not the thought of certain death that frightens me the most, but the fear of getting caught instead.

There is too much at stake today. Too much to lose.

My limbs begin to seize, and I know that if the danger doesn't pass soon, staying hidden will no longer be within my control. I take a chance, peeking up to see that everything seems clear for now.

I quickly set to work again, increasing the pace of my descent. The closer I get to the ground, the sloppier I become, and finally, I lose my grip altogether. I bump down the side of the rock face clumsily and land on my back with a thud, suddenly thankful for the rushing water behind me that swallows my pain-filled groans.

I roll over and pull myself onto my knees, examining my weary hands, now covered with cuts and blisters. I quickly rub them against my pants and stand up, looking around cautiously before running for the patch of Lemoncrest. Its bright yellow petals welcome me like an old friend, and I let out a sigh of relief. The tunnel is around here somewhere. I know it is!

My eyes run over the landscape, settling on a dark patch of bushes that aren't in keeping with the rest of the wild plant life in the area.

The foliage is now so dense and thick that I cannot get through it with strength alone. I stop in my tracks, holding my hands up to the tangled mass of weeds. I concentrate on finding that power within me, pulling it from every cell in my body, drawing it up into my fingertips.

My exhausted state threatens to swipe the legs from under me, but I'll never give up. Instead, I hold as steady as I can, my knees wobbling ever so slightly, my teeth gritting in determination. Soon my hard-headedness pays off, and I hear the slither of the vines and crack of the branches as they begin to fall from my path.

My eyes snap open, and I stare into the mouth of the deep, dark cave, equal parts ecstatic and terrified. I take one last look at the dying sunlight before entering, knowing it will most likely be gone when I arrive on the other side.

* * *

I edge my back along the wall, waiting for the corridor to silence. The servant's footsteps disappear, and I peek around the corner to look at my target. The large green door of my parent's bedroom.

Getting myself here without being noticed has been no mean feat. Luckily for me, the palace hallways are quieter than usual. Many high elves of importance have possibly already made their way to the mausoleum, while others with less social standing will have started to congregate in the great hall for the rest of the ceremonies this evening. I can only hope that my father is running late as usual. I quickly emerge from my hiding place, rushing toward the door.

It's locked.

I tug on the handle ferociously, bile rising in my throat as I consider the consequences of my failure.

"Come on! Come on! Please!" I plead desperately, lifting my fist to bump it against the door on repeat.

Suddenly, the door swings open, and I find myself standing face-to-face with my mother. The stunned look on her face quickly changes, and she immediately begins to sob.

"Eden!! Eden, is that really you?!" she cries as I rush into the room, closing the door behind me.

"Shhh...it's me. It's me," I reassure her as she lifts her hands to rest them on my face.

"I can't believe it!" she sobs, pulling me into her arms to hug me tightly.

I close my eyes, her touch comforting my aching body ever so slightly.

"Mother, where's—"

"Are you okay? How did you get here?" she interrupts hurriedly, leaning back to hold me by the shoulders. "Look at you! You're so dirty and skinny! What did they do to you?"

"Wait, please, I need you to listen. This is important," I plead, peeling her hands from my shoulders to hold them tightly. "Where is my father?"

"What?"

"Where is he? Did he leave already for the procession?" I ask with wide, wild eyes.

"Uhh, no! He's still in his study. He told me he would walk me down to the great hall before he left for the procession, but you know what your father is like."

I breathe out a sigh of relief and nod my head anxiously. "Good."

"Eden, what's going on?"

The door opens behind us, and I swing around to see my father looking straight at us. "EDEN!"

"Close the door!" I demand in a hushed tone.

He does as I ask before rushing over to envelop me in his arms. "Oh, my daughter! My daughter! I feared we would never see you again!" he says while battling tears.

Feeling my father's loving arms around me makes me want to break down in complete heartache.

How could this man, who has shown me nothing but gentle kindness all my life, have committed such horrid war crimes?

I cannot fathom it for one single second! My arms wrap around him tightly in return as my own tears finally fall from my eyes.

"What happened? Were you rescued?" he asks, looking at me with eyes full of a hundred questions.

Little does he know I have many questions of my own.

I shake my head vigorously. "No, Father, I wasn't rescued. I was set free."

His eyes widen in response, but I have no time to elaborate. "I have come home to stop you from attending that ceremony tonight."

I grip the sleeves of his tunic as he looks at my mother in confusion. "What? Why?"

"There's too much to explain."

My heart hurts that I must be so vague, but I know I still cannot fully trust him.

"Eden, I must go, my dear; my absence will be noted. Especially because I am to accompany our new king-to-be."

"New king?" I ask just as the door rattles loudly.

My mother and father look at each other again, and my body turns rigid. "Leave it," I whisper, tugging my father's sleeve again.

"Eden, I can't. They will know something is wrong."

My brain races frantically before I nod my head in acceptance. "Fine...answer it, but get rid of them! Don't tell them that I'm here. Please, if you love me at all, you'll do this for me," I say, staring into his eyes.

The door rattles once again, and my dad looks over his shoulder in a fluster.

"Please, Father," I urge him.

"Okay, okay, then you better hide."

I slip into the bathroom, closing the door to leave only a slither of light.

My father's footsteps come to a stop.

"Aubrun, apologies for the delay. I'm afraid I've come down unwell—"

My heart near stops in my chest at the sound of his name.

Aubrun? Aubrun is the new king?!

I cannot help but steal a glance through the doorway, my mouth dropping open in shock as he enters the room. He looks around, and I pull my head back out of sight as I press myself against the wall.

"Forget that, Haleth. I need your help with something," he says hurriedly.

"Oh?" my father replies, nerves ringing in his voice.

"I've just been informed that an attack on Morween is imminent. Queen Siofra, our lords and elders have already made their way to begin the procession. I need your help with this. I'll ready the guards, but I need you to warn as many people as possible in the great hall. See that the hall is cleared immediately!"

"This is awful news indeed! An attack?! An attack by who?" my father asks.

I squeeze my eyes shut as I listen. My father is an intelligent man. To hear him question Aubrun in such a way sounds off and completely out of character.

"The werewolves, of course, Haleth!" Aubrun answers with an arrogant air of authority that seems to betray his usual gentle nature. "We must go now.

Time is of the essence!"

I hear my father fumble his words as he tries to hide his reluctance.

"Why, uh, yes of course! I'll be right behind—"

"You must go now. We must make haste!" Aubrun cuts in.

Their footsteps then rush for the door, and it slams closed behind them.

Shit!

If Aubrun knows the attack is minutes away, he could ambush Conall and the others before they even break through Morween's defenses. His men will stand no chance against the full force of the vast Elven army! They will be captured without question!

I realize immediately that I need to warn them somehow, and my father's study immediately springs to mind. I know there has to be something in there I can use to give them some kind of signal.

I rush into the room to see my mother standing with her hand on her forehead. "This is what you were talking about. You knew about this?" she questions me tearfully.

"I did, but we cannot let this happen. I have to warn the wolves—"

"Warn them? Eden, why must you warn them?!"

"I can't explain it all right now, but they are not the enemy. Not at all. I can explain everything when I'm back. Stay in the room until then," I say commandingly.

"Eden, if you think I'm going to let you run into their clutches then—"

"Stop, Mother! I was never in their clutches! I stand *with* them! Now if you trust me, you'll do as I ask and—"

I am instantly distracted by the sight outside the window behind her head. White smoke. The funeral is about to begin.

I head for the door, carefully opening it to peek into the empty corridor. I quickly edge my way out, rushing for the staircase. Just as I reach it, a hand shoots out, grabbing me by the arm. I try to wriggle free, but the grip is firm and strong. It's then that I turn to look up into his eyes. His expression tinged with a mixture of sadness and betrayal.

"Aubrun, you must let me go. Please, there's so much I have to tell you."

He shakes his head, taking a step closer to me. "No, Eden. I won't be letting you go. Not this time," he answers quietly, looking around before he drags me off down the hallway.

Terms

Eden

"Aubrun... Aubrun, you're hurting my arm," I say as he ushers me quietly to a bedroom door.

"Quiet," he snaps, opening the door to thrust me inside.

I stumble a little catching myself before I hit the ground. I turn around just in time to see him lock the door behind him. "Aubrun, what are you doing?"

"What am I doing?!" he hits back, taking a quick step forward. "What are *you* doing, Eden? That's the question!"

"My father...he told you," I say sadly, my heart sinking.

Aubrun shakes his head. "No, but it didn't take much to see he was hiding something. Your father never gets flustered. As soon as I walked into that room, I knew something wasn't right! So I waited!"

"Where is he?"

"Carrying out my orders because that is his duty, and he knows it!"

I look around the room, my eyes shifting over the exits quickly.

"Don't even try to think of a way to slip past me, Eden. Do you think I am a complete imbecile?"

"Of course, I don't think that," I say sincerely. "But, please, you must let me go. We have to stop this."

"Stop what exactly?" he demands, walking forward threateningly as I stare back at him in shock.

Since the last time I saw him, it's as though his whole persona has changed. The once quiet, gentlemanly, obedient soldier is all but gone.

"I assume you are referring to the attack on Morween? Since you are, in fact, a high elf."

"I am not, and you know that," I hit back in return through narrowed eyes.

"But you aren't one of them either! Are you?!" he seethes.

I breathe in deeply, preparing myself to launch into the whole explanation.

I *have* to make him understand.

□

There is no other way.

"Aubrun, this is going to sound crazy, but everything they told us about *The Culling* was a lie. There is so much more to the story. King Ciridan had no reason to kill the wolves all those years ago. The lords manufactured the attacks on Elven villages for their own selfish reasons. I know they did. The whole hierarchy is corrupt! Together we can stop them—"

"Listen to yourself, Eden!" he barks, looking over my face in both disgust and astonishment. "Did you forget that they killed your aunt? And what about Erix? What on earth have they done to you?!"

"I could ask you the same question!" I snap defensively.

His nostrils flare in anger. "What's that supposed to mean?"

"The Aubrun that I knew would listen. He would hear me out. "

"Hear you out? Do you think I've forgotten that day in the woods, Eden? Do you think I've forgotten what your so-called innocent *friend* did to me? I could have died!"

I swallow as I remember Conall's vicious attack. "That was different. He was just trying to escape. He was trying to protect me!"

"From your own kind? Eden, he KIPNAPPED you. Kept you prisoner for weeks!" he yells in disbelief. "They have manipulated you and warped your mind! How can you not see that?!"

I run my hand over my face in frustration, and his eyes soften as he reaches out to rest his hand on my face.

"You know, even after everything that happened... I still care about you. That's the only reason I'm here right now and not out there with my men. I couldn't let someone catch you trying to warn the wolves. I couldn't bare it if they charged you with treason."

I reach up to cover his hand with my own. "Aubrun, look into my eyes," I plead desperately. "I appreciate that, but I'm telling the truth. Siofra and the lords have committed war crimes. They must be held accountable."

He shakes his head, his hand dropping back down to his side. "Queen Siofra is a noble and generous woman. Yes, the lords can be conniving, but that is the way of it here. Royal politics are always at play, and you know that. However, I do not believe them capable of harming their own people."

"It's true! The Elven towns were attacked by rogue wolves, and they know it!"

"Rogues? What does that even mean? Wolves are wolves, and they are all just as dangerous and just as deadly—"

"No, they aren't. That's not true! "

"Then tell me why they are coming here to attack us at this very second?"

I look into his eyes and swallow. "Because they lost everything, Aubrun."

"And so might we if we do not take action now."

Something about his tone sets me on edge immediately. He walks past me to the window and stops to look outside.

"Take action now?"

He turns around to look at me.

"Aubrun...who have you been talking to? How did you find out about the attack tonight?"

"Do you think I would share that information with you right now? When you are defending these beasts so staunchly?" he says, his voice lowering to a whisper. "I know about the pack hidden in the mountains."

I try to keep my face neutral while my insides scream in panic. "I don't know what you—"

"DON'T lie to me!" he snaps back with a hurt look. "Harmony... That's what they call it, right?"

My lips close as I try to think what to say, but my mind is blank.

He turns and shakes his head from side to side. "It doesn't matter anyway. When we have defeated the wolves tonight, I will order my men to march on the pack immediately."

He stalks past me, heading for the door, and I know I have to act fast.

"No, no, please! You can't do that! Those people are peaceful! Innocent women and children! Please!" I beg, grabbing him by the arm. "If you march on them, you know the lords will demand their heads."

He shakes me off quickly, looking down at me intensely. "Do you think I want to do this?"

"Then don't," I say sincerely, appealing to the old Aubrun as best I can. "You haven't told anyone about the pack yet, have you? You can leave them be. You can do the right thing, and no one has to die."

"No, I cannot, Eden, because I have a responsibility to our people and Morween! I am to be king in twenty-four hours!"

"And your first act as king will be sentencing all those people to death?" I ask desperately. "That isn't who you are! I know you!"

He looks down briefly before his eyes lift back up to meet mine. "My mind

□

is made up. I'm going to tell Queen Siofra and everyone else that it was you who warned us of the attack tonight. You escaped the wolves and came straight here to alert us. This way, you will be protected."

I shake my head in defiance. "I do not want your protection! I want you to make the choice that you know is right in your heart."

"I can't, Eden."

"Then, so help me Goddess, I will shout it from the damn rooftops that I not only knew about the attack but also helped keep it secret!" I yell frantically.

He stares at me in shock. "You would do that? You would die alongside them? You would die for nothing?"

I hold my head high and nod. "I would rather die than betray them."

His head tilts up to the ceiling in defeat. "Then why don't you live for them instead?" he asks, his eyes meeting mine again.

"What do you mean?" I ask, my brows creasing as I examine him.

"You take on the role you were meant to all those years ago. Agree to be my queen, and I will spare Harmony in your honor. It will remain a secret between us."

"What?" I gasp, looking into his hopeful eyes.

"You cannot pretend to be oblivious to my affections for you. All these years you have known. Even before Erix, you know I have only ever seen you."

Indeed, I could always sense that he had some sort of feelings for me. When I think back to the night of *The Culling* celebration, I remember how he attempted to ask me out, but I never considered that his affections were this strong. Perhaps I didn't want to.

"You have a choice to make, Eden. The attack tonight will be stopped either way, but you can save Harmony for now if you agree to my terms."

I cannot even bear to even think of letting Conall go.

"Aubrun, I can't. I'm sorry."

"Then I'm sorry too," he answers, his eyes filled with sadness.

Suddenly, frantic screams ring out from behind me, and I can tell the battle has already begun. I'm too late. All I can do now is hope with everything in me that Conall and the others make it through.

"I must go now. I have much to attend to," Aubrun says.

He turns to walk to the door, and my heart pounds, images of the children playing in Harmony flashing through my mind.

"Wait," I say quietly, causing him to stop. "How do I know you won't march on the pack as soon as I am sworn in as your queen?"

"You'll have to trust that I won't," he answers. "The same way, I must trust that you'll let *him* go."

A lump forms in my throat, but I know that at this very moment, I have no other option. I need to buy time for Harmony and for Con until I can get back to him. No matter what it takes.

"Then my answer is yes. I will stand beside you." I gulp, looking into his eyes. "I will be the next Queen of Morween."

Hero

Eden

I lie there staring at the ceiling, unable to stop the frantic thoughts racing through my mind. The last time I stood on that balcony was for Erix's funeral seventy years ago. I remember the feeling of helplessness as if it were yesterday. However, tonight, if possible, was one hundred times worse. The way Conall looked at me as I stood there staring back at him from Aubrun's arms tore my heart to shreds.

I'm not at all naive. I know exactly what he must have been thinking of me at that moment. Damn, the thought of him hating me makes me feel sick, but what other choice do I have right now? To protect Harmony, I must play by Aubrun's rules, at least until I can find a way to get back to the den and tell them what I know. How and when I'll manage to get back there, though, is the real question. I glance at the door to see the faint shadow still patrolling the hallway outside my room. I guess I shouldn't be surprised that Aubrun assigned a guard to me for my "protection" while he deals with the aftermath of all of this. He probably distrusts me just as much as Conall does right about now.

It's then I wonder what must have happened with Conall and the others once they all got back to the den...because they must have made it back. My heart can't consider any other possible scenario right now.

I'm sure the men will be pissed that I disappeared, but for all they know, I could have escaped on my own. If Conall is smart, he will tell them that's the case, but I know Rocco and Samuel will probably demand that he be punished anyway.

Will he be whipped mercilessly like Mateo when I first arrived at the den?

I close my eyes and pray that he's not in any pain right now because of me.

There is a soft knock on the door, and my shoulders tense. No matter who the hell it is, the encounter is guaranteed to be uncomfortable.

"Come in," I mutter, hauling my tired body up into a sitting position.

The door opens, and my mother offers me a gentle yet strained smile from the doorway. "Can I come in, dear? I didn't wake you, did I?"

"Come in," I answer. "Where's father?"

"He's very busy, dear. I'm sure you both can catch up tomorrow."

"Oh."

A few moments of silence stretch out between us as she sits on the edge of the bed. It's clear that neither of us really know where to begin.

"Uhh, you go first," I offer her quietly.

She smiles, reaching out to take my hand as tears fill her eyes. "Oh, Eden, your father and I are truly so happy you are home. We missed you so much and were so worried. You have no idea the hell we have endured."

"I can imagine," I sympathize. "But as I said, I'm fine. So there's no need to be upset anymore."

She nods, but her tears begin to fall anyway. "Yes, you are fine," she says, squeezing my fingers. "I'm just so happy that you are home."

I wish I could return the sentiment, but instead, I say nothing. Of course, I'm happy to see her, but my heart is somewhere else.

She begins to look around silently. "You must have missed your bedroom?" she asks with curious eyes.

I look around myself, my gaze settling on the bookshelf in the corner. "I did."

"Good," she smiles softly. "Tomorrow morning, I thought you might wish to accompany me to the seamstress. You will need a dress for the ceremonies—"

"We have to talk about what happened earlier, Mother, we can't avoid it," I interrupt.

She looks down at our hands uncomfortably for a moment before her eyes flick back to mine.

"It's okay, Sweetie, I understand. You were stressed. Confused. We understand that you were trying to stop people from getting hurt. I'm just glad Aubrun could get through to you before you did something that you would regret."

I pull my hand from her grip, my brows knitting together in irritation and frustration. "No, Mother. I wasn't confused. When I told you that the wolves are not our enemies, I meant it. Queen Siofra and the lords are the real liars and murderers."

□

"Eden!" she scolds me, looking to the door fearfully. "You cannot speak that way in this castle! You could be sentenced to death for making such a speech!"

"It's the truth, and if you'll listen to me—"

"I will not," she cuts in sternly before letting out an exhausted sigh. "Eden, you have been through a lot, but you must stop this. Bringing up what happened all those years ago will not help anyone. Least of all, your father."

"Why? Because he feels guilty?" I ask plainly.

"I beg your pardon?" she asks in astonishment. "The past haunts your father to this very day, but he did what he had to do for the Elven people, and you bringing it up is only going to tear open old wounds about your Aunt Felou. Is that what you want?"

As I look into her eyes, I can already tell that the conversation is going nowhere. As the saying goes, you can lead a horse to water, but you cannot make it drink.

"Okay," I reply meekly. "I'll drop it."

I have no intention of dropping it, but it seems there may be more work I have to do before I can help her, or anyone else for that matter, see the damn light.

"You have been through a lot this evening," she continues. "The funeral proceedings are to go ahead tomorrow morning, which means Aubrun's coronation will likely be the day after. It will be a hectic couple of days within these walls. You need to get some rest."

I gulp at the mere mention of it all. "I will."

She kisses my cheek, and I watch as she walks back to the bedroom door to let herself out. A strange feeling immediately begins to settle in the pit of my stomach. I didn't tell her about Aubrun asking me to be his future queen. I'm used to telling my parents everything, yet here I am, with so many secrets that I can hardly keep track anymore.

I throw the sheets to the side, tiptoeing across the floor to the open window. The gentle wind ripples against my skin as I fold my arms over my chest, looking over the forest from high above.

I never got to say what I wanted in the forest earlier when Conall let me go. The whole day is such a blur, but the one thing I remember vividly is the look he gave me when he told me he loved me. My gaze drifts up to the moon, and I sigh heavily, wishing I had seized the moment when I had the chance. I should have told him just how much I love him in return. Since I didn't, I'll now have to settle for whispering it to the moon, hoping that wherever he is right now, he can hear me.

"I love you, Conall," I say quietly into the breeze. "I love you too,"

* * *

I straighten out the black dress, clasping my hands together as I look around the enormous, busy hall that is filling up fast. Now that the funeral procession is over, everyone will head here for the rest of the traditional ceremonies. I notice right away that there is a strange kind of atmosphere in the air. Emotions are running high, as evidenced by the looks on the faces of those all around me. The Moreeen people are indeed shocked and horrified at what transpired last night. I don't blame them; of course they would be. I would feel the same way if I didn't know the truth myself.

"Shall we take our seats for the ceremony?" my mother asks, looking over me carefully.

"Sure," I reply, following her lead.

To say the tension between us has been awkward would be an understatement. Since she showed up in my room this morning, funeral attire in hand, I've barely been able to speak two words to her.

A few friends and acquaintances nod and wave in my direction as we cross the hall, and for the first time, I wonder what they know of my sudden disappearance.

We take a seat in the fifth row, facing center stage. "Mother, what did you tell people when I was gone?"

"Nothing, dear," she answers quietly. "Your disappearance was kept as a closely guarded secret. Apart from the king and his advisors, it was only Aubrun and some of his trusted men who were made aware," she explains. "King Ciridan did not want to spread unnecessary panic, so people were told you had traveled for your studies instead."

"Oh," I answer, an odd sense of relief washing over me.

Knowing that I won't have everyone looking at me as some sort of victim is a weight off my mind, at least.

It is then that two of my mother's friends shuffle into their chairs next to us.

"Morning, ladies," my mother says brightly, nodding at them both in turn.

"Morning Iriel. Morning Eden," one of them answers hurriedly, her expression and body language giving her away instantly.

Shit, here we go. Here comes the fucking gossip. I force myself to smile at the two ladies before focusing on the empty stage.

"It is an awful business all of this. Is it not, Iriel? I heard they killed six noblemen before the guards got to them...six! I can only imagine what damage would have been done if our guards had not intervened when they did."

I blink slowly, breathing in deeply to settle myself.

"Oh, it does not bear thinking about!" the other woman screeches, clutching her hand over her chest.

"Yes, it is awful," my mother answers, glancing at me worriedly from the corner of her eye.

"Iriel, has Haleth told you anything? Did they capture any of the savages before they managed to flee?"

"Uhh, I'm afraid I don't know."

"My nephew works for the Guard," the second woman chimes in. "He said that the beasts completely vanished into thin air! The search lasted all night, and not a single one of the wretched creatures was caught! Can you believe it?!"

I almost snap my neck, turning to look at her, my crowded mind overcome with relief. They made it back to the den. Thank Goddess for that!

"Are you okay, honey?" one of the ladies asks, tilting her head at me curiously.

"Yes, sorry I—"

"It's all so much to absorb, isn't it?" she interrupts, giving me a sympathetic nod.

At that moment, the room quietens, and everyone takes their seats. The side doors are opened, and the lords, nobles and advisors all begin to enter the grand hall, adorned in their finest tunics and robes. I catch sight of my father in the crowd, his head bowed respectfully as he makes his way to his seat.

Finally, the queen enters, accompanied by Aubrun, who holds his arm out for her. You could hear a pin drop as he leads her onto the stage to her seat. Even with her sheer black veil covering her face, she still holds the undivided attention of the entire grand hall. She sits down, and her partially shrouded eyes instantly fall on me. I stare back, matching her determined gaze with my own.

I then turn my attention to Aubrun, scanning over him as he readies himself to speak. This man appears to be a different Aubrun from the one I grew up with. He was the shy guy who followed Erix around, the one who got embarrassed if a woman so much as smiled in his direction, who followed every rule to the letter. Now, it's as though he has changed into a different being altogether. I have to give him credit in some ways. He has been thrust into this job out of nowhere, and yet he seems so determined and confident. However, no matter how much he has tried to alter himself, I can see his soft eyes remain the same when I examine him closely. As though the real Aubrun is still in there somewhere. At least, I pray that he is.

"My Lords, Ladies, People of Morween and our gracious Queen," he begins, looking to Siofra to give her a gentle bow. "It brings me no pleasure to stand before you today under the present circumstances. By now, I'm sure you will all know that we faced a vicious attack on our kingdom yesterday by the beasts we thought we had eradicated a long time ago."

Whispers begin circulating the room, and Aubrun holds his hand up for silence.

"I understand both your worry and concern, but I assure you, as your future king, that this attack will not go unpunished. These beasts will be defeated, and our peace will be restored."

Everyone begins to applaud around me. I look around awkwardly before I sense Siofra's icy blue eyes trained on me once again. I lift my hands and join in reluctantly with everyone else.

"Now, it is also incumbent on me to inform you how we obtained knowledge of this attack in the first place," My heart stills in my chest as Aubrun looks straight at me. "You see, one of our very own was captured by these beasts in the forest on the night of *The Culling* celebration. We did not know it at the time, but she was being held captive by them."

The room fills with the sound of gasps and frantic whispers.

"Eden Nestoriel, would you come up here please?" he says, his words a direct command rather than a request.

I stare at him in shock for a few seconds before my mother nudges my arm.

What the fuck is he playing at announcing this to everyone without as much as a single warning?

I swallow hard, standing up from my chair to make my way down the center aisle. As I do so, I can feel every single pair of eyes in the room watching me. The feeling has both my stomach churning and my jaw clenching in anger.

Aubrun walks over to the stairs, making his way down to meet me halfway. His eyes connect with mine as he puts out his arm for me to take. I make sure he can tell exactly what I'm thinking, my glare conveying my complete disdain for his little stunt.

"Through the mercy of our Gods and Goddesses, last night, Eden was able to escape the wolves who have so viciously tortured her over these past days. She immediately made her way straight here to find me and alerted me to the incoming danger," Aubrun lies convincingly, twisting his head to look at me. "She saved us all from having to endure the painful loss of our queen, our lords and elders. We truly do owe her so very, very much."

The crowd instantly begins to applaud in enthusiastic agreement, their expressions full of sympathy and gratitude.

It makes me feel completely sick, and I swallow, trying not to let my uncomfortableness show. My father watches me with a shocked look on his face. It appears that he is also surprised by this turn of events. At least I am not the only one.

"Please show Eden Nestoriel your appreciation!"

The room erupts into applause, and I glance sideways to see Siofra on her feet, slowly clapping her hands. Our eyes connect yet again, but I see no gratitude within their icy depths, only burning suspicion.

"Thank you all. Now without further interruption, we are here today not to dwell on last night's events but to celebrate the life of an extraordinary king. One who ruled this land with intelligence, grace, integrity, bravery and loyalty. Let us now think of him as we move forward with our ceremonies."

Aubrun nods in finality, leading me by the arm over to the empty chair at his side. As we take our seats, we look at one another for a moment. So many unspoken words communicated with a single glance. I eventually turn away, sitting there seething on the inside as a high elf elder takes to the stage to begin the ancient readings.

Haleth

"What the HELL are you playing at?!" I snap as Aubrun closes the door behind us.

"I do not see what the issue is here, Eden. I told you that I would be telling Siofra and the lords that you alerted us to the attack."

"Yes! But you failed to mention that you were going to announce that to the whole of Morween! It won't be long before every creature in the damn realm hears the news!" I protest, shaking my head as I pace back and forth. Then it hits me, and my neck twists to look straight at him. "That's what you wanted. You want everyone to believe I betrayed the wolves."

He shrugs his shoulders in reply. "Does it matter?" he answers. "You agreed that you would give up your alliance with them. You agreed to the terms, Eden."

I stare into his eyes, knowing I don't have a leg to stand on.

"Anyway, it's not the only reason I did what I did."

I frown, folding my arms over my chest. "No?"

He swallows awkwardly, placing his hands on his hips. "Look... The people were already pretty puzzled when Ciridan chose me as the new king; how do you think they will react to hearing that I have chosen a wood elf to be their queen?"

My mouth falls open in indignation. "Wow! So you are ashamed of my birth and rank now?"

He shakes his head vigorously as he moves closer to stand in front of me. "No, of course not, but I must be realistic, Eden. I have to think of how all of this will play out. Announcing to the people that you saved Morween will endear you to them. They will love you for it! In their eyes, there will be no one more worthy!"

I clench my teeth and close my eyes, flinching slightly as Aubrun's hands take mine.

□

"Trust me. It's better this way."

I open my eyes to look into his, which are soft and pleading. "How can we trust each other, Aubrun? You declared war on the wolves. How do I know your words won't lead to the destruction of Harmony?"

"Because I only want the wolves who attacked us last night. I will keep my word to you regarding Harmony so long as they remain hidden and peaceful," he says adamantly. "Eden, things between us may be messed up right now, but if we believe in each other, this could work. *We* could work."

I find myself wondering how anyone can be so deluded.

How can he possibly believe that we will ever be happy together?

"Then you have to take the guard away from my bedroom door. It's unsettling," I demand calmly.

He thinks it over for a second before he agrees. "Fine."

I step back, and he drops his arms by his side. "Then you must do something for me...give up the location of where the Alpha wolves are hiding."

My brows automatically knit together. "Aubrun, even if I wanted to, I couldn't—"

"Because of their protection enchantments?" he interrupts.

I nod my head, and he walks away in frustration.

"Perhaps your informant can help?" I ask, watching his every move closely.

He shakes his head. "No, they can't."

Just then, the door knocks, and Aubrun and I look at each other curiously.

"Enter," he responds.

The door opens, and Queen Siofra's personal servant enters, bowing her head respectfully. "Apologies for the intrusion, but I have a message for Miss Nestoriel."

"Go on," I reply carefully.

"Queen Siofra has requested both you and your mother's presence at high tea tomorrow morning in the royal palace gardens."

Aubrun turns to look at me expectantly.

"Uhh, yes, of course," I answer dutifully, much to his delight.

I watch as a grateful smile touches his lips. "Will that be all?" he asks the servant, who nods, bowing again before leaving the room.

I wait for the footsteps to fade before I speak.

"Does Siofra know that that we are be to married?" I ask quietly.

Aubrun shakes his head, and I can tell by the look on his face that this notion makes him uncomfortable. Clearly, he considers her a close confidant now.

"Why haven't you told her?" I ask challengingly. "If she is to be one of your main advisors from now on?"

He swallows and shrugs his shoulders. "I respect her opinion, and her experience will be invaluable to us. However, despite what you might think, to me, this union is a matter of the heart, not palace politics," he answers, his eyes connecting with mine sincerely. "She will find out when the time is right, and I am confident she will support us both in any way she can."

It's no longer a mystery why Ciridan chose Aubrun as his successor. If he had his way, he would have named Siofra as ruler. This...this is the next best thing. Siofra has him right where she wants him. He's so blinded by his loyalty to his former king and queen that there is no way he will go against her. Not without proof. Proof which I must somehow provide.

* * *

I wander down the familiar staircase, stopping at the bottom step. I'm not entirely sure I'm prepared for this conversation, but I know it's one I must have anyway.

"Father?" I ask gently, walking into the dimly lit room.

Straight away, I see him sitting in the corner by his desk, surrounded by books and messy bundles of paper as usual.

"Pia Náre!" he replies, looking up at me from beneath his spectacles.

"Haven't you been taking your Wild Gessopweed supplement?" I ask, raising my eyebrow at him as I point to his glasses.

"Ahh," he smiles, removing them to set them on the table. "I guess I have been forgetting recently."

"You mean I wasn't here to remind you?"

He looks at me for a moment before nodding.

I then turn my attention to the rest of the study, which, unsurprisingly, is messier than usual. My father, although brilliantly talented, has always been pretty chaotic. Many of my years spent here as his apprentice included me spending vast amounts of time organizing his books and ingredients.

"It's a mess in here."

"Yes, I have been meaning to clean up. I—"

"Why have you been avoiding me?" I cut in, the words leaving my body in a painful breath.

"Eden, my dear, I've been swamped."

"Don't lie to me, Father," I say, moving closer to his desk. "You are avoiding me for a reason, and I need to know what it is."

He stands up behind his desk and drops his head but doesn't say a word.

"I know, Father... I know what happened all those years ago—what you did."

"Eden—"

"I need to know why," I snap back angrily, my chest heaving. "Were you forced? Because if that's the case, we can do something about it."

"No, I was not forced."

"THEN WHY, FATHER?" I demand, my eyes watering of their own accord. "Why did you give them the means to wipe out an entire species?"

"Because that species was responsible for your aunt's death and the death of many other innocents."

"So you chose to bring death to other innocent people in return?" I ask defiantly. "Women... *Children?*" A tear falls from my eyes, and I quickly wipe it away. "How could you?"

His face turns pale as he leans his hands on the desk. "Eden, you do not understand. The attacks on Elven towns were devastating."

"And you know fine well that rogue wolves carried out those attacks!" I say, his eyes widening in shock. "Yes, Father, I know you were there that night when Alphas Lincoln, Conall and Zeke came to speak with Ciridan. I know that you heard them."

"Yes, we heard them out," he answers. "We listened, and Ciridan was more than eager to believe them; however, the very next day, another attack took place on the outskirts of Morween. Those Alphas in question were witnessed fleeing the scene. Ciridan and Erix were enraged, to say the least."

"Witnessed by who?" I ask in disbelief.

"Lord Faenor and his men."

"HA!!" I gasp in complete astonishment. *The Culling* was the result of that crooked man's testimony?!"

"Not only his. Siofra, who was also in attendance visiting a friend at the time of the attack, claimed that she also recognized the attackers as those Alphas who came to Morween."

This news now confirms Siofra's involvement in all of this. I cannot say I'm surprised.

"This has got to be a joke! The "attack" was clearly staged. They lied!" I snap with narrowed eyes.

My father sighs, running his hand over his face exhaustedly before taking a seat.

"Father, you must believe me. I have gotten to know these men and *know* they did not do these awful things. They went to Ciridan in good faith. They believe that the lords paid rogue wolves to attack their own people, therefore forcing Ciridan's hand. They all became very wealthy afterward. Father, they tricked you. The same as they did to every other elf out there."

He doesn't reply, his eyes looking away from me entirely, but I can see they are filled with pain. "The enchantment was never supposed to kill every wolf," he says quietly, taking me by surprise.

"What?" I ask, lowering myself down onto a chair across from him. "What do you mean?"

He brings his hand up to his head.

"Father?"

"It wasn't right! The enchantment was not ready yet! I didn't have the chance to make my final checks! It was taken from me, and there was nothing I could do about it!" he says, looking up into my eyes. "It was only supposed to target and kill the Alpha wolves."

I stare back at him. Stunned.

"Ciridan wanted to end the war by taking out the leaders. But instead, the enchantment backfired. It killed everyone, and, I'm assuming after seeing them in action last night, it left the Alphas behind, altering their DNA somehow."

My heart aches as he chokes back his emotions. "It was an accident?" I ask in shock.

He nods his head in response. "It was. I made an error with the ingredients. It was a terrible accident, and I was horrified. King Ciridan and Queen Siofra were less affected. Erix had just died, and they were hungry for revenge. The People of Morween were satisfied with their justice. The lords were appeased, and peace was restored to the kingdom. Everyone else was thrilled with the outcome. However, there hasn't been a day that has gone by in seventy years where I have not thought about those poor innocent people. The people that I killed."

I reach my hand out to take his, feeling his pain in the process.

"Father, if this is true, then those people deserve the truth to be uncovered. If it was Siofra or the lords that paid the rogue wolves to attack their own people, then shouldn't they be exposed for their crimes? Their treachery caused this."

He shakes his head adamantly. "No, Eden. Unfortunately, there is no way to undo what has already been done. The proof you seek simply does not exist, and I cannot let you get hurt trying to pursue this. Please, you must let this go and let it go now before you get yourself into trouble."

I let out a deep breath, realizing once again that I will not gain the help I need. "I don't understand, Father. Why stay here after everything that happened?"

He clears his throat awkwardly. "Because your mother had made her home here, and you were receiving a valuable education with the best resources available. It made sense to stay."

His answer doesn't satisfy me in the slightest. I can already tell that there is another reason why he decided to stick around here. A reason that he doesn't want to tell me.

"Eden, I apologize, but today has been a long day. I think I ought to go to bed."

I nod, and he stands up from his desk, walking around the edge to lean down and kiss my head. I watch silently as he leaves, closing the door behind him.

I lean back in the chair, my eyes running over the study carefully as a plan begins to form in my head. Tomorrow, after high tea, I will make it my mission to return to the den. I must speak with Conall and let him know the danger coming his way.

Gauntlet

Eden

I glance at the Elven Guard standing to attention all around us.

"I've taken high-tea with Queen Siofra many times, and it's always such a lovely experience," my mother says, secretly scrutinizing my outfit for any visible flaws. "You don't have to be nervous, dear."

"I'm not," I reply determinedly as we stop by the edge of the royal gardens.

"Ladies, could you please follow me," a voice states from behind. I turn around to see the familiar face of the royal servant from yesterday. "This way," she says kindly.

We follow her through the maze of perfectly groomed little hedges which encase beautiful gardens filled with wild and exotic flowers. I cannot help but be utterly fascinated by them. Under any other circumstances, I would be in heaven, but I must remain focused right now.

We turn the last corner to be greeted with a stone archway decorated by the growth of pretty little soft-pink flowers.

"Queen Siofra and the rest of the ladies are just through here," the servant smiles, leading the way for us.

She gestures toward a circular stone gazebo over by the lake, where there is already a table full of women sitting together in the midst of lively conversation.

As we get closer, my eyes run over the stunning gazebo structure. The stone pillars are intricately designed with impressive carvings. The dome roof is weaved with all kinds of vines adorned with flowers and plants of multiple colors and species.

It's magical, really, and I cannot deny it.

Suddenly, I am knocked out of my reverie by the sound of enthusiastic applause. My head snaps to the table, where I see that the high elf women are now watching our approach with smiles on their faces.

Instantly, my eyes connect with those of Siofra, who claps her hands politely as she greets us.

"Ahhh, here she is. Our precious guest of honor this morning," she says, offering me a sickly sweet smile.

My mother and I stop in front of her, and I force my rigid body into a curtsy like my mother taught me many years ago.

"Your Majesty, many thanks for your invitation to join high tea with you. We are so very humbled," my mother gushes, bowing respectfully.

Siofra offers her a polite yet somehow dismissive smile before her gaze falls on me again. "My dear Eden," she coos, walking over to place her hands on my upper arms. "How lucky we are to have you back with us again."

She leans in to land a kiss on either side of my face. It takes everything in me not to recoil at her touch, but I'm determined to remain unperturbed by her vomit-inducing presence.

"Thank you, Your Majesty."

She nods at me with a raised eyebrow, her thin lips contorting into a tight smile again. She sits at the head of the table and gestures for me to sit on the opposite side. "Please sit, Eden."

I walk over to the chair, which is quickly pulled out for me by the royal servant, who then dutifully begins to pour me some tea.

"Thank you, uhh...?" I ask, waiting for her to tell me her name.

Her expression turns fearful for a second, and she looks at Siofra nervously for permission.

"Go ahead," Siofra orders, her shoulders tensing slightly as she lifts the tiny, delicate, floral teacup to her lips.

"Cassendra," the brunette servant woman replies, nodding at me kindly.

"Thank you, Cassendra, for your help," I say sincerely as she finishes pouring.

She steps away from the table, and I look around at the stunned faces of the pompous women staring at me in disbelief.

Siofra's light laughter then breaks the tension as she places her teacup on the table. "These young elves today do bring me much diversion," she says, her words allowing the other women permission to laugh along with her. "Always in such a hurry to thank everyone around them. It's funny, really."

Her gaze lands on me again, her eyes flicking over me critically. "I suppose, though, that is why we are here today! To thank our wonderful Eden here for her service to the crown."

The atmosphere turns lively once more as the high elf women all nod and chatter in zealous agreement.

"Oh, dear girl. The horror that you must have been through! Being captured by those utterly wretched beasts!!" one blue-haired old witch comments, clutching her chest dramatically. "How on earth did you survive?!"

"Quite easily, actually," I reply, picking up the sticky pastry in front of me to nibble a small piece.

Her mouth falls open in shock. "Oh?"

"Well, I wasn't harmed. I mean to say," I correct myself, giving her a fake smile.

"Thankfully," Siofra adds, raising her eyebrow at me.

"What were they like?" another woman asks, her curious orange eyes as wide as saucers beneath her gold and purple-rimmed spectacles. "The wolves?"

They all nod their head, each of them hanging on my every word.

Without delay, images of Conall begin to flash through my mind.

His honey-colored eyes the moment we first met.

His strong, wet, muscular body as he trained in the rain.

The touch of his large, rough, skilled hands as they grasped my body in both pleasure and ecstasy.

The rise and fall of his sculpted chest as he mercilessly plunged his solid cock inside me.

"Oh... so very, very savage indeed," I answer, making all the women look at each other in both horror and wonder.

I can't help but find it rather humorous how much they have demonized these men. If only they knew just what they were missing....

"I can imagine!" the blue-haired old witch says. "So they held you captive all this time since *The Culling* ceremony?"

I nod my head in reply.

"Oh, how dreadful and—"

"Pray tell," Siofra cuts in directly. "How on earth did you manage to escape, dear?" she asks, her question akin to a gauntlet thrown at my feet.

I clear my throat, glancing at my mother, who is staring at me through nervous eyes.

"Their leader," I answer with a shrug of my shoulder. "He lowered his defenses, and I climbed over them," I reply, the cryptic meaning holding steady and true to my heart.

☐

"I see," Siofra says, waiting for me to continue.

Time to get creative, it seems. "I managed to make my way through the forest and went straight to find Aubrun."

"It is amazing..." Siofra begins. "...that you did not run into any of *my* guards. There were, after all, many on your journey here, I would assume?"

"Not that I saw," I reply unfalteringly.

"You came in through the usual entrance?" she hits back in challenge.

"Of course," I answer. "I wanted to get to Aubrun uninterrupted since the news I had to share was so very important. There wasn't a moment to spare."

"What made you go to Aubrun?" another woman asks inquisitively.

I can hear the cautious edge in her tone. Clearly, the woman wants to know why I didn't go to our gracious queen instead.

"Because he is a valued friend of mine. One that I knew could be trusted," I say controversially, looking straight at Siofra without fear.

She smiles that same sickly sweet smile again. "Ahhh, now you see, ladies. My Ciridan, rest his soul, knew this when he chose our Aubrun to take his place," she gushes as all the women smile and nod in agreement. "He is a gentle and *loyal* nobleman," she finishes with a glare.

It doesn't take a genius to read between the lines of her words. Aubrun is in her pocket, and she wants me to know it.

"He is a great man," I answer, lifting my teacup to my lips. "I look forward to supporting our new king in any way I can now that I'm back," I say smugly, deliberately choosing my words.

The women look at each other in excitement.

"Ohhh...do I sense a hint of romance in the air?" the blue-haired woman questions playfully, kickstarting a chorus of excited giggles.

"Perhaps." I smile at them before returning to Siofra, whose picture-perfect facade has cracked ever so slightly to reveal the fury underneath.

"Let us change the subject," she then interjects sternly. "Eden has been through enough this week, and I am sure she is not thinking of such matters right now. Let us turn our attention to the coronation tonight! Can any of you guess the theme I have gone for?"

The ladies, who are now suitably distracted, dive into a heated and passionate debate about color schemes and flowers. Siofra's eyes stay with me for a few more seconds before snapping away in obvious distaste.

Game on... *Queen.*

Return

Eden

I tightly wrap the black cloak around my shoulders, tying the velvet cord around my neck. High tea took longer than I expected, and I now have very little time to carry out my plan. I race over to my dressing table to pick up the black swiveldrop flower, placing it carefully into my small, handwoven pouch, which I tie to my belt.

Suddenly, the door knocks.

"Just coming," I answer, fixing myself as I walk across the bedroom.

"It's just me," Aubrun's voice calls out from the other side.

My shoulders drop slightly in frustration before I open the door to see him standing in the hallway. "Hi."

"Hi," he replies, bowing his head to me before taking in my appearance. "Are you going somewhere?"

"Uhh, yes," I answer, leaving the bedroom to close the door behind me. "I'm in a hurry, actually, since my mother has arranged for someone to dress me for the ceremony tonight."

"Eden," he says, his voice dripping with disapproval. "You aren't going to Azealea, are you? Security is too tight right now around Morween, and I don't think you should visit your grandmother without my escort."

"No, I'm not. Although, I wish I was. I've missed her so much," I say honestly. "I'm just popping down to Morween village for some supplies for my father's study. It seems he has let standards slip in my absence," I add, throwing in a disapproving head shake for added effect.

"I see," Aubrun replies with a hint of suspicion. "Well, I have a little bit of time. I'll come with—"

"Excuse me, apologies, Sir Aubrun," a man calls out from behind us.

We both turn around to see Lord Faenor heading our way. The despicable asshole....

"I was just wondering if we might review some things before the coronation

◻

this evening? I know the other lords are keen for a meeting, and you said that you would make time for us today," he says, his eyes drifting to me.

From how he lifts his nose in the air, I can see that he considers me beneath him, even with my so-called hero status.

"Ahh, I did say that. Eden, would you mind?"

"Not at all. I can see you are busy. I will see you at the ceremony this evening."

His eyes run over me one last time before he nods. I watch cautiously as they both disappear down the corridor.

* * *

I navigate the market in the center of Morween Square slowly, occasionally stopping to look at the produce on offer from the various enthusiastic vendors.

"Ahhh, you'll not see better wild berries than these this side of the river, missy."

"They are beautiful," I reply, offering the seller a smile as he passes me a juesberry to try.

I lift it to my lips, casually glancing sideways to see that Aubrun's guard is still firmly on my tail. He has been trying to blend into the crowd, but I spotted him as soon as I left the palace walls.

"Hey, wait, aren't you the woman who saved the palace from the attack?" the seller's wife asks excitedly, hurrying around the wooden cart to get a closer look at me.

"Oh, I—"

"It is! It is! Mommy, look!" a little girl squeals, tugging on her mother's hand.

The seller puts out his hand, shaking mine with such excitement that he almost pulls my arm out of the damn socket.

"Thank you, my lady! We are all so grateful to you! You are a true hero!"

"A true hero!" his wife agrees, pulling me into a hug.

"Uhh, thanks," I answer, gulping awkwardly.

I hazard a look at the conspicuous guard again. Seems like I have more than one set of eyes to evade this afternoon....

"Here! You must take these for free! Please choose anything you want."

"I couldn't possibly," I reply, pulling some coins from my cloak. "Really, I'd much rather pay."

The seller offers me a beaming smile as I take the bag of berries from his hand to walk away hurriedly.

Fuck!

After that display, every set of eyes in the damn square are now on me. People wave in my direction, men take off their hats in respect as I walk by, and children point at me eagerly.

I realize quickly that if I'm going to get out of here, I no longer have time to waste. I take a sharp turn down a quiet alleyway, taking off in a run as soon as I'm out of sight. I head directly for the little bookstore at the bottom, swinging open the door, which causes the bell to ring. I'm not worried as I know the place well. The old man who runs this store is half-deaf and asleep most of the time. As suspected, he is resting in his high-backed chair, completely oblivious to my presence. I head for the back of the shop, whipping off my cloak to turn it inside out, changing its black color to a soft powder blue instead.

I rush out into the next alleyway, pulling my hood over my head as I make my way to my next destination. My heart leaps in my chest when I see her sitting there. The young raven-haired beggar woman who sits outside the bakery most afternoons. I head straight for her, pulling out some coins to prepare for my next move.

"Good afternoon," I say softly, kneeling in front of her.

She gives me a kind nod in return, and I take her hand in mine, closing her fingers around the coins.

"May the Gods bless you," she whispers as I hold her hand firmly for a moment longer.

I then let go, looking over my shoulder carefully before taking off in a jog. I stop by the doorway of an abandoned shop, pressing myself into the wall out of sight. Then I reach for the black flower in my pouch, cupping it gently in my hands as I close my eyes. I focus all my energy on picturing the beggar woman in my head. Her gray eyes, her long raven hair, her pale complexion. I paint a picture in my head so vivid that she could be standing in front of me right now.

□

When I open my eyes, I look down to grab a piece of my hair which has turned as black as midnight. A wave of relief washes over me, and I quickly spin around to examine my changed appearance in the shop window. I don't waste any more time, replacing my hood as I walk back into the village square. I keep my head down low as I scan the faces of everyone around me, finally locating Aubrun's guard, who is stretching his neck, scouring the crowd in a mild state of panic.

I head over to the stables, clearing my throat to get the attention of the young, distracted, stable boy who is currently chatting with a pretty pink-haired girl.

"Yeah?" he asks in irritation.

"I'll take the white one. Half a day," I say, holding out a handful of coins.

"You'll need to have a chaperone."

"I won't be requiring no one," I answer quietly, holding out my other hand, filled with an extra handful of gold.

He nods, looking around before taking them from me. He walks over to unhook the horse from its station, passing me the reins before returning to his conversation. I gently rub the horse's nose, leading it through the village to the forest trail before mounting.

"Let's go, boy. We have no time to lose!" I whisper, patting him before flicking the reins.

He takes off in a speedy gallop, and I hold on tight, navigating toward the most discreet path I know. We pass some guards on the way, but none bat an eyelid in my direction. After all, they are much more concerned with those coming into the kingdom than those leaving it behind.

The thick forest soon approaches, and before long, we find ourselves racing through the trees deeper into its beautiful depths. I lead the horse over a little bridge, heading for the same place Mateo captured me on the night of *The Culling* celebration. As soon as I get close, I slow down to a gentle gallop again and peruse the surroundings. It's silent, except for chirping birds in the high tree tops. I then carefully reach down for my woven pouch, removing it from my belt.

Finding my way back to the den *should* be an impossible task. Not only do their enchantments make the large house invisible to the naked eye, but they are sophisticated in design. They lead the seeker elsewhere, discombobulating them entirely and sending them off on the wrong path. As far as I'm aware, only the Alphas know its exact location. For outsiders to find it, their defenses would have to be temporarily lowered. As long as I can get somewhere close by, Con will find me. He'll be watching the forest. I know he will.

I reach into my little bag, gripping a handful of its contents.

Pathfinder powder.

I stayed up late last night putting together the painstaking potion. Of course, it's utterly useless for finding the den but highly useful for tracking your own previous movements.

I toss a handful of the powder into the air, watching as it slowly descends back down. At first, nothing happens, and then, just as I am about to panic, the powder does its job, illuminating a sparking path in front of me. A smile takes over my face, and I grab the reins again, jolting the horse back into action.

As we race through the trees, my raven hair wiping in the wind, I look back to see the trail disappearing behind me. I continue following it onward, the minutes ticking by one after the other. The sun's movement tells me that time is getting on. Luckily, the horse beneath me is strong and capable of the lengthy journey.

Eventually, the silvery trail stops, and I pull on the reins. "Whoa, boy," I say gently, patting his neck.

I look around at the unfamiliar area of forest, my eyes settling on a little patch of water. I hop down from the saddle, leading the horse over to take a drink. As it rests, I reach into my pouch again, ready to grab my next handful of powder.

Suddenly, I hear a rustle in the trees behind me, and I spin around to see a wolf staring back at me. I hold my hands up in surrender, closing my eyes to concentrate on dropping the spell surrounding me. As soon as my appearance returns to normal, the wolf moves closer.

"It's just me," I say cautiously, waiting for his next move.

Then, right before my eyes, he transforms, leaving a man standing in his place. My shoulders instantly relax, and I let out a puff of air. "Mateo!!" I yell, thanking my lucky stars. "Thank Goddess, I found you."

"What the *hell* are you doing here, Eden?" he barks, looking around shiftily.

My mouth drops open a little in shock. His tone sounds nothing like him.

"What? Mateo, please. I know things look bad, but I can explain. I had to find you all and tell you what I know. You are all in danger—"

☐

"Eden... *You* are in danger. You need to leave. Get out of here now!" he says adamantly, grabbing my upper arm to rush me back over my horse.

"What? I don't understand. If you'll let me explain—"

"Explain what? How you left the den and told the high elves about our plan?"

"No, Mateo. It wasn't me! I swear," I protest ardently. "You have to believe me."

He stops and looks into my eyes carefully before taking another look around. "The others are convinced you betrayed us."

"What do you believe? Do you think I would betray you all like that?" I ask sincerely. "You know that I would never do that."

"I want to believe you, Eden, but what I think doesn't matter because you'll never convince the others. Fucking Rocco, Henrick, Samuel and Hunter are on patrol right now with me. If any of them see you—"

"Anton will believe me too. I know he will! And Henrick and Hunter!"

He shakes his head quickly.

"The men are beyond furious. You must leave and get as far away from here as possible."

"No, I can't. This is what I'm trying to tell you. It wasn't me who told the elves about the attack. You have a leak, and we need to find out who it is. Harmony is in danger. You must take me to Con right away! We can't waste any more time."

Immediately his face falls, his expression turning solemn and guilty.

"Mateo?" I ask, searching his eyes. "This is important. I need to see him."

"You can't," he answers, looking up at me, swallowing hard. "He's dead, Eden."

The words tear through me like a razor-sharp sword ripping through my insides.

"What?" I gasp, the word stealing the last of the air from my lungs.

Tears automatically spring to my eyes, and I shake my head in disbelief and complete denial. "No, no. You're wrong!! I would know!! I would know if he were dead!"

I throw my shaking hand over my mouth as the tears begin to fall thick and fast down my cheeks.

"I saw it happen. We all did," Mateo says, his head dropping shamefully.

"How could you do this?!" I cry, anger boiling my blood on the spot. "He's your leader!! He sacrificed so much for all of you! Kept you all safe!! HOW COULD YOU DO THIS?!" I demand, hitting my fists off of his chest.

"He broke the code," Mateo says sadly, grasping my wrists. "He suffered the consequences of his actions."

His answer makes me fall to my knees in pain. A pain so formidable and overpowering that I am certain it will break me for good.

Mateo drops down beside me to hold me by the shoulders.

"Eden, please. You must go—"

"This is all my fault," I sob, clasping my hand over my aching chest. "None of this would have happened if it weren't for me."

"He didn't regret what he did," Mateo says adamantly, looking into my eyes. "I was wrong all along," he admits. "He loved you. More than anything. He knew what would happen when he let you go and he made his peace with it."

I shake my head frantically as Mateo hauls me onto my unsteady feet. "Eden, please. If you don't leave now, Con gave up his life for nothing. He wanted you to be free."

"I don't- I can't-he can't be-" I mutter incoherently.

Mateo puts his hand under my foot to help me onto the horse, taking one last look around before his eyes find mine. "Good luck out there, elf. I hope we'll meet again someday."

I don't get a chance to answer before he slaps his hand against the horse, springing it into life.

As I race back toward the palace, I can barely see where I'm going.

My tears cloud my vision. My pain swallowing me whole.

Fuck!

My eyes snap open, my body struggling to draw breath into my tar-filled lungs. The sunlight spewing in the window stings my eyes, making them squeeze shut of their own accord. My mouth is so fucking dry that my tongue gets stuck in the back of my throat. My chest's violent rise and fall draws my eyes downward to run over the bandages wrapped around my waist.

What the fuck?

Despite the immense pain searing up my spine, I force myself to sit up, looking around the small unfamiliar room.

Where am I?

I blink slowly, my narrowed eyes making their way to the circular window by the bed. It's then I see the forest outside. Peaceful and calm.

"Don't worry. You're not dead, my boy," a voice says in amusement.

I twist my stiff neck to look at the old woman.

"It's you," I say gruffly, my mind suddenly hit with a million fucking questions all at once.

"Yes, it's nice to have you back with us... Alpha Conall," she smiles.

Numb

Eden

As I stare back at myself, all I feel is numbness. As if my body is running on autopilot without any input whatsoever from my messed up mind. When I arrived back at the palace a couple of hours ago, all I wanted to do was lock myself away and cry. Cry for the devastation I've brought the wolves. Cry for my mate who paid the ultimate price for setting me free. My mate who gave up everything for me.

How can I ever move on from this knowing he's gone because of me? Knowing I'll never see his face, hear his voice, or feel his touch again?

I stand there staring at my reflection in the mirror.

Frozen.

Alone.

Heartbroken.

Eventually, the door knocks.

"Miss Nestoriel! The coronation is about to begin. Sir Aubrun requests your presence!"

I close my eyes and take a deep breath, summoning every fiber of strength in my body, every minuscule shred of energy I have left.

And with that... I turn around and leave the room.

* * *

"Wow, wow, wow!! This is beyond stunning!" The high elf woman in front of me gushes as she holds her husband, Lord Agar's, arm. "Is there anything Queen Siofra cannot achieve?"

"I don't believe so, my sweet," he chuckles, picking up a golden flute from the servant's tray.

I do my best not to roll my eyes, following their lead by picking up a drink for myself. Reluctantly, I look around the grand hall that has completely transformed since yesterday. The high ceilings are draped in expensive silk the color of midnight navy blue, and scatted with millions of tiny diamonds that look like twinkling stars in the sky. Everything else in the room is opulent gold, from the chandeliers to the damn candle holders. The ballroom floor has been polished to a shiny black that perfectly reflects the tiny "stars" shining in the "sky" above our heads. It's stunning, like walking on the waters of a calm river in Azealea.

"Eden! Eden, my dear!"

I turn around to see the blue-haired woman from high-tea this morning rushing toward me in her puffy pink gown.

"My dear, you look simply divine," she states in an overdramatic fashion I have gotten used to over the years here.

I nod respectfully, unable to commit to any fake conversation right now.

"Come! Come! I must introduce you to my sons and daughters! They are dying to meet you!" she grins manically, gesturing to a group of onlookers in the corner.

My eyes immediately find the tall, slender blue-haired Elven man who is eyeing me up like a piece of meat.

Good grief!

"I uhh can't right now. I'm sorry I have—"

"She has to assist me with some preparations, Lady Hilda. I'm sure you understand?" Aubrun's voice cuts in as he walks over to my side.

The woman's face lights up in response. "Oh, but of course I do!" she replies, already halfway through a dramatic curtsy.

Aubrun smiles at her charmingly before she rushes off back to her family.

"Hope I didn't interrupt?" he asks, raising a knowing eyebrow.

"No, you definitely didn't," I reply, eying him up and down.

Despite his cool façade, I don't miss how his hand shudders slightly or how he tries to disguise it with the other as he looks around the room.

"Nervous?"

"I'd be silly not to be," he answers, a humble smile crossing his lips.

His expression reminds me of the old Aubrun. The shy, protective friend I used to have.

"It will be alright," I say, my tone not entirely combative for a change.

He senses this instantly and looks into my eyes. "Are you alright?" he whispers, a look of concern on his face.

"I'm fine,"

He nods his head, swallowing uncomfortably.

"Sir Aubrun, it's now time to begin," a high elder elf announces, bowing gracefully before walking to the stage.

"Well, good luck," I murmur as Aubrun's eyes meet mine again.

"Eden, I don't want to spring it on you like last time, so I'm telling you now," he says seriously. "I'd like to bring you up alongside me on stage again. I will announce your up-and-coming appointment as queen once I'm crowned. I know you might say it's too soon, but I think—"

"No, it's okay," I interrupt, ignoring the pain gnawing at my insides. "You have to announce it sooner or later, right?"

"Right." A boyish smile lights up his face. "I've sat you in the front row with your parents. I'll see you on the other side."

He then lifts my hand, giving it a gentle kiss before he walks off to get ready.

Immediately after his departure, I sense all eyes on me. I look around to see elves whispering in hushed tones in every part of the room.

I guess I better get used to this kind of attention; it's about to become a permanent fixture in my life.

* * *

The room erupts into applause, and Aubrun rises from the throne, his crown positioned perfectly on his head by Queen Siofra. I clap my hands with everyone else, bracing myself for what will come next.

"Thank you, People of Moween, for placing your trust in me. I will endeavor to do right by you. To be the king that you deserve, as Ciridan was before me. I must first begin by thanking Queen Siofra for her faith and support during this time. She has been an invaluable mentor, and I hope this will continue long into my rein," he states, nodding at Siofra, who is now standing by the edge of the stage observing with a broad, smug smile.

"However, I believe that a great kingdom such as this deserves a strong ruling couple, which is why I'd like to announce this evening that I am indeed engaged to be married!"

Siofra's smile immediately begins to drain from her face, and her eyes shoot to me, fire swirling in their depths as her nostrils flare subtly.

"Take that, you bitch," my subconscious snarls as I narrow my eyes at her.

The gasps of shock and intrigue ripple across the room, creating an atmosphere of anticipation and excitement.

"People of Morween, Your future queen, Eden Nestoriel!"

Once again, everyone cheers and claps frantically, and I step forward, my father's hand shooting out to grab my arm. I glare at it before my eyes flick up to meet his.

"Eden?" he asks, both concern and confusion written over his face.

"If you won't help me take them down... Then I'll do it myself," I whisper determinedly.

His eyes widen as I slip my arm from his hold to join Aubrun on stage. As I walk past Siofra, I feel her fury as if it's some kind of invisible poison, seeping out to taint the air around her. I do not hesitate in turning my head to look her straight in the icy eyes. She steps forward to take me by the shoulders, a fake, performative smile suddenly appearing on her face before she leans in to kiss me on the cheek. "My my, how quickly you work, little wood elf," she whispers.

"I look forward to relieving you of your duties soon, my queen," I reply, stepping away from her to continue my journey to Aubrun.

The smile on his face is beaming from ear to ear, his happiness appearing wholly genuine and heartfelt. He takes my hand, kissing it before holding it in his.

"A beautiful future queen deserves a beautiful ring!" he declares, looking over his shoulder to his servant, who comes forward with a small golden cushion.

I swallow as I look down at the delicate gold band clutching a colossal midnight-blue rock with flecks of silver inside. Auburn removes it from the cushion, smiling at me as he slides the piece of metal down my finger. The noise in the room is amplified again, and I look up into Aubrun's eyes.

Only this morning, I would have been horrified by this whole thing, but now I don't feel anything.

No anger.

No pain.

Just complete nothingness.

His brows furrow ever so slightly before he clears his throat, turning to the crowd to give them an appreciative wave.

I follow his lead, respectfully bowing to them before holding my head up high.

* * *

The day's events have left me completely exhausted. Thankfully, I was able to escape conversations with my parents by sticking to Aubrun's side for most of the night, playing the doting wife and queen-to-be as I listened to greedy lord after greedy lord sucking up as if they wouldn't have looked down on a man like him this time last week.

Of course, Aubrun is blind to their insincerity.

I kick my shoes off by the bed, my gaze dropping to examine the ring on my finger. It feels heavy, its weight dragging me down further into my pit of utter despair.

Suffering the loss of a great love once before in my life has altered my viewpoint on grief altogether. I know already that this pain will never go away. It will always be ever-present. A bruise on my heart that will never heal.

I walk across the room to stand by the window, my eyes finding the full moon in the obsidian sky. My mission now is the only thing stopping me from falling to my knees and shattering into tiny pieces. I'll protect Con's legacy with my life. I'll do whatever is necessary to finish what he started. There is no other path for me now. No other purpose than to expose the truth and save Harmony once and for all.

Just then, from the corner of my eye, I see a shadow form against the transparent window pane. I open my mouth to scream, but it's too late.

The scream never comes.

Instead, I lift my hands to claw at the thin wire that has been tightly wrapped around my neck.

Allies

Conall

"How did I get here?" I murmur, taking another look around the tiny bedroom.

"It seems you still have friends out there, Alpha."

My brows knit together in confusion before I settle my feet on the old floorboards. Instantly, a shooting pain travels up my spine, and I wince as I bring my hand up to rest on my bandaged stomach.

"I wouldn't do that if I were you," the old woman says, turning to smile at me.

It's then I examine the tray in her hands, which is filled with bloodied bandages alongside ancient-looking metal medical utensils.

"You fixed me up?" I ask, running a hand through my dirty hair.

"Yes," she answers, the skin around her bright eyes crinkling. "It wasn't easy, though. The bleeding was extensive, and my stitch work isn't what it used to be. That is why I would prefer if you lay back down."

I don't take her advice, but I do remain still for a moment as I try to get my head straight. I drop my head down to the floor and close my eyes as those last few moments back at the den race through my mind. Zeke stabbed me before Rocco could. That much, I know. After that, all I remember is thinking of her... Thinking of Eden before I slid into the darkness.

The door in the corner of the room opens, and an old Elven man pops his head inside. "Supper is ready," he declares in a friendly tone.

The old woman nods, turning to face me again. "Well, since you aren't going to take my advice and rest, you might as well eat instead."

"I'm not hungry."

"It will help," she insists, giving me an authoritative stare. "You must try to build your strength up."

It doesn't take me long to determine that she's right. I need to figure out what's happening and where I go from here. I nod in defeat, grunting as I push myself up onto my unsteady legs.

"Woah there!" the man chuckles, rushing forward to throw my arm around his shoulder. "You can lean on me for support. Just bear in mind I have a few hundred years on you!"

I try my best to hold myself upright as we walk across the room and through the doorway into a cozy-looking cottage. My eyes shift around the place quickly, taking it all in. A square wooden table is in the center of the room, not far away from a stone fireplace blazing with crackling flames. The crowded kitchen countertops and shelves are filled with glass bottles and jars of all shapes and sizes. The little window over on the right-hand wall affords a view of the wild forest, which is beginning to get dark. My eyes travel upward to the wooden beams above my head that are draped with the vines of various plants. It's a wood elf's house if ever I saw one.

"You like our little home here? I know it's not much compared with the den," the old woman states, placing the tray down to wash her hands.

"It's nice," I answer awkwardly, dropping down onto a chair by the table.

Her husband sets out some bowls, ladling some kind of stew into each one. "There you go, boy, get some of this into you. You'll be right as rain," he says, sitting across from me.

I nod at him gratefully before my eyes follow the woman again as she sits by my right side.

"So how long has it been, Alpha Conall, since we last saw one another face-to-face?" she asks with a knowing grin.

"I'd say seventy years or so now," I smirk.

"I'd say you're right, and my, you have not aged a day, my boy."

"Neither have you," I answer in reply.

She smiles in return as I cast my mind back to all those years ago when we first met...

* * *

SEVENTY YEARS AGO

"You take the west side, and I'll take the east. Zeke and the others can handle

□

everything in between." Lincoln says as we walk down the pack house steps.

I nod, looking at the dark trees all around us.

"What's wrong? You see something?" Lincoln asks, following my gaze.

"No," I reply. "But it's only a matter of time."

We begin walking to the tree line and, before long, find ourselves in the heart of the forest. "We might have to start thinking of a plan B. It's a fucking miracle the Guard hasn't stumbled on us already," I state seriously.

"They don't even know we are alive, Con."

"Not yet."

He nods in uncomfortable agreement. "That's true. One fucking impossible problem at a time though, right?"

"I suppose. I'll meet you back here in an hour."

He then shifts into his wolf before speeding off into the woods. I get ready to do the same when the bright glimmer of a floating orb suddenly appears in the corner of my eye. I stare at it in confusion for a second, looking around the silent darkness for its source, but there is nothing to be seen. Not a sound to be heard.

What the fuck?

I can't help but follow it, my feet moving through the bed of leaves carefully as I go. The orb twists and turns continuously, carving a path deeper into the forest before slowly drifting to the ground.

"Hello," a gentle voice says from behind.

I twist around speedily to see an old Elven woman looking back at me, a burgundy-colored cloak draped over her head.

I immediately step away from her, readying myself to act if necessary.

She smiles kindly, lifting her wrinkled hands to remove her hood. "Please do not worry. I'm here because I want to help you."

My brows knit together as I examine her suspiciously. "I don't need your help, elf," I seethe, making a move to walk away.

"Oh, but you do, my boy. If you and those other wolves want to stay hidden in that den, you most certainly need my help."

I stop in my tracks, my eyes connecting with hers. "What did you just say?"

She gives me a sympathetic look in return. "You do not need to worry about me. I do not care for war or violence. I only wish for peace and harmony in our realm."

"So you want to help us?" I ask for clarification.

She nods gently.

"And why the hell should I trust you?"

She steps forward, and I watch on high alert as she pulls a small velvet bag from inside her cloak. "This enchantment will protect the house from prying eyes," she says, holding it out for me. "I can tell you how it works, and you can see the results for yourself."

I take the bag from her hand, looking down at it as I think over her proposition.

"No," I eventually say in finality, stretching out my arm to hand it back over. "There's no way on this earth I'll ever trust any of your kind again."

"Then you'll all meet the same fate as your loved ones," she answers sadly, grabbing hold of my fist with both of her delicate hands.

I try to pull away from her grip, but she refuses to let go. Instead, she looks up into my eyes pleadingly, closing my hand around the velvet bag. "You must take this, my boy, if you want to survive."

Something in her expression makes me pause, the sincerity in her eyes appealing to a part of me that I thought was long gone.

Against my instincts, I decide to take a chance, and I nod my head slowly.

She smiles a sad smile, removing her hands from mine.

"Who are you?" I ask, looking her up and down, committing her image to memory.

She shakes her head. "My name is not important," she answers. "But my intentions are. If you trust me, you can remain hidden from sight for as long as you wish."

"Using magic?" I question, my stomach twisting at the mere thought of it.

"Magic must only be feared when it is in the wrong hands, Conall."

My eyes shoot to her face again.

"How the fuck do you know my name?" I growl.

"Because I've been watching you all for a while," she responds calmly. "That is why you must use this enchantment before anyone else discovers your hiding place."

After her worrying admission, part of me wonders if I should put an end to this right now.

If she knows our hiding place, how can I let her wander back into the forest?

How do I know that she won't tell the guard as soon as she gets the chance?

"You need not worry about my silence. I have no interest in the politics at

□

play in Morween," she states insistently as though reading my mind. "Now, this enchantment will only last for seven full moons exactly. When it wears off, you must repeat the process all over again."

"How do I do that?"

"I will teach you, and from here on out, I will leave the enchantment right here waiting for you on the seventh full moon, along with anything else you might require."

"Like what?" I ask curiously.

"We do not have much, but I can provide books, medicines and protection enchantments. You need only leave me a message and ask."

"Why?" I ask, looking into her eyes again. "Why would you do this for us? Do you not think us monsters as they do in Morween?"

Her expression turns from soft to determined in a heartbeat. "No, I do not believe the attacks on our Elven villages were as they seemed," she answers, her bright eyes glistening with tears under the moonlight. "Dark intentions emanate from that palace; I can feel their energy descend upon our lands."

Her reasoning is strange, to say the least. Perhaps she's some sort of witch.

"You're right," I answer. "The attacks were carried out by rogue wolves, not us... They were probably paid for by your own king and his lords."

Her shoulders drop as though her suspicions have been confirmed. "Do you have any proof of this?" she asks hopefully.

I shake my head, and she frowns sadly.

"What happened to your species was wrong. My boy, violence is never the answer. Someday I hope you shall once again live freely in this realm. Someday, I hope that peace will be restored."

With that final speech, I nod, examining the bag in my hand again.

"Tell me," I say quietly. "Tell me how this works."

Guilt

PRESENT

"Now that I have taken a bed in your home, perhaps you'll tell me your name?" I ask, taking a mouthful of stew which burns my throat slightly on the way down.

"Perhaps, although first, you may want to tell me how you came to know where I live?" she questions in mild amusement.

I smirk in reply, lowering the spoon. "I followed you one night." I answer honestly, "After my friend Lincoln...passed. I had to know where you lived in case my second-in-command ever needed to find you."

"Well, I'd say that was a wise decision on your part," she answers with a subtle wink.

The door to the small cottage then opens to reveal Zeke standing in the doorway with a stupid grin on his face. "So sleeping beauty finally woke up then?"

I push the chair back, struggling onto my feet, and he throws his arms around me in a tight hug.

"Goddess," I grunt in agony. "There's a reason why we don't hug, you prick."

He laughs, and I feel his relief as he steps back, holding me by the shoulders. "You look like shit, Con."

"Yeah? You try getting stabbed in the back."

"No thanks. It looked fucking awful. You should have seen the blood," he grins.

"Curious fellows, these wolves," the old man says to his wife as Zeke and I turn around to look at them both.

"Take a seat, my dear," the old woman orders to Zeke, who quickly does as

□

he is asked.

As soon as I sit back down, the atmosphere in the room shifts, and I look into his eyes. "What the fuck happened, Zeke? What did you do?"

"I did what I had to," he replies insistently.

I shake my head, running my hand over my face. "I broke the code. I chose this path, but you didn't. If the men figure this out—"

"If they figure it out, then fuck them, Con," he answers defiantly. "It wasn't right, and they all knew it, but no one had the balls to say it. Without you as our leader, there's no way we would have gotten as far as we have. I know it, and they bloody well know it too."

I lean my elbow on the table. "So...your solution was to stab me?" I question, raising an eyebrow in his direction.

He grins again, pulling a knife from his pocket to flip it in his hand skillfully. "I'd have thought you'd have more faith in me by now. I know what I'm doing—and hey—better me than that asshole Rocco."

"It appears you do know what you are doing, Zeke," the old lady confirms. "If the wound was a fraction to the left or the right, then there would have been no saving him."

He winks at her in thanks before giving me a cocky smile. "You hear that?"

"Tell me what happened exactly," I ask.

"Well," he begins, clearing his throat. "After you went down, I gave the guys a piece of my fucking mind. I could see they felt guilty, so I sent them back inside the house. Told them they didn't have the right to lay you to rest. I asked Anton to stay behind, and when everyone was out of sight, we brought you here. You said if we were ever in trouble, this woman would help, and thankfully, she took your sorry ass into her home in the middle of the night."

My eyes drift back to the old woman, and I give her another grateful nod. "So the men still think I'm dead?"

"Yeah. Except Anton. He's the only one that knows the truth."

"Why him?"

"Because he doesn't believe it either."

"Believe what?"

"That Eden would betray us," he answers plainly.

The mention of her name creates an ache in my chest so vast that the wound in my back pales into insignificance. I lift my hand to my face, pinching the bridge of my nose, images of her beautiful face flashing before my eyes. "Zeke...I saw it in Morween—"

"It doesn't matter what you saw," the old woman interjects stubbornly, her gaze drifting to Zeke.

I frown in confusion. "What the hell aren't you telling me?"

"Alpha Conall, I didn't tell you my name all those years ago because I knew you would never trust me if I did. My name is Citrine Nestoriel, and this is my husband, Erwin," she admits. "Eden is our granddaughter."

My eyes widen in shock as I stare back at her, stunned into silence.

"Yeah, I had the same reaction," Zeke adds.

"Your granddaughter? But that means—"

"Haleth Nestoriel is our son, yes," Citrine finishes for me.

I look to Zeke, who shrugs his shoulders. "I knew you and Eden had your problems, but I didn't know it was this bad," he jokes in an attempt to lighten the mood.

"Fuck," I mutter, running a hand through my hair again. "Then you knew...you knew when you came to see me that night that your son was involved in *The Culling*."

She nods in return. "I did."

"Then you also know the attack we planned was designed to kill him and everyone else involved?"

"Yes, shortly after your arrival here, word traveled from the palace to the village that an attack had been foiled. By my own granddaughter, no less! My granddaughter, who was apparently kept prisoner by wolves."

I can sense a hint of hostility in her tone for the first time.

"You are angry," I say, stating the obvious.

She lets out a sigh as she looks at me intently. "As I told you many years ago, Alpha Conall, I only desire peace. I was disappointed to hear news of the attack but not surprised. However, the news of Eden's capture was very upsetting to hear. My son never even told me. If he had, perhaps this whole mess could have been avoided."

"I didn't hurt her," I say insistently. "I would never do that, but when she was brought to the den, I had no choice. I couldn't let her go.

"You couldn't let her go, or you didn't *want* to?" Citrine asks, her knowing eyes staring into my soul.

"You know she's my mate," I state quietly. "How?"

"Because he told me," she says, waving a finger to Zeke. "I can't

□

just *know* everything."

They all begin to laugh, and I shake my head, unable to make jokes right now.

"Look at me, Alpha," Citrine says adamantly, causing me to lift my head. "I *do* know my granddaughter, and if she was as much in love as Zeke here says, then I know in my heart that she would never betray you. She is loyal, kind and the most headstrong young woman I have ever met," she smiles, reaching out her hand to rest it on mine. "If she did not love you, she would not say it. If she were to betray you, she would not hide it."

I look to Zeke, who agrees before a worried expression falls over his face. "There's more," he says seriously, looking around the table. "Just before I came here, Mateo told me he met Eden in the woods. She told him she had nothing to do with the plan going awry. She said we have a leak. Mateo was worried the others would see her, so he sent her away before he learned anything else," Zeke finishes. "She was looking for you, Con."

As soon as the words leave his lips, guilt rises in my chest. Its weight piling down on me, making it hard to fucking breathe.

I stand up from the table, walking over to the fireplace to rest my hand on the stone wall. I try to catch my breath as my anger toward myself battles to take hold.

How the fuck could I doubt her?

How could I think her a traitor and a liar when she was exactly who she said she was?

"Is she safe now? Is she protected?" I ask, looking to Citrine, who nods her head reassuringly.

"Yes. It was just yesterday during the king's funeral ceremonies that Eden was named as the hero who helped foil the wolves' plan. It seems someone is protecting her, and now she is being hailed as a hero in Morween."

"Good," I answer in relief. "It's safer for her if everyone thinks she is on their side. This must be her father's doing," I say matter-of-factly.

Citrine nods. "Haleth loves Eden with all he has. I'm sure he will do his best to protect her, but she now has the support of someone with even more power than he."

I look at her questioningly.

"Eden's friend Aubrun is to take the throne any minute now when he is named as King Ciridan's replacement."

Aubrun... The name immediately strikes a chord as I recall that day in the forest when he stumbled across Eden and I. Even from that short encounter alone, I could see in his eyes that he cared for her. He was with her on the balcony the night of the attack.

"You think it's him who is looking out for her?"

"I'm not sure yet what is going on, but I do not trust the queen. I never have. I have always suspected her of having her hand in the attacks on Elven villages during the war. Perhaps even more so than King Ciridan himself," Citrine explains. "And I do not think for a minute that she would allow Eden to integrate back into the palace unless she knows for sure that Eden is firmly on their side," she adds with a look of concern.

Silence follows as everyone gets lost in their thoughts for a few moments.

"What are we going to do, Con? What's our next move?" Zeke then asks as each of them looks to me for answers.

I take a second to think. "Did you tell Mateo I was here?"

"No."

"Good. Keep it quiet. If we have a leak, you must find out who it is, but be discreet."

"You think Rocco had a hand in this?" Zeke asks.

I shake my head. "It doesn't make any sense. Every single one of them hates the high elves. Him more than most."

"I'll do some digging." Zeke nods, stuffing the knife back in his pants.

"Also, if Eden is right about this leak, then Harmony could be in jeopardy. It's too dangerous to move the pack, so step up security around the perimeter instead. Send half the men to protect them and keep the rest to send the army on a wild goose chase."

"That's just the thing, Conall; the Elven army hasn't gone anywhere near Harmony. It doesn't even seem like they know it exists."

I think his words over for a few seconds. "Eden..." I turn to Citrine. "You think she found a way to keep them from taking Harmony?"

"If she did, then she must have made a deal of some kind."

Straight away, I can sense something is wrong. "We have to think of a way to get to her. I need to know that she's safe. I need to speak to her."

"Then I will try to make that happen as soon as possible," Citrine agrees, looking into my eyes.

Assassin

Eden

I'm so damn disoriented and shocked that I can't think straight. My burning lungs scream for air, but I cannot satisfy them. My mouth opens and closes like a fish out of water, quickly suffocating to death, but there's no way I'll give up. I throw my body backward against my attacker, my fingers still desperately grabbing at the tight wire. They stumble back, but their grip remains strong. Then, I glance to the side, my bloodshot eyes catching sight of her reflection in the mirror.

It's Cassendra. The royal servant.

Fury boils in my blood at the sight of her, and I lift my elbow to shove it as hard and as fast as I can into her abdomen. She lets out a light squeal, and I push back further against her, knocking us both back onto the bed. Her grip loosens just enough for me to fall to the side, my fingers finally sliding under the wire to relieve the pressure on my neck.

I gasp for air as soon as I am able, thrashing around wildly to free myself from her hold. I use every ounce of strength I have to pull the wire further from my neck, slipping my head through the gap to fall onto the floor.

She shrieks in anger, immediately pouncing on top of me, straddling my waist. She unleashes a tirade of furious punches, and one stray fist connects with my eye painfully before I hold my arms up to defend myself. I bide my time, waiting for the moment to strike, grabbing her fist to twist it as hard as possible.

She lets out a cry in agony, and I push her off of me, jumping back up onto my feet. I blink to clear the blood seeping down from my eyebrow, holding up my fists, ready to fight. She pulls herself back onto her feet, clutching her wrist for a moment before taking her fighting stance.

"Why are you doing this? What is the queen giving you in return?" I snarl, Siofra's smug image taunting me from inside my head.

Cassendra's eyes narrow on me instantly. "I don't do anything for that bitch!" she snaps back. "You fucked up a plan that was years in the making, and for that, you'll die."

My brows knit together in confusion before she lunges at me again with an outstretched arm. I grab it, swiftly spinning her to securely wrap my arm around her shoulders.

"You're with the wolves?" I question in her ear as she flails around to free herself from my grip.

"With them? I'm one of them, you elf bitch!" she growls.

It's then that it clicks just who she is, and I toss her forward away from me. She stumbles a little before spinning around to look back at me in bewilderment.

"You were Conall's connection to the palace," I say, my fists dropping slightly.

"He told you?" she questions scornfully.

"He told me that Ciridan died because he planned it. It was you, wasn't it? It was you who helped him kill King Ciridan?"

Her nostrils flare as her eyes flick over me suspiciously. She then spits at my feet in disdain. "You're a liar! You're the *hero* of Morween."

I lift my finger to point it at her in warning. "You do that again, and I swear I will kick your ass. I don't care who you are."

She keeps her eyes firmly on me, her face contorted in rage.

"Listen... I know this seems hard to believe, but hear me out for a minute before you go all deranged assassin on me again. I'm on your side," I say, looking at her sincerely before holding my hands up in surrender. "See?"

Her chest rises and falls as she listens to me, but still, she doesn't let down her guard.

"I didn't tell the elves about the plan, and I didn't escape the den. Conall let me go. He let me go to come back here and save my father."

"Why would he do that?" she snaps back doubtfully.

"Because I was his mate," I answer, a lump forming in my bruised throat.

A look of shock covers her face. "Was?"

"He's dead," I blurt out matter-of-factly, holding in my emotions out of necessity. If I don't, I know there's no way I'll get through everything I have to say.

"No. You're lying. It's not true! The guards didn't capture anyone. I asked

☐

around and—"

"It wasn't the guards," I interrupt. "He broke the code when he let me go. He was punished because of it. He died because of me."

Her jaw tenses, and her fists tighten. "If it wasn't you who told the elves about the plan, then who was it?"

"I don't know," I answer honestly. "Aubrun found out about the den somehow, and he knows about Harmony too."

She gulps, the look in her eyes shifting from fury to concern. "He knows about Harmony?"

"He does, but he's not going to hurt anyone. I have his word."

"Oh, you have his word? The new king gave you his word, did he? Just like that?" she questions skeptically.

"No. I had to give him something in return."

She frowns as I hold up my hand, the shiny ring gleaming in the moonlight.

"Oh," she mutters, a slight hint of understanding touching her expression.

"It's where you're from, isn't it? The pack in the mountains," I say carefully.

"How do you know about Harmony?" she asks defensively.

"Because I'm not lying about Conall and I. He loved me, and I...I loved him too." I answer, my emotions finally getting the better of me. I turn away from her, slumping down to sit on the edge of the bed.

There's silence for a few seconds before she walks toward me, cautiously sitting by my side. I see her looking at me with suspicion from the corner of my eye, but I no longer have the energy to defend myself.

"I grew up there," she says unexpectedly, looking straight ahead out of the window. "Harmony is my home."

I lift my head to look at her, and her eyes flick to meet mine.

"How did you end up here?" I ask curiously.

"Years ago, I could tell the Alphas were planning something—something big. I went to Conall and told him I wanted to help in any way that I could. Being half-elf, I knew that I could be of use."

"Let me guess, he refused?"

She grins slightly and nods. "Yeah, said he didn't want to put me in danger, but I was persistent. I trained hard. Studied Elven culture in my free time. Eventually, I was able to prove to him that I could do this. I was ready."

"So you became a palace servant? A spy for the wolves?"

"Yes, and it wasn't easy. I've been here for years, working my way up to get closer to the royal household. I had to be the first servant up every morning. The last to go to bed every night. I had to learn everything about those assholes: their favorite foods, what time they go to bed, how Siofra likes to wear her fucking hair. Everything!"

"Sounds like hell," I answer honestly.

"Oh, it was, but when I was promoted to a royal servant, our plan could truly take shape. I began slowly poisoning King Ciridan's food for the sole purpose of aiding the wolves' attack. It wasn't easy. He had various tasters who would try his food before every meal. I had to be careful, and it took a long time. I left a note for Conall in the woods when the job was finally done, and then...."

"Everything was ruined." I finish the sentence for her.

She nods her head, her frustration evident. "All those years...sacrificed for nothing."

"I'm sorry. No wonder you tried to kill me."

"I guess I'm sorry too," she replies awkwardly.

We sit together in silent thought for another few seconds.

"You could go home? I could help you?" I offer her genuinely.

She refuses, shaking her head in determination. "No, I can't go home. From what I've seen, Aubrun seems like a decent man, but Queen Siofra is a piece of work. She'll dig her claws into him, and even if Harmony is safe for now, it won't be for long."

"You're right," I answer back. "It's why I intend to take her down. Her and all of the lords who lined their pockets after *The Culling*."

A smirk crosses her lips, and she nods her head in approval. "Now I see it."

"See what?" I ask curiously.

"Why the Moon Goddess paired you and Conall together."

I try to smile in return, but I can't. The pain of losing him is still too raw.

"Then we will help each other?" I ask, putting my hand out to hers.

She looks at it momentarily before firmly placing her hand in mine. "Yes. I'll help you. What do we need to do?"

"We have to find a link between Siofra and Lord Faenor. Their testimony forced Ciridan to use the enchantment that killed the wolves. If we can prove they did it together, we can expose them."

Cassendra thinks for a moment before standing up to pace the floor. "I overheard Siofra and Ciridan arguing before he died. She wanted him to

□

appoint Lord Faenor as king, but he refused. He said Faenor would be hard for her to control, so he chose Aubrun instead. I thought it was unusual at the time. Ciridan often obeyed Siofra's demands, but he was insistent."

"Siofra would only suggest Faenor if it suited her," I reply. "Could they be more than allies?"

"Lovers?" Cassendra questions. "They could be. They seem pretty well acquainted with one another, but I've never seen any evidence."

"She's too smart for that. If they have been communicating under Ciridan's nose this whole time, we might find what we need in her chambers?"

"No, I've already been through her belongings," Cassendra answers in disappointment.

"But perhaps a little magic might help," I say, raising my eyebrow.

"Perhaps," Cassendra replies with a sly grin.

"Meet me back here tomorrow morning," I say confidently. "I have a plan."

Mistake

Aubrun

I stand there staring straight ahead out of the window in a deep trance. It's my first full day as king, yet I cannot focus on anything other than Eden. To place that ring on her finger last night meant the world to me, but despite her lack of protest, I could see indifference in her eyes. I haven't been able to think of anything else since.

When she arrived back here a few days ago, I cannot deny that the extent of her betrayal hurt. She was willing to sacrifice Elven lives for those of our mortal enemies. For those beasts that took Erix away from us along with so many other innocents.

When I first learned about the attack and the hidden pack in the mountains, my sense of duty told me that I should act immediately. Still, when I saw how fiercely she defended Harmony, I knew I could use it to my advantage. I knew I could use it to get closer to her in ways I never thought possible.

I look down at the book in my hands, the one I have spent the whole morning choosing from the royal library just for her. I never intended to *force* her into marriage, but once I had her in my grasp, I couldn't let the opportunity pass me by.

High elves and wood elves finally united as one.

The match is good for our kingdom and, dare I say it, good for us. If only she would open her heart to me. If only she would give me a chance, she would see that I genuinely care about her, and then maybe someday, she'll feel the same way. After all, love can blossom in mysterious ways. We could be happy if only she'd allow it.

The sound of footsteps from behind knocks me out of my daydream, and I turn around to see Haleth making his way into the room.

"Haleth."

"Good morning, Your Majesty," he says, bowing his head respectfully.

☐

I nod in return before our eyes meet. "I suppose you have questions for me?" I ask, feeling rather guilty about keeping him in the dark regarding the engagement.

"I do, Your Majesty," he replies, his face completely devoid of emotion.

I gesture for him to come forward, and he does so, stopping right in front of me.

"Your Majes—"

"Please, we are to be family very soon. Call me Aubrun," I say insistently.

He lets out a labored breath. "As you wish, Aubrun."

"Will Eden like this one?" I ask, holding up the book to show him. "She hasn't read it before, has she?"

"I do not believe so, but then, she has read so many," he answers.

I smile a little, memories of Eden lying in the grass over the years with her head in a book filtering through my mind. "Yes, that's true and—"

"Forgive me, Aubrun, but I have come here to discuss your engagement with my daughter. Not books."

It's unusual to hear Haleth use such a forceful tone. I set the book down on the table, nodding for him to proceed. "Go on...."

"I find this sudden engagement very unsettling. First, Eden arrives back here under the circumstances that she did, and now suddenly, she has agreed to be your wife."

"Yes, well—"

"I want to know why," he interrupts sternly with a protective edge to his voice.

I look into his eyes and can't help the shame that eats away at my insides.

How does one tell their father-in-law that they blackmailed his daughter into an engagement?

There's no way that he would understand.

"You need not worry about her, Haleth. I care about Eden more than anyone. Believe me. Our marriage alliance will bring the kingdom together."

"Your alliance will put her in danger!" he snaps insistently, his jaw tightening.

My brows scrunch in confusion. "There is no safer place for her than in this palace with me—the King of Morween. Would you rather she was still with them? With the wolves?"

He shakes his head. "Of course I don't, but Aubrun, you are young. You are new to this and have not yet learned the ways of royal politics. I told you that you must become your own man, and so far, I see you falling into the trap of letting others around you dictate your actions."

"Are you talking about Queen Siofra?" I question. "Because I've told Eden already, and I will tell you too. She wants nothing but the best for us."

"That woman cares about her own interests alone. She is ruthless, and you would do well to remember that," Haleth replies sternly.

My eyes narrow. "Do you care to elaborate further, Haleth? As king, I refuse to condemn a person on hearsay alone."

He swallows before looking down at the floor. "Many years ago, I created a powerful enchantment at King Ciridan's request."

"Yes, *The Culling* enchantment. You saved our kingdom, Haleth—"

"You do not know the whole story," he interjects in frustration, his body visibly tense and shaky.

I stop talking to let him continue.

"The enchantment was only supposed to take out the Alphas of each pack. Therefore, stopping the war in its tracks."

I stare at him in complete shock for a few moments. "What went wrong? You made a mistake with the potion?"

He then looks around the room, stepping closer to me to lower his voice.

"The enchantment *should* have worked as was planned. I used every ingredient that was needed. It was perfect. Or so I thought. After *The Culling*, my guilt was so overwhelming that I examined the enchantment myself. I then discovered that one of the ingredients used was substituted for another. When I checked the jars in my study, the nearly identical ingredients had been placed in the wrong jar. To put it plainly, a mistake was made."

I bring my hand up to swipe it over my face, the realization of what he is saying settling in. "Eden...she was your apprentice at the time," I say in understanding. "She must have accidentally put the ingredients in the wrong jar?"

He nods his head in reply. "Yes, and she can never know," he answers, tears pooling in his eyes. "It was my decision to work for the king. My decision to create the enchantment for him. I believed in him and Siofra and truly thought I was doing the right thing for the Elven people. This is *my* fault. However, knowing this information would tear Eden apart."

"Then why are you telling me?" I whisper carefully. "Haleth, why tell anyone?"

"Because Siofra figured it out. She knows I do not make mistakes. After *The Culling*, I wanted to leave the kingdom far behind, but she threatened to tell Eden everything unless I stayed—unless I continued in service to the crown. It was then my eyes were opened to the kind of woman she is, Aubrun. You must be careful around her."

The enormity of his admission leaves me speechless for a moment, and I walk away, taking a seat by the window.

"Do you believe Eden's claims? Do you believe Siofra and the lords set up the Elven attacks all those years ago?"

Haleth shrugs in return. "It's possible. I have been working on something myself, although I do not have conclusive proof yet. Eden is determined to find the evidence, Aubrun, and she is unwilling to be patient. If we do not protect her from herself, then I truly fear the worst."

I nod in understanding. "Thanks for coming to me with this. You have my word that this stays between us. I'll protect her."

He nods his head respectfully in return before turning to head for the door. The thought of Queen Siofra as some sort of villain does not sit well with me. She was my best friend's mother. Gentle and kind. Respectable and admirable.

My Queen.

I look down at the book on the table, placing my hand on it gently. Maybe Haleth is right. Perhaps I'm not ready for this. But one thing is for sure; I'm now part of the game, and I intend to learn how to play it well.

Proof

Eden

I pace the bedroom floor, anxiously waiting for her arrival.

Where the hell is she?!

It's then that the door opens, and Cassendra rushes inside. "Sorry, high-tea ran on longer than expected this morning. You may want to hazard a guess at the main topic of conversation?"

"Could it have been me by any chance?" I ask, folding my arms over my chest.

"You got it," she grins. "There were MANY opinions on your up-and-coming appointment as Queen of Morween, put it that way."

I rush over to the dressing table to open the drawer.

"Don't you want to know what they were saying?" she asks curiously.

"I couldn't give a shit, Cassendra," I shrug, still rummaging around for what I need.

She scoffs. "I'm starting to like you, elf. You can call me Cass, by the way."

I turn around and nod. "Cass...if we pull this off today, we can get rid of Siofra and her harem of phonies for good. It won't matter what any of them think."

"You really think Aubrun will listen to us?"

"If we find the proof we need, then yes. I'm sure I can bring him to our side," I answer, opening the little pot of clear gloop to dab it on my cut brow and bruised neck.

Cass watches over my shoulder as the bruising miraculously disappears. "Wow...."

"It's just temporary," I answer hurriedly. "It won't last long, so we must do this as fast as possible."

She nods, dropping a little bag onto the bed before pulling out a dress exactly like the one she is wearing. "Here. Is this okay?"

"Yes, help me into it," I order, slipping out of my gown to step into her

□

dress instead.

She buttons it up the back, and I grab the brown plant from the table, holding it in my hand as I take one of her hands in mine.

"Uh, am I about to see something freaky?" she asks, wriggling her fingers in my tight grip.

I don't respond to her question. Instead, I close my eyes and focus on the energy rushing through my veins, letting it soar into every part of my body. A few seconds pass, and then I hear her gasp in a mixture of shock and awe.

"What the fuck?! This is too creepy," she says as I open my eyes to meet hers.

I turn around to look in the mirror, and we stand beside each other, identical in every way.

"I need you to keep Siofra away from her chambers while I look around. Can you do it?"

"It's taken care of. A friend of mine in the kitchens owes me a favor. I'll tell Siofra the kitchen staff need her input. She loves nothing more than going down there to boss them all around anyway," Cass answers in disgust.

"Good. As soon as she's on the move, then I need you to blow into this. I'll go to the chamber to start the search once the coast is clear."

She raises her brow immediately. "A whistle, Eden?"

I can't help but smirk in reply. "It's enchanted. Don't worry; only I can hear it."

"Really?"

"It's silly, I know, but my father made it for me when I was a child living in Azealea. When I heard it, I knew it was time to come home for supper," I answer, the fond memory allowing a brief smile to touch my lips, if only for a second.

She smiles in return, placing it safely inside the pocket of her dress. "Good luck out there," she says, lifting her hand to squeeze my forearm.

"You too," I reply, watching as she makes her way out of the room.

I begin to pace the floor again, waiting for the signal. It takes a few minutes, but then I hear the familiar light ring echoing through the corridors.

Here goes!

I begin to navigate my way to the royal quarters of the palace. On the way, some servants offer me a smile, and I smile back, trying to imitate Cass' mannerisms in any way I can. Eventually, I reach the large doors of the royal chambers, and I nod at each guard in turn.

"Back again, Cassendra?" one of them asks curiously.

"Queen Siofra forgot her shawl," I answer confidently.

He nods, leaning over to open the door for me. I smile at him sweetly in thanks before entering the empty throne room. I cast my eyes over it, ensuring no one is around before I make my way to Siofra's chambers. Just as I reach the door, it opens, and Aubrun steps out in front of me.

I freeze on the spot, my heart pausing in my chest.

"Ahh, Cassendra, have you seen Queen Siofra?" he asks, a determined look etched on his face.

"No, Your Majesty," I reply, bowing respectfully.

"Okay. I'll find her later, but I'm glad I ran into you. Can you do something for me?"

"Of course, Your Majesty," I answer dutifully.

He leads the way down the corridor, and I look back at Siofra's door in frustration before following after him.

"I'd like you to have this chamber made up for Eden Nestoriel," he says, opening the door to a huge, beautifully decorated room. "It's right next to mine, and I wish to keep her close now."

I look around, trying my best to keep my expression neutral. "I will take care of it immediately, Your Majesty."

"Thanks," he answers, holding out a book toward me. "Could you leave this on the table for her? And make sure you put some fresh pink Lillydrops by the bed. They are her favorite, if I recall."

I stare back at him for a second before bowing once again. "As you wish, Your Majesty."

He exits the room, and I stand there, looking down at the book in my hands. "Oh, Aubrun..." I murmur, walking over to set the book down on the table.

I don't have time to dwell on my new living situation, so instead, I rush back to the door to press my ear against it. I hear the throne room doors opening and Aubrun's voice disappearing as he greets the guards. I leave the room, making a beeline for Siofra's chamber. It's large in size, and everything is perfectly placed. Something tells me that the woman probably knows the exact location of every item, and I will have to be careful to leave it exactly as I found it.

I make my way over to the center of the room, pulling the potion I made this morning from the pocket of my dress. I carefully cup one of my hands, pouring a tiny amount of gold dust onto my palm. Then, I close my eyes, holding both hands out in front of me.

"Reveal your secrets," I whisper into the silence.

Nothing happens, so I try again, clearing my mind of all thoughts.

"*Reveal*...your secrets."

Slowly, I feel the gold dust rise from my palm, and I open my eyes to see it morph into a bright orb gleaming in front of me. I stand completely still, not even daring to blink as it hovers in place. It then begins to float, drifting around the room at a painstakingly slow pace.

Suddenly, I hear the familiar whistle sound in my head.

"Come on. Come on, please," I whisper, willing the orb to move quicker.

It ignores my pleas completely, taking its time as it dances and pirouettes gracefully in the air. My heart begins to beat faster, my eyes glancing at the doorway intermittently. "Please!" I beg, my voice tinged with desperation.

Finally, it stops directly above the bottom corner of the bed. I rush over to the spot, dropping to my knees to look underneath, but I see nothing. I feel around the edge of the bed frame with my fingertips and freeze when they meet a small ridge in the wood.

This has *got* to be it! Her hiding place.

I try to open the little compartment, but the damn thing won't budge. I look back to the doorway and hear Siofra's voice from the corridor outside ordering a guard to fetch her horse for riding.

Shit!

After pulling the sharp pin out of my hair, I jam it in the small crevice, using it as a lever to pry the secret compartment open. Thankfully, it gives way, and I bend to take a closer look at the pile of letters and envelopes stuffed inside. I grab them quickly before closing the compartment and fixing the bedspread back in place.

"And have Cassendra take my blue jeweled gown to the seamstress for alteration," Siofra orders from the other side of the door. "She's in the kitchens at the moment."

"The kitchens, Your Majesty?"

"Yes, you fool! Isn't that what I just said?" Siofra snaps back angrily.

"Of course, Your Majesty."

I rush for the balcony, passing through the archway before her bedroom door swings open. I push my back against the stone wall, peeking around the edge to see Siofra waltz into the center of the room. She then sits at her dressing table, picking up a hairbrush to begin fixing her appearance.

I spot the gold orb still floating by the edge of the bed. Its gleaming light is dull but still glowing.

Fuck, fuck, fuck!

I lean back on the wall, concentrating as best I can.

"*Cease*," I whisper under my breath, as quietly as possible.

I pray to the Goddess that it has worked, peeking around the doorway once again to see that it has. I breathe a sigh of relief, looking down at the letters in my hands before stuffing them down my corset.

I tiptoe to the balcony's edge to see the empty gardens below. Swinging one leg over, I carefully lower myself, dangling by my fingertips for a few nervous moments before letting go. My feet hit the ground with a gentle thud, and I race under the balcony to take cover, standing completely still as my eyes drift to the sound of footsteps above.

It's Siofra.

I wait patiently surveys the gardens, her footsteps then retracing themselves as she enters her bedroom again. Closing my eyes, I place my hand over my racing heart. It's done. Now I have to find out if I found anything useful. I take another cautious look around before returning to the palace, heading for my bedroom as fast as I can.

* * *

I slam the door, closing my eyes to let the spell around me drop. I unzip Cass' dress as I move across the room, snatching a handful of papers from the bodice to toss them on the bed. The dress falls to the floor, and I quickly get changed into my own clothes.

"Oh, my Goddess, Eden! I'm sorry! I couldn't stall her any longer!" Cass declares worriedly as she enters the bedroom.

"It's okay... I think we got something," I answer hopefully, gesturing to the bed before picking up her spare dress to stuff it back in her bag.

Her eyes widen as she looks down upon the fruits of my labor. "The magic worked?!"

"I hope so!" I reply as we both look into each other's eyes.

Slowly, she reaches down for the first piece of parchment, which is tied around the middle with a thin piece of red twine. I watch anxiously as she opens it, casting her eyes over it in silence.

"Well?" I ask impatiently. "What does it say?"

Her shoulders slump in disappointment. "Absolutely nothing."

"What? No! You can't be serious?" I protest.

"Take a look for yourself," she offers, collapsing dramatically on the bed before tossing the piece of paper down in front of me.

I immediately pick it up to examine the blank parchment closely. Then I pick up another, unraveling it to reveal exactly the same thing.

This doesn't make any damn sense! Why the hell would she hide blank pieces of parchment?

Then it hits me... She wouldn't.

"What are we going to do now?" Cass groans.

"These are what we have been looking for!" I announce adamantly. "The ink...it's invisible. It's pretty common. You can even buy it in the market in Morween."

"How do we read it?" Cass asks excitedly, snatching the blank parchment out of my hands.

"That's just the thing; only the intended recipient can," I smile.

"And you know a spell to overcome this?" she questions with a raised brow. "Is that why you are grinning like an idiot?"

"No, I can't. But I know someone who can. My—"

Suddenly, the door rattles, and I hear my father's voice on the other side. "Eden? Eden, are you in there?"

"Shit! Hide!" I whisper to Cass, who quickly picks up her bag and runs to the window to cocoon herself in the thick drapes.

I stuff the pieces of parchment under my pillow, tucking them in frantically as the door knocks again.

"Coming, Father," I yell, straightening myself out before opening the door.

It's then that I almost collapse at the sight in front of me.

"GRANDMA?!"

Rat

Zeke

"Zeke, you've been gone hours. Rocco is going crazy. He called a meeting. Says you can't avoid the subject any longer," Anton explains quietly as he approaches.

"Why doesn't that fucking surprise me?" I mutter in response.

"Did you see Con? How is he?"

"Alive and kicking," I answer with a grin.

"Thank Goddess for that. So the old elf woman fixed him up?"

"I mean, he's not exactly fighting fit. He looks like shit," I reply honestly. "But he'll live."

"What did he say about what Mateo told you?" he then asks, a look of concern on his face.

"He says we have to try to find the rat. We know now that it's not Eden."

"How the fuck are we going to do that, Zeke? There's no way Rocco will own up to it."

"Con doesn't think it's Rocco, nor do I."

His face scrunches in confusion. "Are you serious? You saw what he was like the other night. He couldn't wait to kill Con off."

"Yeah, but the betrayal doesn't make sense. There's something else going on. I know there is."

We begin to make our way back to the den.

"So what's the plan then?" Anton questions seriously.

We stop at the front door, and I look around cautiously again. "Well, if we indeed have a rat, then we make him think we are onto him. Sooner or later, he will out himself. Preferably sooner. We don't have a lot of time."

"What do you mean?"

"It's Eden... Con and Citrine seem to think she might have made some kind of deal with the elves to protect Harmony. She could be in danger. Citrine is going to Morween tomorrow to find out. We need to sort this whole mess out, and we have to do it fast."

"Shit," he growls, nodding his head in agreement. "Set the fucking trap."

I give him one last look before opening the door to the living room. Immediately, the noise decreases, and I notice the men gathered around the table, waiting.

"And where the fuck have you been?" Rocco demands with a sneer.

"Getting what we need to keep this place protected. Is that alright with you?" I snap back, making my way to the head of the table.

"Ahhh, so it's like that, is it?" he asks before looking around the table. "You see? Just as secretive and sneaky as his predecessor."

"Don't speak about Conall like that. You've got a fucking nerve," Hunter interjects, pointing his finger at Rocco accusingly.

Rocco only snickers in return. "Feeling guilty there, Hunter? Didn't see you defending your almighty leader when Zeke knifed him in the back—"

"Shut the fuck up!" Hunter shouts in return, bouncing up from his chair.

"Enough," I order authoritatively. "All of you."

Everyone continues to argue amongst themselves, and I sit down, lifting my hand to my aching forehead.

How the hell did Conall deal with these assholes for years?

It's been two days, and I'm already fucking demented!

"Can we get on with the meeting?" Jarek interjects, gesturing toward me before pushing his glasses up his nose. "Zeke's waiting."

I rub my hand over my face, pulling myself up straight. "Okay, Rocco, you have my attention. What is so important that it can't wait?"

His jaw tightens, and his shoulders grow rigid. "It's about time we talk about leadership and who will take Conall's place."

"Is this a joke?" Henrick asks with a raised brow. "Zeke was the second-in-command."

"I don't care if he was the fucking King of Werewolves! The code states that if the leader is executed, a new leader will then be voted in to take his place and—"

"Fuck the code," Mateo grumbles quietly, shaking his head in irritation as he leans back in his chair.

"Really?" Samuel responds with narrowed eyes. "Are you still salty about the elf bitch? You do realize she was never going to fuck you, right? She was too busy with Con's cock in her mouth."

Mateo springs up out of his chair, and Samuel does the same, both facing up to each other across the table as they are pulled back by the others around them. The noise escalates, and I know it will reach boiling point quickly if I don't calm the situation.

"Goddess above," I mutter under my breath before standing up and leaning my fists on the table. "SIT DOWN! BOTH OF YOU!"

It takes a few seconds, but eventually, both take their seats, staring at each other in disdain.

"You want a vote, Rocco?" I ask confidently. "I'll give you a vote. All those in favor of my appointment as leader, raise your hand." Instantly, the majority of the table lifts their arms in the air in solidarity. "Happy?" I ask smugly.

His nostrils flare as his face turns red in sheer anger.

"And if you want to challenge that vote...you know what to do, but we all know you're too chicken-shit to try it. You never could pluck up the courage to go against Con."

"Maybe you'll be a different story," he snarls.

"Then I'll be waiting," I hit back, staring into his eyes without fear.

Silence falls over the table, and my eyes flick over to connect with Anton's.

"Now that's settled. There's something more important we need to talk about. I have reason to believe that Harmony could be in danger."

"WHAT? Did the elf know about Harmony too?!" Samuel questions in a rage.

"I'm not talking about Eden," I snap back, looking around at their stunned faces. "The elves have information. Information that came from within these walls."

"What does that mean, Zeke? Does this have anything to do with where you have been all night?" Evan asks in confusion.

"We have the right to know," William states as others nod in agreement.

"I'm not saying a word until I get to the bottom of this shit, but I do know that someone in this room talked," I say carefully, lifting my finger to move it slowly around the table. "And mark my fucking words, I'm closing in, and the asshole who did this will get what's coming to him."

No one says a word. Instead, they all look around uncomfortably before I turn around and head upstairs. Leaving the rat to stew for a little bit longer.

* * *

I wait by the edge of the window in Eden's room. My eyes are stinging in my head, and my body is aching all over. I haven't been able to sleep since the night of the attack. Stabbing Con in the back was one of the hardest things I've ever had to do, but I knew at the time that it was the only option to keep him alive. Thank Goddess, I got the placement of the knife right. To be honest, I wasn't sure I had when I saw his body fall into the grass. The whole experience made me think back to what happened with Con and Lincoln all those years ago. I knew at the time what was going on, but talking about it is not something Con would ever do.

Not with me, anyway.

That's why I was happy for him when he found Eden. Sure, it took me a while to get used to the elf thing, but I pride myself on being a good judge of character. Most of the time, anyway.

My eyes close as I reflect on tonight's conversation and how the men reacted to my revelation. I looked each one of them in the eye individually, and I still couldn't pick out the rat. Even Rocco seemed completely shocked.

I bring my hand up to my face, pinching the bridge of my nose before rubbing my eyes. Then I hear it. The quiet click of the door downstairs followed by the creak of the steps on the front porch. My eyes snap open, and I peek around the edge of the thick drapes at the scene below. I see the figure of one of the men, his identity concealed by the pitch-black evening. The figure stops at the bottom of the steps as he looks around, swinging a bag over his back before heading toward the tree line.

Not on my fucking watch. You traitorous bastard!

I head for the door, making my way downstairs as quietly and quickly as possible. I peer out the downstairs window to see the figure disappearing into the trees.

Opening the door, I take off in a run, my heart pounding as I examine the darkness around me. Whoever it is, I can't underestimate him. If he was willing to betray us all and let Con die, then he may be willing to kill me to escape.

I burst through the trees, coming to a stop when I see nothing up ahead but empty forest. I listen carefully. Only the sound of my own rapid breathing fills the air around me. Suddenly a twig snaps to my left, and I take off again, rushing through the trees as I ready myself to shift if need be.

Then I see him, his hooded figure looking over his shoulder before he flees like the coward he is. He's fast. As all of us are. But there's no way on this damn earth that I'll let him slip through my fingers.

No fucking way!

I'm closing in, my speed and determination now putting me within touching distance of the rat. "IT'S OVER!" I growl angrily, throwing my body forward to slam against his, bringing him to the ground. "IT'S OVER! YOU FUCKING COWARD!"

We grapple on the ground as I take hold of his cloak by the neck, lifting him to slam him against the thick trunk of a tree. It's then I rip the hood down, my wolf itching to tear his fucking head off where he stands.

My eyes widen as I take in his face. "Jarek!"

I stand there with my hands around his neck, my breathing erratic and wild as my brain struggles to comprehend the sight before me. "What the fuck?!"

His pupils dilate in fear, and he lifts his hands in surrender. "Zeke... Zeke, I'm sorry. Please."

I shove him into the tree trunk, stepping back to try catch my breath.

He takes a step forward, his facial expression pleading and desperate. "Please, just hear me out. I—"

"Hear you out?" I snarl, burning venom coursing through my veins. "You're the leak! You're a traitor!"

Without thought, I lunge forward, slamming my fist into his face, knocking his glasses onto the forest floor. I grab him once again, hauling him upright to continue my attack. "You told the elves about the attack! About Harmony! You let the men believe Eden was the traitor! You let Con fucking die!"

"No, Zeke. I didn't!" he protests adamantly. "I can explain everything."

My wild eyes stare into his. I want nothing more than to strangle him to death, but I need answers.

I *need* to understand.

"You have one minute," I seethe, letting go of him reluctantly.

He swallows hard, lifting his hand to his throat.

"SPEAK!!" I roar into the silence, causing him to jump slightly.

"Zeke. I never meant to let Con and Eden take the fall the night the attack went awry. Trust me. When I woke up and heard what happened, I was horrified. It made me feel damn sick."

It's then that it hits me. Jarek was injured on the night of the attack before the ambush even began. When Con was "executed," he was still out of it, unconscious due to his injuries.

"If I had been there, Zeke, I would have told them everything. I would have taken Con's place, I swear it. I wouldn't have let him die for my mistake."

"Mistake?" I bark, still practicing restraint the best I can manage right now.

"Mistake," he nods in reply. "Zeke, I didn't tell the elves about Harmony and the planned attack, but I did tell someone outside the den," he admits, guilt pouring out of him in bucket loads. "Everything that happened the night of the attack... I think it was all my fault."

Letters

Eden

"What are you doing here?" I ask, clasping my hand over my mouth in shock as I look over the small frame of my grandmother.

She laughs, opening out her arms. "Can't a grandmother visit her granddaughter because she has missed her terribly?"

I smile, embracing her tightly in my arms. Her familiar scent immediately calms my racing heart. Her healing energy brings me some semblance of peace for the first time in what feels like forever. "I'm so happy you're here!"

"Oh my dear...me too," she answers, patting my hair.

I lean back to look into her eyes. "Both of us know that isn't true," I laugh, raising my brow. As far as I'm aware, my grandmother hasn't stepped foot in Morween for at least one hundred years.

She grins, awkwardly glancing at my father, who clears his throat. As strange as it is for me to see Grandma here in Morween, I know it must be even more shocking for him. Since *The Culling*, their relationship has been strained. The fact that he chose to live here over Azealea has never sat well with my grandparents, and as a result, they don't see each other often. Apart from a few awkward visits to Azealea to present birthday gifts, I can count their encounters with each other on my fingers.

"So, can we come in?" my father asks expectantly.

I look over my shoulder, ensuring that Cass is still hidden out of sight. "Uh, sure. Sorry, come in," I say with a smile, gesturing for them both to enter.

"Grandma, I'm so sorry I haven't had a chance to visit. I've just been so busy," I begin, offering her a seat on my bed.

"So I've heard," she comments, her brows rising.

"You heard about the kidnap?" I ask, an edge of guilt lacing my words.

"Yes, I did," she replies, throwing an accusing look at my father. "The news traveled to the village a couple of days ago."

"As I said, Mother. Iriel and I decided it was best not to worry you," my father explains defensively. "Everything was being done to recover Eden."

"She is my granddaughter. It's my job to be worried," she responds calmly yet firmly.

He nods his head in recognition. "Of course."

I look between them both, the tension in the room making the tiny hairs on my arms stand on end.

"Grandma, I don't want you to fight over this. Really, I'm okay."

She smiles gently, resting her hand on mine. "Better than okay, I hear. You're engaged? To the King of Moween no less! You must be so thrilled, my dear?" she questions, her knowing eyes breaking my barrier down without any difficulty whatsoever.

I look down briefly before plastering a smile on my face. "I am. Thank you."

It's then she turns to my father. "Haleth, would you mind if I spent some time with my Eden alone? I'm sure we have much to catch up on."

He nods, but I can see the reluctance in his eyes. Perhaps he's worried I'll tell her how much I know about *The Culling* or how I've been on the side of the wolves this whole time.

"Please, send for me if you need anything."

He leaves the room, and my grandma and I silently look at each other.

"Who's your friend?" she asks, a sly grin upon her mischievous face.

"What? Who do you—?"

"The person behind the drapes," she interrupts, amused.

I let out a breath and shake my head. I should have known I couldn't hide a thing from Grandma.

"Cass, you can come out."

Cass steps out from behind the curtain to examine my grandmother critically.

"It's okay; we can trust her."

"Oh, can you now?" my grandma laughs, turning her attention to Cass. "Hello there."

Cass nods warily, looking at me for my next move.

"Grandma, I'm so sorry to have to bring you into all this, but there's so much I have to say. You were right that the wolves are not our enemies. There's so much I have to share with you about the war times, about the king and queen and *The Culling*—"

"I know," she interrupts calmly, patting my hand again.

"You know?" I question, my brows creasing.

"Yes," she answers, smiling at Cass and I. "Eden, my dear, you know I always suspected foul play in the palace. I was never on board with *The Culling* or what happened to the wolves. So...a long time ago, I did something about it."

"I don't understand, Grandma. What did you do?"

"I helped them the best way I knew how."

My mouth drops open in shock, but as I stare back into her bright eyes, I realize I should have seen it all along.

"It was you. You've been protecting them. Protecting the den and protecting Harmony."

She nods her head, a gentle smile crossing her lips.

Tears spring to my eyes, and I hug her tightly, my gaze meeting Cass' as she lifts her hand to her mouth.

"Goddess, thank you. Thank you so damn much!" Cass states in admiration.

"Oh, come on now. It was nothing," Grandma replies kindly. "I just wish I could have done more."

"Maybe you can," I add eagerly, springing up from the bed to snatch the parchments from under my pillow. "Cass and I have been working on taking Siofra down from the inside. I found these today in her chambers."

"Eden..." she begins, a hint of worry in her voice.

"Don't worry! We were discreet. I promise," I say quickly, handing her the papers. "Grandma, these letters have proof of what we need. I'm sure of it. Queen Siofra has been communicating with Lord Faenor using invisible ink. I know that you have the spell to break the enchantment."

She nods carefully as she gathers the loose parchments into a neat pile. "And you wish me to reveal the information these hold?"

"Yes. We need you to do this. It's the only way."

"What do you plan on doing with the information once you have it?"

"I'll take it to Aubrun," I say confidently. "He's the only one with the power to confront her. He can make her pay for her crimes."

"And you trust the new king...your husband-to-be?"

I gulp carefully, realizing that she knows something is wrong.

"Grandma, it's true that he blackmailed me into this engagement. I said yes to save Harmony. But...I know him. He won't ignore this. I'm sure of it."

She looks down at the blank parchment and nods, stuffing them inside her cloak. "If you are sure, my dear, consider it done."

I smile, looking to Cass, who closes her eyes in relief.

"So when can you have the letters ready?"

"Oh, I don't see why I shouldn't have them ready for tonight."

I begin pacing the floor as I try to figure out a plan. "It might be hard for me to get to Azealea to collect them. There are lots of guards stationed around that part of the forest."

"What about Kelna cliffs? In your grandfather and I's special place. Do you remember it?" she asks.

"Of course I do!"

"Then I'll send a trusted messenger with the letters to meet you."

"No, grandma. We can't trust anyone."

"Perhaps here in Morween, my dear, but your old grandma is not easily tricked."

I nod, deciding that if she trusts my judgment, I should trust hers in return.

"You should take the back path out of the palace before sunset. It will be safer," she adds adamantly. "Do you have a means of getting out of here undetected?"

My eyes drift back to Cass, who rolls hers in amusement. "I guess you'll still be needing this then?" she asks, holding out the bag containing her spare dress.

"Thanks, Cass."

"Anyway, I better get going before Siofra notices I'm gone."

"Oh, that's right," I say hurriedly, my brain kicking into action. "A guard is looking for you to take Siofra's gown to the seamstress, and Aubrun asked "you" to make up the chambers by his room."

"For you?" she asks in slight horror.

"Unfortunately, yes," I reply with a shrug.

"Got it."

She nods at us both in turn before heading for the door, closing it behind her.

"Hmmm, lovely girl," my Grandma says, looking back at me. "So...now that she is gone, how are you?"

The familiar crushing pain returns to my chest, but no matter how much I want to talk, I just can't. For my mission to succeed, I must remain focused and clear. Thoughts of Conall right now will only break me, and that's something I cannot allow. "I'm fine, Grandma," I mumble unconvincingly.

Just then, the door knocks, and my father reappears. "I'm just wondering if you would both like some tea. Iriel says she can arrange—"

"Oh, that won't be necessary, Haleth," Grandma interrupts, pushing herself onto her feet as I put my hand out for support. "Our Eden here is very busy. I don't wish to keep her any longer, however, I do hope to see her very soon for a visit," she says, turning to look at me knowingly.

I smile back in return. "I wouldn't miss it."

She then takes my father's arm, and I watch as he leads her out of the room and down the corridor.

I stand there watching for a few moments with newfound hope in my heart. Tonight, I may very well have what I need in my hands, and the prospect is the only thing keeping me sane in this crazy situation.

I am about to head back into my bedroom when suddenly, the sound of a loud cackle echoes through the corridor.

The sound makes me freeze on the spot.

I recognize that laugh. I'd recognize its shrill, high-pitched tone anywhere.

I close the door, stalking through the corridors as I follow the sound to the floor below. I stop as the door to Aubrun's study is thrown open, pressing my back against the wall to hide from sight.

"Thank you very much, Your Majesty. I'm happy to hear that you will be upholding your end of the bargain, and I look forward to visiting the royal palace very soon with the best I can offer. I can promise your high lords and noblemen will *not* be disappointed."

"Thank you, Madam Piffnel. Until then," Aubrun replies swiftly, his voice detached and seemingly uninterested. "Now, please, let my man here escort you quickly. I'm sure you understand the need for discretion."

"Certainly, Your Majesty! Discretion is my middle name!" she screeches with another loud, obnoxious cackle.

My blood immediately begins to boil when I realize what is happening.

Fucking Madam Piffnel!!

Madam Piffnel is the leak!!

The study door closes, and I peek around the wall to see the ridiculous woman being led away by the guard.

I know I shouldn't, but I can't help myself from following behind them, being careful to stay hidden from sight. He leads her through the palace and eventually stops at the back entrance, where deliveries for the kitchens are usually made.

"Please wait here. I will retrieve your horse."

"But of course, darling," she smiles in approval.

As soon as the guard is out of sight, I storm forward in her direction, my body shaking from a mix of pure, unfiltered rage and adrenaline.

"You sly bitch!" I yell, grabbing her from behind to throw her up against the stone wall.

Her eyes widen in shock as she lifts her hands to pry my arm away from her chest. "Get off me at once! Get off me, or I will scream this palace down!"

I shove her against the wall again, stepping back, my fists balling. "You conniving...evil...sneaky—"

"Oh, for heaven's sake, stop there, elf," she tuts, pulling a compact from her purse to fix her makeup.

"It was you! You went to Aubrun and told him about the den! About the attack! About Harmony! Why?" I snarl angrily.

She snaps the compact closed. "It wasn't personal," she shrugs. "You see, my girls and I work hard to make a living. I *adore* the Alphas. Believe me, I do. But business is business. I saw the opportunity for my girls to have all of this again," she says, gesturing all around her. "I only want the best for my girls!"

"Rubbish! You wanted the banishment lifted so you could use your girls to line your pockets!" I spit back.

"Is it my fault that Elven lords pay the best money? This is an opportunity that could not be missed! Besides, I'm wondering why you are so upset about this. From what I hear, you are now hailed as the hero of Morween. The king's apparent infatuation with you has earned you a royal title, and your little wolf pack in the mountains is protected."

"Until you decide to tell someone else!"

"Why would I do that?" she chuckles. "I have what I want now. A contract for my girls to work here and more suitable accommodations for myself. I do not require anything else, my girl."

My eyes narrow. "How did you even know about the attack? Not one of those Alphas would have told you a damn thing."

"Oh, sweet child, you underestimate the power a woman has over a man," she says, taking a step forward. "My girls are not only trained in the art of seduction. They are not thoughtless airheads, as some men may believe. They are more than capable of enticing a man into sharing his deepest secrets."

My brows knit together.

"It didn't take much for one of my girls to convince an Alpha that she had fallen for him. After that, he was dying to impress her with his accomplishments."

I gulp as I listen to her explanation. The leak was accidental. That makes the whole thing even more heartbreaking.

"That's disgusting," I utter, looking her in the eyes.

"Oh, come on. She didn't force him to do anything he didn't want to. Just gave him some light persuasion!"

"And what about me? What did you tell Aubrun about me?" I ask, my jaw tightening.

"I saw you that night at the den. Did you and Alpha Conall really believe the little stunt with Rose and the necklace would work?" she asks in disbelief. "As soon as I saw the necklace around Rose's neck, I knew the silly girl had been used somehow. Alpha Conall barely shows interest in my girls, let alone gifts them with jewelry. No...as soon as I questioned Rose and she told me what happened, I knew why he did what he did. He loves you," she states matter-of-factly. "And if he loves you, then I do believe you know all his secrets."

"Well, you'd be wrong because he's dead," I answer scathingly, a lump forming in my throat. "And you're part of the reason why."

"I am indeed sad to hear that."

"Shut up!" I snap, the rage inside slowly taking over me.

I take a threatening step forward.

"What are you doing?"

I see the shock cover her face as she begins to back away from me. "Giving you *exactly* what you deserve."

Suddenly, the sound of a horse's neigh cuts through the air, its hooves approaching the archway.

"That would be my horse," she announces, her shrill voice hiding her fear. "Good day to you, Eden."

I grit my teeth in hatred, however, I can do nothing but watch her leave.

Soon, it will almost be time for me to make my way to the cliffs to meet Grandma's messenger, and something tells me this day is yet to yield even more damn surprises...

Reunion

Eden

I pull my hood down, shaking out my stolen brunette locks until they return to my own shade of soft lilac.

I can't help it when a small smile touches my lips. The sight up ahead unlocks the most meaningful of childhood memories.

In the distance, on the edge of the stunning Kelna cliffs, are the ruins of an old Elven temple. The very one, my grandparents, were married in hundreds of years ago.

Sure, I've never seen the building in all its former glory, but even the ruins themselves are beautiful. The large towering archways that remain to overlook the cliffs are like windows to an exciting new world. A world with magical skies and formidable seas.

I walk through the grass, looking around in awe as I move. The sky this evening is painted with swirling orange and purple. The colors becoming more pigmented around the sun that is slowly beginning to edge its way down behind the horizon. The breeze feels warm but gentle on my skin as I breathe in the salty air, watching the birds overhead circle and swoop before heading out over the ocean.

Soon, I arrive at the ruins and step through the archway, letting my fingers graze against the rough stone. Grandpa Erwin used to tell the story best. When I was a child, he and Grandma would take me here, and after we collected supplies for her enchantments, he would sit me down and tell me about the moment he stood by the altar of this old temple, waiting nervously for his beautiful bride. He said the moment she appeared through the archway was something he would remember for the rest of his life.

I walk forward to the edge of the cliff, the gentle wind capturing my hair, the last remnants of the bright sunlight bouncing off my face, and for the first time since this nightmare began, I start to think about the future—about the rest of my life.

When Siofra has been defeated, what's next for me?

It may be time to move on from here altogether. To start fresh, someplace where no one knows my name. Where no one has ever heard of Morween or Azealea.

Don't get me wrong, I love my family dearly, but the palace hasn't felt like home since Erix died, and the thought of living in Azealea so close to where I lost Conall causes my chest to ache.

I let out a breath and close my eyes, conjuring up his image in front of me. As an elf, I know I will probably live for many years, but no matter how much time I spend on this earth, I never want to forget his face or what he gave up for me.

"I miss you," I whisper into the wind, a tear rolling down my cheek. "I swear... I'll never forget you. Never."

I lift my hand to swipe my tears away, folding my arms over my chest as the ocean waves gently lap against the shoreline below.

I then turn to look back toward the trees, waiting nervously for the arrival of Grandma's contact.

Will he have what I need?

I hope so because, beyond this night, I have no plans. No other avenues to go down. But no matter what, I will not stop. That I know for sure.

It's then, through the stone archway, I see a figure appear from the forest. The outline of a man.

My first thought is that this must be Grandma's messenger. However, something in the way he moves causes me to freeze. Causes my mind and body to become entranced as I watch him get closer.

I force my feet forward a little, my eyes transfixed on his body, watching every single movement, taking in every specific detail of his rugged form. The familiar slope of his broad shoulders, the air of power and strength in his imposing stature, and finally, the distinctive features of his handsome face.

I gasp, shaking my head in utter disbelief.

All coherent thoughts drift away, taking my sanity with them. I must be going crazy. Going out of my damn mind! It can't be him.

It just... It *can't* be!

My brain tries to cling to reality, but I've already lost the battle. I've been swept away in a sea of perfect, dreamy fiction. I give in to the tide, allowing it to sweep me up and engulf me entirely.

"Conall?" I whisper, my heart filling with rebellious, desperate hope.

I move forward, lifting my dress to break out into a run through the grand archway.

"CONALL?!"

I've never felt so unsure and yet so crystal clear in my whole life.

It is him!

He's alive!

My feet take me closer and closer, and then, for the first time, I see him clearly. The bright orange sun beating against his golden skin, making his honey eyes shine.

"CON!" I scream, watching as his face contorts into a beaming smile.

He begins to run in my direction, and my brain scrambles to catch up with my rapid pace. My hair whips in the wind, and my chest rises and falls under the weight of my heavy breath.

And then, on the edge of the Kelna cliffs, our bodies collide together as one. I leap into his outstretched arms, slamming against his hard chest with so much force that it brings us both down to our knees.

My arms wrap around his strong neck, refusing to let go as I frantically breathe in his comforting scent.

It's him!! It's him!!

I break down in his arms, tears now streaming down my face as his warmth surrounds me. His energy washes over me; his love overwhelms me as he showers the side of my face in intense, powerful kisses. Finally, he buries his head in the crook of my neck, holding on to me tightly.

We stay like this in perfect bliss until I lean back, holding his face between my trembling hands. My eyes find his immediately, and my brain finally accepts the impossible.

"It's you!! It's really you!!" I sob, looking over him in a complete state of wonder. "I don't understand! You're alive!"

His large hands cover mine.

"It's me. I'm here," he whispers reassuringly, his eyes flicking to my lips. "Eden, I love you. I love you so damn much."

I don't have a chance to respond because, within a split second, his lips are on mine, moving in sweet, perfect motion with my own. I fall into his kiss like it's the air I need to breathe. I hold onto his shoulders, griping the strong muscles as one of his arms wraps around my waist, pulling me closer. His other hand tangles in my hair at the back of my head, holding me in place.

We cannot get any closer, and yet we still try. Our bodies push against one another, our lips unwilling to part, desperate to make up for lost time.

Eventually, he pulls away, his intense kisses now moving downward, landing on my face and down my neck. My head dips backward, my eyes opening to the painted sky as his tingling, healing touch begins bringing back together the pieces of my broken soul.

It's him! My mate has come back to me!

His hands reach for mine, and our fingers intertwine, his grip remaining strong and powerful while his kisses grow slow and tender.

Then he stops. His head bowed to lean against my chest.

I listen for a moment to the sound of his breathing. A sound I thought I would never hear again.

"I'm so sorry, Eden," he says quietly.

I look down, placing my hand under his chin, returning his gaze to mine.

"How?" I ask carefully. "I- I thought you were gone."

"I thought I was too," he replies, a slight weary grin touching the edge of his lips. "But that Grandma of yours had other ideas."

I can't help but laugh, tears filling my eyes again as I shake my head from side to side.

"What happened?" I ask, trying and failing to come up with some kind of explanation for all of this.

"It's a long story," he answers, touching my cheek softly. "I promise I'll tell you everything, but not right now. Right now, I just want to look at you."

I smile softly, leaning further into his touch. The rough pad of his thumb rubs over my skin, making its way down to my lips to trace over them lightly.

Not once do his eyes leave my face. I've never felt so calm and so at peace. Every thought, every worry disappears as though we have been transported to another world entirely. One where Siofra and Morween do not exist.

Only he and I.

Together.

"You're so beautiful," he says quietly, an edge of pain in his voice. "How could I have doubted you? How could I believe—?"

"It doesn't matter. None of it matters now you're here," I reply honestly from the bottom of my heart, my eyes pleading with his. "Conall, about what happened the night of the attack...."

☐

"Shhh," he interrupts gently. "I'm not ready for this to end yet. Call it crazy or selfish, but I don't care about anyone or anything else right now," he says decidedly. "Eden...all I want...all I *need*... is you."

His words melt me instantly. "Then take me," I whisper as he moves closer again.

Our eyes connect, and then he kisses me fiercely, igniting the flames of pure burning desire just like that. He lays me down beneath him in the grass, his body covering mine as his intoxicating touch does things to me that no one else ever could. In between kisses, we stop to look at one another in both love and awe. It seems neither of us can't quite believe we are here.

If this is a dream, then I know that I never want to wake up.

"Goddess, how I've missed this face," he says quietly. His strong hand holds my chin for a second, his thumb tracing the outline of my jaw tenderly before his hand moves down over my breasts. "How I've missed this body," he rasps, his darkening eyes looking down as he slowly loosens the laces of my bodice.

He throws it open to reveal the soft white chiffon material underneath. His hand immediately grasps my breast, and I moan in pleasure and delight, arching my back and pushing myself into his touch.

His head dips to my neck, kissing downward before he tugs the soft material to the side. His tongue flicks against my nipple, swirling in delicious motions as his hands push my breasts together, kneading them lustfully. I can sense his desire increasing as our love for one another manifests physically.

His touch grows rough and desperate. The beast that I have come to love and require so much resurfaces, ready to join us, and I moan in appreciation, his presence unlocking a deep yearning and hunger that only he can satisfy. Unlocking the passion that has been missing since we last were in each other's arms.

"Oh, Con," I moan, feeling my core tighten, my panties beginning to soak with my arousal.

He kneels up, eyes scanning over my bare, reddened breasts in approval before removing his shirt.

Immediately, my eyes find the bandage around his waist, but I don't question it. Instead, I focus my attention back on his striking face.

"Tell me..." I say, with a naughty smile, my body now burning under the surface. "What else have you missed?"

A slow, sexy grin touches his lips, and he lowers himself down to lie beside me, leaning on one arm. "You really want to know?" he asks, his low, deep voice turning me on even more.

I bite the corner of my lip, my head falling to the side to nod in reply. My dress begins to pull upward as his hand moves up my leg, stretching out over my shivering skin as it moves. His touch grows firmer as he reaches the top of my thigh. Then his hand moves across my panties, entering inside to let his finger slide down my aching, wet pussy.

Oh my...

"I suppose you think I'll say I missed this the most. That I miss its addictive taste or how it feels to have it wrapped around me."

His finger finds the small pulsating bud, and my mouth drops open, my brows knitting together as he holds my gaze prisoner.

"But what I've missed most are your eyes," he continues quietly, looking into mine deeply.

His body moves in closer as his finger circles in a thrilling rhythm.

My hips begin to buck ever so gently against him.

"These eyes give me everything I need," he whispers, watching me. "They show me how much you enjoy my touch...."

I nod in ardent agreement, my desperation for him building with each skilled stroke of his hand.

"They show me what you truly desire...."

I moan loudly as his finger enters me, my eyes flickering as pleasure racks every nerve in my body.

"Open them, Eden," he orders, causing my eyes to snap open again.

His body then smothers mine in an instant. He grabs my panties, pulling them down quickly as I frantically tug at the edge of his pants. The sight of his hard cock makes my eyes widen in anticipation; at this moment, there is nothing I want more, and he knows it.

His fingers meet my wet core again, and another incoherent, spontaneous moan bursts from my lips. My teeth then clench as he brings me closer and closer to the brink, but I'm not ready yet. Not until I have it all. Not until I have all of him

His face moves closer to mine, and we stare at each other intensely.

"These eyes...these eyes show me how much you want me," he growls, that raw animal quality now present in his guttural tone as he readies himself to ravage me.

☐

I stop him in his tracks, my hands reaching for his face. "Then let them also show you how much I love you, Con," I say breathlessly. "Because I love you so damn much it hurts."

He stares back at me for a second.

Speechless and still.

And then, he loses all control, gripping my waist as he pushes inside me.

"YES!!" I call out on instinct, the full, satisfying feeling taking hold of me immediately.

I throw my arms over my head, and he lifts his hands to capture mine, pressing them into the cool earth.

I lift my head to look down and see his cock sliding in and out of me.

"Connn...!" I moan just before his lips find mine.

His tongue invades my mouth desperately, and I welcome his vigor, kissing him back with every fiber of energy and love I have to give.

His hands leave mine, one resting on my cheek while the other moves over my body, touching me in all the right places, driving me wild.

His pace gets a little faster, his thrusts becoming more determined and intense. His nose grazes mine as we stare into each other's eyes.

The connection I feel with him right now is beyond words or explanation.

I begin to spiral under him, and he gets faster again, sensing my all-consuming need to come, reading my mind and body like an open book.

Goddess, how does he do this to me?

Before long, the dizzying combination of his tenderness and powerful strength culminates in an explosive orgasm that hits me like a wave of immense pleasure.

I call out his name, but the sound gets lost, swallowed by him as he kisses me passionately.

I struggle to breathe.

To think.

I only feel.

I throw my head back in delirious relief, and eventually, his pace relents, allowing me to float back down to earth to reclaim my useless limbs.

"Are you okay?" he whispers breathlessly.

"More than you know," I murmur, a wondrous smile appearing on my face.

I press my hands against his chest, and he allows me to guide him back. I flip over on top of him in one smooth motion, straddling his lap as I waste no time grinding on him.

His hands grip my waist, his chest tightens, and the muscles in his thick neck tense. My eyes settle on the crook of his neck, and I suddenly have the urge to kiss him on that very spot. I lunge forward, my lips pressing against his hot skin.

"Fucking hell," he groans, his hand wrapping around the back of my neck, holding me in place.

I feel his cock swell impossibly hard inside me before he grabs the back of my head, tilting me roughly to one side as his wild, hungry mouth finds the skin of my neck.

I move up and down his length, closing my eyes, growing more excited when I hear him groan in pure approval and satisfaction.

I've never heard him so vocal. So incredibly needy.

Knowing he wants me this much sends me soaring toward another orgasm faster than I can comprehend.

Then, I feel a sharp pain. His teeth grazing my sensitive skin. The pain, however, is overcome with overwhelming pleasure, and so I dare not move a muscle. I moan, stretching my neck to allow him greater access and permission to do what he wants with me.

But then he stops.

"Fuck!" he groans again loudly, a hint of frustration in his voice.

His hands move down to grip my waist hard as his head falls back to rest on the grass. He pats my ass in warning, but I don't move. I don't stop. I can't. "I love you, Con," I say quietly.

He looks at me through primal eyes, his hand reaching up to touch my face, bringing me closer. And with that, he explodes, taking me over the cliff edge with him.

I rock back and forth until the unbelievable feeling subsides. Then I fall on top of him, his arms wrapping around me, holding me protectively against his chest.

Where I belong.

Leader

Eden

"What are you smiling at?" I ask suspiciously, submerging my shoulders below the surface of the calm water.

"What? Can't I smile at my mate?" he asks, wrapping his arms around me to bring me closer.

"You can, but you don't do it that often," I shrug in jest.

His brows raise, and he snickers. "Goddess, you make me sound like a hard bastard. Am I really that bad?"

"Did that little dance with death make you forget that you took me prisoner and forced me to be your house slave for weeks?" I hit back with a chuckle.

"You know...one of these days, you'll probably have to get over that," he grins cheekily.

"Never," I laugh, wrapping my arms around his neck.

He lands a gentle kiss on the end of my nose before his head turns toward the horizon. "We are going to lose sunlight any second now," he says, his voice reflecting exactly how I feel.

I nod in reluctant agreement, leaning my head on his shoulder. "It's time for real life again, isn't it?" I ask, worry beginning to creep up on me all over again.

"Hey, we have each now. It's going to be okay."

"But it's not, Con," I reply adamantly, lifting my head to meet his gaze. "We need to end this. Once and for all. For Harmony."

His eyes flick over my face, and he smiles softly again. "You are incredible. Do you know that?"

"Sure, but it doesn't hurt to hear you say it," I laugh, jumping into his arms.

He grips my legs to carry me through the soft, lapping ocean waves back to shore.

"Are you sure you should be doing this?" I ask, my eyes flicking down to his injury again.

"You think a knife in the back is going to keep me down for long?" he asks jokingly in return.

Despite his jovial tone, I can sense the hint of anxiousness in his voice.

"Con, what's wrong?" I ask as he puts me down on the sand.

"Ahh, it's nothing," he answers, pulling his pants up over his wet thighs.

As soon as we got down here earlier, I made him tell me everything that happened the night of the attack. At first, I was angry with Zeke for taking such a gamble with Con's life, but now I realize if he hadn't taken that risk, then I would have lost Con for sure.

"Do you miss them? The other Alphas, I mean."

He looks at me in mild amusement. "Fuck, no."

"Then what is it because I know there's something?" I ask insistently.

The smile drains from his face, and he exhales in defeat. "I haven't been able to shift since it happened."

"Oh no, are you okay?"

He rests his hands on my upper arms gently. "Don't worry about me. I'll figure it out."

I nod, lifting the white underdress from the sand to throw it over my head.

"I'm more worried about you anyway," he states, reaching into his pocket to pull out three rolls of parchment paper.

My eyes widen. "Shit!! How could I forget?" I squeal, reaching out to snatch them.

He immediately lifts his hand further in the air, a serious look now covering his face. "Eden, where did you get these?"

"From Siofra's chambers."

"Fuck," he says on a sigh, shaking his head. "This is too dangerous. I'm putting a stop to this—"

"What?! You can't! We are too damn close, and Harmony's safety is still at stake!"

"Then I'll find another way, but I don't want you involved in this anymore," he answers firmly.

"Con, I'm already in deep, and I wouldn't have it any other way!"

"In deep? What else has been going on at the palace? What are you not telling me?" he questions, stepping forward.

Shit... I can already tell that Grandma hasn't told him the whole story about Aubrun. It's just like Grandma to allow us to work it out on our own.

□

"She didn't tell you?" I ask guiltily.

"Citrine? No. She said that you would explain."

"Uhh, okay. You might want to sit down," I murmur, folding my arms across my chest.

"Just tell me."

I swallow and nod my head. "Well...the night of the attack, I *was* being protected by Aubrun."

"Yeah?"

"But I had to promise to give him something in return."

His face grows hard. "What did he do to you, Eden? What deal did you make?"

"I- I promised him my hand in marriage."

Conall immediately growls in anger, stepping back to pace away from me.

"Con—"

"I'll kill him," he interrupts, shaking his head from side to side. "I'll fucking kill him. Did he lay a finger on you? Did he hurt you?"

"No, he didn't hurt me. I know his actions were wrong, but he's not a bad man. He's just... lost."

"Lost?!" he spits out, his face scrunching. "Eden, the man is trying to force you to be his wife! His damn queen! He's a fucking disgusting little runt, and if I ever come face-to-face with him, I won't hesitate to kill the bastard!"

"Con, I'm not letting him off the hook for what he has done, but when it comes to Harmony, I don't think he will attack. If he was going to, he would have done it already. It's not the type of person he is."

"So you were going to marry him? That's what you've been doing? Playing his damn wife-to-be?"

"Yes, I have! I did it for Harmony!" I answer sincerely. "I thought you were gone. Protecting Harmony was the only thing I had left."

He looks down at the sand for a second before his eyes return to mine.

"Harmony is not your responsibility, Eden. It's mine," he says firmly. "And the truth is... I let them down, and I let you down too."

"No," I say defiantly, taking his face in my hands. "Look at me, Con."

His eyes lift to meet mine. "We are in this together. I told you back at the den. Let me help because I can do this. You just have to believe in me. Can you do that?"

He swallows, nodding reluctantly.

"Now tell me, did Grandma find anything in the letters?" I ask, nerves and adrenaline churning in my gut.

"I don't want you putting yourself in danger anymore—"

"Con!" I plead. "Please, I need to know. Did she find anything?"

He then nods, his palm opening out to reveal the rolled parchments. "Oh, she found something alright."

I could cry tears of happiness right now I'm so damn elated. I grab one of the letters from his hand, throwing my ass down onto the sand to open it out hurriedly.

I begin scanning the swooping calligraphy, bypassing the vomit-inducing lovely-dovey drivel until I get to the good part—Lord Faenor telling Siofra that he has arranged another rogue wolf attack when they next meet. One that will finally force Ciridan to take action against the "filthy" wolves once and for all.

"This is it!" I say, looking to Conall as he sits down beside me. "This proves they planned the attacks together! That they paid the rogues!"

"Yeah, it doesn't stop there," he says, holding up another letter. "This one is dated just before Ciridan's death. Lord Faenor responds to Siofra's offer to have him finally installed as king. Of course, the asshole jumps at the chance."

He hands it to me, and I unravel it quickly.

"But this one..." he says, holding up the last letter triumphantly. "This one dates back to the days of the war. It discusses their plans to take over the werewolf territories and make the kingdom of Morween the biggest and most profitable in the realm. In it, Faenor asks Siofra if she has paid the rogue wolves yet. It even names a whole heap of other lords who got on board with their plan," he explains. "Eden, it confirms everything. It proves that they were in this together right from the beginning. That they staged the wolf attacks and killed their own people."

I let out a breath in sheer relief. "We did it! We found the proof!"

"No. *you* did it, Eden," he says, his lips tugging at the corner.

I wrap my arms around his neck, overcome with so much emotion.

"So what was the next stage of your master plan?" he asks interestedly as I pull back to roll the parchments up carefully.

"Well, now I have these, I'll take them to Aubrun and—"

"Eden, no."

"Con, listen. Aubrun is only loyal to Siofra because he is loyal to Morween.

☐

When he learns she killed innocent elves for her own gain, he won't rest until she is punished."

He looks at me intently, and I can tell he has his doubts. "He doesn't seem like a man with morals to me. I can't stomach the thought of sending you back in there with these," he says adamantly. "I'll take the letters to him."

"Con, you won't even make it through the door. He won't listen to you, but he *will* listen to me. Trust me on this," I insist. "I know what I'm doing, and I'll be careful."

"What about your father?"

"It has to come from me," I say with certainty.

He nods in defeat, looking out to the horizon as the last of the sunlight disappears, plunging us into darkness.

"Once I show Aubrun these, the whole Elven army will descend on Siofra, Faenor and the rest of their accomplices. They stand no chance at all."

"Then what?" he asks quickly.

"What do you mean?"

"What happens to your deal with Aubrun?"

"Once he and the whole of Moween know the truth, Harmony will pose no threat to him. I don't have to protect it anymore." I smile a little as I reach out to touch his face. "I'll come back to you, and we will finally be free."

"I'll drive myself fucking crazy just waiting for you to return, Eden. I can't."

"Then maybe there's something else you can do while you wait," I offer.

"What do you need me to do?" he asks reluctantly.

I take his hand and squeeze it in thanks; happy he can find it in himself to let me take the reins on this one. As a natural-born leader, I know how hard it must be for him to let me be the one making the moves.

"I found out this afternoon who leaked news of the attack and the existence of Harmony to Aubrun. It was Madam Piffnel."

"Madam Piffnel?" he asks, lifting his hand to swipe it over his face. "One of the men... They told a nymph, didn't they? Fell for her charms and spilled their guts?"

I nod my head sadly. "Yes. I don't know who, though."

"Fucking idiot... Zeke's on it right now. He'll come through and find out who it was," Conall answers in frustration.

"Maybe don't go too hard on whoever it was. After all, you also told me," I grin.

"That was different," he replies adamantly. "You are trustworthy."

"Conall...."

"Okay, fine. I'll take care of Madam Piffnel and the leak. I'll sort it out."

I smile gratefully before looking up at the night sky. "I really don't want to say this, but it's time I returned to the palace."

"I'll take you."

"It's too dangerous for you to come anywhere close. Don't worry about me," I say, picking up the blue servant's dress. "I'll be okay anyway. Thanks to Cassendra."

He grins guiltily, lifting his hand to rub the back of his neck. "Fuck... I probably should have warned you about Cass."

"Yes, you should have!" I scoff as he stands up to join me. "She almost killed me!"

His eyes widen in surprise. "She what!?"

"To be fair, she thought I was a traitor." I shrug. "Don't worry. We are all good now."

"Glad to hear it," he grins. "She's a good kid...look after her, won't you?"

"I will," I promise, lifting my arms to rest them around his neck. "We're almost there," I whisper. "Just a few more hours."

"I love you, Eden," he replies, looking back into my eyes.

"I love you too," I smile happily in return.

Demise

Eden

"Damn, you sleep like a mountain bear."

I roll over, opening one eye to look up at Cassendra.

"How did you get in here?" I question before yawning loudly. "The door is locked."

"It might be about time you put an enchantment on that thing," she answers, holding up her hairpin, which she then slides back in her hair.

My eyes widen a little in surprise. "You might be right."

"Well?" she asks eagerly, taking a seat on the edge of the bed. "What happened last night? Are you going to tell me, or must I kick your ass again?"

"You hardly kicked my ass," I hit back, raising my brow with a grin.

"You may want to tell that to your face," she chuckles, pointing to my eye.

"Shit," I mutter, tossing the sheets aside to head over to the dressing table.

I dab my bruised eye and neck with the clear gloop while she waits impatiently.

"Edennnnn," she groans, her head tilting to the side. "Come on! Put me out of my misery!"

"We got her,"

"We did?!"

"Take a look for yourself," I say, nodding my head toward my pillow.

She tosses it out of the way, practically pouncing on the parchments to scan them over one by one.

"Oh, my Goddess! We got the bitch!"

"Yep!" I grin. "What's more is the messenger who delivered the letters was just...well, he was everything."

Her brow scrunches in disgust. "You elf women move on fast, huh?" she replies in a snarky tone.

"Stop it," I laugh, shaking my head. "It was Con."

"He's alive?!" she answers, bouncing onto her feet excitedly.

I nod, standing up to accept her tight hug.

"You have no idea how happy that makes me, Eden!"

"I think I'm still in shock," I answer, biting my lip as I think back to last night at Kelna Cliffs.

It was perfect in every way, except for the part when I had to leave him. However, knowing that Siofra will soon meet her downfall is a sweet consolation prize.

"So what now?" Cass asks hopefully.

"I'll get dressed and go straight to find Aubrun and—"

"Ahh," she interrupts awkwardly with a wince. "That might be a problem."

"Why?" I ask in confusion.

"Because I've been sent here to escort you to your new room for dressing."

"Dressing for what?" I question in irritation.

"Queen Siofra has decided to throw a last-minute engagement luncheon for you and Aubrun in the great hall this afternoon. Aubrun already accepted the invitation on your behalf."

"Shit," I groan under my breath. "Where is he now?"

"I'm not sure. In a meeting with the lords, I think."

I let out a puff of air and nod reluctantly. "Fine,"

It's then that it hits me that this celebration may be a blessing in disguise. All the lords here in the palace, under one roof, will make it easier for them to be intercepted by the Elven guard in front of a palace full of high elves.

"Why do you have that look on your face?" Cass asks suspiciously, interrupting my thoughts.

"Because we can take advantage of this, Cass," I say, gripping her shoulders. "All I need is time to speak to Aubrun beforehand. Then it's sure to be Siofra's most eventful ball yet!"

* * *

"Did you find him?" I ask Cass eagerly as she steps into my new chambers.

"Yes. He's on his way! What do you need me to do?"

"Nothing, just stay on alert. I'll take care of the rest."

She nods her head and readies herself to leave. "And Cassendra..." I say before she turns to look at me. "...thank you."

"It's been a pleasure," she smirks, winking at me playfully before opening the door to leave.

I pace back and forth, reviewing my speech again in my head. It took me hours last night to think of the right words. After all, how do you tell a king that his mentor is a lying, murderous traitor, and you have the evidence to prove it?

Around the third hour, I realized that to speak with the old Aubrun, the man I know and trust, I have to talk to him as I always have done. Honestly. As his friend.

The door knocks, and I take a deep breath, straightening out my dress as I prepare to lay it all out on the table. "Come in!"

I wait in anticipation as the door opens to reveal Aubrun behind it. He smiles at me warmly, and I smile in return, my eyes drifting down over his cream and gold tunic, the material identical to that of my dress.

"Wow, we are going for the matching look this afternoon," he says, a hint of nerves in his voice.

"It looks like it," I chuckle.

"Cassendra told me you were looking for me. Do you like your new chambers?"

I follow his line of sight, scanning over the bed draped in light pink and cream silk, overlooked by a grand, golden headboard that stretches up to the high ceilings. "It's beautiful," I answer honestly, taking a step forward. "But Aubrun, I must speak with you about something incredibly urgent and important."

He lifts his hand, moving forward until he stands directly before me. "Please let me go first, Eden," he says insistently, looking down over my face. "I know this isn't perhaps what you wanted from the beginning. Being queen or being with me." A flicker of vulnerability flashes in his eyes before he continues. "But I will prove to you that I would do anything to make you happy. Anything." he finishes, a hopeful smile then crossing his lips.

A slight edge of guilt stabs at my gut, but I know I can't let it distract me. "Aubrun," I begin, swallowing a little in preparation. "Just to hear you say that means so much to me. Truly."

The smile drains from his face. "But?"

"There's something I have to show you, and it's not going to be easy, but I want you to know that I trust you with this," I say honestly, lifting my hands to rest them on his shoulders. "You are a *good* man. You always have been, and I believe you'll be a great king too. I need you to remember that I'm here for you as your friend and always will be."

His eyes run over my face before they flick up to connect with mine. "What is it, Eden?"

I turn away from him to walk over to the desk by the window, opening the small wooden box as he watches over my shoulder. "It's empty," he says in confusion.

I wave my hand over the box and whisper the old Elven word, channeling my power skilfully.

"*Advenor.*"

He gasps when the parchments appear in front of us, sitting neatly inside. "What are they?" he asks, taking them from me as I hand them over tentatively.

"They are proof that Siofra, Lord Faenor and others paid rogue wolves to attack Elven villages," I say gently, looking into his wide eyes. "They are written in Siofra's hand and marked with her seal. You can read them for yourself."

He swallows carefully, nodding his head in slight shock as he takes a seat at the desk. I wait by his side as patiently as possible, watching over him as he reads the details of her treachery. All the while, I consider what his reaction might be.

Will he be upset? Devastated even, by her betrayal?

Eventually, he drops the last letter onto the table, placing his face into his hands. "How could I have been blind?" he murmurs in quiet frustration.

"We were all tricked," I say sincerely, kneeling to take his hands in mine.

"Not you! And not Haleth either!"

My brows scrunch in confusion, but I don't have time to question him further about my father.

"Who else knows about these letters?" he asks quickly, his eyes meeting mine.

I shake my head, deciding that bringing Con, Grandma or Cass into the equation right now would help no one. "Only you and I," I lie.

"Good," he replies, glancing at them again as his hands ball into fists.

He falls into silence, and I immediately begin to grow nervous. "Aubrun—"

□

"So that's why I was chosen. Ciridan thought I was weak enough to control, and Siofra…well, she didn't even want me as king in the first place," he snarls, hurt permeating his words. "She wanted Faenor so they could continue whatever disgusting antics they have been up to for all these years!"

"Well, yes, but they both made a mistake because they underestimated you," I say, sensing his need for reassurance.

"You're damn right they did." he rages, abruptly standing up from his chair. "I'm going to confront her. Tell her I know exactly what she's been up to."

"You *can* do that in time," I reply firmly. "But we should remain cautious. She's dangerous, Aubrun. First, we should show these letters to the leaders of the Guard and have them prepare to arrest her and the others."

"No," he answers angrily, shaking his head. "I want to see the look in her eyes when I tell her she's caught. When I tell her that this so-called weakling is going to bring her and Faenor down once and for all!"

It's then he takes off, marching for the door.

"Shit," I mutter, stuffing the parchments back in the box and reactivating the spell as quickly as possible. "Aubrun, wait!"

I rush off after him as he stalks through the throne room determinedly and through the large doors into the palace corridors.

Of all the reactions I expected him to have, I must admit this one has taken me completely by surprise. He's utterly furious and ready to take action, but I know that fury is not an emotion that will yield results in this instance.

"You have to calm down!" I implore, catching up with him to match his strides. "We must come at this tactically. Listen to me!"

"I need answers, Eden."

"And you'll get them. But think about this rationally for a second."

He ignores me completely, continuing until we reach the grand hall, which is filled with people. He stops to look down into my eyes, and I plead with him silently as the crowd claps politely in our direction.

"His Majesty, King Aubrun and Miss Eden Nestoriel!" the royal announcer booms loudly.

Aubrun takes my hand in his, and I try my best to smile calmly as we enter together. The music begins to play, and my eyes flick over the room, decorated in cream and gold to match our outfits.

"There you both are," Siofra smiles, walking over to us, champagne in hand. "Aren't you both a sight for sore eyes?"

She leans in to offer Aubrun a kiss on the cheek, and I watch nervously for his reaction. His jaw clenches, but he doesn't say a word.

Siofra looks over him with suspicion, and I know already that she can sense something is wrong. However, before anything can be said, a group of high elf lords and their ladies surround us in a swarm, greeting us with fake smiles to mask their distaste.

"Aren't they just a beautiful couple?" Siofra asks with a wide disingenuous grin.

The rest of the group practically fall over themselves to agree with her, reaching out to shake our hands and offer their congratulations. "Quick, someone fetch our new king and soon-to-be-queen a drink!"

Then, a servant appears with a tray filled with champagne flutes. Aubrun takes a drink, and I follow suit before tugging discretely on his hand. "Could I speak with you a moment, Your Majesty?" I whisper, looking into his eyes. If I can just get him alone again, we can discuss this carefully, as I had hoped.

He stares back at me for a moment before nodding. "Of course. Siofra, would you mind joining us? Eden and I are eager to thank you personally for all of this," he says politely, gesturing to the general splendor around us.

"Actually, Your Majesty—"

"Eden," he interrupts, looking at me sternly.

Fuck. I can see he is not going to change his mind. I take another drink of champagne before placing the glass on a nearby table.

"Oh my, of course!" Siofra chuckles, smiling at the other lords and ladies. "No need for thanks, though. I do live to serve the Kingdom of Morween!"

She gestures through the doorway. "Let's go to the parlor, shall we?"

Aubrun nods, and I glance at him sideways, trying to communicate with my eyes.

I understand his want to confront her. To get answers from the mentor he trusted implicitly, but he's going about this all wrong! I half consider making a run for the stage to announce Siofra's guilt to the world myself, but I doubt I'd be taken seriously. Aubrun has to be the one to lay down the orders. To bring the guards up to speed before Siofra and the lords have a chance to react.

Thankfully, Aubrun seems to take my warning glances on board, and as we pass by the door, he stops to order two of his guards to accompany us.

We walk silently the short distance to the parlor room, and Siofra opens the door to allow us to walk through first.

"Wait here," Aubrun orders the guards quietly.

They do as he asks, standing to attention outside the room.

"Is everything alright?" Siofra asks innocently as Aubrun closes the door.

He lets go of my hand and walks toward her. "No, it's not," he answers plainly.

Siofra smiles sinisterly, her eyes flicking to me. "Perhaps you'd care to explain further if you can manage it, *Your Majesty*."

It's not hard to detect the sarcasm in her voice. She's gone from sucking up his ass to mocking him outright to his damn face.

"Siofra, you have been exposed. Evidence has been found that proves your involvement in war crimes seventy years ago. You will be tried and sentenced with your accomplices under the full weight of Elven law," Aubrun explains in anger. "I do not fancy your chances of survival, Queen Siofra, when the Elven people hear of your disgusting treason."

Siofra only looks back at him, mildly entertained by his outburst. "Wow...what a speech, Your Majesty," she begins, walking over to stand in front of the fireplace. "Perhaps I did underestimate you," she says, turning her head and raising her brow as she looks over him critically. "But then again, here you are. Dear simple-minded Ciridan was right about one thing. You are very predictable and very emotional. Just as he was really."

Aubrun takes a deep breath. "That's all you have to say? You have no defense to make? No explanation to give?" he snarls, narrowing his eyes. "Don't you think you owe me answers?!"

"Oh no, how can I defend myself?" she replies. "After all, my letters were perhaps a little too well-detailed. It is my fault for keeping hold of them for all these years. Call it sentimentality!" she laughs, her eyes then drifting to me.

My brows scrunch in confusion. She knows we have the letters, and she's far too calm. "Aubrun, call the guards. She up to some—"

Suddenly, I gasp as my body begins to shake violently all over.

"You really are a clever little wood elf," Siofra says, walking over to me. "I may not have even noticed the missing letters had I not randomly checked on them today. I assume you must have stolen them this morning after your move to the royal quarters of the palace? It was silly of me not to consider you capable of such a stunt."

I lift my hands to my neck in a panic, trying my best and failing to fill my lungs with the air I need to breathe.

"Eden!" Aubrun calls out frantically, charging over to my side as I crumble onto my knees, my limbs growing more rigid by the second. "What the hell are you doing to her? Stop it now!" he demands, readying himself to call the guards. "HEL—"

"Oh, I wouldn't do that if I were you." Siofra laughs, shaking her head from side to side. "She has already ingested the poison. The first stage is paralysis, and then her organs will fail rather rapidly. Only I know how to stop it. If you call the guards, she'll be dead within mere minutes."

I can feel my brain giving up, black spots appearing in my vision as I fall helplessly back onto the floor.

"Please, stop this! What do you want?" Aubrun begs in dismay.

"I simply want my letters back, Your Majesty."

I immediately try to shake my head, my wide, bulging eyes looking up at Aubrun in an attempt to communicate my objection. There's no way she'll stop this. No way that she will let me live when he gives her what she wants. He cannot just give away the only piece of evidence that we have for nothing.

Aubrun stares at me in a mixture of pure panic and frustration before jumping up onto his feet. "I'll get them! Please just stop what you are doing!!"

"Call off your guards and get me what I need now," Siofra snaps back in return. "Oh, and Your Majesty... I would hurry."

Aubrun takes off in a rush, heading for the door before disappearing from sight.

My limbs have now frozen completely, and I lie there.

Helpless.

Siofra kneels to look down over me. "Awww. Poor little Eden," she says, her head tilting to one side. "It is a shame you put your faith in such a silly, predictable little boy. But never mind. He won't be around for much longer, and neither will you," she smiles wickedly. "Don't worry about the poison. It won't kill you, my dear, but it will serve a purpose. Two birds, one stone. It is one of my more clever ideas, I have to say. I do thrive under pressure!" She lifts her hand to push a strand of hair away from my face. "You know, I was not lying when I said I was impressed with you. I can see how you managed to dig your claws into Erix and then into Aubrun. Two attempts to become Queen of Morween is not to be sniffed at," she chuckles. "I understand the need for power more than you know. How it feels to come from nothing. We are more alike than you think."

It's then she puts her hand inside her bodice, pulling out a necklace. A necklace with a symbol that I recognize all too well.

"Us wood elves are not as stupid as they think we are, are we?" she whispers with an evil grin.

I want to shout and scream back at her, but as hard as I try, I cannot move a damn muscle. I'm a prisoner in my own body. Powerless to stop the disaster which is about to unfold before me. I can only watch on in horror as she tucks the necklace back inside her bodice.

At that moment, Aubrun reappears with the wooden box, handing it over to Siofra willingly. "The guards are gone, Siofra. Now give her the antidote. Stop whatever this is. NOW!!" he demands, his panic-stricken eyes looking down at me.

Siofra casually walks over to the table in the center of the room, examining the box as she moves. "Ahhhh, I see what this is. As I said, you are very clever, Miss Nestoriel," she says in amusement, opening the empty box. "I may not quite have the same powers or talents as your father, but I believe I can manage this."

She holds her hand over the box, closing her eyes.

"Advenor."

I watch in complete despair as she pulls the parchments from the box, her eyes flicking back to mine briefly. "Your Majesty, who else knows about these letters? Bear in mind I can tell when you are lying."

"No one. Eden told only me, and I came straight to you. No one knows." Aubrun replies assuredly. "You have to believe me!"

She examines him, and a smile covers her face. "Oh, I do," she chirps in satisfaction before she tosses the letters onto the raging fire. "Oops...would you look at that."

If I could cry, I would. But instead, I lie there as the pages curl and wilt before me in the burning, orange flames.

All hope is lost.

Justice will remain a distant dream, and it's all my fault.

Aubrun bends down at my side, holding my face in his hands as I slip into darkness.

"SIOFRA!! You have what you want; now stop this!! Stop it now!!"

The last thing I see before darkness takes me are his helpless eyes.

* * *

I gasp loudly for air, sitting bolt upright as my body and mind come back to
life in a thunderous burst.

What happened? Why the hell am I not dead?

It's then that I realize I'm holding something in my hand, and I look down,
my eyes bulging when I see what it is.

A blood-covered dagger.

I begin to breathe heavily, my heart pounding as I look down over my cream
gown, which is saturated in crimson red.

I yelp in horror, my reluctant eyes looking to my side where I see him.
Aubrun, lying on the marble floor, facing the other way.

I toss the dagger aside, scrambling onto my knees, crawling desperately to
his side. "Aubrun!" I sob, pulling his shoulder, causing his body to flop back.
"AUBRUN!"

I grip his face desperately with my blood-soaked hands, but I can already see
it's far too late.

His bright-blue eyes are wide open—lifeless as they stare back at me. His
body is cold and saturated in his own blood.

"NO!" I cry in utter despair, throwing myself down onto his chest. "I'm so
sorry, Aubrun! I'm so sorry!"

Suddenly, the door in the corner of the room flies open, and a small army of
guards rush inside to surround me.

"OH MY. THE KING. SOMEONE CHECK THE KING!" Siofra screams
in fake outrage and shock, clutching her chest in dismay.

I'm hauled backward, kicking and screaming like a mad woman, as Lord
Faenor waltz into the room to kneel by Aubrun's side. "I'm afraid he's gone!"
he announces loudly. "The king has been murdered!"

"NO! It wasn't me!" I scream as I am dragged away from Aubrun's body.
"THIS IS HER DOING! PLEASE, YOU MUST LISTEN TO ME! PLEASE
LISTEN TO ME!"

Not a single person answers my pleas, and instead, I am dragged by my arms
out of the room, looking over my shoulder to see Siofra smirk in triumph.

Finished

Conall

I flinch as I pull my fist back from the tree trunk, examining my bruised knuckles before landing another punch.

"What did that tree ever do to you?" Zeke laughs on approach, folding his arms over his chest.

I'm too tense to laugh. Instead, I pick up the cloth from the grass and swipe it over my sweaty brow. "You going to joke around or help me train?"

He shrugs his shoulders, pulling off his shirt to discard it on the grass. We begin sparring, and I can tell my reactions are slower than usual but not entirely useless, which is somewhat of a comfort. After a while, Zeke stops to take a breath, and I have to say, I'm more than happy to take a break myself.

"You alright?" he asks, looking me up and down curiously. "Seems like you're working through some issues."

I run my fingers through my hair and shake my head. Honestly, I'm not in the mood to talk about it. Last night I decided to give Eden the final say on what to do with the letters. It fucking made me sick to my stomach to see her go back to that place, but at the same time, I know that I can't control her. She's a woman who makes her own decisions, and I can't be the one to take that away from her.

"How did it go down back at the den?" I ask, changing the subject.

"Oh, it went down alright," Zeke answers breathlessly, taking a seat on a fallen log.

"Well...who was it?" I ask impatiently. "Who was the rat?"

"Guess."

"Are you fucking serious, Zeke? Just tell me who the damn leak—"

"Alright, alright. Calm down," he snorts. "Nice to see you're back to your usual asshole self."

"Zeke...."

"It was Jarek," he then answers with a look of pure disappointment on his face. "But it's not for the reasons you might think. He—"

"Told one of the nymphs," I say, finishing the sentence for him.

His brows scrunch in confusion. "Yeah, how did you know?"

"Eden. She spoke with Madam Piffnel at the palace."

"Shit. Con listen, I know Jarek fucked us over. I realize that, but he didn't do it on purpose. He made a mistake." He sighs, rubbing his forehead. "He just got caught up in the thought of having someone. Some kind of connection."

I take a seat on the log, nodding my head in return. "I guess I can relate."

Zeke looks at me with relief in his eyes before grinning widely. "Don't get me wrong. I'm pissed at him, but I'm even more pissed there'll be no more nymph visits to the den from now on."

I can't help but snicker back. "I'm sure you'll survive. You dirty-minded bastard."

"Me?" he asks, raising his eyebrows. "So I'm assuming your reunion with your mate was all strictly business then?"

I shrug dismissively, and he laughs. "Yeah, that's what I thought."

"So what did you say to Jarek?" I ask curiously.

"Nothing yet. He tried to leave, but I took him back to the den. He's riddled with guilt over your so-called death, Con. I feel bad for the guy. I think if he was around that night, he would have owned up to what he did."

I lean my forearms on my knees, clasping my hands together. "Yeah, I think you're probably right."

"Anyway, where is Eden? Did you find out what's going on with her and Harmony?"

As soon as he asks the question, I can't help but picture Aubrun's little fucking weasel face. I've spent the whole night trying to avoid thinking about the asshole. Don't get me wrong, I understand why Eden has trust in him. She always tries to see the best in people. It's just the kind of person she is. Then there's the fact that she's known him for the better part of a century. However, she must also realize that even good people can do shady shit sometimes.

"Eden entered a marriage alliance with the new king in exchange for Harmony," I explain, my temper simmering beneath the surface.

"Shit," Zeke answers in shock. "That's...that's rough. Is she okay? Is she safe?" he questions, giving me a cautious look.

"She seems to think so, but I don't like it. She has evidence to take down Siofra—a bunch of letters admitting her guilt and part in *The Culling*. She'll probably be sharing them with the king any minute now."

"Wow," Zeke laughs, shaking his head from side to side. "That's amazing! She's not one for giving up, is she?"

"Doesn't look like it," I answer in irritation.

"Come on, don't try to pretend you don't love that feisty thing she has going on," Zeke grins. "You two might have fooled everyone else back at the den with all that enemies-to-lovers bullshit, but I knew you were into her straight from the beginning. All those intense stares and screaming matches... It was clearly foreplay."

"Fuck off, you liar." I scoff, sitting up straight.

"No, really! I could see you both together, and here is the reason why." he states adamantly. "Elf or not. She's a damn Luna, and you know it."

I can't deny that he's right. Eden is the most determined and impressive woman I've ever met. Outspoken and fierce in her protection of others, not to mention loyal with a heart of pure gold.

"You're right," I concede, offering him a slight smile. "She is."

He nods, standing up abruptly. "So where does that leave us? We should help in some kind of way, right?"

"I was thinking we could pay a visit to Madam Piffnel."

He smiles slyly in return. "Sounds good to me."

"Business," I say, raising my eyebrow at him as I stand up. "Keep your head in the game and your damn cock in your pants."

He holds his hands up in mock surrender. "Of course. Wouldn't have it any other way."

It's then I take a deep breath, looking around the forest. "There's just one problem."

"Oh yeah?"

"I can't shift."

"Can't shift?"

"That's what I said."

"Shit. Why is that?"

"I don't know exactly, Zeke, but it's most likely got something to do with literally getting stabbed in the back."

He snorts before glancing at Citrine's cottage. "Can't the old lady help you with your performance issues?"

"No, but she's looking into it. Also...performance issues?" I question threateningly as I begin to make my way back to the cottage.

"Listen, I'm sure once you've fully healed, your wolf will come back. It happens to a lot of guys, apparently. I mean...never *me*, but I hear it's common. Nothing to be ashamed of!" he calls out after me, clearly very impressed with his own joke.

* * *

"Is this the place?" I ask Zeke, looking over the shabby exterior of the Inn by the side of the mountain.

"Yeah," he answers, folding his arms over his chest.

At that moment, a drunk wood elf wanders out the front door, practically tumbling down every step to land in a pile of mud.

"It's charming, huh?" Zeke grins. "I guess it's no longer a mystery why Madam Piffnel seeks the great riches of the palace."

I step over the drunk man before making my way up to the front door.

"I just feel sorry for the nymphs. I mean, trading in sex with an Alpha wolf for a high elf is like trading a fucking sword for a... I don't know...a spoon?"

"Money is King," I reply, opening the creaky wooden door which leads into the noisy, rundown tavern. "These women are trying to make a living, Zeke."

"I guess," he mutters as we both look around.

Fiddles play out across the room, and joyful laughter and drunken voices fill the air. The man behind the bar stops cleaning glasses to glare at us. By the looks of him, he seems to be some sort of elf/goblin hybrid, but I can't be sure.

I give him a nod, and he nods in return, his expression remaining suspicious as he watches Zeke and I take a seat.

"Two of your finest ales, barkeep!" Zeke shouts loudly over the ruckus noise while I look around at the rest of the clientele. The place is peppered with passed-out drunkards amongst tables filled with slightly less drunk men who are being entertained by nymphs.

Then, we catch the attention of some familiar faces in the corner of the room. Within seconds, a swarm of scantily-clad women descend upon our table.

"Alpha Zeke, Alpha Conall, is that you? What are you doing here?" one of the nymphs squeaks, taking a seat on my knee eagerly.

"Where is your boss?" I ask, lifting my hand to remove her palm from my face.

She pouts, leaning forward to whisper in my ear. "Are you not here to play with us?"

"No," I reply firmly, guiding her off my lap. "We are here on business."

"Oh really?" one of the other nymphs giggles, nodding toward Zeke.

I look over to see him grinning like an idiot as two nymphs playfully nibble at his earlobes and kiss his chin. "What? I'm a very deprived red-blooded animal. Give me a break."

I throw him a stern glare, and he rolls his eyes, shooing the girls off of him. "Sorry, ladies. Not happening today."

I then spot Madam Piffnel descending the staircase in front of us, her eyes landing on our table before she turns to rush back upstairs.

"Let's go," I order determinedly, getting up from the chair to follow her.

"Where the hell do you two wolves think you're going?!" the goblin man yells, drawing a large sword out from under the bar. "No one goes upstairs without paying!"

"Zeke," I bark in command.

"On it!" he answers, grabbing the goblin's head to smash it on the bar counter.

The fiddles stop immediately, and everyone looks at each other in shock, but I'm too furious to give a shit. I take the stairs two at a time until I reach the top to find a long staircase with multiple rooms. A clatter rings out from the room at the end of the hallway, and I watch as a shadow flickers through the gap under the door.

I stalk forward angrily, grabbing hold of the doorknob to throw the door open. Immediately, a flying arrow from a crossbow comes whizzing at me, and I move out of its path.

"Ahhh. Fucking hell!" Zeke groans in pain, looking down at the arrow protruding from his shoulder. "Little heads up would have been nice, Con."

I shrug as he pulls the arrow out in frustration, tossing it to the floor.

Madam Piffnel fumbles with another arrow as I march over to snatch the weapon from her hand. "Are you fucking crazy?"

She begins whimpering in terror, slowly backing up against the wall with her hands up. "Gentlemen, please. We can sort this out."

"You think?!" Zeke asks sarcastically, pointing at his wound before covering it with his hand.

"I'm sorry. I- I panicked!" she answers hurriedly. "Alpha Conall, I thought you were—"

"Dead? No, no such luck Madam Piffnel," I reply coldly.

"Please, gentlemen. Forgive my mishap. How about I invite some of my girls to meet your needs today. Free of charge, of course?"

"Why don't you do that," I snap with narrowed eyes.

"Wait...what?" Zeke asks in confusion.

Madam Piffnel nods frantically, running over to the doorway. "Oh, girls!"

After a few seconds, the room fills with nymphs, most of whom I vaguely recognize from their presence at the den over the years.

"Girls, won't you see to—"

"Your girls aren't going to get you out of this one," I interrupt, taking her by surprise. I firmly grab her by the arm to sit her on a chair in the corner of the room. She gulps as I sit across from her, her eyes flicking to the women watching us silently. "I think you know why I'm here, Madam Piffnel."

"Alpha Conall. Please, you don't understand. I was forced to give up that information."

"DON'T LIE TO ME!" I yell, smacking my hand off the table as she jumps in fear. "You went after that information to sell it to the high elves. Don't dare deny it!"

"I did it for my girls!" she protests, her true sentiments completely transparent.

"You did it for yourself!" I snarl back.

She closes her lips as I stare her down.

"Where is the contract?"

"I don't know. Perhaps I—"

"Where is it, Madam Piffnel?" I question, standing up threateningly.

She stands in front of me, dusting off her gown before she walks over to a cabinet, opening it up with a key from her pocket. I take the parchment from her hands, opening it to look over its contents. Premises paid in full in Morween and exclusive rights to private palace functions.

□

"What are you going to do with it?" she asks worriedly, her eyes widening.

"Oh, you don't need to worry," I reply, glaring at her. "Because you are leaving here tonight."

"What? But I can't leave my girls! They need me."

"Do they?" I question, walking over to the women to hold up the contract. "It's all here, ladies. This new contract gives you only twenty percent of the profit made in Morween. Does that sound fair to you?"

They look at each other in uncertainty, whispering.

"I told you she would try to rip us off."

"She promised we would get more this time!"

"She told me I could work behind the bar."

"We can't let her do this to us again!"

"Whatever the woman says cannot be trusted," I explain, causing them to fall silent.

"Girls," Madam Piffnel begins. "Surely you do not believe him?!"

It's then a blonde-haired woman steps forward, her eyes steely and determined. "You've taken advantage of us for too long, and you're only getting worse! We won't have it anymore!" she yells as the other women nod in agreement.

"There you have it, Madam," I say triumphantly. "I'm sure they can manage in Morween without the likes of you."

"Without me?" she asks in shocked outrage. "You are very much mistaken, Alphas! You cannot do this!"

I take a step forward, looking her straight in the eye. "Madam Piffnel, you put my men in danger. You put the lives of innocent wolves in danger. I can do whatever the hell I want." I lift my hand to grab her neck aggressively, and her eyes bulge in fear. "Do not underestimate how far I will go for my people. If you don't leave here by nightfall or if you dare to step one foot in Morween again...I'll kill you. Do you understand?" I ask in a low, threatening tone.

"Yes, yes, I understand," she concedes, shaking in fear.

I nod at Zeke, who gives her an equally terrifying glare before we leave the room, making our way back downstairs.

As soon as we enter the tavern, the goblin who Zeke knocked out earlier takes a run at us.

"No, stop! Saldan. It's okay. They finally got rid of her," the blonde-haired nymph says, holding her hand up in front of him. "Madam Piffnel is to leave here immediately. Escort her out of here, will you?"

He narrows his eyes in our direction but nods obediently, heading for the staircase.

"You've wanted rid of her for a while I take it?" Zeke asks interestedly.

"Yes. Some of the girls were scared to go against her, so this has finally given them the push needed," she answers nervously. "Alpha Conall, I have something to say. It was I who told Madam Piffnel what Jarek said," she admits, tears clouding her eyes. "I didn't want to tell her! Honestly! I really did fall in love with Jarek, and I believe he loved me too. Madam Piffnel blackmailed me into giving her information. The women weren't getting paid until I came through and told her what she needed to know. Some of them were going hungry. I just...I had to protect them, but I know it was wrong. Please, if you must punish someone. Then let it be me. I won't put up a fight. The girls know nothing about Harmony, I swear."

Her head bows shamefully before I put my hand out to give her the contract. "Go to Morween with the rest of the women and take this with you, but give it a few days until things settle," I instruct.

She looks up at me through shocked, tear-filled eyes. "What?"

"Take it," I insist, handing it over. "Use it or don't, but you all at least have a choice. Don't make me regret this."

She takes the contract from me carefully. "Thank you. I'll look after them. I promise," she cries, smiling at me sadly.

I turn around to leave, and she grips my arm tightly. "I know I may ask for too much, but can you...can you tell Jarek I'm sorry? I'm so so sorry, truly. If he can find it in his heart to forgive me, then I'll be waiting."

I simply nod, heading for the door with Zeke following me.

"You think Piffnel will stay away from Morween?" he asks as we walk down the wooden stairs.

I look up at Madam Piffnel's window, listening to her shriek in terror as she is forcibly removed from the house. "No, she's finished. Without the women's support, she's got nothing. She won't step foot in Morween again."

"Even if she does, we will just set Eden on her. Right?"

"She'd enjoy that, I think." I snicker in reply. "Now, let's get back. I need to find out how she got on at the palace. Hopefully, this whole fucking mess is about to come to an end."

Ankorord

Conall

I run my hand through my hair, watching the sun disappear behind the trees. It's getting dark, and my worrying about Eden has reached new levels. If only I had marked her last night when I had the chance, then I would at least have some kind of indication that she's safe.

I wanted to.

Goddess knows I came so close, but I knew it wasn't the right time. I'm not even sure if she knows about the marking process in the first place, and I would never force that on her without speaking to her first.

But fuck—the urge to do it—the desire to finally make her mine was one of the most powerful feelings I've ever had in my life.

It's a fucking miracle that I was able to push past it.

As I approach Citrine's cottage, I notice multiple shadows crossing by the window, immediately putting me on edge.

I look around carefully, edging toward the kitchen window to look inside. I see Citrine and Erwin sitting at the wooden table with a lilac-haired woman. She seems to be crying, her head in her hands as Citrine gently pats her back.

Fuck, this isn't good.

I take off in a sprint, throwing the front door open to enter the small living room/kitchen.

"Where is she?" I question frantically as everyone turns to look at me.

The lilac-haired woman only begins to sob louder, and it's then I take in the features of her face.

She's Eden's mother. She has to be.

"And this would be Alpha Conall. The man I was telling you about," Citrine says, looking me over sympathetically.

"Citrine..." I say, taking a step forward. "Where the hell is Eden?"

Her sad eyes look over my shoulder, and I spin around to see Eden's father, Haleth Nestoriel, standing behind me.

We stare into each other's eyes for what feels like a damn lifetime. My wolf snarls inside my head, itching to rip the fucker to shreds. It's just as well he can't burst out right now, or I might lose control altogether. This is the man who brewed the potion responsible for the loss of all those innocent lives. Quite simply, none of this would have been possible without him. My jaw tenses, and my hands ball into fists.

"Where is she?" I growl aggressively.

He swallows, his head dropping slightly in submission. "Eden has been taken prisoner in Morween," he answers, his voice riddled with shame and guilt.

"FUCK!" I yell, barely clinging to my sanity. "I knew this would happen! I knew that weasel couldn't be trusted! He arrested her? That fucking COWARD!"

Citrine clears her throat gently. "No, Alpha Conall. I'm afraid it's worse than that. King Aubrun is dead, and Eden has been accused of his murder."

"What?" I ask in disbelief, looking back to Haleth. "He's dead?"

He nods in answer. "Yes, unfortunately."

"This is Siofra's doing," I bark, pacing the floor as I try to control my rage.

"Oh, there's no doubt about that," Haleth agrees sadly. "I do not know the full circumstances, of course, only what Cassendra was able to share with us before—"

"You spoke to Cass?" I interrupt. "Is she okay?"

"She's fine. They have no idea that she's involved," he answers reassuringly. "She found Iriel and I immediately after Eden's arrest and warned us that the guards were looking for us. She explained the plan Eden had with the letters they found."

"Where are the letters now?" I ask frantically.

"That I do not know, but I would guess Siofra has already intercepted or destroyed them if she has managed to create this situation to make it look like Eden murdered the King of Morween."

It's then, I snap, striding forward to grab him by the scruff of the neck and pin him to the stone wall. The others gasp in horror, but no one says a word. "You fucking let this happen to her! YOU LET THEM THROW HER IN A DAMN CELL?!" I yell in explosive anger.

I immediately see the guilt in his eyes and realize it is nothing but a reflection of my own. I am as much to blame for this as he is, and I cannot deny it. I should have gone with my gut instinct on this. I should have stopped her from going anywhere near that damn castle last night! Eden is clever and brave, but she's not a soldier. She hasn't seen war the way I have.

"I failed to protect my daughter. You're right," Haleth admits, ashamed. "This is all my fault."

I shove him against the wall taking a step back before I do something I might regret.

"So what now? What does this arrest mean?" I question Citrine.

She swallows, squeezing Eden's mother's hand. "Well, she will be tried. Perhaps even as early as tomorrow and...."

"AND?!"

"If she is found guilty, she will be sentenced to death."

My blood runs cold at the thought of losing her this way. I already know that I'll do anything to get to her. Anything to save her.

"We have to get her back," I snap, walking toward Citrine. "Surely there is some kind of enchantment you can do to get me inside the palace? The shapeshifter trick? Anything?"

She shakes her head. "Unfortunately not, Alpha. Inside the palace walls is a fortress; besides, you are a wolf. If you cannot use magic, I'm afraid those enchantments do not work for you."

I shake my head in frustration. "Then I'll have to get in the old fashion way—through the fucking entrance."

"And take on an army?" Haleth questions. "Even with your altered genes, it wouldn't be long before you are captured too. The Elven Guard is huge, and they will not make the same mistake they did at Ciridan's funeral."

"Eden is also being held in the dungeons with no visitors in or out. Siofra's personal guards are keeping watch. It's impossible to get in," Iriel sobs. "My poor girl. She must be so scared."

"I wouldn't worry too much, my dear," Citrine insists. "Eden is stronger than you know. She will cope. We just need to find a way to get her out and do it fast."

"Then what would you suggest?" I retort, looking between each of them for answers.

Haleth clears his throat a little before stepping forward. "We finish what Eden started and bring Morween the proof of Siofra's treason. Once they see it for themselves. Eden will be released, or at least her trial moved."

"How?" I ask through narrowed eyes. "If you say Siofra has already got rid of the letters, then we are back to square one!"

"Well, not entirely. I have always had my suspicions about Siofra and—"

"Really?" I question in disbelief. "I find that hard to believe. You wiped out an entire species at her command."

His head drops before he looks back up. "I only mean to say that I came to suspect her and Lord Faenor's involvement in the Elven attacks after the war had ended."

"You did?!" Iriel shrieks, aghast. "Why didn't you tell me? Why didn't we get out of there, Haleth?"

His eyes flick back to mine shiftily. "I had my reasons which are not important at the moment," he explains. "However, I did begin to do a little digging."

"What did you find?" Erwin asks curiously.

"Not much. Siofra and Faenor were always discreet in their interactions, but I could still detect their closeness. I think, on some level, Ciridan did too, but he didn't want to admit it to himself. He was so devoted to her," he explains. "I often observed the queen and Lord Faenor walking together outside in the palace gardens, and it struck me as unusual."

"So you tried to find out more?" Iriel asks for confirmation.

"I did, but I wasn't as successful as my daughter, put it that way," he says, a tinge of pride in his voice. "They were very careful in their interactions around the castle, but I tried to listen in on their conversations with the use of an enchantment."

"You used the Auddrubble charm," Citrine interjects.

Haleth nods. "Yes, mother."

"What's that?" I ask impatiently.

"It's a very complex charm. It forms a small glass ball, which, when left in earshot of a conversation, will pick up the sound of individual voices and store them inside."

"So you heard them? You heard them talk about their crimes?" I question, hopefully.

"Unfortunately, no. Many conversations yielded nothing at all, but one I captured a couple years ago stuck with me."

We all look at him silently, waiting for further explanation.

"In their conversation, Faenor states that Siofra should meet him at

Ankorord for their usual evening together."

"Ankorord?" Erwin asks in confusion. "Why would they meet there?"

"Possibly the chosen location of their lovers' trysts?" Citrine suggests, raising her brow. "After all, where is more secret than the abandoned ruins of an old civilization?"

"Ankorord... I've never heard of it," I state honestly.

"No, it is not a place anyone would choose to go." Citrine begins. "It is nestled in a deep valley and believed to be cursed."

"Cursed?"

"Many hundreds of years ago, the people of the city all came down with a mysterious illness. A plague that killed a large proportion of the population. Those who could, fled, and survivor accounts state that even nature had begun to die off in the once vivacious valley," she explains.

"Some believed the wrath of gods themselves was responsible for the city's demise. Legend has it the gods were unsatisfied with the level of greed, corruption and debauchery in the city," Haleth adds.

"Sounds like the perfect place for two snakes to meet then," Iriel comments angrily.

I nod my head in agreement. "Did you go to King Ciridan with this find?

He shakes his head in return. "No. He would have only asked Siofra directly, and I couldn't take that chance, so instead I went to check it out for myself."

Iriel gasps in shock. "Haleth! You went to that place! To Ankorord?!"

"My dear, do not worry; the myths about the city are just that. I observed the place from afar, and what I saw was enough to convince me that the old castle is, in fact, still in use."

"What did you see?" Erwin asks with wide eyes.

"I recognized some of Faenor's men standing guard."

"You didn't think to tell someone about this?" I ask scathingly.

"I wasn't sure who I could trust. Besides, I'm not entirely sure that there is anything there. I did not want to risk Siofra finding out about me snooping around."

"Are Faenor's men still guarding the place?" Citrine asks.

"I have no idea, but I do believe it's the only lead we have."

"If Siofra kept her letters from Faenor, perhaps he kept her letters too?" Iriel says hopefully. "The place has got to hold some secrets! Otherwise, why would he bother to guard it?!"

"Then we should check it out," I answer decisively. "But if we are going to go up against Faenor's men and win, then we need help," I say, looking to Citrine, who swiftly agrees.

"I will do what I can, although I think, Alpha Conall, it may be time for you to return to the Den of Alphas."

Homecoming

Eden

I throw my arms around my knees, taking in my disgusting surroundings once again from the cold dungeon floor.

How could I have been so stupid?

I should have known Siofra was capable of this.

Con was right; I should have thought of another way. I lift my hands to my head, stopping when I catch sight of the bright red blood that still stains my skin. I close my eyes and take a deep breath, unable to shake the image of Aubrun's lifeless face.

Poor Aubrun. He was a pawn in their game all along, and he didn't deserve this. It makes so much sense to me now why Siofra was so pleased with her plan. If she had killed Aubrun outright, then there would have been questions and suspicions. This way, she can take out Aubrun and me in one masterful act.

It's just as she said. Two birds, one stone.

I already know that her master plan is to have Faenor sworn in as king. It is no longer a matter of if but when.

Suddenly, a familiar sound hits my ears, and I jump up onto my feet.

It's coming from outside.

I look over to the doorway to make sure the guards are not watching before I scramble over to the stone wall, clinging to the bricks in an attempt to haul myself up to the barred window. My fingertips shake in rebellion, but I refuse to let go, pulling myself up until I can just about see down to the ground below.

Just as I thought, I see Cass standing there looking up at me, the whistle in her mouth. "Psst, Eden!" she stage-whispers, looking around cautiously. "Are you there?"

"Yes!"

"Your Mother and Father escaped. They will get help!"

I let out a sigh of relief to know that they managed to get out of the palace in time. I have gone from hero to zero in the blink of an eye, as they say. No good could come of them still being here while the entire Kingdom of Morween hates me.

"You have to get out of here too," I suggest quickly, taking a cautious look over my shoulder. "It's not safe."

"No, I'm not leaving until you are out. I'll be fine. Trust me!"

"No, wait!"

"Trust me!" she insists before dashing off quickly.

I let go of the wall, slumping back onto the floor to think about what will happen next. No doubt, my father will go to Azealea to seek help, but that means he will come face-to-face with Conall. I hardly know what prospect is worse. My inevitable death sentence or the thought of my father and mate meeting.

Conall

I exit the dark forest, staring up at the house before me.

It's only been a matter of days, but it feels like a lifetime ago that I stood here in this front yard or, should I say, *died* here in this front yard.

I have a fair idea how the men will react when I walk through that door, but I know I have no other choice. Battles are fought by soldiers, and there are none more well-prepared nor suited to this job than these men. I trained them myself, for Goddess' sake.

I walk forward, taking the steps two at a time, pausing for a moment before I push the door open.

Here we fucking go....

As soon as I step inside, I see the men sitting around the table eating dinner as usual. At first, no one notices, then eventually, the sound of chatter disappears, and every set of eyes are now on me.

The house is as silent as the grave as they all stare in a mixture of confusion and utter disbelief.

Even Rocco is too stunned to say a word, his face contorted in a look of pure shock.

It's then that Zeke, who is sitting at the head of the table, stands up, his eyes searching mine before realization falls over his face. He knows that if I'm here without warning, it's an emergency, and I have no other option.

"WHAT THE FUCK?!" Hunter shouts out, breaking the tense silence. "Did Con just walk through the damn door, or am I having some kind of fucking breakdown?"

I shrug nonchalantly, taking a step forward. "Nice to see you all too."

"WHAT THE FUCK IS THIS?!" Rocco eventually chokes out, slamming his fork down to get up from the table.

"I DON'T UNDERSTAND? YOU'RE ALIVE?!" Mateo questions in disbelief.

"WELL, HE'S NOT A FUCKING GHOST, IS HE?!" Samuel roars, standing up to follow Rocco, who is now stalking forward in my direction.

I stand my ground waiting for his approach. Zeke runs over to join me, lifting his hands as the men crowd around us in a swarm of anger and general confusion.

"EVERYBODY JUST NEEDS TO CALM THE HELL DOWN!" Zeke orders loudly.

"CALM DOWN??" Rocco snarls. "You want us to calm down when a damn dead man just walked through the fucking door?!"

"Yeah, Zeke... This is crazy!" Henrick interjects. "What's happening? We have the right to know!"

"I can't believe this," Neville adds, shaking his head in shock.

"SOMEONE NEEDS TO EXPLAIN WHAT THE HELL IS GOING ON. NOW!" William yells over the sound of men arguing and shouting.

Zeke nods in agreement, twisting his head to look at me briefly before looking around the men. "Listen, I know you'll all be pissed, but I don't give a SHIT anymore, so here it is," he snaps. "I didn't kill Con the night of the attack. The truth is...I took him somewhere to get help. It's a choice that I alone made. So if you want to go bat-shit crazy on someone, then it might as well be me."

"And me," Anton adds, stepping out from the crowd. "I helped, and I would do it again."

"Goddess above! This can't be happening," Evan comments, pointing at

Zeke. "You lied to us."

The men then stare at us silently. No one seems to know what to say until finally Rocco finally pipes up.

"FINE! If that's what happened. Then all three of you are fucking traitors! You all broke the code and—"

"Oh, enough with the fucking code already!" Hunter yells in annoyance, stepping into the circle. "What do you suggest we do? Kill them all?"

No one answers; they just look around at each other doubtfully.

"What? Someone had to be the one to say it," Hunter continues. "I know it wasn't just me who didn't want Con dead on the night of the attack. Most of you assholes felt the same way, yet none of us had the guts to stand up and do anything about it," he states. "Except Zeke. He was the only one with the balls to dare challenge the damn code!"

Mateo nods his head in agreement, stepping into the middle. "We should hear them out. Code or not. Too much has happened over these past few weeks. We should be trying to stick together."

There is a small whisper of sound as the men confer with each other for a few moments.

Hunter turns around to look at me, and a smile appears on his face. "It's good to see you, Con. Sorry about the initial shock. No offense."

I nod my head in return, looking back around the room. "None taken."

"Alright. I'm fucking listening," Rocco snaps angrily. "Let's hear this pile of shit then."

Zeke points to the table, and everyone heads over to sit down. Zeke gets ready to speak, and I hold my hand up to stop him. He looks into my eyes and takes his seat instead.

I walk around the table, stopping near the center as the men watch me intently. "I didn't come back here to defend myself. I told you the truth the night of the attack. I did let Eden go. I also didn't come back here to beg for your fucking forgiveness either," I explain plainly. "I did, however, come back because I need your help."

"You've got a fucking nerve!" Samuel snorts. "Waltzing back in here like you own the place—like you can just order us around."

"I'm not planning to order you around," I interrupt calmly. "All of you are your own man, you can do whatever the fuck you like, but I'm going to ask for your help anyway."

☐

"What do you need help with, Con?" Hunter asks curiously, scrunching his brows.

I look around them carefully, my eyes settling on Jarek, who stares back nervously.

"Eden has been taken prisoner at the palace—"

"OH, YOU HAVE GOT TO BE JOKING?!" Rocco booms furiously. "You came here to ask us to help your traitor girlfriend?"

"Prisoner? What happened?" Mateo asks worriedly, ignoring Rocco's outburst.

I glare at Rocco, who is seething in his chair, his face bright red with rage. "She has been accused of killing the King of Morween."

"Really?" Samuel snarls. "Last we heard, she was ready to marry the fucker!"

"It was a deal she made," I grit out between my teeth. "To save Harmony and TO SAVE ALL OF YOU ASSHOLES!"

"BULLSHIT!" Rocco growls, throwing his chair back. "She screwed us all over!"

"She didn't," Jarek interrupts, looking into my eyes before standing up. "Eden wasn't the one who told the elves about the attack. It was my fault."

I fold my arms over my chest as he continues telling the truth. About the nymph, Madam Piffnel...everything.

When he is finished, everyone stares at him in silence.

"I understand if you cannot accept my idiotic choices, but I need you all to know that I take full responsibility for this," Jarek adds. "We can't let an innocent woman suffer because of me and the mistakes I made."

"Goddess, fuck," Evan says on a sigh, rubbing his forehead. "This is a lot to take in."

"How are we supposed to get Eden out of this?" Neville asks with concern.

I take a deep breath and explain the story starting from the beginning. Siofra's letters, Aubrun's murder, finally ending with Faenor's hideout at Ankorord.

"So you want us to storm the place? See if we can finally find proof to show the elves?" William confirms.

"Yes, there is no one else who can do it but us, and if we find the proof we need, Eden's grandmother will take care of the rest," I explain. "We can bring the queen and the lords down for good."

They listen to me intently, nodding along in understanding.

"Then where do I sign up?" Anton asks, clasping his hands on the table.

"Me too."

"I'm in."

"Wait," I say, holding my hand up. "There's more I have to say, and you're not going to like it," I confess honestly. "Eden's full name is Eden Nestoriel, and she is the daughter of Haleth Nestoriel."

The sound of gasps fills the room, but I ignore them, walking around to stand at the head of the table. "Her father's crimes are not hers. Eden has gone out of her way to bring the queen and the lords of Morween to justice for what they did to us all those years ago. It's the reason they turned on her. It's the reason why she will be sentenced to death tomorrow." The words stick in my throat, but I know they must be said. The men have to know the whole truth once and for all. No more fucking surprises. "Despite the danger, Eden made it her mission to protect all of you, and in the end, it could be the thing that gets her killed if we don't help her. Eden Nestoriel is loyal to *us*. She's one of *us*," I declare without a shadow of a doubt. "She sacrificed her freedom for all of us, and we will *not* abandon her now!" I say determinedly, leaning my fists on the table. "She's my mate. She's a fucking Luna, and she needs our help."

"That's right!" Anton shouts, standing up to join me. "Count me in!"

"No one left behind," Henrick agrees with a nod. "I'm in too."

"You know I'm game," Hunter adds, looking around the table.

I look at each man, eventually stopping at Rocco, whose jaw tightens. "I'm not doing it for you," he snaps angrily. "But I'm in. It's time to take these sons-of-bitches down once and for all."

"Good," I answer, standing up straight. "Let's get to fucking work."

Concealed

Conall

"Look at this place...it's like something out of a dream," Mateo whispers, casting his eye over the valley below.

"More like a fucking nightmare," Anton adds quietly.

Hunter and I walk up behind them and take a knee to examine the scene for ourselves.

"Did you enjoy your ride here?" William snickers, giving me a side-eye.

"Don't you worry about him. I gave him the ride of his damn life, didn't I, Con?" Hunter grins as the others laugh.

"Focus, assholes," I order sternly.

Their attention is then drawn back to the ancient palace nestled in the middle of the dark valley, which is only illuminated by the light of the full moon.

"There are definitely signs of life inside the ruins. They have torches burning," Mateo observes, moving closer to the edge.

"Stay back, you fucking idiot!" Rocco snaps quietly, running up behind us, hunched over.

"What did you see?" I ask, waiting for his report.

"It's not great. Twenty guards to the rear and another twenty at the front."

"Yeah, and Goddess knows how many inside," Hunter adds, shaking his head.

"At least that confirms that they are hiding something. Why else would anyone come here? It gives me the damn creeps," William states, shivering animatedly for effect.

Then, Jarek runs up behind us, laying the leather bag on the grass. "Zeke is in position. He will set off the old woman's enchantment three minutes from now."

"Good," I answer, stuffing two purple vials from the bag into my pocket. I watch the rest of the men emerge from the forest, shifting from wolves to their human forms.

"Damn, the landscape is pretty open, Con. There's no cover down there in the valley. We will take at least three arrows each before any of us even get close enough to attack," Neville states doubtfully, observing the old abandoned palace for himself.

"There are a lot of elves down there too," Rocco says. "We're outnumbered."

"When has that ever stopped us?" Hunter grins before they all look to me for their orders.

"In a couple of minutes, Zeke will create a distraction using an enchantment—"

"It's not more sleeping potion, is it?" Henrick interrupts worriedly.

I shake my head. "These are Faenor's men. I don't want them put to fucking sleep. I want them dead. I'm not taking any chances."

"Nice," Samuel grins in satisfaction.

"When we see the distraction, we all head for the main entrance of the palace. You see the doorway over there?" They follow my line of sight, nodding their head in understanding. "By the time we get there, the distraction will have drawn some of the guards away, but not all of them. We take down the remaining ones, and Team A will wait behind to deal with the second wave of guards when they return. Team B, you'll follow me inside the palace walls. From there, we will have to fucking wing it. Citrine had no information for us about what's inside there," I explain. "Everyone clear?"

"Crystal," Anton chuckles. "I'm looking forward to this boys."

There is a murmur of agreement as I cast my eyes over to Zeke's position, far away in the distance. "Good. Now get ready to move down the cliff edge."

"Wait," Mateo whispers. "What is the distraction?"

"Trust me. You'll know it when you see it."

We then break apart, the men shifting into their wolves while I stand up to follow them to the edge of the steep valley.

I look down at the sword strapped to my waist, pulling it out of its sheath slightly. It's hardly how I would choose to fight, given the option, but there's not much I can do about it right now.

"Fucking hell," Neville whispers in awe, causing me to look up.

In the distance, on the other end of the valley, is a small army. Some soldiers are on horseback while others stand with swords and bows ready.

The Alpha wolves all stare in wonder at the illusion that looks more than real. I watch Faenor's men below, pointing up to the faux army, who are poised and ready to "attack." They immediately scatter to take action, half of them running to join the guards at the rear of the ancient ruins while others stay to watch over the main entrance. They pull out their bows, firing at will toward the army in the distance. They've taken the bait. Citrine's army stands its ground without moving an inch.

"Go," I order the wolves, watching them pour down the hill around me. I follow behind, navigating the rock face as fast as possible on human legs. It's steep, but luckily I just about manage to stay on my fucking feet.

As soon as we hit flat ground, Faenor's men spot us coming. Some run at us while others draw their swords. Archers get ready, and mere seconds later, arrows are flying our way thick and fast.

I channel my wolf's energy that still runs through my veins, dodging the flying arrows with laser focus.

We get closer, and I pull a purple vial from my pocket, launching it at the group of guards by the palace entrance. Instantly, the air fills with a burst of purple haze, and the arrows stop as the archers struggle to find their bearings. The simple trick works, and within seconds, we reach the entrance to the ruins, bursting through the haze to get within touching distance of Faenor's men. I pull the sword from my waist, thrusting it through the stomach of the first elf who comes running my way.

Suddenly, I feel someone grab me around the neck from behind. I throw my head backward to hit his face, spinning around to take a fighting stance. The Elven man begins swinging around his sword in fancy swoops and whirls as he glares at me through narrowed eyes.

"Arggggg!" he yells, charging at me in anger.

Our swords clang repeatedly as we counteract each other's moves, ducking and diving out of the way.

It takes a few frantic swings, but eventually, I fight him down to his knees, slashing my sword across his damn throat before he has the chance to get back up again.

He falls onto the ground at my feet, and I look around to see the purple haze is now beginning to subside. Faenor's men have been practically torn to shreds by the Alphas who have unleashed seventy years' worth of fury on their victims. A few remain, but I know there will be more guards on the way any minute now.

I look to the top of the valley to see Citrine's army begin to wane and fade away as if on cue.

"TEAM A, BE READY FOR INCOMING ATTACKS. TEAM B, FOLLOW ME!"

I run for the stone steps, dodging a flying arrow from an archer who attempts to reload his bow as I charge at him. He manages to take aim, but I slice his whole arm off before he gets the chance to fire. He screams in agony, rolling around on the ground as I drive my sword through his chest.

The team of wolves run past me to enter inside the stone walls of the palace, and I notice Zeke's wolf now joining Team A to fight off the rest of Faenor's men behind us.

As soon as I enter the imposing, crumbling building, I hold my sword up in preparation. The place seems to be abandoned and lifeless, but I'm not taking any chances. I take a few seconds to survey our surroundings instead, realizing I've never seen anything like it before in all my life.

The decrepit structure has similar features to the palace of Morween, but the level of destruction and decay gives it a different appearance and feel entirely.

Colossal stone statues adorn the expansive entrance as if they have stood their own silent guard for hundreds of years. The ceiling is now practically nonexistent, the moonlight pouring in through enormous holes above our heads. The stone floor is covered with overgrown vines with only a small path cut through leading to the right-hand side.

I point my sword in command, and the Alpha wolves move in that direction, spreading out across the wide corridor. We move forward on high alert, and I look at the walls on either side of us to see they are illuminated with fire torches.

We arrive in the center of the corridor, and it's then that more of Faenor's men appear from their hiding places, attacking us from all angles.

Suddenly, I hear a rock clatter to the ground beside me, and I look left to see a high elf jump out from a hidden alcove. His long dagger slices my upper arm, and I drop my sword accidentally. He takes another run at me, and I grit my teeth in anger, grabbing his weapon-wielding arm to twist it up his back. He yelps in pain, and I swipe the legs from under him, taking his dagger from his hand to run it across his neck in one smooth swoop.

I pick up my sword with my other hand and charge on, cutting down any asshole who tries to stand in my fucking way. Whatever is at the end of the corridor—whatever they are hiding—I'm going to find it.

The Alphas around me do their jobs, and I take off in a determined run with Mateo's and Hunter's wolves now joining me at my flanks.

We battle our way through the chaos, finding ourselves at the end of the corridor and the end of Faenor's men. We stop in front of a set of stairs illuminated by the same fiery torches. "Down here," I mutter, tossing the bloody dagger to one side to lift my sword again.

Cautiously, we head down the steep staircase, opening the large wooden door at the bottom to reveal a dark, damp dungeon.

As soon as we step inside, my eyes widen at the sight.

Behind the bars of a series of large jail cells are groups of high elf men who are staring back at us in shock. I take in their skinny, unkempt appearance as we move, identifying the crest of Morween on their Elven Guard uniforms.

I approach one of the cells slowly, and a guard walks forward. "Who are you?" he demands from behind bars, his expression filled with both suspicion and curiosity.

I check out the contents of the cell behind him to see small wooden tables, chairs and uncomfortable-looking bunkbeds.

How long have these men been here?

How the fuck did they get here? And why was Faenor holding them prisoner?

I narrow my eyes at the man in return. "I could ask you the same question." I hit back.

He swallows, holding his head high. "My name is Walden. Commander of the Second League of the Morween Elven Guard."

I raise my eyebrow, looking down at his torn, old, shabby uniform. "Is that right, Walden?"

His jaw tightens. "Why have you come here?" he asks directly.

"I've come..." I begin. "...to take Lord Faenor down."

A slow smirk spreads over his face as he turns around to look at the other men in his cell. The bars of the cells all around us begin to rattle loudly as the men go crazy in celebration.

It's then that a loud voice cuts through the noise. "THE TIME HAS COME, MEN! TIME FOR US TO TAKE BACK OUR CITY FROM THE CORRUPT. IT'S TIME TO TAKE BACK MORWEEN!"

The men part, and a figure walks forward from the back of the dark cell, stopping at the bars directly in front of me.

"I never thought I would see the day that we would meet again, Alpha Conall."

I stare back into his familiar eyes.

"Nor I...Prince Erix," I answer in return.

Retaliation

Erix

SEVENTY YEARS AGO

I straighten up my tunic, waving to Eden one last time before her bedroom door closes. Damn, I can't help the smile that touches my lips. I'm the luckiest man in the kingdom to have her love and I know it.

"We're running late, lover boy. We should probably hurry up," Aubrun comments worriedly as we head to my father's study.

I chuckle a little, shaking my head. "Relax, Aubrun, the lords always have plenty to say at these meetings. I doubt we have missed anything important."

"I guess you're right. Are you prepared for the attack on Whiteclaw?"

"Uh, as prepared as I'll ever be."

He frowns. "You don't sound so sure."

"It's not that. It's just ambushing an entire pack of wolves is not something we have done before. It will be tricky. They won't go down without a fight. Still, it's the only path we have left now after their attack yesterday," I answer, my anger reappearing once more.

When those Alpha assholes turned up here in Morween a couple of days ago with their claims of "rogue wolves," I was ready to give them a chance. Don't get me wrong, I was suspicious of their intentions, but I listened to what they had to say. My father did too, allowing them time to track down these so-called rogues and provide proof of their involvement. Then, within a matter of hours, the same Alphas were seen killing more of our people! The thought of it leaves me infuriated.

How could I have been so fucking naïve?

Clearly, our leniency was taken advantage of. They were probably laughing about our gullibility as they left the palace walls! I won't let that happen again, that's for sure.

"Yes. It is a different kind of mission, but necessary, unfortunately," Aubrun states matter-of-factly. "We must trust in your father. He knows what he is doing."

I smile at him in amusement as we come to a stop outside the study.

"What?" he asks, scrunching his brows.

"Nothing. I'm just hoping you'll be this loyal to me when I'm your king."

"Of course I will, Erix. Always," he replies faithfully. "My loyalty is always with you and Morween."

I put my hand out to grab his in thanks. "You're a good friend, Aubrun, and I appreciate you saying that because I've been meaning to ask you for a favor."

"Sure, anything," he answers immediately.

I clear my throat, my thoughts drifting back to Eden's beautiful smiling face. "I want you to keep an eye on Eden when I'm gone. She's uncomfortable with this new path we are taking with the war, and I just feel she could use a friend right now."

He swallows and nods his head respectfully in reply. "Of course. I'll look after her."

"I knew I could count on you," I smile. "Okay...let's get this shit over with."

We enter the busy room, and instantly, the sound of heightened voices fills my ears.

"How many guards will be attacking Whiteclaw?" Lord Algar asks my father forcefully.

"Enough," my father answers sternly. "Here is their leader now. I'm sure he can attest to the readiness of our men."

He looks at me expectantly, and I give him a respectful nod. "Yes, Your Majesty. My men are prepared and ready to march on Whiteclaw within the hour."

"Excellent," he answers, looking around the lords.

"I must ask, Your Majesty, why we are even bothering to attack in the first place?" Lord Faenor adds from his seat at the table. "If your wood elf here—"

"Haleth," I interject loudly, sitting across from Faenor. "His name is Haleth."

"Of course, Prince Erix, forgive me," Lord Faenor says, pausing before he looks from me to Eden's father with thinly veiled contempt. "If *Haleth* here has been working on an enchantment to kill off the Alpha wolves of each pack, shouldn't we just go ahead and use that instead? We have given them enough chances already."

"I have to agree with Lord Faenor, my dear," my mother comments, putting her hand out to rest it on my father's. "We already know these Alphas are vicious liars. They begged us for mercy, then attacked our people several hours later! In front of my very eyes! We cannot abide it any longer."

My father nods as he considers their opinions for a moment. "Haleth? What do you think?" he asks, looking at Eden's father.

Haleth clears his throat to speak. "I think, Your Majesty, that any enchantment we use must be a last resort. I agree with your plan to send guards to Whiteclaw. Perhaps they might be able to uncover more truths about these recent attacks. After all, it does seem odd that these Alphas would ask for mercy only to attack hours later."

"You didn't see them!" Faenor snipes back. "Those horrid beasts tore innocent elves to shreds in front of our queen! How dare you defend them?!"

"Lord Faenor," my father interrupts calmly. "I do not think that Haleth is defending them. He advises we proceed with tact and caution, and I agree."

The table falls into silence before my father looks at me directly. "Son, you are to march on Whiteclaw as previously planned. You can question their Alpha on what he knows. You have permission to use the force you deem necessary, but if you can preserve the lives of women and children of the pack, then you should do so," he orders. "I trust your judgment and leave the details of the mission in your capable hands."

I bow my head to him graciously. "As you wish, Your Majesty."

There is a murmur of quiet discontent around the room. Still, my father ignores it, lifting his hand to dismiss everyone. Lord Faenor is the first to leave, striding out of here as if he has someplace to be. Asshole.

I've never trusted the man. In fact, I could say the same of several of the men in this room. However, the Court of Lords is a necessary evil, as I have learned over the years. Each of them has their own wealth, armies, estates and agendas. Keeping them onside is an essential part of keeping Morween stable and prosperous.

"I'll just go and make some arrangements for the families of the attack victims," my mother says quietly.

"Yes, my dear Siofra. Make sure they have everything they need," my father answers, leaning in to kiss her cheek.

She departs with the rest of the men, and I remain in my chair, offering Haleth a respectful nod as he closes the door to leave my father and I alone.

"You want to earn that wood elf's respect, I see," my father comments, amused, as he heads over to his chair behind his desk.

I grin, shrugging my shoulders as I stand up. "Is it that obvious?"

"You do realize that you are to be his king one day? He doesn't have to like you to respect you."

"I'd prefer if my father-in-law both respected me *and* liked me, Father," I answer honestly, giving him a sly smile.

He chuckles in return. "Well, you cannot make your intentions any clearer than that, my boy. So you wish to marry the young wood elf? Eden, is it?"

"I do, Father," I answer sincerely, a hint of nerves in my voice.

"Ahhh. Well, good for you."

"You mean...you approve of the match?" I ask curiously, raising my brow in surprise.

"My son, your mother is both my sun and my moon. If your grandfather had told me I couldn't marry her—"

"You would have done it anyway," I finish with a laugh.

He nods his head. "Yes."

I snort, looking down at the floor to shake my head.

"So, you are prepared for this mission?" he asks seriously, changing the subject.

I straighten my shoulders. "Yes, Father."

"Good. Unfortunately, it has come to this. It is not what I wanted."

"Nor I," I answer honestly. "But you are right in your orders, Father. We cannot lie down and allow them to attack our people at will. Suitable and tactical retaliation is required."

He then stands up from his desk, walking around the edge to place his hand on my shoulder. "Good luck. We shall see you back here soon, my son."

$$* * *$$

After delivering the final orders to our men, Commander Walden and I begin preparing our horses to leave Morween.

□

"I'll ride on ahead with the First Batallion, and you will remain with the Second League," I confirm in finality. "When we arrive at Whiteclaw, we will attack first from the north of the territory, and then you should intervene from the east as discussed."

"Yes, Your Majesty."

"You know that when no one's around, you can call me Erix, right?" I ask with a grin, securing my sword around my waist.

"Your Majesty, I did not call you Erix even when you were the height of my knee. Do you think I am about to start now?"

I laugh, putting my hand out to shake his. "See you on the battlefield, Walden."

"Yes, you will, Your Majesty," he laughs, mounting his horse to lead his men on the journey ahead.

I prepare to leave myself when one of my mother's servants suddenly appears at my side. "Your Majesty! You are needed. Come quickly, please!"

"What's wrong?" I ask, perplexed as I follow him to the edge of the forest.

"It's young Eden Nestoriel. She fell while retrieving flowers in the woods. She has been badly injured! I heard her cries! She's just through these trees!"

My stomach twists upon hearing his explanation. "Go and fetch a doctor! Now!" I order, bursting through the tree line. "EDEN! EDEN!"

It's then that I see two figures in the distance—my mother, talking with a man who has his back to me.

"Mother?" I yell in surprise. "Mother, what are you doing out here?"

She ignores my calls, putting her hand on the man's shoulder. "So you understand what you must do?" she asks him softly.

"I do, Your Majesty. I will not fail you. I promise."

"Good. Your family will be proud, and they will be waiting for you on the other side."

The man then turns to face me, and I almost fucking collapse on the spot when I take in his appearance. He looks exactly like me in every way. The same hair, eyes and facial features. Hell, even his tunic and armor are an exact duplicate of my own.

"What the fuck is going on?!" I yell, receiving no reply.

My mother lifts her hand, looking at me sympathetically before muttering something under her breath. Immediately, my eyes droop, and I fall to the cold forest floor.

Schemes

Erix

I awake to a murmuring sound and open one eye to look up at the non-existent ceiling above my head.

Where the hell am I?

I stay completely still, staring at the stars in the sky for a few seconds before my head falls to one side to take in the rest of the room. If you can even call it that. It is the ruins of an old sitting room of sorts. Broken furniture litters the floor, piles of rocks are stacked up in every corner, and fire torches hang from the walls illuminating the darkness with a soft glow.

I sit up carefully on the broken chair, holding my aching head as I try to piece together what happened before I ended up here. I was ready to leave for Whiteclaw with my men. A servant told me Eden needed my help, and then I saw my mother in the woods, talking to my fucking doppelgänger! The whole situation is bizarre. I'm positive I must be losing my damn mind!

It's then that I pick up on the sound of voices again, and I twist my neck to focus on the hushed tones.

"You mustn't worry."

"But I am worried, Siofra. What if he does not comply? What if he is not with us?"

"My son is not a coward. He will see sense. I will make him see things our way. Trust me on this!"

"And if he doesn't? What next—"

I listen as best I can, but snippets of the conversation are now entirely inaudible. I stand up to move closer, my foot accidentally tipping over a pile of rocks in the process.

Fuck.

"Shhh! He's awake. You must leave us. And have faith!"

I stand up straight as my mother enters the decaying, old sitting room, and our eyes meet. "Oh my boy, you are awake. I'm so happy to have you back with us," she coos gently, resting her hands on my face with a smile.

"Mother," I repeat firmly, lifting her hands. "Explain what the hell is going on. Now."

Her smile falters, and she steps back from me, bowing her head. "Of course, son. I'll explain everything, but first, I want you to remember how much I love you. I want you to listen to what I say before you comment."

I stare at her in complete confusion, but I know that right now, I have no option but to comply. "I'm listening," I answer, placing my hands on my waist.

"Erix, my son, I have brought you here today out of necessity because we must take immediate action to protect our kingdom from those disgusting beasts who have invaded it."

My brows scrunch in reply.

"The wolves are now taking over enormous amounts of land. Their numbers are increasing vastly each year. It will not be long until they outnumber us, and what then? Morween will no longer be the stronghold it is now. Our people will suffer. The territories around us will suffer. *They* will be the dominant species in our realm! Eventually, they will have the power to wipe us out if they choose, and we cannot let that happen."

I exhale after hearing her paranoid speech and shake my head. "Mother, you must remain calm. You sound hysterical. My father is handling the situation with the wolves appropriately. I know the attacks on Elven people have been difficult to deal with, and you have also been through a lot, but this war will not last forever."

"Perhaps not, but how many innocent elves must be lost in the meantime?" she asks adamantly. "Your father has heard of these attacks, yet he does nothing!"

"Nothing? Mother, I was on my way to Whiteclaw to engage in a retaliation ambush upon his order!"

She tuts, losing her gentle expression as she folds her arms over her chest in irritation. "Attacking one pack will do nothing, Erix, and you know it. More decisive action must be taken to rid our lands of these beasts once and for all. Your father has already proven that he doesn't have the stomach for it. So now the job must fall to other hands."

Immediately, alarm bells start ringing in my head.

Surely my ears deceive me, and my own mother hasn't resorted to treason?

"Mother...what have you done?"

She turns to face me and holds her head up high. "The lords and I have taken steps to ensure that your father can no longer dismiss the threat to our realm. We have taken steps to *help* him see sense."

"What the fuck does that mean? What steps have you taken?" I ask, unable to hide the horror in my tone.

Her eyes look deeply into mine again, and her shoulders relax. "Erix, you are a good son. Your father loves you more than anything in this world. More than me. More than the realm. We can use that to our advantage."

"Use me?" I ask indignantly. "How are you going to use me?"

"By letting him believe you are dead."

"What?" I gasp, taking a step away from her in disgust.

"Erix, if your father believes you were killed at Whiteclaw mercilessly this evening along with your Battalion, he will finally take the action we require."

At first, I'm completely baffled by her revelation. Then it occurs to me precisely what "action" she's talking about.

"You want him to use Haleth's enchantment. You want to force his hand. To make him go up against the wolves blind with rage!"

She nods unashamedly. "It is the only way."

"It's a dirty trick, Mother!" I shout back in anger. "How could you even suggest this? How could you betray him like this? You are supposed to be his loyal subject! His confidant and advisor! His damn wife, for crying out loud!"

"I have been his advisor for many years, but he refuses to listen to reason! This is the only way that Lord Faenor and I—"

"FAENOR?!" I question furiously. "That's who you have concocted this ludicrous plan with? Well, now this all makes sense! You cannot trust the man, Mother. He's a snake, and he's manipulating you."

She swallows a little, raising her brow. "He is not manipulating me. I am the Queen of Morween and know what is best for *my* kingdom. Lord Faenor knows too. He is a strong man. Loyal to his own species. Loyal to his own people," she replies with such admiration that it makes my damn toes curl.

"You are in love with him." The words make perfect sense as they tumble from my lips.

She doesn't respond to my claims, but I already know them to be true.

I put my hands on my hips again, shaking my head in disbelief. "Mother, whatever you have planned…it's not right. I will not be a party to fooling my father. You must stop this craziness now."

"I'm afraid I simply cannot do that," she answers with a casual shrug of her shoulder. "This is bigger than you or I. This is for Morween, and it must be done. If you try to understand, you'll see I am right."

Fuck!

Who is this woman? It's like I don't even know her at all! I stare at her in frustration as my mind drifts back to that moment in the forest before I ended up here. I passed out after she muttered something under her breath. Some sort of spell or incantation. I've seen Eden perform them enough to know what they sound like.

"Wait. Back in the forest…did you…did you use magic on me?" I ask carefully. "You said something that made me collapse, and that man I saw you with…he looked exactly like me!"

My voice trails off as I then consider the crazy possibilities that now swirl around in my head.

Magic.

Shapeshifting.

Those are skills possessed by some wood elves. Eden being one of them. She's shown me before how she does the shapeshifting thing, and not only is it fascinating, but it scares the shit out of me.

"My son, there are some truths I must share with you about myself," my mother says, walking over to stand by the decaying fireplace.

Curious, I watch as she pulls a necklace from beneath her dress. "You know that your grandparents raised me in Morween before I married your father."

"Yes, and?"

"Well, what you do not know is that your grandparents are not blood-related to you or me. The fact is, they found me in the forest when I was just a child." My eyes widen in surprise as she looks down at the necklace in her hands. "They found me with nothing but the clothes on my back and this necklace. The ancient symbol of wood elf magic."

"You're a wood elf?"

"Yes."

I'm completely shocked by her revelation. If anything, I thought she despised them. I never once suspected she was one of them!

"What happened to your real parents?"

She lets out a deep sigh. "My parents were savages, Erix. They were despicable vermin. A plague on Elven society! They lived off the land in the forest. Begged for or stole any possessions they had and eventually got themselves killed when they tried to steal from the wrong person."

"So you were an orphan?" I ask, a slither of sympathy gnawing at my insides as I consider what that situation must have been like for a young child.

"Yes, I was alone for a while before your grandparents found me and took me in as their own. They educated me as a high elf. Taught me the ways of their culture, and from then on, I vowed that I would never have to resort to begging for anything in my life. I would make my own way in the world. I would do what my lowlife parents never could. I would rise to heights that the realm had never seen before."

As I listen, I can't help but feel her intention behind every word. Her determination to succeed by any means necessary makes me question her very position as queen and as my mother.

"You wanted to be Queen of Morween? You chased that goal?" I ask.

Her eyes shoot to me with a hint of anger. "Of course I did. As many young Elven women did at the time. It's the reality of royal politics, son, and you would be wise to remember that."

"It's disgusting," I reply scathingly.

"Disgusting? So you think that little wood elf, whom you have been dating, is not doing the same thing? Erix, I did not believe you to be as naive as your fath—"

"Eden doesn't care about titles!" I snap back defensively. "She loves me—"

"No! I love you!" she yells, stepping forward. "That is why I do all of this! For you! Your kingdom and your legacy!!"

"No, none of this is for me, Mother. You are kidding yourself! This is all some sort of wild, deranged plan that has stemmed from your own childhood trauma!"

She walks forward to grip the collar of my tunic forcefully. "Erix, you will be king of the most prosperous nation in the whole world! No one will dare challenge us. We can have it all!"

I stare back into her cold eyes, unable to formulate a response. My mother has never been the most hands-on parent, nor is she particularly warm or maternal, but she has never shown me cruelty or given me a reason to doubt her character. This woman seems completely different from the mother I have grown up with my whole life, yet sadly, I know that it is her. For the first time, she has revealed her true self to me, and I cannot accept it.

I cannot accept *her*.

"No," I answer sternly. "The answer is no. I will not be part of your scheming."

She exhales, a look of pain crossing her eyes for a brief second. "That is unfortunate. I never saw this coming. I anticipated that you would be reasonable," she mutters sadly. "Anyway, it is now out of your hands. It is done."

"What is?" I demand. "Where are my men?"

"Dead," she answers simply in return. "Along with the man who took on your likeness. The plan is already in motion."

"WHAT?! Mother, you can't—"

"I CAN, AND I DID!" she snaps back angrily. "Tonight, as far as everyone else is aware, you marched your men into battle, and you were killed at the scene."

"So you staged my death?" I ask, swallowing the lump in my throat. "You used magic to send someone to die in place?"

"Yes. The man who took your likeness was happy to volunteer for the mission. He lost his entire family in one of the wolf attacks. Once I explained to him what had to be done, he understood. As you will too someday."

"THAT'S FUCKING SICK!" I yell in anger. "You exploited an innocent man's grief for your own personal agenda. If you can do that, then what else are you capable of?"

She ignores my question, instead continuing with her explanation. "Witnesses will tell your father that you died heroically, and he will do what he should have done already. He will finally get rid of their kind once and for all."

"Their kind? Even if Haleth gives him the potion, the wolves will regroup and choose their new leaders. The enchantment may delay them, but it won't eliminate them."

"We shall see," she answers ominously.

The chilling words send a cold shiver down my spine, and it's then I realize that her intent isn't just to kill Alpha wolves.

It's to kill them all.

"This is immoral, Mother. Sheer madness! Think about what you are doing!" I plead, trying to appeal to any shred of decency left inside her. "You made an epic mistake, but if you let me go, maybe I can fix this before it gets out of hand. Before you do something you'll regret."

"I do not and never will regret my actions."

My jaw tightens, and I swallow hard. "And what about me?" I ask quietly, searching her eyes. "Where do I slot into all of this? A dead man cannot be king."

Her eyes turn soft, and she walks forward, resting her hands on my face. "After the deed has been done, you can come home to Morween. Lord Faenor will say his men found you in the forest, disorientated from battle. We will tell the people that your body was misidentified. Your father will be so delighted to have you home that he will not question it, Erix."

"And then what? Do we carry on life like normal? My father remains king, and you and Lord Faenor continue to scheme behind his back? Behind my back?"

She shakes her head gently. "It will be a different world, my dear. I will convince your father to step down, and you shall have the throne with me at your side as your faithful advisor. The lords will have their riches and their lands restored. They will owe us immensely. The war will be no more. We will be indestructible."

Her eyes plead with mine, and my heart drops in response.

"No, Mother. I will not be part of this. Any of it."

It's then that her gaze drifts over my shoulder.

I spin around to see Lord Faenor by the door, a group of men at his side. "Perhaps this might convince you, Prince...."

Within seconds, his men march on me, grabbing me securely as I struggle wildly to fight them off. "Let me fucking go! YOU TRAITORS! YOU COWARDS!"

My mother does nothing to stop them, standing back to allow them to drag me across the stone, vine-covered floor through an old corridor and down a set of dark steps.

My eyes struggle to adjust to the darkness, and then I see them. Commander Walden and around thirty of his men locked in a series of cells.

"What the fuck?!" I yell in fury as we come to a halt.

"Prince Erix, these men have been captured and sentenced to death. You have two choices. Join us as your mother has offered, and I will award these men a quick death, or don't, and they will die painfully."

My eyes meet with Walden's through the bars of the cell, and he shakes his head subtly, communicating my own sentiments exactly.

I twist my head to Faenor, staring at him in disdain. "Go fuck yourself, Faenor!" I snarl, spitting at him in disgust.

He moves out of the way, his eyes darting to my mother. "Very well. Have it your way. Guards...arrange for these men to be killed—"

"Then you better add me to the fucking list," I hit back angrily. "Because I won't stand by and let my men die without me."

My mother's eyes widen in horror, and she shakes her head, walking over to Faenor to take his hand. "My Lord, a word."

He allows her to lead him to the other side of the corridor, and I see them locked in an intense conversation before he breezes back toward us. "Very well, Erix. Your mother and I have agreed that some time in the cells might change your mind."

Just then, the doors to the cell in front of me are unlocked, and I'm tossed inside at Walden's feet.

"If I were you, I'd make up your mind sooner rather than later," Faenor states quietly. "You're fortunate you have a mother that loves you. If it were up to me, you would be dead already, along with your weakling father."

I reach out to snatch his neck, and his men immediately grab my arm, loosening my grip enough to toss it back into the cell.

Faenor narrows his eyes at me, straightening his collar before turning to leave. "Come, my dear, we must get back to Morween. We have a funeral to prepare for...."

I stare at my mother one last time before she turns her back and leaves, hand-in-hand with him.

There is now complete silence. I close my eyes, and a veil of complete and utter shame tumbles over me instantly.

This is my fault.

I should have seen this coming.

I should have spotted the signs that something was amiss.

Then, a hand drops onto my shoulder, and I turn to look at Walden.

"What happened?" I ask him simply.

He looks around the other men. "We arrived at Whiteclaw during the attack and were about to intervene when I spotted something unusual."

I wait silently for him to continue.

"You, Your Majesty," he says quietly. "I watched you leading your men into certain death. Your tactics were shoddy, your sword work was even worse. As soon as I saw their brute of an Alpha kill you with one strike, I knew it was not the prince I had trained since he was five years old. I ordered my men to turn back to Morween, and we almost got there before we were intercepted by Faenor's men and brought here to Ankorord."

"Ankorord?" I repeat in shock.

He nods his head sadly. "I'm sorry I failed you, Your Majesty. I was too late in my assessment of the situation," he says, bowing his head.

"There's nothing to be sorry for," I answer sincerely, looking around all the men. "All of you... You have shown your loyalty to Morween, and in return, I pledge my loyalty to you."

They bow their heads solemnly.

"What do we do now, Your Majesty?" Walden questions. "Our chances of escape do not look good."

"Then we wait," I answer, glancing at the door. "I'm confident this will not last long. Soon they will make a mistake, and my father will notice. Someone will find us—and when they do—we will make them rue the day they ever dared to betray their king."

Rivals

Conall

PRESENT

The silence surrounding us is deafening, and for a few moments, no one utters a single word.

I'm in total shock, and I can't hide it.

The dead Prince of Morween is standing right in front of my face.

Eden's ex-boyfriend and former love of her life.

Of all the things I expected to find here...he was not one of them.

"I thought you were dead," I eventually say, looking Erix up and down suspiciously.

"Well, I'm not. As you can see," he answers plainly in return.

It's then that Mateo and Hunter shift into their human form, their faces contorted in confusion as they take in our intense showdown.

"Con, what's going on?" Mateo whispers.

Erix glances at them both before his eyes find mine again. "So they didn't do it after all? My mother and Lord Faenor... They didn't kill the wolves off?"

I raise my brow. "Oh, they killed off the wolves, alright." I snarl in reply.

"And yet you are alive?" he questions dubiously.

"They made a mistake," I answer with narrowed eyes.

"Clearly," he mutters as he looks between Mateo, Hunter and I. "Are these men of yours Alphas too?"

I nod.

"Where's your leader?" he asks. "The one who came with you to Morween that night to speak with my father." He lifts his hands to rest them on the bars of the cell.

I ignore his question entirely, deciding to get straight to the point instead. "What are you doing here in this place, Erix?"

"You first," he snaps back.

I smirk, shaking my head from side to side. "I'm not the one in the fucking cell."

His jaw tightens, his eye twitching in blatant frustration. "I'm here because I wouldn't go along with my mother and Lord Faenor's plan to kill the wolves. They faked my death to force a reaction from my father after YOUR disgusting attacks on our people."

I force the sword through the bars to jab at his neck threateningly.

His men jump forward to his defense, but he lifts his arm to hold them back.

"Those attacks were a fucking lie," I growl in a dangerously low voice. "Your mother set them up from the beginning."

He swallows, and from the look in his eyes, I can see that he already suspected this was the case.

"But then...you know that already, don't you, Prince Erix?"

He glances at the Commander at his side before he nods. "We had our suspicions. Seventy years of imprisonment leaves you with a lot of time to think things over," he answers.

I remove my sword from his neck and step back from the cell.

Just then, the dungeon door opens, and the other Alpha men spill into the corridor.

"Con, what did you find?" Zeke asks, coming to a halt at my side. His eyes immediately widen at the sight in front of him. "Wait, what the fuck?!"

Erix only stares back in return.

"No, no, no. This is impossible," Rocco's voice interrupts as he barges to the front of the group.

Erix frowns for a second before he nods in understanding. "I take it from your reaction that you are the Alpha of Whiteclaw?" he questions calmly.

"Your damn right I am!" Rocco fumes, hitting the bars with his hand.

"What is he talking about?" Anton whispers to Zeke. "Who is this guy?"

"The Prince of fucking Morween," Zeke answers, running his hand over his face.

The men look at each other in stunned silence before their eyes fall on me.

"I killed you! I fucking killed you! You piece of shit!" Rocco snarls ferociously, jutting his head forward aggressively.

"Obviously, you didn't," Hunter quips, trying to hide his amusement amidst the building tension.

"Shut your face, you asshole," Rocco growls, pointing in his direction.

"All those years you held the title of the great 'Prince Slayer.' Now we find out it was nothing but a lie," William accuses, causing Hunter to snort.

"It wasn't a lie! I killed him!" Rocco protests, making a move to attack.

"ENOUGH," I order in irritation, turning my attention back to Erix, who looks straight at Rocco, unfazed by his claims.

"It wasn't me who attacked your pack that night at Whiteclaw. It was a trick set in motion by my mother, and I can explain everything if you let me out of here."

"Why should we?" Samuel questions in anger. "Your mother destroyed our lives. She took everything from us. How do we know we can trust you?"

"You think I've been locked in this cell for a fucking seventy-year-long vacation?!" Erix questions sarcastically. "Let me out of here, and I'll go straight to my father and tell him everything. He's a good man. He'll do the right thing—"

"Your father is dead," I interject, matter-of-factly, not bothering to sugarcoat the honest truth.

Erix's expression remains stoic, but his eyes give him away. I can see the pain swirling in their depths. "He's dead?"

"He is, and I was the one who killed him."

Erix stares at me for a long, weight-filled moment.

"Shit. You probably shouldn't have admitted that," Neville says quietly under his breath.

Immediately, Erix loses his cool, throwing his arm through the bars to try to get at me. "You fucking asshole!" he yells. "I'll kill you!"

"Ohhh...sure, well, give us the keys why don't you? We will let you out right away!" Hunter mutters sarcastically, raising his brow.

"My father did nothing wrong to you!" Erix protests.

"Regardless of your mother's crimes, your father ultimately gave the order responsible for releasing the enchantment that killed every wolf in my pack. Innocent women and children included," I answer.

"But he was a good man! Manipulated by the lords and my poisonous mother!" he snaps defensively through gritted teeth before he looks down in shame. "This wasn't who he was."

I stare back at him intensely. "We know that now."

"You do?" he questions angrily. "So that's why you're here then? *You* figured it all out, huh?"

I shake my head. "Not me," I answer, preparing myself for what I must say next. "You have Eden to thank for that."

His breath catches in his chest, which then rises and falls quickly. "You know Eden?" he asks a hint of desperation in his tone.

It's impossible to ignore the look he had in his eyes the moment I said her name.

He loved her...and he loves her still.

I try my best to hold onto my self-control. The mere thought of another man even thinking of her in that way is enough to send me off a cliff edge. But now is not the time for jealousy. No matter how much it gnaws at my brain, I know I must push past it.

"Yes, I know her," I respond, preparing myself for Rocco or one of the others to make a smart remark. However, to my surprise, they say nothing.

"Where is she now?" he asks, worry permeating his voice.

"She has been imprisoned. Falsely accused by your mother and Lord Faenor of killing the king."

"Killing my father? You let her take the fall for that?" Erix snarls.

"Not that king," Zeke interjects. "After your father's death, Aubrun was made king."

"Aubrun?!" Erix questions, clearly bemused by his father's choice. "They picked Aubrun?"

He looks at his Commander, who rolls his eyes. "Let me guess, Ciridan named him as heir. The young lad gets himself killed, and Faenor is now in the perfect position to take the throne?"

"Once Eden is sentenced. It's only a matter of time," I explain.

Erix lifts his hands to rest them on the bars of the cell again, looking down at the ground before taking a deep breath. "Fine. Then you must get me back to Morween," he pleads. "I'll expose my mother and the lords for their actions. I won't let them harm another innocent person, especially her."

The room falls into silence again as the men wait for my verdict.

Am I sure Erix is the honorable man he claims to be?

No. I can't trust the asshole as far as I can throw him. He may very well even try to kill me in retaliation for his father's death, but I know I have no other choice. Saving Eden is the priority, and it requires a leap of faith. One that I'm willing to take to save her life.

"Let them out," I order, nodding to Zeke.

He walks over to examine the lock, and I stay firmly in place, staring into the eyes of the man who loves my mate.

* * *

I stand by the edge of the forest, my arms folded across my chest, waiting patiently as Erix catches up with Haleth, Iriel and Citrine.

"Shit, looks like the ex has already got the edge with the in-laws," Zeke states, nudging my arm with his elbow.

I'm too fucking tense to reply, so instead, I watch as Iriel embraces Erix with tears in her eyes.

It's true that they know him a heck of a lot more than they know me. They know how happy he made her back then and how much Eden loved him.

He's the love of her life in their eyes.

Whereas me... I am the man who took their daughter prisoner. Who dragged her into all this mess in the first place. I can't exactly blame them if they show a preference for him.

"Don't worry, Con," Hunter says reassuringly. "He seems like a bit of a pussy to me. I mean, imagine spending seventy years in a jail cell without figuring a way out."

"Is it any different than seventy years locked in the den?" I interrupt, raising my brow.

"Hmm, Touché," he shrugs. "I guess that means you're fucked then," he grins, smacking me on the back.

The other men laugh in response, but I don't bother to reply.

It's then that Erix approaches, along with Eden's family and Commander Walden. "Citrine thinks we should head inside and come up with a plan."

I nod, instructing Zeke to come with us.

Erix and the others walk ahead, and I notice my men and the guards looking over at each other in mutual distrust.

"Hey...play nice, assholes," I warn seriously. "Do not fuck this up."

"Don't worry about us, Con. We'll be as good as gold," Henrick smirks.

426

I shake my head, making my way into the cottage to join everyone inside.

"When I arrive at the doors, they will let me through. We should time it for when Eden's trial begins as the lords will all be in the one place—"

"Wait," I say, interrupting Erix in his tracks. "You're not suggesting that we just walk up to the fucking gates of Morween and demand entry?"

"No," he answers snappily. "I'm suggesting that I do."

"Has seventy years in exile caused you to go fucking insane?" I question in disbelief. "You walk up to that door, and the guards will seize you before you get anywhere near Eden. Then, if you're lucky, your mother will send you right back to where you fucking came from!"

"I'm not an idiot!" he hits back, taking a step toward my face. "I am their rightful king! I have the respect of my people!"

"No, you had their respect," I correct him adamantly. "You've been gone for seventy years."

"Then what would you suggest, Alpha Conall," he says, narrowing his eyes.

I look away from him to address the others. "We use the secret tunnel Eden used to get back into the castle the day of Ciridan's funeral."

Erix's jaw tenses. "Get back *in* the castle?" he questions suspiciously.

"Do you know the tunnel that I mean or not?"

He swallows, nodding his head reluctantly. "Yes, I know it. I didn't think she would remember it though. It was a long time ago...."

Everyone looks at us awkwardly, and it's clear to see no one wants to be the first to pick sides. Eventually, Haleth clears his throat. "I think, Prince Erix, a more discreet entrance into the castle is needed. We must get you inside that hearing room where the elder high elves and the people of the realm can hear what you have to say. We cannot give Faenor the chance to intercept you."

"Whatever we do, we have to do it quickly," Zeke adds. "It's only a matter of time before Faenor realizes his men in Ankorord are all dead."

"Okay, so we use the secret tunnel to get in. Then how do we get inside the hearing room?" Erix asks.

"We do what it takes, and we fight. Wolves and elves together," I say determinedly.

He thinks for a second before he nods, putting his hand out toward mine. "For peace."

"For Eden," I answer, taking his hand in return.

Revelation

Eden

I pace back and forth in the cell, my mind working overtime as I try and fail to devise some sort of escape plan. The fact is, I'm pretty much at their mercy without access to nature or my father's study, and there is nothing I can do about it.

I stop and look up to the small, barred window to see the sun is now shining high in the sky. It's officially mid-morning by my count, and I'm sure it won't be long until the hearing begins in the throne room.

Just then, the dungeon door opens, and I walk over to the bars of the cell to have a closer look. Two guards appear inside, swiftly taking their positions on either side of the door to allow Siofra to enter between them. The very sight of the woman makes me want to scream in rage. I wouldn't say that I particularly possess a killer instinct, but I would no doubt take great pleasure in killing this woman slowly.

"Eden," she says with an unmistakable air of joy in her voice. "How are the dungeons treating you? Are you being attended to? Have you had something to eat? Something to drink?"

I scowl at her, and she stops in front of the cell, smiling as she looks me up and down. "Oh dear, dear, dear. What terrible choices you have made, Eden," she says, shaking her head. "Once a promising young woman and now nothing more than a traitor to her people. I must admit I never saw it coming," she continues, tilting her head. "And neither did our poor Aubrun, it seems."

"You disgust me," I growl. "You'll pay for what you did to him, Siofra."

"What I did to him?" she asks in mock indignation, glancing back at the guards on the door. "My dear girl, you were found with the murder weapon and the blood of our beloved king all over you. You were simply caught in the act. I'm sorry to say that the hearing today will certainly not lean in your favor."

Her false sympathy and lousy acting are as plain as the nose on her face.

How can no one else see her for who she truly is?

"Why are you here?" I snarl. "What do you want from me?"

She straightens her shoulders and holds her head up high. "Oh, you have nothing that I want, dear girl. Your trip to the gallows this afternoon shall suffice. Nevertheless, it would seem the high elf elders believe you should change your attire before the hearing. It would not be pleasant, shall we say, for the people to see their king's blood still staining the clothes of his ruthless murderer."

She gestures to my blood-stained dress, but I don't bother to look down. Instead, I look her straight in the eye. If she wants to see me suffer, then she can keep wanting. I won't show a damn shred of fear in her presence.

"I'm going to tell them what you did," I threaten quietly. "I'll tell them all of it, Siofra. Everything that I know about you and Lord Faenor."

She takes a step forward, lowering her voice to a whisper. "And who, my dear, will believe you?"

"Perhaps no one," I shrug. "But those claims will be out there. In the guards' barracks, on market street, in the taverns of Morween and beyond the kingdom itself. Someone out there will know something. It might not be today or tomorrow, but your web of lies will eventually suffocate you, and you will be held responsible for what you have done."

She shakes her head. "I'm not worried one bit."

"You should be." I snap back assuredly.

If my family and Conall fail to get to me in time today, they will not rest until Siofra is brought to justice. That thought alone will keep me going through this day ahead. Whatever it may bring.

"And what about the part *you* played in all of this?" Siofra asks with a wicked expression on her face.

"My part?"

"Are you telling me that you never stopped to wonder about your father's choice to stay here after the horrors of *The Culling*?"

I glare at her, her question unwillingly creeping under my skin.

"You see, it appears that some ingredients became muddled in your father's study. Key ingredients that changed the entire enchantment in ways that your father could not have foreseen," she says with false sadness. "Not to worry though, your poor father dealt with the guilt and covered for your fatal error for all these years by pledging himself and his capabilities to Morween."

☐

"You're lying," I grit out, my stomach churning.

"Am I?" she chuckles, clearly enjoying every moment of this.

My mind swirls with the possibility that the killing of all these innocent wolves stemmed from my mistake. It makes sense, after all. Why my father stayed here. Why he was so secretive about his involvement in *The Culling*. Why he has been avoiding me since the moment I started asking questions. He was trying to protect me from the truth. The truth that it was I, not him, who made the fatal error all those years ago.

Just then, another set of footsteps enter the dungeons, and I see Cassendra approaching. "Your Majesty," she says dutifully, bowing her head to Siofra. "The dress that you requested."

"Oh, this will do nicely," Siofra answers, her eyes lighting up with wicked glee.

She lifts the dress from Cassendra's arms, holding it up in front of me. However, I can barely focus on what is going on right now. I feel so sick. I try to push my guilt-ridden shame aside, even if it's just for a few moments.

I flick my eyes over the dress, immediately recognizing it as one typically worn by the wood elves of Azealea. It has no lace or delicate silks. No frills or bright colors. Its design is plain, woven from tough wool and brown in color.

Siofra cannot hide her extreme amusement, but little does she know that I couldn't care less about the clothes I'm wearing today.

It's insignificant.

All of it is.

"We cannot allow Morween to forget who you truly are. Eden Nestoriel...*wood elf* of Azealea."

I glare at her before she walks over to the guards, instructing them on what to do with the dress.

As soon as they are conversing, Cass looks straight into my eyes, her hand resting on the pocket of her dress. The pocket in which she placed the whistle yesterday. Her hand taps three times, and I nod subtly in return. Her head then turns quickly to Siofra as she makes her way back over to us.

"Now, we shall leave you to change into more suitable attire," Siofra declares with a sly smirk. "May the gods have mercy upon your damaged soul, dear Eden."

I fold my arms over my chest, watching her and Cass leave the dungeons together.

One of the guards then approaches the cell with the dress in hand while the other opens the door to allow him inside.

"Here, put this on, wood elf," he orders, tossing the dress on the floor at my feet.

I stare at him for a long moment.

"Now!" he barks, pointing at the dress.

The other guard by the door grins creepily, and I know I won't get rid of their leering eyes anytime soon. I undo the silk laces, allowing the blood-stained dress to fall at my feet. The filthy men continue staring at me unashamedly. Still, I continue unfazed, picking up the new dress to step into it carefully. I pull the scratchy material up my bare legs and tie the bodice around my bust.

I then look at both men before closing my eyes and muttering some utter gibberish under my breath. There's silence for a moment before one of them speaks.

"Hey, what the hell are you doing?" he questions, his voice tinged with suspicion.

My eyes snap open, and I shrug casually. "Do you mind? I'm trying to remember the words to the enchantment that makes a man's dick shrivel up and fall off."

They both look at each other in a state of panic, exiting the cell and swiftly heading for the door of the dungeon.

"Idiots," I mutter as the heavy door closes behind them.

I then begin to scour the woolen dress. I know that Cass was trying to tell me something earlier by gesturing to the whistle. She will blow it three times; that was clear.

What does she have planned?

I check the pockets of the dress to find them empty, eventually resorting to patting my whole body down an inch at a time. Then, I finally grab the hem and run my hand along it carefully. My fingers meet with something hard sown into the lining, and I tear at the threads to release what's inside.

A long iron key.

I exhale deeply before slumping down onto the cold, stone floor.

Resurrection

Conall

I drop down low onto my knee, examining the quiet forest around me. There's no sign of any guards, so I lift my arm to gesture for my men to move forward. Immediately, they appear around me from their positions amongst the trees.

"The river is just up ahead, over the cliff edge," Erix whispers.

He moves first, and as soon as he leaves the tree line, an arrow comes flying his way.

"LOOK OUT!"

I leap out from my spot, tackling him to the ground as the arrow blade slashes across my back.

"Zeke, go!" I order, pointing in the direction of the archers who have now revealed their position behind a large rock.

Zeke and Mateo run at the pair of Elven guards in wolf form, dodging their flying arrows before taking them down.

"WAIT! Conall, call your wolves off!" Erix orders as I drag him back up onto his feet. "Remember, no killing guards if it can be avoided!"

"Didn't we talk about this already? My men know what they are doing," I snap back in irritation, looking over my shoulder to see Zeke and Mateo drag the two guards off by their feet, kicking and screaming.

After a few seconds, the forest around us falls silent again, and Zeke pokes his head out of the trees, lifting his thumb with a stupid smile on his face.

"Satisfied?" I ask as Erix glares at me.

I wouldn't say that preserving the lives of Elven guards is high on my priority list right now, but Erix insisted, and in the name of peace, I agreed. I guess my strongly-held hatred of their kind is now beginning to weaken slightly as it has become more apparent to me in recent days that the guards who serve the kingdom are victims of their leaders' lies too.

Commander Walden then appears behind us from the forest. "Don't worry,

Your Majesty; we knocked the guards out and put them with the others. I've got men watching over them now."

"Good," Erix answers, dusting himself off and picking up his discarded sword from the grass. "Hopefully, we won't run into any more guards until we are inside the palace walls."

I glance back at my men, signaling them to head for the cliff edge. As they move, Erix turns to me, eyes narrowing. "Alpha Conall, I don't need a bodyguard."

"Really? Because you were about to get an arrow shoved up your ass a second ago," I mutter, stalking past him. "I need you in one piece if this is going to work."

He sighs in frustration, swinging his sword around before stretching his neck from side to side. It's possible that after all that time stuck in a jail cell, his combat technique is rusty. All I know is he better fucking pull himself together. We are relying on him to get this done.

We come to the edge of the steep cliff, and the men look down curiously.

"How the hell did Eden get down there?" Anton says in wonder.

"Forget wood elf; she must be part spider-monkey," Hunter jokes.

Jarek then pulls out the small vials given to us by Citrine, passing them down the line for everyone to take a quick swig.

Eventually, a vial of pink liquid reaches me, and I swallow a mouthful, passing it to Erix who does the same.

"Alright then, who's going first?" Henrick asks in amusement.

Erix immediately puts his foot out over the edge, and I slap my arm over his chest to stop him. "Not you," I growl.

His jaw tightens, but he doesn't fight me on it.

"Okay, fuck it. I'll go, you bunch of wimps. Not like it can kill me, right?" Hunter smirks before jumping into the air dramatically.

We all watch as he floats over the cliff's edge, his large body drifting to the ground like a feather in the wind.

"Damn, that's got to be the ugliest fairy I've ever seen," Zeke snorts as we all watch on in amazement.

"This is fucking awesome!" Hunter calls out, earning a warning look from me.

"Everybody, move," I order.

They do as I command and step over the edge, each of us following Hunter down to the ground at a slow and steady pace.

I look to my right side to see Anton flapping his arms like a fucking enormous, confused bird and cast my eyes upward to see Jarek closing his eyes in fear and muttering something about heights under his breath.

Goddess above, it's just as well wolves don't do magic. It would be a fucking disaster waiting to happen.

My feet hit the ground, and I examine our new position by the fast-flowing river. There isn't a guard in sight around these parts, and I smile to myself slightly, realizing how clever Eden was to think of this entrance in the first place.

"Over here," Erix calls out, heading for a thick patch of vines covering the rock face.

He pulls out his sword and begins chopping the foliage to reveal a dark passageway.

We follow his lead through the twisting stone corridors, and he finally stops, holding up his arm to bring everyone to a halt. Up ahead, I can see the flicker of torches and know that we must be close to the inner walls of the castle itself.

"You all know the plan," I whisper, "Walden's team head for the throne room and enter by the royal gardens. Stick together and be as quiet as possible. No shifting unless necessary."

Walden nods, gesturing to the tunnel at his right side. Zeke and a mixture wolves and elves follow on behind him.

"The rest of us will take the throne room by the main entrance. We will meet guards on the way, so stay vigilant and remember we need as few casualties as possible," Erix states seriously as we push on down the corridor.

I catch Rocco rolling his eyes in irritation, but he doesn't argue.

As soon as we turn the corner, I spot two guards ahead. I signal everyone to stop and look at Erix, who nods in understanding. We run up behind the guards who hear us at the last second and draw their swords, but it's too late. I've already secured one in a tight headlock, cutting off his air supply. At the same time, Erix elbows another in the face before punching him to knock him out cold. The man in my arms goes limp, and I shove him aside.

We push on again through the palace, and it doesn't take long to see that Erix was right in his prediction. Our mixed team come across guards at every turn, but between our fighting skills and their knowledge of the castle, we fight the guards off together like a well-oiled machine.

Before long, we have left the underground passageways and reached the palace's doors. The ornate gold detailing decorating the white marble hallways tells me we must be at least getting close to the royal quarters. We stop at the bottom of the corridor when we hear voices coming from inside the throne room.

The hearing is about to begin.

I squint around the edge to see two huge doors closed tightly, lined by a group of around fifteen Elven guards standing shoulder to shoulder. I signal to Erix the number we are facing, and he nods. Jarek hands me the familiar vials of sleeping potion, and I step out from behind the wall, tossing them across the floor to release at the guards' feet.

Immediately, they start dropping like flies, just as they did on the day of Ciridan's funeral.

"Go," Erix orders the others, waiting for them to push ahead.

We step over the limp bodies of the guards, and I look at Erix. "Ready?"

His jaw tightens, and he replaces his sword in its sheath. "Yes."

"Wait here until it's time."

I throw the door open, and our team filters in through the throne room, rapidly spreading out to cover the entirety of the space. The guards inside react quickly, some of them taking a fighting stance while others run toward us, ready to fight.

The room descends into panic as the citizens gathered for the large hearing scream in fear and confusion. I storm down the center aisle of the room, and a guard runs in my direction, swinging his sword at my head. I duck out of the way and punch him in the gut. He stumbles back, allowing me to send an uppercut straight to his chin. His head tips back, and the armored helmet falls from his head, hitting the floor with a clang. He swings his sword again wildly, but I jump out of the way, snatching his throat to throw him down onto the marble floor with a thud. The blade falls from his hand, and he lies unconscious at my feet.

It's then I look up to see that our men have now secured the room. Some guards lie on the ground while others are being held at the point of a blade. The citizens continue to scream and yell in panic, and I know I must silence the chaos before things get out of hand completely.

"SHUT UP! ALL OF YOU SIT BACK DOWN, AND NO ONE WILL

GET HURT!"

The room goes quiet, save for the whimpering of some scared Elven women. I stride over to the table at the top of the room, where I see the jury of elder high elves sitting in a row. My eyes then shift to my side, where the lords are watching me wide-eyed. I immediately find Siofra and Faenor, whose expressions convey a mixture of fear and rage.

"People of Morween," I begin, twisting my body to look around the silent room. "My name is Alpha Conall, and I am here today not to reignite the flames of war but to share with you the treachery and heinous crimes of your leaders," I explain. "Your queen and lords have lied to you for too long. Have ravaged your towns—killed their own people—in the name of greed and—"

"ENOUGH OF THIS!" Siofra yells, springing up onto her feet. "These are vicious lies! Someone detain this beast immediately! As the last remaining sovereign of this realm, I demand it!"

It's then that the doors at the back of the room open once again, and Erix walks in. The sound of shocked gasps and murmurs fill the space.

"It can't be!"

"It's not him! Surely it's not!"

"He looks just like him!"

"Prince Erix?!"

He stops at my side, turning to face Siofra directly. "Hello, Mother. It's been a while."

Her mouth falls open in disbelief, her hand visibly shaking as she lifts it to her face.

"Surprised to see me?" Erix continues, walking forward to look over the faces of the stunned lords.

"THIS MAN IS AN IMPOSTER!" Faenor yells desperately, rising to his feet. "How dare you rabid beasts impersonate our beloved prince?"

Erix smiles, shaking his head from side to side before clearing his throat. The room quietens further as the Elven people gawp at him with uncertainty. "People of Morween, your eyes do not deceive you today. It is I, son of King Ciridan—your prince—your rightful ruler and servant to the realm," he proclaims, addressing the entire room. "I can assure you. I am who I say I am!" he continues, pulling a ring from his finger to toss it to one of the elders.

"The Royal Prince's seal," the elder confirms, holding it up to show the others.

Erix then pulls his sword from its sheath holding it up to present it to the table of elders.

"You now have my seal and my sword, and you shall also have the truth."

The elder elves nod for him to proceed.

"This wolf tells the truth of my mother's treason. The fact is that she and many of these lords in front of you now have sullied our once great city. Their corruption runs deep, and I shall tell you every last detail of their disgusting betrayal, starting with my own wrongful imprisonment. An imprisonment forced on me by my own mother, who sought to use my staged death—as well as fake wolf attacks—as a means of destroying an entirely innocent species."

The people in the room begin to mutter amongst themselves, a strong aura of anger and frustration building up in the tense atmosphere.

Erix walks forward, standing directly in front of Siofra, who stares at him, her face as white as a ghost.

"You disgust me, Mother," he snarls lowly. "You *will* be punished for what you have done."

Suddenly, the throne room doors open, and a river of Faenor's men come flooding into the room.

"SEIZE THEM ALL!" Faenor orders loudly.

I get ready to fight when suddenly, I see a man run straight at Erix's back, sword in hand.

Shit!

"ERIX!" I yell in warning.

He turns his head but has no sword to defend himself. Then, out of nowhere, Rocco's body flies through the air, taking the incoming sword straight through his gut. He hits the ground at Erix's feet.

Erix's eyes widen, and he runs for his sword, snatching it up to fight off another attacker. Commander Walden enters the room with the rest of our team, and it's clear that many palace guards recognize him as their former leader.

"GUARDS OF MORWEEN! DEFEND OUR CITY! BY ORDER OF YOUR COMMANDER AND YOUR PRINCE!" Erix yells into the chaos.

The palace guards immediately join us in the fray, and Faenor's men are now more than outnumbered.

I finish off the man I'm fighting, looking to the guilty lords who have now attempted to scatter and flee like the cowards they are.

☐

"STOP THEM! SEAL THE DOORS!" I bellow, but it's too late.

I see the tail of Siofra's dress disappear behind the closed door as she and Lord Faenor make their escape.

Fuck!

I run in their direction, swinging open the doors into the empty palace corridors. Erix appears at my back. "This way!" he shouts, running down the hallway to our left.

I follow him, and we catch Siofra and Faenor in our sights, splitting up to run in different directions.

"FUCK! FAENOR IS GOING FOR THE DUNGEONS!" Erix yells breathlessly.

"I'll take him! You take the queen!" I order.

He nods, and we part ways, running after our intended targets.

Ghost

Erix

"MOTHER, STOP! IT'S OVER!" I call out, running after her as she disappears inside my father's study, slamming the door closed behind her.

I grab the knob to find it locked, but with so much adrenaline coursing through my body, I don't let it hold me back. I lift my foot, kicking the door until it bursts open to reveal the familiar room on the other side.

My mother yelps in surprise, pulling back from the desk drawers to stand still. Her hands then rise slowly in the air, and tears roll down her cheeks.

I slam the broken door behind me, and we stare at each other silently.

For all these years, I have wondered what it would be like to look her in the eye again.

Would I be overcome with blind rage?

Would I break down in a fit of despair and sadness?

I had no idea what to expect, but right now as I look into her icy blue eyes, I feel nothing at all. No warmth for the mother who raised me. No hatred for the woman who imprisoned me.

Just *nothing*.

"Erix! My boy! My beautiful son! I'm so happy that you are here. I've missed you so very, very much—"

"Enough," I interrupt. "I've had enough of your lies to last me a lifetime."

"I'm not lying!" she argues adamantly, shaking her head. "I wanted to see you. I swear. I have dreamed of the day we would meet again."

"Well, you know where I've been all along," I answer. "For seventy long years, you know where I've been."

Her head lowers, and she blinks in shame.

"You do not understand. I wished to come and see you, but Lord Faenor forbid it. He said we mustn't make contact until you saw some sense—"

"So now you are claiming he is the mastermind behind all of this?" I ask, moving closer. "That he forced you to exile your own son?!"

"He wanted to kill you!" she yells back, her tear-filled eyes finding mine again. "But I said no! I stopped him because I knew we would be reunited one day, and here you are now, my dear sweet boy! You have come back home, and now I realize there is nothing that I wanted more than this!"

She rushes forward to rest her hands on either side of my face. "I have made so many mistakes, and yes I have lied, but my love for you is true, and it is strong. You are my son, my flesh and blood. Now that you are home, we can be a family again. Just you and I."

I close my eyes, and she leans her forehead to mine for a long moment before reaching her arms around my body in a firm hug.

Part of me wants to believe the lie. Wants to believe that she can change, but I know in my heart that she is beyond redemption.

It's then that she proves me right, sprinkling some kind of powder over me before muttering under her breath.

"*Caderes.*"

The quiet incantation leaves her lips just as I suspected it would. I already know it is meant to incapacitate me somehow, so when nothing happens, she tries again. Her voice rushed and desperate.

"*Caderes...*"

"Not this time, Mother." I step back to look into her confused eyes, pulling the crystal from my pocket, the one given to me by Citrine. "Your magic may be strong, but there are many out there who possess more talent than you ever will."

She gulps in realization and defeat when the door of the study is thrown open, and Commander Walden appears with a troop of guards behind him.

"Siofra, former Queen of Morween, you are hereby under arrest and will face trial where you will answer for your crimes committed against the realm. The people will decide your fate, your sentence carried out immediately after the trial," I say carefully, looking into her eyes. "Take her away. I want her locked in insolation under your watch Commander Walden."

"My pleasure," he retorts, grasping her wrists, securing them in iron cuffs behind her back.

"No! No, Erix! Please! I'm your mother!" she protests as she is dragged out of the room. "I love you! I love you!"

Eden

I look down at the key in my hand, twirling it around with my fingers as I wait for Cass' signal.

The last hour has felt like torture.

Imaginary images conjured by my brain have plagued me in the form of vivid flashbacks.

Lincoln clutching the bodies of his family.

Conall attempting to wake his dead mother and father.

Whole packs, silent as death falls upon them like a dark shadow from the sky.

I close my eyes and try to breathe past it.

I'm not entirely stupid. I know that what Siofra said may very well be a lie concocted to make me suffer, but somewhere in the back of my mind, I have this niggling feeling that there could be truth to her words.

My years spent as my father's apprentice taught me a lot, but the fact is that I was still learning back then and more than capable of making mistakes.

If what siofra said to me is true, then how could I ever look Conall in the eyes again? How could he ever see me the same way?

The whole scenario is enough to make me want to give up. To throw in the towel and allow them to drag me to my death.

Suddenly, I hear commotion from the floor above my head and notice dust and rock fragments come loose from the ceiling.

What the hell is going on up there?

I barely have time to consider the possibilities before I hear the sound of the whistle.

One.

Two.

Three times.

I take a deep breath and stuff the key inside the lock, twisting it to free myself from the cell. I run for the door of the dungeons and gasp when I hear a loud thud from the other side. The door opens, and I look down at the ground to see the two guards lying dead.

□

"We have to go," Cass whispers, tossing the crossbow to one side to grab my hand. "This way. Maybe we can escape through the gardens while they are all distracted in the throne room."

I nod in agreement, ready to follow her lead when I hear it. The sound of yelling and shouting coming from the royal quarters of the palace.

"Wait!" I order, coming to an abrupt halt. "What is that? What's going on?"

"I don't know!" Cass replies frantically. "But I don't want to hang around to find out!"

Then, it dawns on me exactly what the noise is and where it is coming from.

"It's the throne room! Con must have got in!"

"What? How?"

"I don't know," I admit, shaking my head. "But we have to help him!"

We turn back the way we came heading for the throne room as fast as possible. Cass turns the corner first, and her body is shoved back through the air, her head cracking against the marble wall with a thwack.

"CASS!" I shout, running to her aid to find her unconscious.

Just then, arms wrap around me, one holding me around my chest whilst the other covers my mouth.

As I am dragged backward, my screams leave my body in a distorted muffle. I manage to steal a look at my attacker, my eyes widening when I see that it is Lord Faenor.

I struggle against him wildly, pushing my back against his chest before he pulls a knife from his cloak.

"Enough!" he snaps, holding the blade to my neck.

At that moment, Conall appears at the end of the corridor a few feet away from us. His eyes, filled with fury, find mine, and he takes a few slow steps forward. I look over him to see his chest heaving, a sword held firmly in his hand.

"DON'T COME ANY CLOSER, YOU FILTHY BEAST!" Faenor roars, pressing the cold steel against me harder in warning.

"Don't listen to him, Conall!" I shout. "Kill him!"

Faenor presses the knife into my neck, piercing the skin. "Shut up!!"

I breathe through the pain as a warm dribble of blood begins seeping down the column of my neck.

Conall's eyes light up with rage, but he does not speak. Instead, he lifts his hands in surrender, slowly bending down to the ground to put down the sword.

"That's it, you disgusting dog. Now get up," Faenor orders. "Eden and I are going for a little walk now, and if you dare follow us, I'll kill her."

Conall's eyes meet mine again, and I will him to do it. To do what he must to end this son-of-a-bitch once and for all.

I tip my chin, and his eye twitches before he grabs a dagger from his boot, rising to his feet quickly to send it flying down the corridor at Faenor's face.

I squeeze my eyes closed, feeling the blade graze my cheek slightly before it sinks into Faenor's face, hitting him square in the eye. He screams in pain, releasing me from his hold to fall backward. His body grows still, blood pouring from his mouth as he slides down the white marble wall to land in a heap on the floor.

Dead.

I gasp for air and turn my head to see Conall running to me. "Eden!"

In a split second, his arms encompass me, and I sink into his warm body. "It's over. It's over," he chants reassuringly, holding me tight as his eyes skim over my face. He lifts his thumb to rub the dribble of blood from my cheek.

"You came for me," I murmur, staring into his honey-colored eyes with tears in mine.

"Always," he answers, holding my face in his hands.

In return, I offer him a weak smile, and his forehead touches mine as we close our eyes.

"Eden...I have something to tell you," he murmurs, his hands falling from my face, pain flickering in his eyes as he takes a step away from me.

"What?"

His brows knit together, and his lips part, but no words emerge.

"Conall...what is it?"

"It's about Erix."

"Erix?" I question in confusion.

"Eden?"

My heart stills in my chest, my eyes growing wide at the sound of his familiar voice. I turn my head to the side and take a sharp breath when I see him standing there looking back at me.

My Prince.

My Erix.

□

Declarations

Eden

"Erix?" I question breathlessly, my brain struggling to comprehend the sight in front of me right now. "Is that you?"

He nods his head softly, a weak smile touching his lips. "Yes."

I lift my hand to my mouth as complete and utter shock racks my whole body. My heart kicks back into gear, pounding in my chest aggressively, causing my head to spin out of control.

The hallway suddenly fills with people as guards and wolves appear around us. The noise echoes in my brain, making me feel like I might pass out any second.

"Cass!" Zeke says, bending down to lift her flickering eyelid. "Come on, Kid. Wake up!"

She groans, pushing his hand out of the way. "Get off of me, you ass!"

"Con, the throne room is secure. The guards are now escorting the citizens to the great hall as we speak," Jarek reports to Con, whose eyes have not left me. "The elders are waiting for you and Prince Erix when you're ready."

Con nods in return, and I swallow, my eyes drifting back to Erix, who stands at the end of the corridor like a ghost of the past.

A figment of my imagination.

I hold onto the wall for support, making my way toward him slowly but steadily. He moves forward to stand before me, his eyes flicking over my face. We stare at each other as I try to pull myself together, and the hallway quietens around us as everyone watches with curiosity.

"I don't know what to say... You haven't changed a bit. You're just as I remember you," he whispers, lifting his hand to touch my cheek.

I cannot speak.

I have not a single coherent sentence in my head.

Instead, I just study him.

His blue eyes are bright and twinkling. His warm sandy-colored hair is swooped back from his handsome face. The face that I kissed a thousand times before he was so cruelly taken from me.

"How?" I ask gently.

He exhales, his hand dropping from my cheek.

"I can't explain it all right now. But I will. I promise."

I nod automatically, and his hand reaches out to take mine. I remember his gentle touch as if it were only yesterday that I felt it; the softness of his skin touching mine is a feeling I have yearned for for countless years.

I look down at our intertwined fingers and then lift my head to look back at Conall.

He stands there watching us from afar with his arms folded over his chest. Unmoving. Unreadable.

"Can I borrow you? Just for a few minutes. I know that you need your rest," Erix asks carefully, drawing my attention back to him.

"I uh... I'm sorry. This is just a lot to take in."

"Please," Erix pleads, his eyes filled with so much sadness that my heart aches. "I won't keep you for long."

I nod, unable to refuse, letting him lead me away from the busy corridor into the empty library.

Silence falls on us like a heavy weight as soon as the door closes.

We stare at each other, and still, I have no idea what to say, but I know I need to try. "Where have you been?" I ask carefully, my voice quivering with nerves.

"My mother... She had me locked away."

I gasp in horror, my brows scrunching as I look over his body again. It is then I see just how thin he looks, his clothes old and tattered.

"Erix, I'm so sorry," I murmur, tears filling my eyes. "You've been alive all this time, and I- I didn't know."

"Hey," he whispers. "This is not your fault. Don't you dare say you're sorry. Especially not after everything you have done for my people."

I can't help the flood of emotion that washes over me in a tidal wave.

The guilt, the anger, the sheer unjustness of it all.

He wraps his arms around me, cocooning me in his familiar embrace, kissing my head before resting his head on mine. "Shhhh."

We stay like this for a few moments, and then he leans back to look into my eyes. "You have no idea how much I missed you, Eden. I thought about you every day. In my darkest hours, thoughts of you pulled me through. Thoughts of someday having you in my arms again," he says quietly before lifting my chin. "Eden, I still love you as much as the day I left this palace."

My heart breaks at his declaration; the outpouring of his love takes me back seventy years in the blink of an eye. His eyes search mine hopefully and then flick to my lips, his head inching closer.

"I can't," I whisper, staring into the pools of deep blue.

He stops in his tracks, his jaw tensing as he nods in pain. "You've moved on?" he asks. "Are you married?"

I shake my head gently. "No, but there's someone else...and I love him, Erix."

He looks over my face, waiting for me to continue.

"Alpha Conall...he's my mate."

He immediately looks away, stepping back to rub the back of his neck.

I stand watching helplessly as he paces the floor. "Your mate?" he asks again for clarification. "But you're not a wolf; how does that work? Is it even possible?"

I shrug my shoulder, unable to give him answers. "I'm not sure how or why it happened, but it's true. We *are* mates, and I love him."

It is hard to say these words to him, knowing that he has been through hell, but I also know that I must be honest with him.

Erix nods, putting his hands on his hips as he looks down at the floor. "How long have you been together?"

"Not long," I answer truthfully.

His head snaps back up. "Then you have to think things through, Eden. Please?"

"Erix...."

He takes my hands in his, gripping them desperately. "Our love was real, Eden. It meant something. I was ready to marry you and spend an eternity loving you for every part of who you are. I still feel the same way," he explains. "Our happiness was stolen from us, but we can have it all back because I still love you, and I can see in your eyes that you still love me too. I'm not ready to give up on you yet or to give up on us."

He then brushes my hair from my face softly. "Just allow me to show you how happy we could be."

The door knocks, and when it opens, I see another familiar face appear behind it. "Sorry, Your Majesty. The people are growing restless in the great hall. You may want to address them now if you can," Commander Walden states.

"Of course, make sure the elders are there too, Commander. I'll be right there."

Walden nods and closes the door.

"Come," Erix says gently. "It's time for Morween to know the truth and to heal."

I follow him to the door, and he lets me walk into the empty corridor first.

I immediately look for Conall, but he is nowhere to be seen.

Erix and I walk in silence to the great hall, which is bustling with people who immediately grow quiet when they see us approaching. I'm met with suspicious and curious looks, but I don't let that scare me.

"Eden!" my mother cries, pulling me into a warm hug.

My father follows her lead, throwing his arms around us both.

Erix gives me a soft smile, nodding at my father respectfully before he heads for the stage at the front of the room.

My mother releases me, and Grandma Citrine appears at her back to take my hands. "My beautiful girl, what a journey you have had," she says sadly, lifting her hand to my face. "But happiness is on the horizon. I can see it."

I nod, taking a deep breath as everyone faces the stage to listen to Erix.

Still, my eyes scan the room looking for Conall, but I've yet to find him. Instead, I see the rest of the Alphas standing near the front of the hall.

"People of Morween, you have been through a lot of turmoil today," Erix begins. "I understand your hurt, confusion and frustration, and I say to you all that it is now time to close this chapter of our history and heal together. However, before we can do that, we must go back to those dark days of war, and I must tell you all the truth of what really happened...."

As Erix launches into his passionate speech, my mind drifts off as I look to the door. Wherever Conall is, I need to find him.

I slip away from Grandma Citrine, quietly making my way back through the empty hallways of the palace. The large entrance is open wide, and I nod to the guards as I slip through the doors.

I then see him leaning against the palace gates, looking toward the forest in the distance.

"Planning on going somewhere?" I ask softly.

☐

He turns his head and smirks. "Thought about it," he answers, twisting around to face me.

"You did?" I ask, unable to hide the disappointment in my voice.

"Harmony needs to know what happened here today. I'll need to check on them as soon as I can."

I nod in understanding. "Of course."

An awkward silence lingers between us, and he looks down at the ground before his eyes return to mine. "He told you he still loves you, didn't he?"

I nod my head carefully in response.

His jaw tightens, and I sense the pain and anger in his aura.

"It doesn't matter though, Con, because I told him that I love you—"

"But you love him too, Eden," he interrupts. "I saw it in your eyes as soon as you looked at him."

I shake my head quickly. "No, it's different," I protest. "Erix and I have a history, and I'm just... I'm just trying to process all of this as best I can, but I don't even know where to start! Everything I say is wrong, and I don't know what to do!"

I begin to pant heavily in a state of panic, and he grabs my arm, pulling me into his body. My skin tingles on contact with his, and I breathe in his scent, which immediately calms my flustered mind.

"It's okay," he whispers. "You don't need to have all the answers right this second. You need time to think."

Then he lifts my chin to look into my eyes.

"But Eden, listen to me," he says seriously. "Erix might not be ready to let you go, but neither am I. I'll fight for you with every last fucking breath in my body because even if I don't get to call you mine yet, I'm already yours. Always have been. Always will be."

I stare at him as he releases me from his hold, brushing past my body to enter back inside the palace.

Leaving

Eden

"I've been looking for you everywhere," Cass says, perusing the study curiously.

"Hey," I answer, placing the jar in my hand back on the shelf. "Sorry, I just had to find somewhere quiet to think."

She wanders over, examining the busy shelves as she moves. "Wow. So this is the famous Nestoriel study. I have to say, it kinda gives me the creeps."

I smile in return. "How's the head?" I ask, gesturing to the small green velvet chairs by the window.

"It's fine!" she laughs, sinking into her seat. "I feel like I should be asking you that question." She raises her eyebrow at me before offering me a sympathetic smile.

I can't help but let out a puff of air, sitting down to place my head in my hands. "Urgg, Cass, this is such a mess. No matter what I do, I'm going to really hurt someone, and my heart breaks every time I think about it."

"So don't think about it too much, Eden," she says plainly. "You have to follow your heart and do what you want. Both these guys have been through hell and back. Sure, someone will get hurt, there's no avoiding that part, but they will survive."

I nod, leaning back in my chair to look into the forest. It's getting dark now, and the negotiation talks are still ongoing in Erix's study. My mind has been going crazy, wondering how it's all playing out.

"Are you looking forward to going back to Harmony?" I ask Cass in an effort to occupy my muddled mind.

She shrugs a little. "Yes, it will be nice to see people again, but it's been a long time. I feel like I'm ready for a new adventure."

The thing that strikes me about Cass is she doesn't seem the type to settle into village life. She's destined for more, and she knows it. "Where will you go?"

"I've not decided yet," she answers with excitement. "But wherever it is, I am NOT going to cook, clean or serve anyone ever again!"

"I guess that's fair," I chuckle, pouring us both a drink as the sound of footsteps meets my ears.

"Mateo!" Cass calls out excitedly, jumping up from her chair.

"Hey, Cassie! It's so good to see you again," he grins, opening his arms to envelope her in a hug.

"How did you find us?"

"Eden's mother said you guys might be down here," he answers, looking around. "This place is...uhh, it's really something."

Cass looks at me, vindicated, and I laugh. "It's okay; you can call it creepy if you like. Cass has already made me well aware of the fact."

"Oh, thank Goddess for that," he laughs, his eyes connecting with mine for a long moment.

"Sooo...I think I'll go bother Zeke and the others for a while since the meeting is over. Catch up with you later, Eden?"

"Course. Thanks, Cass." I answer sincerely.

"Ahh, it was nothing," she laughs, punching Mateo's arm before heading for the stairs.

"She's great," I say to Mateo as he sits down in front of me.

"Yeah, she is. One of the strongest women I know. Just like you."

I smile in return, and he throws me a playful wink.

"So, uh, how did the meeting go?" I ask, unable to hide the nerves in my voice.

"You really want to know?" he asks, raising his brow. "I noticed you were invited and didn't come along."

I clear my throat and shuffle uncomfortably in my chair. "I've had enough palace politics this week, I think."

"True, although we both know that's not the reason that you didn't go," he states knowingly.

"Was it civil?" I ask hopefully.

He grins, nodding. "I'm not going to lie, it was tense, but everyone left with a sense that things were heading in the right direction. That's the best we can hope for right now."

"Yes, you're right," I say, waiting for him to continue.

"Erix is currently working on a peace treaty with Conall. He is committed to spreading the truth to the wider areas of the kingdom and the surrounding villages, but now the news has hit Morween, I don't think it will take long for everyone to learn what happened."

"Good," I answer, a little weight lifting off my shoulders. "What about Harmony?"

"They are free to stay where they are if they like or move if they wish. The land is officially theirs now. They are safe and free, which is all we ever wanted for them."

I smile, leaning back in my chair again to take a deep breath.

"I haven't told you the best part yet," Mateo states with a wicked glint in his eye. "Erix has seized all of the corrupt lords' lands and riches. We have the choice to take our pack lands back if it's empty, or if it's already occupied by Elven citizens, then Erix offered reparations instead. He also threw in the little added sweetener that we can be the ones to carry out the lords' sentences after trial if we choose to. I'm fairly certain some of the guys will take him up on that offer."

"And everyone is okay with all of that?"

"I mean, Rocco is pissed."

"Oh fuck," I reply worriedly, my brows knitting together.

"Although, that's more because we have been calling him the 'Prince *saver*' now instead of the 'Prince *slayer*.' I don't think he can handle what his heroics have done to his beloved asshole reputation."

I giggle before looking at him thoughtfully. "Really though, you think everything will be okay, Mateo?"

He shrugs airily. "Only time will tell, but at least everyone has the decision to do what they want now to move on."

"What are you going to do?" I question, tilting my head as I examine him.

"My pack lands are still empty, but they aren't much use to me now so I'll probably take some gold too. I think I might go home for a while and figure out what I want from there. Maybe I'll go traveling for a bit. Call me unsociable, but spending seventy years with the same damn assholes has left me with itchy feet which are ready to explore."

"I think that sounds like a good plan."

We look at each other for a moment, and his face suddenly turns solemn. "I think I owe you an apology."

"Mateo...."

"I liked you, Eden," he interrupts quickly. "I think I got caught up in having someone there to protect again. It's in my blood, after all. But I crossed the line when I tried to come between you and Con. It wasn't my place."

"You were just trying to look out for me. You've been a good friend," I answer sincerely. "I don't know if I would have survived those early days in the den without you!"

"So you forgive me for the whole hitting you over the head with a rock thing?"

"Would any of us be here now if you hadn't?" I ask with a light laugh.

"No, I guess not," he murmurs in realization, standing up from his chair. "In that case, you were the best mistake I ever made, Eden Nestoriel."

"I'll take that as a compliment... I think," I laugh, standing up to meet him.

He gives me a warm hug, patting my back firmly. "Keep your chin up. Things can only get better from here. Surely."

He then leaves me alone in the study, and I let out a deep sigh, walking over to the shelves filled with hundreds of ingredients. Siofra's words still haunt my thoughts, no matter how much I try to stop them. Whether she is telling the truth or not, Con has a right to know her claims. I decide to stop putting it off, heading for the stairs leading back into the palace.

It's dark now. The citizens have long left the palace walls, and there is an air of calm I haven't felt in a long time around here. Then, I hear the sound of loud, rough familiar voices speckled with laughter and the occasional obscenity. It's funny how the sound once irritated me beyond belief, and now I find it oddly comforting. I open the door of the large drawing room to find the Alphas sitting together having a drink.

"Uhh—oh boys, look who it is. Trouble has arrived," Anton announces, grinning like a madman as he walks over to scoop me up into a bear hug.

My feet dangle as he swings me around like a rag doll.

"Alright Anton, give her a break. Hasn't she been through enough?" Hunter laughs, grabbing me into a similar style hug. "How's our hero doing?"

"I'm fine," I answer vaguely in return. "Hi, everyone."

Mateo gives me a reassuring nod while the others smile warmly.

"So turns out you weren't a backstabbing bitch then," Samuel shrugs, earning him a look of disgust from Henrick.

"Goddess, you're such a dick. Just apologize to the woman already."

He glares at Henrick and shakes his head in refusal. "I'll admit I was wrong."

"Then let's just leave it there, huh?" I ask, looking between him and Rocco where he sits on the couch, bandaged around the waist.

"Truce," Rocco grunts in return, giving me a curt nod.

"That's probably the best you'll get out of those pricks," Zeke says from behind.

I spin around to greet him, hugging him as the rest of the men return to their drinks.

"Zeke—"

"Con has just finished up with Erix," he answers, anticipating my next question. "He will want to speak with you before he heads out."

"Heads out?" I ask with a frown.

"Con and a few others are going to Harmony tonight to deliver the peace treaty news. I'm going to stay here and work on some more of the details with Erix."

My eyes widen, and I let out a surprised breath. "Oh, okay."

"Go on, go find him," he says with a smirk. "He'll be outside. Brooding, most likely. You know how he is."

I squeeze Zeke's arm in thanks, rushing for the door.

As soon as I burst into the hallway, I bump straight into Con's hard chest. "Shit!" I yelp in fright.

He lays his hands on my upper arms, and my shoulders relax on cue. "I was just on my way to track you down."

"Me too!" I squeak a little too eagerly.

Calm. Yourself. Down. Eden!

"Is there somewhere we can talk?" he asks, looking into my eyes seriously.

From the tone of his voice, I immediately feel that whatever he has to say may not exactly be what I want to hear.

"Sure," I answer, swallowing worriedly.

I turn around and lead him down the hallway in silence. As we walk, I see him looking around curiously, taking it all in. I've been living in this palace for so long that I forget what this ridiculous opulence must look like to an outsider.

"It's a little different from the den, huh?" I ask in an attempt to lighten the mood.

"Yeah, you could say that."

I come to a stop by the door and turn to him slowly. "This is my room."

He glances at the door behind me, his jaw tensing a little as he swallows.

□

My cheeks begin to warm as I open the door to let him in first. He walks inside, looking around before stopping in the middle of the floor.

There's something about him being here that instantly makes my temperature rise. That makes me want for his touch.

"It suits you," he comments, gesturing to the abundance of flowers and stacks of books placed everywhere.

I try to hold myself together, pushing my lustful thoughts aside. "I did what I could with it."

He laughs slightly, nodding his head.

I take a step forward, and he does too.

I rest my hands on his chest, lifting my eyes to meet his, and I can't hold myself back any longer. I launch myself at him, grabbing handfuls of his shirt as I pull his lips down to meet mine. He throws his arms around me, lifting me off the ground as he devours my mouth with his own.

There's no feeling that even comes close to this.

To being in his arms.

To have him want me so completely.

I feel whole when I'm with him. Like myself, but stronger and more powerful than I ever was before.

I tear my lips away from his, and our eyes fix on each other intensely as I drag him over to the bed. I sit on the edge, and he stands in front of me, watching with laser focus as I lie back on the mattress.

His dark, hooded eyes scan over my body, and I return the favor, memorizing the grooves of his muscular forearms and those large, capable hands.

I drop my hands to my dress, tugging it up slowly, my legs spreading as I invite him to come to me. To satisfy this burning need that I have. A thirst that only he can quench. "Con..." I whisper desperately, biting the edge of my lip.

He swallows again, lowering his body down on top of mine.

I feel his hardness straining against his pants and subtly push my throbbing core against him.

He doesn't react. Instead, he remains still, studying my face.

"What's wrong?" I ask, my brows knitting together.

"This is not what I intended to happen when I came looking for you—"

I shake my head gently, leaning up a little to land soft kisses on his jaw.

His eyes close, and I feel his cock swell against me, a stifled groan leaving his chest.

"Doesn't this feel right to you?" I murmur in his ear. "Don't you want this?"

His body stiffens, his hands balling into fists on the bed as he tries to control himself. "You have no idea how much I want this..." he answers in a low husk that has me all but begging for more. "But I can't. Not tonight."

I stop, my head resting on the bed as I look at him questioningly.

"Eden, I'm going to Harmony tonight. I have things I have to take care of."

I gulp in disappointment, unsure of what to say next.

"This isn't me stepping aside," he adds assuredly.

He lifts himself from my body and sits on the bed beside me as I sit up to join him.

"Oh? It sure feels that way."

"That day in the forest when I let you go, I told you that no matter what happened, I was glad I found you."

"Yes, and I'm glad I found you too."

"But you didn't find me. You were *forced* to stay with me. Forced into a bond that you didn't ask for. That your kind doesn't recognize or fully understand."

"I don't see it that way, and you know it," I argue gently.

He nods and looks away for a moment. "I just need to know you've taken the time to think this through. If you choose me, it's for the right reasons. Not because of lust. Not because I forced you. Not because I held you captive." he explains. "I took your freedom away from you once before, and I won't do it again. The least I can do is let you figure this out on your own terms."

I reach for his hand, holding it tightly. "I don't need to figure it out."

"Then tell me that when I come back in a couple of days," he says calmly, looking into my eyes. "Tell me when you've had time to process everything, and then I'll know you're sure."

As I stare back at him, I can see the pain in his eyes. I nod in agreement, and he lifts my hand to his lips, kissing it softly.

"I'll be back soon," he says quietly, standing up to head for the door.

"You better be, wolf," I whisper, the words out of my mouth before I can stop them.

"Just try and stop me...elf," he smirks, closing the door to leave me alone once again.

☐

Nostalgia

Eden

"It's kind of Erix to do that, isn't it?" my mother asks, breaking me from my daydream.

"Hmm?" I answer distractedly, picking up the teacup to take a drink.

She looks from me to my father carefully. "I can see you have other things on your mind today."

"Sorry," I murmur, shaking my head. "What were we talking about?"

She smiles softly. "That's okay. I was just saying it is kind of Erix to give your father the choice to remain working here if he wants."

I look at my dad questioningly. "What are you going to do?"

A shadow of a smile touches his lips. "Well, the hospital wing has been asking me to look into various remedies for some time now. I haven't had the opportunity to help because I served the crown, but now that I can, I think this would be time and effort well spent."

"I'm glad, Father," I say sincerely,

"I'm sure Citrine would like to help out too, Haleth," my mother says encouragingly. "You should ask her!"

"Maybe I will," he answers with hope in his voice. "Perhaps my daughter would like to assist as well?"

I smile in return. "I haven't really thought about what to do next,"

"Of course. And there's no rush."

He and my mother go back to eating and discussing new plans together. As I observe them both, I realize that this is the first time in so many years that I have witnessed my father somewhat content in life. It's strange really, that I never noticed before how unhappy he was. How miserable he seemed to be working here at the palace. I know that he will forever carry guilt within himself for the part he played in all of this, but to see him look to the future gives me hope.

Can there be hope for me too?

Will I ever be able to move on from the past?

At this point, I don't know.

"Sorry to disturb you, Miss."

A servant hands me a note, bowing his head respectfully before taking his leave. I open it up and brush my fingers lightly over the delicate, familiar script.

*

*

*

Meet me as soon as you can in our spot.

*

*

*

"Is everything okay?" my mother asks, examining me worriedly.

"Uhh yes, I've got to go though. Thanks for lunch," I answer, saying my goodbyes before strolling through the palace gardens.

As I take the route, I think about how long it has been since I trod this path. After Erix's death, I couldn't face coming here anymore. It held too many beautiful memories.

The first time we watched the sunset together.

Our first kiss.

The first time he told me that he loved me.

All are special, meaningful memories that were just too painful to relive after he was gone.

It's a beautiful day today. The sun is shining, and the flowers are in full bloom. If this were any normal day, these factors would soothe my soul, but this is anything but normal. I've felt odd since Conall left last night. Like I'm in limbo.

I pause for a moment to take in the view up ahead. The stunning circular, carved stone structure of the lake house. The rays of sun bouncing off the walls make it appear golden, and the array of flowers and vines make it seem like it has spontaneously sprouted from the ground.

I breathe heavily and make my way upstairs, stopping at the small balcony when I see him looking out over the calm, shimmering water.

"Hi," I say softly, wandering over to his side.

His head turns, and his handsome, newly-shaved face lights up. "Hey."

☐

I cast my eyes over the water, and I can see from the corner of my eye that he is watching me.

"You look beautiful today, by the way," he says, a slight nervous edge to his voice.

"Thank you," I smile, leaning against the stone balcony. "You don't look so bad yourself."

He laughs, nodding his head. "I'm not going lie; it felt pretty good to bathe again."

"I bet it did," I grin, looking over his perfectly positioned tunic.

"It's not too much, is it?" he asks, swallowing as he looks down over his attire.

"For a future king? I'd say it's perfect."

He smiles in return before clearing his throat. "I'm glad you came, Eden. I'm sorry we didn't get a chance to speak again last night."

"Don't be silly, Erix. You just inherited responsibility for an entire kingdom. I understand you're busy."

"Yes, it has been a bit of a whirlwind. Trying to get my head around everything that has happened here...."

"I can imagine," I say sympathetically.

"I'm sorry about what happened with Aubrun. I heard what he did to you."

I exhale gently and look up to the sky. "He was a good man but wasn't cut out for any of this."

"Maybe. Perhaps the same can be said for me."

I immediately shake my head at the mere suggestion. "That's not true at all," I argue, placing my hands on his shoulders as I look into his blue eyes. "What you have achieved here in less than twenty-four hours is incredible. The kingdom *needs* you as its king. There's no one else who could do the job better."

There is no need for me to embellish or offer false praise. I mean every single word. Erix was the perfect king back then, and he still is. He's the man I always hoped he was, and it makes my heart sing to see it.

"Thanks," he answers gratefully.

I squeeze his arm, dropping my hands by my side as he steps closer, his light breath fanning my face.

"You know, the people also need a queen. One who is gentle and kind but also clever and wise. They need you, Eden." I swallow as he takes my hands in his. "Just look at this place!" he says, gesturing to the pretty lake. "It was made for you...you and I together. Remember what we did here on the night of my father's awful 300th birthday party?"

"Erix..." I warn as he begins to laugh playfully.

"What? I can't help it if I still replay the memory!" He taps his head, and I smile.

"You wore your hair up that night. Your dress was blue with gold trim, and your panties...well—"

"Stoppp," I groan, pushing his shoulder.

His eyes fix on me, his smile wide as he lays his hand on my face. "I'd do anything to go back there again," he whispers quietly, his sadness filling the space between us.

"I wish none of this ever happened to you, Erix. Truly, I do."

He nods, letting out a puff of air before grabbing my hand tightly. "Come on... I have something to show you."

He begins dragging me eagerly back downstairs, and I look around curiously as he takes me through the winding corridors of the palace. "Where are we going?"

"You'll see!" he laughs. "Your patience hasn't improved in the seventy years I've been gone, it seems."

"I beg your pardon?!" I scoff jokingly in reply.

We stop at the doors, and I immediately know exactly where we are. "You know we're not allowed in there."

"Didn't you hear? I'm the new King of Morween."

"I might have heard that," I chuckle, opening the door to step inside the large palace greenhouse. Until now, it's been strictly off-limits, reserved only for Siofra. It always struck me as odd, but now I know why she was so interested in flowers. She was a wood elf all along.

As I amble down the winding path, I stop to admire each individual flower in all its glory. "Wow, this one isn't even native to Morween or anywhere near here, for that matter!" I squeal excitedly, touching the bright yellow petals of the sun-thicket. "You know it can aid in healing wendal-pox, right?!"

"I did not know that," Erix smiles, watching me flit from flower to flower like an overgrown kid. "My father has to see this," I exclaim in wonder, looking up at the tall, overarching blue-blossom tree.

"He can...because it's yours," Erix says matter-of-factly.

I spin around, and he beams at me. "I love seeing you like this, Eden. If you become my queen, you'll want for nothing. You'll have an entire palace at your fingertips. An army of staff at your beck and call. You can carry on your work in peace, and you'll be able to help people the way I know you've always wanted to," he says hopefully. "Just think about that, won't you?"

"Okay," I agree.

"Listen...I hate to do this, but I have a meeting to get to with Zeke, and I don't want to cancel—"

"No! You absolutely shouldn't. Go. Do what you have to do."

He gives me a wink before he leaves, and I stand there for a moment longer looking around the grand surroundings.

∗ ∗ ∗

I tilt my head as I examine the red velvet gown in the mirror.

It was lying on my bed when I arrived back earlier, along with a note inviting me for a private dinner with the prince this evening.

The dress is stunningly luxurious. Fit for a queen, some might say. I guess many women in Morween would kill for a chance to wear such a gown; I, on the other hand, can't help but focus on the slight itch of the heavy material over my body.

The door knocks, and I find a palace servant waiting for me. "Follow me please, Miss," he asks respectfully.

I do as I'm told, navigating the palace hallways until we end up in the royal quarters.

"If you just take a seat, the prince will be with you shortly."

"Thank you," I answer, taking in the new setting.

I recognize it vaguely as the royal dining area, but it's not an area of the palace I have been to often. All of the tables have been removed, bar one situated near the window under a huge, elaborate golden chandelier.

I sit at the table, running my fingertips over the solid gold cutlery. It occurs to me that one simple spoon from this table could feed a family in Morween for months. It's silly, really....

"Eden, sorry I'm late!"

I fumble with the spoon, which bounces onto the floor with a clang. "Shit...sorry," I mumble, getting out of my chair to pick it up.

Erix reaches it before I do and hands it back to me. "That's okay, I've got it," he says chirpily.

As I stare back at him, I'm suddenly transported back to the Alphas' den the night I entered Conall's room for the first time. I dropped a piece of cutlery then too. My mind conjures the intense look in his eyes as he handed it back, the soft light around him, and the warmth of the blazing fire.

It feels like an age has passed since then.

"Are you alright? I can have them fetch a new one. Geralt!"

"No, don't," I say, shaking my head with a smile. "I'm sure we both have eaten from a lot worse."

"You can say that again," he laughs as we sit down together.

"Uhh...thank you for the dress, by the way."

"It looks amazing on you," he answers, taking his time to examine me.

I raise my brow playfully. "My face is up here, Erix."

"Oh, yeah," he replies cheekily. "Forgive me, it's been a while."

I chew at my lip uncomfortably.

"So what's on the menu?" I ask, attempting to change the subject.

"All of your favorites, of course," he grins, passing me a small handwritten menu card.

I can't help but laugh as I look over the mishmash of meals. "Looks incredible!"

"What can I say? I know you, Eden Nestoriel."

I can sense the seriousness in his words. He wants to remind me of our past and how well he knew me back then.

As the food comes to the table thick and fast, we spend some time catching up. Mainly I talk about my work and research. It's nice, but it's more than obvious that neither of us wants to bring up the elephant in the room.

"So, how are you feeling about the trials starting?" I eventually ask as Erix swallows a spoonful of Posey cake.

His eyebrows lift, and he huffs out a breath. "It's going to be tough, but it has to be done, and as king, my people have to see me as strong. They need to believe in me to deliver the justice required. The realm is fragile right now."

I nod in reply. His words are true, but we both know it's not as simple as that.

□

"Have you been to see her?" I ask carefully.

"No, and I don't intend to. There's nothing more I have to say to the woman. She is not a mother. She never was."

I reach out to touch his hand, offering him an encouraging squeeze. "Look at the man you have turned out to be regardless. Be proud of yourself. She can never take that away from you."

"You always know what to say, Eden."

"Do I?" I snort. "I don't particularly think that's true."

"Well, it is," he insists.

I take a drink of wine as he looks at me carefully. "So, I guess it's not just me who has a lot going on... The whole mate thing must have come as a shock?"

I almost choke, spluttering as I swallow the burning alcohol. "Uh, yes. It was."

"Something is holding you back though. I can see it. I know you say you love him, but maybe—"

"I do love him, Erix," I interrupt. "It's not that."

"Then what is it?"

"Your mother...she said I made the error with *The Culling* enchantment. I haven't told Con yet," I explain sadly, shrugging my shoulder.

Erix looks at me for a long moment. "Eden, it would be easy for me to sit here and say nothing, but I wouldn't want you to live with that guilt. My mother lied to you," he says sincerely.

"Really?" I ask, my voice tinged with desperate hope.

"Yes. She told me she intended to eliminate *all* wolves the night I was imprisoned. She just couldn't do it on her own. She needed your father's enchantment, but trust me, she knew what she was doing when she altered it."

A shaky breath leaves my body, and I bring my hand to my head in relief. "Thanks, Erix."

He then reaches over to take my hand. "Come on, let's get some air."

I look around in confusion as he leads me out onto the royal balcony overlooking Morween.

Gentle music floats through the night air, and I'm surprised to see a small band playing instruments just for us.

I swallow a gasp as Erix lifts my hands to rest on his shoulders. "Dance with me," he whispers under his breath.

I do as he asks, swaying with him slowly in time with the music as his arms snake around my waist.

"If you pick me, Eden, we will live a lifetime of happiness. You'll never hear a cross word from my lips. You'll never shed a tear. I'll honor you like a queen. Forever. You'll have everything you could ever want."

I look into his eyes, and my stomach twists painfully. "Erix—"

Before I can finish the sentence his lips are on mine, and for a very brief moment in time, we are that young, bright-eyed couple who were madly in love once upon a time.

Our lips part, and he smiles softly, pulling me in to rest my head against his chest.

Haven

Eden

"*You* invite *us* to breakfast, and then you spend the whole time staring into space?" Neville asks, nudging Anton for backup.

"Oh, sorry," I apologize, picking up my fork to dig into my fluffy scrambled eggs.

"This food is good, but I'd argue— in our heyday— ours was better." Anton shrugs cockily.

I laugh and nod in agreement. "Here, here!"

He picks up the glass of sparkling wine and freshly squeezed orange juice. "I could get used to this, though!" he says jovially, downing the whole drink in one.

"You can take the Alpha out of the den, but you can't take the den out of the Alpha," I tease.

"Morning!" Zeke says happily, walking toward us with parchments in his hands.

"There he is. The boss man," Neville laughs. "Watch out...anyone would think you're after a job here."

"Nah, you know this pompous life isn't for me. Soon as this shit is sorted, I'm out of here."

I do wonder what's next for Zeke. He has spent many years dedicated to his job. Maybe he's itching to travel like Mateo.

"Yeah, yeah. So what do you need from us today, boss?" Anton asks, eyeing the parchments.

"I need you to sign on the dotted line. Erix has given you all that you requested in the negotiations, so these seal the deal," he explains, dropping the pile on the table save for one. "I'm taking this one to Harmony today. I'll be back tomorrow with Con and the others."

Immediately, my ears perk up. "You're going to Harmony?!"

"Yeah."

"Can I come?"

"You do know Con will be back first thing in the morning?"

"Please, Zeke," I beg, my eyes pleading with his.

Since last night on the balcony with Erix, I've had a growing pit in my stomach. Sure, the kiss was brief, and nothing else happened, but it's not how a woman with a mate behaves.

It's not how *I* want to behave.

"Alright then. Twist my arm, why don't you. But if Con gets pissy over this, you're taking the fall."

"Hand on heart!" I reply animatedly.

"Okay then, hurry up. We leave in ten."

* * *

Zeke's wolf stops at the edge of the forest, and I climb off his back, dropping the leather bag down in the grass.

His wolf looks at me expectantly, and I lift my hands in surrender. "I know, I know!" I twist my body around to look the other way as he shifts back into his human form. "You know I have zero desire to see you naked, right?"

"Oh, I know. You have enough men on your plate without adding me in to spice things up," he scoffs.

"Asshole," I laugh in return.

"No, seriously though. This is self-preservation, Eden. I don't want to be the guy caught naked with Con's woman in the woods. He might just pay me back for that knife in the back after all."

I shake my head and smile in amusement.

"Ready," he declares.

I spin around as he sits on a log to put on his boots.

"I'm not sure he would mind, you know," I suggest nervously. "Con said he wouldn't give up on us, and then he left—"

Zeke snorts as he stands up to meet me. "The man just entered a peace treaty with the bright-eyed king-to-be. Your former flame. Did you think he was going to stay while the guy tried to woo you back? Con would snap his neck if he saw Erix so much as try to kiss you. Leaving was for the best. We don't need another war."

I gulp in understanding as he puts his hand on my shoulder. "Trust me, I'm right. Anyway, you're here now. I dare say that might cheer the moody asshole up a little."

I swallow anxiously as Zeke leads the way out of the trees toward the valley nestled between the mountains. I breathe in the clear, crisp air, looking up at the sky as the birds swoop and dive overhead. My ears meet the sound of the babbling stream as we approach the village, and I watch the crystal-clear waters in awe. The natural landscape is wild in its rugged beauty. Not preened to perfection as it is behind the palace walls of Morween. This...this is nature at its finest.

The little houses capture my attention next, reminding me of Azealea in a way. However, I can also see the contrast. The fusion of werewolf and elven styles coming together as one.

As soon as we enter the small village, all eyes are on us.

"Looks like you're a hit," Zeke whispers with a grin.

Goddess, I hadn't thought about how the people here would react to my presence. I'm sure they have heard about the peace negotiations by now, but that doesn't mean they won't be wary of me.

Why wouldn't they be?

"Well, hello there, Alpha Zeke," an old man says, walking over to join us. "It's good to see you again."

"And you, Nikon,"

The old man turns his attention to me, looking me up and down carefully. "And who is this pretty young woman you have with you today? Has the famous Alpha Zeke decided to settle down?"

"Me, Nikon? Never... This is Eden. She's Conall's mate."

Nikon's eyes widen as he laughs gently. "Of course, I should have known. You are just as he described you."

"Described me?" I ask in surprise.

"Well, yes. He told us all about his brave Elven mate who fought corruption and evil on our behalf. He's very proud, you know."

I can't help but smile a little in return.

"Thanks, Nik. I tried to tell her." Zeke grins, elbowing my arm.

"I'm sorry, but do you know where Conall is?" I ask, suddenly impatient to see him.

"Oh, he'll be working on his cottage, no doubt."

"He has a home here?" I question, unable to hide my surprise. It's not something that he ever mentioned before.

"Well, he's never *lived* in the place," Zeke shrugs. "But I think he hopes to someday."

"You'll be very welcome here, Eden," Nikon says with a gracious smile. "We are a wonderful pack if I don't say so myself."

"You *would* say so yourself, Nikon. You were the first one here!" Zeke laughs.

It's then that I remember the story Con told me when he brought me here to Harmony. The story of how he and Lincoln found a young hybrid boy wandering in the woods after *The Culling*.

"Wait..." I say, stopping to stare at Nikon in amazement. "You were just a young boy when Con and Lincoln found you. He told me all about it."

"Oh, don't remind an old man," Nikon laughs. "These non-aging Alphas like to point it out often enough."

"He was a really annoying kid," Zeke states matter-of-factly.

"Now I'm old enough to give you a clip around the ear, young man!" Nikon laughs.

We stop in the middle of the street, and Zeke points to a small tavern. "I'll be spending most of the day here with the others if you need me, Eden."

"Wha—"

"So to get to Con's cottage, just keep heading straight. Cross the little wooden bridge and take a right by the big oak. Trust me, you'll know the one."

"You aren't coming to see, Con? I thought you had paperwork for him?"

"Nahhh, you can manage. I wouldn't want to get in the way," he smirks, patting me on the back. "Besides, Nikon owes me a beer. Isn't that right OLD MAN?!" he yells jokingly.

"Oh, hurry up before I change my mind," Nikon answers. "Eden, I hope we will see you again later."

"I wouldn't count on it, Nik," Zeke states, wriggling his brows suggestively.

I hit him with the parchment before they both disappear inside the small tavern. I then look around the little street again, clutching the parchment in my hand as I follow Zeke's directions. As soon as I turn at the oak tree, I see the outline of a cottage in the distance. It's a little further out than most of the houses and is burrowed amongst massive, towering trees.

I close my eyes for a second, and the scents and sounds whirl around me in the most comforting way, like a blanket I could snuggle into for a lifetime.

I stop in front of the house, my ears picking up on the sound of hammering that stops almost instantaneously.

"Eden?"

I spin around to see him shirtless. A look of shock etched on his handsome face.

"Surprise!" I announce, attempting to sound casual and light when in reality, my heart is doing somersaults.

He grins a little, shaking his head as he places the hammer on a wooden bench. "I guess I shouldn't be too surprised. You never were good at following my orders."

I lift my brow, and he laughs. "I'm kidding."

"Hmm, really?" I ask, walking toward him slowly. "I do seem to recall you telling me once upon a time that you were my Alpha and that I should do as you say."

His eyes flick over my body as he shrugs his shoulders. "And I seem to recall you telling me to get fucked...or words to that effect."

I can't help the big smile that makes its way to my lips, and I rush forward the last few steps to sink into his arms.

He holds me tightly, his muscular arms like solid steel, caging me in his embrace. My cheek presses against his bare chest, his steady heartbeat holding me as his willing captive for a few seconds longer.

"Why did you come?" he asks carefully. "I told you I'd be back in Morween tomorrow."

"Perhaps I just couldn't wait that long," I answer, looking up into his eyes.

He swallows and nods his head.

"Should I go back?" I question jokingly.

"Not a chance," he answers, lifting his hand to touch my chin.

I hand over the parchment, then check out the house, taking in all the little details. "You didn't tell me about this place," I state in a semi-accusing tone.

"I didn't know if I'd ever get to use it. As you can probably tell, it has been a work in progress for a long time."

He rubs his hand over the back of his neck as I move closer to the door.

"Can I?"

"Go ahead."

I smile in thanks, opening the door into a small living room with an open-plan kitchen.

"It's not much, but—"

"Oh wow, look at the beams...and the windows too!"

His eyes brighten as I rush across the room to check out the view. "It's like you can see into the heart of the forest from here."

"That was kind of the idea." He walks up behind me, his bare chest brushing against my back. "You know... I'm glad you're here," he husks, lifting his hand to brush my hair from my shoulder.

"Oh yeah?" I ask breathlessly. "Why is that?"

He drops his hands to my waist, twisting me around slowly, my ass grazing his crotch as I turn around to meet his gaze.

"Because maybe you can help me with something?"

"Anything," I breathe out, fixing my eyes on his daringly.

He smiles the sexiest smile I have ever seen, turning around to saunter across the room. My body aches as I wait, my eyes drifting to the bedroom in lustful hope.

"Come on then, what are you waiting for?" he asks, gesturing back outside.

I'm not opposed to the suggestion and follow him eagerly back outdoors, where he picks up a hammer and thrusts it into my hands. I stare at it in confusion.

"If you're here, you might as well make yourself useful," he grins, bending down to pick up a plank of wood from the grass.

"You are an ass!" I yell, pointing the hammer at him playfully.

"You've called me worse," he shrugs, throwing me a wink. "Come on, this house isn't going to fix itself."

I follow him around the cottage to the back door, where there is the beginnings of a small terrace.

"Well, I can see now why you need my help," I mutter sarcastically.

"Shut up and get to work," he orders, handing me the wooden plank.

I laugh before sinking to my knees, picking up a nail to hammer the board in place.

He watches over me carefully while I work.

"There..." I say, tilting my head. "That looks great!"

"Not bad. Keep moving, elf."

"Alright, alright. I'm not your slave anymore, Alpha," I laugh, narrowing my eyes at him.

"What a shame that is..." he answers, raising his brows suggestively.

"Oh, I'm not falling for that tease again. Next, you'll have me chopping the damn firewood."

"Now there's an idea," he grins, picking up a saw to begin cutting planks.

We get to work together, making small talk about the negotiations, the other Alphas and my conversation with Nikon.

I must admit how good it feels to be with him like this. No complicated plans to make. No secrets to unravel. No tension or uneasiness. It's just us doing regular everyday things that regular everyday people do.

"So tell me something about you that I don't know already," I challenge him, taking a break from hammering to sit on the half-built terrace.

"I'm not a very complicated man," he retorts, sitting beside me.

"Uhhh. I'd like to disagree," I smile, bumping my shoulder against his. "Come on, there must be something I don't know about you yet."

He laughs and shrugs his shoulders. "I can draw. Does that count as something interesting?"

My mouth falls open in shock. "You can draw?! Like portraits and things?"

He screws his face up a little. "More like still life kind of drawings, but it's not something I've done in a long time. Who knows, I might be shit at it now."

"Well, there's only one way to find out."

"Yeah, let's not bother," he states, shaking his head.

I laugh hysterically as he watches me with a smile.

"So, what do you want to do next?" I query, standing up to stretch out my sore limbs.

He pauses, standing up as a playful smile plays on his lips. "There are a few things I can think of."

"Really?" I ask, lifting my hands to rest them on his chest.

"Really," he answers, his eyes looking into mine.

I blink at him seductively, standing on the tips of my toes as I reach up to nibble the edge of his earlobe before landing a gentle kiss on his neck. His body shivers ever so slightly, and I grin in triumph. "Revenge is oh so sweet," I whisper, running my fingers across his chest as I walk away slowly.

"Well... fuck," he moans as I sashay away from him back toward the village.

"That was cruel."

"Come on, Alpha! Keep up!"

"Care to tell me where we are going?!" he asks, amused.

"To get drunk!" I laugh in reply.

* * *

"After you," Con grins, opening the door of the little tavern.

I smile nervously, heading inside to take a look around.

It's not unlike the taverns we have in Morween, but it's a lot smaller, with perhaps only twenty or so people dotted around the place. Some of the faces I know instantly, my eyes drifting to the bar to find Zeke, Hunter, Henrick, Evan and Cass sitting on high stools.

"Hey, hey! Look who it is! The power couple!" Zeke says, lifting his beer enthusiastically.

"Goddess, we thought you both would be breaking in the bed right around now." Hunter winks before Con smacks him on the back of the head.

"Shut the hell up, idiot."

"Okay, okay! You say that like we have never heard you two going at it before," Hunter laughs.

"You...are a pig," I accuse him, throwing him a rude hand gesture.

"Wowww, has this elf got sassier, or is it just me?"

Cass looks at me seriously. "We should kick his ass, Eden."

"Absolutely," I smile, sitting on the stool beside hers. "Although I'll settle for a drink. Hunter, you're buying."

"I've got you covered," he concedes, holding his hand up to the barman to order Con and I a drink.

I can't believe how unbelievably easy it is to fall into sync with this group. It's like I've somehow known them my whole life. My cheeks ache from laughing at Cass and Zeke, who banter back and forth, and my sides hurt from watching Hunter attempt to jig in time with the fiddles on his shaky, drunken legs. I sit on Con's knee, and he holds me around my waist, his thumb rubbing my skin gently as he is entertained by the drunken antics around us. I lay my head against his as he laughs heartily at Evan and Henrick, who are impersonating Rocco and Samuel to a tee.

Before long, it begins to get dark, and I can feel myself completely unwind into a state of pure contentment. I turn my head to look at Con appreciatively. His smile wide as he points his beer at Zeke, who is twirling Cass around to the music, dipping her back and forth frantically, much to her annoyance.

For the first time, I see him in a new light, and it's so beautiful that it literally brings tears to my eyes.

Eventually, he sees me and examines me worriedly. "Are you okay?"

"Yes," I nod frantically. "You're just *so* beautiful," I mumble.

His brows knit together before he begins to laugh. "Uh-oh, someone's drunk."

"I'm not!" I protest as he scoops me up into his arms. "I'm just living in the moment!"

"I've got to get this one to bed, guys. She's talking shit now," Con jokes, smiling down at me.

"It appears elves c-can't handle their liquor!" Henrick stutters drunkenly as I slap Con's chest. "I'm not drunk, I swear."

"Let's go," he winks, saying his goodbyes to everyone in the tavern as he carries me out the door.

I give in to him, wrapping my arms around his neck as we head off into the moonlit night. He glances at me, and I smile. "I had fun tonight," I declare, meaning every word.

"Good."

I pat his chest for him to let me down, and he releases me from his arms, watching me stumble ahead of him, humming a tune as I dance around under the moonlight. I feel lighter that I have done in years. Whether that's down to the wine or the excellent company, I'm not so sure.

"And you say you're not drunk...."

"I'm not!" I yell unconvincingly.

We enter the forest, and I cast my eyes up to the enormous oak tree, taking in the starry night.

"Wait!" Con calls out, bending down to pick up a flower. "For you. It's lilac, like your eyes."

I bite my lip and look down at the plant, shaking my head in refusal.

"What?" he asks in confusion.

"It's a Lilac Niffle Blossom, Con."

"And?" he asks, studying it for a second before looking back at me in realization. "It's fucking poisonous or something, isn't it?"

I nod my head and snort uncontrollably.

"Shit," he huffs, tossing the flower on the ground. "That's the last time I try to be romantic."

I give him a sympathetic look, still chuckling under my breath. "Do you have any butter in the cottage?"

"Butter? I think so."

"Then you'll be fine!"

We arrive inside the house, and he sits at the table as I head to the pantry. "Ahh, you're in luck!"

He watches as I take a tiny blob of butter in my fingertips, rubbing it into his palm gently. "This will do the trick."

Immediately, the small itchy rash begins to disappear.

"You're amazing," he says in awe, staring at me lovingly.

"This was an easy one," I smile, walking over to wash my hands at the sink. "Although, you're lucky I didn't finish that last wine at the bar! I may have forgotten about the butter!"

When I sit back down, the look in his eyes has changed completely, and silence lingers between us. "Why did you come here today, Eden?" he asks calmly, his words stripping me bare in seconds.

I flick my eyes away briefly before looking back at him. "Erix kissed me last night."

He nods his head, his jaw tightening.

I watch as he stands up from his chair, pacing the floor in front of me.

I stand up to meet him.

"So..." he says, looking at me with those intense honey eyes.

"So what?"

"How was it?"

I pause for a second, ready to tell the whole truth. "It was...nostalgic. It was nice, I guess."

"Nice?" he questions, his eye twitching slightly in anger.

I nod, taking a step forward. "But I don't want nice, Con."

He looks down at me, his eyes trailing over my face slowly. "You want rough?"

I shake my head in return. "No." I then rise onto my tiptoes to curl my hand around the nape of his neck, pulling him in closer. "I want the same as you, remember?"

His brows knit together questioningly.

"I want to feel alive," I whisper.

There's another silent pause, the air sparking between us like a bolt of pure electricity.

"Fuck this..." he growls, giving up whatever game he's been playing. He pulls me hard against his chest, and he kisses me.

Oh Goddess, does he kiss me.

My skin tingles all over.

My body aches.

My mind races.

There's not a single part of either of us that holds back.

I'm so caught up in the moment that I ignore the warning signs. The alarm bells ringing in my mind letting me know that at any moment now, I'm going to—oh fuck!

I tear myself away from him, and he stares at me in confusion before realization covers his face.

I run to the bathroom, arriving just in time to puke my guts up.

Con rubs my back gently, holding my hair as I sink into a state of complete and utter embarrassment. "I'm so sorry," I mumble, sitting back on the floor to wipe my sweaty brow.

"I did try to tell you," he laughs. "Come on, you little drunkard," he jokes, lifting me up to carry me into the bedroom.

I groan as he places me on the bed, and the room begins spinning around me. "I'm sorry I ruined the moment," I mutter guiltily. "Will you still stay with me?"

"I guess I'll have to," he shrugs sarcastically, climbing into bed beside me as I smack his chest again.

He chuckles as he pulls me in close. And in blissful silence, we lie in each other's arms.

"Eden..."

"Yeah?" I ask groggily, looking up at him.

"I want this," he says quietly.

"You want *this*?" I question in confusion.

"This... today... is the life I want," he says insistently, looking into my eyes. "I know I can't give you diamonds or gold. There won't be any grand parties or celebrations. Hell, I can't even promise that I won't be an asshole sometimes or that we won't piss each other off now and again." He smiles as I laugh softly. "But I can promise you, Eden, that I'll love you more than anything. Everything that I have... everything I am... will belong to you."

I take hold of his hand as he kisses my forehead. "Now go to sleep. And for fuck sake...don't puke on me."

I snort loudly, squeezing my eyes closed as he holds me tightly in his loving arms.

Trial

Conall

I take another drink of water, looking over Eden again, where she sleeps soundly. Waking up beside her this morning, here of all places, felt like a strange dream. Even though I've been working on this house for some time now, I never let myself fully commit to the idea that it would someday be mine. That it would someday be the place where I could settle down with the person I love. Perhaps it's wishful thinking, but she seems as taken with Harmony as I am. Her reaction to the village and this house were even better than I expected, but I know better than to get ahead of myself. A fucking lifetime of disappointment and pain has taught me as much.

There's a knock at the door, and I enter the living area to open it.

"Morning!" Cass says brightly, bursting inside to take a nosy look around the cottage.

"Morning," I mutter in return, nodding to Zeke, Hunter and Henrick as they follow behind her. "Where's Evan?"

"Throwing up in the forest," Zeke grins, slapping his hand against mine.

"My head is pounding. There's no way I'm carrying your ass all the way to Morween, Con," Hunter declares, walking over to the kitchen to pour himself a drink of water.

"You guys are a bunch of babies!" Cass remarks, throwing herself down onto a wooden chair. "I'm as fresh as a daisy!"

"You try carrying him then, Cass! He weighs a damn ton!"

"I can hear you, you know," I say, folding my arms over my chest.

"Still no sign of your wolf then, Con?" Henrick asks with a frown.

I shake my head in reply.

I'd be lying if I said it's not beginning to worry me at this point. My wound is almost fully healed, yet whenever I try to shift, something is blocking me from doing so.

"You know my theory," Zeke shrugs, grabbing a piece of bread from the table.

"What's that?" Cass asks curiously.

"Don't get him started," I groan.

"He needs to mark Eden," Zeke says matter-of-factly. "And pretty fucking soon, I would say—"

"What does that mean?"

My eyes immediately shoot to the doorway to see Eden standing there with a puzzled expression.

Shit.

I knew this would happen eventually. I've been meaning to tell her about the marking process since that night at Kelna Cliffs when I almost lost control of myself, but I haven't stumbled on the right moment yet.

Zeke twists his head back to me and grimaces in silent apology.

Yeah, thanks for that... You prick.

"Wait, you haven't told her about marking?" Hunter smiles, pointing between us both. "It's supposed to be fucking awesome! What are you both waiting for? I don't know how you have managed to stop yourself, Con."

"Okay, that's enough. All of you get ready to leave. We'll be out in a minute," I order quickly.

There's an awkward silence before Cass bounces up from her chair to break the tension. "Eden, you'll ride with me today, won't you?!"

"Sure," Eden smiles, her eyes flicking to me.

I open the door to let them shuffle outside, and when I turn back around, Eden is staring at me with a raised eyebrow. "So, do you want to tell me what that was all about?"

I pinch the bridge of my nose and let out a breath. "It's nothing that can't wait until later. I don't want you to worry about it," I say honestly.

"But I—"

"We'll talk about it later," I interrupt insistently.

I'm not sure how much of the conversation she heard, but telling her that my wolf has gone into hiding because he hasn't had a chance to claim her doesn't seem like the kind of thing I should say right now. Knowing Eden, as I do, I'm aware that she would do anything to help me get my wolf back, and it's not the reason I want her to choose me over the fucking Comeback Prince.

"Uhh, okay, if you're sure," she mumbles, lifting her hand to swoop her wayward hair out of her face.

I nod, moving closer to lift her chin gently. "So, how's that hangover of yours?"

She scoffs, shaking her head from side to side. "Put it this way, I'm never going drink for drink with a bunch of wolves EVER again."

I smile back before turning to open the door. "Well, no time to sleep it off if we want to be back in time for the trials starting. Let's go, we better get a move on."

* * *

Eden

"Hey, you look a little better," Cass grins as I sit beside her in the crowded throne room. "It's amazing what a wash and change of clothes can do, huh?"

"That and my Grandma Citrine's hangover remedy," I answer honestly.

She looks at me with a stern expression. "Do NOT let me leave Morween without a bottle, Eden. I swear."

"I won't," I chuckle in return.

I then carefully look around the busy room. It's filled once again with citizens of Morween (as it was the day of my own trial) with the same long table at the front filled with the elder high elves.

"Where's Con and the others?" I query anxiously.

"The Alphas are sitting together near the front, and as for Con..." she points her finger off to the right-hand side of the room, and my heart stills in my chest when I see him standing talking one-on-one with Erix.

Shit.

Zeke's words from yesterday bounce around inside my head as I take in the unsettling scene.

"Don't look so worried. I doubt they are talking about you. They have a bunch of lords to kill," she says with a vengeful snicker. "Trust me, their attentions are seriously diverted, at least for now."

"Damn, I wish that made me feel better," I mumble, swallowing the lump in my throat.

Erix walks across the room, sitting at the elder elves' table. His eyes scan the crowd, settling on me before he offers me a sad smile. I return the gesture.

Goddess, I can't imagine what he's going through right now. The pain of reliving everything that happened while his evil mother sits in front of him will surely be traumatic.

Then there's Conall... My eyes flit across the room to see him sitting next to Zeke and the others. His hell is just as bad, if not a hundred times worse!

"Let the show begin," Cass whispers as the side door to the throne room opens wide.

Commander Walden storms inside with a posse of guards on his tail, surveying the room before they bring in the chained-up lords.

Faint whispers fill the air as they are dragged across the room to sit on a wooden bench. Each of them looks completely disheveled and exhausted. Their grotty appearance is a clear reflection of their sheer desperation and helplessness. I, for one, have not a single iota of sympathy for any of them. They deserve everything that's coming their way.

The entire room then falls into silence, everyone watching with bated breath as Siofra appears next through the doorway. Unlike the lords, she has attempted to fix her appearance for today. Her hair has been combed through, and her dress is spotless, but it's her attitude that makes the most significant impact. She looks around the throne room in apparent disdain, her head held high as if this whole situation is beneath her.

How can anyone be so hard? So stone-faced and shameless?

As she is taken across the room, she glances at Erix, and he stares right back at her. However, despite the determined look in his eyes, I can see the shadow of pain in his expression. The sight makes my stomach twist in knots.

The trial begins with various witness accounts from the people involved in this long, sordid part of our history.

My father is called to talk about *The Culling* enchantment's original purpose and testify that he had no idea of Siofra's plan to steal or adapt the spell.

Conall is called to talk about the rogue wolves and their part in the invasion of Elven towns.

Commander Walden spends an angry half hour explaining precisely what happened the day he and the Second League were intercepted by Faenor and taken to Ankorord.

And then, finally, I hear my name being called loudly across the busy room. I sit there frozen for a moment before Cass gives my arm a slight nudge to

□

bring me back to reality. I stand up slowly and walk forward to take a seat in front of everyone. My skin crawls beneath the surface, and my throat dries up as the crowd gawps at me expectantly.

"Miss Nestoriel," the elder high elf begins, "Could you please tell us what happened the day of King Aubrun's death?"

I nod, my eyes drifting to Siofra who is staring at me with burning hatred. I swallow hard, looking back to the crowd, where I find Con's face a few feet away. His eyes connect with mine, and he holds my gaze, nodding at me reassuringly. As I stare back at him, it's as if the nerves dissolve and disappear. I straighten my shoulders and look back at Siofra. Her awful face reminding me of every disgusting crime she has ever committed.

It's time for this bitch to finally receive her just desserts. I smirk slightly in victory.

"Of course," I reply to the elder elf. "I'll start from the very beginning...."

Execution

Eden

When the trial is over, the elders, with Erix's blessing, sentence the entire group of lords and Siofra to death. The lords are to meet their demise at the hands of the Alphas as part of the peace treaty agreement, while Siofra is to be hanged in public as per Elven law for treasonous members of royalty.

The outcome is no surprise to anyone, but I can see from the look on Erix's face that it doesn't make things any easier for him.

The lords are led out of the throne room to the sound of jeers and applause all around us, and then the Alphas stand, following after with severe and determined looks on their faces.

On the night of Ciridan's funeral, they were denied their long-awaited vengeance, and it looks like they are about to receive it. I watch Con leave with the others with his head held high. He finds me in the crowd, and I offer him the same reassuring look he gave me. Whatever happens now, I can only hope that it brings him some kind of peace. That it helps to ease some of the pain that will forever live inside him.

Cass reaches for my hand and squeezes. "He'll be fine."

"I know he will."

The truth is that I know how strong he is already. It's not Con that I'm worried about at this moment.

It's Erix.

My eyes drift back to Siofra, who is now being taken to face her fate.

"ERIX!" she calls out, finally breaking her steely outer facade. "Do not do this!" she screams as she struggles against Commander Walden. "These people have turned you against me! I am your mother! I showed you mercy, my son! Show me mercy in return!"

His eyes close, his chest rising and falling slightly as the stress of the moment finally catches up with him. The noise around me amplifies as the entire throne room descends into furious protests. These people have been lied to. They are livid and are not about to stand for Siofra's attempts to wriggle out of her punishment. If Erix backs down now—and overrules the elders—I'm sure his reign will end before it even gets started.

I observe him carefully, willing him to stay strong with every fiber of my being.

Then he raises his hand, standing up to demand silence. Siofra stops struggling and looks up at him hopefully as he steps out from behind the table. The unruly crowd quietens to hear what he has to say.

"Come on, Erix. You can do this. Don't listen to her!" I plead silently in my head.

"You have disgraced this kingdom for the last time. Your sentence shall stand, and I will watch you leave this world alongside my people. You are no queen, and you are no mother of mine."

There is silence for a long moment before Siofra lets out a vicious screech. She begins to thrash around once again as Walden and another guard restrain her desperate struggles. "I should have let them kill you! You are just like your weak father! The realm will see it soon enough! The crown will not sit on your head for long—"

Her screams trail off into the distance as she leaves the room, and Erix returns to his seat.

"This hearing is now concluded. Siofra's execution shall be carried out within the hour," a high elder elf announces, bringing the trial to a close.

Immediately, the room comes to life again as people begin to leave. Erix's eyes fix on mine as I try my best to communicate my support.

"Eden, are you coming?" Cass asks, breaking me from my trance.

"Uhh, yes, I'm coming," I answer, standing up to follow her.

Erix frowns, springing to his feet to make his way toward us. "Eden, can I speak with you for a moment?"

"I'll leave you to it," Cass says, nodding at Erix before she swiftly disappears.

I stand there waiting as Erix watches everyone leave the room, and before long, we find ourselves completely alone.

Looking at him now, I feel his pain so completely, and I wish I could do something to help.

"I know I have no right to ask you this, but I don't know how I will get through the next hour without your help."

My brows knit together, and I step forward to place my hand on his arm comfortingly.

"Please, come to the balcony with me? Because if you're not there, Eden, I'm not sure I'll be able to hold myself together," he explains worriedly. "I need you to help me with this."

"Erix, you know that you do not need to watch. There is not a person out there who would blame you if—"

"I must, Eden," he interrupts insistently. "Morween needs to see her king standing in unity. It's something that I must do. There is no doubt in my mind," he explains. "Please, I need this. Promise me you'll be with me."

"I promise. I'll be there," I answer without delay.

"Thank you," he whispers, clearing his croaky throat before stepping back. "I've got to go speak to the elders. I'll send for you in a moment."

I wasn't particularly planning on watching Siofra's demise. Just knowing that she will finally meet her end is enough for me, but how can I turn down his cries for help? After what he has been through, it's the least I can do.

I let out a breath and walk out into the corridors of the palace, where to my surprise, I see Conall standing with Jarek, Mateo and Neville.

My eyes connect with Conall's right away, and I realize that just seeing his face makes me feel better, just as it did during the trial.

"What are you guys still doing here?" Cass asks them all in confusion. "Aren't you supposed to be handing out the ass-kicking of the century right about now?"

"I think I would prefer to give it a miss," Jarek says, looking around at the others, who nod in agreement.

Conall remains quiet.

"Can we talk?" I ask him carefully.

He nods, and I gesture to the nearby library, opening the door to lead us inside.

"Eden, you did a good job up there. I know you were nervous," Con begins, closing the door behind us.

"Why aren't you going with the other Alphas to kill the lords?" I interrupt, searching his eyes for answers. "If you aren't going because you think it might upset me, it won't! This is your right, and I fully understand that."

"I know that you do," he says calmly.

"Then what is it?" I ask again. "Is it because of your wolf?"

As soon as the question leaves my lips, I see him shift uncomfortably.

For the whole journey from Harmony this morning, all I could think about was what Zeke said in the kitchen. He said Conall needs to "mark" me to get his wolf back. In the back of my mind, I can picture the book I began reading back in the den. It mentioned that wolves usually mark one another, but I must confess that I didn't get to read much further. The thought of him losing this massive part of himself because of his connection to me makes me feel awful, and I already know I would do anything to help.

"That's not the reason," he answers plainly, interrupting my thoughts.

"Then what is it?"

He looks away for a second before his eyes return to mine. "I'm *tired*, Eden. Tired of this bullshit. Of being obsessed with revenge and tired of death. Meeting you has changed everything," he explains. "I thought vengeance would be the one thing that brought me peace, but it's not...."

He takes a step forward, his eyes running over my face. "It's you."

Goddess.

I have no words to say.

I stand there staring at him, filled with so much love and admiration that I could burst on the spot. I wrap my arms around his waist to hold him tightly.

Just then, the door knocks in interruption, and a royal servant appears.

"Excuse me, Miss. Prince Erix requires your immediate presence."

I nod, waiting for him to leave before looking up into Con's honey eyes.

"You should go," he says calmly. "It's the right thing to do. And if I know you at all, Eden Nestoriel, then I know that you want to do what's right."

"I do," I whisper, looking at him with appreciation. "Thank you for understanding."

Reluctantly, I release myself from his embrace, holding onto his hand for a second longer before I leave to fulfill my promise.

* * *

I walk onto the balcony to see Erix standing there looking over the sight below.

A vast crowd has formed in Morween, or rather an angry mob has gathered from all corners of the realm to witness the demise of their once beloved queen. I've never understood the attraction of watching someone else die, and even though this form of punishment is rare, I still find it hard to stomach.

The sound of music is carried on the air. The noise from the crowd a mixture of laughter and jeers. The overall joyous yet ominous atmosphere sends a shiver down my spine.

I stop at Erix's side, and he puts his head down momentarily before turning to look at me. "I'm doing the right thing... This is the right thing, isn't it?"

"I wish I could tell you what to do, what to think or how to feel, but I can't. You are king and must decide on your own, but I'm here for you. Trust your judgment, Erix."

He nods, closing his eyes for a moment.

I cast my eyes over the crowd again and see more than a few Elven people looking up at the balcony curiously. Erix was right when he said people would be watching him. His reign is just beginning, and they want to see how he reacts to all this.

It is then that the sound of the palace drums begins to beat, and the guards filter out of the entrance to clear a path into the village square. Even from this distance, it is not difficult to see Siofra make her way out into the mob who are baying for her blood. The gold trim on her black velvet dress catches the remnants of the fading sunlight as she marches slowly toward the gallows to receive her fate.

The crowd stills as she climbs the steps, and the rope is placed around her neck securely. Only then does Erix look up, his body tense as his eyes remain fixed. I see his hand tremble, and he reaches for mine discreetly.

"I need you, Eden," he whispers lightly under his breath.

"I'm here," I reassure him, squeezing his hand in return.

And then it happens.

The lever is released, and Siofra's body falls through the wooden panel, disappearing from sight.

The crowd reawakens raucously, and Erix's grip grows tighter as he stares at the empty space where his mother once stood.

We remain silent for a moment before he backs away, walking into the royal chambers behind us.

I look over the curious faces again, who watch from below, before I follow him through the doorway, unsure what to do or say. I can only watch as he paces the bedroom floor in turmoil.

"What can I do?" I ask sympathetically. "Is there anything you need my help with?"

He stops and shakes his head. "No, I'm fine. I'll arrange a burial with Walden. We will find somewhere discreet. No one will know the location," he answers in a slight daze.

"Okay, well, if you need to talk or—"

"I know I said I wouldn't rush you into anything, but I can't *not* say this," he begins. "I know you went to *him* yesterday, but Eden, think about the connection we shared the other night. We belong together. We always have, and I- I need you. On days like today, it's you that I need to get me through. Ruling this kingdom without you by my side—"

"Erix, you know I'll support you, but it's is not the time to discuss this. You've just been through hell, and I—"

"Don't," he says." shaking his head. "Don't say anything else until you think it through, okay?"

I nod, and he rushes forward, throwing his arms around me to hold me in a tight and intense hug.

I can't deny that his words make me feel trapped, but I can feel how much he needs this right now. He isn't thinking clearly. I stretch my arms around him, focusing all my strength and support on him in the only way I know how.

"It's done," he says in finality, leaning back to look into my eyes. "This whole nightmare is over, and I won't think on it for another moment longer. We have the coronation tomorrow, and there's still much to prepare."

"You don't have to rush this, Erix. The people can surely wait another few days."

"No, I would rather get this over with. We need stability, and this will help. Don't worry; I'm keeping it as low-key as I can." He leans in to kiss my forehead. "Thanks, Eden. For everything. I better go," he says just as the door knocks on cue.

"Your Majesty, Commander Walden would like to speak with you."

"Of course, I'm coming right now,"

And just like that, he buries the pain and leaves to carry out his royal duties.

Mark

Eden

"So what does this do?" Conall asks, picking up a jar of brown Dirkweed to examine it.

"Well, nothing on its own," I chuckle. "But pair it with some Whickerwillow sap..." I continue, holding up the jar of red goo. "...then you've got yourself an explosion waiting to happen."

"An explosion?"

"Yep. It can be dangerous stuff," I laugh, replacing the jar and folding my arms over my chest.

"Where was this when we were taking Ankorord? That's cool as fuck. Does Citrine not approve?"

"Not really. She's one for more sophisticated enchantments instead of a large bang."

He grins, shaking his head as he replaces the Dirkweed.

There's quiet for a moment before he looks around the study again. "So this is where you spend most of your time?"

I shrug a little. "I guess so. This place was a comfort to me when I first arrived here in Morween. I never really fit in, so this study was like home."

"Then I take it, it's a place you wouldn't want to leave?"

I look at him for a long moment and shake my head. "I can work anywhere there is nature. This place...it's different now. Things have changed."

"They have," he answers, his eyes scanning my face. "Have you thought any more about what I said last night?" he asks, a touch of uncertainty in his voice.

"Harmony is amazing. The cottage is—"

"I know it's unfinished, and it's a bit rustic—"

"It's perfect," I interrupt, offering him a sincere smile.

He moves closer to brush some hair from my face. "You made it perfect when you stayed with me last night," he rasps.

I stare into his eyes as his hands lift to my face and his lips brush against mine. Feeling warm and giddy inside, his magic touch soothes my aching muscles from the stressful day we have both endured. I sigh in satisfaction as he lands gentle kisses along my jaw, trailing them down my neck slowly. His strong, broad shoulders begin to tense, the muscles flexing as he presses his chest against me ever so slightly. I gasp as his kiss becomes more intense and curl my hands around the nape of his neck wantonly.

"I want you, Conall," I whisper softly.

He pauses, his grip on me tightening as his kisses against my neck grow more intense.

"You can do it, you know," I continue, my voice dripping with desire. "You can mark me."

Immediately, his entire body stills, his head lifting from the crook of my neck to look straight into my eyes.

"What?" he asks, his brows knitting together.

"I said you can mark me," I repeat, studying his blank expression. "It's what you need, isn't it? What you were talking about this morning when I walked into the kitchen."

His expression turns dark and severe in a heartbeat, reminiscent of those early days in the den. He takes a step away from me. The cold dismissal leaves my lips parting in utter confusion.

"Con, what—"

"So you are offering to do this out of pity?"

"No! I don't pity you, Con, but I do want to help."

"See, this is why I didn't tell you about Zeke's theory!" he says, rubbing his hand over his stubbled jaw. "Because I knew you would do this!"

"Do what?" I ask defensively.

"I knew you would jump in and tell me to mark you without thought."

I shake my head as my bemusement begins to turn to anger. "Conall, isn't that what this "mates" thing is all about? We take care of each other and—"

"Do you even understand the marking process or what it means for us?!" he interjects sternly.

I swallow a little in return. "I haven't had a chance to read about it, but I can—"

"Read about it?!" he fumes. "Eden, not everything comes out of a damn book."

He takes another step away, beginning to pace the floor in front of me. I grit my teeth together and narrow my eyes at him. "Maybe if you just told me about it, I could understand what it means. I'm not a mind reader, Conall! You have to talk to me."

"Yeah, well, that's been a little hard lately with your fucking ex around every corner."

"And that's *my* fault?" I ask in equal anger. "I never wanted any of this! Do you think this is easy for me?"

"I don't know, you tell me because as far as I can see, I'm on standby like a fucking asshole while my mate is kissing another man!"

His words slice through me like a knife, and I shake my head in disbelief. "I can't believe you just said that to me."

He looks down at the ground guilty, lifting his head to look into my eyes again. "Eden, I shouldn't have said it. I'm sorry."

I fold my arms over my chest, hugging my body as a tense silence hangs in the air between us.

Just then, footsteps and laughter sound out from above, and Cass, Zeke and Anton descend the staircase to join us.

"Hey guys, we've been looking for you," Anton chirps joyfully, slapping Con on the back. "We thought you'd want to know how much the lords squealed for their pathetic lives."

Con doesn't respond. His eyes stay firmly on mine as Cass and Zeke look between us awkwardly.

"Con, are you alright?" Anton asks cluelessly. "Zeke, tell him how epic it was."

Zeke shrugs. "Fucking brilliant, but we don't need to talk about it right now. I'm all tortured out for the day."

Clearly, he and Cass have picked up on the mounting tension since she quickly changes the subject.

"So we are going into Morween for a little bit tonight. Do you guys want to come?"

"Oh?" I answer distractedly. "What for?"

"Well, poor Jarek has been completely miserable. We think it's because of the nymph. You know, the one that he fell in love with," she explains.

"We thought we could go on a little nymph hunt," Anton adds. "Zeke said they have probably arrived in Morween by now. Maybe we can convince her to meet with Jarek."

"My mission is to find the woman and play ultimate matchmaker," Cass smiles widely.

"Yeah, and if we happen to have a little fun along the way, then so be it," Zeke adds, winking at Cass.

Cass's face contorts in disgust, and she slaps his arm. "Urggg, forget it! I don't know why I told you two big oafs that you could come along in the first place. This mission requires a tender touch! Eden...that means you. Let's go. I won't take no for an answer," she states challengingly.

I glance at Con before I agree. "Okay, let's do it."

"Yesss!" she laughs, grabbing my hand to drag me away.

"Eden, I'll come find you later," Con calls after me as we make our way upstairs.

"No need! Don't wait up!" Cass answers, closing the door behind us.

When she turns around, the smile drains from her face, and she takes hold of my shoulders. "Eden, are you okay?"

I shake my head a little, Con's words echoing in my head. "No. Today, it's just...."

"It's been a lot," she finishes for me, pulling me into a hug.

"Yes. I'll be fine. Con and I just had a silly fight."

"I knew it. What did you fight about?" she queries, releasing me from her hold.

"Uhh, I'm not entirely sure if I'm honest. Everything was fine, we kissed, and I told him he could mark me if he wanted to—"

"Oh..." she interrupts, wincing.

"What?" I ask in confusion, biting my lip. "Did I do something wrong?"

"You told him he could mark you? Like...in the middle of your father's study?"

I nod, my exhausted brain now beginning to recognize my clumsy error.

"Did you tell him you wanted it or...?"

I think back for a moment and eventually shake my head in return. "I guess I still don't know what it really is."

"Yikes. I suppose people are fools when they're in love."

"Shit," I mumble, shaking my head. "I made a mess of this, didn't I?"

Cass smiles sympathetically. "Well, it's not all your fault, but let me just say, marking is sacred to a wolf, especially an Alpha. It's not something you do on a whim. It's got to be special. But he should have told you all of this! There was no excuse for him to be an ass. You can only work with the information you have so he needs to be more open with you, even if he isn't used to being that way with someone yet."

It feels so good to have someone who understands what I'm going through right now. Both Erix and Conall have suffered so much pain, and I feel the pressure of both insurmountable loads resting on my shoulders. I guess the pressure has gotten to me today.

"Both men are hurting. They want you more than anything, but they both need to realize that being stuck in the middle is no walk in the park either. If you want me to, I swear I'll give them both a piece of my mind!" she growls, gesturing to the door of the study. "Just say the word, and I'll go back down there and tear him a new asshole."

I can't help but laugh. "It's fine. I just need to clear my head for a bit. Maybe getting out of the palace will be a good thing."

"Of course, it will! Let's get going. Jarek and his miserable little face are depending on us."

"Thanks, Cass."

"Oh, it's no big deal. It's actually kind of nice having a girlfriend."

I smile and nod along enthusiastically. "It kinda is...."

* * *

Conall

As soon as the door closes at the top of the stairs, I pick up an empty glass jar and toss it across the room to hit the stone wall.

"FUCK!" I roar, squeezing my eyes closed as my chest heaves up and down.

Zeke glances over his shoulder at the mess and then back at me. "Feel better?"

I shake my head, resting my hands on my waist as I let out a breath.

"This is why you should have come with us earlier," he shrugs. "Let out some of that rage."

"I fucked things up," I state, swiping my hand over my face.

"How?" Anton asks, folding his arms.

"You got jealous, didn't you?" Zeke states knowingly as Anton and I look at him in surprise. "Hey, hey, listen! I might not *do* relationships, but I can see what's going on. I have fucking eyes."

I run my hand through my hair. "I said some stupid shit. Shit that I didn't mean."

"Well, I'm not surprised you lost it," Zeke says nonchalantly. "You've had the pressure of the trials, you lost your wolf, and now you've got to play nice with the elf king for the sake of peace. Not only that, but you have to watch while the smooth fucker attempts to win back your mate! It's got to be rough, Con. I mean, the guy is a *king*. Look at everything he can give her! Look at this place!"

I glare at him as Anton clears his throat quickly. "Uhh...I don't think that's helping, Zeke."

"My point is, Con, there's a lot going on. You've been bottling that shit up, and it's unhealthy." Zeke explains. "She's your mate, so act like it."

"What do you suggest I do, Zeke? Club her over the head and drag her back to Harmony with me? I said I would give her space to make up her mind, and that's what I'm doing."

"Yeah, but you also told her you'd fight for her. Why haven't you marked her or at least talked about it?"

"I haven't had the chance. Besides, I don't want her to choose me because she feels like she has to fix me like I'm some fucking wounded animal!"

"Bullshit. You're scared. You're not familiar with the concept but here it is. Just tell her how you feel. Step out of the shadow of the last seventy years and leave it behind. We all have to."

I stare back at him, and Anton does the same, slowly clapping his hands together. "I've never seen this side of you before, Zeke; that was bloody beautiful."

Zeke screws his face up, and I can't help but scoff subtly at the pair of assholes.

"Alright, so you've got a point," I concede.

"Course I do," Zeke says with a casual wink. "Now, let's go drink, shall we? All this lovely- dovey talk is giving me a headache."

"Yeah, but you're so good at it, though," Anton says, staring at him in wonder.

Zeke stops and glares at him seriously. "Don't you ever say that to me again."

I watch them both head for the stairs and smirk. I always looked at the guys from the den as associates rather than friends, but I suppose somewhere along the way, they became both.

"I'm going to stay here and clean up this mess first. I'll find you."

I look around quickly to find a broom in the corner and begin sweeping the broken glass into the corner.

What a fucking idiot.

It's not Eden's fault that I lost my damn mind for a second. After all, how can I blame her for offering to help when I haven't told her about marking and its importance? Zeke's right. I have to man the fuck up and speak to her about it properly; regardless of whether it's the right time or not, she has the right to know.

"Oh, forgive me. I didn't realize that you were down here," I hear a voice say from the stairs, breaking me from my thoughts.

I turn to see Haleth standing there, looking at me cautiously.

"I was with Eden," I answer dryly, setting the broom against the wall. "I'm just leaving."

Shit. Talk about awkward as fuck....

He nods, and I move toward him, ready to slip back upstairs.

"Alpha Conall, might I say something?"

I stop in front of him and he blinks anxiously, a slight look of fear in his eyes.

"I realize that I have never personally apologized for everything that happened all those years ago," he begins. "I just want to say that there isn't a day that goes by where I don't regret what happened. I am truly very sorry."

I stare back at him, unsure of how I should respond. My anger toward him has, of course, dissipated under the circumstances. Still, I'd be lying if I said I was ready to forgive the man completely for everything he did.

"I fully admit that I was fooled by the wrong people. I was blinded by anger and grief upon losing my sister, and I should have been more perceptive to everything that was going on around me. I should have realized that something was wrong much sooner than I did. I'm well aware that none of this would have happened without my input. And so, if you can never forgive me, I understand. I just needed you to know." He looks down at the ground as silence falls between us.

"You didn't kill my people. Siofra and Faenor did," I then say bluntly as his eyes flick up to meet mine. I give him a curt nod and continue walking.

"Alpha..." he interrupts, stopping me in my tracks. "I wanted to let you know my mother and I will be working on an enchantment to break the curse you and the other Alphas have endured. It may take some time, but mother is very skilled. I think she will have a potion ready in the future if anyone should wish to take it."

I cannot hide the shock in my expression. The curse is not something I had even been thinking about up until this point.

"Oh, and another thing," he adds, clasping his hands together. "It's about Eden."

I wait for him to elaborate with a questioning look.

"I can see that my daughter loves you very much and that you love her too. I hope you'll have a happy life together when all of this is over."

I furrow my brows. "And what about Erix? He also loves your daughter and can give her all of this," I say, gesturing around the room.

Haleth smiles, taking a step closer. "Erix is a good man. And you are right; he would give her everything she could ever want, but then, Eden does not need any of this. I think deep down, you already know that."

He smiles politely, and I nod my head, turning to make my way upstairs.

Decision

Eden

I place the basket on the grass while I examine this morning's treasures. I pinch some of the little orange seeds, laying them out in my hands. Dragon-Flower seeds have been on my grandma Citrine's ingredient list for a while now, so I know she will be delighted with this find. I smile to myself, letting out a gentle sigh. It's funny, really. How such simple things can bring you comfort when you are feeling overwhelmed. Which is exactly how I've been feeling these past few days.

Don't get me wrong, getting out of the palace last night with Cass to track down Jarek's mystery girl was a great distraction, but I still lay awake for most of the night afterward.

I look around the quiet forest and breathe in the fresh air.

I needed this.

Being back here amongst nature always helps to settle my mind. At least for a few hours anyway. Tonight we will attend Erix's coronation, and I already know that the tension will be unbearable. The way I'm feeling right now, I'd happily hide out at Grandma's house for the evening, but I know that isn't an option. Sooner or later, I have to face up to this mess.

I pick up the basket and head for Azealea, soaking up every peaceful moment I can while I still have the chance.

When I arrive at Grandma's house, Grandpa Erwin is baking bread while she sits at the table, grinding herbs and plants together in a crazy concoction.

"Morning," I say with a smile.

"Eden!" Grandpa exclaims. "We weren't expecting you!"

"I know. I thought I'd drop by. I brought some gifts," I say, lifting my brow at Grandma Citrine.

"Then you had better come in, dear!"

I laugh as I close the door, walking across the room to sit at the table with Grandma.

"Breakfast?" Grandpa asks expectantly.

"Of course," I grin, pulling some plants from the basket to show Grandma.

"Beautiful! Beautiful!" she declares happily. "Thank you, dear."

"What are you working on?" I ask, hopeful she will feel comfortable sharing her work with me again.

She looks at me for a moment, and a soft smile covers her face. "A remedy for the Alphas' curse. Your father and I hope to find a cure for those who wish to take it."

My mouth falls open a little in shock. "Oh...."

Her bright-blue eyes turn sympathetic. "Are you okay, dear?"

"Yeah. Sorry, I was just surprised. That's all."

She reaches her hand out to pat mine gently. "It's still going to take a while. I'm at the highly experimental stage!"

I laugh wearily, swallowing the lump in my throat as Grandpa places a teapot on the table.

"So, how are things in the palace?" Grandma asks, pouring some tea into my cup.

"Uhh, busy," I answer honestly, avoiding the obvious. "The trials are over, and the coronation is tonight, so it's...strange."

She examines me carefully. "And how are you, my dear?"

"Grandma... I don't want to be the reason why anyone feels pain," I answer on an exhale.

She squeezes my hand reassuringly. "Do not take that burden upon your shoulders. This situation is difficult for everyone, and there will be pain; this is unavoidable. But there will also be great joy and love. You must only follow your heart. It will guide you in the right direction."

I nod as I contemplate her words. I know already what I have to do. In truth, I've known from the very start.

"Now, hand an old woman the Stickywillops please," she instructs, her smile widening.

I laugh gently in return. "Coming right up."

* * *

"Are you sure this is okay? I really don't want to cause you any trouble," Lianna says as we walk toward the royal quarters of the palace. "I already feel I've overstepped by staying here last night."

"Rubbish!" Cass responds vehemently. "You are our guest, Lianna!"

She looks around nervously, pushing her long blonde hair over her shoulder. "I'm not sure others would agree. Perhaps the palace isn't ready to welcome a nymph. What if the future king gets upset?"

It's then I spot three Elven women staring at us curiously from the end of the corridor. "I wouldn't worry about it, Lianna. The high elves will just have to get used to sharing this kingdom again. Don't let them get to you. As for Prince Erix, he will welcome you with open arms."

"Eden is right!" Cass adds reassuringly. "Besides, you have other things to think about... Like Jarek's face when he sees you walking into the ballroom later."

She nibbles her lip anxiously, taking a deep breath as we approach the doors to the throne room.

"What are you doing here, Cass? I thought you were out of the servant business?" one of the guards asks with a grin.

"Turns out I have one last duty to perform. Come on, Jocon. Let me through for old times' sake."

He rolls his eyes as she flutters her eyelashes at him sweetly.

"Fine, I'll let you through, but only because Miss Nestoriel is with you, and I wouldn't like to get on the wrong side of Prince Erix."

Cass huffs. "Fine. Whatever helps!"

He opens the door to let us through, and I immediately scan the large throne room for any sign of Erix.

"Are you well acquainted with the prince?" Lianna enquires curiously, causing Cass to snort in return.

"It's a long story," she snickers.

Cass leads the way to the chambers Aubrun had prepared for me, opening the door to let us enter first. "Now, I'm sure there are lots of gowns in here. Aubrun had the wardrobe fully stocked before he...."

Her voice trails off as she looks at me apologetically.

"Oh, are you sure this is okay?" Lianna asks me again, picking up on the awkward silence.

"Of course!" I respond insistently. "Please help yourself."

⬚

She smiles softly, joining Cass by the large closet to flick through the selection of fine materials and vivid colors.

I sigh as my eyes travel the room, finishing at the vase on the nightstand, filled with wilted flowers.

The sight instantly reminds me of Aubrun, and my heart aches a little.

"Eden, I'm not great at this. I need your help," Cass demands. "Do we think pink to compliment her skin tone or green to match her eyes?"

I glance at both options distractedly. "Uhh, maybe try both?"

We spend the next hour or so getting together everything that we need for the coronation celebration this evening. Lianna settles for the pink dress, which looks beautiful on her, and Cass grabs some matching heels to finish off the outfit.

"Oh, this reminds me, Eden, I arranged for the Alphas to receive outfits for tonight's event. I can't wait to see what they think of their tunics."

My eyes widen in response. "You got them tunics?!"

"You bet I did! I can't wait to see Rocco in his daring purple and silver ensemble!" she giggles mischievously.

I select a dress for myself, slinging it over my arm as we get ready to leave the room.

Suddenly, we hear raised voices coming from outside, and Cass stops to look out the window.

"What the hell is going on out there?" I ask curiously.

"At this time? The Guard will be training, but it isn't usually this noisy," she answers.

We wander out of the bedroom onto the stone balcony, and I stiffen at the sight before me.

Duel

Conall

"Hey," Zeke says, walking over to the lunch table. "I take it from that look on your face that you didn't catch up with Eden last night?"

"No, she was out late and hasn't been in her room all day," I answer with a grunt.

"She and Cass didn't get back from Morween until around midnight, but they did track down Jarek's girl. Eden invited her to the palace, so I'm sure she's probably with her now," he explains. "I met Cass on the way back to my room last night."

I raise my brow. "On the way *back* to your room?"

He grins in return, and I shake my head, rolling my eyes.

"Come on! Is it my fault that the Elven ladies are curious about us, Con? I don't fucking blame them. They have been deprived for way too long, my friend."

Two women then walk past our table, one waving at Zeke with a blush covering her cheeks. He winks at her before his eyes drift back to see me glaring at him in warning. "I swear, if this peace treaty goes sideways because you are fucking some high elf's wife, I'll kill you myself, Zeke."

"Strictly single women only," he chuckles, shrugging his shoulders. "Anyway, you have a damn cheek. You're the one stealing their future queen from under their noses."

I narrow my eyes, and he holds up his hands in surrender. "I'm kidding, obviously!"

"Zeke...you're a pain in the ass. I might just kill you for the fucking hell of it," I grumble.

"Yeah, you've got that kind of murder-y look in your eyes today. Why don't you put it to good use instead? The others are out training with the Guard. Fancy a look?" he asks with a glint in his eye.

"Training? Who set that up?"

"Commander Walden was impressed with what he saw yesterday. He asked us to come and show his men a move or two."

"So long as it's only a few."

"You're right. We don't want to give all our secrets away," he laughs. "So, are you up for it? Cass mentioned she and Eden are busy today finding a dress and shit for Jarek's date."

"Fuck it, okay then," I nod in defeat, taking a drink before following him out of the dining room.

We leave the palace, walking past the perfectly trimmed hedges onto the Elven Guard training field. In the distance, we see Commander Walden talking to a group of men while others train on the grounds behind him. Zeke and I take a minute to observe the scene with interest.

"Damn, it's a good setup they have going on here, isn't it?" he comments, gesturing to a group practicing combat with weapons.

"It's organized," I state, looking around the field split into sections, my eyes running over the archers engaged in target practice. "I'll give them that."

We head down onto the field, joining the other Alphas, where they are getting ready to demonstrate some hand-to-hand combat moves for Walden and his men. I'm not surprised to find them here. Elves excel in archery and sword fighting, but this is where we truly have the upper hand. Killing from afar isn't our style. Ours is far more direct, close and personal. If we want you dead, we'll look you straight in the fucking eye when we deliver the final blow.

Hunter and Mateo step forward into the center of the field, circling each other for a few moments before they begin to fight. They both move with speed and precision the way Zeke and I taught them. Taking turns to demonstrate their individual talents and skills. Mateo lands an uppercut that causes Hunter's nose to burst, but still, they don't stop. Their fight grows more vicious, and Commander Walden looks at me questioningly. I can tell he wishes to stop the fight, but I fold my arms over my chest and shake my head. My men don't back down. They know what they're doing, and it's not often that I'll interfere in their training.

"Any barbarian can wrestle and throw wild punches," I hear one guard mutter to another under his breath. "Where are the swords?"

"Swords..." Hunter says breathlessly, taking a break from the fight to point at the guard in question. "...are for pussies."

He grabs Mateo's arm, slinging him over his shoulder until he slams on the ground flat on his back. He then grabs him by the throat, squeezing his windpipe until Mateo's face starts turning a bright shade of red. The surrounding men fall into complete silence as Mateo struggles for air, and Commander Walden shifts uncomfortably on his feet. "Alpha Conall...?"

Hunter twists his neck to look up at me, and I give him a curt nod. As soon as Mateo is released, he rolls onto his side to gasp for air as Hunter slaps him on the back. "I think you broke my nose, Matty you fucker," he laughs.

The men around us murmur in approval as Hunter helps Mateo back onto his feet, and Commander Walden begins clapping. "Well, that was eye-opening, Alpha Hunter. That takedown was very impressive—"

"Impressive indeed," a voice interrupts from behind.

I turn around to see Erix watching on, his eyes flicking to me briefly. "There's no doubt hand-to-hand combat is important, but the skill needed to wield a weapon like this one cannot be underestimated."

The guards bow respectfully as he pulls his sword from his sheath to look over it.

"Do you wish to demonstrate, Your Majesty?" Walden questions, drawing his own sword and taking a dutiful step forward.

"Certainly, but how about a little fun?" he suggests with a grin walking into the center of the training area. "Alpha Conall? What do you say? Are you well aquatinted enough with the sword?"

He looks at me challengingly, and I furrow my brows. We both know that a fight between us, training or not, won't end well.

"Oh shit," Zeke mutters as everyone looks at me curiously, waiting for my response.

Every fiber of my being tells me this is a bad fucking idea, but I can't help the fire that races through my veins. Backing down from an outright challenge is not something I'd ever do, and I'm not about to start now.

"Alright," I answer, stepping forward onto the training ground.

"Oh, so you're really going to do this? Fuck me... Don't kill him whatever you do. Goddess above," Zeke mutters under his breath, swiping his hand over his face before crossing his arms.

The other men, Alphas and guards alike, begin to barter back and forth, making bets amongst themselves. I don't care enough to listen to what they have to say; I'm too busy looking back at Erix as he stretches his neck from side to side in preparation.

"Walden, give the Alpha your sword," he orders confidently.

Walden walks forward, giving me a concerned glance as he hands the weapon over. It seems everyone is scared that I'll lose control. That I'll do something that might jeopardize the peace we have finally restored between our people, but I can hold it together in a fight. Despite my jealousy and anger at the situation, the lessons my father taught me as a boy still resonate to this day.

Emotions can be powerful in a fight when channeled correctly, which is what I intend to do.

Erix takes a fighting stance, and I push my opinions about him to the back of my mind, examining him just as I would any other opponent. I can already tell from the way he holds his sword that his right shoulder is weak, but apart from that, I can see that he won't go down easily. He has a determined look in his eye that tells me as much.

I swing the sword in my hand to get used to the feel of it. It's old-fashioned, slightly heavier than average, but looking at Walden, it doesn't surprise me. The man must have had it in his possession for at least a couple hundred years.

Erix then begins to move, his feet crossing over one another carefully as he circles. Our eyes remain fixed on one another as the crowd quietens down around us. He strikes first, lunging forward quickly with two successive swings of his sword. I dodge out of its path easily each time without raising my own weapon.

He's testing me to see if he can lure me into a panicked retaliation.

But it won't work.

His jaw tenses in realization, and he moves forward again with more force, prompting me to lift the sword to defend against his swings. The metal clatters against the veil of silence, indicating that the fight has begun.

I can already sense the anger and desperation pouring out of him. His emotions have taken control within the first few seconds, which ultimately means...he doesn't stand a chance.

We trade attacks back and forth, each of us gaining more knowledge about the other as we go. Our attacks grow quicker, and I feel my heart pumping in my chest the longer I let this draw out. He's skilled. There's no denying it and part of me just wants to see what he's capable of.

He charges at me again, swiping his sword at my lower body. I block his swing, using brute force to push him back a few steps. I lift the blade to drive it toward his body, and he dodges it quickly, stumbling over his feet just a little. A little is all I need. I swing the sword again, forcing him onto one knee to defend himself. My weapon clangs against his as he holds his sword above his head. His arms shake under the pressure as he stares up at me. I can see he's struggling to hold me off. His teeth are gritting together, and the sweat beads on his forehead as his chest rapidly inflates under the weight of heavy breaths. I use my strength to push down on him harder, and his body eventually relents, causing him to fall back on his ass.

He shuffles back, frantically turning onto his hands and knees to struggle back up onto his feet. I could chop his fucking head off right now if the notion took me. I could make him disappear from Eden's life once and for all with one swing of this fucking sword. I follow behind him like a beast stalking its prey, ready to force him into surrender, and it's then that I hear them.

The whispers.

They begin to circulate all around us, stopping me in my tracks. I scan the guards to see them examine Erix's sorry state intently. Some shake their heads, and others look away in clear disappointment.

I stop where I am for a moment, feigning a shoulder injury as Erix takes a second to regain his balance on two feet.

I swing my sword back into position as he breathlessly makes his way back into the center. He might not know it yet, but it's clear for me to see already that this fight can only end with one outcome.

He's finished.

He's finished unless I decide differently.

I clear my throat. "Come on, *prince.* Is that all you've fucking got?" I taunt, tilting my head to the side. "I was promised a decent fight, or have you lost the fucking ability?"

His brows knit together in renewed anger, and he lifts his sword once again, running at me with a loud, determined grunt.

My words do the trick as our battle ignites quicker than before, our swords slicing through the air skilfully. I bide my time until the moment arrives and brace myself for the blade that slashes across my thigh. Immediately, blood begins to pour from the area, and the guards grow rowdier in anticipation.

"That it, Your Majesty!"

"You've got him now!"

"Finish him!"

Erix's shoulders practically lift in confidence, and he comes at me again, letting out another purposeful cry as he stabs his weapon at my torso. I jump back out of the way, and his sword clashes with mine, knocking it out of my hand to fall onto the dusty ground. He uses the opportunity to thrust his sword toward my neck, stopping just as the pointed edge of the blade presses against my skin.

I stop moving and silently surrender as his eyes bore into mine, widening first in surprise and then again in sheer relief.

The guards around us erupt into applause and cheers, and the noise escalates as they all talk amongst themselves, settling their bets.

Still, Erix stares at me, his blade pressed against my neck. I can tell from the look in his eyes that he is having the same thoughts I did only moments ago. But even the fiercest of rivals must learn to tolerate one another in the name of peace.

He swallows hard, his sword finally lowering away from me. He puts his hand out to shake mine, and I take it firmly.

"Congratulations," I say calmly, offering him a curt nod.

He nods respectfully in return, and I walk past him to pick up the discarded sword, handing it back to Commander Walden.

"Thanks for that, Con. You just lost me twenty pieces of silver!" William declares in irritation.

"Care to explain what that was all about?" Zeke asks knowingly.

I glance across the field to see Erix happily celebrating with his men, who are eagerly patting him on the back.

"No," I answer.

He smirks, raising his brow. "Fair enough."

"I've never seen you lose a fight, Con," Henrick adds suspiciously. "What got into you?"

"Just not my day," I answer with a shrug, and he grins.

I feel her presence in the air before I see her. Her subtle but fucking intoxicating scent carries on the wind making me breathe in deeply. I turn my head to look up at the palace, and my eyes find Eden's, where she stands on a small balcony alongside Cass and the blonde Nymph. Her face is awash with shock, her pink lips parted as she stares back at me.

Coronation

Eden

"What if he's still furious with me?" Lianna asks anxiously as Cass smoothes down a strand of her perfectly positioned blonde hair.

"He won't be," I answer assuredly, patting her arm.

"It's Jarek we are talking about," Cass adds. "He doesn't get furious. In fact, he's possibly the only Alpha I know that doesn't have the odd temper tantrum."

"Really?" Lianna questions.

"Eden, back me up,"

"Drama kings. All of them," I confirm with a grin. "Except Jarek, of course."

Lianna laughs, her bright smile bringing some color back to her cheeks.

"So you're ready?" I ask her gently.

Cass tuts. "Of course she is! She's flawless; look at her. Now let's get a move on."

I roll my eyes in Lianna's direction, and she giggles. "You both look beautiful too."

"Thanks! For a minute there, I thought neither of you were going to mention it," Cass jokes as we begin the journey down to the great hall.

"Do you have a partner, Cass?" Lianna asks curiously.

"Partner? *Bleugh!*" she answers animatedly. "I have lovers."

"Plural?" I question, raising my brow.

She smiles wickedly in reply. "I'd say you should try it, but I don't think either of your men are the sharing type, Eden."

"You've got that right," I groan under my breath.

Although I have love for both men in my heart, I know that ultimately, I'm not the sharing type either, nor would I enjoy *being* shared. Goddess, even the thought of it stresses me out rather than turns me on.

We reach the bottom of the staircase to find the enormous foyer bustling with excited people. The place is decorated beautifully, as always. Erix did say that he was aiming to keep things low-key, but in Morween that never seems to be an option.

"Oh, Goddess! There they are," Cass smiles, gesturing to the Alpha men across the room.

My eyes follow her line of sight. All of them are grouped together, talking amongst themselves, except for a few stragglers entertaining some giggling Elven women.

I vaguely hear Cass commenting on their tunics, her high-pitched laughter telling me she finds the whole thing hilarious. However, I'm too distracted to care right now, my eyes searching for the only Alpha that matters.

My Alpha.

Henrick steps out of the way to lift a glass from a server's tray, and it's then I get a glimpse of him.

My breath hitches slightly as I drink him in.

He's dressed in a burgundy tunic embroidered with muted golden thread in a subtle floral design. It fits his large frame like a glove, accentuating his broad shoulders. The tight sleeves showing off the curves of his rounded biceps. The outfit is more formal than anything I've ever seen him wear, but damn, does he do it justice. I examine his face appreciatively. The two or three day-old stubble shadows his strong jaw in the sexiest of ways, and his hair sits perfectly imperfect on top of his head. He looks so damn handsome that it's impossible to focus on anything but him.

A small smile makes its way to my lips when I see him make warning eyes at Zeke, who is chatting to an Elven woman, curling his finger flirtatiously around a tendril of her red hair.

"Okay, let's do this," Cass grins, encouraging Lianna forward.

We make our way through the crowd, and I finally tear my eyes from Con to watch Lianna, who looks like she might pass out at any moment.

"Hey..." I say gently, tugging her arm. "Breathe. It's going to be okay."

She swallows hard, nodding her head.

"Hey, Cass! I've got a fricken bone to pick with you!" Hunter calls out through the crowd when he sees us approaching. "Why did I get the *worst* tunic out of everyone?!" he whines, looking down over his lime green and pink outfit.

"For this precise reason, asshole!" she laughs, taking in his pissed-off demeanor in triumph.

"Yeah, well—"

"Lianna?"

Jarek's shock-filled voice cuts Hunter off mid-sentence.

"Hi," Lianna replies, lifting her hand to tuck her hair behind her ear.

Jarek's eyes widen, and he takes a step forward. "W-what are you doing here?" he asks breathlessly, scanning over her in disbelief.

She smiles, her eyes turning glassy with unshed tears. "I-I didn't know if I should come. I probably shouldn't have. I just missed you so much." She bobs her head, and some tears spring free before her hand lifts to swipe them away quickly.

Jarek breathes, twisting his neck to glance at the Alphas around him.

At first, no one says a word and the awkwardness mounts. I can only imagine how Lianna feels right now.

I clasp my hands together in front of my body, my eyes finally settling on Conall again, where he stands a few feet away. He's already staring at me with his trademark unreadable expression, and my shoulders tense as I consider what he might be thinking.

Is he still mad at me for what happened last night?

I wouldn't know, of course. I've pretty much avoided the situation all day today in order to clear my head.

"Jarek, please say something," Lianna whispers.

He lifts his hand to push his glasses back up his nose. "I'm not sure what to say, Lianna. Perhaps you are right, and you shouldn't have come."

Her face instantly falls in disappointment, her gaze dropping to the floor. "I understand," she says, desperately trying to disguise the pain in her voice. "I'm so sorry to have intruded." And with that, she turns, rushing back through the sea of people who stare at her curiously.

"Seriously?" Cass scowls, turning to chase after her.

My mouth opens, and I look at Con with pleading eyes. He immediately responds to my silent request, sauntering forward to stand beside Jarek who is frozen in place, watching Lianna leave.

"What the hell are you doing?" Con asks.

"She betrayed me," Jarek answers quietly, his voice uncertain. "She betrayed all of us."

Con's brows knit together, and he shakes his head. "Do you love her?"

Jarek swallows, looking around the other men before he nods. "Yes."

Con shrugs his shoulders casually, lifting his arms to fold them over his chest. "Then I'll ask you again... What the hell are you doing?"

Jarek stares at him briefly, blinking quickly before taking a few slow steps forward.

"Yes, Jarek!"

"Go get her, my man!"

"Fucking run, you idiot!"

The men burst into applause and teasing taunts as Jarek runs across the busy foyer to catch up with Cass and Lianna. The elves in the room stop their conversations to watch as the scene unfolds. The Alphas whoop and yell, letting out wolf whistles as Jarek spins Lianna around, taking her face in his hands as he kisses her.

A huge smile covers my face, and I laugh, clapping my hands with everyone else. It's then I look to the side to see Conall turn at the same time. Our eyes meet, and I thank him without a single word. His mouth turns up at the corner, and he uncrosses his arms, making his way over in my direction as everyone in the room goes back to their own business. My stomach fills with butterflies the closer he gets, and I suck in a breath as he stops right in front of me.

"Hey." I smile softly, looking up into those honey eyes.

"I've been looking for you," he answers, his gaze drifting over my face.

"I'm sorry, I had to visit Grandma today, and then Lianna needed my help. "

He nods, taking another step closer to close the gap between us. "I need to speak with you about last night."

My breathing intensifies. "Of course," I say on an exhale.

Just then, the palace trumpets begin to sound, signaling that it's time for the ceremony to begin. I break our intense eye contact first to look around as everyone enters the great hall behind us.

I then feel him lean into my ear, his breath tickling my neck. "Don't go too far. As soon as I have the chance, I'm stealing you."

I shiver in delight, remaining rooted to the spot.

"Eden! Eden, darling!" my mother's voice calls out on approach.

Con takes a step back, acknowledging her respectfully.

"Alpha Conall," my mother greets him in return. "How nice to see you again."

I can tell by the tone of her voice that she doesn't wholly mean it. It's not that she dislikes him, but if she were to choose a side, it's a given to say that Erix would receive her vote.

"And you, Mrs. Nestoriel," Conall answers.

"Well, I must say, you wear a tunic extremely well," she smiles, examining him briefly before turning her attention to me. "Eden, I'm sorry to interrupt you both, but the prince has requested that we sit at the front. He wishes your father to play a small role in the ceremony, assisting Elder Gideon with the Royal Oath."

I glance at Conall sideways, and he smirks.

"You understand. Don't you, Alpha?" my mother asks him with another polite smile.

"Of course," he answers, his eyes holding mine for the final time. "Ladies..." he nods, turning around to return to Zeke and the others.

I let out a puff of air and glare at my mother, who is watching them with interest.

"Could you be any more transparent, Mother?" I ask with a raised brow.

"Me?!" she asks innocently. "I'm not taking sides, I swear."

"Hmmm," I respond, tugging her arm toward the great hall. "Let's head inside."

* * *

I watch proudly as the crown hovers above Erix, the elder elf finishing his speech for the waiting crowd. Erix's bright blue eyes shine like sparkling diamonds, his chest puffing out confidently as the precious gold finally lowers to rest gently on top of his head. As soon as it does, I exhale a breath of relief, lifting my hands to clap enthusiastically. After everything this realm has been through, it is now that peace has been finally restored. As I look upon our new king, I do not doubt we are all in good hands. We are all under the care of a man who will rule with honor, integrity, passion and kindness. He was made for this moment, and seeing it makes my heart burst with pride.

His blue eyes flick to me and I offer him a genuine smile, lifting my hands even higher to clap in appreciation. He smiles at me before he casts his eyes over the rest of his people.

"LONG LIVE THE KING!" a royal crier calls out, eliciting an eager chant from the crowd.

"LONG LIVE THE KING!"

"LONG LIVE THE KING!"

The palace music begins to play, and Erix rises from his throne, holding still as a long cape is draped over his shoulders. He then follows Elder Gideon down the marble steps, holding his head high as he walks down the center aisle of the great hall.

"May the gods bless your rule!"

"Congratulations, Your Majesty!"

The genuine outpouring of emotions and joy in the room is palpable, and I know every elf here feels it as I do. For the first time ever in the palace, I look around and see the beginnings of a new age. High elves and wood elves existing in harmony. Hell, we even have some wolves and nymphs thrown into the mix!

As Erix disappears from sight, I spot Con a few rows back, clapping his hands along with everyone else. This whole situation wouldn't be possible without him either.

How can it be possible that in this lifetime, I have been blessed with meeting two of the best men that have ever walked this realm?

Goddess, I'll never know.

"Thank the Gods for this day!" my mother cries gratefully, dabbing her tears away before she leans in to hug me.

I hold her in return, looking over her shoulder at the buzzing crowd again. There's an unmistakable shift in the dynamics in the palace already. Without the interference of the greedy and corrupt lords, at least for now, the future looks bright and peaceful.

Bond

Eden

As we head inside the ballroom, I hear my name being called out from behind. "Eden! Wait up!"

I turn around to see Lianna and Jarek approaching me hand-in-hand. The sight automatically makes me smile.

"We missed the ceremony." Lianna blushes, looking to Jarek, who lifts her hand to land a gentle kiss.

"That's understandable," I grin, shrugging my shoulders.

"I just wanted to say thank you for everything you have done for me."

"No, please don't thank me. It was all Cass' idea."

"Oh, she told me that," Jarek laughs.

"Your generosity and encouragement meant a lot to me too, Eden," Lianna continues, looking at Jarek, whose face is beaming with a huge smile. "I wouldn't be here without you."

"No problem at all. I wish you guys the very best."

"Lianna has agreed to come with me to Harmony," Jarek explains enthusiastically. "I hope to begin working there as a pack doctor soon."

"That's amazing!"

He nods happily, glancing over his shoulder at Conall and the other Alphas as they enter the ballroom. "Perhaps I'll even see you there. You know, I still need to brush up on my knowledge of plants. I could use an expert to turn to for advice."

"I'd happily teach you how to treat Blue Thistle burn anytime!" I laugh in reply.

The busy room begins to settle, and trumpets sound as the palace servants open the large doors at the top of the stairs.

My gaze trails up the path of marble and gold to see Erix make his way through the doors, lifting his hand to wave to his adoring audience.

As he walks down the staircase, I notice that he has changed his outfit.

□

Instead of the heavy cloak and long ceremony garments, he now wears a silver, fitted tunic that shines under the twinkling lights of the chandeliers.

When he reaches the bottom step, music begins to play, and he scans the sea of faces until his eyes find me. I swallow hard as he makes his way over in my direction.

Lianna and Jarek side-step out of the way awkwardly.

The eyes of the entire room are now on us as Erix stops in front of me, laying out his hand. "May I have this dance, Miss Nestoriel?"

There's no way that I can refuse. To do so would be highly embarrassing for us both.

"Of course, Your Majesty," I respond, resting my hand in his to let him guide me to the center of the room.

As we move, I can't help but look at Con, who is watching us with a serious expression. I don't miss how Zeke leans in toward him, whispering something in his ear before he shoves him slightly in the direction of some drinks.

My body tenses all over. This is what I was afraid of. The reason why I've been MIA all day.

Erix holds my hand tightly, placing his other on my waist as we glide around the dancefloor in time to the music. He looks at me intensely, those pools of blue studying my face. I shoot my gaze away to thankfully see other couples taking to the floor all around us. It eases the tension, if only a little.

"You look beautiful tonight. As always," Erix says quietly, drawing my attention back to him.

I smile, looking down over his tunic. "As do you, Your Majesty."

"You know you can call me by my name. To you, I'll always be Erix."

"Oh, I know. But I'm just so proud of you that I had to say it."

His hand tightens around mine. "You are?"

"So very much," I reply honestly from the heart. "The people of Morween are lucky to have you."

"No, Eden. They are lucky to have you. You made this happen."

I smile softly as we fall back into silence. He watches me for a few seconds before his eyes then travel the room. "I'll be happy to get this night over with."

My expression turns soft in understanding. "You're the king. If you order the music to stop playing and the drinks to stop flowing, they will."

"And deny my men their first proper night of celebration in seventy years?

How could I live with myself, Eden?" he jests.

"Well, look at you... You're sure to be a hit with your people already!"

"I'll say," he agrees. "I already promised Elder Gideon's wife the next dance, followed by their four daughters, one after the other. Then I apparently have to greet some high elves who have traveled from Tipreon to be here. The list is never-ending."

"You are a very gracious king indeed," I say in amusement. "I'm sorry. that you're in for a busy evening. I'm sure you're exhausted."

"I am," he answers. "But not too exhausted to be with you."

It's then a royal servant appears to tap him on the shoulder gently. "Your Majesty...."

"I have to go, Eden, but you'll come to find me later?"

I clear my throat and nod, watching as he kisses the back of my hand.

He walks away, and I stand in a daze, startled when I feel a hand wrap around my wrist.

"Eden? Shit, sorry. Are you alright?"

I look up to see Anton's large frame, clad in an emerald green tunic with blue swirls.

"Yes," I practically squeak in reply.

"Yeah...sure seems like it."

I quickly look back to the side of the dance floor to search for Con, but he and Zeke are nowhere to be found.

"Fancy a dance?" Anton asks with a lopsided grin.

"How about a drink instead?" I counter.

"That's a much better idea," he guffaws. "I'm guessing we'll be making yours a double?"

"I'm thinking triple," I answer, leading him to a table with drinks.

He hands me a glass, and I proceed to look nervously around the room.

"So that was pretty cool that you tracked down the nymph."

"Yes, she's amazing. She's perfect for Jarek."

"They look good together," he comments. "Makes a man rather jealous, actually."

I look to him in surprise. "You'd like to settle down?"

"Sure. Is that so hard to believe?"

I shake my head with a smile. "No, you'll make someone very happy someday, Anton."

"A catch like me? An Alpha who knows how to make the best pancakes this side of Morween? There's no doubt about it!"

"I take full credit for that!" I laugh, smacking his arm.

He grins, watching me closely as the smile fades from my face. "Yeah, love is messy, huh? But I'd imagine it's worth it."

"I dare say it is," I agree, swallowing another burning mouthful of alcohol.

Suddenly, I see Con enter the room again, and I freeze.

He searches until he finds me, flicking his head to the door leading out to the west wing corridor. I nod eagerly, placing the glass on the table to follow him.

"Where are you going?" Anton asks in confusion.

"Off to make a mess," I reply with a smile.

"Good luck!"

I reach the door and peer around the corner to find the softly-lit corridor empty. I walk forward amongst the glow of the candles, looking up to the starry sky through the glass domes on the ceiling. I find the door directly in front of me open wide, and I make my way outside to the palace gardens. There's total silence out here, save for the gentle hum of the music from inside the palace walls.

"Con?" I ask the darkness.

It's then that I feel his presence behind me, and I turn to see him standing, looking down over my face.

I smile softly, and he returns the favor, stepping forward to close the gap between us. "Conall, about the dance—"

"I get it, but I wasn't going to watch it happen."

"I know it must be difficult."

"Difficult? I want to break his neck when I see him touch you, Eden."

"You had your chance today," I say with a gulp. "I saw you out there on the training field. You had him beat. You know it, I know it, and I think deep down Erix knows it too." He looks away for a moment while I search his face for answers. "Why did you do it?"

He shrugs his shoulders, his gaze returning to mine. "Sometimes people just need the win more than you do."

I can't help the joyful smile that touches my lips upon hearing his words. His confession confirms my thoughts from earlier when I watched them fight. He knew that losing would cost Erix the respect of his men in a time already filled with so much uncertainty. He put the need for peace above his own ego, which I know for a dominant man like him, is not an easy thing to do.

"Why are you smiling?" he asks quietly, studying my expression.

"Because of you, Conall, because of who you are."

"And who am I to you?" he continues, his chest pressing against mine.

"You're everything a true Alpha ought to be," I explain adoringly. "Nobel yet humble at the same time. Strong but also restrained. Wise but spontaneous. Powerful, and yet, gentle. To put it simply, you are amazing."

He pauses for a long moment, and I wonder if anyone has ever told him these things before. It's safe to assume the answer is most probably no.

It's then that he clears his throat purposefully. "Eden, I should have told you sooner about the marking process. What I said last night when I was angry...it was wrong, and I'm sorry."

I hold his gaze. "I know you are, and I am too. I should have realized how special a moment like that is. I wish I had understood."

"That's my fault," he insists.

"It's okay. We've been busy, caught in a whirlwind, and it's been tough to find the time to talk."

He shakes his head in refusal, his brows knitting together. "No...that's not why I didn't tell you. I tried to convince myself that it was, but the truth is that I was afraid," he explains. "As it turns out, I was scared to want happiness. I was scared to want you, but I'm here now, Eden, wanting you anyway because I realize that I want it all. A life. A future."

I want *us*.

And if I'm lucky enough to have all of that, then I'll never want for anything else in this lifetime. I'll have everything I need and more.

I tilt my head, my heart squeezing in my chest.

"I was afraid that this bond between us, this perfect piece of happiness, would be taken from me. That it would be ripped out of my grasp just like everything else in my life," he explains. "I was feeling sorry for myself. Guarding the last broken piece of my heart, afraid that if I gave it away completely, I'd crumble."

"Oh, Conall...."

"But I should have remembered my heart is already yours, and so if you choose me, I'd like to mark you as mine. In fact, it would be the single greatest thing I've done in my life."

My eyes widen as I rein in my overwhelming emotions.

He smiles softly, lifting his hand to lay a finger on my neck. "When a wolf marks his mate, he sinks his teeth into her skin right here," he explains. "The mark left behind is permanent. It not only acts as a visual display of their love but also establishes their unbreakable bond. It cements it firmly for the rest of this life and beyond. Once a wolf marks his mate like this, they become one and the same."

I stare into his honey eyes, blown away. "That's beautiful," I say on an exhale. I lift my hand to rest it on his cheek, feeling him jolt subtly in response to my touch. "What does it feel like?" I whisper curiously, realizing that I've never asked the question before. "What does it feel like when I touch you?"

He leans into my hand, blinking slowly before opening his now deep, dark eyes. "I can't describe the feelings I get around you, Eden. No words can ever do them justice."

"Please try," I whisper hopefully.

"Let me show you instead," he says, lifting his hand to mine, peeling it from his face to place it gently on his chest.

My entire body stills in anticipation as his hands reach up to my shoulders before he trails them softly down my arms.

A shiver runs down my spine.

"The first thing that happens is my skin tingles and sparks underneath your fingertips," he husks lowly. "It's as though I'm on fire and on ice at the same time."

His large hands rest on my waist, holding it firmly before he slides them up the contours of my body. My eyes close, and my back arches subtly as they move over my breasts.

"My body comes to life. Every nerve is awakened. Begging for your attention. Begging for more of you."

His hands slide up the column of my bare neck, his thumbs pressing my pulse points under my jawline to elicit a small, needy gasp from my lips.

"You steal the breath from my lungs. You suck the wind from me in the most addictive, all-consuming way, making me forget my own damn name."

One of his hands flicks my hair behind my shoulder, and he leans into my neck, pressing his lips against my hot skin. The small action sends shockwaves running through me, resting in my core that now aches with desire.

"I'd run through stone walls just to feel your body pressed against mine. I'd take a thousand punches just to taste you. When you touch me, Eden... I burn for you."

I arch against him further, desperate for more. More of his touch and more of his words. "Please don't stop," I say breathlessly, a state of delirium possessing me.

His head lifts, his impossibly dark eyes finding mine as his hand lifts to splay firmly across my rising chest. "My heart beats faster whenever you're near. One look, one smile, one kiss is enough to send it racing," he continues, turning me into a panting mess in his arms. "It's as if it's calling out to you, Eden," he says passionately, his lips moving within touching distance. "It knows that its missing piece is right here. Right here with you."

Our eyes close, his nose grazes mine in a playful, lustful, breathy dance, and I can't take it any longer.

I throw my arms around his neck, ready to pull him in, when I hear my name being called.

"Eden! Eden, are you there?!"

My eyes snap open, my jaw tensing in frustration as my mother appears by the door. "Oh...sorry to interrupt."

"What?" I snap, unable to hide my annoyance at yet another intrusion.

"I was just looking for you as Commander Walden is leading a toast to King Erix from the Guard. I thought you might want to be there."

I let out an exasperated breath. "Mother...."

"It's fine, Eden. I was just leaving anyway. I've said everything I had to say," Conall announces, his eyes tearing from mine before he walks over to my mother. "Mrs. Nestoriel, I realize you have no reason to trust me with your daughter, but you need to know that I would die for her. I love her, and that's never going to change."

My mother stares at him in disbelief, too shocked to respond. She merely nods her head at him in reply.

It's then he looks back at me. "If you need me...you know where I'll be."

As soon as he finishes the sentence, he leaves, taking my heart with him.

Complete

Eden

I stand outside in the corridor, resting my head on the wall as I psych myself up for the night ahead.

I don't know what to expect. I'm a ball of mixed emotions. Emotions that threaten to overwhelm me once again, sending me running for the protection of the forest, but I know that there can be no more running. No more excuses or interruptions.

I lift my hand to knock on the door, waiting to hear his voice. "Come in."

I twist the knob, making my way inside to find him standing there looking back at me.

"Eden," he says, a huge smile crossing his lips. "I was hoping you'd come." He approaches with his arms outstretched. "I can't believe that you're here!"

His arms wrap around me, holding me in the warmth of his chest. I close my eyes, my heart aching as I reach around his body to hug him back.

"Thank Goddess—"

"Erix," I interrupt, peeling myself from his body. "We need to talk."

The bright smile drains from his face, and he nods, gesturing to the sofa in the corner of the room. We sit in silence, and I blink, taking a deep breath before opening my mouth.

"Don't do this, Eden," he pleads, with a wounded expression. "You've hardly had any time at all to think this through! I was impatient before, but I can wait. I swear—"

"But I can't," I interrupt, resting my hand on his. "This isn't fair to you, and it isn't fair to Conall either. The truth is that I don't need any more time. I already made up my mind."

"And you choose him," he states, his gaze dropping to the floor.

I nod my head softly in return. "Everything I said to you tonight... I meant every word. I'm so proud of you, Erix. I'm so proud of the man you've become. I'll forever be proud to have you as my king and my friend."

He shakes his head. "Friends is not what I want."

"But it's all I can give you," I answer honestly. "I'm sorry, Erix, but I have to follow my heart, and it now belongs to someone else."

He nods, turning away to rest his head in his hands. "I've already lost so much. I don't know if I can take losing you too, Eden."

"You can handle anything," I say adamantly, hooking my finger under his chin to bring his eyes up to meet mine. "You've already proven how strong you are. Now you have your whole life ahead of you. A brand new life just waiting to be lived and I *know* you'll live it to the fullest."

"Where do I even begin? How can I even think about replacing you?"

"We don't have to replace one another. The love we felt for each other was real. It helped make us who we are today, and I'll never forget it for as long as I live."

"But it's in the past?" he asks quietly, his blue eyes searching mine.

I nod my head. "Now it's time to look to the future."

He exhales deeply and I stand up, readying myself to leave.

"I take it you'll be leaving Morween?" he questions, rising to his feet.

"Yes, I will," I answer without a doubt.

"Then I'll miss you, Eden."

"I'll miss you too, Erix."

He takes a cautious step forward, putting his arms around me once again; only now, we both know that it's for the last time.

From this moment onward, our paths have separated. He has his own journey to make, and I have mine.

Conall

I take another drink as I look out of the window over the forest below. Now that the peace treaty is signed and everything is in order, I'm itching to leave this place behind once and for all. If I had my way, I'd pack up and go first thing in the morning and never look back, but how can I leave while a huge part of me is here?

Tonight I laid it all out on the table. No more lies. No more secrets. That part of our journey is over. I never once imagined I would say the words that came out of my mouth tonight, yet every single one of them is true.

I've never been more open. More bare.

But then again, every time I think I'm done, she strips me of another piece of my armor. Another layer that I didn't realize I had.

I glance at the clock above the fireplace to see it strike midnight. It's been a while since I left her in the gardens, and now this is it. It's time to see if my mate wants me as much as I want her. It's time for her to make her choice.

Come what may, I know that I'll survive.

Because that's what I do.

I survive.

But I don't want that to be my life any longer. I want a home. A future. And I can only see that happening if she's right there with me by my side.

It's then that the door knocks, and my heart thumps in my chest. I turn around and head toward it, deciding that if this is a drunken Zeke or any one of those other assholes, then I'll have no choice but to punch them in the fucking face for getting my hopes up.

As soon as I approach, I catch onto her scent. It instantly soothes my nerves, and I close my eyes briefly, breathing in before I open the door to find myself face-to-face with her.

She smiles gently, her eyes trailing up over my bare torso. "Can I come in?"

I nod, standing aside to let her walk into the center of the room.

"You came," I say quietly, breaking the tension.

"It's you, Con," she answers softly. "It's always been you."

Her words take immediate effect, stirring something deep inside of me.

"I never really needed time, but I think you did," she says, taking a step forward. "You needed to know that I was sure. That I wasn't just choosing you because of the bond."

My heart thuds in my chest as she moves closer again.

"I do believe in fate. I believe I was meant to meet you, but I also believe that our fate can be dependent on the choices that we make. And I choose you, Con. With everything in me, I choose you because why wouldn't I?" she continues. "When I met you, I met a new version of myself. A woman that was brave, determined and powerful. You are the one who gave me that gift, and I can't thank the stars enough that I was hit on the head with a rock that night."

I smirk, and she laughs gently, tilting her head to the side. "I want to be yours, Con. Make me yours tonight... and tomorrow...take me home."

With her declaration, the last barrier in our way crumbles at our feet, and I clamber over the rubble to get to her. To take her in my arms and never let go.

Our bodies crash against one another with a force that almost knocks her off her feet. I catch her in my arms, dragging her into my atmosphere. Now she has given me her word; I'll hold her here forevermore.

My lips devour hers in a fierce, possessive kiss, and somewhere in the back of my mind, I know that I'm acting on primal instinct. But it's hard to care. She said she wants me to take her, to make her mine, and it's all I can do not to mark her where she stands. My hand reaches around the back of her dress, tugging the zipper down forcefully to cause the fabric to loosen around her body. She drops her arm and shimmies the dress off, allowing it to land at her feet. My hand automatically reaches for her breast, grasping it roughly as she pushes herself into my touch, chasing it.

Goddess, how I love to have her chase it.

My mouth lowers, and I sink my lips around her peaked nipple, swirling my tongue, licking and sucking like a deprived beast.

My hands drop to her ass, and I squeeze her hard, causing her to yelp in a mix of both pleasure and pain. She pulls herself back from my tight grip, her lilac eyes connecting with mine. "Hey...hey...it's okay," she whispers, lifting her hands to hold my face. "I want you and only you. I'm not going anywhere."

There it goes again. That feeling stirring in my gut that makes me want to growl fucking out loud. A red-hot sensation travels up my spine, working its way through my body limb to limb.

"Say it again," I groan, pressing my lips against her racing pulse. "Say that you're mine."

"I'm yours," she breathes out, her body rubbing against me as she grabs the nape of my neck for more.

A pang of pure pleasure rushes to my cock, making it ache like hell to be inside her. She reaches for my pants, pushing them down over my ass to release my dick that yearns for her. Her breath hitches when she grabs hold of my shaft, feeling how hard I am for her right now.

□

"Oh my...."

We look into each other's eyes, and I lift her under her thighs, wrapping her legs around my waist as I carry her over to the bed.

Her arms wrap around my head, pulling me in to kiss her. Our kisses are messy and passionate, and I groan into her mouth as she massages my tongue with her own.

I put her down on the bed, and she shuffles back, her ravenous eyes looking into mine as her head rests on the pillow. My gaze rakes down over her body, honing in on her stomach, which sways in motion with her gentle, needy thrusts.

Fuck...

I'm bending over her now, my mouth traveling across her midriff, my tongue dragging upward between her breasts, which she grabs lustfully as she looks down at me. "Mmm... yesss," she moans, sucking her bottom lip.

She watches me, hypnotized, as I reach down to tug her underwear off, tossing them to the side before I notch my solid cock against her. She nods, and I sink inside her, both of us groaning in tandem in a mixture of want and relief.

It's been too long since I've felt her wrapped around me. Too long since I've had her body underneath mine.

"You feel incredible," I growl, working my hips back and forth slowly at first, savoring this mind-blowing feeling.

"You do, too," she breathes back, her face twitching with every thrust. "I've missed this."

"Not as much as I have," I counter, my hand splaying across her cheek and into her soft lilac hair.

I begin to move faster, and her legs drop open wider, inviting me deeper inside. Her walls draw me in repeatedly, seizing my cock in her tight grip.

Damn, I can't get enough of her. Her pussy drives me fucking wild.

To think that I once tried to fight these feelings for her makes me feel like a completely idiotic asshole. There's no way I'll ever deny myself again. Whenever she wants a piece of me, I'll be more than happy to fucking provide.

She lifts her hips to meet my thrusts, and we begin moving in sync. Her whimpers and moans fuel my desire as I work to build her orgasm. Tonight she'll come like never before, and I'll make sure of it. I lean back on my knees, lifting her leg to throw it over my shoulder. It presses against my chest, and I pin her to the bed with untamed thrusts.

The new angle has her eyes rolling in the back of her head, and I drive into her with more power, watching her intently as I press my thumb inside her hungry mouth.

She grabs my fist, sucking on my thumb until it's coated in her warmth. I remove it quickly, sliding it down her slick wetness to press on her clit. Her body convulses against the mattress, her head lolling to one side as she grabs fistfuls of the sheets.

"Yes, Con...that's so good. What... are you... doing to me...?"

"I'm staking my claim...Eden, because this body...is fucking mine. It's mine; do you hear me?"

"Y-yes!" she stutters, yelping as I grasp her perfect tit in my hand.

My cock pulses dangerously inside her. If I let go even a fraction, I know I don't stand a chance. I'll explode inside her without warning, and I'm not done.

Not yet.

Not even close.

I release her silky leg, leaning over her once again. My eyes connect with hers intensely, her nose brushing against my own. I suck in every breath she takes, committing every damn detail of her face to my memory.

My beautiful, brave, sexy, clever, stubborn, loving mate.

Goddess, look what you gave me.

She's everything.

My whole fucking world.

Out of nowhere, I feel my teeth extend in my mouth, my wolf coursing through my veins as though he's just been dropped inside my body from above.

Eden's eyes widen, her breathing intensifying as I lean down into the crook of her neck. I kiss her skin softly, and her hand lifts to hold the back of my head in place.

I swell inside her, my mouth opening to sink my teeth into her. She shudders under me, and I remain fixed in place. My thrusts growing wild again, building to a crescendo that neither of us are ready for.

She cries out in ecstasy, her pussy gripping me as her orgasm crashes over us both. I can't hold back any longer, and I release inside her, my cum filling her up to claim her body while my mark claims her soul.

□

I get lost.

I'm stuck somewhere between fucking paradise and euphoria and have no desire to find my way back just yet.

Eventually, my vision begins to clear, and I open my eyes to look into hers.

My wolf claws at my consciousness, and I realize that she's all I needed to bring him back.

My dark soul has claimed hers, and with that, her light has permeated through me. It has changed me in ways that I never imagined.

In her arms, I've found happiness.

In her arms, I'm complete.

Packing

Eden

"I'm never going to get all of this stuff packed if you keep doing that," I smile, folding the dress in half as Con kisses my neck.

"Then don't bother," he replies, continuing his tantalizing journey to my shoulder. "Leave this stuff," he orders, his teeth grazing my skin lightly. "Once I get you home, you won't need clothes for a long time anyway."

"Is that a promise?" I question, laughing as I turn to look into his eyes.

"You're damn right it is," he answers, a sexy grin playing on his lips as he wraps his arms around me.

I smile in return as I reach up to hold the back of his neck.

His gaze then drifts downward, his hand lifting to flick my hair over my shoulder. "Show it to me," he demands, his irises darkening.

I tug the neckline of my top to one side to reveal my mark. The symbol of our love and our bond.

Goddess, last night was the most amazing night of my life. As soon as his teeth sunk into my skin...as soon as I felt him release inside me...I was on cloud nine. It was as if the whole world shifted, and I suddenly understood why I've felt like I never truly belonged for all these years.

Eden Nestoriel, the 'Nowhere Elf,' is the 'Nowhere Elf' no longer.

In this remarkable man, I've found exactly where I'm supposed to be, and there's no feeling like it.

He lifts his hand to the column of my neck, holding it gently as he brushes his thumb over the sensitive patch of skin.

"Fuck, look at you..." he breathes wantonly, staring at the mark he made. "...all mine."

The possessiveness in his voice gives me butterflies, and a shiver runs down my spine.

"The packing will have to wait," he insists, pressing his body against mine as his hand runs up to my face.

□

I gasp when I feel him hard against my hip, and a satisfied grin makes its way to my lips. "Does touching my mark make you hard for me, mate?"

"Why don't I show you?" he offers.

A rush of excitement floods my system, and I flick my eyes to his, holding his gaze as I drop onto my knees.

His hands run through my hair, and I close my eyes as I tease the edge of his pants with soft kisses. A few seconds pass, and I feel his urgency growing, his right hand tightening to a fist at the roots.

"Don't tease me anymore," he orders, tugging my hair back to bring my gaze back to his. "You want to feel my cock in your mouth, don't you?"

I exhale a little, nodding my head needily.

"Words," he commands, his black eyes boring into mine.

"Yes. Yes, I want it," I whimper, a throbbing ache beginning to grow between my legs.

"Then take it. It's all yours."

My eyes light up with desire, and his grip loosens a fraction as I turn my attention back to his pants, tugging them down to set him free.

I sink my lips around his thick tip, flicking my tongue over the small bead of pre-cum awaiting me.

A low, rumbling groan leaves his chest. The sexy-as-hell noise alone is enough to make me moan in return. I slide him further inside my mouth, pushing him deeper and deeper until I can't physically take any more of him.

"Fuck...."

He holds my head in place, his hips thrusting forward slowly as he hits the back of my throat.

My eyes water as my gag reflex tries to take over, but I don't care.

My desperation for more of him is carnal. Primal even.

It's as though being claimed by his wolf has awoken something profound within me. A part of me that was hidden deep down for the longest time.

My hands reach up to grab his ass, my fingernails digging into his firm, heavenly skin.

"That's it...You take my dick so fucking well," he praises, his hands reaching down to my face as he fucks it over and over. "Let me see those eyes."

My lashes flutter as I look up at him, and my head moves quicker. Sucking him in and releasing him in a steady rhythm that has him throbbing against the walls of my mouth. His upper body tightens, his muscled neck straining as his head drops back in pleasure.

Goddess, I can't take anymore.

My hand drops to my pants, and I slide it inside, moaning when my fingertips meet my wet folds.

Still, I maintain my relentless pace. Sucking, licking, worshiping his perfect cock.

It's then he pulls my hair back forcefully. I pant for air for a brief second before his hand grips my chin, tugging it upward. He bends over to smash his lips against mine, and I feel my whole body jolt in lustful delight.

My back arches as my finger works its way over my clit. My tongue battling his for dominance.

It's a fight that, on this occasion, I'm happy to lose.

We break apart, and he straightens up, thrusting inside my mouth once again.

"You see what you do to me?" he growls lowly between gritted teeth.

I groan in approval, nodding as I smother him with my lips all over again.

It turns me on beyond belief to know that I'm the only one who will ever do this to him from here on out. I'm the only one who will make him feel this way.

His breathing intensifies. He hisses in pleasure, and I grip his thighs that tense under my touch. I begin to work faster, knowing I have him close to the edge.

Just then, the bedroom door knocks. My eyes widen slightly as I glance sideways in distraction. His fingers lace through my hair as he brings my attention back to him.

"Don't stop," he grits out quietly, looking directly into my eyes. "Don't you dare fucking stop."

The door knocks again, but I do as I'm told and ignore it, hollowing my cheeks to suck him harder.

"I'm coming now, Eden," he says calmly, his hips beginning to jerk toward me with more desperation. "Are you ready for me?"

I answer his question with a needy moan, readying myself to swallow.

A few more thrusts are all he needs to release inside of me.

The door knocks again as I taste him on my tongue, swallowing greedily as I stare up at his handsome face, which is set in a look of pure lust.

"That's it, Eden," he groans. "Swallow every drop."

The warm liquid runs down my throat, and he pulls out of me, allowing a drop of cum to land on my bottom lip. His hand lifts to my face, his thumb swiping over my lip before he pushes it gently inside my mouth.

I suck on it for a second, another knock on the door fading into the background as we look into each other's eyes.

Then he reaches for me, pulling me back onto my feet to kiss me softly on the cheek.

"Wait here," he orders quietly, fixing his pants in place as he walks across the room to get the door.

I watch him go, slumping down onto the bed like I've just run to Tipreon and back again. Goddess, this man leaves me so damn breathless.

"Yes?" Con asks the mystery caller.

"I was sent by Mrs. Nestoriel, Sir. She's waiting for Miss Eden in the palace gardens for lunch."

Immediately I roll my eyes, falling back onto the mattress.

"No problem. Tell Mrs. Nestoriel she'll be there."

The door closes, and I hear Conall's footsteps get closer.

"Urggg, do I have to?" I question, leaning up on my elbows.

He smirks and nods his head. "Time to tell mommy dearest you're leaving with the Big Bad Wolf."

I grin, letting out a gentle laugh. "Are you sure? There are better things we could be doing right now...."

I raise my brow suggestively, and he scoffs, folding his arms over his chest. "Better luck next time, elf."

"Goddess, I should have left you on the edge, you ass."

He laughs as he walks over to the bed, pulling me up onto my feet to settle his hands on my waist. "Do you need me to come with you?"

I shake my head and smile. "No, I'm one hundred and twenty-seven years old, Con. It's time my mother realizes I'm a grown woman who can choose to do whatever she likes."

"Or whoever she likes," he corrects me in amusement, sweeping a wisp of hair behind my ear.

"Right," I chuckle, biting on my bottom lip. "I won't be long. What are you going to do while I'm gone?"

"I'll pack this stuff up, then I have something to take care of in Morween with Zeke."

"Okay," I answer, patting his chest. "Don't forget all my books too." I nod toward the filled bookshelves, and his brows knit together.

"You're taking the books?"

"Of course! They are more essential than the clothes!"

"Well, you've got that right," he smiles. "But still...you're going to make my poor wolf carry that shit all the way to Harmony?"

"Number one. Don't ever call my beloved books shit.' Number two. If you loved me, you would."

"Guilt-tripping...nice touch. Day one as bonded mates, and this is us already?"

"You better believe it," I laugh, patting his chest again.

"Wouldn't have it any other way," he answers, his eyes trailing over my face lovingly.

I smile in reply, leaning forward to kiss him. "I'll see you later."

He winks at me as I tear myself from his embrace. "Later."

I load the last of Eden's bags onto the cart before handing the coachman some silver. "You have the directions; just leave the bags at the tavern in the village. I'll take care of it from there."

"Yes, Sir." He nods, dipping his hat respectfully.

I take a step back as Zeke appears behind me. "All packed up and ready to go? You two aren't messing around."

I turn to look at him, and he grins widely. "Congratulations, man. I'm happy for you both. You deserve it."

"Thanks, Zeke," I answer, slapping my hand against his as he pats me on the back.

"I'd like to think I helped, you know."

I snort, nodding my head. "Can't say I disagree."

"So are we going to go do this thing then? You big handsome, romantic bastard."

"Just shut up, and let's get on with it. We don't have long,"

"Okay, the place isn't far from here—"

His voice trails off as he looks over my shoulder, and I turn my head to see Erix walking toward us.

I immediately take in his tense demeanor and glance back at Zeke, who raises his eyebrow. "Trouble on the horizon?"

I shake my head in reply. "I can handle it. You go. I'll catch up with you."

He nods before heading off in the direction of the town.

"Alpha Conall, might I have a word?" Erix requests, looking into my eyes seriously.

I nod, crossing my arms as he stops in front of me.

There's silence for a few moments as his eyes watch the horse and cart disappear down the dusty road. "You sorted transport? I was going to offer."

"It's sorted," I reply matter-of-factly.

We stare at each other again, and he lets out a puff of air. "I hope you realize how lucky you are, Alpha."

"I do," I say assuredly.

"Then I wish you well for the future."

"Likewise, Your Majesty," I answer, giving him a curt nod. "I'll take care of her."

He nods in return before turning around to return to the palace.

Beginning

Eden

As I approach the table, I see my mother already sipping her tea.

"Hey, sorry I'm late. Lunch slipped my mind," I say truthfully, sitting across from her.

"Oh, that's okay dear. I've just been enjoying the sunshine. It's glorious today, isn't it?"

I look around the pristine gardens and smile as I see two birds dancing around one another by the blossom tree. "It is."

Just then, a palace servant approaches, laying out a small platter of food. I give him a polite nod in thanks as my mother selects a dainty yellow pastry. "Come on then, don't make me eat all this alone," she chuckles.

I smile, leaning forward to rest my arms on the table. "Mother, I'm not staying long."

She swallows, placing the cake down to clear her throat. "Oh? Where are you going?"

"You know where I'm going," I answer softly.

She nods her head, leaning back in her chair. "And you're sure about this, Eden?"

I can hear the worry in her voice, and although it irritates me a little, I try to put myself in her position. Although she knows Con's true character now, she still doesn't know him like I do.

She only sees the rough exterior. The front he puts on for the rest of the world while I see the rest of him.

His tenderness.

His compassion.

His love.

I reach out to take her hand in mine, squeezing it tightly. "I've never been so sure of anything in my life."

She stares back at me for a moment before nodding her head. "Then you are making the right decision, my dear."

I sigh in relief as she rests her other hand on mine.

"But that doesn't mean I won't miss you."

Her eyes begin to well with tears, and I can't help but shake my head in amusement. "Mother, must I remind you of my age?"

"Exactly! You're still just a baby! I didn't leave home until I was one hundred and forty-three!"

I let out a laugh, beaming at her widely.

"When do you leave? There's no rush, is there? Must you go so soon?!"

"I want to," I reply insistently.

A small whimper leaves her lips, and she nods, smiling sadly. "Then I suppose I must let you get on with it."

"You must," I confirm as she pulls her hand from mine to wipe away a tear.

"I'm excited, Mother. I can't wait for what's to come my way next. With Conall, I feel like I've finally found my place in this world."

"Then you go out there, my dear, and conquer it together."

I smile, and she straightens herself up in her chair. "But first...we have tea."

"Of course," I grin, bringing the little teacup to my lips.

* * *

I stand by the palace entrance, watching the path to Morween anxiously. It's been a while since high-tea finished. It ran on longer than I thought it would, especially since my father appeared unexpectedly to join us. In the end, though, I'm glad Con insisted I go. My parents and I have been a team since we arrived here from Azealea all those years ago. When no one else accepted us, we had only each other for a time, and I know it must be hard for them to see me leave. Don't get me wrong, it's not like I'll never see them again. We've already arranged for them to visit Harmony next week once Con and I have settled in. My father is keen to explore the forestry in the area, and I am too. I'm sure between us both, we will find some interesting new ingredients to share with Grandma Citrine.

I rest my back against the stone wall, my eyes drifting over to the training field in the distance that is filling up with the Guard as they begin training for the day. At the top of the steps, I see Erix appear from the doorway, engrossed in conversation with Commander Walden.

A gentle smile touches my lips as I watch him. Last night, although difficult, was also incredibly liberating.

Since he arrived back in my life, I've felt this weight around my neck. Sadly, his love (which was once my everything) became an anchor, tethering me to a past I had long left behind.

Of course, none of that was his fault, but the tether had to be severed at some point, for both our sakes.

I find myself wondering what the future might hold for him now.

Will he find his true love as I have found mine? Will he have children who will rule this kingdom for centuries to come?

Every part of me hopes so.

Perhaps years from now, when all of this drama is a distant memory, we may be capable of being friends again. I know that I would like that very much.

"Hey, Eden!" Zeke's familiar voice breaks me from my reverie, and I see him rounding the corner with Conall by his side. I can't help but grin like an idiot as I watch him approach.

"Have you been waiting?" Conall asks, stopping in front of me. "Careful, anyone might think you missed me."

"I was, and I did," I say adamantly, wrapping my arms around his waist.

"Goddess, you guys are sickening," Zeke jokes, looking between us both. "I might have liked you both better when you were pretending to hate each other."

"Oh, we weren't pretending!" I state, looking up at Con. "I hated his guts."

"Right... I guess I just assumed that enemies *don't* end up in bed together every other night, but hey, what do I know?" Zeke shrugs with a playful wink.

I laugh, releasing Con from my grip.

"Did you smooth things over with your mother?" he asks with concern.

"Yes, I did. Don't get me wrong, I don't think she's ready to hand my former kidnapper a 'Son-in-law of the Year' award just yet, but she's happy for us."

"Good," he smiles. "So long as you're happy."

"I will be. Once we get to Harmony. Shall we go say goodbye to Cass and the Alphas?"

He shakes his head. "Can't. They left already."

"They left?" I ask, my mouth dropping open in shock and disappointment. "Even Anton? What about Hunter?"

"All of them," Zeke says plainly, folding his arms before throwing Con a grin.

I look between them both suspiciously. "What's going on?" I demand, raising my brow.

"How do you fancy taking a detour on the way to Harmony?" Con asks.

I throw him a puzzled look in return. "Where?"

He smirks. "Back to where it all began."

Hereafter

Eden

As I stand in front of the den once again, I feel a whole heap of mixed emotions.

At one time, this place was my prison. A fortress that held me in her grip so tightly that I feared I'd never feel the sun on my skin ever again. At one time, I even considered the possibility that I might even die here.

"Are you okay?" Con asks, examining me carefully.

"Yes," I whisper, my eyes meeting his for a moment before looking back at the house.

What horrors this place has seen.

The dark days of *The Culling.* A seventy-year-long exile. The capture of an unassuming, little Nowhere Elf. Not to mention Conall's extremely close brush with death.

It's crazy how somewhere with such a dark history has also given me something I never thought I'd ever have.

A true mate.

"Come on," Conall slips his hand into mine, intertwining our fingers as he guides me toward the steps.

Zeke opens the door, and we are immediately greeted with loud chatter and laughter. I look around the large sitting area to see that it has not changed a bit. The usual bunch of Alpha men fill the room, some sitting around on the dusty, worn sofas while others sit at the table, drinking.

"Weyy heyy! Look who it is! Nice of you all to show up!" Hunter calls out, rising from his chair to make his way over.

Conall glances at me with a knowing look, and I can't help but laugh. This sort of thing is really not his style, and we both know it. More than likely, it was Zeke who arranged this little get-together.

The noise level in the room climbs as everyone says their hellos, and Conall leads me over to the table to pour a drink for us both. That's when Cass and

Lianna make their way over, each of them grabbing me into a firm hug.

"I knew you'd make the right choice in the end!" Cass laughs. "You're a Luna, and there's no denying it!"

"I don't know... It was touch and go there for a while, I'd say." Hunter teases, knocking back his drink while Con glares at him. "I'm just messing. I was never in any doubt, boss."

He makes a face behind Con's back, and I laugh, shaking my head from side to side.

"So you ditched the king and the chance to be Queen of Morween for this asshole?" Henrick asks, throwing his arm around Con's shoulder.

"I see some time away from this place has made you both grow a pair of balls. Get your arm off me," Con retorts in amusement, drawing a loud guffaw from Anton.

"Yes, I did," I answer Henrick's question proudly, giving Con a small wink. "Who needs a damn crown anyway?"

"Here, here!" Neville chimes in, filling up my cup again. "I don't know about all of you, but I'm glad to get out of Morween."

"Too many elves," Rocco adds plainly, tossing back his drink. "No offense," he adds, glancing at me sideways.

"None taken," I answer, shrugging my shoulder.

"What you talking about Rocco? You're the 'The Great Prince Saver.' Remember?" Mateo teases, followed by a howl of laughter.

"I told you pricks to stop calling me that if you know what's good for you!" Rocco growls, taking a threatening step forward.

"Hey, hey, hey, dial in your inner asshole for at least a couple of hours, Rocco," Jarek orders, taking us all by surprise.

"Oh...doctor, doctor," Evan laughs, biting his lip jokingly.

"Sorry, but I'm spoken for," Jarek answers, lifting his cup before wrapping an arm around Lianna.

"You guys are too adorable," Cass coos, her eyes then lighting up as she examines Con and I. "But... I need to know about Con and Eden. I know it's personal, but damn it, I don't care. Eden, Con, did *it* happen?"

Everyone looks at us expectantly, and I grin, tugging the neckline of my tunic to one side to reveal my mark.

"AHHHHH!!!" Cass squeals, pulling me into another hug.

Everyone begins to offer congratulations, shaking his hand and mine in excitement.

"Can you believe we are all congratulating these two for doing the deed?" William asks in amusement. "Like, 'Hey, congratulations on your amazing sex!'"

I laugh as Hunter takes a step back from Con. "Don't hit me, Con, but I have to know too..." he begins, lifting his hands in surrender. "Is it as good as everyone says it is?"

I hold in a smile, looking to Con and raising my brow. "Well, mate...is it?"

His brows crease just a little, and I know he's replaying the moment in his head right now as I am.

The connection. The warmth. The love. The pleasure. Urggg! I wish we could do it all over again!

"No," Conall finally answers, flicking his eyes from me to Hunter. "It's not good. It's fucking mind-blowing."

His confession elicits cheers and more congratulations from the rowdy men around us.

Cass rolls her eyes. "Men. Will they ever change?"

"This bunch? I don't think so," I laugh as Anton nudges my arm.

"Hey, Neville! I'm starving! You said we could eat when Con and Eden got here," William complains.

"Oh shit, yeah, take a seat everyone! The guests of honor have arrived."

"Just Con and Eden? What about me?" Zeke questions jokingly as everyone begins to shuffle in around the table.

"You were head Alpha for about five minutes," Samuel sneers in his usual unpleasant tone.

"Five minutes more than you, dickhead," Zeke hits back, shutting him up.

"I don't want any bad vibes tainting my bacon, eggs, and pancakes," Anton warns, pointing between them both. "Come on, Neville. Let's get a move on."

Con sits down at the head of the table, and I pause for a second. "Wait for me!" I call out after Anton.

"Eden, you don't have to. We've got this."

"Are you kidding? I want to!" I insist. "Back in the kitchen with my two favorite men—"

"Careful," Con warns.

I shoot a look over my shoulder and smile. "Sorry, my two favorite *cooks.*"

"Wow, that downgrade stung like hell," Anton jests, pressing his hand over his heart.

"GUYS!! Food!" William demands, earning a few calls of agreement.

"Okay, okay! I'm going! Calm down, you Alpha assholes!" I laugh on the way to the kitchen.

* * *

Serving dinner tonight has taken on a whole new meaning. Once we put down all the plates, we fell into a relaxed atmosphere. Everyone is now talking amongst themselves, and Conall grabs me to sit on his lap. I giggle as I bring my drink to my lips, and he stabs at his pancakes one-handed.

"I think I'll go somewhere exotic, you know. Fuck it. Sand, sea, and sunshine. Maybe I'll meet myself a siren on the other side of the world," Hunter declares before stuffing his mouth with bacon.

"Count me in!" Henrick agrees, slapping William's arm questioningly.

"I'll think about it!" he laughs in return.

"Well, I won't be fucking going anywhere but back to Whiteclaw," Rocco mutters, giving them all a look of distaste.

"Just as well you weren't invited then," Hunter smirks.

"What will you do, Rocco?" Cass asks curiously.

He shrugs his shoulders. "I don't know, maybe I'll get myself a farm—"

Hunter snorts, and Cass throws him a disapproving look. "I think that sounds lovely. Maybe the animals will soften that heart of yours."

His brows knit together, and he shakes his head as he takes a drink.

"What about you, Zeke?" Mateo questions. "Are you going to Harmony with Con and Jarek?"

Zeke turns to look at us and smiles. "Nah, I fancy a change. I was thinking I might find some work in Tipreon, although I'd like to travel around a bit first."

"Work?" Henrick questions in amusement. "You've got a pocket full of gold, and you want to go find work?"

"Goddess forbid anyone puts in a solid graft around here, you bunch of lazy pricks," Zeke answers with a grin.

"It's not lazy! We have earned it. Look at the Conall. Even he's going to retire!" Evan adds.

"Hmm, we'll see," Zeke murmurs, looking at Jarek.

Conall narrows his eyes as he examines them both in turn. "Do you two know something I don't?"

Jarek clears his throat, taking a cautious look around. "It seems the people of Harmony have already discussed your move to the pack, Con. Nikon said they plan to ask you to take on the Alpha title. Sole Alpha, that is."

The room grows quiet, and Con looks at Zeke who smiles with a shrug. "I don't know if you were expecting to go there and fade into the background, but the people aren't having it."

"I think it's a great idea," Cass adds encouragingly. "Just because there is now peace doesn't mean that the people no longer need you. You should do it."

There's a strong murmur of agreement amongst the men, and Con turns his head to search my eyes for my input.

"Don't look at me," I smile. "This is your decision, but if you want my opinion, then I think you should do it."

"Really?"

"Definitely," I nod, lifting my hand to touch his face. "You were made to protect people. It's what you do best."

He nods slowly in reply.

"Then that settles it. Let's make a toast!" Zeke announces, standing up to hold his cup in the air. "I'd like you all to raise a glass. To the new Alpha and Luna of Harmony!"

"To the Alpha and Luna!" everyone replies enthusiastically, taking a drink in our honor.

Happiness

Eden

We crowd around the doorway as everyone begins to take their leave. The moment is bittersweet for many reasons. Bitter because it is time to leave each other behind. Sweet, because it's time for everyone to move on to bigger and better things.

There is no doubt that since *The Culling*, these men have been stuck in their own personal form of hell. I would even go as far as to say that some of them will never break out completely. What they experienced was a trauma like no other. An event so gut-wrenching that the mere thought of it is enough to evoke tears and heartache in a perfect stranger.

However, today is the dawn of a new era for these men. A time when they can take back control of their lives that have thus far been ruled by duty, vengeance and suffering.

"I'm going to miss you, elf," Anton says, pulling me into a bear hug.

"I'll miss you too, but you know where we are. Please come and visit! All of you," I say sincerely, looking around the group who are all hugging each other in goodbye.

"I won't be taking you up on that," Rocco says, stepping in front of Conall and I. "But I will say that you are alright."

I nod, and he puts his hand out to shake mine. "Thanks."

He turns to Conall and puts his hand out once more. "If I ever see you again, it will be too soon."

"The feeling is mutual," Conall answers, shaking his hand firmly.

Rocco nods, heading for the door to disappear with Samuel behind him.

"And off they went... Good riddance," Mateo says under his breath, turning to smile at me.

We hug each other goodbye, and everyone moves out onto the yard, leaving Conall and I standing at the top of the stairs.

I wave with tears in my eyes as everyone shifts into their wolves, some heading south while others heading east and west.

"See you at Harmony!" Jarek calls out, shifting last to allow Lianna to climb onto his back.

They disappear into the trees, and the dark forest descends into silence.

Con wraps his arm around my waist, looking down over my face. "Are you okay?"

"Yes," I answer with a sniff. "But you know I'm a crier!"

"I might have noticed," he grins in return.

"Should we go home now too?"

He thinks for a moment, looking around the forest. "I think we could stay for one more night."

"I agree," I answer, looking into his eyes.

In a split second, the mood changes.

He knows it, I know it; hell, even the damn woodland animals know it.

His grip on me tightens, and he pulls me back inside the den. "My bedroom...now," he orders,

The door slams closed behind us, and I laugh giddily as he drags me upstairs to the next floor.

We rush down the hallway past the Alphas' old bedrooms until we reach those forbidden stairs. Those stairs that once filled me with a strange mix of fear, anxiety and lust.

Con lifts me up quickly, tossing me over his shoulder. I yelp in surprise, beating my hands against his back in feeble protest. "Let me down!" I laugh, my core tightening as he smacks my ass.

"Struggle if you like, but this only ends one way."

His promise increases my excitement tenfold, and I dangle over him willingly until we reach his bedroom.

He drops me onto my feet, and I look around the familiar setting.

He gets to work, lighting a fire as I walk around slowly, running my fingers lightly over the bedspread.

Images of that night he first pleasured me in here race through my mind. The words that he said I still remember so clearly.

"Wolves are blessed with a mate. A mate who is destined to be theirs forever. Theirs to kiss...theirs to touch...theirs to claim...theirs to fuck...."

I kick my boots off and sit on the edge of the bed, my heart beating faster as I watch him stand up in front of the fire, which is steadily growing behind

□

him.

"What are you thinking about?" he asks, stepping forward.

I smile teasingly. "Oh, just about the first time you touched me... Do you remember that night?"

"Remember it?" He raises his brow. "I still think about it every damn day."

My eyes light up with his confession.

"Do you want to repeat it?" I ask, biting the edge of my lip.

"No," he answers, shaking his head.

"Oh?"

"I'm not looking to go back. Especially not to a time when you weren't fully mine," he explains. "From now on, I want it all. Every part of you."

I breathe deeply, and he moves closer, towering over me as I lie back on the edge of the bed.

"Wait," I demand, looking up into his eyes.

He examines me questioningly as I wrap my hand around the nape of his neck. "I'm in charge tonight...mate."

A hungry look spreads over his handsome face. "Is that right?" he asks, his eyes raking over me.

"Oh yes," I answer confidently.

"Then tell me what you want... I'm more than willing to take orders," he rasps with a sexy smirk.

I move further back onto the bed, pulling him along with me. "You had your fun this morning. Now it's time to return the favor."

I peel the top from my body, discarding it on the floor by the bed as he stares at me. "Well?" I ask challengingly.

"I thought you'd never ask."

I bite the edge of my lip as he reaches for the hem of my pants, pulling them down with my underwear simultaneously. I thrust my hips upward to allow him to slip them off me easily, my legs closing automatically to hide my exposed body.

He reaches for my knees, prying them apart slowly as his eyes devour me. "Fuck...you are perfect."

There's something exciting about lying here completely bare before him while he is fully clothed. It makes me feel strangely vulnerable and yet powerful at the same time.

I blush a little as he rests on his knees, taking hold of my ankle to kiss it.

Slowly, he makes his way up my leg, peppering my sensitive skin with tender, passionate kisses.

He lowers himself between my thighs, teasing my midriff with his lips as my desperation for him grows.

"Con, do it," I command breathlessly. "Let me feel your tongue."

"Patience. I'm taking my time with you tonight." His lips curl up at one side, and I gasp when I feel his finger slide through my wetness.

The sensation of the small act already has my eyes rolling. My back arches against the mattress, and he tugs me sharply toward him, holding my ass firmly as his tongue glides over me.

This exact moment sums up why he drives me so damn wild.

I *adore* how his touch turns from delicate to rough in the blink of an eye. Both his tender care and brute force marry together to create the perfect blend of hard and soft. I'm certain no other man on this earth could make me feel the way he does.

I squirm in delight as his tongue flicks against my clit, pushing myself against him as my hand drops to his head. I run my fingers through his hair, my nails grazing his scalp causing him to groan into me. The slight vibration elicits a gasp as pleasure ripples through my body. "Mmm...yes."

His movements grow wilder as he presses his lips against me harder, his enthusiasm making me moan uncontrollably.

I grip a handful of his thick, brown hair, lost in ecstasy, as I practically ride his face.

He pulls away from me, and I pout in frustration, my orgasm lingering on the edge.

He lies down on the bed, tugging me by the hand to straddle his waist. My bare, wet pussy grinds against his hardness as he grips me by the neck to pull me down for a desperate kiss. My eyes close as his kisses land across my jaw and down my neck, where he sucks on my mark.

His hands then grip me behind my thighs, encouraging me to move upward over his body. I look into his eyes in nervous excitement as he positions me over his face.

"Let me taste you again, Eden."

I lower myself down gingerly onto his waiting mouth, gasping as his tongue brushes against my pussy. Instantly I relax into him, using my knees to support my gentle movements.

□

His hands lift to grip my waist, pulling me down over him with more delicious pressure.

"Oh my..." I moan deliriously, my hands reaching down into his hair again.

His hand smacks against my ass, his chest rumbling as he runs his hands up firmly over the contours of my body.

I throw my head back when his hands grasp my breasts, palming them roughly before teasing my hard nipples between his fingers.

"Fuck... I'm going to come," I groan as my hips jerk back and forth of their own accord.

His stubble grazes my skin, amplifying the satisfying feeling that's now taking over my pussy, and his hands grip my waist, his fingers digging into my skin with delicious, painful pressure.

I let myself go completely, calling out as I spiral into my orgasm.

He pulls me down on top of him, ravenous with need as his mouth claims mine. I taste myself on his lips as he flips me over to lie beneath him.

I'm caught in a rapture, barely aware of him standing up by the bed to remove his clothes. He towers over me again as my senses begin to return to my body.

My clear head doesn't last long as he thrusts inside me, tugging my wrists above my head with one hand to pin me in place. His other hand rests on my waist, his head ducking to capture my nipple in his mouth as I roll my hips beneath him to fuck him back.

He growls in pleasure, his movements growing wild and fast.

"That's it! Goddess, that feels so good!" I moan, my head falling to one side as another orgasm builds. "Again. Please!"

He lets go of my wrists, leaning back on his knees to tug me up onto his lap, impaling me in place on his solid cock. I groan in inexplicable pleasure, throwing my arms around his neck as I ride him repeatedly, our sweat-covered bodies molded and writhing together as one.

It's then that my eyes spot it, and I stop in my tracks, my ragged breath catching in my throat.

"Wha-"

My eyes lift to meet his, and we stare at each other while he continues to thrust gently inside me. He says nothing as I look at his body again with overwhelming emotion.

Right there, at the bottom of his neck, just above his collarbone, is a small black and white tattoo of a little flower.

"When did you do this?" I ask in a whisper, searching his eyes.

"Today," he answers, his hand reaching up to hold the back of my head. "You have your mark, and now I have mine."

Only this man could make something so delicate and pretty look so incredibly masculine. I tilt my head to gaze at its soft petals ripping under his hot, tanned skin. "Can I touch it? Does it hurt?"

He shakes his head. "It doesn't hurt."

I lift my hand to rest my fingers against it, brushing over it lightly. His torso shivers against mine, and I smile in sheer wonder, a tear dropping from my eye. He wipes it away, pulling my head down to his neck. My lips press against his mark as his thrusts quicken just a little. I grip his shoulders, bucking my hips against him as his chest heaves.

"I love you," he husks, drawing my eyes back to his face one last time.

"I love you too," I answer, my heart bursting with joy.

"Then marry me, Eden."

My mouth drops open a little, my eyes clouding with tears.

"Say you'll marry me."

I nod my head lifting my hands to hold his face. "Yes, with all my heart, yes."

We look into each other's eyes as we come together at the same time. Neither of us look away. Neither of us close our eyes.

We are here together in blissful happiness.

The moment is perfect in every way.

Forever

SIX MONTHS LATER

"Oh, it's a disaster! It's so hot out today that the icing on the cake melted, and I will have to do it all over again! Please, I need you to taste it and let me know what you think, Alpha!" Gelda, the village baker, says in a panic.

"That's the least of our problems, Gelda. The chairs we ordered from Morween haven't arrived yet. At this rate, there will be nowhere for all the visitors to sit," Temal, my young but enthusiastic Beta, adds.

"Oh Goddess, what kind of impression will that make?" his mate Jesika questions worriedly. "All of these visitors aren't going to think much of our pack if we can't put on a wedding for our own Alpha and Luna!"

I look around each of them in turn, taking a deep breath before I begin. Goddess knows I've been through many stressful situations in my life, but who knew that wedding planning would be right up there with the worst of them?

Six months ago, when we moved to Harmony, Eden and I thought nothing of telling everyone about our engagement. Little did we know that it would create mass excitement within the pack, who have hardly talked about anything else since. It seems that all these years lived in isolation have left them more than ready for a celebration. One that they don't have to hide from the rest of the world. It became clear to Eden and I pretty quickly that our desire for a small wedding was no longer feasible.

"Listen, no one panic. This is not a crisis," I say calmly, looking to Gelda first. "Don't worry about the cake. Even if it's a little melted in places, it will still taste damn delicious if I know you, Gelda."

She smiles, her tense shoulders dropping. "Thank you, Alpha. It's a chocolate sponge. Your favorite."

"You know me too well," I grin, patting her back. "Don't waste any more energy worrying. Everything will work out fine."

My mollycoddling is enough to set her on her way, and then I turn to Temal and Jesika. "You two need to stop worrying what people think of us because I can tell you right now that I couldn't give a shit. As for the chairs, don't worry. We can make do with whatever we have in the village already."

"But they won't match. It won't look as pretty," Jesika says sadly. "Won't the Luna be disappointed?"

"Fuck no," I scoff in amusement before I take in their stunned expressions. "Erm, what I mean to say is Eden will be happy with all the work you have put into this. She won't be disappointed. I promise you that."

Jesika smiles in relief before leaning in to kiss Temal on the cheek. "Okay, well, I'm off to check on the flowers. They should be pretty much ready to go now."

"I'll see you at home later, Baby," Temal answers squeezing her hand before she leaves us.

I look around to see a few pack members decorating the little village square for tomorrow. The place does look amazing; I have to hand it to them.

"What's next on the list, Alpha?" Temal asks dutifully. "I've already checked with the Inn, and they can provide rooms for those visitors who are staying over tomorrow, and some pack members have offered to act as hosts too. I've made sure the seating plan is in order, and I've postponed training sessions this week—"

"Stop," I order him sternly, lifting my hand. "You've done enough, Temal, relax. Take the night off and enjoy it."

He nods, looking around us anxiously. "I guess everything is in order."

"It sounds like it. Now go catch up with Jesika and take a break."

"Thanks, Alpha. I'll see you tomorrow for the big day."

"See you then," I finish, watching him leave.

I continue through the town square, stopping to compliment pack members on their hard work as I go. Goddess, to see all the effort going into this wedding tomorrow almost makes me feel bad for what I have organized for this evening, but I'm not about to change my plans now. Not when I know deep down that I'm doing the right thing.

I arrive at the cottage and open the door to find Eden over by the sink washing dishes.

"Hey there," she smiles. "So you managed to escape, did you?"

☐

"Just," I answer, walking up behind her to snake my arms around her waist. "I thought Gelda was going to force-feed me chocolate cake at one point, but I handled it."

She laughs gently, lifting her delicate hands from the soapy water to grab a cloth. "And what about Temal? Is he still—"

"Panicking? Big time," I answer as she looks at me sympathetically.

"You must miss Zeke a lot, huh?"

I smirk, nodding my head. "Don't worry... Temal will come through. I just need to break his youthful spirit first."

She snorts, dropping the cloth to rest her hands behind my neck. "That won't take you long, Alpha. I believe in you."

"Thanks for your support," I grin as she laughs along.

I take a deep breath and rest my forehead against hers. "I'm sorry. I know this has been a lot, but the madness will be over tomorrow, and we can get back to normal."

"I know," she answers softly. "There's still so much to do."

We have been working hard to expand Harmony these past couple of months. Not because we want it to change but because, with each passing week, we are welcoming more wolves to the pack. More distant pockets of survivors heard about the peace treaty with the elves, and it encouraged them to come out of hiding.

As their Alpha and Luna, it's our responsibility to ensure everyone who comes here gets off to the best possible start and remains safe. I've even begun training some pack members to fight, should we ever need to protect ourselves in the future. It has been a busy few months, to say the least, but it has been satisfying too.

Eden has been amazing. As I always knew she would be. She helped Jarek get his doctor's practice up and running and has since been stocking up his medicine cabinet with everything needed to take care of our people. She has now started having work done to the den to restore it to its former glory. Every time we go back to check on the progress being made, I can sense Lincoln and Fern's presence more and more. It's an odd but comforting feeling.

"Fancy getting out of here for a bit?" I ask, leaning back to look into her questioning eyes.

"Tonight? It depends on what you have in mind. We have kind of a big day tomorrow, in case you've forgotten," she laughs, raising her brow.

"I know," I shrug. "But my wolf is itching for a run, and you know he likes to take you with him."

She strokes my skin, standing up on her tiptoes to gently kiss the little flower on my neck. I close my eyes, my grip on her waist tightening as her sweet breath ripples over me. "Are you sure you don't want to just spend the night in bed instead?" she asks between teasing kisses.

Fuck, I'll never get enough of her teasing ways, but right now, I have to resist temptation. "You're insatiable," I state, placing my hands on either side of her face before kissing her forehead. "But I want to go that run. Come on, it will do us good."

She purses her lips and narrows her eyes suspiciously as she scans my body. "Who the hell are you, and what have you done with my horny mate? I want him back now if you don't mind."

My hands splay into her hair, my fingers tangling around the soft lilac curls as I tug her head back to meet my gaze. "Be careful what you wish for."

Her eyes widen, her back arching slightly as she presses her body against mine.

"Now let's get a move on...while we still have some sunlight."

$$* * *$$

I follow Conall out into the thick of the forest, both of us laughing together as we discuss the madness of the past couple of days. I must admit he was right about leaving the cottage for a while. I already feel so much more relaxed, and he hasn't even shifted yet.

I absolutely adore this place.

I love our little home, our wonderful pack members, my work, and I love this.

Our forest.

Our own little patch of heaven on earth.

Since we moved here, life has just seemed so effortless. Despite being busier than I ever have been, I now have a purpose that is rewarding on so many levels.

I glance at Conall as he talks passionately about warrior training, and I can't help but smile. Our relationship has continued to grow from strength to strength these past months, and every day, I find I learn something new about him. Some tiny facet of his being that was once undiscovered.

Sure, some days I could kick his grumpy ass up and down the village, but I can say hand on heart that I love the bones of this man. That's why when my father announced last month that he and Grandma had concocted a cure for the Alpha curse, I had a mild panic attack.

Taking the potion would make Conall mortal again, and with that, he would begin to age at the normal speed for a werewolf. The prospect of losing him in as little as sixty or seventy years is a hard one to accept, but I know already that it's not my place to make this decision. Only he can do that.

We come to a stop, and Conall begins to undress. He hands his clothes to me, and I stuff them into the bag, slinging it over my back. "Where are we going anyway?"

"You'll see," he answers with a casual shrug.

I lift my head to throw him another curious look. "What are you up to? Why are you acting so strange?"

He smirks. "Don't you trust me?"

"I don't trust you as far as I can throw you, Alpha," I joke playfully, raising my brow.

"Too bad," he winks.

Before I can argue, he steps back to shift into his wolf.

I'll never *not* be amazed when watching him do this. At one time in my life, it would have sent me running for the hills, but now, Conall's wolf is one of my favorite things about him.

"This isn't fair. You can't just shift to avoid talking," I say accusingly, dropping onto my knees.

He nudges me, and I hold his furry head as I scratch him behind the ears. "You're lucky I love your wolf more than you, asshole! Okay then, Alpha, whisk me away if you must. I'm ready for you!"

He drops his body low for me to climb onto his back, and I grip on tight as he takes off into a speedy run.

The cool wind whips across my face, sending my hair flying wildly behind me. The scents and sounds of the forest fill my senses as the fresh air pumps into my lungs. This freeing sensation is one I've come to thoroughly enjoy. Rarely a day goes by now when I don't accompany Conall on one of his runs.

I relax entirely as he weaves his way in and out amongst the trees, navigating the terrain as though he knows it like the back of his hand. I hold on tighter as he gets faster, my ears eventually picking up the sound of the crashing sea in the distance. I look around at the whizzing blanket of green, trying to decipher exactly where we are, when it hits me.

We are heading for Kelna Cliffs.

My body hugs his back with a squeeze, letting him know I've figured out his master plan after all.

We finally slow down to a stop, and he lowers to let me climb off. I step back, a knowing smile covering my face as he shifts back to his human form.

"I should have figured it out," I laugh, shaking my head from side to side. "Will you ever stop surprising me?"

"I hope not," he grins, taking the bag from my hand to get himself dressed. "I just thought it would be nice to watch the sunset on my last day of freedom," he states jokingly, pulling his pants up his thick thighs.

My mouth drops open in indignation, and I smack him across the chest. "Last day of freedom? You ass!"

He laughs, tugging his shirt over his head.

I smile as I look up at the sky through the canopy of trees. It's already beautiful shades of mixed orange and purple. Just as it was the night I was reunited with Conall.

Goddess, that feels like a lifetime ago.

"You ready?" he asks, smiling at me cheekily.

"Lead the way," I answer, sliding my hand into his.

I lean my head on his bicep, curling my arm around his as we trudge through the long grass to leave the forest behind.

I smile widely as the salty sea air billows around us and briefly lift my head to look at him. "This was the best surprise. I'm glad you convinced me to come out tonight."

His honey eyes hold mine for a few quiet seconds before he tears them away. "I was hoping you would say that...."

I turn my head to follow his gaze, my mouth dropping open as we get closer to the old ruins.

☐

There, through the archway, against the backdrop of the stunning sunset, are a small group of people.

Our people.

I twist my neck to look back at Conall, and he stops in his tracks, turning to face me as he takes my hands in his.

"What's going on?" I ask him in confusion.

He smiles, his eyes trailing over my face. "I thought I'd marry you tonight if you're up for it."

Stunned, I look back to the archway as I take in the scene again.

My mother, father, grandma, grandpa, Cass and Zeke have spotted us and are now clapping and waving enthusiastically in our direction.

"Wait, what about the pack? They were so excited about the wedding," I ask with a slight frown.

"They will still have their wedding, but this will be our little secret."

A smile spreads across my face. "*You* are a very, very bad man," I say, laughing in disbelief as I hold his face in my hands.

"Isn't that part of why you fell in love with me?"

"It is," I answer, staring into his eyes adoringly. "It sure is."

"But Eden, if you don't love this, then—"

"I love it," I interrupt adamantly. "It's perfect, Con."

His handsome face beams, and he throws his arms around me to hold me tightly in his embrace.

"WHAT DID SHE SAY?!" Zeke calls out in the distance.

I let Conall go, and he lifts his thumb to give him the go-ahead.

Tears spring to my eyes as cheers ring through the air, and Conall squeezes my hand as we begin walking in their direction. As we enter through the archway, everyone comes rushing toward us, offering us hugs, smiles and congratulations.

"Thank you all so much," I sniff, looking around at their smiling faces. "Thank you for being here."

"We wouldn't miss this for the world, my dearest." Grandma Citrine smiles, lifting her hand to my cheek.

I lean into her touch, covering her hand with my own.

"You take good care of our girl, Alpha," my father says, putting his hand out to Con, who takes it firmly.

"I will."

My mother mumbles incoherent emotional blabber as she grabs me into another tight hug.

"Let's get this show on the road before we lose the sun!" Zeke laughs, shaking Con's hand before giving me a wide smile. "You ready, Eden?"

"Absolutely," I answer with a grin.

Everyone takes a step back as Zeke takes his position in front of Conall and I.

"Wait!!" Cass interrupts, rushing forward to place a flower crown on my head.

I laugh joyfully as I lift my hand to touch the delicate flowers, and Con smiles as he stares at me. "You are so beautiful," he whispers, the fading, soft sunlight making his eyes shine bright gold.

"So are you," I answer sincerely, taking his hands again.

"Ladies and gentlemen, we are gathered here today to celebrate the marriage of Conall and Eden," Zeke begins, looking at us both. "Life can sometimes pull us in directions we never thought possible. I'm sure the pair of you will agree that a few months ago, this would have seemed fucking as impossible as impossible could be."

"Language..." Con warns him, causing me to giggle.

"Shit. Sorry," Zeke grins in return. "What I'm trying to say is that these two found their way to one another against all the odds," he explains. "Overcame their differences with a few, shall we say, hiccups along the way. Am I right?" He makes a face and laughs a little as I nod vigorously in agreement. "But now, as they stand before us, they have everything they will ever need. They have true love."

I smile at Con as he lifts my hand to kiss it gently.

"And when you find a love that's *this* perfect, you hold on tight, and you never let go."

"Never," I agree, smiling as I shake my head.

My mother sniffs loudly, holding onto my father, who kisses her head in return.

"Can we have the rings?" Zeke asks, looking to Cass, who steps forward with her hand outstretched.

Con lifts the delicate band to my fingertip, staring into my eyes.

"Conall, do you take Eden to be your wife."

"I do," he answers, pushing the ring on slowly.

☐

I flick my eyes to the sparkling diamond, reflecting the orange sky.

"Eden..." Zeke encourages, breaking me from my momentary trance.

I reach for the silver band in Cass' hand and hold Conall's large hand above mine.

"Eden, do you take Conall to be your husband?"

"I do," I confirm without a single doubt in my mind.

Conall smiles, his eyes communicating everything with one solitary look.

Everything that Zeke said is true.

Neither of us went looking for love, but when we found it, despite everything, we clung to it for dear life. We triumphed over every obstacle thrown our way, and in the end, here we are....

The luckiest elf and wolf that ever did live.

I push the ring onto Conall's finger, and immediately, he envelopes my hand in between his, his thumb brushing against the ring that now sits proudly on my finger.

"Then, without further ado, I pronounce you husband and wife! You may now kiss the bride!"

My parents and grandparents clap joyfully while Cass and Zeke take a more rowdy approach. Cass whoops at the top of her lungs, and Zeke wolf-whistles as Con takes me in his arms to press his lips lovingly against mine.

Epilogue

Conall

Eden lays her head on my shoulder as we sit alone, watching the sunset. I hold her hand in mine, twiddling her ring in blissful silence as I contemplate the success of my risky plan.

"I really don't want to take it off tonight," Eden says quietly, lifting her head to look into my eyes.

"It won't be off for long," I smile, lifting her hand to my lips.

She stares at me intently, her eyes running over my face. "Thank you for all of this. You just...you blew me away again."

My brows knit together. "It's no more than you deserve," I say honestly. "I wish I could give you the world, Eden."

She shakes her head, a soft smile on her lips. "It's like Zeke said. All we need is each other."

I nod, pulling her into my embrace once again.

"Conall, what are you going to do?" she asks, her voice tinged with nerves.

There's no need for her to elaborate. I already know what she's asking.

A few weeks back, Haleth broke the news that he and Citrine had a potion ready to break the Alpha's curse. It's there waiting for anyone who wishes to take it. At the time, Eden didn't ask me what I wanted to do, but I could see the look in her eyes. She has the same look right now. Her lilac irises pierce through me, desperately looking for answers.

"It's strange..." I begin, taking a deep breath as I look out to the ocean. "The moment that it happened—the moment I became practically immortal—I've never felt so dead inside. I'd lost everything important to me. I was a shadow of the man I once was, and the thought of spending forever roaming around on this earth made me cold and bitter."

I turn inward, lifting my hand to wipe away a tear from her cheek.

"But now that I have you, Eden. Now that you're mine. Forever...it isn't enough."

Her hopeful eyes lift to connect with mine, and she takes a labored breath. "Does that mean you aren't going to take the cure?"

I shrug airly. "I think it could wait a couple hundred years or so, don't you?"

"Yes! Oh Goddess, yes!"

She smiles that beautiful smile again as I lean forward to kiss her on the head.

* * *

"Alpha, the chairs finally arrived, and we have everyone in their seats ready to go," Temal states, enthusiasm and loyalty pouring out of him like an overgrown puppy.

"Thanks, Temal. We'll be out in a minute."

Zeke watches him disappear out the door before he glances at me in amusement. "I see you've gone in a different direction with your new second-in-command," he grins as I walk over to the mirror to fix my collar.

"Yeah, he's a good kid. Loyal and hardworking. Plus, he doesn't hump everything that moves, so there's that."

Zeke snorts, nodding as he puts his hands in his pockets. "Fair enough."

"He has a lot to learn, but he'll get there," I add, turning to look at him. "Where are you headed after tonight anyway?"

"If you must know, I'm taking a break from- how did you put it? *Humping everything that moves.*"

"Really? Let's hear it," I order, amused. "You aren't heading into dragon territory with Cass, are you?"

"Dragons? Nah, fuck that! They are crazy. I got myself a job in Tipreon. I start next week."

"Tipreon? The fae aren't much better than the dragons," I chuckle as we leave the tavern to head for the busy town square. "What is there for you to do in Tipreon?" I ask curiously.

"Bodyguard work. I'll be protecting some rich woman. It's easy money."

I stop in my tracks and raise my brow. "Protection? For a woman?"

"Don't look at me like that. She's married," he shrugs. "I have my morals!"

"Yeah, well, make sure you stick to them. I don't need you getting yourself caught up in a battle with the fucking fae."

He laughs, shaking his head from side to side. "Don't worry. I hear she's a real brat, anyway. Burns through a bodyguard a month, I hear."

"Then why take the job?"

"I can handle her," he states confidently. "I put up with you for seventy years, didn't I?"

"You better watch what you're saying. You might not make it to fucking Tipreon." I joke in return, causing him to laugh. "So I assume you won't be taking Haleth's potion?"

"No. I'm pretty sure the "immortal wolf" part got me the job in the first place. Haleth gave me a vial, though. I'll keep it for when the time is right."

We stop at the edge of the ceremony space, and I look around at the hundreds of people who have gathered to watch Eden and I marry. A couple of kids shout my name, and I lift my hand to wave back.

"Goddess above, take the damn ring off, you idiot," Zeke scolds, nodding at my hand subtly.

"Shit," I scoff, pulling it off my finger to hand it to him.

"Poor Temal. Kid's got his work cut out for him now that you're losing your edge."

"Losing my edge? I could still kick your ass, brother, and don't you forget it," I say in jest as we walk up the aisle with the eyes of the entire pack and its visitors on us.

"Yeah, yeah," he grins as we stop in front of the elder elf.

We both shake his hand and take our positions as the music begins to play.

A few moments later, I see her emerge from the inn on the edge of the square. She's holding onto her father's arm, her eyes looking straight at me as he leads her to the end of the long aisle.

I smile like a fucking lunatic as I take in her stunning beauty.

As she walks, the soft material of her pure white dress floats behind her, giving her an ethereal quality that I can only describe as angelic.

My *wife* is a fucking angel, and I won't hear otherwise.

She draws closer, and we beam at each other like naughty children, my jaw hurting from smiling so damn much.

Haleth shakes my hand, and I give him a respectful nod.

As Eden stands in front of me, I lean forward to take her hands in mine, the sparks dancing over my skin where we touch.

"Are you ready to marry me all over again, elf?" I ask her playfully.

She smiles, hypnotizing me with those mesmerizing lilac eyes.

"Bring it on...wolf."

END

Follow Me

Join my Facebook group *Meet me at Molly's* for up-to-date book information, new realeases, character mood boards, giveaways and so much more!

You can also follow my social media pages below.

Facebook: Molly Cambria
Instagram: Molly Cambria

Announcement

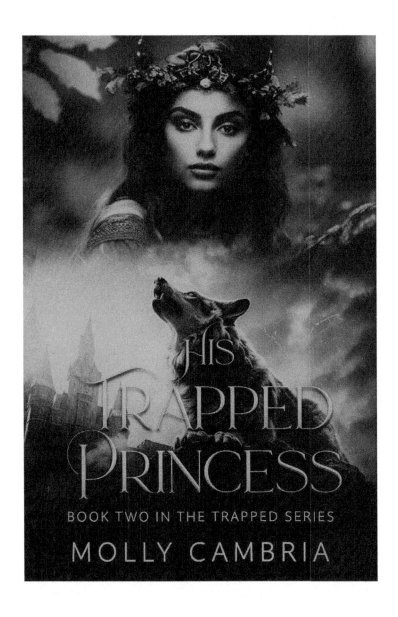

Book two in the 'Trapped' series. Coming soon...

Author Bio

Molly Cambria is a romance author based in Scotland. Discovering a new found love for reading during the pandemic, she was inspired to create her own stories and began writing for various reading apps. She has now moved into self-publishing and is looking forward to bringing more stories to her readers. She particularly enjoys writing paranormal romance where she has the opportunity to create new and exciting worlds filled with interesting and complex characters. As well as this, she has a love for strong female leads who know how to give their swoon-worthy love interests a run for their money! Interact with the author in her Facebook group 'Meet me at Molly's' and stay up to date with all the latest book news.

Printed in Great Britain
by Amazon

36240997R00320